P9-DNT-879

NOT AS A STRANGER

NOT AS A STRANGER

*

by Morton Thompson

CHARLES SCRIBNER'S SONS
New York

PRINTED IN THE UNITED STATES OF AMERICA

For FRANCES PINDYCK THOMPSON
to whom this book and this author
are dedicated

NOT AS A STRANGER

⋆ CHAPTER 1

The doctor came out of the house and he closed the door gently behind him. He looked up and there was a little boy.

"Hello, Luke," he murmured.

The little boy lowered his eyes humbly and when the doctor reached the top step of the porch the little boy turned and put out his hand, the doctor relaxed his grip on his bag and they walked down the steps together and across the sidewalk to the buggy.

The doctor got in on the driving side. The little boy held the doctor's bag with both hands. The doctor seated himself. He took up the reins. The little boy raised the bag and gently lowered it to the carriage floor.

"Thank you, Luke," the doctor said. He smiled absently. He nodded.

The boy looked silently up at the doctor. The doctor flipped the reins. The buggy drove off at a smart trot.

The boy watched the carriage disappear. When it was gone he took to his heels. He ran across town, never slacking, always as fast as he could go. He came to an empty street. When he saw that it was empty he slowed instantly. He walked directly to a wooden house in the middle of the street. In a window of the house was a porcelain sign, a rectangle of white, three and one-half inches high and fourteen inches long. On the sign was lettered severely and blackly, "Chester Kellogg, M.D."

The little boy sat down on the top step of the porch of this house. He waited a long time. He waited nearly two hours. He sat very still in the warm July afternoon, blinking a little sometimes and thinking his own thoughts. From far off, the air of the small town of Milletta brought to the porch occasional faint shouts of children at play. Once a door slammed. Once a trio of dogs burst into a hysterical shrill yapping and their yelps died in the distance. The little boy heard everything and he heard nothing. The sounds funnelled into his ears and drained away. He was listening for something else. The sound he was waiting for came at last. It was the sound of a horse clip-clopping. The carriage turned into the street. The little boy rose. He walked down the steps. When the carriage stopped in front of the house the little boy was at the horse's head. His hand went up as the reins were dropped. He held the bridle. The doctor got slowly out of the carriage. As he straightened, his bag in his hand, the little boy was at his side. He put out his hand. The doctor surrendered his bag. They walked up the steps together. They walked across the porch. At the door the doctor put out his hand for his bag. The little boy held it up so that he could take it. His eyes never left the doctor's face.

"Thanks, Luke," said the doctor. He noticed the little boy staring. He shook his head. "Not today, Luke," he said gently. Then he turned and went into the house.

The little boy walked gravely down the steps and into the street. He began to walk toward home. He had had high hopes, but tomorrow was another day. He had made seven calls this day. It was a good day. Tomorrow was another day. Great days did not come often. But they came. When they came Doctor Kellogg let him come right into the house, and the minute the door opened there was that wonderful smell, that smell, that smell, that wonderful smell, ether and iodine and alcohol and carbolic acid and salve, one smell. And through this smell, right into the office, and there the smell was strongest and there he could stand and gaze and gaze and gaze his never filling fill. He could stand quite still, his hands straight at his sides, hoping with a prayer that the doctor would never think he would touch anything—it would all end, then. It would never happen again. But once Dr. Kellogg had put his hand on his shoulder and led him to the white case, the shiny glass, the instruments, the curves, the glisten, the straight, sharp reach of the scissors, the thin, cold knives, the precise meaningless, meaningful, odd, direct, and incomprehensible shapes that were beautiful and nameless. And Dr. Kellogg had named them.

"This is a bistoury—"

A bistoury . . . a bistoury . . .

"And this is a tenaculum—"

Tenaculum . . . tenaculum . . .

"And here is a curette—"

Curette . . . curette . . . Bistoury. Tenaculum. Curette . . .

He would never touch anything. They all knew it. Dr. Kellogg, Dr. Dwyer, Dr. Alexander. He would never touch anything and he would seldom say anything. He didn't have to. What was there to say?

The little boy's name was Lucas Marsh. He was seven years old. There wasn't anything he had to say.

Dr. Kellogg was the best call and always the most hope. But once Dr. Dwyer had sat down on his porch and opened his bag and rummaged and brought forth a bottle.

"That's an appendix, Luke. Vermiform appendix. Appendix vermiformis."

He offered Luke the bottle. Luke held it. The alcohol in the bottle tilted. The length of white tissue emerged, gleaming. Then Dr. Dwyer put out his hand. He took the bottle and put it back in his bag. He rose, patted Luke on the shoulder, and went into the house.

Once Dr. Dwyer let him ride many blocks beside him in the carriage. Dr. Alexander had been a long time letting him carry his bag, but he had always let him hold his horse. And then there was the day when Dr. Alexander trusted him. He let him carry the bag from the carriage right up to the front door. Now he thought nothing of it. Often as not he'd let Luke lift it right out of the carriage.

There was always hope. The little boy began to think about tomorrow. He thought about tomorrow all the long way home. After a time he decided his first call would be Dr. Dwyer. He quickened his steps. He would have to get up early.

He sighed contentedly. He ran into his house.

For all humans there is a common beginning in the known mechanics which provide their presence. And this beginning is the instant in which a single sperm of one hundred and fifty million, travelling a relative distance of more than a million miles, reaches the ovum to which its unbrained intelligence has directed it. A human begins then.

If any of the other hundred and fifty million sperms had reached the ovum instead, a different human would have begun, for in the universe man comprehends no two living things are alike and sperm are living things.

If man has a mundane destiny, it begins here. If man is mundane chance, it begins here. Man knows no more. But it is conjectured that there is no chance. In the year Lucas Marsh was conceived and began, twenty-nine million other humans began.

Some of these, by the choice of one sperm in a hundred and fifty million, were born with their viscera outside the body. Some were born without a head. Some began with two hearts, some with six fingers, some with three eyes, some with a penis and a vulva, some without lungs, some without any members whatever.

In most, the characteristics, visible and invisible, would fall within the limits of the majority or the normal.

But the body is not all, and in some there would be profound differences in the spirit, there would be emphasized pathways in the brain, there would be mutations of the mind. And scientists would begin from the loins of ditchdiggers, and mathematicians would begin from the sperm of savages, a violinist would be born to the deaf, a hunter to the sightless.

And for some of these their urges would be dim, troubling impulses and for some they would be strong and for some the impulses would be irresistible and their life, itself. Their very life.

Lucas Marsh was born in the town of Milletta in the early 1900's, to Job Marsh, owner of a harness store, and Ouida Marsh, daughter of a druggist. He was to be a doctor. No more is known.

✶ CHAPTER 2

At the kitchen table Ouida Marsh looked up, hearing him enter, smiled as he charged at her, and deftly turned her cheek to him an instant before his kiss would have landed on her mouth.

"Get washed, Lucas," she said after a moment and he disengaged himself and went to the sink. Ouida Marsh removed her rimless glasses with the long black ribbon and put them carefully in a case. The glasses were without optical significance, she had bought them in a notions store and she wore them for reading as a costume suitable to the occasion. The magazine she had been reading was *The Phrenologist's Gazette,* sent for from Chicago, and when Lucas had washed his hands she called him and when he had shown her his hands she sat him down in front of her and looked at him carefully.

Lucas looked back at her curiously.

"Where's Papa?" he asked.

"Your father will be late," Mrs. Marsh said briefly. "Let me look at you, Lucas."

He sat obediently still.

She studied his slim, oval face, his high forehead, his dark eyes, his cheekbones, his thin neck, his thin hands, his lithe and wiry body. She studied him as a stranger, noting with inward surprise significances she saw now for the first time. According to this new and wonderful science Lucas, her boy, her property that she had made, was of a pronounced North American type, and she had not known this before, nor even known the existence of a classification. She opened the magazine. She glanced from it to Lucas, then back again. He was also dolichocephalic and dolichoprosopic and, in general, dolicho. In some excitement she opened her lips to tell him so. She recollected, as the thought formed, that she did not know how to pronounce these strange and wonderful words, and smiled instead, and clicked her tongue mysteriously.

"Come over here, Lucas. Sit down beside me. Pull your chair around so your back is to me."

Lucas obediently did as he was bid. Mrs. Marsh turned a page and following the printed instructions placed her fingers on the little boy's head.

"You're very spiritual, Lucas," she said almost instantly. "Very, very spiritual . . ." She moved her fingertips over his skull. "Great reasoning power . . ." she glanced at the book . . . "pronounced memory . . ." She came to a new bump, read, recoiled, frowned, felt again, compressed her lips. "Pronounced amativeness," she said with cold emphasis. She bit her lips. "We will have to do something about that, Lucas."

The little boy turned fearfully. He did not know what he had done but he knew he had done something. Guilt tightened his belly.

"That means our baser impulses, Lucas." Mrs. Marsh leaned toward him. Her face was very serious and stern and it seemed to have swelled a little. "Do you understand, Lucas?"

He looked back at her, waiting, fearful, depressed.

"We will have to be very careful, Lucas. The bump is there. We will have to guard ourselves, all our life."

"Yes, Mother."

"Do you know what 'amativeness' means, Lucas?"

"No, Mother."

The little boy crimsoned. He turned his head away in an agony of embarrassment.

"Look at me, Lucas."

He forced his head to turn.

"Yes, Mother." He writhed.

"You'll come straight to Mother and tell her?"

"Yes, Mother." He put his hands on his head to feel the bumps she had felt and desperate to change the subject leaned over to look at the magazine.

"You wouldn't understand it, dear. Mother will explain it to you. It's a great new discovery, all based on scientific fact, and it tells how we can change our whole lives and become completely new human beings by understanding our own characters through the bumps the brain makes on the skull."

He felt the bumps on his skull.

"Each one of them means something, Lucas."

"Can we change them really?" To his fingers the bumps felt very hard and permanent.

"Oh, yes. We can change them completely."

Lucas marvelled.

"Are we going to eat dinner, now?"

"Your father will be late. You don't mind waiting, do you, Lucas? You don't mind practicing with Mother subduing our baser animal impulses?"

"No, Mother."

"Each time you fight it the battle is a little easier."

In a sudden access of affection she leaned forward and stroked his face. Her fingers wandered over his chin and she frowned. She smiled sadly. She began to knead his chin outward.

"Your chin, Lucas. Have you been massaging your chin as Mother asked you?"

"Yes, Mother."

"First thing in the morning? Last thing at night?"

"Yes, Mother."

"Always outward, over and over. More and more every day. You have a weak chin, Lucas. You must have a strong chin. The chin is the sign of character."

Lucas sighed, ashamed. He tried to divert her attention from himself.

"Is that a spiritual magazine, Mother?"

"Oh, yes, dear. Very spiritual. Very, very spiritual. Tell Mother—what did you do today?"

"I made seven calls," he said excitedly.

"You didn't make any calls, Lucas. Only doctors make calls. You just played a game."

"I ran around a lot," he said carefully.

"Can't you play more spiritual games, Lucas? Mother has such great dreams for you, darling. You're Mother's whole life, you know. Never forget that. Mother wants the little boy she suffered such agonies to bring into the world to be a great artist, a spiritual being the whole world will look up to." Her dark, handsome face leaned to him earnestly. Both heard the sound of footsteps. Both started. Mrs. Marsh rose to put away the phrenology magazine.

The footsteps died away.

"Your father is very late."

The little boy's face fell.

"Are you hungry, Lucas?"

"No, Mother," he said manfully.

"Take a drink of water."

"I'm not thirsty, either," he boasted.

Her heart warmed to his effort. Her eyes filled.

"Come here, darling."

He went to her instantly. She pressed his head to her full and finely formed breasts.

"Do you love Mother?"

He buried his face in her neck.

"You're all Mother has. Remember that. Remember, won't you, darling? I carried you under my heart for nine long months—would you be lonely without Mother, Lucas?" She tried to draw him away to look at him, but he dug his face deeper into her neck and nodded his head fiercely. "Mother won't be with you always, sweetheart. Mother will die, someday. Mother will be dead and gone." His small body tensed. He began to sob. She pulled him free of her, still resisting, and examined his face hungrily down which the tears fell like gouts of clear blood. "Will you miss me, Lucas?" His eyes closed in an agony of grief, his face wrinkled helplessly. Now he sobbed uncontrollably.

"Oh, Mother's darling." She drew him to her again, she hugged him fiercely, hungrily. "Mother's not going, darling. See? Mother's right here. Mother's not going to die."

He cried a long time.

Afterward she dried his tears with her handkerchief.

"Aren't you ashamed?" She smiled at him tenderly. "A big boy like you?"

He nodded obediently, not trusting his voice.

"You're so short, Lucas." She surveyed him. "I wish you'd grow taller."

He looked down at his small length.

"We'll think of a new exercise, shall we?"

He nodded vigorously.

"I know you can stretch yourself. I know you can if you try. If you really try. Will you try for Mother, Lucas?"

They looked up.

The footsteps were unmistakable now. An instant later the door opened and Job Marsh entered.

"Hi!" He grinned blithely. He ran the palms of both hands over his fine, straight blond hair, crossed the room to put his lips dutifully to the cheek Mrs. Marsh dutifully offered, straightened, reached out and pulled Lucas' nose. Mrs. Marsh had already begun to set the dinner on the table.

"Have a good day today?" she asked mechanically.

"Absolutely," he carolled. "And likewise palm de tare and likewise pross de toot."

"Job!" Mrs. Marsh cried out. She looked at him furiously, with hate and contempt.

He chuckled and seated himself.

"In front of the child!"

Job Marsh winked at Lucas. He smiled deprecatively. Lucas smiled back.

"I've asked you before—" Mrs. Marsh said bitterly.

"I know it. Let's eat."

Mrs. Marsh looked at him witheringly. Her glance emphasized that he was seated and she was standing behind her chair. She made a small noise of contempt, slowly took her eyes from him, compressed her lips and lowered her head.

"Don't you say grace," Job broke in. "You take too long. I'll say it." He lowered his head. Mrs. Marsh and Lucas lowered their heads. Job waited a moment.

"Grace!" he cried suddenly, and instantly fell to eating.

Lucas laughed in delight.

"Lucas!" cried Mrs. Marsh.

Lucas guiltily bent his head and slowly began to eat. He ate, with the accompaniment of occasional sidelong looks at his mother, by raising placatively small forkfuls of food to his mouth and by keeping his mouth obediently closed until the fork was about to touch his lips. Job Marsh ate heartily, he put as much food on his fork as it would carry and he bent his head as he lifted the fork to receive the food as quickly as possible. Mrs. Marsh watched her husband deliberately and each spoonful he lifted was a frank avowal of lust and his appetite was a happiness in lust; there was lust, she could not expunge lust from things as they were, from the world, but there were manners concerning lust, manners making lust acceptable to the female. Job's entire lack of concern with these glosses made of her days many small blazes of hatred and rebellion and an intense desire to escape the world and to begin again, to be cleanly reborn. She watched her husband. She ate more slowly and more reluctantly. Her movements became more mannered, her feeding became an exaggerated ritual of delicacy in which food was not food but an opportunity for delicacy. She exaggerated her movements to make her disgust plain. This never troubled Job. It made him laugh. And he laughed Mrs. Marsh into speechless fury.

Lucas ate with an eye to both his mother and father. He watched his mother fearfully, hoping not to incur her inexplicable wraths. He watched his father, trying to discover what the essential act was in his father's habit of eating that so enraged his mother. He had become accustomed to scenes between them and he hoped dully that this time there would be no new scene.

"What's the matter?" Job looked up suddenly. "Don't you like your own food?" he grinned.

"You think that's funny, don't you," Mrs. Marsh said coldly. "Lucas, put your fork on your plate! Well, I don't think it's funny at all."

"Seems funny to me," Job teased.

"What you do to my appetite doesn't matter. The least you could do would be to set a good example. I know you think nothing of me."

Job looked curiously at Lucas, who was plying his knife and fork clumsily but with determined delicacy.

"He's doing all right, ain't he?"

"Isn't—if you don't mind—"

"Isn't he?"

"Finish your dinner, Lucas! It's late. I want you to go right upstairs to bed."

"I brought something home for him, first."

"What did you bring, Daddy!" Lucas leaped from his chair and ran to his father. "Where is it!"

"Lucas!" cried Mrs. Marsh. He looked at her rebelliously. "Go back to your chair and sit down and ask permission to rise and leave the table!"

"There's something out in the hall," Job told the boy as he retreated to his chair. Lucas sat down. "You'll find it on the table."

"May I please be excused?" Lucas implored.

"Use your napkin."

He dabbed at his face.

"Put your fork on your plate."

He put his fork on his plate.

She nodded her head. "You may be excused."

Lucas rushed to the next room. On the table was a small paper box, the lid perforated.

"Careful how you open it!" Job called from the kitchen.

In the box was a newly hatched chick. Astonished, wordless, Lucas bore the bird in his hands into the kitchen.

"It's mine," he said, helpless. He touched its softness with his fingers. He set it reverently on the table. The bird evacuated.

Mrs. Marsh leaped up, her face wried in disgust.

"Put him on the floor," said Job gently.

"Take him off my table—where we eat—" cried Mrs. Marsh.

Hurriedly Lucas lifted the tiny chick and set it on the floor.

"I'm going to call him Chickie," he said softly.

"You want to take care of him," said Job. "Don't go handling him too much, he'll die."

Lucas looked at his father, alarmed.

Mrs. Marsh returned to the table with a wet rag. She cleaned the bird's droppings, angrily washed the cloth. The chick followed her, peeping. Lucas watched every movement of the downy yellowness with adoration.

"You've got to feed it regular," said Job.

The little boy knelt on the floor and put out his hands.

"Here, Chickie," he called, "come on, Chickie."

"Where's the box it came in?" Mrs. Marsh demanded. Without waiting for an answer she strode toward the next room. The little chick followed her. The little boy looked at his father with delight.

"Look, Dad! Look at the little dickens following Mother!"

They beamed at each other.

Mrs. Marsh pushed angrily through the swinging door. The chick followed. An instant later Mrs. Marsh pushed through the swinging door again, the box in her hand. The chick followed tardily, the door caught him. He was crushed. His bill opened wide. His legs fluttered. He peeped feebly and died.

The three watched. It was over. And still they watched. Suddenly Lucas gave a great shout:

"You killed him!" he screamed, incredulous. "You killed my Chickie!"

Job walked to the bird and stood looking down at it. As he watched, it stiffened, elongating one leg as if to push away death.

"That's too bad," he said, and shook his head. "That's—that's too bad . . ."

"I didn't see it!" cried Mrs. Marsh. "Why didn't it keep out of my way!"

Lucas rushed to the bird. He threw himself to the floor beside it. It was quite dead. He stroked it without hope. He looked up at Mrs. Marsh.

"Why did you kill it, Mother?"

"I didn't mean to kill it, Lucas. I'm sorry."

"I'll get you another one," promised Job.

"Of course if your father hadn't brought this home it never would have happened—"

The little boy began to cry at last.

"I'm sorry, Lucas. Come to Mother, darling."

Lucas cowered away. He wept uncontrollably. He could not stop. Job tried to raise him.

"Come, darling, come to Mother—Mother's sorry—"

Lucas raised his face. It was very white.

"Why did you kill it?" he begged. "What did it ever do to you?"

"It's time for bed, Lucas. Come on, darling. Mother will tell you a story. Mother's sorry, darling—"

"It was an accident," said Job.

Lucas rose, coffining the bird in his hands. He put the bird in the box. He walked to his father and put up his face to be kissed, he offered his mother his cold lips. Without another word he went up to bed carrying the chick with him.

"Getting a little headstrong," said Mrs. Marsh.

"Too bad," said Job. "It hit him hard."

"If you hadn't brought it home it never would have happened."

"A boy needs a pet. He's got a right to a pet. Any boy. I had one. I had a dog."

"We've been over that. I'm not going to have any filthy, vile dog to clean up after—no animals of any kind." She looked at him pointedly. "That's what I'm trying to get away from—animals!"

"Oh, now, Ida—"

"My name happens to be Ouida."

"Why don't you just relax—you're tensed up all the time and you're getting him that way. Look how thin he is. Why don't you just stop monkeying from one diet to another and let him grow up like a normal, healthy boy!"

"You make him stop running around like a maniac all day, running from doctor to doctor, and I'll show you how thin he is."

"Now, Ouida, a boy's got to chase after something. Let him alone. That's just a phase, that doctor chasing. All boys go through phases. When I was a boy—"

"Never mind telling me about when you were a boy. I know what you used to chase after and so does all the county. I'm not going to have my son growing up like that, if you don't mind."

"Just let him alone."

"He's my son and he'll grow up decent. He's got great things in him."

She looked at Job contemptuously. "The kind you'd never even know about."

"She's off again," said Job and spread his hands resignedly.

"Perhaps you'd like to see him grow up a doctor? Perhaps his harness-maker father thinks that would be fine!"

"No, I don't want to see him grow up to be a doctor. And I know he won't. There's no money in it. He's got better sense. It'll come out when he's older. He'll look back and laugh at it. But there's nothing *wrong* with being a doctor—except he won't be one—"

"I have nothing but contempt for doctors."

"Notice you call one when you need one."

"I don't need them. I've got my own methods."

"Well, keep them to yourself. And don't go practicing them on any-body else—"

"Has it ever occurred to you for one moment what vile diseases he might pick up just being around them?"

"Oh, for Christ's sake, Ouida!"

She looked quickly at the ceiling. Then she glared at Job.

"He can hear you, you know. If you're going to be common you might at least think of the son you profess to love so much—"

"You make a man—"

"I don't make you anything. You're what you are, a filthy, disgusting beast, and nothing'll ever change you."

"I notice you don't mind eating what your filthy, disgusting harness maker brings home, Miss Lahdeedah fine lady."

"You actually don't care whether he hears you or not, do you!"

Job studied her a moment, then turned and went upstairs to bed. On the way he stopped at Lucas' room and opened the door gently. Lucas was on the floor at his bedside. He kneeled beside the box. He had a rag which he had soaked in water and with his free hand he held the chick's beak open and was squeezing drops of water carefully and lovingly into the chick's dead throat.

"Won't do much good, son," Job said quietly.

"It might," said Lucas in a small voice. He did not look up nor inter-rupt himself.

"Your mother didn't mean it," Job said after a while.

"I know it," Lucas said dully.

He squeezed out another drop of water, never taking his eyes from the dead bird.

"I'll get you another one," Job said.

Lucas looked up quickly. There was fright in his eyes.

"I don't want another one," he protested. "Please, Daddy!"

"All right, son."

Lucas resumed his ministrations.

Job watched a while, then quietly left the room.

The door closed behind him. Lucas continued to drop water into the bird's opened beak. He began to cry again, the tears fell on the bird and he wiped them tenderly away. He cried without sound. After a long time he crept into bed. He brought the dead bird with him. He put it on the pillow. He thought a long time, trying to forget the door closing. Finally he slept.

In the morning, instead of going out on his calls, Lucas tried again to revive the bird. The bird was by now cold and stiff. He tried to warm it by breathing on it, then by putting it inside his shirt against his bare belly. Mrs. Marsh, going about her household tasks, shuddered with disgust but said nothing. Lucas could not warm the chick and next he tried to make it supple, to dissolve its rigidity by exercise. He sat it on the floor and forced its stick-stiff legs into a walk. At noon Mrs. Marsh called him to lunch. He nibbled at the curious fare of beets and spinach with egg, a diet she was then committed to; he ate little and she did not coax him or threaten him. They ate silently.

"I think you'd better bury Chickie," Mrs. Marsh said after the table was cleared.

Lucas looked at the dead bird he was trying again to resuscitate.

"He's not doing any harm," he said mildly.

"He's dead, dear. He's beginning to smell."

Mrs. Marsh brought forth a pretty box she had been saving and they put the bird in it. Lucas held the lid and they went into the back yard.

"Here's a beautiful place," Mrs. Marsh said, narrowing her eyes as she had seen artists do, "right under this tree."

She got a shovel and dug a shallow grave. It was very kind of her and Lucas watched her gratefully.

When the grave was dug they sat down a while at Mrs. Marsh's bidding, and she used the opportunity to talk to him of life and death, trying to explain things to him beautifully. But Lucas watched the chick. When she ended talking he sighed. The chick had not moved. She took the lid from him and fitted it gently to the box. Then they buried it.

Lucas dug up the box three times during the afternoon, but the chick was still dead. In the evening he brought his father out to look at the grave. Mrs. Marsh, unbidden, followed them, and the three stood at the grave sadly. After they stood a while Lucas stopped suddenly and dug it up again. But the chick was quite dead. Reluctantly, he put it back in the box and covered it with earth again. He was not burying a bird, he was burying love.

"We'd better put a marker on it," said Job.

He got a heavy stone, too heavy for a little boy to move, and set it over the grave.

"That's his tombstone, Luke. Just like folks."

Lucas had not gone on his calls at all that day. The next day he wandered off on a mission of his own. He hung about chicken pens. He watched chickens, alive, studying how they moved, wondering each time they moved at the difference between moving and not moving. In two of the chicken pens he saw dead chickens, they lay where they had fallen. He poked at them with a stick but they did not move. They were dead. The other chickens moved about them unconcernedly. They moved, it was nothing to them, they were living. He reached a conclusion on states of matter. Both types of chicken were alive, the living and the dead. Dead was just a name applied to a different status of living. His attention was now diverted to still another phase of living, an intermediate phase. In one coop he found a chicken with an injured leg. This chicken hopped as best it could, it moved, it was alive, but it could not move as much as the other chickens. He studied it minutely. When the chicken came close to the fence he seized it. He forced the retracted leg to the ground and tried to make the chicken walk on both legs. The bird pecked him and he let it go.

Late that afternoon he came upon a dog. The animal in an agony of bliss and pain was scratching itself endlessly with one hind leg. Lucas watched it a while. Then he moved in swiftly and held the dog's leg. The dog promptly transferred his scratching to the other hind leg. Lucas sat on him. He held both legs. The dog yelped helplessly.

Dr. Alexander, driving by, stopped his carriage.

"Boy!" he shouted angrily. "You boy! Stop abusing that dog!"

Lucas, abashed, rose, still holding the dog's legs.

"What are you trying to do to that dog?"

"He's hurting himself," Lucas said shyly.

"How is he hurting himself?"

"He kicks himself with his leg."

Dr. Alexander blinked. He stared at Lucas thoughtfully.

"Get in, boy," he said, moving over. "Come with me."

Lucas lifted the wriggling dog into the carriage and got in after it. Dr. Alexander drove to the drugstore. He came out with flea powder.

"Now watch this, boy. Drag that dog out of the carriage and watch this."

He sprinkled the dog liberally with flea powder. He stood up. The dog ran quickly off.

"Now that dog is cured, boy."

Lucas, who had been watching the dog run off, turned to the doctor, open-mouthed.

"He's cured. I sprinkled powder on him. Flea powder. Now he won't kick himself any more. Do you understand? That's flea powder, son. He wasn't kicking himself. He was scratching. The fleas made him itch. The powder kills the fleas."

Lucas stared in wonder at the box of flea powder. Dr. Alexander watched him a moment longer, then abruptly put the container into his hands, climbed into the carriage, and drove off.

For the rest of that day Lucas went about Milletta hunting for scratching dogs. He found dozens. In an hour the box was empty. He refilled it with sand.

The next day he went back to his rounds again. He arose especially early. He went first to Dr. Alexander's home and office and he was in time to carry the doctor's bag all the way from his front door to the carriage. Then he raced across town to Dr. Dwyer's, but here he was too late, the doctor had gone. From Dr. Dwyer's he went without much hope to Dr. Kellogg's, but Dr. Kellogg also had gone. Thereafter he prowled the streets. Much of the doctors' practice was in the outlying farm area but much of it was also in the town, and there were days when most of their travelling was in the country and then there were days when most of it was in the town, sometimes for all three and sometimes for two and sometimes only for one of them. Lucas prowled the streets looking for the doctors' carriages. Whenever he saw one he sat down on the curb and took up his vigil. When the doctor emerged from the house Lucas was ready. Sometimes he carried the bag. Sometimes he had time only to hold the horse's head. By noon he had made four calls.

It was time for lunch. Before going home he walked toward his father's shop. The sign, "J. Marsh & Co., Harness," hung flat against the false front of a small building on Main Street. Lucas stood in a corner in the semidarkness while his father sold a farmer a checkrein. When the farmer moved out Job walked eagerly across the shop to the boy.

"Hi, Luke!"

"Hi, Daddy."

"What can I do for you that your mother hasn't done twice as good already?"

"I'd like some money, Daddy."

"Money! Good gracious, who ever heard of money!"

"Yes, sir."

"How much money you want, Luke?" Job brought a handful of coins from his pocket and extended them to Lucas. Lucas looked at the coins, then up at his father.

"I don't know," he confessed.

"Well, tell me. What do you want to get, Luke? Maybe I can help you."

"Some flea powder."

Job blinked.

"You want flea powder? What on earth do you want flea powder for? You gonna put it on me? You think I got lice?"

"I want to put it on dogs."

Job stared at his son inquisitively. But the little boy volunteered no more and Job thereupon understood it was something to do with doctoring, a subject on which both knew the other's views, and delicately forbore to question him further.

"All right, son," he said gravely. "Here's a dime. That's for you. Go buy all the flea powder you want."

Lucas stared at the dime then raised grateful eyes to his father.

"Time you had an allowance!" Job said loudly. "Boy your age needs pocket money. Ten cents a week. Every week, this time, Luke. Ten cents. All right?"

"Yes, sir," Lucas said, dazed.

"You like leather some, son?" Job blurted.

Lucas looked about the dim shop.

"I like the smell," he admitted.

"Like the way it curls? And supples?"

"Yes, sir."

"All right, son. I'll see you at dinner. Run along. Get your flea powder. Some day this summer maybe you'd like to spend a day with me. Here in the shop, maybe? How'd you like that?"

"Yes, sir," Lucas said obediently.

"You'll like it!"

"Yes, sir."

Lucas walked sedately from the shop. Outside, he broke into a run, the hard, wiry run he used to get from doctor's office to doctor's office. He pelted into the drugstore, waited docilely for other customers, shyly tendered his dime, and was given a quantity of flea powder, put it carefully in his pocket and jogged home for lunch.

It was beets and spinach with eggs—"they contain all the minerals"—and he ate quietly and sparingly of this miracle health food.

This day somehow he was released. Unaccountably he was no longer part of the household tensions, a part of their machinery. He was a separate machine in himself, congruent with the other activities but no longer a shuttlecock between and among them. He was separate and distinct and contacting, but unconnected. Something had happened. He did not know what it was and he did not trouble himself with its origin. But he relished it tremendously, he felt free—a little furtive, but free. The death of a man or a god has done this for others. For Lucas it took only a chicken. Life and death are neither more nor less in quantity or quality for whatever is living or dead. It is not a deep nor a difficult truth. Lucas did not ponder. The effect of the truth had already become part of him. He had now allied himself with life and against death. His confused and anguished yearnings to be with doctors had now an identifiable part. The doctors, too, were aligned with life and against death. When he carried their bags or held their horses' heads he was one with a part of them.

This afternoon perhaps he would encounter Dr. Alexander. Perhaps he would take him into his office. There wasn't much chance of this. But it could happen.

"Bistoury—curette—tenaculum—" he said to himself.

He ran off to begin his afternoon rounds.

He ran furiously.

He never stopped.

✶ CHAPTER 3

At the boundaries of Milletta a sign proclaims the community's height above sea level: 785 feet; its population: 2,600; and its position: "MILLETTA—HUB OF THE WORLD."

Job Marsh had not been born in Millettá. He was an alien to the hub of the world. He accepted misfortune lightheartedly and he was almost always cheerful. These provocations to fortune, these flyings in the face of Providence, were enough to keep a man alien in a farming community in the early 1900's. There were other ways in which he differed markedly, but the principal fact which made him bizarre and separate and talked about and forever wondered at was that he owned, not one store like the normal man, but four. They were small stores, three were located in communities near Milletta, and one store, the main store, was in Milletta.

Job Marsh had lived in Milletta since he was sixteen, he was a fixture of Milletta, but he was an addition to it rather than a member of it.

The years had not much aged him. He was of something less than medium height. He was thirty-four years old and as spare, as wiry, as agile as he had been when Milletta first saw him at sixteen. He had added a mustache, a thin line of blond hair, carefully trimmed. His face was long and oval, his lips were wide and thin, his eyes were light blue, his nose was thin and prominent. His hair, combed straight back, clung to his skull, and here the tiding years showed a slow recession of hair on either side of his high forehead.

He let his nails grow long and they were usually dirty. He was always scrupulously shaved. His face had character and distinction and he was handsome. When he was carefully dressed, and he liked to dress well, he was out of place in Milletta. He looked like a *boulevardier*.

Job viewed the other members of the community detachedly. He followed their rules with good humor.

Privately he lived in a simple world whose rules were things as he found them. In this world he moved surely, blithely, seriously. He was not bound by community rules but he observed them scrupulously and publicly. They never deflected him from the direction in which he moved.

Job Marsh intended some day to own a harness store in every principal city in America. He intended to own a tannery to supply these stores with leather. He intended to possess a mine to furnish ore for a steel mill he would own which would supply all the nails, bits, rivets, tongues, and other metal relating to harness.

Only a part of this dream was known to anyone else. His wife knew he planned to own more harness stores and that his ambition was to be the largest harness dealer in the county. Sometimes it seemed to her that he might have such mad dreams as being the largest harness dealer in the state. But she had no real basis for such suspicions and did not mention them.

Other merchants in Milletta, and particularly Banker Purvis Benjamin, realized vaguely that although Job owned four stores he might perhaps be thinking of one day acquiring another one.

To Milletta security was sufficiency. The future was what would occur within the next week. To Job Marsh there was no quantity, no substance he could name total security, and in his world it did not exist and because he was what he was he could not reasonably invent it. Insecurity was a fact, a cheerful, present fact. In all his life it never shook him, never made him fear. He was almost always affable; he joked easily and he preferred obscenity; he never forgot an expression that took his fancy and he never relinquished it and got the same enjoyment from it as when he first heard it. Adversity did not move him deeply. He was not surprised by it. The simplest food contented him and in small quantities. If he slept on the floor he did not marvel at its hardness. He was indifferent to unpleasant scents. He loved all the odors of a woman's body, he loved them strong. He was never free of a craving to sleep with a woman, with any woman. He was unsuited to idleness. He loved work.

He regarded young Lucas' life and young Lucas' future with satisfaction. The boy's life was softer than his own had been and Job wanted the boy's whole life to be thus. He did not feel that life would be changed, for its fabric and its pattern were immutable and he knew this well. He intended the boy to see life as he saw it. But he meant Lucas' living to be easier than his own youth had been.

Job Marsh had been one of five children. They had been orphaned while they were very young. Even if his parents had lived and continued to work the rocky Upper New York State farm, Job's life would have been extremely hard. It would have been a life hungry with poverty and emaciated with need and shamed by lack. But when the parents died the children fell to the only living grandmother. Upon this one old woman and five small children fell the necessity of pecking from those barren acres what chance might surrender to them.

The children were invariably hungry. Their days began in exhaustion, were houred by exhaustion, and ended by exhaustion. Their sufferings produced in them a precocity for enduring. They attended school until need plucked them from school to defend their bellies against hunger and their skins against cold. Job quit in the sixth grade.

Despite their poverty and the improbability of their survival the grandmother from time to time clutched aside a few pennies. These she frantically hid. Invariably these minute sums disappeared in some new need. Stubbornly she began again. When she had collected a new hoard, seldom more than a quarter, she hid the coins behind a loose brick, the fourth brick in the corner of the fireplace.

The children quickly enough learned how things were ordered in the world in which they had been born and they accepted the world as they accepted the seasons. None of the Marsh children was ever ashamed of patched clothes, of broken boots, of uncut hair, never, as long as they lived. When other children mocked their raggedness they saw what the children mocked, and grinned, too.

As soon as they could, the children left the loose association of their group, the girls marrying quite young and the boys foraging quickly away from the miserable farm to seek easier survival.

At sixteen Job found his way to Milletta. He went from store to store along Main Street, looking for work. It was nearly dark when he came to the harness store, owned by Andreas Plenkin.

"I'll clean up your shop, mister, sweep it all down nice, wash the windows, if you'll let me sleep in the back." He grinned at Plenkin.

Plenkin brooded.

"Just for tonight."

That was the beginning. Plenkin did not really want him around, he wanted the shop to himself, and himself to himself; he was a foreigner and he lived alone and unspoken to, except in the course of trade. But the next morning his shop had been transformed and he looked about him incredulously and then at Job, a thin, weedy, blond boy, grinning at him in the midst of it.

"I'll run errands, carry stuff, do whatever you tell me all the rest of today. And you give me breakfast."

Plenkin, still staggered, blinked at him uncertainly.

"Just for today," Job said confidently. "Tell me what to do. Want me to oil up some harness?"

Thereafter he worked for Plenkin. He could not be dislodged. Smiling, watchful, respectful, quick, obedient, and utterly tireless, he did what he was told earnestly and thoroughly and then looked for more.

In two months Job was earning a dollar a week, a noon meal Plenkin shared with him, and his lodging, the benches in the back of the shop. This was his salary, his end of childhood, his start in adult life. At seventeen Milletta summed him as a tireless worker with a perpetual hunger for girls, an odd youth who lived with that foreigner Plenkin. He received now three dollars a week.

And Job had summed and studied Milletta. He knew the history of each merchant. He knew all progress, who was fighting up, who was hanging on, who was falling to extinction. He weighed all opinions. He studied every least business deal.

He knew that for Blacksmith James Waters, who fashioned almost nothing now and who lived on horseshoeing and repairs—for Samuel Hasper, who owned a grist mill—for Edward Haines, whose defeated mill still wove a few textiles—for Saunders Hale, whose tannery seldom tanned—for all the other one-time factories of Milletta, survival was no longer in doubt. They were through. The railroads had come a few years before and they had by-passed Milletta. The railroads brought to other towns about Milletta everything that men in Milletta could make, produced faraway by cheaper labor, of material bought at quantity prices, fashioned into finished articles that sold for less than the artificers of Milletta paid for raw material.

And that was the story of these merchants and Job Marsh knew that story well. He knew the facts which pulled them down. He knew the history of those who still survived and he knew their survival was fortuitous and that they knew it was fortuitous. He was alien to all these, a man untribed. His kin of the human family was another group, a vague group, faraway, scattered men who saw things as they were, with neither liking nor resentment, saw things, saw what they meant, moved naturally to possess themselves of the railroads or to control the possibilities they offered, and who were now through the commerce of the nation attempting the ownership of everything necessary for man's survival. In far-off Milletta, Job Marsh, at eighteen, followed their progress with the delight a man has for a joke which it is not polite to laugh at openly. He heard of their legal setbacks with incredulity. He waited with confidence for their rebound from defeat and followed their prompt, brisk conquests of the law with admiration. He read of their redoubled success with delight. He grinned happily over the inevitable.

When he turned to his own affairs he saw his situation with the same joy. Accident had given him a stake in life, a rich starting point. He was launched in the harness-making business. Farmers would always need harness. He was located in a farm area. Plenkin would fail, it was just a matter of time. Plenkin was doomed. Like the others, the railroads had doomed him. He had not the slightest inkling that he must use the railroads, that they could make him rich instead of putting him out of business.

It was obvious to Job that he must buy harness, not make it. The days of making were over. The days of little men were done. He planned happily. Plenkin would fail. Before the failure was complete he must somehow get the shop and start his fortune.

He had become indispensable. Plenkin had aged. He had worked a long time. The time was spent. The man was spent. He was obsolete. He was worn out.

This year Job received the first letter he had ever gotten in his life. It was from his eldest sister, Liza. The grandmother was dying. Job arrived too late. Liza greeted Job wordlessly. She put her arms clumsily around him. She began to cry. They went together to the old farmhouse in which he had been born and the grandmother had died and they talked for a while of their childhood, they talked dutifully, straining to remember how it had been, how they were to each other.

Liza rose finally. It was very late.

"I'll stay here," Job said diffidently.

Liza's eyes filled.

"You can't stay here, Job," she said protectively. "You come with me. I've got your bed all ready for you. Come on, Job."

"I'd better stay here." Job shook his head. "One of us . . ." He let the sentence trail.

"I've got to go home," Liza apologized. "I've got Tom to look after. . . . But Job—you shouldn't—"

When she was gone Job took a lamp and went from room to room. Occasionally he opened a bare closet. He pulled out a few empty drawers. After a time he tired of this and found a bed to his liking. He sat on the edge of the bed and undressed, dropping his clothes where they fell. When he had stripped to his long underwear he reached for the lamp, raised the chimney, and blew out the flame. He put the lamp on the floor. He sat on the edge of the bed, waiting. His eyes became accustomed to the darkness. He rose and felt his way downstairs. He walked leisurely, without excitement and without any real hope. But when he reached the fireplace his pulse quickened. It was quite possible that Liza, despite her opportunity, had not been to the hiding brick at all. He removed the brick very carefully. He put his hand into the aperture. He started. His fingers contacted coins and paper. He removed everything. When he was sure no more remained he brought that which he had taken out up the stairs to his room, entered a closet, shut the door, struck a match, and counted it. His eyes glistened. There were one hundred and seventy-eight dollars. He pondered. He separated twelve dollars and a few coins. Then he left the closet, found his trousers, put all the rest in his pockets, and went downstairs again to the fireplace. He put the twelve dollars and the coins in the aperture. With the greatest care he replaced the brick so that all was as it had been. Any of the children could have done this as well. Over and over, times without number, they had explored the grandmother's hiding place. It had been a deliciously frightening game to remove the brick, to count what few coins were in the hiding place, then to replace the brick so carefully that the grandmother had never been aware of their meddling.

Job remembered this as he replaced the brick affectionately, he smiled, remembering it, all the way upstairs. The grandmother was dead. The hiding place was anyone's hiding place now. The money belonged to no one, it belonged to the first person who could arm himself with it. He fell asleep marvelling a little at Liza, that she had not thought to look.

Months later, when the old farm was sold and the money distributed, Job received a letter from Liza. It contained a draft for one hundred and sixty dollars, his share from the sale.

"You remember Grandma's hiding place," Liza wrote. "I opened it but there was only twelve dollars and a few cents in it, the poor soul I guess this was what all she could put by so it was used up in the funeral expenses no sense to divide it."

Job waited a week, then took his hoard to the bank.

"Looks like quite a deposit," Purvis Benjamin said, strolling to the teller's window.

"Yes, sir, Mr. Benjamin." Job grinned. He expunged the grin decorously. "My grandmother," he said soberly. "God rest her."

"I'm sorry," Mr. Benjamin said piously.

"Very old," Job deprecated.

"We all have to go."

"Yes, sir. All of us."

"Ah, well."

The teller pushed the deposit book through the window grille.

"Money belongs in the bank," Job said virtuously.

"Drop in any time," Benjamin said warmly. "Any time at all."

He watched Job pass through the bank doors. "How much'd he put in?" he asked.

"Little over three hundred dollars."

Benjamin licked his lips. He thought about three hundred dollars.

"That's the way to do it," he said aloud. He looked about the bank a moment. He turned and walked to the back, to his office.

Job, who had kept out twenty-five dollars, walked directly to Potter's Furnishings. It was a large sum of money and he proposed to be extravagant. He bought two new shirts and four pairs of socks, three neckties and a pair of yellow shoes with mother-of-pearl buttons.

"I guess I'll buy a suit," he said diffidently. He looked up. The salesgirl was not listening. She was smoothing her hair back and looking over his shoulder. Job turned to see what male she was tidying herself for. It was not a man. Standing a few aisles away, looking discontentedly about her, was a brunette young woman, a beautiful woman, shapely, dressed as few Milletta girls ever managed to dress, even on Sundays.

Job stared respectfully.

The salesgirl left him and hurried to the young woman.

"I'll be right with you, Miss Bushwah," she stammered. "I'll be with you in just a minute—"

The young woman looked about her languidly.

"I am in no hurry," she pronounced carefully. She bent her head in a little nod, half bow, and turned away.

"Isn't she wonderful?" the salesgirl whispered, flustered. "She must have just got in."

"Who is it?" Job demanded.

"Who is it? Why, it's Weeda Bushwah, that's who! Francis Bushwah's daughter."

"Bushwah?"

"The druggist! That's his daughter. Spends most of her time in

Cleveland," the girl said reverently. "Look at her. Look at her dress, look at her hair. That's style! Nobody hardly dares talk to her. She knows everything. . . . Just look at that dress . . ."

Job stared.

"What do you call her Bushwah for?" he demanded. "Why don't you call her—"

"Because that's her name!" the girl whispered fiercely. "Don't ever let her hear you pronounce it any other way!"

"Her pa's name is Boor-goys. Everybody calls him Boor-goys—"

"You better not let her hear you! That's all! It's a French name. B-o-u-r-g-e-o-i-s. Bushwah. That's how to pronounce it. She told me herself. She gets awful mad if you don't. Isn't it wonderful? Her first name is Ida. One day she put an Ou in front of it and changed it to Ouida. Weeda Bushwah! Isn't that just like her? Isn't she wonderful? What else did you say you wanted?" She looked apprehensively at the waiting Ouida Bourgeois' back.

"I want a suit." Job's face brightened. He glanced covertly at the young woman. "I want a suit," he said loudly.

They walked to the suit rack.

"Size thirty-six! That's me! Perfect thirty-six!"

"Shh!" the girl hissed. She looked quickly toward Ouida Bourgeois.

"The only thing I can't figure out is what color!" Job continued loudly. "What I need is somebody with a good idea in color. Somebody who really knows!"

Miss Bourgeois stirred slightly.

"We haven't got but so many colors," the girl said, looking at Job angrily.

He jogged the girl with his elbow.

"Ask her!" he whispered. "Go on!"

The girl stared at him, scandalized.

Job walked to Ouida Bourgeois.

"I beg your pardon, Miss Bushwah," he addressed her back. She turned slowly. She looked through Job. "I want to beg a favor of you. Your taste—you understand. I want to ask you a favor . . ."

"This is Job Marsh." The salesgirl came forward, crimson. "He moved here while you were away. Works for Plenkin." She looked at Ouida, beseeching pardon for him, then glared at Job.

Ouida inclined her head slightly.

"I understand your name is Bushwah," Job said ingratiatingly. "Glad to meet you. My name is Job Marsh. I work for Plenkin. I heard about you. I got to buy me a suit, I'd like to ask you a favor, no offense meant."

Ouida raised her eyebrows, then raised her chin slowly, looked at Job and waited. One of her subjects, the female, stammered:

"He wants to ask you what color suit, Miss Bushwah."

"That's right." Job looked at Ouida cheerfully. "I guess we need an expert."

The salesgirl trembled. But without a word Ouida led the way to the suit rack. She eyed Job as though he were a post she intended to paint. She inspected the suits.

"This one," she said slowly.

"That one?" asked Job.
"That one."
"It's gray—"
"You should wear gray. You should wear gray always. It's in good taste. It is also a very spiritual color."
"Won't go with those yellow pointed shoes you bought," the salesgirl said spitefully.
"No," said Ouida. "No yellow shoes."
"Anything you say, Miss Bushwah. Grateful for your opinion. Put myself right in your hands. Grateful for the chance."
Ouida smiled reluctantly, she was so pleased she could not help herself, she smiled a full, warm smile of approval on him. And Job blinked and had the sense to be silent.
"It is my pleasure," Ouida said gravely.
The clothes he bought were put back. She selected others. She was very happy.
Thus Job Marsh and Ouida Bourgeois encountered each other. In Milletta the encounter was mildly mouthed and briefly pondered among the minutiae of the day's happenings. Ouida's father mentioned it that evening, and her mother apologetically recalled all that was known of Job Marsh. The attention was minor and passing. But Ouida felt invaded. She was alarmed, then irritated. She desired to punish, to strike back and at the same time to amaze and be justified. She looked at Job Marsh with interest. As an instrument he was an unlikely human. This quickened her. She was bored. Her speculation, always quixotic, became resolve, and decision forthwith made her project reasonable. She decided to take up Job Marsh, to show Milletta's clods what a being so superior as she could create of a thing so completely unlikely, so entirely and remotely inferior as Job Marsh.
Thereafter they met frequently. They took decorous walks. She talked extensively and Job listened. He was as obedient as possible. She corrected him endlessly. He admired her the more. Her culture amazed him. He considered her as valuable as a diamond ring. Her good looks and her appearance bemused him. He waited cheerfully for the day when he could begin by taking her hand. Meanwhile he kept scrupulously on his good behavior.
"You're so different, Miss Bushwah," Job said once. "How do you account for how different you are?"
She stopped walking then and turned and faced him.
"You couldn't have said a nicer thing," she said slowly.
"Well, it's true," he shrugged.
"All my life I've wanted to be different. I look about me and the humans I see disgust me."
"Me too."
"I believe there is a God in each of us. Do you believe in God, Mr. Marsh?"
"God? Oh, sure. I don't go to church much—"
"Of course you do. Deep down there is something very spiritual in you. I can feel it . . . There's a God in each of us, I believe that." She opened her mouth to speak, then closed it. Opened her lips again: "I

wonder, sometimes—perhaps some of us have a little more God in us than others . . ."

"I think so," he said readily. "You bet! I ain't saying—"

"I'm *not* saying—"

"I'm not—"

"So you see we must take care—we must be free—we must be secure—"

"Money!" Job brightened.

"Not money. I've never lacked for money, like you, poor boy! My father gives me what I want. It's not money. It's more."

"I bet you read all the time. Day and night."

"It's not books. I don't have to read. I *know*. It comes to me." She pressed her chest. "It's in me. In myself. I know. I don't know how. I just know."

This was the Ouida Bourgeois, the Ida Boorgoys who, Milletta women were sourly and happily sure, would never find a mate, and this was the Job Marsh from whom they kept their daughters.

For a long time they met thus and she reformed him and shaped him to her heart's content and he proudly accepted her changes and cheerfully bore her contempt and was virtuous with her praises. She was happy to have her subject but she kept him carefully in his role, for all to see. Months later she let him hold her hand, she saw no harm in it. They did not profane their relationship with kisses.

Job waited.

CHAPTER 4

The town of Milletta watched, as it watched all movement, chewed, meditated, watched.

On the farms the days flowed slowly through the countryside and what had been planted grew to be harvested and flowed out in exchange for tokens to buy what had been worn or broken and for new seed to be planted, to be harvested. And in the town, along Main Street, the merchants sent tokens to New York and Chicago in exchange for things which were sent them and which they sold to each other and to the rest of Milletta, adding a sum to the sum they had paid, and thus they paid each other what they had earned from each other and thus they survived, and in the town the days flowed quietly also.

The life of Milletta was a day and then another day, a birth and a birth, a death and a death, and the mechanics of their survival was that each man bought of the other what he needed and sold the seller what he needed and ate and slept and was housed and procreated and this was each man's purpose. The two lawyers of Milletta untangled the community's quarrels, the doctors mended the sick, the priests of Milletta guarded the customs and once a week were vigilant to raise the question of an old fear.

One day in late fall Plenkin fell from his bench to the floor. He lay there unconscious, his lips blue, breathing the hard sounds of an old man. Job ran for Dr. Kellogg.

"He should never be working," Dr. Kellogg said angrily, kneeling beside Plenkin.

"I've told him, I've begged him!" Job said eagerly. "Is he bad, Doctor? Is he real bad?"

"Got any relatives?" Dr. Kellogg opened his bag. He began to fit the parts of a syringe together.

"I don't think so. I never heard of any. Maybe . . . Maybe in the old country."

"Ever do this before? Fall over?"

"No, never. But he goes slower and slower. All of a sudden the last few months he's almost come to a stop. He's got rheumatism, he says. In his shoulder."

"Yes—" Dr. Kellogg dissolved a pill and drew the fluid into the syringe—"I know that rheumatism. In the shoulder!"

"Gets so bad he can't move. 'Take it easy,' I told him. 'I'll do the work. Stay home a few days a week.' He's got to work. That's how he is. Every day. Pain so bad he can't move his left arm."

"Heart." Dr. Kellogg jabbed the needle into Plenkin's arm.

"In the shoulder?" Job queried, awed.

"In the shoulder. And he's through. He's through working."

Plenkin opened his eyes. He peered at them dimly. He wondered where he was.

"There he is!" cried Job. "He's awake!" He bent down. "You hear that, Mr. Plenkin? You've got to stop like I've been begging you. You've got to stop working! Here's the doctor!"

The old man's eyes had been dim. Fear cleared them. He grunted and tried to rise. Dr. Kellogg pushed him back.

"Can you get him home?" he asked Job. He turned to Plenkin. "You lie still, now. You're all right. You've had a little attack."

The going forth of Plenkin through the front door of his shop, supported into a buggy by Job and Dr. Kellogg, the driving home, all was watched by Milletta, by as many as could see, staring from their shops, peering from their windows, a working animal fallen, one of their number, felled by age, unable to battle for survival any longer, surviving still but his future not in his hands but in the hands of fortune and chance, the issue over, decided, the span ended, led forth from his shop, on his way home. They watched with pity and dread and excitement and fear and gratitude. Not them, not yet them, it was Plenkin, not them, not, not, not yet. They muttered uneasily, they went back to work harder at their task of exchanging with one another that which they needed for survival.

Plenkin was forced to bed and Dr. Kellogg gave him a sedative. He closed his eyes and slept.

"He'll want to get up and work tomorrow," Job warned.

"Not him. Not tomorrow. No relatives at all?"

"That close? Really that close, Doc?"

"You can't tell. He's an old man. He's been going on habit, not body. The machine's gone. One thing—he's through."

"I'll take care of him."

The doctor walked to the door.

"Just keep him quiet."

"How you gonna keep him from getting up and going to work?"

"His body will keep him. If he wakes up give him one of those pills. I'll be by tomorrow."

He clucked to his horse and drove off.

Job walked to Plenkin's bedside and stood for a while watching him curiously. Then he let himself quietly out and walked back through the late afternoon sunlight to the shop.

He entered by the back door. He stood for a moment in the gloom. He began a slow and methodical tour of the small premises. He inspected everything. At the cash drawer he took out the money, stacked it abstractedly, counted it, put it back. He looked about the shop again. He sighed. His time had come.

He put on his coat, left the shop, hired a rig. Two hours later he was in earnest conference with Eric Seltzer, proprietor of a harness shop in nearby Pocanic. Seltzer listened, blinking. Job finished. Seltzer shook his head.

"Why don't I just wait until he dies and then step in and buy—and *then* buy?"

"Might be ten years." Job grinned affably. "On the other hand if he died tomorrow there's others want it. Maybe you'd get it—maybe you wouldn't. Maybe you wouldn't like the price."

"Hell!" Seltzer said with finality. "He won't sell! He won't sell to anybody! I've tried four times before ever you got here."

"He'll sell to me."

"He won't sell to anybody."

"All I have to do is quit him."

"I don't think so."

"To him it'd be different. Not like to a stranger."

"I don't like it."

"What don't you like?"

"It ain't businesslike."

"You want the business?"

"I don't like the way I got to go out on a limb to get it."

"Look, Mr. Seltzer. I come here with a fair proposition. I could have gone to Quarles at Roundtree, or Ames at Los Santos. They'd have jumped at what I'm trying to hand you on a silver platter. I've told you how things are and I've told you how you can get a prosperous, going harness business at less'n it'd cost you for the worst farm in the county. Now there it is, take it or leave it. Maybe it won't work at all. Only remember—I came to you first."

"Let me hear you tell it again."

"All right. First you sign my note."

"Why don't you get the money from the bank yourself?" Seltzer cried suddenly.

"I'm too young," Job said detachedly.

"I seen other fellows younger'n you get loans to go into business," Seltzer said virtuously.

"Fellows known, maybe. Not fellows only been in town long as me. Maybe the bank knew their family. Anyway, I already sounded them out."

"How?"

"Little ways. Words here and there."

"Yup," said Seltzer, satisfied. "All right, then. I sign your note."

"You sign my note and the bank gives me the money and I buy the business—"

"In your name," Seltzer said indignantly.

"That's the only name Plenkin's going to sell to. But it'll be your business. On the quiet I turn over the profits to you. Out of the profits I take my salary, ten dollars a week, plus ten percent of the net—which is what I get for running the place and thinking up this arrangement and handing it to you on a silver platter. Someday the old man'll die. Maybe it'll be today, maybe it'll be ten years from today. But when that happens we put a new sign over the store: 'Seltzer & Co.' And there's where I got to rely on you. I got to rely on you not to fire me the minute you take over. All I got's your word."

"I'm not worrying about *my* word. What I want to know is what assurance have I got you'll step out when the old man dies? My God, boy! I don't know even what I'm sitting here talking to you for!"

"Make it a demand note—"

"What's to prevent you turning around and selling the shop and paying off the note?"

"And suppose I did? What would you be out?"

Seltzer licked his lips.

"We could sign a paper," he said. "We could do that."

"What for would we sign a paper, Mr. Seltzer?" Job asked coldly.

"I need *some* protection!" Seltzer exploded. "What do you think I am! Anything could happen to you! Anything! Now, look. Let's look at it this way. We could sign a paper—just between ourselves—absolutely secret—setting down all we talked about. That way you know, and I know, and we both know. That way we're protected. You, as well as me."

"A paper—" Job stared at him.

"Just a private agreement, a contract between you'n me nobody ever need hear of."

"You know what that kind of paper would be, Mr. Seltzer?" Job said in a hushed voice. "You realize you're asking me to set my name to a conspiracy to defraud? And you're going to set your name to it too?"

"And who'd know about it?"

"No, sir, Mr. Seltzer! Not me! I don't want anything illegal. I thought there was a chance here for both of us to make an honest dollar. A fellow has to look out for himself in this world. But no illegal business. No sir! I don't go into anything like that!"

He rose. He forced a smile.

"Well," he said, "it's been a pleasure—"

"Where you off to?"

"I got to get back. I want to stop in Milford."

Abel Smith owned a harness shop in Milford.

"Just take it easy," Seltzer said irritably. "Sit down! You come in here like a clap of thunder, put a proposition, and run off before a man can think."

Job did not sit down.

"You want the store, Mr. Seltzer?"

"Certain, I want the store!"

Job said nothing. He waited.

"What's your proposition?" Seltzer demanded at last.

"I've just told you."

"Well, tell me again."

Job told him again. When he had finished, Seltzer fell to thinking.

"I got to have some kind of paper," he said finally.

"What kind of paper?"

"Something that says the place is mine and not yours. Something that says in name only."

"What the hell kind of paper can I give you! Excuse me, Mr. Seltzer, but just tell me that. What kind of paper wouldn't be conspiracy to defraud?"

Seltzer gnawed his knuckles.

"Let's go over it again," he said.

"You think about it." Job shook his head. "You just think about it," he said wearily. "I've got to get back before I'm missed." He turned toward the door.

"How about you giving me a note?"

"I'm already giving you a note."

But Seltzer's face had cleared.

"I've got it," he cried. "Now I've got the way out."

Job watched him warily.

"You give me a note, you understand—"

"I'm already giving you a note!"

"All right. That note. I mean another note. A note saying you owe me the shop."

"Another demand note—?" Job parried.

But Seltzer swept on triumphantly. "You might drop dead after all. You might run away, you might—God knows what can't happen to you. That's what I'm trying to get at. But if you give me this *second* demand note doesn't matter what happens. If anything happened to you or you just happened to change your mind or anything, I present the second note—and I'm protected."

Long before he finished Job was waiting.

"Sounds all right," he shrugged. He thought a moment. "All right with me, if that's what you want . . ."

"Certain—that's all I've been trying to make you see—now how about it?"

Job pretended to muse a moment.

"Right!" he decided. "All right, Mr. Seltzer! That's the way we'll do it, then!"

They shook hands happily.

Plenkin was conscious when Job returned. Job had brought with him the day's receipts and the account books. He busied himself with these. Plenkin watched.

"Vant paper, pencil," he said after a while.

In his bed Plenkin scrawled laboriously. Job watched him. He was tense with the day's happenings.

"Vant envelope," Plenkin said.

Plenkin addressed and sealed the envelope. He let it lie on the bed. He pondered. Finally he picked it up and handed it to Job.

"Go mail," he said. "Mail in morning."

In the morning men drifted in from other stores along Main Street to hear what had happened. With each Job shook his head wryly.

"Plenkin wants to work—Doc Kellogg says no. Plenkin's bound to work. Doc says if he does—" Job paused, let the sentence drop delicately. He smiled ruefully. "Seems like a fellow's got to know when to quit." He sighed. He shook his head.

At noon the shop was empty and he took the letter to the back shop and examined the envelope. It was addressed to a Mrs. Thaddeus Mikulicz. Plenkin never wrote letters. Job weighed the letter. He struggled with temptation. He desired mightily to scan the pages, even though it was written in a foreign language. Virtuously he put the temptation from him. He opened the door of the stove and tossed the letter into the fire.

During the next week Plenkin tried twice to get out of bed to go to work. Each time Job had to summon the doctor. Plenkin now lay in bed and stared at the counterpane in silence. He was at bay and he knew that he was at bay. He knew that Job knew it. Job had been too polite, too anxious to serve him. Plenkin waited for the inevitable.

"About time you stopped work, ain't it, Mr. Plenkin?" Job said diffidently one night.

He tried to get out of bed. Job held him back. Next morning, after Job had gone, Plenkin tried again. When Job returned from the shop at noon he found him lying on the floor. This time Dr. Kellogg offered no anger. He said only that if Plenkin did this again he must get another doctor. The door closed firmly behind him.

"What do you think we ought to do about the shop, Mr. Plenkin?" Job asked anxiously.

"Pretty soon voman come. Take care of me. I write granddaughter."

"All right. Fine. Who takes care of me?"

"You young, strong fella."

"Now's the time I got to look out for myself. I got to do something, Mr. Plenkin."

There was a silence.

"Vot you vant?" Plenkin asked finally.

"Sell me the shop."

"Sell? You crazy!"

"Sell me the shop and I'll run it and give you ten percent of what I make. You can live on that and rest and get back on your feet."

"Don't talk no more!"

There was silence again.

"Vair you get money buy shop?"

"The bank'll lend me."

"You crazy!"

"They'll lend it."

"I never sell shop. Never!"

"I know you'd never sell to anybody else. I've lived with you long enough. I know that."

"I give you job—I give you place sleep—"

"Mr. Plenkin, I'm going to tell you something. Do you know what the doctor says?"

Plenkin tried to raise himself from the pillow. He failed, tried again, sank back.

"I never sell shop!" He said it with finality.

"That's all right." Job nodded. "I worked for you pretty hard, Mr. Plenkin. But that's all right."

"You vait. You vork shop, voman come take care for me, you vait."

"I'm going to work for Seltzer, Mr. Plenkin. Over in Pocanic. I'm sorry. I wish you the best of luck. I'll go over and see him tomorrow."

Plenkin said nothing. Job returned to the shop.

That night he brought home a contract by which Plenkin agreed to sell him the shop for $1,500. He read it to Plenkin. He laid it on the bed. Next morning he dressed in his best clothes and packed his carpetbag.

"Here's the keys, Mr. Plenkin." Job put them on the bureau. "I hope you get someone to run the shop for you real soon. I want to thank you for everything you've done for me." He smiled politely, picked up his carpetbag, and started for the door. He reached the door and opened it. He was over the threshold.

"I sign," Plenkin muttered tiredly.

When Purvis Benjamin saw Job enter the bank and walk directly toward his office he smiled grimly. When a young man was sparking a girl he generally wanted a horse and carriage.

"What can I do for you?" he asked, trying to estimate how much of a horse and carriage a fellow like Job might want to court a girl like Ouida Bourgeois.

"I want to borrow fifteen hundred dollars."

Benjamin blanched.

"Fifteen hundred dollars! What kind of a rig—you want to borrow fifteen hundred dollars?"

"I'll tell you, Mr. Benjamin. Very confidentially. I want to buy out Mr. Plenkin."

"You want to borrow fifteen hundred dollars to buy out Plenkin—how's he feeling?"

"No better. Worse. I want fifteen hundred dollars."

"Andreas Plenkin selling out—?"

"To me."

"Never!"

Job opened the contract of sale, smoothed it, laid it on the desk between them.

"I never, I never. No sir, I never."

"I'll have to know, Mr. Benjamin."

"And you want fifteen hundred dollars. No sir, I never . . . Well, let's see. Got that much inventory?"

"Say about seven hundred. And there's the good will."

"The good will . . . Yes, of course . . . No . . . not fifteen hundred . . ."

"How much?"

"I'll tell you. Let's see now . . . Yes, that's just about it—you can have seven hundred."

Job picked up the agreement of sale, folded it carefully, put it carefully in his pocket.

"Going to Tyre won't do you any good," Benjamin said earnestly. "I don't care, but I doubt they'd let you have that much. Local business. I'm stretching it. But an out-of-town bank—"

"That's all right. That's about how I figured. Forget that. Now suppose somebody signs my note for $1500. Seltzer, say, over in Pocanic."

"All right! You got a contract of sale. Now, how you going to protect yourself from Seltzer? Do you know why he's willing to sign your note?"

"He's going to try to take the shop away from me."

"That's exactly what he's gonna do. He's been trying to get that shop for years."

"I kind of figured maybe you'd give me a little protection . . ."

"Any deal you go into with him you need protection!"

"Yes, sir."

"You can make a go of it, can't you?"

Job grinned.

"That's right. I don't know what Plenkin would have done without you. If Seltzer figures to pick it off like a grape off the bush maybe this time he's overreached himself. You're young, you see. He figures on that. . . . Think you can keep up your payments?"

Job grinned.

Benjamin nodded.

"No reason why not. I'll back you. Personally. Here's a form. Get it signed—"

Job produced a note, endorsed by Seltzer.

"Lend me your pen," he said briefly.

Thus Job at eighteen became the owner of his own harness shop. Now his days were endless. He worked indefatigably. He cut prices. No labor was too small or too trivial for him, and what he did he did with enormous cheerfulness. The shop bustled. Business swelled. There was never any doubt of his success. He had not even a small failure. He never gave failure a chance.

A week after Job became the owner of the shop Seltzer drove over from Pocanic. He entered the shop victoriously, called Job, and scanning the interior, ordered changes. Job listened patiently.

"Now, where's the books? Let's see the books," Seltzer commanded.

"You don't care about that," Job said diffidently.

"Let's see the books!" Seltzer frowned.

"There's something you'd better understand, Mr. Seltzer. This is my shop. Mine . . ."

"*Your* shop—!"

"That's right, Mr. Seltzer. I own it. You signed my note for $1500. And I bought the shop. The bank'll get its money regular."

Seltzer gasped. His face reddened.

"You told me—why, you know perfectly well what our deal was, you little thief! What are you trying to pull? Now you get the hell out of here! Go on! Git!"

"Maybe you got something says I got to get out of here? Says you own this shop? Is that it, Mr. Seltzer?"

"I don't propose to argue with you. I've got a paper signed by you agreeing to turn this shop over to me, agreeing to pay me fifteen hundred —demand note—I demand it! I demand it, right now! Now don't waste my time. Just get out."

"That agreement, Mr. Seltzer—that demand note—it ain't worth the paper it's written on. I'm sorry. But that's the way it goes. Business is business."

"I've got your signature—"

"You've got my signature to an agreement. And not a dollar changed hands with that agreement and no agreement's worth a cent unless both of us get something out of it. To say nothing about me being a minor."

The bank note was slowly and regularly paid off. Job Marsh who at eighteen had forced Plenkin to sell him his beloved shop, who had forced the Milletta Bank to put up the money, who had outwitted Seltzer into signing a note which gave Job the shop Seltzer wanted was now and henceforth a Milletta prodigy. He was a prodigy and he was feared and his saga was wonder.

It was the way things were properly done in the world, the manner in which a man justified his parents and his upbringing and his schooling, the way he survived, the way his survival became a model for his community. It made true all the maxims man had invented and most of the reasons he had decided upon for his presence on the planet. It was an occasion for chattering.

That which followed happened obviously and logically and tribally. Plenkin grew stronger and able to care for himself, and Job moved to a boardinghouse. Another month passed and now the shop was running smoothly. As he sold harness Job replaced it with merchandise bought from the cities. He used his personal funds. He no longer made harness. He bought harness cheaper than he could make it. He sold service. He worked long hours at repairs, and in time the shop's work product, always behind because new harness had to be made and repairs effected concurrently, became available very promptly. He began to draw trade from farmers waiting on other harness shops.

At this time, arriving at the shop early one morning, he found Plenkin there before him. Plenkin was waiting for the shop to be opened. He stood stolidly outside the back door. He had been thin before his attack, now he was emaciated and quite bent.

"Vant to vork," he stated.

Job grinned a welcome.

"Why, sure, Mr. Plenkin! Come right on in! Guess you know your way around," he chuckled.

He put his arm around the old man's shoulders. He was Plenkin's blood brother in one clear respect. They loved work, their days were modelled on it and shaped to it faithfully. Job understood completely. The old man wanted exactly what he stated. He wanted to work, he could not live without it. He was adrift in a lonely world, terrifying and crazing; with work between his hands, the thoughts of work all his thoughts, there came order and comfort and a morrow without chaos. In the shop Plenkin did not even look about him to see what Job had done, what changes he had made. He found his bench, he sat down, he pulled a hame strap to him, he began to work immediately. He worked silently, greedily, all that day. The day ended. They stood outside the shop as Job locked up. Then Plenkin lifted his head and peered at Job.

"Come tomorrow?" the old man asked hopefully.

It is true that Job was in many ways different from other men in Milletta, but he had one characteristic which made him different from most men, everywhere. He never in all his life hated those to whom he had done an injury. He treated them just as he treated everyone else.

He smiled at Plenkin, smiled fondly.

"You bet!" he said protectively. "You come tomorrow and next day—whenever you feel like it—"

"Feel good."

"You work here all you please."

When this month ended he paid Plenkin the very salary he used to receive from him. But when the next month came he shook his head.

"I want to keep you, but you'll have to help me."

Plenkin bowed his head to hide the fear in his eyes.

"Vant to vork," he said humbly.

"I know it. But I got bank payments to make. I hadn't figured on paying any salaries. And on top of that I got to keep paying you ten percent. Pretty soon it'll be ten percent of nothing. We're in this together. See what I mean?"

Plenkin looked up at Job, waiting.

"What am I going to do?" Job asked ruefully.

Thereafter, Plenkin signed a release foregoing the ten percent due him from the business. Job raised his wages a dollar a week. Plenkin worked on. He worked feebly. He now worked for Job.

Job was on a new footing with Ouida Bourgeois. To her he was no longer young-man clay to be shaped, but adult clay. He spoke with greater assurance.

"A poor old man like that, working," she said one night.

"Plenkin? Why he likes to work! Honestly! He'd be lost if he didn't work! I believe he'd pay me to let him work. I'm actually doing him a favor."

"I have no illusions about you. You live in a jungle. You do no one any favors."

Job grinned happily. He knew this was as far as Ouida could go in acknowledging his victory.

"You live in another world, Ouida," he said mildly. "I'd like to live in the kind of world you live in, too. Somebody's got to bring home the bacon."

Ouida was mollified.

"Straighten your tie," she said. "Why do you wear such ties?"

"Pretty, ain't it?" Job grinned.

"Really, Job!"

"Isn't."

He moved closer to her on the porch swing.

"I've got a book I want you to read. I want you to study it from cover to cover." She produced a slim volume.

"I read that book. You gave it to me two months ago. Ruskin, isn't it? Hell. I can't make out what he's talking about!"

"This is not Ruskin, Job. And please don't be a boor. I don't tolerate profanity. This is Emerson. And I want you to read him."

Job hefted the book.

"Like Ruskin?" he asked with distaste.

Ouida controlled her irritation.

"I'll make it easy for you," she said. "I'll read you a little."

She opened the book. She began to read melodramatically. She gestured. She paused frequently to peer at Job to see the effect of her reading and Emerson's prose. She tried to make her tone thrilling. She endeavored to make her voice throb with impact. She became excited.

Job put his arm around her waist. He had never done this before. She did not notice.

"You see?" she cried. "You see?"

Job crossed his legs.

"I never realized—" he said unevenly.

She soared on. The words excited her. The spirituality of her enterprise swept her away. She was moved deeply. She was exalted. Her senses quivered. Job put his hand on her knee. Infinitely slowly he began to caress her thigh.

"Now, Job," she said gently.

She looked at him, her eyes moist. His eyes met hers hungrily. Inexplicably, her lips raised and offered to him. He seized her. His mouth devoured her. His hands explored her greedily. Impatiently one hand was suddenly on the bare flesh of her thigh, caressing, moving upward. His body leaned upon her. He freed a hand for an instant to lift one leg in the hammock.

Dazed, her body clamoring, blood pounding thickly, she drew away and pulled herself upright.

"Job! Job, dear . . . don't . . ."

Job forced his eyes to focus. They blurred again. His nostrils widened. There rose above them thickly the odor of her femininity, of her body. He reached for her tentatively, again.

"No . . . no, Job . . . no more . . ."

"We'll get married," he said thickly. "Let's get married, Ouida. Come on."

She pressed his hand. She bent and kissed his cheek.

"Go home now. Go home and let me think."

He rose. He noticed the volume of Emerson on the seat. He put it in his pocket. It had served once and it might serve again.

For hours that night Ouida sifted what had happened. At the beginning of her thinking she trembled at the thought that her body had moved her, that she had surrendered to her body. The thought accused her. Suddenly it was plain. She sighed with relief. It was Emerson. Her body and Job's body had been made incarnate with the spirit, lifted with the spirit, moved into the unknowable, soared into the apogee of spirituality. He must then be her soul mate. Their marriage, then, was inevitable. She knew it must be. He was a boor, a conventional Milletta bumpkin, uncouth, a grinning lecher, a ruthless and unscrupulous pillager, without any moral sense, blatant, loud, tasteless. These things he was, standing beside the dim and vague outlines of her ideal man, her ideal of that which was man.

But men were crude clay. And they were clay. And somewhere in this man was a great, a dizzying, a marvelling, an unsuspected ocean of the mighty spirit. Around that incredible fund, that greatest of funds, she could build, she could shape the clay. The world would bow before her in admiration. Given the spirit, everything was possible. Someday he would dream greatly. She would hold him by her side. She would comfort him. She would plan with him. She would direct him slowly, surely upward, ever upward, to the empty throne beside her, to reign with her. Her body shivered at the memory of his hands. She said her prayers with fervor. She slept deeply.

⋆ CHAPTER 5

When they were married it was almost, for Job, like winning another shop. He had now acquired Ouida, all of her. And all of her was of great worth, a prize. He knew she was passionate. He felt that her face and her figure would ornament any man living. He knew she was reckoned far above any woman in Milletta for her taste, her manners, her graces, her mind. It was a tremendous acquisition. And he was very fond of her.

He was not unkind, he was far from cruel, he was not unpracticed. But he had waited so long that on their wedding night, on his wedding night, he could not wait. He seized her cold, when they were alone, seized her without preliminary, smothered her mouth with kisses, bore her backward to the bed; her knees touched it and crumpled and he threw himself upon her, he flung up her dress, in an instant he had penetrated her, in another instant he was spent.

He stood and tidied himself abashedly. She smoothed her dress, sat up and looked at him coldly. Her cries of pain and disgust were still wet on her lips.

"I'm sorry," he breathed. "You get me, Ouida."

"You beast!" she cried. She hated him with all her heart. "You filthy boor! You beast!"

"Ah, now, Ouida," he moved toward her, "don't pay any attention to—"

"If you touch me," she said levelly, "if you dare to touch me . . ."
She slept on a sofa that night. He shrugged and waited for time and the next morning and the morning after. And the months. And the years.
Occasionally in the months that followed and became years, when he could artfully exalt her, she opened her thighs to him, delirious as he. Afterward she always repented, he had taken her unawares, he had dragged her down to his level, he had aroused in her the body all men must put down, the body that filthied all that was best and noblest in man's nature, in his holy spirit. She rose shamed, dirtied, angry, and deflowered.
There were not many such occasions, but from one of them Lucas was conceived after they had been married many years and after she had faced fully, large and small, all that Job was and all that he might do.
Her life was a fragmented chaos, an agony of imprecations to Heaven. "Why me?" she would scream. "Why, why, why?"
Meantime, she refuged in whatever avenue of the spiritual presented itself. She explored Buddhism, and Bahai-Ullah, and Fletcherism, she spent hours over a crystal ball sent all the way from Chicago. She delved deeply into Spiritualism and tried to commune with the dead, the dead great, seldom her own parents. She read Emerson and Ruskin and Pater and tried china painting, using spiritual motifs only. She explored the Book of Mormon, the Bhagavad-Gita, the Talmud, she sought spiritual enlightenment on the unknown cipher of Francis Bacon. She had no friends. She kept to herself.
Her hope and her world were now Lucas. She was against meat at this time, with repugnance she cooked it and served it to Job, she fed Lucas and herself only vegetables. She believed in herself as she believed in the right. She believed that she possessed an instinct and an intuition for all knowledge and that what her mind owned was hers because of unshakable faith, pure thoughts, and indomitable will and that these things were so strong in her that she was superior to all life about her. She believed devoutly and humbly in God. It was impossible for her to distinguish between the God she worshipped and the God in her.
When Lucas was six weeks old Ouida brought him to Dr. Alexander.
"He keeps getting thinner," she said reluctantly.
"What does he do, specially? Cry? Cry a lot?"
Asking me a lot of questions, she thought contemptuously to herself. If he's so smart why doesn't he know. Doctors!
"He throws up," she said, looking at the doctor with hostility, the smoldering of one doctor compelled to go to another. "That's what's the matter with him. He gets the best milk. I get it from Potter's, there's nothing better."
"Maybe that's the trouble . . ."
This was idiocy. She forced herself to be patient.
"He won't keep a thing on his stomach." She tried putting it another way.
"Potter's got Jerseys."
The baby began crying thinly.
"Well, what about Jerseys! Look at him. Skin and bone. I thought you could help him. Don't you even want to examine him?"

The doctor took Lucas from her, unwrapped him, patiently and idly went over the small body.

"I'll tell you something about milk, Mrs. Marsh, it's got butterfat and water in it and one thing and another, but—"

"There's no chemicals in the milk I get from Potter's. None. And no water. None. Whatsoever."

"I don't think you understand, Mrs. Marsh—"

"I understand perfectly well. I understand perfectly and completely."

"Then you know Jersey milk is the richest—"

"Precisely!"

"And the fat globules are probably too big for his little stomach to digest—"

"There's nothing the matter with his stomach. It's perfect. I see it as perfect."

"Well, I'm afraid I can't do much for you. My advice is to give him some downright poor milk, thin stuff, maybe Holstein. I think you'd better try that, Mrs. Marsh."

Ouida silently swaddled Lucas, and silently left the office. Her eyes were bright with anger and her lips were thin. She went directly to Potter's dairy.

"I want richer milk than you've been giving me. I want the richest milk you've got," she said coldly.

"Richer?" Mrs. Potter straightened indignantly. "There just ain't any richer! This here is the richest milk there is! Jersey cows don't give down no richer! No cow does!"

Ouida controlled her anger.

"I just thought there was some you kept for yourselves," she said carefully. "Something special—"

"There ain't no special. We drink what you drink. Every mouthful." A thought struck her. "You want more cream in it? We can add some cream . . ."

"That's it! That's it, exactly! From now on give me twice as much cream in every bottle!"

For a week Ouida fed the baby on the richer milk. He ate greedily, vomited, screamed. The next week Ouida fed Lucas almost pure cream. Now he vomited even while he sucked voraciously, screamed, sucked more, vomited, screamed until he was blue. She yearned over him, she hugged him to her fiercely, terror came to her. The child's crying penetrated the house night and day.

"Take him to a doctor," Job fretted. "You don't know everything. Let a doctor see him."

"For your information, I have had him to Dr. Alexander," Ouida said coldly.

Next morning she pushed back an edge of her panic and deafening herself to his cries, holding back her fears, tried to think. She decided on a complete reversal. She skimmed the milk for his feeding. As usual, he fed voraciously. Then he threw up, but only half his feeding. He cried during the day, but now fitfully. He retained at least half of what he had been fed and next day he did not vomit at all. Reassured, Ouida now resumed command of the situation. She added cream. He began to throw up again. She went back to skimmed milk. He stopped throwing up. She added only a few drops of cream. At the end of ten days she had evolved a formula which was approximately that of Holstein milk. The crisis, the trouble, was over. Lucas began to gain weight.

"Looks good, don't he!" Job chuckled.

"Doctors!" Ouida spat contemptuously. "Of course he looks good!"

She was haggard. She had lost weight with the child. Her nights had been sleepless. Her mouth was wried with torture, she held the child to her desperately, protectively. But in her fatigue-reddened, drawn black eyes was invincibility.

"Mrs. Marsh don't hold much with doctors," Job told Milletta proudly. "She's a doctor all by herself. By God, you should have seen what she did with that kid of ours!"

He was very proud of Ouida. He admired her profoundly.

"Nothing she can't do she sets her mind to. And not just do it, mind you—be in a class all by herself! Nothing, by God! Just nothing! Beats anything I ever saw!"

Ouida withdrew into her private world, which was peopled by herself and the baby, Lucas. She poured out upon the child love and hungry affection. While he slept she read to him from Emerson. He was housebroken at six months. His toys were picture books, not of kittens and red barns, but of great masterpieces of painting. When he was one year old she began to teach him table manners, holding his small hands in hers, guiding him resolutely through those digital maneuvers of replenishment which the primate had decided were prideworthy. Her patience was limitless. The child was her entire life. They inhabited a world of their own, removed from the world about them by the distance of their superiority and the spirituality of their aim. When he asked questions she was beside herself with joy. She spent hours answering a single question. She delighted in the sound of her voice, in the manner in which she was at all times ready to fill his slightest intellectual need. She loved him with all her heart. She would very cheerfully have died for him.

When he was three years old Lucas screamed sharply one afternoon and held his hand to his ear. His agony was beyond moral suasion and Ouida took him reluctantly to Dr. Dwyer.

"Mastoids," Dr. Dwyer said briefly. "May have to operate."

"You'll not lay a finger on this child. He's not going to be cut—"

"May have to. Looks bad. We'll see. Get some rubber tubing with a small catheter and run hot water into his ear—at least once every hour. That means every hour. Night and day. Once an hour. Try it. We'll see."

"How hot?" Ouida's face was white.

"Be very careful. Test it like his milk. Now, don't let it be too hot. Because here's where it's going . . ."

He drew from his bookcase an anatomy book and opened a page to the anatomy of the ear.

Ouida looked impatiently at the maze of red and blue lines and colors.

"I know, I know!" she said curtly.

She rushed the child home. Faithfully, every hour of the day Ouida douched Lucas' ear with hot water. Every hour during the night she rose, went to his bedside, ministered to him. On the fourth day she was stumbling with fatigue. She leaned against doorways, her eyes closed, sleeping for seconds. She would arouse herself as she stood at the stove, cooking, finding she had been asleep. At about two o'clock of the morning of the fifth day she failed to hear Lucas crying. This time she was in a near-coma. At three o'clock the cries penetrated her semiconsciousness, she lumbered groggily to her feet. She stumbled to the kitchen, reeled, boiled water. Dazedly she filled the hot-water bag. She lumbered into the room where he lay screaming.

"Now, darling, now . . . Mother's here," she said thickly.

She fumbled the tube into his ear. She held him so he could not move. She released the stopcock. The water, boiling hot, rushed upon the painfully inflamed membranes of the child's inner ear. He emitted a prodigious scream, without pause a series of maniacal almost adult shrieks. His body convulsed out of her grasp. She held him tighter, forced the tube in deeper. The scalding water flowed on. Suddenly on the threshold of her numb brain black realization loomed, she shrieked, faint with horror. She jerked out the tube. Now he sobbed endessly, his head rolled from side to side. Ouida wept helplessly. She crushed him to her breast, she crooned over him, she cried and could not stop. She writhed to tear herself, to kill herself.

Stumbling, barely able to see because of her tears, she ran with the child to her bedroom. Job was sleeping deeply. She roused him. He ran for Dr. Dwyer. She sat down on the edge of the bed, folding the child to herself, kissing his feet, sobbing, imploring.

Dr. Dwyer peered into Lucas' ear. He injected slowly a little warm oil. Lucas continued to sob, occasionally to cry out, then to resume sobbing.

"I don't know," said Dr. Dwyer. "I can't tell. He may be deaf for life."

Ouida closed her eyes, her body leaned to oblivion. Job stepped to her side, put his arm about her.

"You can't tell, though, can you?" he said determinedly. "Too soon to tell about a thing like that, could have happened to anyone . . ."

"Don't know," said Dr. Dwyer. "I was trying to avoid operating. One-in-a-hundred chance. Now—" He shrugged.

"Can't tell!" insisted Job.

The doctor nodded cooperatively.

"We'll see . . ."

"You did your best," Job said when the doctor had gone. "Don't worry. Get some sleep."

Ouida wrenched free from his comforting arm.

"What do you know about it!"

"It's all right, Ouida—"

"Sleep! That's all an animal like you can think of! Sleep!"

She sat by Lucas' bed the rest of the night. She stroked his forehead. Her touch was infinitely light. She talked to him in a barely audible voice.

"You're going to be all right," she said over and over. "Mother's here, darling . . . mother's right here . . ."

After a while Lucas slept. She crouched beside him, still. She stroked his forehead, gossamer-light, on and on. Her low monotone never ceased. Job got up, tiptoed from the room and went to bed.

Within forty-eight hours Lucas' mastoid inflammation was mending. Two days later he was almost well. In a month it was as if he had never been troubled. In another month Ouida's life had a new credo.

"He was at death's door," she was to say all the rest of her life, "and by mistake, by the sheerest accident, half dead for sleep, I poured boiling hot water—hotter than boiling—right—into—his—ear! The doctors gave him up. And two days later he was on the mend . . ."

"How do you account for it?" Job asked her once, privately.

She sighed. She shook her head over the immensity between them.

"Did it ever occur to you—can't you possibly comprehend—that I was guided?"

She asked it sighing, a human alone, among strangers.

"You don't have to get sore," Job said, impressed. He looked at her warily, with admiration.

The First World War troubled Milletta only so deeply as had the Spanish-American War some fourteen years previously. For a time it seemed that Job would be drafted. He was at this time a member of the school board, a director of the Chamber of Commerce, and a pew holder in the Methodist Episcopal Church. At the possibility of his being drafted his misgivings became open fear. He was not afraid of fighting nor of privation nor of regimentation. The thought of being killed or wounded never occurred to him. But he had an empire growing, a thing so complex, even though small, that it would collapse the moment he ceased to manipulate it. He turned all his wits to evade the draft. Simultaneously he tried openly, vigorously to obtain a lieutenant's commission.

The war ended before he could be called up. During the early part of the war he made a great deal of money selling harness through his four stores. His profits became enormous. But he never got out of debt. He did not permit this.

Much of the time Lucas felt himself a stranger to his mother and father. They were so unlike. He could be like neither without feeling a traitor to the other. Beyond this problem there was life as he knew it, the things in living that were exciting and important. And these things were entirely different from the important things in the lives of his parents. They were so different that he knew reluctantly he could never explain himself to them.

What he loved, what he needed, he had to seek in some secrecy. It was plain to Lucas that Job and Ouida, each for a different reason, housed a definite antagonism to doctors and the profession of Medicine. There was no doubt of this antagonism. There was no doubt they disapproved.

When he was eight, Dr. Dwyer loaned him an anatomy book, the doctor's own anatomy book, from his own bookshelf. Lucas could not believe the glory of that day. He brought the book home. Holding it reverently he showed his mother the magnificent pages.

"It's very kind of Dr. Dwyer to lend a little boy like you such a valuable book," Ouida said shortly. "Mother could tell you all that," she gestured at the charts. "Now, be very careful that you return it in the same condition you brought it. Put it away, now. It's time for your lessons, Lucas."

He put the book on the table on which his homework was spread. From time to time he glanced covertly at it. At bedtime he brought it to his bedroom, and slept with it. Next afternoon he came directly home and attacked his homework. He worked fiercely. When he was done he had more than a golden hour remaining until supper. He reached hungrily for the anatomy book. He drew it toward him savoring the moment. He opened it. He began to pore over the pages. He was lost, utterly lost.

Ouida watched in silence.

The hour passed.

"Put your book away!" she said sharply.

Job had come home.

Lucas looked up, dazed.

"See what your son is reading," Ouida said shortly.

"What you got, boy?" Job leaned over him to read.

"Doctor Dwyer loaned it to me." Lucas looked up fearfully, hopefully.

"He did, did he?" Job grinned. "Sure it wasn't Dr. Alexander? Or Dr. Kellogg?"

"What do you mean?" Ouida started.

"Oh," said Job, "you've got to watch this fella! He knows every doctor in town!"

"I just run errands for them, sometimes—"

"Say he *does* run errands! And holds their horses and carries their bags, runs from one to the next—anytime you want to find Luke you just call the doctor—any doctor!"

Ouida frowned.

"*That's* why you're so thin—" she began uncertainly, using the first weapon that came into her mind.

"I don't run much, honest!"

Job rumpled Lucas' hair.

"Got to watch him!" he chuckled. "He'll be a doctor before you know it! If you ain't careful!"

Ouida sniffed.

Later that evening when she had put Lucas to bed, she sat on the edge of the bed and stroked his forehead.

"What is this?" she asked softly. "What have you been keeping from Mother?"

"It isn't anything, Mother! Honest!"

"Chasing around after doctors—holding their horses—never telling Mother—"

"I thought you knew—"

"Lucas! Now, that's an untruth! How could Mother know?"

"I don't know. I thought you knew. I've always liked—" It was incredible to him that they were not aware.

"You promised never to keep anything from Mother," Ouida said mechanically. She sensed the power of this claim on Lucas. She considered how to oppose it.

"I didn't keep anything from you! Honest! I thought you knew!"

"How long has this been going on?"

"Ever since I can remember, Mother. When I was little."

"And is this how you spend your days? When you should be studying? Or just being with Mother? Running after doctors?"

"I thought—"

"Answer me!"

"Yes, Mother."

She looked at him, thinking.

"I don't do any harm! Honest! I just—"

"Stop saying 'Honest'!"

"I just like to be with them. And sometimes—"

"What?"

"Just now and then they teach me. When they've got time. Just a minute, now and then. The names of things. And why things happen. And—and—about Medicine—"

"Mother can teach you all those things," Ouida said jealously.

"Yes, Mother."

"Mother knows more than all the doctors!"

"Yes, Mother."

"Why don't you come to me, Lucas? Why don't you ask me?"

"I like the smell around them, I like the instruments, I like the *feeling* around them—I don't know what to ask you—I'd ask you if I knew . . ."

"You don't want to be a public mock, do you?"

"No, Mother."

"Well, just think what people will say about you—about your own mother—when they see you running after doctors all the time, waiting on them hand and foot—"

Nothing definite was said. He examined each sentence carefully. Nothing definite was said. For a while he carefully pruned the time spent lingering around the doctors' offices. He came home earlier.

That night Ouida sought Job.

"How long have you known this was going on?" she demanded.

"God, the whole town knows it! Don't tell me you're just waking up?"

"I have enough to do running this house and wondering where our next cent is coming from and whether you've beggared us between breakfast and the time you come home to keep up with every breath a child draws!"

"Well, don't get mad at me! I haven't done anything. The kid's just doctor-struck, that's all!"

"What are we going to do?"

"What do you mean: 'what are we going to do'?"

"You know *exactly* what I mean!"

"About him chasing the doctors?" He looked at her incredulously. "For Christ's sake, we're going to do nothing! What in the hell do you think we're going to do? Bury him?"

"It may seem nothing to you—I know what comes first with his father, so you needn't tell me—but I'm his mother! I'm interested in the child, strange as it may seem!"

"You ought to be proud of him, then! The docs say he has quite a head on his shoulders. What's the matter with hanging around doctors? You want him hanging around poolrooms?"

"It so happens that my son isn't going to be a doctor."

"Who said he was? Look, Ouida! Kids go through all that. It's a phase, y'understand? Just a phase. Forget it. Leave him alone. Pay no attention to him whatsoever. Let him go his own ways. I know what I'm talking about. Hell, he isn't even in high school yet. By that time he'll want to be an engineer, or a fireman, or Santa Claus! Forget it."

Ouida wavered.

"Don't let on to him, Ouida! I'm telling you! Laugh it off! A kid's bullheaded. Just show him opposition and he'll trick you! He'll make a game of it! And before you know it, it's deadly serious! I'm telling you, now, Ouida—!"

"You don't have to tell me anything," Ouida cried indignantly. "I guess I know children. I guess I know my own son!"

Gradually, Lucas resumed his day-long vigils. As often as not, nowadays, he would be invited into the buggy to accompany the doctor into the country. He said little on these trips. He listened greedily. And the doctors, knowing why he was with them, talking obediently about the case they were jogging toward, about Medicine in general, about studying Medicine, about the names of things.

All of this Lucas now kept to himself. Sometimes he was so full with that which he had learned that he trembled with the excitement. His mother noticed and understood, but she never mentioned it. His father looked at him kindlily and winked. Lucas was full of love for both of them.

"Ever see a carbuncle, Lucas?" Dr. Alexander asked suddenly one day. He had just come out onto his porch and Lucas was waiting.

"No, sir!"

"Well, hop in."

The doctor flopped the reins and they were off.

"Now, I'll tell you the difference between a boil and a carbuncle. Git up! Now, do you know what a boil is?"

He waited expectantly.

"A boil is an abscess. It starts in the skin. Microbes get into a sweat gland. They eat a pocket under the skin. The pocket gets swollen with pus. You got to cut through the skin to the pocket to let it out."

"That's fine. That's fine."

"And the most dangerous place for a boil is on the end of the nose or in the nostrils. When you poke around the microbes can get spread into the blood stream and maybe into the brain. You can die from a boil."

"That's good. That's fine. Now how about a carbuncle?"

Lucas looked at him helplessly, mortified.

"A carbuncle is another name for boil. The difference is, with a carbuncle the pus pocket spreads out into a lot of channels—like a starfish. See?"

"Yes, sir."

"When a boil breaks—there's one opening. When a carbuncle breaks there's a lot of openings."

"How do you open a carbuncle?"

"Same way. You cut the skin down to the pocket."

"A cut shaped like an X. Two cuts."

"Fine."

"And people get boils from not eating the right foods, and from kidney trouble and diabetes and living in bad air."

"Not all of them at once."

"No, sir."

They rode a while in silence.

"But you *could* have all of them at once!" Lucas burst out.

"You could. But not likely."

"You wouldn't be worrying about boils, then."

"That's right. Git up!"

Far down the road a house came into view. The doctor pointed.

"We're going there. Got to see the woman of the house. While I'm there I'll take a look at the man. He's got a carbuncle. Now pay attention. I'm going to lance his carbuncle. Here's what I'm going to do. I'm going to paint the area with iodine. I'm going to lay wet gauze around where I'm going to cut. I'm going to cut. I'm going to poke in a drain. Then I'm going to put on a bandage. Do you understand?"

"Yes, sir."

"You've got it clear?"

"Yes, sir."

"Fine."

The buggy had reached the house. The doctor stopped the horse. He got out. He reached for his bag. He looked at Lucas.

"Well, come on, come on!"

Lucas stared at him, open-mouthed.

"Come on, Luke!"

Lucas scrambled over the side of the buggy. The doctor held his bag toward him. Lucas grabbed it gratefully.

They pushed past the gate, the front door opened immediately. The woman of the house smiled a wan greeting.

The doctor stepped over the threshold. He turned to Luke, who stood waiting, holding the bag toward him.

"Come on, son. Come on in," Dr. Alexander said. There was no possible chance of a mistake. He had said it, he had really said it. Numb with delight, Lucas entered the house.

"My helper," Doctor Alexander said courteously. Lucas looked at her anxiously. But the woman did not laugh. She only smiled a welcome and nodded.

My helper! It rang in Lucas' ears. It thundered. The hairs at the back of his neck prickled. Stiff with pride he followed the doctor into the kitchen of the farmhouse.

The doctor turned to the woman.

"Well," he said, "guess we'll go upstairs if you're ready."
"All ready." The woman turned obediently.
The back door opened and the farmer clumped in. He held his neck stiffly bent away from his body.
"Hi, Doc," he said, sideways.
"Be right with you," Dr. Alexander said. He gestured to Luke. "Brought my helper along."
The farmer promptly pulled out a chair and set it near Lucas.
"Sit down," he said. "Glad to have you." He, too, said it seriously, there was no mockery in it. There was in his manner that if the doctor saw fit to bring Lucas, the doctor knew what he was doing. All the tools of a doctor were mysterious. The boy was young, but the doctor had a reason for bringing him, and however it was the boy was going to help, the doctor knew best.
"Set," he adjured Lucas, smiling a welcome. And there was even a little respect in his tone. It was unmistakable. There was definitely respect.
The farmer poured himself a cup of coffee, recollected, put the cup in front of Lucas, poured himself another cup. After a wild moment of indecision Lucas took the coffee resolutely, following the pattern of maturity the doctor had established for him.
"Got boils. Got 'em bad!" the farmer confided.
Lucas swelled with pride at the confidence.
"That so?" he said guardedly.
"Got 'em bad."
"Boils can be pretty serious."
"So I heard."
Lucas nodded.
They drank their coffee in silence. The doctor came downstairs. He entered the kitchen briskly. The man stood up.
"Well, Charley, might as well get started!"
"Okay, Doc. How's the missus?"
"She'll be all right. Going to have to operate one of these days. I think that cyst's getting bigger. Big as an orange, now." He turned to Lucas. "Uterine cyst," he said politely. "Probably quite a few adhesions."
Right in front of the farmer.
"Yes, sir," said Lucas.
"Guess we'll get started."
"What do you want me to do, Doc?"
"You just sit in a chair, any of these kitchen chairs'll do nicely. Sit facing the back. Did you boil some water, Luke?"
Lucas' world collapsed.
"No," he said, ashamed to his depths. "I—"
"Doesn't matter. We'll flame the knife." He looked about him. "Now —my bag—"
Lucas rushed for it. He brought it to the table, opened it, stood aside. The farmer watched interestedly. But now Lucas was almost unconscious of the farmer's presence. Now he was committed to do what the doctor required, to the job in hand. Now he and the doctor were one, a unit, speaking the same language, apart, and this man was a stranger. He was

animate tissue which was to be treated thus and so, for which a part of one's consciousness must be reserved, a small part, a part to deal with the direct cries, the supplications the tissue might utter, and this part would deal with these manifestations mechanically, making the conventional sounds of sympathy and reassurance.

The doctor unfolded a clean towel and put it on the table. Lucas watched intently. He was memorizing each action so that he might do it next time. When the towel was opened the doctor laid upon it a lancet. Then he brought from the bag an alcohol lamp and assembled it. Lucas quickly went to the stove and brought back a match. The doctor nodded. Lucas ritually lit the lamp. Next from the bag came a small vial and a long curved tweezers. In the vial were three twists of gauze covered with vaseline. Now came a vial of iodine, a small heap of snowy gauze squares. Now the doctor was ready. There was a pause. The doctor looked at the back of the farmer's neck. Looked down at the array of materiel on the towel. He looked at Lucas. Lucas breathed quickly.

"All right, now," the doctor addressed the farmer, "I'm going to open this carbuncle for you—it's going to hurt a little."

"Can't hurt worse," the farmer said stolidly.

"Maybe I better freeze it . . ." The doctor hesitated.

"Don't worry about me," the farmer assured him.

"Don't want you jumping around—"

The farmer gripped his hands tighter.

"I'll set!" he promised.

The doctor made up his mind. He returned to the open bag, brought forth a fat tube with a nozzle at one end.

"I'm going to freeze it," he said to Lucas.

"Yes, sir," said Lucas confidently. He did not know what was about to happen but he strove to put all the approval he possessed into his answer.

The doctor now carefully and slowly removed the soiled bandage which had concealed the carbuncle. For the first time Lucas saw that which they were to treat. His assurance left him. His fierce pride of being one with the doctor fled thinly, left him a small boy gaping at the back of a human neck on which an ugly inflamed lump the size of a monstrous marble presented itself. Lucas fought the shock of aversion which had made him look down at the towel as if there were something there which interested him more. He forced himself to look at the carbuncle again.

"That's a bad one," Dr. Alexander said. He swabbed the region with iodine. He looked at Lucas appraisingly. "You see—the infection entered a pore hereabouts, worked its way down to a sebaceous gland—and here's the result."

Lucas' mind seized gratefully on this planned distraction. He now looked at the carbuncle steadfastly. It was really a neck, just like anybody else's. The doctor placed wet gauze pads around the boil. Now everything looked better. A germ had gotten into a pore and the pus and inflammation beneath the surface had raised the skin on this part of the neck, forced it up, made a mound of it. And the red was blood, the same blood that made the man's skin pink, only a lot of it, a lot of it in one place.

The doctor lifted the fat glass tube and held it two inches from the carbuncle. His thumb pressed down on the handle back of the nozzle. There was a hissing noise. A thin, fine stream sprayed the huge carbuncle. The inflamed red had become white. Soon the entire carbuncle was frosty white. The doctor put down the tube.

"Now it's frozen," he said.

He waited, picked up the tube again, resumed spraying.

"Light the lamp."

Lucas hurriedly seized the match, struck it, held it to the lamp wick. Blue flame appeared. He stared at it, fascinated.

"Pick up the lancet."

Lucas looked at the doctor, then obediently picked up the lancet.

"Hold it in the flame."

Lucas held the knife uncertainly over the flame.

"Just the cutting end—hold it close—heat both sides—"

With infinite care, Lucas did as he was bid.

"Now hand it to me—hold it by the middle—don't touch the end—put the handle in my fingers—"

With his other hand the doctor put down the tube.

"Ethyl chloride," he said. He turned back to the man's neck. "Now—you see—"

He cut down on the swelling. The white tissue parted promptly, gaped like a thin pair of white lips.

"And now—"

And he cut down at right angle, a cross of gaping white lips.

Lucas swallowed, his eyes glowed with excited admiration.

The doctor cut again, deepening each incision. Suddenly there boiled up in each slash thick, ropy, greenish-yellow pus. An instant later the white, the snowy carbuncle, no more human than snow, was red with dark blood, the blood and pus mixed, a thick, soupy blood coiling sluggishly out to the surface, spreading.

A gush of black-green-yellow followed. Lucas retched. Horror dazed him. He could not look away.

"Hand me the pads—"

Lucas stared on.

The doctor turned his head to look at him.

"The pads—" He pointed to the gauze squares.

Lucas looked numbly at the pads. He forced himself to take one, to put it in the doctor's waiting hand.

"More! More pads!"

He seized more. He handed them up. The doctor was wiping away the exudate. It flowed on. Soon there were no more pads.

"There's more in my bag. Hurry!"

Lucas wrenched his limbs into movement. He walked to the bag. He looked down into its black mouth. His head began to reel. A spasm of nausea sickened him. The bag blurred.

"In the left hand corner—"

The doctor's voice was cold, commanding, his hand went automatically into the left corner, his fingers felt gauze, he brought up a handful of pads. The doctor took three. He placed them around the oozing carbuncle.

"Here! Hold them in place!"

Lucas looked at the doctor helplessly. The doctor took one of his limp hands. He placed it on the gauze. Gingerly, reluctantly, Lucas put up his other hand, pressed his fingers on the rest of the gauze. He waited, standing dizzily, averting his eyes.

"Feeling better?" The doctor had stepped around to face the farmer, peering up into his face.

"Fine," the farmer said stolidly.

"Didn't hurt much, did it?"

"Beginning to hurt a little now."

"Almost done."

The wife walked into the kitchen.

"Glad I had my assistant here," the doctor said cheerfully. Lucas straightened. The appeal was irresistible. He began to endure what was to be endured, resolutely. Now he forced himself to look full upon the oozing carbuncle, the stained gauze, his own fingers. He felt the farmer's neck beneath the gauze.

"All right–" The doctor was at his side again. He put his fingers on the gauze. Lucas stood aside. "Now we'll see if we can get a little more out." He pressed down as he said this. Another spoonful of the thick stuff squeezed out and overlaid the gauze. This time Lucas had three more pads waiting before the doctor removed those that were drenched. The doctor smiled at him.

"Hand me the drains–in that vial there–and the tweezers–"

The room was still spinning, but the woman had moved beside them to watch and Lucas kept his eyes on the carbuncle with such a surge of will that he felt the will and his own determination and not the impact of what his eyes were set upon. The doctor placed a drain in one of the apertures he had cut, thrusting it deep into the neck with the tweezers.

There was a small groan from the farmer.

Lucas started. The woman looked at him. He controlled himself.

"Almost done," the doctor said abstractedly.

On a square of gauze he spread vaseline, quickly pressed it over the wound, took the two strips of adhesive, laid them over the gauze, pressed the ends on the man's neck.

"Done!" he said.

The woman began to clean up.

The lancet and the tweezers, the unused gauze, the bottles and vials went quickly back into the bag. The farmer stood up. He still held his neck gingerly awry.

"Feels a lot better," he said.

"I'll be back in a few days, change the dressing." The doctor snapped the bag shut, handed it to Lucas.

"Can I get you a cup of coffee? Piece of pie?"

"Not a thing," said the doctor.

"Piece of pie for your helper?"

They all looked at Lucas.

"No—" the doctor smiled—"we've got to get on. Save a piece for him, for next time."

They walked to the door, there was a small mirror in the hall and Lucas got a glimpse of his face. He noticed with dismay that it was quite pale.

Then they were in the buggy, homeward bound.

"Wasn't so bad, was it?" the doctor said.

Lucas did not answer.

Around them the fields stretched, the world was a prosaic field, humdrum, meaningless, exasperating. That which really mattered, the most exciting stuff of which life could be fashioned, that which was all-absorbing and all-meaning, they were driving away from, it was in that farmhouse, in the kitchen, the bag opened, the instruments emerging, a carbuncle about to be opened.

Lucas looked adoringly at Dr. Alexander.

"I should have had the water hot," he said humbly.

"Next time—"

Next time. . . . There was to be a next time . . . His eyes filled.

"Yes, sir," he said.

Existence was cored by those two words. He said them quietly to himself, testing the sweet anguish. His heart beat faster. Next time. When he rose in the morning he began to hope excitedly. When school was over he burst into a world in which this day might be *the* day, he raced to Dr. Alexander's, he sat on the steps. He waited day after day. Each day opened happier, more excited than the drab day fled. Next time.

Perhaps tomorrow.

There was another boil, soon, another carbuncle, there was a cut sewn, there was gunshot removed, a torn scalp, an amputated finger. There was next time. There was another next time. There were days and weeks and months of next times. And Lucas' life was a patient waiting, a fulfillment, a waiting again.

This was the stuff on which his days were fed. This was his hunger. This was his necessity. This activity of Hominidae was for him its prime activity and all the rest were corollary, this was his meaning and his whole desire and his purpose. This had been so from his beginning. The minor surgeries neither awakened nor quickened him. They fed him. They fed the hunger which was Lucas Marsh, a named mechanism of cells in which by accident or design this hunger was the summed and ordered craving of the cells themselves.

On this day, riding through the countryside with his father, he groped for words to bridge the alien terrain between them, words with the reassurance and the bridging of love.

He sat thinking of what he should say, thrilled to be taken for a ride with his father, sensible that his father did not idly invite him for a ride but would sooner or later say something which would make the purpose of the invitation clear. And Job, for all his bland and breezy and confident dismissal of Luke's excitement about Medicine, had determined to create, from time to time, prudent opportunities in which to point out the excellences of his own way of life, the charm of it, its excitement, its sterling worth.

"Looks like we're going to have a good year," he confided.
"That's fine!" Lucas was hungry for Job's approval.
"I just paid off the six-thousand-dollar mortgage on the Tyre store yesterday." Job grinned.
Lucas belabored his small wits for a reply to show he understood.
"That's wonderful."
"I should so say," Job chuckled.
"I should so say so," chimed Lucas.
Job's face sobered.
"Now I'm going to slap another mortgage on it."
Lucas looked up, astonished.
"Yep! Gonna slap another right back on!" Job was pleased with the boy's amazement.
"Doesn't that mean going back into debt, Father?"
"That's right, son!"
"But you just got out—!"
"And now I'm going right back in!"
They rode a while in silence. Lucas was troubled.
"Don't get it, do you? Remember this all your life, Luke." He put his hand on the boy's knee. "When I get out of debt it means I'm free—free to borrow again. See?"
"Doesn't everybody try to get out of debt?"
"We're not everybody. We're you and me. See? Now, I'm going to borrow six thousand dollars more from the bank. And I'll have to pay them six percent for the use of it. Now if I can't turn around and make *eight* percent on the six thousand, why, I better quit, see? I'm just no businessman."
"Yes, father," Lucas said dully. He had heard a lot about that six-thousand-dollar mortgage from his mother, he had heard her worry and fret over it, and here was his father, just as his mother had predicted, plunging in all over again.
"You can get eight percent and more on any good farm mortgage. Nothing safer than a farm mortgage."
"Yes, Father."
"Money's just a thing, Luke. It's only merchandise, like any other merchandise. Don't save it. Make it! Keep making new money! I don't save harness, do I? I put it out to sell. That's all money is. Just like harness."
"But everybody saves money!"
"No, no. Saving just means don't waste it. Don't throw it away any more'n you would harness. But don't go sticking it away in a box down the cellar where it can't do any good, like sticking it in a bank. Get it out where it can work—make more for you. Never forget that. Don't pay any attention to people. People are stupid. Mob-stupid. When they do something long enough they make a rule about it and when they've got it all down pat and a lot of people do it then they call it smart and respectable."
"How about the people that are always in debt and never have any money? Those people, Dad?"
"You can't tell. Luck is what was bound to happen only you didn't

figure on it. I'll tell you a funny thing, Luke. You listen to me. I'll tell you the truth about people. Nine hundred and ninety-nine out of a thousand are full of ambition and drive. Pay no attention to them. Those are sidewise people. They push out sidewise. Any human's got just so much drive. These people got so many ambitions there isn't drive enough to cover them. So all their efforts are little efforts. They whoosh out—sideways . . ."

They drove a while in silence.

"You see, Luke?"

"Yes, Dad." Lucas wondered how he summed up to his father.

"They'll never get anyplace. They just sit there like vegetables. Sideways people. The most of the human race. Salt of the earth. Voting for people on the chance who they vote for will lead them somewhere. Working for each other, talking, making rules which say the kind of life they lead is the right one."

"They make the rules?"

"That's their consolation prize."

"How about the others?"

"Well, there's not many of them. But you be one."

"Yes, Father."

"The one-track fellows. The Morgans, the Rockefellers, the Carnegies. The ones that're born knowing. I mean—how things are. They see what to go after. Whatever it is—what a man—one of them—has to have. They put everything else out of mind. And they don't think anything else. And they don't sleep anything else. And they don't eat anything else. Other people? They just hear them far off, dimly, a kind of bleat that don't mean anything. *They* know what life is. *They* know!"

"They fail, though. Some of them do."

"You've been listening to your mother, son. Your mother is a fine woman. But she don't know much about life. She thinks she does. And we'll never tell her different. But life is life, Luke. Don't forget that. Don't ever go pretending it's something else, some game or something. Those people don't fail. Not ever. What they're working on fails. They keep right on a-going. They never stop. All the rest—the herd—are sideways. *They're* straight up. Now there it is, Lucas. It's plain. It's simple. You've got to see it. You've got to see it *now!* You've got to forget the rest. You've got to get. That's your only hope. People are nice. But they just don't matter."

Now Luke knew there was a world of the flesh and a world of the spirit. He knew this. He knew it well. There was his father's world and there was his mother's world. He wanted with all his heart to please them both, to be on their side, in their world, to be what they wanted him to be. He tried diligently to show them that he was trying. And all the time he knew he could never be what they wanted him to be, not if he tried forever. It was impossible. There was no doctor in their worlds. And in his world there was nothing else.

One day he would listen to Job, straining to appear beguiled while Job tried cunningly to enchant him with the fun of business, smiling brightly, hoping his father was happy with him. Or he would listen earnestly, in the same hour, to Ouida while she spoke and gestured lovingly to him of the future she knew was his.

"Mother's got great dreams for you, Lucas. Great, great visions." She half closed her eyes. "I see you a leader among men, a mighty leader, a leader of the spirit, upward, upward, ever upward."

He would frown earnestly, so that she could see he was following every word.

"A great artist, perhaps—"

And he would nod quickly, hopefully . . .

"A great musician . . ."

He would cock his head as if to think, then nod more briskly than before . . .

"The world—the whole world bowing down to you . . ."

He would lower his head to show that despite this he was modest as Mother would have him be. And all the while, with Job or with Ouida, he knew, he knew himself, he knew what he was, he was sick with the sense of having failed them, of tricking them, of acting, of leading a secret life. He thought surely they must read his mind for the very weight and clearness of his guilt.

Sometimes they found him out.

He was eight when Ouida discovered his hoard of bottles and the fascinating refuse he collected back of the drugstore.

"Don't you want me to tidy these up?" she asked evenly. She smiled at him sweetly with her eyes and mouth.

"No, thank you, Mother. No, don't. Don't bother." His face flamed with shame and embarrassment. He hugged her and kissed her, hung over her all the rest of the day to show that he loved her, that she mustn't be hurt. But he kept the rubbish. He moved the magic bottles, the empty boxes, to another place. And she did not look for them again.

When he was eleven Job opened by mistake a package addressed to Lucas and found a glorious, shining new book on anatomy for which he had saved nearly two years' allowance.

"I didn't mean to open it, Lucas," he said apologetically, handing the book to the boy in its torn wrappings, "I never thought of anything being for you—in the mail—"

And Lucas had taken it quickly, burning with guilt, ashamed to look at his father. He fled with it, lest his mother come in and discover it also.

There were no reproaches. And he knew they looked at each other with understanding, patiently waiting, waiting for a change he knew would never, never come.

He was a lonely child. But he did not know this. He watched other children playing, bewildered at their raptures. He lived his life alone. It was another life. He read hungrily. The doctors saved for him the medical literature and advertisements that flooded their mail. These he read over and over, saving them lovingly, fingering them, deciphering them. In study periods he would stand at the big dictionary in the corner, hunting, hunting, reading absorbedly, now sidetracked by some new word, now consulting the list of medical words he had copied laboriously on a slip of paper, words in the pamphlets, in the medical bulletins. Sometimes when there would be a word the dictionary did not contain he would ask one of the doctors for the meaning. Sometimes he would be ashamed to ask, lest they remember suddenly that he was a child and withdraw their favor.

At the same time a new cosmos had enveloped him. His tastes had become suddenly keener. Foods he liked he became inordinately fond of. He discovered a strangeness, a sharp newness, in the sense of touch, his hands lingered caressingly over the bark of a tree, his fingers explored cloth, paper, iron, all the substances he encountered, for the feel they would reveal, and all these things were a great strangeness in the commonplace, a great newness, a new dimension. Then odors, the odors of cooking, his mother's few scents, the smells of cloths, of leather, the smell of a skunk; he analyzed them, he weighed them, he worried them, why did they smell as they smelled, why did they feel as they felt? And he stared at them more sharply and brooded and looked long and hard. And they were different. Sights, smells, touches, tastes, these were the substances of the world about him, important and relevant and new. And as for sound, his heart beat to the sound of a doctor's horse clip-clopping up the street to the porch on which he waited; and the miracle sound, the beatitude, the clink of an instrument.

He did well in school. He was liked. He played sometimes with other children. He was liked and pitied. Adults found him quiet, well behaved, abstracted.

"What are you going to be someday?" they would ask brightly.

And if his father was with him he would look at his father.

"He's got a lot of time for that," Job would say confidently. "I guess we won't be too far apart, eh, son?" And he would put his arm about Lucas.

And if his mother was with him, Lucas would look down.

"He hasn't made up his mind yet," Ouida would smile. She would look at him serenely, confidently. She would smile. And Lucas would smile too.

And if he was with both of them, he would say nothing and they would say nothing, merely wait for him to reply. And in the silence the visitor would laugh heartily and delightedly, and clap him on the shoulder.

"Bet you'd like to be a fireman, wouldn't you, sonny? Or a cowboy! How's that, now! A cowboy!"

When the war ended, Job owned the four stores; there was, to be sure, a mortgage on each. But there was money in the bank, there was a new home, there was comfort and even the beginnings of luxury.

Job bought a shining Winton.

"Don't worry you, Mr. Marsh?" a townsman would ask slyly.

"Me? Like cows worried when margarine was invented! This thing? People'll buy 'em, of course. Like to sell me any your horses cheap?"

"I guess there'll be horses a while."

"I guess there will be. Not more'n a million years or so."

"Yep."

"Or as the Frenchman says: 'Palm de tare—and likewise—pross de toot'! . . ."

* CHAPTER 6

But there were times in school when he was lonely. There were times when he felt keenly the differences between himself and the mingling, babbling, and sharing groups about him. There was never a time when he would have exchanged his life and its meanings for theirs but now and again he wished that his mother was more like other mothers and that his father and mother were more like other paired members of the tribe about him.

It was during one of these lonely periods that Lucas came home from school very late one day, late and sweaty and dirty.

"They want me for track!" he cried. "I'm supposed to come out for the track team!"

"Well, good!" Job rose and clapped his shoulder.

"What track?" demanded Ouida, furious and bewildered.

"I want some track shoes! Good leather ones!" Lucas cried.

"Guess we shouldn't have any trouble in the leather line," Job said comfortably.

"Don't be so intense, Lucas! You're too intense!" Ouida frowned.

"I used to be quite a runner myself." Job grinned. "What kind of race you gonna run?"

"The half-mile! Coach says I'll make a quarter-miler. But *I* like the half."

Ouida listened to this suddenly established rapport between Job and her son with dismay and alarm. She forced a set smile.

"When did you ever run!" she scoffed.

"Oh, I used to run around the farm. I ran faster than anybody. Every time there was a church ruckus I used to get in all the races. Won 'em all. Every one."

"Every one!"

"That's right."

"Did you like to run distances, Dad?"

"Sprints or distances—it was all the same to me. Won 'em all."

Later, Ouida came into the living room, where Lucas sat studying. She sat down beside him.

"I want to talk to you a while."

He searched his mind guiltily.

"Yes, Mother . . ."

"I have been to see your principal, Mr. Prescott. He agrees with me. He says you have great aptitude, Lucas. But you won't apply yourself—"

"I'm all right, Mother—"

"You're a dreamer, Lucas. That's what he says. When you should be studying you dream. You have no application."

"I got 94 in Latin—I got 86 in—"

"You like those things! You like Latin, you're like myself, I love languages! I could be a great language scholar, I would love to know them all—you like French, you like history. But you don't even bother to study them."

"Now, Mother! I got 94—"

"You could have gotten a hundred."

"A hundred!"

"There's absolutely no reason why you could not have gotten a hundred. The child I carried in my body, the little life I carried underneath my heart and bore in agony—"

Lucas twisted.

"Not under your heart, Mother. In your—your abdomen—you couldn't carry me under your heart—"

"Under my heart, Lucas."

"Yes, Mother."

"You're going away from me, Lucas. I feel it. You're drifting farther and farther away."

"Don't say that—"

"I can feel it . . ."

"It's not true! It's just not true!"

"The little boy I knew and loved—"

"I'm here, Mother!"

"I have to tell you this, Lucas. I have to tell you the truth. I won't always be here to guide you. I'll be gone, someday, Lucas. I'll be dead. Mother will be dead. You'll be alone."

Her face was lifted to his a little. Her lips were open. Tears streamed down her cheeks.

"Will you miss me, Lucas?"

He threw himself on his knees beside her, his arms tight around her, his face pressed against her bosom, his eyes shutting out her voice, tears involuntarily squeezing between the shut lids.

"Don't—don't, Mother! Don't! Please . . . Please don't! . . ."

She caressed his head gently, her hands passing over his hair. She gazed off into the distance.

"I've got to tell you, Lucas." She began to sob a little, helplessly. "You've got to see . . ."

"I'll try, Mother. Don't die. Be with me . . ."

"You're all I've got, Lucas."

"I'll be good. I'm sorry, please—"

"And now games, Lucas. Now it's something else to take your mind off your studies. My Lucas! My boy playing *children's* games. You—with your mind, your fine mind that I gave you . . ."

"I'll stop—"

"Games are not for Lucas. Kangaroo shoes. And yelling. Leave those things for the clods. They don't matter. You have Mother. You have the brain Mother gave you. I won't always be here, Lucas. I'll be dead and gone. I'll be far away. You'll be lonely. Then you'll see. Then it'll be too late—too late . . ."

He clung to her harder, the tears flowed faster, he could not stop them. He loved her, he knew what she was doing, and he could not stop. At length she forced a laugh.

"Look at us," she cried. "Two boobies sitting here crying!"

She pressed him away to look at his face, to drink his tears. He averted his eyes. He put her hand to his cheek.

"What is it you want, Lucas? What do you really want to be?"

He hesitated.

"Whatever you say, Mother."

"No, let's talk! You and Mother! Tell me. Tell me truly. Tell me from your heart."

He sighed.

"You know."

"I *don't* know!"

"I want to be a doctor."

"A doctor! You really want to be a doctor, Lucas?"

He twisted helplessly.

"That's what you still really want—in your heart of hearts?"

"I can't help it. I'll do whatever you say. But you asked me. You told me to say—"

"Have you sat by yourself and concentrated and let the Divine Light pour through you in all its great and mighty shining waves?"

"I've tried, Mother. I've tried and tried—"

"You're a very old soul, Lucas. Mother is a very old soul too. We go back, back, back into time, we two, back to the Pyramids. . . . I was a priestess once, a Princess in Egypt—"

Lucas swallowed.

She turned her face slowly. Her eyes were grave. She smiled with her mouth.

"If that's really what you want, Lucas . . ."

He looked at her, not breathing.

"If you have searched your soul and asked Almighty God for His guidance . . ."

She waited as if listening. She nodded.

"So be it. I do not know why or how, for their wisdom is beyond me. My guides have spoken. Now I know. You will be a doctor."

He stared at her, white-faced, not believing, holding his breath.

"You will tell your father that you will not need those—track shoes!"

"Oh, yes, Mother! Yes! Yes!"

"And you will study? You will apply yourself? In the things you don't like as well as the things you do?"

"I'll make a hundred in math! Medicine's full of math! They use it for everything! X-rays, physics, chemistry—everything!"

She rose, uplifting him with her. She kissed his cheek. He kissed her and she turned her head barely in time, for he would have kissed her on the mouth.

"You can go to bed now. You've studied long enough. Your face is tired."

"No, no!" He sat down quickly. "Now I've got to study. Now I've got to really study. Now you'll see."

"There are no limits for you, Lucas. You can be the greatest man in the world."

"Yes, Mother."

He flung himself upon his books.

In the kitchen, after she had carefully closed the door, she stood still, her hands folded. After a time she twisted her shoulders stiffly, moved to the kitchen table, sat down. She picked up a book on reincarnation. She began to read.

When she looked up, hearing Job come home, an hour had passed. She heard him enter, heard Lucas call to him, heard his excited young voice telling his father the news. She heard Job exclaim. His voice was mechanical. Her face hardened. She heard them talk a while, heard Lucas go upstairs to bed.

Job entered the kitchen. His face was white with anger.

"What the hell do you think you're doing!" he demanded furiously.

"Were you by chance referring to me?" Ouida asked icily. "It's not necessary to shout."

"Did you tell that boy he could be a doctor?"

"If you are referring to Lucas—my son—"

"Your son! A poor thing like you! You happened to have a belly to breed him in. I'm surprised you had that, I'm—"

"Moderate your voice," Ouida said shakily.

"You're a lunatic, that's what you are. You ought to be put away! You and your crystal balls and your spirits. Now you leave that boy alone or I'll—"

"You'll what!"

"I'm warning you, now—"

"Who are you—a lout like you!—to say that fine boy shall or shall not study Medicine?"

"You've been as dead set against it as me. Where do you get off all of a sudden to—"

"He's my son and I know him through and through. I know him as you can never hope to know him. I bore him. I know his every thought. He wants to be a doctor. I've looked into his eyes when he told me so. I don't expect an animal like you to do anything but scoff at the fine things, the things you can never understand. And I say if he wants to be a doctor that's what he's going to be. Now just exactly what do you think you're going to do about it?"

"You've got the world all doped out, haven't you, Ouida. Do you know people laugh at you? They always have, you know. You're a big joke. They snicker behind your back. Half the town thinks you're crazy. They're sorry for me. Because I'm married to a crazy woman. That's what they think of you. I'm married to you. I've got to put up with a certain amount of your pretending you're better than anyone else, and your crystal balls and your quarrelling with the very food a man eats. Because I have the damned bad luck to be married to you. That's all right. I married you with my eyes open. You were a halfwit then, and nobody'd have you and I knew it and I married you. But don't get the idea that because I let you get away with it that that gives you the right to say what a boy's whole future is going to be. Don't ever get that idea."

"You married me! Oh, when I think what I've done, what I've done!"

"You've done pretty well, if you ask me!"

"Ask you! Why would anyone ever ask you anything? You're a liar and every human that knows you knows you're just a dirty liar. You're a liar and a thief. You're an animal. There isn't a spark of human decency in you. You're filth. Pure, human filth. You came from filth, you live in filth, and you'll die in it. Don't you ever tell me what people say. This whole town knows you, Job Marsh. And despises the ground you walk on."

"That's how everybody is to you. The whole human race. That's that dreamworld you live in. Suit yourself. You live where you please. Just leave that boy alone."

"So he can grow up like his father? And someday rip a decent girl like an animal on her wedding night? So he can steal a store from an honest old man that befriended him? So he can grow up an ignorant swine who can't live unless he lies and steals from decent people? That's your world, is it?"

"It's kept a roof over your head and bought Ouija boards for you and kept him fed and clothed and not ashamed. You go ahead, go your own way. Just keep your nonsense to yourself. Don't infect him. Don't try to pull that stuff on him that this world is a spiritual place to live in. Because you're all alone, Ida Boorgoys! The world knows better. And he's going to amount to something in the world. Not *your* world. Not the lunatic asylum. Leave him alone, you bitch, you dumb excuse for a woman. Or I'll have you locked up. Committed!"

"You'll have *me* locked up—!"

"I'm warning you—!"

"Do you know what would happen if I ever opened my mouth about you? Do you know?"

They were both shouting now, careless and alone. Ouida's face was death-white. Her eyes glittered. Her voice had become hoarse. Job studied her, uncertain.

"I'm just telling you, now Ouida—I'm warning you—"

She walked to him. She gathered saliva in her mouth. She spat in his face.

"You'll warn ME! YOU! You degenerate dog!"

Trembling, unnoticed, Lucas entered the kitchen.

"I've had enough!" Job roared. His fist crashed into Ouida's mouth. She fell sprawling.

Her hand crept, dazed, to her lips. A bloody tooth dropped into her fingers.

"Father!" wailed Lucas. He rushed at Job to hold him. His father struck him out of his way with a sweep of his arm, without turning his head from Ouida.

"Lay there!" he snarled. He looked at her with raging satisfaction. Then he strode from the room.

Lucas knelt beside his mother.

"I'm glad you saw," she said thickly. Blood poured from her lips. "Now you saw. Now you know what I've had to put up with. Now you saw for yourself." He tried to help her rise. "Get away from me!"

She struggled clumsily upright. Lucas ran for a towel, wet it, rushed back to her. She struck it wildly from his hand.

"I've had enough!" she screamed. "I've had enough too! I've had enough of all of you." She ran coughing to the sink. She began to vomit.

Lucas watched, desperate, withered, sick with pity, guilty, longing to escape, impotent, alone. There had never been anything like this. Always before he had had a secret sympathy for his father, a resentment for his own embarrassment at his mother's naked rages. Sometimes he and his father had looked at each other covertly. But this, this was too unlooked for to be believed. He shrank from both of them, his bonds with them ripped, the breach stuffed with shame; adrift in a world which peered and listened and must know all.

In the days that followed Job did not speak to Ouida and only in rare monosyllables to Lucas. When he noticed them at all he looked at them remotely, coldly, and with contempt. He left the house quickly and came home late. He enveloped himself in the harness shops. He worked fiercely and resolutely. He devoted himself to repair the breach in his defenses, in the wall of his world, to thrust out his home, his wife and his son, these aliens and their alien problems. The revelation that they had somehow insensibly gathered power to penetrate his world, to influence and disrupt it, amazed and frightened him. He was aghast at himself and angry and he cursed bitterly the undefended highway in his life over which these intruders had marched to assault him.

He must never let this happen again.

As to Ouida, Job knew best how to retaliate. The quarrel had freed him. He was free with a new freedom. He was free, now, to plan as he chose, to maneuver, to consult no one. He wondered, alarmed, how many opportunities he had missed. The family fortunes were comparatively stable. Rather than risk scenes Job had contented himself with the management of the four stores. These, this career they represented, hardly taxed his capacities. He surveyed himself with disgust and anger. He unleashed himself, his thoughts leaped the safe ramparts and quested for spoil. It was at this time that he made plans to buy four other harness stores, one a very large establishment in the city of Meridian.

It was outrageous, it occurred to him a moment, and in another moment he was launched upon it.

The Meridian store was imposing. Its history was troubled. No one had been able to make it pay. This was almost the greatest challenge life could offer Job, and the best loved. He plunged into assaults on the owners.

Now he was himself again, and now the shy animal that had won the planet, whose cells had evolved in conquest and flight, was pure in him, simple and entire. And the planet was his prey and everything that existed upon it. And time and the moment were willows to weave in a trap. That was the simple business, there was nothing more, nothing except the delightful pretense that this was not so.

Job smiled happily.

He lived three days in Meridian. He fastened upon the Derickson brothers who owned the store, he whittled at them remorselessly. He lied tremendous lies, simple lies, confusing lies, exciting lies, and lies so complicated only he could unravel them. Also, sometimes he told the truth. It was all one. Late at night, when he reluctantly left them, he went out into the streets, still exhilarated, pent, and sleepless. In a bar was a streetwalker, he was delighted, he made for her directly, he grinned obscenities in her ear and she smiled at him and he hugged her, exultant, the bartender frowned at him and Job grinned wider, he and the whore were wed by that frown, Job sighed and grinned wider. Now the drinking began.

Next morning he left her to go directly to the Dericksons. He was renewed. He plunged avidly into his unlikely battle to split the Dericksons, to twist them, to cajole them, bully them, to frighten them and entice them into surrendering their property to him at a price so low that Job himself smiled fiercely at the audacity and the possibility of it all.

In the evening his whore was waiting for him again. He wallowed with her gloriously and rose as before to return to the assault and the siege on the Dericksons.

Toward noon of the third day he resolved to return to Milletta. He was happy. He had spent a fulfilling time. He relaxed. He prepared to say his farewells. An hour later he very suddenly won. He was completely surprised. Once again he had won by his wits and his wits alone, but this time the stakes were larger and sobering. Relatively small as the purchase price was, the sum was still huge, the property involved was larger than anything he had ever owned. To raise the money he would have to put second mortgages on the four stores, borrow on everything he owned. Now a new battle began, in which he persuaded the owners to accept stock for a portion of the purchase sum. He gave them a check for the balance. He rushed home to raise the amount and deposit it before the check was presented for payment.

A few moments with Charley, his helper, borrowed the old man's life savings—that was four hundred dollars, and from a salesman come on a regular selling visit he borrowed three hundred more. He was irresistible, his momentum hurled him faster, he went to merchants, to farmers; before the banking day ended he had raised within a thousand dollars of an amount large enough to encourage the bank to allow him an overdraft. For the final thousand dollars he forged Ouida's name to a note secured by four vacant lots her father had left her.

Job walked out of the bank, stable and serene, out into the world, his world now, a new world, a new man. He paused briefly at the shop, it had dwindled, become in three days a little shabby, a poor thing. One of eight.

"Take the day off, Charley," he said unexpectedly.

"Me? Oh, I don't think I'd better do that. Thanks all the same—"

"Go on. Go ahead."

"Well . . . I'd as soon not . . . I—"

"Got an interest in the business, now, eh?"

"I want to thank you again, Mr. Marsh. I don't know how to put it, I guess it don't mean much to a man like you—but letting me invest that four hundred dollars—"

"That's all right, Charley. No need for thanks. You earned the privilege. Fair's fair . . ."

Job Marsh went home. He had not changed his shirt, his socks, or his underwear in four days. He was beginning to feel grubby and uncomfortable.

While he had been gone Ouida had been happy. She was indifferent to his whereabouts. That he had simply dropped out of her world did not bother her at all. The respite gave her Lucas, she had Lucas all to herself, the house was free from tension, she was free, completely free, to do as she pleased. The possibility that Job might never return did not occur to her. He had become like an illness to which she was subject. She knew she would have it always. She assented to this illness. She knew how much of her life was sacrificed to it. She was determined only to preserve her spare life in the pursuit of that which kept her whole and which was the only world that really mattered.

Her first intimation of Job's departure came a few hours after he left Milletta to go to Meridian. There was a knock at the door and Charley looked at her, troubled. She hid her still-bruised mouth with her hand.

"Fellow wants to see Mr. Marsh," he said. "Thought he might be here."

"Hasn't he been to the shop at all?"

"Oh, sure. He up and left and I thought–"

"No, he's not here, Charley–"

"Took the rig–"

He was gone, then. She relaxed. She smiled happily, gaily, keeping her face half averted to hide her bruises.

"Guess we'll just have to expect him when we see him."

"Guess so. Thought you might know . . . Got a toothache, Miz Marsh?"

"I'm afraid so. I was getting ready to go to the dentist."

"Well . . ."

"He'll be back, Charley."

"Yes, ma'am."

She closed the door. She stood savoring her freedom. The freedom grew, swelled in her, she was intoxicated with happiness. She ran to the kitchen, put away the basin from which she had been putting hot cloths to her face. She rushed upstairs to change her clothes. In the midst of her dressing she smelled something burning. She rushed downstairs again, gazed wildly about the kitchen. Smoke was eddying slowly from the oven door. She wrenched it open. Smoke poured out, choking her. She had forgotten a bread pudding. A fit of coughing overcame her and she sank into a chair, gasping for breath, powerless. Recovering a little, she fumbled the back door open, leaned against the doorpost. The fresh air revived her. Still coughing, she turned back, snatched up one of the wet cloths she had been using, covered her mouth and nose and ran unsteadily to the open oven. She dragged forth the burning pudding, threw it in the sink. She turned on the water. She stumbled to the door again, rested a moment, sat down on the back steps .

The smoke cleared. She went upstairs and finished dressing. She continued to cough a little. Her throat felt raw. She mixed salt and water, gargled, put on a hat, muffled the lower part of her face in a scarf, and set out for the dentist's office.

"I had a fall." She laughed remorsefully.

"I see you did, Mrs. Marsh," he said expressionlessly, who had treated hundreds of such falls. "We'll have a new tooth for you in a jiffy." He peered closer. "Got kind of a sore throat there, haven't you!"

"I guess this was bound to be a bad day. Burned a bread pudding. The whole house was full of smoke. I must have swallowed enough for a county."

"Pretty red, all right. . . . Now, there's a root in there we'll have to go after. I'm sorry, Mrs. Marsh, you'll have to set yourself . . ."

She smiled at him brilliantly, confidently, proudly. She opened her mouth wider. Ouida Marsh knew how to stand pain.

A half-hour later he was finished. He shook his head at her admiringly. Not a sound had passed her lips.

"It's all in the mind, Dr. Sorenson. The mind controls the body."

She went home, she set her house in order and waited for Lucas. When he returned from school she took him for a long walk through the countryside.

They had the evening to themselves, a long evening. She sat quietly by while he studied, made him sandwiches after a while, insisted he drink warm milk, which he detested, and which he drank with a smile, to please her. They were marvellously close. The next day they were rich with themselves. Ouida laughed like a girl. Lucas' eyes swam, adoring her.

On the third evening she drew out a Ouija board. She bade him sit with her at the kitchen table. She drew the blinds. She lowered the lights.

"Now we shall see," she smiled, seating herself as at a feast. "Now we shall see what flows through you."

He looked away embarrassed.

"Oh, no, Mother . . . not that stuff . . . please . . ."

"Not stuff, darling. You don't really mean that. I want you to try this. Try it with Mother. Just for me."

"But I don't know–anything about it! Boogies and spirits and–"

"Do you remember fairies, darling? Do you remember how when you were a little boy they used to talk to you?"

"Yes," he said, flushing and ashamed.

"Look at me, Lucas. And how you used to come to me and tell me about it? And how Mother explained to you? You weren't afraid of fairies, were you, Lucas?"

He sighed.

"Well, they weren't fairies, Lucas. They were spirits. Good spirits. They don't come to every little boy. Only a few, a very few, a chosen few. But you–they hover about *you* always, Lucas. I see them hovering about you now."

He looked about apprehensively.

"You mustn't be afraid, son. This is one of God's greatest gifts to us . . . for the spirit of man is mighty, Lucas. The spirit of man is God Himself . . . and these who have passed over are waiting, waiting about us, protecting us, waiting to tell us . . ."

She placed his hands on the planchette. She shut her eyes. Her face lifted in the gloom. He looked away from the bruise on her mouth.

"Lightly, Lucas . . . lightly . . . lightly . . ."

The silence gathered about them and seemed to solidify. The darkness contained movement. Fear prickled the back of his neck. He breathed faster. The planchette had moved.

"Ask it a question, Lucas." Her whisper frightened him. "Ask . . . ask . . . ask to yourself . . ."

How soon will I be a doctor? he thought. He made it a sentence and said it silently. Will Dad help me? Must I run away?

The planchette moved under his fingers. He lifted his finger tips until they barely touched the wooden tripod and it drifted from beneath his hands. He followed it quickly. His mother's eyes were shut. The planchette stopped. It rested upon the word "yes," it drifted on, moved waveringly about the board. His eyes widened and tears of fright flooded them. Over and over the board the planchette moved, now dashing to a letter, now halting, irresolute. Could one believe? Could one really believe? The darkness pressed closer. In the silence there was only the sound of the tripod, moving on felt, sibilant, small. . . .

In the darkness Ouida spoke at last and her voice and her words caromed in the silence.

"They're all about us," she said tiredly. She cleared her throat. "Do you believe, Lucas? Do you believe, now?"

"Yes, Mother," he whispered. He looked toward her with fear, trying to make out her face in the gloom.

"Did they tell you what you wanted to know, dear?" She took his hands.

"I think so," he said uncertainly.

"They told me something too," she said slowly. She waited a moment. She listened. "No," she said, "No . . . we won't talk about it . . ."

Lucas stirred.

She rose. She turned on a light.

"Well!" she said smiling. She coughed. "That was fun, wasn't it! Wasn't that wonderful, Lucas?"

"What did they tell you, Mother?" he asked eagerly.

Her mouth continued to smile but her eyes stopped smiling and became distant.

"We won't discuss it," she said brightly. She walked to him and kissed him. She hugged him to her. Her arms relaxed, stayed about him, began to rock him slightly.

"You must never be frightened, Lucas."

"No, Mother." His love for her hurt him, it was a mighty pain.

"The love of God surrounds you. It surrounds you, always. Peace and eternal love. Open your heart, Lucas. There is a part of you that knows this, always, that waits for you to know too. The body does not matter, Lucas. This, and only this, matters. Within you is a world, the only real world, my son. The rest is only illusion. The shell. Man is a part of Almighty God. Man is God. Man is spirit. Man is soul. Man is mind. The rest is animal."

She rocked him slowly, gently, infinitely.

"Within you is truth, you have all power, power to command, power to rule, power to see, and understand . . . within you, Lucas . . . within *you* . . . nothing else matters. . . ."

They had never been so close.

When Job returned Lucas awaited him guiltily, wanting him, heavy with disloyalty.

Job was in excellent humor. His smile faded when he saw Ouida.

"I want to say something," he said. Lucas turned to disappear from the room. "No, son, you stay. I want you to hear this too. Ouida, I'm sorry. I did a terrible thing and I'd give anything I've got not to have done it. You can say what you like to me, I deserve it, and I'd welcome it. I beg your pardon. I deeply beg your pardon. I apologize."

Lucas stared at the floor, not daring to look at either of them.

"Well, it was a terrible thing," Ouida said uncertainly.

"It was a terrible thing and I'd like to cut off my arm if it would do any good to undo it, and I apologize."

Job appeared deeply and sincerely moved.

Ouida looked at him, amazed.

"Well . . ." she began. She faltered. "Well . . . we all make mistakes . . ."

Job walked forward and took her humbly in his arms.

"I missed you," he said honestly. "You don't know how I missed you."

Ouida thought desperately, wildly.

"We've been walking in the country!" she cried. "In the beautiful, beautiful country—"

"Why don't you run down to the shop, son!" Job called. "Your mother and I have something to talk about."

Lucas started to the door.

"I'll go right down," he said eagerly.

"See how everything's going!" Job called after him, grinning.

He turned to Ouida.

"What do you say, Ouida? Shall we make up for lost time?"

"Please, Job." She twisted away. "Everything's been so nice—so calm —so peaceful—"

"I came to you on my knees," he said humbly. "Aren't we man and wife? Do you despise me that much?"

"It isn't that, Job. I just don't—I never— Let's sit down shall we? And you'll tell me where you've been and what you've done, and I'll tell you about the walks we took, do you know what Lucas said?"

"Ouida! Please! I'm your husband! I've come back to you! Is this how you're going to treat me? I'm a man—must I go outside my own home—"

He put his arm around her waist. He drew her, unwilling, to the stairs.

She bit her lip, she closed her eyes, he led her upstairs.

Afterward he bathed and changed his clothes.

He could do anything now. Nothing could stop him. He had won everywhere. It was impossible—everything was impossible—and he had done it.

Lucas returned. There was dinner. The house was at peace again.

⁎ CHAPTER 7

Now this was the home and the community, the cave and the tribe, these were the drives that forged the gambits of survival, the rules and the customs that controlled what was basic in living.

And from these essentials and from this place, which was any place, Lucas Marsh had been dowered with reaction and living pattern and shaped and circumstanced, clothes hastily flung over him as his vector embarked him toward his heritage.

He was alone now, that which motivated him set him apart. The pattern of those who begot him differenced him, made him more separate. His apartness, his loneliness, catalyzed his hunger.

There was no doubt that Lucas was going to college. Job had set aside a fund for this, Lucas' college fund. The harmony which marked his return lasted barely two days.

"He'll come to, all right," Job said confidently.

"He's never wavered an instant. I wish you'd realize that, Job. He's young. But part of him's grown up. It's beyond us."

"There's no hurry. No hurry at all. You'll see."

"I'll see! What do you ever know about him! I was the way you are. I didn't want him to be a doctor either. But he's set! And if he wants it with all his heart—"

"I don't care what he wants. I know what's best for him."

"How can you know what's best for my boy!"

"Your boy!"

"Yes, my boy! He's mine, not yours! I carried him under my heart—"

"Look, Ouida! Why don't you just shut that big mouth of yours and mind your own goddamned business!"

"You'll teach him! He'll grow up to be a degenerate like his father! You miserable—"

But Job was gone.

"You'll have to see your father, Lucas," Ouida told him later. "I talked to him but it was no use."

"But I thought it was all settled. He'll just get mad—"

"He's the one you'll have to see."

"But—"

"I'm tired of fighting your battles for you. I'm tired, tired, tired. Fight for yourself. . . ."

"I have to see my father about being a doctor," Lucas told Professor Glenn, who taught him chemistry.

Professor Glenn looked at him wearily over the chemistry counters littered with glassware. From out-of-doors the sound of classes dismissed for the day rioted faintly back to the deserted classroom.

"There shouldn't be any difficulty," the professor considered. "Your marks are high—"

"I thought maybe you could tell me something I could say."

"I think you're setting up obstacles. If Medicine's what you want to do, if you really think you've made up your mind—"

"Yes, sir," said Lucas miserably.

"Would you like me to speak to him on your behalf? I don't know your father but I'd be glad to speak to him—"

"No, no! Oh, no! Thanks, Mr. Glenn."

"Yes . . . Well . . ."

"I guess my fatal time has come," Lucas said to Henry Moffatt, who fought him point by point for scholarship.

"What's the matter?" Henry thought in terms of decimal points of advantage, he thought coldly, school was grades, they were rivals but their distance from the remainder of the class placed them together in a perpetual guarded and armed truce.

"I got to have a talk with him."

"Your grades are all right. What are you worried about?"

"It's about being a doctor."

"Well, doesn't he know? Just tell him, that's all."

"Sure. Just tell him."

"I'd tell him. I'd tell him, quick."

"Yes-s-s—sure, you'd tell him."

"What's the worst he can do? Just tell me that. You tell him and what's the worst he can do?"

"I don't care what he can do—"

"He can beat the tar out of you!"

"He's never laid a hand on me. No, that's one thing about Dad. No, I'm not worried about that . . ."

"Well then tell him. What are you bothering about?"

"He's just so dead set. I'd do anything to please him. But I don't know how to *want* anything else. If I only knew I could—"

"Gosh! They must have got used to it by this time. Everybody knows you're going to be a doctor! What's the matter?"

"They think I'll change. I just can't make them see. They just don't know. I hate it. I dread it. It's gotten so I can't study or anything . . ."

Henry looked at him watchfully, alerted.

"That's a shame, Luke," he said, trying to hide his satisfaction. "That's a plain shame. . . ."

As he had when he was a boy, Lucas waited outside Dr. Alexander's office, sitting on his front porch. The doctor, emerging, looked at him, surprised.

"I wanted to get your advice on something," Lucas said to Dr. Alexander.

The doctor shifted his bag to his other hand and waited.

"I have to see my father about something . . ."

Girl in trouble? Gonorrhea? wondered Dr. Alexander. He scanned Lucas closely.

"I thought I'd come by and maybe you'd give me a little advice. Something you could tell me, maybe."

"What's the trouble, Lucas?"

"I want to be a doctor."

"Well?"

"I have to tell him so."

"But everybody knows you're going to be a doctor!"

"Yes, sir. I thought there was something you could tell me I could tell him—"

"Tell him what?"

"Explain to him—"

"What is there to explain?"

"I have to kind of break it to him."

"Oh, Lucas! He knows! How could he help but know?"

"I guess he knows, all right. How I feel. But he thinks how I feel will change. He's sure of it."

"Maybe you will change, Lucas. Ever thought of that?"

"Yes, sir. I tried to imagine. There wasn't any way I could imagine."

"Well . . . I've got a few calls to make, Lucas. Talk it over with him . . . I'm sure he's reasonable . . . if you want I'll drop by."

"Oh, no! I'll do it."

"I don't know why you're so apprehensive. He's never seemed to me particularly violent."

"It isn't that, I just want a way to make him understand. I have to see him, I have to talk to him and I thought maybe there was something you could tell me—"

"You'll be a doctor, Lucas. Don't worry about it."

"Not without his help."

"No . . . not without his help."

"You can't work your way through Medicine."

"You know that, don't you?"

"I know."

"Not any more."

"Yes, sir."

"Go see him. Just talk to him reasonably, don't antagonize him . . ."

"Yes, sir . . ."

Doctor Alexander nodded and was gone.

After that there was nobody else.

The rest of the day he studied how to begin. He tried opening statements. He spoke them aloud, discarded them, selected new ones. There was a small sum of time remaining and the half-hours of this time alternately rushed panicky or dragged and would never end. His dread mounted. Desperately, desirously, he pondered escape. He would run away. Always, like a thing of granite was this, that he was of Medicine, that he must be a doctor. Around this granite his thoughts were mists and they eddied and swirled about this immovable fact, this stone, this upreared and unalterable and uncaring granite and in a flash they were gone and the excitement whirled him into eagerness for the interview. A moment later he was helpless with dread again.

"He's going to talk to you tonight," Ouida warned Job.

"I'll take care of it," Job said.

"Don't be a fool, now. He loves you—"

"You just mind your business, Ouida. I'll handle it."

Job pushed back his dinner plate.

"Well—" he grinned—"got to take a drive tonight. Got to see Miller. What do you say, Luke? Like to take a little ride with me?"

Lucas rushed to get his hat and coat.

For a time they drove without speaking.

"Country looks nice this time of year, don't it?" Job said after a while.

"Oh, yes! Yes, it does!"

"Wants a little more rain." He clapped the boy on the knee. "What do you say, Luke? Got something on your mind?"

"Yes, sir."

"Something you want to tell me about? About college, maybe?"

"That's it. I wanted to ask you—"

"Well, you're going to college. That's all there is to that. Rest your mind easy. Your mother and I have made up our minds. You're going to college."

"Yes, sir. That's wonderful! Thank you, Dad!"

"Never failed you yet, have I?"

"Oh, no! No, never!"

"Don't worry your mother, Luke. She's fretting, she's losing weight over you. Everything's going to be all right. You just go ahead and study and enjoy yourself all you can while you're young and let me do the worrying."

He clucked to the horse.

"And when you're through—when you've had all the learning you want—why, there'll be your place waiting for you. Right beside me. You and me together. How's that strike you, Luke?"

There was a little silence.

"The point is, you'll change, Lucas. You'll look back on all this and laugh. You've got to remember, Luke, I know what's best for you. That's all I'm after. Not what *I* want. You're like your mother in some ways. You don't know the world. It isn't what you think at all. The way you are it's all plans and dreams and ambitions. It's different. It isn't that way by a damned sight. It's what's born in us and what we are. That's what the world is."

"I know. I know what you mean. At least I try to know. But it's just the way you say. Everybody is different, Dad. Not everybody's in the harness business."

"I don't care what business you go in, particularly, boy. I'd like to see you in with me. Any father would say that. But you've got to go into business. That's the main business. That's life. All the rest is hogwash. If you could corner the doctor business—but you see you can't do that. They trade in knowledge and what kind of business is it when there isn't enough knowledge to get the trade? And keep it? Sure you treat sick folk and maybe that makes you feel good. That's kid stuff. Look at the farmer and look at the vet. The farmer needs the vet of course, one of his cows gets sick he calls the vet in a hurry. Pays him a good fee, too. But when the farmer goes home he's got thirty cows and when the vet goes home he hasn't even got one cow, all he's got is a little money for treating one of the thirty cows the farmer's got. Do you see what I mean? You be the farmer. Pay some other poor dog for his services. See? Now that's the way it is, Luke. Nothing will ever change it."

"Yes, Father."

"You speak up. You speak right up and speak your mind. Don't be afraid."

"I am afraid."

"What are you afraid of? Me? Why me?"

"I'm afraid you'll think I'm stubborn. I don't want you to get mad."

"I'm not going to get mad. Not the slightest chance of it. That's what we came out here for—to talk."

"You see—it's hard for me to explain to you—"

"Go right ahead, boy . . ."

"I—I don't know anything else except being a doctor. That's all I've ever thought of. I can't imagine how it would be not to feel that way. Just like I'd say I *am* a boy—and can't understand being anything else—it's hard, it's very hard to explain—"

"You get it off your chest. You go right ahead. Talk it out."

"Well, that's about all, Dad. I don't really want to go into the harness business . . ."

"There's lots of businesses—"

"I don't want to go into any business. Even if I did want to—but I can't want to. I've tried. I want you to believe that. There just isn't anything else."

"Well, you haven't got any great problem there. You can always make it a *second* ambition. Make all the money you can first. Then, someday when you're rich and can afford to amuse yourself any way you're a mind to, cut loose and take a vacation and study to be a doctor, if you want to. You can always do that. Meanwhile, let me be your guide, Luke."

"But you can't do that, Dad! You can't put it off!"

"Then make it your hobby. Take up some business you like and make a go of it and make Medicine your hobby. Lots of people do that. Any number of successful men—"

"Who?"

"Who? I don't know who! They just do!"

"It's different, Dad, with Medicine. You've got to throw your whole life into it—you've got to start and never stop—it's your whole life—it's—"

"All right, Lucas, you've talked long enough. I've heard everything you had to say, you've got it all off your chest, I've tried to be patient, I've tried to show you how things stand. It's all right for a boy to dream, I can understand that. But you're no boy any longer. You're a young man. It's high time you took stock of yourself and the world you've been born into and put these silly schoolgirl schemes and dreams behind you. You've had your fling and it's time to settle down. When I was your age I was up at four o'clock every morning and I worked until I dropped and I was hungry and cold most of the time and ragged the rest. Now I'll tell you this, Lucas. And it's the last I'll tell you. And I've had my say. If you want to be a doctor you can be a doctor. I'll not lift a finger to stop you.

You go right ahead and be whatever you want. But don't expect me to help you do something I know is dead wrong. For I won't do it. I won't have any part in it. I've gone along, been reasonable. Waited for you to come to your senses. You talk like a child. Now do as you please. But don't forget this. Tack it up in your memory and don't forget it. I'm not sending you to college and paying my good money so you can learn to make a living telling some rich bitch why she has to take a shit once a day!"

Therefore Lucas made his plans to run away.

He did not plan with resentment or anger or indignation. He planned with fear. He was afraid that if he did not run away he would not become a doctor. He went to Dr. Alexander again. He asked for advice, where to go, what to do. He was humble, he was anxious, and he was inflexible. Dr. Alexander listened. When Lucas left he clapped on his hat and went to the harness shop.

"I'd like to have a talk with you and Mrs. Marsh," he said shortly.

"Absolutely. Nothing we can't straighten out, I guess. Wait a minute and we'll go see Mrs. Marsh. Or would this evening do just as well?"

"I've got my calls. As you say, it won't take long."

Ouida opened the door. She stared from Job to the doctor.

"What's wrong? What's happened?"

"Now, take it easy, Ouida, nothing's happened, doctor feels there's something we ought to know." He pushed past her into the house.

"Is it Lucas?" Her hand flew to her throat. "Is something the matter with him?" Her voice had become husky. She coughed, swallowed hard.

"Nothing has happened, Mrs. Marsh." Dr. Alexander sat down. "We are three adults and between us we can see that nothing does. Lucas is about to run away."

"Now I think of it, it's the best thing that could happen to him," Job cried. "Make a man of him."

"But he's never given any sign—!" Ouida protested. She cleared her throat impatiently. "He's happy in his home—his school life—he's a good boy—is he in trouble?"

"He wants to study Medicine," said Dr. Alexander.

"He wants to study Medicine?" Ouida echoed.

"He wants to study Medicine," Job said impatiently. "And if we don't let him study Medicine he's going to run away."

Ouida looked at the two men unbelievingly.

"That's right," said Job angrily. "So the doctor has to take time off from *his* work and I have to take time off from *my* work—I ought to be in Meridian right this very minute—"

"Yes," said the doctor. "Well, there it is. Tell me, have you got anything against Medicine?"

"You know how it is, Doc. A man wants his kid to have the best. I've had to make my own way, I've had to work hard all my life. And you and I know that Medicine isn't exactly, well—"

"It's not a field a man goes into to make his fortune."

"That's what I say. That's all I say."

"I've known Lucas since he was a little boy. I've never known the time he didn't want to be a doctor. Some men are born to be doctors. I shouldn't be at all surprised but Lucas is one of those men."

"But you're not sure!"

"No, I'm not sure. I'm not really too sure of anything. But as sure as I *can* be of anything, I'm sure Lucas was meant to be a doctor."

Ouida started to speak but was overwhelmed by a storm of coughing. They waited for her to subside.

"I'm not what you'd call a hard man, Doctor. Mostly, I've left the whole care of the boy to his mother. That's right and proper. But this is a decision for men. It isn't a choice left up to children and women. You know what the world is. And I know what the world is. It isn't any dream-world. I'd like it so, well as the next. But it isn't. It's what it is. You've got to have money. The world revolves around it. You've got to have it. There's only one way to get it, you've got to get it from the next fellow. There's folks think that isn't a pretty picture. I don't see anything wrong with it. And if I did, it wouldn't matter a damn. For that's the way it is. Right or wrong, that's the world we're born into, whether we're born with a hankering for this or that or God knows what."

"You mind your manners!" Ouida cried.

Job ignored her.

"Now, don't go getting mad if I tread close to the bone."

"You keep a civil tongue in your head," said Ouida angrily.

"This is between Doc and me. You just sit back and keep your mouth shut. Now then, Doc! Can a man be a rich doctor?"

"There's no reason why he shouldn't—"

"No pussyfooting, now! The real truth. It'll never go out of this house!"

"I'm going to answer what I think is in your mind. The highest ideal of a good doctor doesn't includes riches. Many a doctor has invested the money he's made through healing and become rich that way. In the purest sense of the word, if he'd been devoting every instant to his patients he wouldn't have had time for investments. And if someone had made the investments for him he should, ideally, have plowed the money back into his practice to provide better equipment and care for his patients. There are also men who fight to establish a practice in a fashionable neighborhood, in a rich neighborhood, and who become rich that way. That conflicts with the highest ideal of Medicine, for healing is for all, and one should not aim to heal only the rich. I'm going to be entirely truthful with you; in the finest possible sense of the word there is no such thing as a rich doctor."

"That's enough for me."

"That is the reason why you do not want your son to study Medicine?"

"That's it, Doc. I could hem and haw and say a lot more. But that's it."

"And I'm his mother! And I say he has a right to follow what God has put in his heart."

"God put in my heart an almighty yen to be a circus rider once," Job said with a grin.

"I think Lucas will be a doctor, Mr. Marsh," said Dr. Alexander. "I think you'd be wise to help him. I don't think there's anything else in life for him."

"Over my dead body."

"He can't do it alone. That's what I must tell you. He knows that."

"I'll tell you what. If he likes it bad enough he'll work his way through."

"Not Medicine."

"He can't work his way through college like any other boy?"

"Not medical college."

"You mean to tell me nobody's ever worked their way through medical college?"

"A few. It's been done. It used to be easier. But the more we discover, the more there is to study. Today the chances of a boy going through medical school without help are hopeless. There isn't time. He has eight hours of classroom work every day. He has to study at least five hours. He has to sleep seven hours. If he spends an hour a day to eat three meals and perform his natural functions, that leaves him three hours."

"That's three hours, though," Job said stubbornly. "When I was a boy—"

"Those three hours are badly placed for a boy looking for work. They come after an ordinary man's usual working hours. They offer part-time jobs, janitor work, dishwashing, maybe tutoring. And there's hundreds competing in those three hours."

"There's Sundays."

"Job!"

"Yes, there's Sundays. And assuming he's so very, very fortunate as to find work on Sunday, assuming he's able to get ten hours work every Sunday, his total hours for a week add up to twenty-eight hours. If he's most fortunate, he'll get as high as thirty cents an hour. It isn't likely. But even then his weekly earnings will amount to eight dollars and forty cents a week."

"Look, Doc! When I was Luke's age I was on my own. If I'd had eight whole dollars every week—"

"Eight dollars a week isn't what it used to be, Mr. Marsh. The hame strap that used to cost me a dollar at your shop now costs me a dollar and sixty cents. But out of that eight dollars and forty cents a week, your son would have to clothe himself, feed himself, and provide a roof over his head."

"Make a man of him!"

"And in addition, he'd have to pay his tuition."

"How much is that?"

"Roughly, around three hundred dollars a term. Say six hundred a year. And add to that about seventy-five dollars for his books, all secondhand, his laboratory fees and supplies. The lowest you can possibly estimate—and I tell you frankly it cannot be done on that—is that the boy has to earn seventy dollars a month. And in the summer, completely untrained, he will somehow have to earn the unheard-of sum of a hundred and twenty-five dollars a month, living at home, of course, and with no expenses. Can you think of some way he can earn in Milletta as much as a bank cashier?"

"It can't be done," said Job.

"I say nothing of what it would do to his health."

"And how do you expect a boy to study with all that? What does Lucas know about working?" Ouida demanded indignantly.

"That's what it means, Mr. Marsh."

"Just to be a doctor."

"That's right."

"And when he's all through, when he's graduated—"

"Then a year as intern at some hospital—the best one he can get into. And the best hospitals take the brightest boys—those who've had most time to study."

"What does he get then?"

"He gets his meals, his uniforms, his laundry, and from ten to fifteen dollars a month."

Job's face darkened.

"That's what it is to be a doctor! That's the big reward, is it?"

"I'm not going to hold anything back. I'm going to give you the whole picture. When he's through with his internship he has to set up in practice. It's going to cost him at least three thousand dollars for his instruments, his office, his equipment. And when he's done all that, probably gone into debt for it, like most of us, he'll have to sit and wait for patients. It'll be five years, all of five years, before he even begins to get out of the red. That's what it is. That's the whole picture. I haven't tried to give you the bright side."

He finished speaking and there was silence.

"Can you imagine yourself a doctor?"

"No offense—I frankly can't!"

"Well, Lucas can't any more imagine himself being a businessman. He just can't imagine it. I don't know you folks very well. I'm thinking of the little fellow who used to haunt my doorstep. He knows you know what's best for him. He knows you love him and you're wiser than he is. He would give anything to be what you want him to be. He doesn't know how. He's what he is. Nothing can change him. It doesn't happen often. It happens once in ten million. He's born to it. Rich or poor, Lucas Marsh was made by God Almighty to be a doctor. The rest is up to you. I can't say more."

"He'll be a doctor," Ouida said quietly.

"I only want to do what's right for the boy," Job said stubbornly. "I still say—"

Job wavered. He was confused. He was alone. It was as if he were losing the boy, as if Lucas were vanishing into another world. There was nothing to share with him. He was on his alien way. He was adrift in a world where he would invent phrases to cover his bare bones and maxims to fill his belly, adrift like millions around him, milling like cattle around the planet, lost and lost and lost and all the while with a father who knew the way, who could help him, who could share the truth with him, open his eyes to it, set him securely on the only way.

"Mr. Marsh and I want only what's best for the boy," Ouida said. "It's just never been explained to us. None of us knew how deep it was with Lucas, it could have been only a child's fancy . . ."

"I've got to be on my calls," the doctor said. He looked at his watch. "I'm late."

"Want to thank you." Job rose numbly. "Glad to pay you for your time—"

"No need for that! I should have come sooner."

"Man's time is worth something—"

"You give that boy his chance and I'll be more than paid."

"I want to thank you, Doctor—" Ouida came toward him. "I want you to know—" A cough interrupted her. "I want—" The cough overwhelmed her, she was racked by a spasm, she groped back to her chair and bent over it, helpless.

"That's a bad cough you've got there." Dr. Alexander walked to her side.

"Got her lungs full of smoke," Job shouted to be heard over the noise of Ouida's coughing. "She's been losing weight, too." He was glad of the diversion. "Better look her over, Doc."

The doctor pressed Ouida into the chair. He tilted her head back. A little blood showed at the corners of her mouth. She bent her head, swallowed, mastered the coughing, drew a deep breath.

"It's nothing. I'm quite all right. Really."

Doctor Alexander stooped, opened his bag, drew out a wooden depressor and a reflector.

"All right, now?"

Ouida nodded.

He opened her mouth. He peered at her throat. He looked a long time. He let her close her mouth. He drew back and waited. Then he opened her mouth again, bent over her and peered again.

He straightened. He removed the reflector from his forehead and put it back in the bag.

"Bad one, ain't it, Doc? She's been coughing like that for almost a month. I told her get it looked at—"

"Smoke—" Ouida swallowed. "Smoke got in my lungs. Burned a bread pudding. Whole kitchen full of smoke—" She waved her hand.

"I think you'd better come to the office," the doctor said. He smiled.

"I rarely go to doctors. I'll come in sometime if it isn't better."

"Yes. No hurry. Still—wouldn't do any harm to come on back with me—get it over—"

"Go on, Ouida! Place sounds like a dog pound!"

"It really isn't necessary—" Ouida searched the doctor's face.

"Might as well catch it," the doctor said indifferently and firmly. "Won't take a minute . . ."

Job drove them to the doctor's office and returned soberly to the shop. In the shop he stood sadly. The boy was not lost yet. He held to that thought. There were two years of premedical training. A lot could happen in those two years. In those two years lay the whole answer. If he couldn't make the boy see reason in two years it would be his own fault. The truth was there, plain and easy. The boy would see it. The scales would drop from his eyes. He'd look up one day, he'd laugh at himself. And he and the boy would be together. Forever. The whole world their oyster. The world waiting for them. It was a lonely world. There wasn't any doubt of that, the world was damned lonely. Ouida was all right but she had a world of her own, she lived in another world. Nobody lived in the right world. Only himself. It was lonely, all right. Sometimes it was damned lonely. Now there'd be the boy. He and the boy. And the boy'd have something to come to, by God! He remembered Meridian suddenly. He reckoned his small empire of eight stores. Eight was just the beginner. He'd been sitting still too long. Time was wasting. He had the store in Meridian now. And who'd ever have believed that? It was easy. The world was easy. The world was made up of fools who played games and mouthed pious noises at each other as they gulped at each other's guts. Little nibbling gulps. Polite gulps. With their little fingers held out, just so. As if they weren't feeding on each other at all, oh no, they weren't doing what they seemed to be doing at all. They weren't even seeming to be doing. Job grinned. The boy and he would have many a chuckle over it. He got together his papers and headed for Meridian.

⁎ CHAPTER 8

In the doctor's office Ouida sat down gingerly in the examining chair and held her mouth open.

"I'm not going to look right now, Mrs. Marsh. I want to ask you some questions."

"I've had quinsy a long time."

"I see you have."

"Caught it so badly last winter I've never been able to shake it off."

"Made you lose weight, too? Dropped quite a bit?"

"Yes. I always stay the same. But lately—" She gathered a loose fold of her dress.

"What have you been doing for this quinsy?"

"I want you to know something, Doctor. I'm here because I'm grateful to you. I don't want to hurt your feelings. That's why I came. I believe in mind over matter. I control my own body. Completely and absolutely. I've never been ill a moment in my life. My body doesn't control me. When I let this quinsy take over I am being punished for my own weakness."

"If everyone was like you where would my practice be?"

"You may laugh at me if you wish—"

"Not at all! Not at all, Mrs. Marsh—"

"I do not permit illness! I have been treating my throat by myself!"

"And you used—?"

"I do not expect you to believe this, Doctor, but there are forces, forces not of this earth, divine forces. I summon them. They cure me."

"Those—ah—forces, they are all you have employed?"

She bent her head slightly.

"Once or twice, when the pain was particularly strong—when I was particularly weak, rather—I used a strong salt gargle. They rebuked me."

He looked at her seriously, his eyebrows lifted inquiringly.

"My forces. They instructed me. They took away my salt water. They told me to use witch hazel."

"You gargled with witch hazel?"

"With the pure infusion of the trees as God made them."

"And did this give you relief?"

"I have been remiss. If I had continued I should be cured."

"You used nothing else?"

"Nothing."

"No strong acids, chemicals of any kind?"

"None. I did as I was told. They have never failed me."

"Yes. Now, if you will open your mouth again . . ."

He searched her throat closely.

"I am going to do something that may cause you discomfort."

She smiled contemptuously. She opened her mouth to him. He bent closer. In a little while she gagged, he continued nevertheless a moment longer.

He straightened at last, looked at her. She looked back at him serenely, questioningly. He sat down at his desk and began to write.

"I won't need any medicine, Doctor," she said firmly.

"No, I know. This is just something to ease that cough a little—"

"Is it witch hazel?" she demanded.

"Sort of witch hazel, something we made from witch hazel—"

"Well—" she said doubtfully.

"You could call it witch hazel, all right."

"I'm not supposed to have anything but witch hazel—"

"This is just the essence of witch hazel, you might say, purified witch hazel—"

"You may think me odd, Doctor, but I assure you there are things not found in books—"

"I encounter those things every day," he said gravely. "You have a perfect right to whatever is—revealed to you."

"Do you think Lucas really would have run away?"

"He would have hated to, but he honestly saw no other course."

"But I'm his mother! Why didn't he come to me! I can't imagine Lucas—"

"Would you have advised him to run away?"

"We could have talked it over. There would have been a way—"

"Tell me, Mrs. Marsh, what did your mother die of?"

"She had heart failure, poor soul. My father too."

"Yes . . . Any throat weakness?"

"Not that I know of. Oh, the usual sore throats—"

"I understand. And you—?"

"I've always seemed to have a weakness here." She put her hand to her throat. "Nothing to bother me, much. But when I caught colds they always seemed to lodge just here. They were the worst of the colds. Not that I've had many," she said hastily. "And lately I've had lumps—these lumps on my shoulder." She pulled her dress to show him. He fingered the lumps expressionlessly.

"And this particular sore throat—"

"I've had it ever since I burned the pudding, the whole kitchen was full of smoke and—"

"But not before?"

"Not that I know of. Oh, it was sore from time to time, little sorenesses, they passed, everything passes, you know, Doctor . . ."

"I admire your courage, Mrs. Marsh."

"Thank you." She flushed.

"I wish more of my patients were like you."

"May I go home now?" She smiled.

He hesitated. He looked over his notes again swiftly.

"Yes. Have this filled."

"Is it a gargle?"

"No, these are pills. You may gargle if you like. Take these pills. When your throat is sore, when you feel you should take them. That will be your best guide."

Lucas, who had been home, then to the harness shop, was waiting for her when she returned home.

"Where have you been?" he asked anxiously.

"What have *you* been up to? What's this I hear—from strangers—that you're going to run away?"

"There's nothing else for me to do," he said in a low voice.

"There's always something else for you to do. You could always come to the mother who loves you."

"You don't know, Mother. I had a talk with Father."

"Tell me what he said. Tell me every word."

"It's no use."

"Tell me, Lucas."

"You'd only get mad at him and then there'd be fighting, and I'd be the cause of it. He'll never understand. Never . . ."

"I don't want to ever hear again as long as I live that you're running away. Do you hear me, Lucas? If you feel you must run away you must come to me and tell me. Now listen! Now you are going to feel foolish." She waited. He said nothing, his head down. "Did you think Dr. Alexander was going to help you? He came straight to us! Why do you do such things, Lucas? Why do you torment me? Going to strangers! Confiding in a stranger and not your own mother! What have I done to deserve such a thing from you! I know I must deserve it. But what have I done! Only tell me!"

He gaped at her. "You mean I can study Medicine now? You mean Dad said I could?"

"Now, Lucas! Don't get excited! He hasn't said so!"

"But there's a chance? A chance?"

"Lucas! Now stop it!"

He groped toward her. She gathered him in hungrily.

"My own boy . . ." She rocked him in her arms. "My darling, my darling . . ." She coughed, held him closer, held back the cough swelling in her by sheer will. She did not understand why Lucas was so moved, the violence of it was beyond her understanding, but he was in her arms and he clung to her.

Dr. Alexander stopped at the harness shop next day.

"I'd like to speak to you for a moment."

"Come in, Doc. Sit down. What's on your mind?"

"I want you to prepare yourself. I have something to tell you, something you must face."

"Ouida?" he asked blankly. Then a sudden thought came to him. "Oh, now, her tongue gets a little loose now and then. I don't know what she's said, Doc, but you mustn't mind it. Why, Lord, she says things to me that—"

The doctor looked at him compassionately.

"It's cancer, Mr. Marsh. Cancer of the throat."

Job sat down. He swallowed. He stared at the doctor.

"Cancer of the throat?"

"There's no possible doubt. I wish there were. I'm afraid it's in the last stages."

"You're joking!"

"Would you like to take her to another doctor? I can understand. I wish there were room for doubt. By all means have someone else—"

"Ouida? You talking about Ouida?"

The doctor nodded sadly.

"But she's still walking around—healthy—same as ever—"

"I know. It's horrible. . . . She'll be dead in six months."

"Six months!" Job cried wildly.

"At the outside. Perhaps in two. It's going very fast. It's out of control now. I'm going to say something to you, Mr. Marsh: it would be the blessing if she died tonight!"

Job licked his lips.

"Haven't you ever noticed she had trouble swallowing?"

"Never—no, by God, never! Wait! Last Christmas a piece of plum cake seemed to choke her. She's been tetchy for soft foods ever since. That's right! Trouble swallowing! Hell, she's always had trouble with her throat, more or less, colds seemed to take her there, quinsy sort of, never gave it a thought, never babied herself any, so naturally I never thought—you can operate, can't you? There's bound to be *some* chance—!"

"There isn't a chance, Mr. Marsh. I can operate. But I know before I start—there isn't a chance."

"Maybe she'll *want* you to operate—"

"I don't think she will. You know Mrs. Marsh. She might. I'll do whatever you say. You're going to have to face it. She's going to have a bad time. And you're going to have to watch it. At first I can give her pills. I gave her some today. I had to tell her they were witch hazel. She's in considerable pain. She's not the type that lets on. They weren't witch hazel, of course. They were morphine. She'll need more and more. In a little while morphine won't help her."

"There must be something—"

"There is. There's one thing. Death."

Toward the end, Ouida Marsh seemed to become younger, young as a young girl. Her body withered rapidly as the doctor had predicted, she complained of quinsy and when her remedies did not help her she turned apathetically to what comfort the doctor could provide. It was not possible to guess what agonies she bore, for she bore them silently, but they must have been very great and, for a lesser person, unendurable. Once, Lucas came home early from school to hear the low noise of her hoarse cries, but she heard the door open and close and an instant after he entered she was silent. She wrote long letters to Lucas and to Job, and toward the end it was evident from these letters that she must have had an inkling of her waiting death. Her throat closed rapidly, then sloughed open, then closed again; her sounds were thick and burbled and unintelligible. For a time she was lonely and frightened. However close Lucas pressed himself to her, however long into the night Job sat beside her watching, holding her hand, they did not seem able to reach her, to be with her, to be in place of the loneliness and the fear. Then the blessing of the morphine took her mind and greater and greater doses pushed back everything but the pain, pain too heavy to be moved, agony too deep to be reached. Toward the end they prayed for her to go. They loved her, a part of Lucas died with her, but it was too much. Too much, too much, greater than all of them, too much to bear, poor soul let her go, let her die, let it end. . . .

The doctor stayed with her very late one night.

Next morning she was dead.

She lay as a young girl might lie, curled, very small, cold, motionless, her haggard mouth a little open, her eyes closed. Where her body had rested the sheet was a little stained.

"No!" screamed Lucas, "you will not bury her! Never! Never! Never!"

"Son, son," snuffled Job. "It's all right, boy, they've got to do it . . ."

"Never! Please, please, never . . ."

Ouida Marsh was gone.

CHAPTER 9

She was buried.

The ritual noises were made. The earth was smoothed. The day ended. The sun rose. The day ended.

Day, day day, and then no more days. Now the weeks came, now a month. Time was a shattered window into the void. And into the void his tears fell. Into the blackness, the mouthing blackness, the tears fell, never stop, I swear it, never, never, never. And the tears stopped, slowly. They were a trickle. And then they stopped. And one day of one week of one month after the breast had healed, after the jags were lonely palisades peering the unknown, one day the glass was whole again. And time was a window. And beyond the window was Ouida, dead.

Beyond the window.

Not gone.

But gone, all the same.

Lucas sat by the grave long, still hours. He sat by the grave and looked into time and shivered and saw nothing. He sat and brooded and now and again he patted tenderly the earth mounded upon Ouida who lay far beneath, patted as if he patted Ouida herself, ran his fingers through the grasses. He brooded nothingness. He had no thoughts. Once he stepped upon a corner of the grave and shrank, cringing, and moaned. Over and over he patted her where he had stepped, where it had hurt.

After a while he returned to school. When the day's study was over he went to the cemetery. He brought his books and there he studied, and sometimes he talked about his problems and sometimes he read aloud. You could not see his lips move. A few feet away and you could not even hear him. Her feet could not hear him. Only her head.

In the evening he would rise, he would walk reluctantly away from her, he would leave this other home, he would sigh and walk to the house, he would let himself in.

They had a servant, now, they had hired a girl who kept the house and looked after them. At first she had gone home nights. Now she slept there, in an unused room.

And Job would enter, after a while, and put on a sober, unsmiling, grave face and when the evening meal had ended he would rise and leave the house and go silently back to the shop. And Lucas would study dully, and the time coming, rise and go to bed.

Job entered the house reluctantly and left it with relief. For in the house and with Lucas the funeral had never ended. And for Job the funeral had ended on the day the first clod fell hollowly on Ouida's coffin, within five minutes the grave was filled, the earth was flat except for the telltale mound, and with it, turning away, there was no help for it, Ouida was gone.

There fell to his lot now a time for sober face, for small speech, for gravity, for decorous acceptance of the tribal noises of sympathy. Work was the same, the demands of the day were the same, everything was to do, everything was to be done, nothing had happened to these things, there was no death here, no caring. But one did what was to be done unsmilingly, putting the smile away, decorous for the season of such things, sad for the time of sadness.

"I guess you're going to college this fall, ain't you?" he asked one night.

"Am I?" Lucas asked dully.

"That's what your mother wanted," Job said quietly. "You'll go this fall." His heart warmed. "Got the money all laid aside. Been saving it a long while. I'm always looking out for you, Lucas. Don't forget that."

"I know, Dad."

"Sometimes it may seem as if I'm not. But I always am. Don't forget that."

Inwardly he groped for a new relationship.

"You all right?" he asked delicately.

"I'm fine," Lucas said, faintly embarrassed.

"Don't need anything?"

"I'm lonesome," said Lucas simply.

"Same here," said Job. He warmed at the confidence. There was, of course, nothing else to say.

Lucas, he confessed to himself next day, he did not understand. All other people were easy. He could almost always foretell unerringly what they would do; within a few moments of meeting them he sensed their limits, their weaknesses, their vulnerabilities.

But Lucas— He sighed.

"I tell you, Charley, if I hadn't married Mrs. Marsh I could have been one of the Morgans."

"Don't doubt it."

"I'll bet I could."

"I'll say this for you, Job Marsh, there ain't anybody in the world, and I worked in plenty of harness shops, there ain't ever anybody knows harness like you do."

"I'm glad I married her, you understand—"

"Naturally."

"I'm only saying—"

"She was a good woman . . ."

"Finer woman never drew breath—"

"Pretty—smart—"

"You know something, Charley? I'll tell you something. She was her own worst enemy."

"I didn't know her good—"

"Her own worst enemy."

If I was a young fellow, Job thought with alarm, I'd be off in the cities right now. New York. I'd be in New York, nothing could stop me, look at me here! And do you know where I'd be? I missed a boat! That's what I did! And never knew it! I've got to get going! While there's still time!

"Hang on, Charley," he said jubilantly, free.

And he departed for Meridian.

"What do you do all day?" he asked Lucas next morning.

"Nothing," Lucas said defensively, "I take walks, I read—"

"Don't want you hanging around the house—"

"I don't—"

"Do you good to come down to the shop, help out a while, take your mind off things."

"Yes, sir."

"Instead of frowsting around."

Lucas looked down at his plate.

"Might as well come down this morning."

"Now?"

"If you're through eating. That's where I'm going."

Thereafter for a week Lucas went to the harness shop with his father every morning. For a time Job and Charley set him to sorting harness, hoping to infect him with interest by the contagion of leather, and if he had shown any interest or even capacity they were leagued to put him to small repairs. But Lucas had no interest in harness, neither in the shape of leather nor in its odor, its repair or its purposes. He sorted badly.

"You blind or something?" Job asked incredulously. Charlie turned away, embarrassed.

"I'm sorry," said Lucas.

"Don't even know what you done wrong, do you! Mixing up check-reins and hame straps and things that don't even *look* like each other."

"I'm sorry. I can see it, now—"

"You're a smart boy, Lucas. You're not that dumb!"

"I'm not doing it deliberately—"

"He don't do nothing else all day, Mr. Marsh. I'll say that for him," Charley seconded.

"I don't know what I've done to you that you should do me that way," Job said remindingly.

"I'll try—I'll do better," Lucas promised anxiously.

"You better just wait on trade," Job said. "Let him wait on the trade, Charley. The prices are marked on everything."

"I'm sorry—I'm really sorry."

Job nodded. He walked out of the shop.

In the next two weeks he was seldom at the shop. The store in Meridian claimed him. Usually he did not come home until late, sometimes not until the next day. Lucas went to Dr. Alexander's house in the evenings after dinner, content to sit on the porch and read his anatomy book as long as there was daylight if the doctor was out, and sometimes he arrived on time to go out on late calls with him. In the beginning he sat silent.

"I want to tell you something," Dr. Alexander said finally. "I know you're grieving for your ma. And this is what I want to tell you. Save your pity for the living. The dead can't use it. And it won't save the dying. You're wasting your time. Pity's valuable. Don't waste it."

After that it was easier. Somehow the grave was dug deeper. Somehow Ouida no longer lay just below the raw mound. But she returned to the house one night. She returned abruptly.

It was on one of the nights Job returned from Meridian very late. This night Lucas heard him enter. He got out of bed. He opened his bedroom door, he was about to intercept Job and suggest a midnight raid on the icebox. His smile faded. Job was tiptoeing into the servant girl's room. He watched, dumfounded, as the door closed. In another moment he heard his father's voice, the servant's giggle, a bed creaking. He returned to his room, leaving his door open. He sat on the edge of his bed. He tried to think but he could not. He felt Ouida present in the house, very strongly present, invincibly present. He choked with a distaste and shame. And then anger, and he sat on, rigidly, coldly committed, waiting, and when he heard the door open down the hall he rushed out to the landing. Job was leaving the servant's room. He was barefoot. He had on only his trousers. He carried the rest of his clothing in his hand. He looked up, startled and then sheepish at the sight of Lucas. Lucas turned immediately and went back to his room, closing his door carefully behind him. He returned to bed. For a long time he tried to sleep. At last he rose with deliberation, turned on his light, picked up his anatomy book, and began to read. Daylight came. He blinked, stretched, regarded the light with satisfaction, read on, heard the house stir, opened his door a few inches so that it could be seen that his light was on. When he had heard the servant and Job go downstairs he dressed leisurely. He sat opposite his father during breakfast. He said nothing. Job read the paper.

Into the shop that afternoon came Dr. Alexander. Job hastened forward. Dr. Alexander shook his head.

"I see you've already got a job," he said to Lucas.

"Not really," Lucas said eagerly. "I'm just in the way here—"

"Thought I'd break him in," said Job. "Got him selling. Had a little trouble at first but now he's doing all right."

"Glad to hear it," Dr. Alexander nodded. "Well—I guess I'll have to look for somebody else."

"Sorry," said Job.

"Wait!" said Lucas. They looked at him. "You don't really need me, Dad." He looked at Job meaningly.

"That so?" said Job, challenged.

"No," said Lucas. "This is work our servant girl could do." He looked steadily at his father. Job looked away. "I'll be right with you," Lucas cried to Dr. Alexander. He scrambled into his coat.

"If you're sure it's all right," said Dr. Alexander.

"Guess he knows what he's doing," said Job. There was a faint smile on his reluctant lips.

The shop door shut behind them. They got into the carriage.

"You might as well start today," said Dr. Alexander. "This is the sort of job that happens once in a lifetime to a fellow in your boots. You're going to take care of a man by the name of Fellowes. Have you ever heard of the Reverend Fellowes?"

The carriage jogged on. Dr. Alexander talked steadily. The Reverend Stephen Fellowes was a retired minister. He lived on the outskirts of the town he had once served and he had a small income which kept a housekeeper for him. Lucas' job was a simple one. He was to be the old man's companion for the next two months, he was to sit with him, to read to him when he desired to be read to, and to be sure that he was served with a urinal every three hours.

"I don't say you'll get rich from the wages," Dr. Alexander admitted. "But you'll have a patient. In a sense this man will be your first patient, there's that element. And being exposed to a man like that for two months is better than a year of college. You'll get five dollars a week and your lunches."

For the next two months Lucas adventured in a world completely different from Milletta. The Reverend Fellowes was a thin old man, given to long silences, to books, and to brooding. The first embarrassment of serving so remote a man with a urinal soon passed, Lucas learned to read aloud, and although much of what he read was incomprehensible to him, the Reverend Fellowes having a taste for religious quibbles of the eighteenth century, he read the whole of Homer that summer and a great deal of Virgil and Horace and Ovid and Suetonius and a history of the Greeks. At such times, and in such literary company, the thin old man's parchment-like skin would acquire a faint rose hue, his eyes would become hard and bright, and the lines of his mouth would play with the letters of indomitable, he would be immortal in another century, he would be a dweller in another land, before another God, in a body that was flesh without mortality.

And some of this beauty was transmitted to Lucas also. Long before the two months were up he discovered why people could follow books so passionately and look at the world they lived in with a superior amusement from behind eyes that had travelled in many pages and in many worlds, and though it bred no hunger in him it bred respect, as a runner watching a weight thrower, or a king watching a president. And this respect became stronger on those nights when Job was home for dinner, although he did not respect Job's accomplishments less for the contrast between the two adults.

But the day that was to remain longest in Lucas' memory of that curious summer, and the image that would all his life be sharpest remembering the Reverend Fellowes and his own youth and his young manhood and the essence of mankind in whom he had recognized himself as a part, came two weeks before the summer ended, as they were reading Xenophon, as the Greeks were coming in sight of the sea.

"Can you see it, Lucas? Do you see those weary heroes, a single hero for all their number, a single hungry man who was all Hellas, all that Greece stood for, born and bred beside the sea's white spume, cradled to its booming roar, the blood of the gods sluicing it wine-dark for the dreaming gaze of young men avid on the cliffs, gone to a far country, fighting among strange rocks, spent on alien sands, through forests and mountains and plains, the months passing, the years, and now come at last, come one day, come one opening of the eyelids of the gods, dumbstruck, disembodied, become eyes and soul, seeing it, seeing it—

" '*Thalassa!*' they cried. Their mouths opened. Their souls shouted. '*Thalassa!* The sea! *The sea!*' "

His face was transfigured. He was all that God could make of this man here in this time, in this place, his soul was clean, his mind was risen.

"*Thalassa,*" he whispered.

And then his face altered. The lines flowed slowly back to plastic, parchment flesh. He licked his lips.

"I waited too long," he said apologetically. Lucas, still dazed, smiled at him, uncomprehending.

"I'm sorry," the old man said.

And suddenly Lucas noticed the wet stain on his trousers. He jumped to his feet guiltily.

"The flesh," the old man murmured as Lucas changed him. "Always the flesh, the flesh. Do you see how we are tied?" he asked, suddenly peevish. "Don't forget that, young man. Don't ever forget it. You'll never be free till you're dead."

"Will there be a Xenophon where we're going?" Lucas asked shyly.

"I don't know," said the old minister. "If it weren't so I would be afraid to die."

The summer ended.

Lucas spent the last days in the small hills about Milletta, avoiding the house, avoiding Job, avoiding the servant, avoiding even Dr. Alexander, content to be unseen, to hatch what he had heard, what he had seen and lived, to watch the shimmering railroad tracks, to disappear with them, into the distance.

The day came and he said farewell to the house, he went to the station, he got into the train like a sleepwalker, while they were still seeking a seat the train moved on, it was over, he was on his way.

In the seat beside him, Job studied a newspaper picture of an automobile. The caption said America was on its way to seventeen million autos. Job grinned. There were more farms than there had ever been, as long as there were farms there would be horses, as long as there were horses there had to be harness.

He remembered, abruptly, gossip about a harness shop in Lankasville, a shop in trouble, a shop run down. He looked at his watch. Lankasville was larger than Meridian.

He patted Lucas' knee.

"Guess we're almost there," he said.

Lucas looked at him warily. His father was smiling at him with friendliness and behind that friendliness was content.

"You be a good boy, Lucas."

"I will, Father."

"If you want anything, you just write me."

"I don't think I'll need anything. I mean—I've got everything—"

"Don't worry about anything."

"I won't."

"That's the main thing."

"Yes, Father."

"You'll be thrown in with a lot of strange people. Well, you were when you were born. Remember that. Every place you go in this world you'll be thrown in with a lot of strange people. So don't think anything of it."

"No, sir."

"Yes . . . Well! . . . Now about women."

"You don't have to—I mean—"

"Don't go getting any nice girl in trouble. That's all you've got to worry about. Just don't go getting any nice girl in trouble. Understand?"

"Yes, Father. But you don't have to—"

"A man's got to have a woman. And I'm not going to be goddamned fool enough to tell you otherwise. You're going to have to have a woman and you're going out looking for one. Just don't go getting any nice girl in trouble. It costs money and trouble. Go get a chippie. Then you'll be safe. Watch yourself. Pick a clean one. Because if you don't you'll find yourself wearing your whatsis in a Bull Durham sack. Clap. Disease. Hurts like hell. Now that's all. I've said my say."

He looked at Lucas and his features relaxed.

"When you're in trouble, come to me. I'm your dad."

The train began to slow.

Lucas rose. He reached for his bags in the rack overhead.

"Think you can find it, all right?" Job asked.

"The school? I—I guess so— Aren't you coming with me?"

"Want me to? Sure! I'll be glad to!"

"I thought—"

"I'll tell you what, Luke, if you can find it yourself it'd be a help. Fact is, I have to get to Lankasville."

"Oh . . . I didn't know . . . Why, sure, Father! Sure I can find it! Don't you worry for a minute! Everything's swell!"

"Because if it isn't—if you want me—"

"No, sir! Absolutely not! I'm glad—I mean—"

"Now you just tell me, Luke! It won't take a minute! It's just that I've just got time to make connections to Lankasville and if I go with you—"

"It's silly, Father. There's no need—"

"I guess you can find it, all right—"

"Of course I can!"

"Just get right into a cab—here!" Job's hand dove into his pocket and emerged with a bill. He pressed it into Lucas' hand.

"I don't need it, Father! I've got plenty—"

"You just take that and pay the man out of it and he'll set you right down at the door. There's ten dollars."

"But it's too much! Honest, Father—"

"Keep it! There's a little extra for you."

The train was stopping. They made their way down the aisle. They stood on the platform.

"Well, Luke—"

They looked at each other uncertainly. They embraced awkwardly, quickly.

"Well, boy—"

Lucas got down from the train quickly.

"Goodbye, Father . . ."

"Take care, now!"

"I will, Father . . ."

"Be a good boy . . ."

"Don't worry—"

"If you need anything—"

The train began to move.

"Goodbye, Father—"

"Goodbye, Luke—"

"Write me—"

Job waved. The car passed. Another car succeeded it. Lucas stood alone on the platform.

A cab driver picked up his bags.

"Take you there and set you down for a dollar'n a quarter."

Lucas nodded. The man turned and slouched toward his cab. Lucas followed him. His home was behind him and he was on his way to school and life had evolved to this, this day, and this beginning. And he remembered where he was and walked more quickly.

⋆ CHAPTER 10

The enrollment he had so long desired and of which he had dreamed with such excitement and longing passed in a succession of clerical progressions through which he moved prosaically and at the end of which he found himself adrift again, trudging toward Saylor Hall and the roommate to whom he had been assigned.

As he walked, one of hundreds of young men swarming erratically over the lawns and gravelled walks of the campus, the severity and ominous exactness of the college buildings penetrated his loneliness. He was dimly aware of the long, the wide, green acres, the river beyond, and behind the campus buildings, the fields and the woods which bordered them. He was jostled many times by the excited youth about him and each time shyness suffocated him and he felt more alien.

He came to Saylor Hall, he mounted the stone steps, he passed inside, he climbed again, he walked down a corridor, scanning doors, he retraced his steps, he read the names on the door cards more carefully, he stiffened suddenly, his own name startled him and beneath his name Alfred Boone, his roommate, a stranger. He looked at the door uncertainly. He read the names again. Finally he opened the door of his home.

There were three persons in the small room. Two of them, adults, a man and a woman, sat on one of the narrow beds. The third, a young man his own age, looked at him from before one of two bureaus.

"I'm Alfred Boone," the young man said after a moment. He came forward, his hand outstretched. Lucas put down his suitcases uncertainly. They shook hands. "This is my mother and father." He gestured to the bed.

"He's hogged the best bureau, he's got the best bed, and if I were you I'd make him start all over again," Mr. Boone said calmly.

"How do you do," Lucas said, confused.

"Don't hit him too hard," said Mrs. Boone, "just hit him once and get it over and we'll all go out to supper together."

The young man bent his head toward them briefly. "Jokers!" he explained. "You can have any bed you want. Any bureau appeals to you. We sat here for a while waiting and then—"

"It's all right," Lucas muttered in an agony of shyness. "I don't care—"

"That's no way to begin with him," warned Mr. Boone. "If I'd beat him early enough I'd still have a tie left. And take this bed, the one we're sitting on—it's the softest."

"Did you come alone?" Mrs. Boone asked.

"Yes, ma'am," Lucas said.

"I'll tell you what you do, why don't you just drop everything and let's go out and eat?" Mr. Boone said quickly.

"Unpack!" cried Mrs. Boone. "Hurry up and unpack! Get it over!"

Flurried, Lucas hastened to open his suitcases, the room was quickly divided, the belongings of both young men were as quickly put away. Lucas covertly examined these strangers.

They were complete strangers. The mother and father did not behave as parents; their behavior was outside his experience. Their good humor and their joking were reminiscent of Job, but Ouida regarded levity suspiciously and rebuked it often. Here there was disconcerting poise and easiness.

And these people liked each other. This was evidently long habit and to them an unremarkable fixture in their relations. He observed them warily. Alfred Boone he could not classify at all.

As they ate together in the small university town Lucas' confusion grew. They talked without preamble of anything, he could not anticipate their next thought. They included him in their intimacy and this equality and regard drew him mightily and at the same time surprised him and made him anxious. He responded timidly. He did his best to join them and to respond as they responded, but he did not know how.

They were very happy together. There was finally no doubt of that. And as it became evident that this was their normal condition he forgot his apprehensions. He saddened; he pitied them, he grew warmly fond of them and he wanted to protect them from the unsmiling world he knew lay about them, the harshness they ignored and the cruelties and the disappointments of which they seemed serenely unaware. Life had taught Lucas that laughter was a brief joy, unexpectedly come and always followed by some reciprocal sorrow or gravity and he was concerned for them because he thought all humans, and especially older humans, knew this.

He looked at the three he had just come to know and it touched him, their kindness, and his heart was wry with pity for what must come to such nice and such kind people. He coveted their affection, their ease, and their incomprehensible happiness.

"You're going to be a doctor too?" Mrs. Boone asked.

"Yes," said Luke eagerly, come to a world he knew. "Yes, I am going to be a doctor."

"You and Alfred. But why?" she asked suddenly. "What is there about Medicine that attracts you, Luke?"

He looked at them shyly, as always nonplussed, unable to form a sentence which would explain clearly to himself how urgent the reason was and how watery the words, an ocean of words, each word a wave, the waves slipping one into another.

"Alfred's a joiner," Mrs. Boone said. "If there's a club or a fraternity Alfred wants to join. Medicine's a fraternity. So Alfred wants to join."

"Listen to her!" said Alfred. They looked at Luke.

They saw a pale young man, the skin a little moist with nervousness, drably dressed, thin, peering at them nervously, anxiously, and uncertainly. There is in most young men the bloom of the year's youth behind them and the mold and set of the year in which they find themselves. On Lucas there was set boy and young man, and the spirit between wavered, made no choice, remained still, waited for further instruction.

He is a handsome thing. Mrs. Boone looked at Luke searchingly. Lovely eyes. Girls are going to like that mouth, the curve of that lower lip, the little line of cruelty there—is it cruelty there at the corners? No mother, poor darling. Pity his father was too busy to come with him. So young. And something in him so old. Something hard, something far beyond Alfred. Force for himself? Or for what he wants? Poor stick! Those clothes! And she looked away then at Alfred.

He's got to get out of himself, Mr. Boone decided. Alfred'll take care of that. Otherwise he'll sit in corners. That's his type. Nice-looking kid. Too shy, though. Goes beyond shyness.

He isn't what I had in mind, Alfred thought philosophically. Looks like a student. Oh, well! I'll have fun elsewhere, and I'll study with him. No trouble, though . . . that's one thing. . . .

He won't hurt me, Lucas thought, peering sidelong at Alfred's face, his large nose, his short brown hair, his thin, angular and tall frame. The impact of these three friendly persons eddied warmly toward him and he abandoned an outpost of his reserve.

"I've always wanted to be a doctor," he blurted.

There was a faint check in the flow of conviviality. It was as if he had shown an arm suddenly naked that ought by rights to be in a coat sleeve.

"Always?" echoed Mrs. Boone.

Luke nodded. He was alone, again. Somehow he had gone too far.

That night Lucas found the darkness comforting. It hid him, it protected him, it made all one. Again the feeling of strangeness, of being a stranger from an outer world, came over him as he thought of Mr. and Mrs. Boone, these parents, these parent quantities, these solid, warm, protecting and protected, these at-ease people.

His wondering slowed. He drowsed in the nearness of sleep. He roused abruptly. His belly was hard with sudden excitement. He was come to the beginning.

A wave of friendship for the creature in the other bed who would share this college living, this great adventure, who was himself, his own counterpart except that his manners were different, who now dreamed the same dreams, made him secure, made him not alone, and he drowsed and sleep washed him warmly onto the dark reaches of unconsciousness.

In the morning he registered for courses with Alfred.

"It's going to be a long wait," he said dubiously when registering was over.

"Two years?" said Alfred incredulously. "Why, it'll be over like that! Then the *real* work begins!"

"Chemistry and physics and math and history and English—what do we need all that for?" Lucas despaired. "That's what makes it so long. Why can't we just take what we'll need in Medicine—and that's all. We could do it in eight months!"

"All I know is we've got two beautiful soft years to play."

"Two years!"

"You act like you want to start Medicine right now!"

"I've been studying with doctors," Lucas confided.

"The hell you have!"

"All that history and English and stuff—"

"That makes you a gentleman, my boy. A gentleman and a scholar and a college man."

"All I want to be is a doctor."

"You're nuts, boy. I'm going to do like the man said—spend the next three days getting acquainted with our fellow convicts."

"Let's walk around, first."

"Hell, the buildings will be there. We'll see enough of them! Gotta make contacts, son!"

He walked with Lucas over the campus. Lucas consulted the small printed map of the university.

"Let's go this way!"

"Wonder where that guy came from—looks like a South American. . . . There's a guy dressed like a college man, that's a sophomore, sure! . . . Boy, look at him! . . ." Alfred examined the humans about him with interest and absorption. Lucas pressed on. At the medical buildings Lucas stopped, open-mouthed. He drew a deep sigh. Alfred looked at him quickly.

"Is *this* what you wanted to see?"

"Look!"

"It looks just like the rest!"

The brick walls of the medical college rose before them, stiff and serene, and, to Lucas, remote as Carcassonne.

Alfred shifted embarrassedly.

"Look at those guys going in and out," he said tactfully, hoping no one would notice Lucas staring thus. "Older fellows, aren't they? Boy, they got a grind. And do they know it! Look at those faces."

Lucas gaped at the privileged and ordained, passing quickly and silently in and out of the medical-college buildings. They talked to each other soberly, in low voices, their foreheads were creased anxiously. That older man, that adult, was surely a professor, and as he watched, the students divided respectfully to let him pass; at the other college buildings he would have been jostled unceremoniously.

"Two years!" Lucas murmured, shaken.

"Long enough! Come on! We've seen it! We got work to do. We got to get acquainted. Let's go where we belong!"

Slowly and unwillingly Lucas moved away, looking to the last, hungering for the place where he belonged.

At Saylor Hall Alfred moved from room to room, making friends, selecting carefully, casting his lot among his own. Obediently, Lucas followed him. They found their eating hall, they moved leisurely about the athletic fields, strolled to the nearby town. On the way Alfred picked up a small covey of other young men. Gradually, Lucas drifted to the outside of the group.

Next day Lucas left Alfred to further acquaintance making. He walked about the entire university. In an hour he was loitering again outside the medical buildings. Late in the afternoon, emboldened by familiarity, he sat on the steps of one of the buildings, straining his ears to catch a stray word from the passing students, words in the Language. Later, he loitered about the hospital, watching patients enter, trying to guess their ailments, watching the doctors drive up at the rear, seeing the brisk, white hustling of nurses.

In the months to come he would linger and hunger often. Occasionally a medical student would greet him, and he would thrill and stiffen with embarrassment, and in a few moments the medical student would discover that he was an outlander and mumble awkwardly and walk on. And Lucas would stare after him, gratefully.

Two years.

But he was in college. Now he was here. Nothing would ever break his hold.

There were some of his fellows who in after life, triggered by certain memories, would leaf with thickened fingers through their recollections and, like a man pawing his pocketbook for a weathered snapshot, produce a happy memory of a happy college life, a single feeling that summed it all, an involuntary smile at the memory of play, of young being young among young. There would be a few, like Lucas, who in after years and as long as they lived would remember college as their home, the first loved home since their birth, the home they preferred to all homes, all caves, all parents, all rules, organizations, hearths, cradles, and hunting packs on the planet.

In this place, subject to a few simple rules, he was free. And he could spend his days, and his nights too, if he liked, it was all up to him, his mind a hone on which his vector sharpened, studying fiercely and endlessly and implacably, deliriously free to follow the direction of his force.

Alfred, who took the same subjects, studied little, threw his books impatiently aside, dressed himself with great care and fled. Once or twice during the first week, estimating guiltily that Lucas was either poor or shy, he was on the point of speaking, of inviting Lucas to go with him, he had almost lipped the words into the air. He checked himself each time. Lucas' face, studying, was unconcealed pleasure. It was inconceivable, seeing him, that he could be happier.

They were very friendly. They liked each other. They were very cheerful together, they became good friends quickly. And Alfred waited patiently for the day when Lucas would be bored with study, when fatigue would provide him with an opportunity to show Lucas the world.

This day never came.

To Lucas, Alfred was incomprehensible. Alfred was a human without a visible plan and without any goal. He was not troubled by the differences between them. Long ago he had found that life as other boys lived it was not his.

In their first days together he was frightened for Alfred and amazed by him. To Alfred each hour of the day was an hour for play, each moment that could be borrowed or stolen or preempted. He played even in classes. He made the most of his freedom.

Little by little Lucas realized that most of the boys at college were like Alfred. The college went comfortably on, the days, the weeks passed. There was no day of reckoning. When Alfred fell behind, as he frequently did, Lucas was relieved to loan him his notes, to work with him. Helping Alfred made him part of the cosmogony of youth, of the youth around him, of the circle he contacted but inside whose circumference he did not live.

He felt no superiority. He felt a difference between himself and them. But as this difference had always existed he did not feel set apart by it; it was his relation to the group.

Little by little Alfred drifted out of his life and out of his considerations. They slept in the same room, they were warm and friendly to each other, they lost their sense of unease and difference. They went their separate ways.

All about him swarmed the life of the college, the young men garbed ritually, speaking ritually of prescribed things, laughing a prescribed laughter, frowning with a prescribed contempt, the young men of the family Hominidae, jealous of their ritual, chosen young men, proudly alert to preserve their difference from the unchosen and from the world from which they had come and from the world into which they were destined, tightly organized chauvinists of prescribed youth, warriors for a four-year custom, the traditionless given a tradition.

When he first came Lucas felt himself an outsider. He walked humbly and looked about him anxiously. He knew no rules and he was self-conscious with the constant fear of offending, of placing himself outside the pack. He soon became aware that almost all the other young men who had been admitted with him walked as gingerly as he walked and were as apprehensive. Alfred was never apprehensive. Alfred had no fears. Alfred was serene.

"It's easy!" he comforted Lucas. "Do as the others do. That's all there is to it. Just do as they do."

The uniform was simple and it was within the reach of even the poorest students. It consisted simply of battered and dirty white shoes with very thick soles, a rumpled raincoat, shirts with buttoned-down collar tabs, trousers of one color and coats of another. No one wore hats.

In a short time he was dressed in this uniform, and now in classes, as he moved about the campus, as he attended the excited rallies of youth, he felt himself to be indistinguishable from the rest. He relaxed. He obeyed the rules youth made for youth.

But there were also ritual noises, ritual thoughts, ritual attitudes, and ritual subjects, ritual amounts of study and play and ritual forays into the terrain of the adult, into the privileges of adult warriors, which included drink, marriage practice, communal smoking, and tribal conference.

And in the vicinity of these things Lucas remained self-conscious, mindful of an audience and aware that while the population of the college presented to the outside world the appearance of a tribe there were little lonely islands in it. And these islands remained lonely and apart. And he knew forlornly that he was one of these islands. He was one of a few dozen such islands, a youth incapable of youth on the common terms of youth.

They saw each other in libraries, inspected each other furtively, spoke rarely and stiffly to each other, fearful of being identified for what they were. They came to know each other by sight, to be able to recognize themselves in occasional newcomers. They kept to themselves. They hoped not to be noticed.

Sometimes in the evenings Lucas thought of Ouida and wondered where she had gone. The impact of her living remained. Her condition was death, she was dead and he knew she was dead. But the impact of Ouida was so strong that he did not think of death seriously in connection with her. She was gone.

The mosaic of mother-days moved across his memory, the face of Ouida, the feel of her, the sound of her voice. But each time his memory was imperceptibly less keen, the sharp stone become rounded pebble.

He longed to be as other boys, to think their thoughts, to have their horizons, to be friends, to have friends, to be one with this enormous family. There was not a week when he was not hurt in some little way or some great way by being excluded, by a casual look, by a conversation made across him as though he were not there, by parties organized in his presence to which he was not invited.

At these times he would remember Dr. Kellogg, or Dr. Alexander, or Dr. Dwyer, and the long hours sitting on the steps, waiting for the sound of the doctor's horse.

It was not difficult to re-enter that old and happy world. It was very real and to enter it was like turning a page in a worn and much read book. It was a place to which he could return at will, a place of need, a sanctuary.

One day, when he had been in college nearly five months, he put aside his studies early and walked to the town. He loitered from street to street inspecting shop windows. From time to time he saw other college boys. For the most part they were in groups or in pairs and they were obviously abroad on errands. They talked animatedly, an aura of excitement and pleasure in their very walk.

Lucas listened avidly. He tried to understand their excitement, to be excited himself. They were completely absorbed in their errand. They were delighted with what they were doing and they were one with each other. If he could just learn the secret, Lucas yearned, if he could overhear some word, see some action, some gesture, the whole structure of their society would be clear to him. He could be one with them. He did not seriously consider the possibility that total absorption in socks could ever root itself in his living and outlook and become part of him. He wanted only to perfect himself in the appearance of interest so that he could pass muster as one of them, be a unit in the organized army of youth about him, enjoy their games, have their fun, and, even not enjoying, still be part, undetected and unchallenged.

It was quickly over. The three went out, talking loudly, headed on some absorbing errand elsewhere. The clerk walked slowly to Lucas.

"Interested in some ties?"

"Some socks, maybe," Lucas said hopefully. He felt bold.

"And what size?"

Lucas obediently balled his fist and held it out to the clerk. The clerk looked at it a moment, surprised, then picked up a pair of socks, wrapped it around the fist, tried another pair.

"That'll be eleven. Any particular color?"

"Gray ones."

"Six gray—that'll be twelve dollars." The clerk turned to wrap the socks. Lucas flinched. Then, resolute to pay the price of fellowship, he put his hand in his trouser watch pocket. The pocket was empty. He had lost his summer wages. He had somehow lost forty dollars. He stared at the clerk in horror. In the next instant he was sick with shame.

"Oh, wait a minute!" he faltered. The clerk turned. "I just thought of something . . ." He started edging toward the door. "I better look mine over . . . make sure I get the right color . . . I just remembered —I'll be right back—"

He wrenched the door open. He smiled, red-faced. He nodded reassuringly. He was through the doorway, he was on the sidewalk, he was safe. He walked rapidly away. Not daring to look back he turned the first corner. Two blocks later he halted before another shop window. He glanced covertly about. He was not being observed. He sighed. He walked slowly on. He could still feel the clerk's eyes. He heard a hail, his own name called. He looked around, startled. Alfred was striding toward him, beaming, trailed by three other young men, strangers.

"Where you been, boy? What you up to?" Alfred slapped the point of his shoulder.

"Just looking around." A warm wave of companionship and gratitude stiffened Lucas.

"Looking 'em over, huh?" He turned to the three. "You see? A fellow doesn't know his own roommate. Here he is out picking 'em over. Hell, boy! I figured you'd be back studying!"

"Seen anything! Any poontang?"

"No good just walking the streets, boy," Latimer said kindly. "We've tried that."

"Imagine old Luke out cruising with the best of 'em!" Alfred said proudly.

"You get much?" Latimer asked anxiously. "Maybe he's tapped a lode! These deep, quiet boys you never know!"

"Not a thing," Lucas said earnestly. "Not a one."

"We're organized," Alfred said. "Travel in packs, that's the only way. System. Latimer's the sex fiend, old man experience. Ellways is the big broad athletic type." Tall and rangy Ellways grinned self-consciously. "Travis is the clothes department." Travis smiled serenely, beautifully and faultlessly dressed, careful and careless. "And I'm just a big-brother, joiner type. Can't miss. One of us has to get in."

"He could be the country-cousin type," Ellways said earnestly, nodding at Lucas.

"The fellow a girl has to trust," pondered Latimer.

"Come on in," Alfred urged enthusiastically.

"I will!" Lucas said gratefully.

"Sure!" said Travis.

A pair of girls passed, talking animatedly, pretending to ignore the group.

"Hey!" called Latimer.

One of the girls turned her head and looked at the group coldly. Lucas shrank guiltily.

"How do you do, how do you do, how do you do!" called Ellways. The girl stared at them indignantly, tossed her head, said something to her companion. They giggled and walked on. Lucas looked about uncomfortably, agonizedly sure the whole street was watching.

"Well come on, come on!" cried Alfred. Latimer was already walking toward the retreating girls, followed by Travis. Lucas hung back. "Hey!" Alfred stopped. "Aren't you coming, Luke?"

"Too many," Lucas said. "You got enough—"

"Plenty for all!" Alfred protested, his head turned to Lucas, his body walking after Travis, Ellways, and Latimer.

"You go ahead," Lucas said. "I'll see you later."

"Try the Goodhue Candy Shop!" Alfred admonished. "It's always loaded—I'll see you—I'll see you back in the room—"

He hurried after the others. The girls rounded a corner. The boys followed. Lucas was alone again. He walked on. He lingered outside the windows of clothing stores looking at the clothes there, clothes that belonged uncompromisingly to young men of another world. Now with the loss of the forty dollars he was incomparably poorer. He sighed and walked on. Now he studied tobacconists' shops, studied the pipes, looked curiously at the brown heaps of tobacco, read the exotic names. Then there were shoe shops and he peered at the smart shoes, hopelessly expensive, made to be scuffed to the college pattern. For as long as he could remember Ouida had made taking care of clothing an article of faith. He came to a book store. He felt at home, he had a right here. He looked at the books in the rack outside, fearlessly picked one up, examined it, casually set it back. He lingered here some time. No clerk came out. Reluctantly he walked on. It was getting late. He had missed dinner. He turned toward the campus. It was twilight when he reached the green, saw dimly the familiar buildings, the gravelled walks. In the gloom he began the long trudge toward Saylor Hall. The college streets were dark now, and deserted. He saw other figures only occasionally. He walked on into the night. To his right he heard suddenly the soft sound of music. He looked ahead. Lighted windows made a golden halo in the night. It was a fraternity house. Concealed in the darkness he walked toward it. He peered furtively at the windows. Inside a group of young men crowded about a piano. They were singing together, a hymn of youth, a hymn of being together, inarticulate with song, rapt, lost in happiness, their arms about each other's shoulders.

Now the night was more lonely and he stood solitary, a small figure in the empty darkness.

A new song began. He walked on. The darkness of the campus enfolded him. The sound of singing dwindled. In a few more paces the light was gone. Then the sound was gone. Beneath his feet the gravel crackled. Ahead was the dark bulk of Saylor Hall. He climbed the granite stairway.

In his room a letter from Dr. Alexander was waiting:

"Hope you are getting along all right, but knowing how much this means to you I am sure you are. I don't know whether this will help or not, at least not right now, but some time ago I promised you a letter of introduction to a former classmate and here it is. His name is Grover Aarons, and he is full professor of pathology at the medical college. Might drop in on him and make yourself known. You remember that farmer with the wen on the side of his neck? Finally took it out last week and found a needle embedded in the tissue alongside. Said he swallowed it when he was ten years old. All good wishes and we expect great things of you. Sincerely, George Alexander, M.D."

⁎ CHAPTER 11

He came into the hospital, the first he had ever entered. He looked about him acolyte-hungry, and all about him was the incense of the temple, the smell of formaldehyde and alcohol, of mercury and iodine and a hundred other chemicals, all subtly blended, suspended, linked to tissue and blood and bone and the skin of man and his inmost fluids.

It was not a boy, not a young man standing there on stones the nameless had joined with cement, the forgotten had quarried. It was spirit, the inner drive of man, of this one man, spirit born and aged in the birth-instant, spirit without years and beyond time, and this stood waiting for the vessel of flesh in which it was contained to carry it forward to the world in which it could be God.

He stood inside the hospital for the first time and what he saw and what he felt, all of this took no second, no interval, but a soul's time, a time without time, as brief as the instant before Creation and as long as all the lives of such as he that had ever been lived before him.

He found his way to the office of Grover Aarons. Grover Aarons, who began life as a Yeshiva student faraway in New York's crowded Williamsburg section, studying Talmudic law, studying, arguing interminably the points some sharp Jew might one day throw at him and he a rabbi and unless he argued now unable to answer that black day. And in the middle of it, well on his way to become a rabbi, he was troubled for an inner speaking. It did not come all at once, but gradually, pushing hard against the vessel of himself until he had to listen. And more or less, a little here, a little now and a little then, so kill him for it, he had always kind of half wanted, maybe—oh, it was an impulse, probably, just an interest—he had always wanted to become a—let us say it—to fool around, to dabble in, to learn a little more about—well, to study Medicine.

And the day came, the middle of his becoming a rabbi, when gradually stopped and imperative began. And if he was an ocean the waves of him heaved, the storms tore, the typhoons reared, the tumult was like death, like a loved one dying that must be prevented, must be held back, shriek, pray, clutch, scream, weep, beg, grovel. And then let go. And he let go. And they let go. All about him let go. And he was dead. And he left the Yeshiva and went to school to become a doctor.

Well, and now he was a doctor, and all he had to do was become an intern, only Jews don't just pick a hospital and at Jewish Hospital there were already too many Jews, and he got in anyway, and then he went away. He didn't set up a practice. He wanted to practice Medicine, not to heal Jews, and he wanted to practice without let wherever and whatever Medicine he wanted, and to do that he had to find some spot on the planet, some spot in the country on the planet where he was nationed, where they seldom thought about Jews, where they thought about Jews just a little.

He came to this backwoods where few people had ever seen a Jew and didn't really know one if they saw one and had only a tribe's, a community's, distrust of a newcomer. And after a year of practice, of no practice at all, he applied for a teaching job at the university. And now he had been there ten years. Now he was professor of pathology. Now he had nothing to do with patients. Now he had only to do with the tissues of patients, of what made them die. Now he had only to do with Medicine. With the books and the instruments and the tissues on which it practices. And what *geist* he had, what vector, urge, impulse, soul and spirit, funnelled itself here, into this pathway, and the pathway developed, and he became a pathologist, not just a name, not just a function, but all its eating, living, and breathing, thinking, dreaming, and aspiring entity.

He was forty-four. He was five feet four inches, he weighed one hundred and sixty-two pounds, he was small-boned, his hair was brown and crisp, his eyes were gray, his face was a pointed oval, his hands were pale again, his face was lined to laugh at himself, his eyes were lined to be rueful, to be wary, to be angry before the blow, to laugh in relief.

He looked at Lucas and his first thought was that here was a student who was about to fail and who had come to plead with him. And the second thought was that he would be easy on him, he was no enemy, he was harmless, he was plainly frightened, desperate, cornered, intense, and it mattered horribly. He would be easy on him.

And Lucas handed him the letter.

"Sit down, sit down." Grover Aarons waved his hand, opening the envelope.

Lucas, sitting, watched him read. He came to the end, began halfway again and read to the end again. Then he studied the desk a moment, put down the letter, looked up at Lucas and smiled.

"Wanted to be a doctor long?"

"As long as I can remember."

"Some doctors make a lot of money. Every man owes it to himself to get security, to lay it up for the day when he can do his own research. There's money in Medicine . . . honest money . . . there's no question of it . . ."

Lucas looked away in embarrassment.

"Yes, sir," he said.

"Every man's got his heart fixed on a sum. A certain sum. How much money do you think you'll need?"

"I don't know . . . I never thought of it . . . I guess I want to make money, all right . . . You have to make money . . ."

And Aarons thought, All right, he's not in it to make money. It isn't money he wants. All right, it's not money.

"Kind of small place, Milletta . . ."

"Yes, sir."

"No hospital?"

"No, none. Sometimes Dr. Alexander puts a patient up at his house. Not often. Children mostly, after a tonsillectomy—"

"Farmers make money too. They must make money or there wouldn't be three doctors in such a small town. But a lot of fellows, me included, don't like farming, never would make a farmer. I guess it's easy to get bored in a small town. All farm kids seem to try to break loose, get away, go to the cities. Any profession must look glamorous to them."

"Maybe so . . . I never thought of it quite like that—do many of them leave to be doctors?"

"I guess not many of them do at that."

"Maybe veterinary doctors."

All right, thanks for saving my face. All right, so it isn't glamor, it isn't let's-get-away-from-a-small-town, it isn't not-be-a-farmer. Whatever it is I'll be easy on you, you tried to put me at ease, that was kind, "maybe veterinary doctors," you were trying to help me out. It isn't money, then, and it isn't running away and it isn't the lure of glamor and position.

"I guess a few of them do become vets, at that. That's probably it. I wouldn't have thought of it. You say this is the first hospital you've been in?"

"Yes, sir!"

"Kind of exciting, eh? What did you think of it?"

Lucas looked at him, his eyes shining. He smiled.

"Really liked it, eh? It does that to all of us. There's something dramatic about a hospital—life and death under your hands—there's something about a doctor, learned, wise, clad in white wisdom, the ancient robe of the seer—healing in his hands—intellect in his eyes, the eyes of the world on him, pleading, hoping against hope, and the doctor is the last resort, awful as Jove, the right hand of God, to give and to take, the last appeal."

"Yes, sir."

"Doesn't it ever hit you that way?"

"Yes, sir."

"Doesn't the prospect of your being one of these doctors thrill you, exalt you? Isn't it a great prospect?"

"Yes, sir," Lucas said dutifully.

All right, so it's not drama, it's not money, not escape, not position. We're coming to it, my boy. We're narrowing it down. You haven't got many left.

"Of course there's some of us who just like to study. And when I say study I mean study Medicine. Many of the greatest discoveries that have ever been made have come from people like that—spending days and weeks and nights and years over a lonely table in a laboratory, failing, starting again, failing, starting again, never quitting, learning, always learning. Learning for the sheer sake of learning. That's one of the things that grips any medical man through and through. You like to study?"

"I love it, sir. Medical study."

"The more you study the more you'll find that all study is medical study—all learning is learning, it's an apple for every man's bite. Engineers, farmers, doctors, musicians—they're all nibbling at the same apple. That's what you like, eh?"

"Yes, sir."

"It's a good thing you do. Now let's take something else. Now of them all which do you like best?"

"Which do I like best—"

"Which part about Medicine draws you hardest? Which of the ones I've mentioned?"

Lucas moved uncomfortably.

"All of them draw you equally? Come now!"

"Well, not money. I need money—but not money. Not to become a doctor just because of money. No, sir. But all the rest." *And those are just words that cover the surface. They tell something of what you feel about something but they're just terms of agreement. So I feel all that. And I say yes. Because there isn't any other word I know that says yes and means the whole iceberg and not just the tip that's showing. And it's all that, all you've said.* "Only there's something more," he blurted.

"Some specialty—some special field—a brain surgeon, maybe—" Dr. Aarons said gently.

"No—I don't know yet—maybe there would be a field. But I don't think so. Not one field. That doesn't feel right. It's something else. It's healing—"

"You feel pity, you can't help yourself—"

I'll say yes. But I don't mean pity. "I'm going to be honest. I don't feel much pity . . ."

"Well, you don't cure patients with pity—"

"I want to heal, all right. That's true. That's pity, maybe. It's more like seeing a picture hanging crooked on the wall and itching to straighten it and no matter what happens you must straighten it—"

"Whether it's a chromo or a Rembrandt—"

"It doesn't matter. And it's something else. I used to feel it when I'd ride with the doctors on calls, Dr. Alexander, mostly, he took me more than the rest. It was interest, that's an awful word, I don't know the word, it's something more, something you have to do—because—because—"

"A monkey climbs—a dog barks—a horse runs—a cow gives milk—"

"That's right! That's it! It's *for* you. It *is* you! It's your whole everything, it's what you do because—"

He looked at Dr. Aarons helplessly.

"Because it comes from inside. Because all the rest comes from the outside to the inside—money, position, dramatics, study for the sake of study, all the rest are surface things to which you react. But this is reaction itself, produced of itself, produced when you start living and your genes tell you: *'Go!'* "

"Yes, sir," said Lucas gratefully.

"That's it, isn't it?"

"Yes, sir . . . and more . . ."

"Yes . . ."

So that's it. One in ten million. One in a hundred million. That's two I've seen. I'm forty-four, now, and that's two. So that's it. You poor, poor son of a bitch, you poor driven Thing, you nebulae of genes and God knows what, you're for it, you bastard, you don't know it, but you're for it. Why didn't you give it to me, God? Instead of only a piece of it? Just enough to recognize it in somebody else? What'll he do with it? Look what I've suffered and I've only got a piece of it! Look at that lucky young, ignorant, shiny-eyed, look at that, look.

And in this silence Lucas looked at Dr. Aarons respectfully.

"That pre-med . . ." he ventured deprecatively.

"The pre-med? Yes, the pre-med. Yes. What you want to do is plunge right in. But you have to know how to talk, after all. A doctor is a gentleman. Culture is important. Two years isn't much. You're almost through your first, right now. Tell me—what did you say your father did?"

"He's a harness maker, sir."

"A harness maker? Are they still making harness? In this day and age? Who would have believed it."

"He doesn't make it, sir. He sells it."

"Enough to see a fellow through medical school anyway!"

"Oh yes, sir!"

"Harness stores! And all I see is automobiles! Tell me, is that a good business, harness? Hasn't it fallen off? Surely it's fallen off a little!"

"You never can tell with Dad. This time next week he may have a dozen of them!"

"He sounds like a clever man!"

"Oh, he is! There's no stopping him."

"And your mother? Ah! . . . I'm sorry. I'm very sorry." It was recent. The eyes were still raw with it.

"Well, you're all fixed then. I'm glad of that. To tell the truth I was worried about that. You can't work your way through, you know. I did. But you can't do it any more. And I only did part way. But you can't even do that now. It was almost impossible then. But now—it's impossible."

Now I'm trying to frighten him. He's frightened already. What do I want of his life? Can he help being what he is, what I remember? And with a father, God forbid, in the harness business.

"You say this is your first visit to a hospital? Come on. We won't see everything, but I've got to go upstairs anyway."

The first impact for Lucas was the first sight, the first floor, the first corridor, the first wheeled stretcher, the first glimpse into corridored rooms, the first white uniforms, the first wasted faces, the first smells, the first sense of another order, another system, another law. After that first impact the next corridors and the next rooms, the next patients, the next equipment, the next strangeness, were only successions upon an undigested first.

On the top floor there were no patients, only a long corridor and a corridor joining this at right angles, making a T. The bar of the T were the operating rooms.

"That's where the mechanics work," Dr. Aarons sniffed.

Lucas smiled obediently. He stared.

"That's what the movies play up." Dr. Aarons paused to let Lucas look. "In there is high drama, men in white fighting swiftly against death, flashing knives, blood flowing, mystery. In there is where little boys with pocket knives and thread do the same things over and over, by rote, like mechanics."

Lucas smiled appreciatively, the smile covering a defensive feeling toward surgeons. He was troubled. Now he sensed that in the temple there were sects and that one sect rivalled another. He felt suddenly adult and self-conscious.

"Up to about a hundred years ago doctors ranked first and surgeons were barbers," he said righteously.

"Hey!" Dr. Aarons stopped and stared at Lucas. "That's right! Where did you learn that?" He was very pleased.

"I read it. I read it in some medical history."

"How long have you been reading that kind of stuff?"

"Medical books? Since I was eight or nine. The doctors in Milletta used to loan me some. I read all I can get."

"Anything special? Or whatever you can get your hands on?"

"It's hard to get any kind of medical book. I just read what I can get."

Dr. Aarons walked on again.

"I'll see what I can do for you." They reached the end of the corridor. Here there were two doors, one marked "Laboratory," and the other "Pathologist." "Here's where I hang out."

They entered a wonderland of gleaming glass, bent in fantastic shapes, crystal-thin, fat and swelling, incredibly complicated instruments, scales, fluids green, fluids red, fluids purple, bottles ranked formally, formally labelled, formally brown.

Lucas' eyes rounded. He sucked in a quick breath. Dr. Aarons glanced at him sidelong.

"Full of junk," he shrugged. "Everything's a mess."

Lucas looked at him incredulously.

"Got to be cleaned up," Dr. Aarons grumbled. He walked to a table, picked up a tall beaker, glanced at the contents critically, set it down.

"What's that, sir?"

"That?" Dr. Aarons turned back carelessly. He picked up a pronged instrument, fished in the graduate, brought up a dripping chunk of tissue. "Liver. Got to section it sometime tomorrow." Lucas stared. Dr. Aarons dropped the tissue back into the graduate. "Make a slice of it—here—" he walked to the microtome and put a careless, loving hand on it—"freeze it with this—" he dropped his hand to the carbon-dioxide tanks—"mount the frozen section—" he picked up a box of microscope slides—"stain it—" he pointed to a row of bottles over a sink—"put it under the microscope." The microscope, the research microscope, resembled no microscope Lucas had ever seen. It was a breathless beauty, the very light which served it was a unit as large as the brass tubes he had until this moment regarded so reverently in Dr. Alexander's office back in Milletta and thought the final word in scientific wonder.

Dr. Aarons was watching him intently and casually.

"Ever seen a tissue slide?"

Lucas looked at him helplessly.

Deftly, Dr. Aarons slipped a slide into the graduated scale prongs, in almost the same motion flipped on the lights. Out of the black, crackled finish of the light box a cylinder of intense light bridged the two instruments. For a moment Dr. Aarons fiddled negligently with the adjustment knobs, peering through the microscope. He straightened abruptly.

"Here!"

Gingerly, Lucas bent to look.

"You'll have to keep both eyes open. We won't worry about that now. Someday you'll have to learn."

For a moment Lucas could see nothing. And then suddenly the field leaped out at him, a paralyzing wonder of purple, shading to red, an infinity of pattern, lines sharply defined, unmistakably cells. His head jerked up. He stared at Dr. Aarons.

"Cancer," Dr. Aarons said briefly. "Those are kidney cells. Look like nails, don't they?"

I've seen cancer. Lucas trembled with happiness. I've seen cancer and a human kidney. I've seen it! I've seen it! I've got to remember!

But Dr. Aarons was walking toward the door. Lucas followed reluctantly. "That'll give you some idea. Here's the stink lab."

They entered a large room. Two women and a young man about three years older than Lucas looked up. The women were seated at microscopes. Nearby the young man was tending to distillation apparatus. Here too, wherever Lucas looked, was an unending wonder of bottles and glass tubing, strange and marvellous machinery, the pungent odor of bitter chemicals.

"This is Miss Dorchester—Miss Jeanette—Mr. Ahrlquist." They smiled, waited, looking at Lucas. "This is Lucas Marsh, young fellow sent by an old classmate. Doing pre-med now. Expect to have him with us soon." Ahrlquist turned back to work. The women waited.

"Pleased to know you," Lucas mumbled.

"Been showing him the wonders of science," Dr. Aarons said carelessly. "What did that blood picture show?"

"High eosinophile, fast sed rate." Miss Dorchester smiled.

Lucas blinked. Her self-possession, the glibness with which she, a woman, a female, talked to Dr. Aarons on his own terms, was privy to the same knowledge, confused him. Her fine, reddish-blond hair wisped softly out of control about her triangular face, framed the prominent cheekbones, made her eyes more blue, her straight nose thinner, softened her wide, rather thin-lipped mouth. Lucas stared at her. Miss Dorchester colored, smiled friendlily, and turned back to her microscope.

"Going to have a late blood sugar for you today, Ruth," Dr. Aarons said cheerily. And Ruth Dorchester looked up from the microscope, her shoulders sagged and she looked at Dr. Aarons in dismay.

"Oh, no!"

"That's the third this week!" Miss Jeanette protested. "Why late? Why are they always late?"

Miss Dorchester was twenty-seven years old, but Miss Jeanette was thirty-six, and where Miss Dorchester was slim and as tall as Lucas, Miss Jeanette was of middle height and overweight. Her hair was black and her oval, kind, plain face had long ago given up the look a woman wears for suitors and the possible.

"We'll never get home. Always at the last minute!"

"How about Ahrlquist giving you a hand—"

"I'm tied up on this alkaloid determination!" Ahrlquist said quickly and stubbornly. He was a thin and weedy youth, his face a little pimpled. At the hostility in his tone the women looked quickly away from him back to Dr. Aarons.

"Somehow you always manage to have some long-winded test under way when something like this comes up, don't you?" Dr. Aarons said wearily.

"You want me to drop it?" There was a faint note of contempt in Ahrlquist's voice.

"Get it over with," Dr. Aarons sighed. "I'm sorry, girls."

"Very glad to have met you!" Ruth Dorchester's clear, high voice reached Lucas, who had turned with Dr. Aarons.

"And you, too." Lucas whirled clumsily. But she had returned to her microscope and, belatedly, he turned again and followed Dr. Aarons out of the laboratory.

"Come back anytime," Dr. Aarons said. "My liver is calling me. You can find your way out all right?"

"Oh, sure—I'll be—"

"Wait! I forgot!" He turned the knob of the pathology-laboratory door. "I wanted to loan you some books." Inside the room he looked at a bookshelf crowded with fat medical tomes. He paused in simulated vexation. "Pathology be all right?" he asked Lucas apologetically.

"Oh, fine, fine!" Lucas breathed.

"Well, I thought I had some others—but here's two—you might look them over—should be a later edition—but you'll get something out of them"—he handed them to Lucas and smiled full at him, friendlily—"with your background."

Lucas' eyes dimmed. "Thank you! I keep saying thank you, but—"

"Just bring them back when you're through."

The door closed. Lucas was alone in the corridor. He walked slowly, lingering. At the landing he looked back once at the laboratory door, then walked quickly to the floor beneath. An orderly moved swiftly and silently toward him, pushing a wheeled stretcher, on the stretcher a long, blanketed mound. Lucas stood aside to let him pass. From the mound came the odor of ether. At the point where the blanket ended there was a waxen, unconscious face, sexless, the head bound in a towel. This mounded being was in an unknown world. It had been sent there, it would be recalled, it had been opened, its dark secrets had been touched, its life had been handled and put back and sewed up. Now the blanket covered what had been done, and the smell of ether. Down the corridor two nurses bustled, their shoes white, their stockings white, their starched skirts moving crisply.

He turned to walk to the main floor. From the corridor in which he had just seen the nurses the crude clamor of shouting rose. He whirled.

Down the corridor an emaciated old man fled, shouting, his short gown flapping behind him. Down the corridor rushed an orderly, pursuing. From her desk in an alcove the charge nurse stepped out, her arms wide to stop the oncoming shouter. She turned to Lucas.

"Stop him!" she cried.

Lucas scrambled to sustain the impact of the escaping patient who charged into them blindly, never ceasing his wild shouts. An instant later the three were on the floor, Lucas' books tumbling, and almost immediately the orderly had plunged atop the mass. The emaciated man struggled wildly and nakedly, then abruptly his hoarse shouts became low grunts. He subsided.

The charge nurse and the orderly led him back down the corridor.

"There's nothing for you here," the disarrayed nurse called angrily to the patients now standing openly gaping in their doorways. "Go back inside your rooms, please. Shut the door!"

They withdrew reluctantly. Lucas watched the trio enter a room far down the corridor. Panting a little he stooped to pick up his books. He picked up the nurse's cap also. He brushed at it clumsily and gently. He held it, looking about him, at a loss what to do with it.

"Thank you very much." The charge nurse had swiftly and soundlessly returned. She put out her hand, took her cap, and put it on quickly as if to cover a bit of nakedness.

"That's all right." Lucas brushed self-consciously at the top of one of the books, suddenly noticed blood smeared on the back of his left hand. He looked up at the nurse.

"He cut himself on a screen trying to get out of the window," she said contemptuously. "You never know when they're going to break out, good as gold days running and all of a sudden— They don't belong here in the first place!" she said angrily. "Plus four! They're mental cases—and that's where they belong!"

She smoothed down her uniform indignantly.

"I'll wipe that off for you—" she looked at the books—"Doctor . . ."

"That's all right." His voice came to him from a distance, he fumbled for a handkerchief, "I'll get it."

But she had magically produced a square of gauze and the hand he surrendered was clean and the pledget was out of sight.

"Thank you, Doctor," she said again, impersonally, and turned away.

Lucas walked shakily down the stairs. Plus four! That was syphilis! And plus four! That was the last stage, that was the stage where it attacked the spinal cord and central nervous system, syphilis, carried by the bloodstream, the blood fresh on his hand, seeking an entrance, blindly seeking, in the divine order of its unsinning, unmalicious, unalterable instinct, a scratch, a tiny scratch. Not infectious! he remembered clearly. It came back to him now. Not infectious in that stage. Almost not infectious at all. A danger to be thought about, to be treasured, and not a danger that could happen, but to treasure.

"It doesn't pay to be morbid about such things," Lucas said jubilantly. He said it aloud, walking. He looked about with concern. No one had heard him. It doesn't pay at all, he reiterated proudly, silently, this time only in his thoughts. It doesn't pay, Doctor. It won't do. One can't be morbid. One handles it, one grows careless. We all run into infection every day, Doctor. One can't be morbid about such things!

He walked exultantly from the hospital. He walked down the steps. The odor of the hospital vanished. The fresh air was another world, but he was a doctor walking down the cement steps into this workaday world, and the place of mysteries, where every sound and every movement and every thought was ritual and concise, this enclosure shut from the world was behind him and the doctor walked away from it, the cord which bound him to it stretching thinner and thinner with each step he took, becoming evanescent, then invisible, then somewhere sundering, fading, gone.

He felt the weight of the books he was carrying. His spirits lifted, surged up as he looked at them, formal, blue, stamped with gold. And suddenly he could not wait to get to his room. He had to open them, to read them. He strode from the path and sat quickly under a tree. He opened the first book. The words ascended to his mind, incomprehensible, beautiful, more beautiful than any words that could be understood, he read with delight words that were old friends, medical words, medical meanings, medical language, and his fingers stroked lovingly the glossy paper, turned the pages tenderly, with reverent, dreaming care. . . .

And the man rushed down the corridor toward him, the old man, the thin gray hair flying, the wild, open mouth, the sparse hairs on his unshaven face, the gray lines, and they were on the floor, tumbling, and the thin body wrenching its bones incredibly. And there was blood smeared on the back of his hand. A thin smear of yellow-red blood.

"I'll wipe it for you—*Doctor!*"

He turned to the book hungrily.

The wad of bills that were his summer earnings had disappeared without trace. He quailed at the thought of writing to Job about the loss of a sum so great and determinedly budgeted the ten dollars that remained to him until the end of the month. In a few days he saw with despair that he had figured badly. Despite his sternest resolves he was spending a dollar a day for food. He was amazed at his lack of resistance and his self-indulgence but his amazement was of little practical use for it was never evoked when he was hungry.

It was apparent that the few dollars he had left would not carry him for the next sixteen days, when his allowance would arrive, and after classes on the day he had determined this he went into the town to look for a job.

There were no dishwasher jobs. There was a sign in the window of one shabby restaurant, but the proprietor peremptorily told him in the presence of a half-dozen disinterested customers that he wanted no college kids. Wherever he went, Lucas quickly saw, there was a prejudice against giving jobs to students. He bought a newspaper. At the beginning of his quest he had slunk from shop to restaurant. Now he studied the want-ad section boldly, standing on a street corner for all to see. There were very few employment ads.

Next day he went to the college administration building and asked for help. They looked at him in astonishment. They explained to him carefully that jobs were spoken for months ahead, that jobs were very scarce, that the town of Winthrop almost never had jobs for college students, having a chronic unemployment problem for its own non-collegiate employables.

He left the building dazed, enviously noting a student-janitor on his knees scrubbing a flight of steps. He walked toward town again. He counted his money. He had four dollars. He walked the streets of Winthrop, trying block after block. When the day ended he had canvassed even private homes. There were no jobs. There were no jobs anywhere. And his hunger was such, sharpened by the miles he had trudged and honed by his fear feeling the lonely four bills, that when he had done eating and turned back toward the campus he had only three dollars left.

The next day he had been looking less than an hour when he saw the sign. It stood in the window of an inconspicuous, small and dingy undertaking parlor. The sad-voiced man who opened the door to him nodded glumly when Lucas spoke of the sign in the window. He led Lucas to the display room and vanished in the gloom. Lucas looked cautiously about him. He was surrounded by caskets, their white-satin intestines blooming from sad openings where the polished lid would close, tilted, all of them, in a coquettish curtsy of the foot end so that their yellow, white, pink, and purple blandishment might be fully eyed in the covert glance they knew would be their portion.

"Sort of reproach you for being alive, don't they?" a voice made Lucas whirl. A chubby man in his late twenties ran his hands lovingly over the soft pleated and ruffled comfort a corpse would never feel.

"You come for the job?" he said.

Lucas nodded.

"What kind of a job is it?" he whispered.

"What are you—apprentice? You know embalming?"

"Apprentice, I guess."

"Gonna live in?"

"I don't know. I don't know anything about the job," Lucas said rapidly. "I need a job—"

"It's a beautiful line, isn't it," the chubby man admired the curtsying caskets and their spilth of foaming velvet. "You see that one over there? Nobody'll ever buy that. Twelve hundred dollars. That's too much. But it's a show piece. Must have cost all of six hundred, just as she stands."

"You're an embalmer?" Lucas asked respectfully.

"But this is what I like," the chubby man said. "Give me a salesman's job—look at this stuff—how could you help but buy it. Do you know what the profit is on an item like this?" He dropped his hand reverently on a sleek brown casket. "That's a seller. Costs two hundred. Sells for six. Just as fast as you can get them in."

"They need a salesman?" Lucas asked hopefully.

"God, I don't know what they need. Couple of Guineas running this place now, just bought in, God knows what they want. This is the one I want! Yes sir, when I go, brother, this is the one for me! Seven hundred and fifty smackeroos!" He patted the wooden friend respectfully. "Look at those handles!"

"You'd have that—knowing what they cost?"

"Somebody's got to pay for them—and you can't take it with you," the chubby man said cheerfully. "You a salesman?" Then he looked past Lucas.

A dark woman stood in the doorway. She looked at Lucas searchingly. Then as wordlessly as she appeared she disappeared past the heavy drapes.

"Sizing you up," said the chubby man. "I got to go. Good luck to you. If you want it."

Lucas waited alone for a long ten minutes. The man who had admitted him reappeared abruptly.

"You an embalmer? Young fellow like you?"

"No, sir," Lucas said. "Maybe I could be a salesman. I'm a student. I'm going to study Medicine. I need a job. I'd work real cheap—"

The man disappeared while Lucas was talking. This time he was gone only a few minutes.

"Missus says no," he called out in a low tone.

"No chance at all?" begged Lucas.

The man stood silently aside. Lucas shivered. He passed through the drapes, he passed the silent man, he felt the black eyes of the woman boring from a recess of the dark hallway, there was no sound to his footsteps, the nape of his neck prickled, he opened the door with a jerk, he was outside and down the steps. A mud-stained newspaper floated down the sidewalk like a harlequin, a small breeze dropped it in the gutter. Lucas turned the corner. He walked quickly. He did not look back.

There were no jobs in Winthrop. There were no jobs at the college. For a man who wanted to work part time, and to select the hours he would work, the prospects were simply nonexistent. There were no jobs, at any price, anywhere.

Lucas borrowed five dollars from Alfred. Alfred gave him the money without comment. Lucas wrote Job. A few days later Job sent him ten dollars. A few days later he sent him twenty dollars more. Lucas repaid Alfred. Alfred accepted the payment without comment. After this he saw less of Alfred than ever. He walked about Winthrop by himself. He kept his money in his bureau drawer, never going out with more than two dollars in his pockets. Sometimes at nights he went into bars where no one spoke to him, he attended campus concerts, where people who did not know him nodded at him brightly and walked on, he browsed in book stores, he prowled the library, he lingered near the hospital. There was a drugstore near the campus and often he spent an idle hour there, surreptitiously watching the people who jangled in and out and wondering what they did and where they were going and whether they knew that he belonged to the college too, and perhaps they were classmates.

✶ CHAPTER 12

The school term ended. The campus hived, swarmed, summer plans were buzzed, release was imminent, and youth busied itself deliriously with the coming explosion.

On the train bearing him home Lucas looked about him with a new self-possession and a new eagerness. When the train slowed he was waiting in the vestibule. He escaped down the train steps. He was home! The hot boards under his feet, the familiar station, the cinders, the sign, the shapes, sights, and odors, he embraced them with his senses, his hunger for them unslaked by the contact, made more keen by their promise of home. He looked about him, grinning. Behind him the train moved off. The station, the platform, were deserted. But home! he cried to himself silently. Home! he said fiercely. I'm *home!*

Hefting his bag he strode heartily toward the center of town and on all sides of him loved things fell into view, the dusty road, the town, the well-remembered stores—the harness shop. The door was closed. He looked through the window. The shop was empty. Charley's off and Dad's home, getting lunch—home. . . .

He made himself not run. He walked the remaining blocks with his head lowered. He looked up. The house was before him. He ran up the steps. He forced himself to walk slowly, he bit his lip for pain to compose his features. He rang the bell.

I'm a salesman, he rehearsed rapidly, got a fine line of leather goods, sir—

He could hear the bell ring. If Mother was here she'd say it's a creditor, he grinned fondly. I'm a salesman, sir—and now he knocked, knocked loud, louder, banged confidently. The grin faded. He waited perplexedly. He shrugged good-humoredly. He tried the knob. The door did not open. It was locked.

He put his bag down. What the hell! he thought resentfully. He went to the back door. It was locked. He tried the windows, embarrassed. No one noticed him. Now he pushed at them, frankly tugged and pushed.

"By God!" he said aloud. "By God Almighty!"

He strode angrily to the shed, found an old table knife, returned to a window, tried to force the lock. The lock did not give. He jabbed harder, scarring the woodwork, careless, glad to be scarring it. The lock stayed fast.

He stood back, hands on hips, panting a little, surveying it.

"Well, I'm going to get in," he said aloud. "I'm going to get in and that's all there is to it!"

He picked up a stick. He weakened. I could go downtown. But what would I do there? I'm home! I want to get in!

He raised the stick and smashed a pane. He put in his hand and wrenched the lock open.

"There, by God!" he said grimly. He climbed over the sill. He walked through the house to the front door, opened it, retrieved his suitcase, looked inquiringly up and down the street. The street drowsed emptily. Far down a man slouched along slowly. He brought the suitcase inside the house. It was cool and smelled pleasant and musty. He shut the door. He dropped the suitcase. He looked about him. He drank it in. He was home.

He walked through all the rooms, treading the roses of homecoming, feeling the carpet here, the bare floor there, seeing the familiar doors, the woodwork, the rooms, the furniture, all dear to him, spoons, a nail, a table cover, a welcomer, a delight. For a while he sat in the kitchen, resting.

Slowly the emptiness of the house began to oppress him. Then faster and faster the oppression rushed in, the loneliness, the aloneness, the empty house. He leaped up. He went out quickly, strongly, the house behind him. He went to the harness shop.

"Your pa's in Meridian," said old Charley. "God, you've growed! Didn't seem to know you was coming home today. Didn't say nothin'!"

"I wrote him!" Lucas said resentfully.

"Didn't say a word."

Didn't say a word! And he knew it! I wrote him over and over again. Not a word! Not to tell Charley, even!

"What time do you expect him back? I went to the house. I had to break a window!"

"By God!" Charley cackled delightedly. "Broke a window! Got in, did ya? No, he ain't coming back today. Nope. Don't look for him rightly, till day after t'morra! God, you've growed!"

In the quiet street Lucas fought down a sense of shame and resentment, a feeling of rejection, a feeling of being covertly observed and his rejection discussed. He looked about him for sanctuary. He remembered Dr. Alexander. He walked briskly in the direction of the doctor's office. As he walked he noticed two new stores. Milletta had changed a little. There were more automobiles. There were few horse-drawn vehicles. Ahead of him, from the Milletta Bank building, stepped the familiar figure of Mr. Benjamin. Lucas slowed, hoping he was unnoticed. But Mr. Benjamin had seen him.

"Glad to see you, Lucas. Looking fine. Home for the holidays?"

"Yes, sir. About an hour ago. No, two hours—"

"How's college?"

"I'm doing fine, Mr. Benjamin. Yes—"

"Glad to hear it. Just pay attention to your work and study. We all expect great things from you. That's right." He cleared his throat. "Your father about?"

"I beg your pardon?"

"I was just wondering if you'd seen your father. I was looking for him and—"

"He's in Meridian."

"In Meridian! I see. Yes, well . . ."

"Charley doesn't expect him back today."

"Not today, eh? How about tomorrow?"

"I think Charley said he'd be back tomorrow."

"Yes, that's probably so. Sure. Did he say what time tomorrow? I mean—about?"

"He just said sometime tomorrow."

"I see. . . . Well, I'm glad to see you looking well, Lucas. Hope to hear fine things of you. Glad to see you home. Good day."

Mr. Benjamin, whatever his errand was, turned and walked back to the bank. It must have been a busy day, Lucas reflected. The banker had been formal almost to the point of queerness. He had a brief moment of concern. He wondered at the banker's transparent desire to see Job. But he had been reared in an atmosphere of concern; whatever it was, his father would maneuver out of it smoothly. People like Mr. Benjamin were his natural prey. He thought of his father as Ouida had thought of him, her outlook on Job was his, now. Out of sight, out of mind, he thought bitterly. I wonder what he's up to now?

The white square of cardboard was on the doctor's door. The arrow pointed to "Doctor Out." Lucas sat on the steps. After a while he rose. There was Dr. Dwyer to visit and Dr. Kellogg.

As he had when he was a boy, Lucas strolled through the streets of Milletta seeking the doctors' carriages. Dr. Dwyer was out. Dr. Kellogg was out. And on the streets of Milletta there were no doctors' carriages to be seen. He walked a little further. He looked out over the ribbons of light brown, the empty roads leading into the countryside.

He gave up. Emptily, except for a sense of desolation, of loneliness, of rebellion, he turned back toward the center of town. He thought of the shop and began to walk faster. Perhaps his father had returned. He reached the shop, breathless. He peered inside. Except for Charley, working away on a long strip of leather, the shop was empty. He turned away. He stood uncertainly.

The street outside the shop was dusty, the grass died at its edge. He looked unseeingly at the remembered store fronts. This was home. He said it mechanically. I belong here. This is where I'm supposed to be. Here. He looked about him hopefully. There was neither welcome nor rejection. The day moved impersonally into time. I've got to go someplace, he said uncertainly. The town . . . the shop . . . the doctors . . . and then there was home.

Reluctantly, he walked homeward. He saw the empty house again. His steps echoed on the porch. He stood inside, in the hallway. The house was somehow stiller. It was emptier than before. It was a house, now. It was wood and plaster and wallpaper. It was a case of wood, full of rooms, smaller than he had remembered them, carpeted, furnished, inanimate, a picture here, a picture there, offering at no one, hanging, an empty house.

He looked about him awkwardly. He had a sudden sense of constraint, it was as if he had opened a door and walked into a stranger's house, walked beyond the front door into forbidden territory, and stood now waiting for someone to appear, surprised to see him standing there. He felt a stranger.

"This is my home!" he said defensively, aloud.

He saw on a small table his mother's picture, an old photograph, a picture of Ouida as a blooming and lovely girl. And at the sight of the stiff cardboard easel, the remembered face, longing and loneliness and yearning hollowed him, and the cemetery rushed into his mind and he turned gladly and fled the house.

He saw it at last, a small field, stone-fenced, on the edge of town. A breeze moved the quiet grasses and fanned his face. He had been walking very fast. He wiped his wet forehead on the sleeve of his jacket. He walked happily into the cemetery.

The cemetery seemed larger than he had remembered it. He walked confidently toward Ouida's grave. He halted. The gravestones were unfamiliar. He must have taken a wrong turning. He had come to the wrong plot. He looked about him, alarmed. And then two plots away he saw it. A moment later he was standing by his mother's grave. There was a gravestone there now. "Sacred to the memory of Ouida Marsh, Beloved Wife and Mother. Born 1880, Died 1921." White stone, new-cut. The tumulus of earth that had pillowed over the form of Ouida was almost flat now. It mounded gently. It was no longer raw earth but sod. And grass had died and grass replaced it and there was no line of separation, nothing to show there had not been grass here always, the grass of the cemetery, as far as one could see.

Carefully, gently, Lucas sat beside the headstone.

He tried to think of what she would not know. There was nothing, actually. If she was right, she would know everything. She was here, she was everywhere. Tenderness flooded him at her nearness. After a while, feeling home with her, he raised his eyes, deliberately he forced himself to look at other graves, at the whole cemetery. He looked back at the small mound which covered Ouida. It was unchanged. And yet something had changed it. It was grass, now, part of the cemetery, the mound was identical with other mounds, that which was peculiar to Ouida, to dearness, to the personal, to privacy, to a place set apart, filled with presence, tangible with love, was suddenly impersonal. It was empty. Ouida was not there. He fought frantically to regain her. For a moment he succeeded, the place was alive with her, the instant was fragile, it broke, she was gone, he was sitting in an empty place, on earth, on sod, in a place used for a cemetery, beside a headstone, beside a hundred headstones, beside a hundred graves, and the wind, the curious, restless wind, rustled the grasses of all impersonally, the common wind, the common grass, the common sod.

He strained desperately to put this from his mind. He strained, aching, for the other feeling, the feeling of Ouida.

It was gone.

He left the cemetery. He walked back to the empty house.

Inside, he waited, looking about him, undecided. He picked up his suitcase. The day rushed through his mind. Step by step, incident by incident, frustration by frustration.

"No, by God!" he cried harshly. He shook with rage. He was blind with it. He smashed his fist against the stairway wall. "To hell with you!" he screamed. "To hell with the lot of you!"

He whirled, then, and walked out, slammed the door behind him, marched to the station, waited a fuming hour, boarded a train back to college.

He saw the buildings again with gratitude. He could not wait to be among them. For this was home now. This was all he needed. This was his. This could not be taken from him. This he had made. This was home.

⋆ CHAPTER 13

When the train stopped he had decided clearly what he must do. He alighted impatiently.

He faced the bursar confidently, smiling.

"I'm in a kind of pickle," he confided. He smiled ruefully, a smile at himself, a smile to share with the bursar the way students were always getting into a pickle, always having to run to the bursar, the poor, long-suffering bursar, but what could a young fellow do?

The bursar permitted himself a half-smile, a movement of the lips, acknowledging the gambit.

"I was supposed to see Dad today—I went all the way home—and when I got there he'd been called out of town." Lucas halted. He produced an embarrassed smile.

"What was it in reference to?" the bursar said warily, patiently.

"Why, you see we'd agreed on a summer term for me. I wanted to catch up on a lot of stuff we'll have this fall—I'm taking a pre-med—and I'd—we'd talked it over and instead of wasting the summer he decided, sure, go ahead and take the summer course! It was only at the last minute—"

"We haven't heard anything from him—" The bursar shook his head.

"I know! That was it! I was to go home, spend a day or so with him—you know how it is! He wanted to see me for at least forty-eight hours! After all, he doesn't see me all year—and he was to give me a check and—"

"I'm afraid I don't see what I can do—until—"

"My goodness! Can you imagine anyone in their right mind trying to get into summer school when he didn't *have* to?"

"Yes," said the bursar. "I can. As a matter of fact—"

"No! You're joking! Actually conniving? When they don't *have* to?"

"There have been cases—"

"Honestly!" Smiling, Luke shook his head in amazement, delighted, bemused, incredulous.

"I don't say we run into it very often," the bursar conceded, reluctantly accepting that Lucas was not one of these.

"It's hard to believe . . ." Lucas shook his head, his voice trailed off. The bursar now believed him, and Lucas spoke with sympathy, helping the bursar to the next step.

"Yes . . . Well, now, in your case . . ." He tapped his teeth with a pencil. He frowned. "I don't see what we can do . . . We'd have to have—"

"Gosh! Now I *am* in a pickle! You've been so understanding and kind, when I first came here—and I thought, well, it *is* a problem but if *any*body can help you, that's Mr. Johnson. So I came right to you. There's nobody home and I came all the way back knowing matters were all arranged and here I am. And I—" He shook his head helplessly. He smiled a smile that was not a smile, that was just not tremulous.

The bursar cleared his throat.

"I appreciate your position. I'd like to help you. But you see—"

"Gosh!"

"If you had a letter, even, anything that would give us something to go by, some formal expression of intention—"

"A letter!" Lucas shook his head, hopelessly.

"Yes, some letter your father has written you, something in which he says—"

"Oh!" Lucas cried. "Oh, wait! His last letter—! Wait!" He searched his pockets feverishly. He looked at his suitcase. He bent as if to open it. "No!" He straightened. "No! I know where it is!" He grinned happily at the bursar, sharing his joy with him. "And it's all there! How he wants me to go to summer school, how he's glad I've agreed to go—it took a little persuading," he confided sheepishly, "and how I'm to come home for two days and he'll give me the check and I'm to have three dollars a week spending money—" He paused to get his breath, excited, relieved; a great sigh of relief swelled from him.

"Spending money?"

"Yes, he keeps me pretty short, doesn't want me to have too much. I've got a couple of cousins, rich father, they're pretty badly spoiled, he keeps pointing them out to me—but that's enough. Goodness! I can do on that very well! Sure! As a matter of fact it took my last nickel for train fare—I'll need the first week's in advance—"

"You go get the letter—"

"I will!" He grabbed his suitcase. "I'll be right back—thank you! Thank you, Mr. Johnson! I won't be a minute—!"

He escaped from the bursar's office. Still wearing the bright smile for all to see, he rushed out of the building, toward Saylor Hall. At a safe distance he discarded the smile. He licked his dry lips. Fear thickened in him. He forced himself to consider the next step, to do what must be done.

He went directly to his room. He unpacked, putting off the moment, holding off the fear. When his few clothes had been put away he turned to face the room. It was empty. The dormitory brooded in the stillness of summer. He had a sudden feeling that except for himself the campus was deserted. Alfred's pennants and pictures were still on the wall. Fulboating, Lucas thought. And he remembered Alfred's laughter, pictured him somewhere in a happy, lazy, intimate shouting group. He looked about the room again, now emptier, now more still, more alien.

And now determinedly he turned to his desk, rummaged there, found a few sheets of Job's business stationery he frugally used for correspondence. He left the room. He walked down the corridor, knocking at doors, opening them, until he found a room still occupied, an occupied room and a typewriter.

He brought the typewriter back to his room. He inserted a sheet of his father's business stationery. "Job Marsh," it said across the top, "Harness of all Kinds, Repairs, Try the Shawnee Line, Only the Best Meets the Test. Branch Offices: Meridian, Tyre, Los Santos, Old Wetherly." He read this carefully. He began to write.

"Dear son:"

He found the letters with care and difficulty.

"I'm glad to hear you're making out so well." How would Job put it? What were some of his expressions?

"Things have been looking up here steadily and business was never better. Have been thinking some of putting in a line over Sherwood way. More of that when I see you. Now in answer to your last letter—"

Lucas paused. He thought carefully. He proceeded with confidence. The die was cast.

"—I am glad you see things my way. I think taking the summer course is exactly what you need and as you know I have always wanted you to take it and been anxious that you see things my way. You make the necessary arrangements and I want you to have four dollars a week for spending money, I think that's enough and as you know I don't want you spoiled. When your term ends I want you to come straight home as I want to spend some time with you. I have been very busy but I am most anxious to see you and see how you've grown and talk over your plans and maybe have a little fun together, father and son. I'm very proud of you and the marks you've made and I don't have to tell you I've missed you. Looking forward to seeing you when term ends and when I see you I'll give you a check to cover your summer tuition and allowance, I remain, your loving Father."

He took the letter carefully from the typewriter. He found Job's last letter. On the back of the page, back of the sprawling signature, he rubbed a pencil. With a pencil he followed the loops of his father's signature. He took the upper sheet away. On his letter beneath were the faint marks of the traced signature. He took a pen and carefully followed the marks. He let the ink dry. With an eraser he removed all pencil traces. He looked at the letter with satisfaction. He folded it, put it in the envelope which had contained his last letter from Job, pocketed it, brought the typewriter back to the room from which he had borrowed it, and walked quickly back to the bursar's office.

"I've got it!" He came in waving the letter gleefully.

The bursar took the letter carefully from its envelope, unfolded it, smoothed it, read it. He pursed his lips.

"Yes," he said, "yes, that will be all right."

"Grand!"

"That's what we needed."

"For a while I thought I'd lost it!" Lucas closed his eyes in mock dismay.

"Now, what courses did you have in mind—"

"English, history, and German. Those three. I'm going to try and do them so I won't have to do them this fall—"

The bursar prepared his papers.

"It certainly must be some job keeping a whole university in order. Boy! When I think of the records you have to keep—the problems—the whole university—"

"It never ends." The bursar nodded. "Well, here you are."

"I'm certainly grateful to you, Mr. Johnson. I was in a real pickle—"

"I've arranged your classes to cover the mornings. I expect you'll have uses for the afternoons this fine weather—" He looked enviously toward the window. "Well—"

"Uh—Mr. Johnson—"

"Yes?"

"The allowance. I'm a bit short and—"

"Oh, yes. You wanted an advance."

"If you could—"

"Four dollars, wasn't it?"

"That's right!"

"Sign this."

"I can't tell you how grateful I am," Lucas said.

"Well, these things do happen. We'll hear from your father shortly—"

"That's right. Or—just send him a bill. That'll remind him—"

"You'll find the summer-session rules in your *Student's Guide.*"

Lucas walked forth onto the campus. He looked over the empty, spreading acres. He possessed it all, now, it was all his, he had the university almost to himself. He walked about until the excitement subsided a little. He walked to his home, to Saylor Hall, he sat on the steps there and scanned the day, the summer, the fall.

Everything fitted, everything was provided, the future was full, tidy, made whole.

He turned his thought to face coldly that which would happen in Milletta. His father would hear of his arrival and learn of his abrupt departure. His father would have to be told what he was doing. There was no alternative. Job's paternity was careless and he would not find his son's absence disagreeable. But he would have to know what had happened and he would have to agree to the expenditure Lucas had forged.

A life with Job and Ouida had dowered Lucas with a sense of prosperity and a sense of uncertainty. There was little in Job's demeanor to reflect accurately whether he was secure or on thin ice, whether money was plentiful or scarce. But Ouida's vigilance was unceasing, her anxieties and her worries sharpened her perceptions, Job could seldom deceive her, and, in time, Lucas, closely tuned to his mother, came to have the same perceptions, the same unconscious habit of observation. He knew now from a score of impressions that matters were somewhat precarious with Job.

He went upstairs to write the letter which must be written. He was calm. He wrote confidently:

"Dear Dad: I was awfully sorry to have missed you, but it was just as well, because the way things have turned out I had to be back at school, anyway, if I wanted to be in time for a chance at summer session. One of the chief reasons I wanted to see you was to talk this over with you, it came up very suddenly so I hadn't time to write before I was due home. I had to make a quick decision and I tried to do it the way you taught me, figuring out all the pros and cons from the other fellow's viewpoint. First of all there is the matter of expense. It won't cost much more to keep me here all summer than it would home, playing around and enjoying myself, which always takes money. And in the second place it shortens my college time considerably so there is a big saving on that. I knew you wouldn't object too much to my being out of mischief all summer and I expect the way your plans are and the things you have afoot you wouldn't have too much time for me and would be glad to have as much of your time as possible free to maneuver in.

"I'm awfully sorry I missed you. I hope you can get up someday this summer, or maybe I can get a ride home. I'm pretty strapped for money but I'm trying to get by on what I have, even though you always told me to come to you the minute I need help. You and I are alone now, and I'd like to spare you all the burden I can. Your loving son, Lucas."

He read the letter detachedly and carefully. He put it in an envelope and addressed it. It had come out even better than he expected. By taking the problem point by point and addressing each point to Job's viewpoint the letter now appeared unanswerable. In addition, he could probably expect from twenty to thirty additional dollars from Job during the summer. With his allowance this would sum slightly more than five dollars a week. But if he could find a spare-time job, if he was able to write Job that he was employed, he would be even more deeply rooted. It was impossible to find a job, but this was summer. Perhaps in summer—

He thought of Dr. Aarons. He stuffed the letter to his father in his pocket and rushed to the hospital.

"Have you seen the bursar? He's a good man to help with jobs," said Dr. Aarons.

"How about cleaning the labs?" Lucas asked abruptly. He sat back, relieved. Where he had felt tension he now felt warmth. It had been said.

"Cleaning the labs? You mean a job? As a job?"

"I streaked right over here to see you. It came to me—I remembered the time you took me through, how you said the labs always needed cleaning—"

"My God, boy! There's no money for that! Why, it's all I can do to keep the staff I've got together!"

"I wouldn't need much money . . ."

"Much money! I can see you don't know anything about money!"

"I'll do all the labs. I'll clean them so they shine. I'll keep them spotless. The staff can get that much more work done. It'll give you the effect of another technician. I'll work every minute I'm not in class. Weekends, too. Nights, if you want me."

"It can't be done."

"For twelve dollars and a half a week."

"You can't do that."

"Why not?"

"It's no pay for a human. An orderly gets more, a cleaning woman—"

"That's all I need."

"I can't let you do it."

"Dr. Aarons, don't you know what it means to me, just to be allowed to work in the laboratory?"

"I know, I know. My boy, there are certain basic realities which you have to face in life. Dreams, ideals, are one thing—but the world about you—"

"And your labs would be spotless. Always. Spotless. And think of the extra volume they'd turn out—freed from janitor work! Will you ask them? Will you? Please?"

Dr. Aarons looked away from the intense young face. If it was a dollar and a quarter a week it'd be just the same. So it won't kill him. It's not spittoons, after all. One dirt is another dirt, and this dirt has the mantle of science to make it respectable. He shrugged.

"It'll be all right," he sighed. "If I have to pay you out of my own pocket we'll make it work, somehow."

"Dr. Aarons—!"

"Now, don't thank me! It's criminal to work for that, I ought to be ashamed to let you, I am ashamed—"

Suffocated with happiness Lucas was helped into a white coat, he wore a white coat for the first time, now he wore part of the uniform. He nodded shyly as Dr. Aarons announced him carefully as the new lab helper. He beamed, wordless, during the pleasantries that followed, conscious of the white coat, impatient to begin.

"I leave him to your tender mercies," Dr. Aarons said at last.

"He'll be a shadow by the end of the week," Miss Dorchester promised.

Dr. Aarons was gone. Ahrlquist, who had been working silently throughout, now came forward.

"You ever work in a lab before?"

"No, I haven't–"

"Well, I'll show you what you've got to do." He turned and walked to the rear of the lab. Lucas followed. The women watched, exchanged outraged looks, shrugged and returned to their microscopes.

The laboratory was a long rectangle, divided into four small rooms and one large room. In the smaller rooms the laboratory animals were caged, there were two rooms for patients and a room for supplies. The larger room was shelved with reagents and chemical equipment which occupied three-fifths of its space. The remainder, the province of Miss Jeanette and Miss Dorchester, was equipped with clinical test apparatus.

Following Ahrlquist, Lucas walked in a narrow aisle on either side of which geometrical vines of glass tubing rose from squat, round, flat, cylindrical, brown, blue, clear, amber vessels, wax-stoppered, glass-stoppered, cork-stoppered, clear, cloudy, stained, colorless, petcocked, coiled, chambered, serene, remote, boundless with function, insistent with surmise, with drama, momentous with curiosity, the extension of his living, the machinery of his vector, the instruments of his mind, the branches for his hands.

"What's the matter," Ahrlquist asked indifferently. He had watched covertly.

"It excites me. I can't help it."

"This? This crap?"

"I mean the shapes of them, their complexity, what they do–"

"Lot of goddamned glass."

"Do you think I'll ever learn how to work that stuff?"

"Is that what he put you here for?"

"Oh, Lord, no! Just to clean up. I meant–"

"It'd be like him!"

"Look! I don't know the simplest thing! It's just that the sight of this stuff excites me. Always has."

"When you've cleaned the five millionth piece of it let me know how much it excites you."

"I guess you're right," Lucas said placatively.

"There's nothing to it."

"Nothing!" Lucas looked at Ahrlquist enviously, admiringly.

"You'll get used to it." Ahrlquist was mollified.

"What do you want me to tackle first?"

"That thing there, for instance." He flicked a tall flask, one of a glittering row, shaped like a pear with a long, long neck, stoppered, the stopper receiving an inverted smaller flask, in turn tubed, leading to another invert, stoppered in a twin of the first flask. A row of these, precise, exactly the same, exactly aligned, all on a stand exactly machined to fit them, beneath each flask a burner, in one end of the stand a spigot. Lucas stared at it, his mouth open.

"That's a Kjeldahl."

"A Kjeldahl!"

"Distillation."

Lucas swallowed.

"And that's a Van Slyke amino-nitrogen deaminizing—"

Kjeldahl . . . Van Slyke . . .

"And that's an inspissator—" He jerked his head irritably in the direction of the women—"I wish they'd learn to keep their goddamned stuff in their own department!"

Kjeldahl . . . Van Slyke . . . inspissator . . .

"That's for titration, they're too goddamned cheap to buy a Coleman —extraction and separatory condensers and tubes—Saybolts, Erlenmeyers, Hempels, Sokhlets with a Friedrichs condenser—junk, junk, junk—"

By the end of the first day Lucas had learned how to clean the animal cages. He had washed flasks, he had learned to ether-dry pipettes, to wash slides, to dust bottles, to sweep floors. He had mollified Ahrlquist, he had avoided the area where the women worked, he had waited sedulously on Ahrlquist.

"You got some fraternity meeting to go to—some college-boy stuff?" Ahrlquist asked as the day ended.

"No, no! I don't go in for that kind of stuff! I don't belong to anything—"

"Well, if you're not doing anything and you don't have to eat in any of those fancy places I eat in a lunch room. It's good enough for me!"

"Me too!"

"Okay, then." Ahrlquist looked sidelong at Lucas. "Ever bowl?" he blurted suddenly.

Lucas blinked. "Bowl?"

"Christ, you know what *bowling* is, don't you. You been in bowling alleys!"

"Gosh—I haven't—I live in a little town, and—"

"Well, for Christ's sake. You don't know anything about bowling!" But Ahrlquist was pleased.

"Do you bowl?"

Ahrlquist glanced at Lucas, twitched his lip elaborately.

"Yeah . . . Some . . ."

At the diner Ahrlquist fed avidly and silently, then pushed the plate away with disinterest. Lucas made haste to finish the sandwich which his budget allowed him. He rose, still hungry, the flat-tasting egg sandwich gave him a sense of virtue, of the better things disregarded.

Ahrlquist's home was in a tattered boardinghouse, a single, narrow room, a strip of torn carpet, a bed with a thin mattress and a worn, patched spread, a second-hand bureau, a chair, a rattan table. On the bureau, on the rattan table were loving cups, bowling prizes, the two surfaces were covered with them. The walls were hung with photographs, pictures of bowling alleys, group pictures lettered in white: "Tacoma Champions, 1919," "Missoula League, 1920 . . ." lettered Lexington and Susquehanna, St. Paul, Winnigatchee, Buffalo, Herkheim, Oneida, Harrison, Multnomah. Lettered towns heard of and unheard of, blaring faces, stern, reserved, proud, determined, diffident, and wild.

Lucas whistled dutifully.

"What—them? The cups? Christ!" He flung open a door. "Got a closetful!"

"And these—" moving to the wall to stare with feigned absorption at the anonymous faces—"these are all you? All winning teams?"

"I could be national champion if I had half a chance." He bent, picked up tenderly a pair of bowling shoes and, sitting on the bed, began somberly to lace them on. "Cost me sixteen dollars," he said briefly.

"Bowling stuff's expensive?"

"I've got everything I need. It's going around. It's going from town to town, working up a reputation, meeting better and better. Until by God one day you're in the big leagues, you're playing champions, you're in the runoffs. National!"

"Those are good-looking shoes. I mean—"

"But how the hell can you save enough on what they pay? How the hell you going to do it? Reminds me—what they paying you?"

"Well, it's not much. But it's not their fault. I get twelve-fifty a week. That's all I asked for."

"Twelve-fifty a week—!" Ahrlquist stopped lacing his shoe to stare at Lucas.

"That's all I asked for. There wasn't really any job—and I needed just that—twelve-fifty a week—it's my own fault—"

"The sons of bitches! It's not their money. It's state money. There's endowments. They got plenty. You'd think it was theirs! The dirty rats!"

They walked out of the dark and musty room, down the dim stairway, out into the somehow luxurious street.

"I'll be free of them someday. And then by God . . . !"

"But you know so much!" Lucas protested. "Do you mean you'd actually throw it over—give it up—for bowling?"

"Look, kid! Don't let the sight of a few twisted hunks of lab glass fool you. It's just glass, see? And the job's just a job. Like any other. You learn it, you do it, you draw your pay. Sure I know it. I ought to know it. I been doing it twelve years!"

They entered the bowling alley. Ahrlquist was greeted with deference. Hangers-on addressed him hopefully. He took it as his due. He went to the office, the manager hurried to produce a small canvas bag, hefted it carefully over the counter. Ahrlquist opened it, pulled out his special bowling ball, inspected it critically, turned away, now became almost jovial.

A small group of bystanders moved diffidently toward the alley, picked what seats they could find, leaned against the railing to watch.

"Gonna kill 'em tonight?" one called out brashly.

"I told my missus about that three hundred—I told her—" another began excitedly.

But Ahrlquist had turned his back and was now wiping his hands with care on a towel slung from the ball-return post.

"Get up!" he ordered one of the sitters. The man rose promptly. "Sit there," Ahrlquist directed Lucas. Lucas sat apologetically in the seat the man had cheerfully quitted.

Ahrlquist now applied chalk to his hands. He inspected them critically. Then he walked to the edge of the alley and squinted down the shining expanse. He returned, picked up his ball. For a moment he stood, poised, lost to all else, looking far down the alley at the triangle of ninepins. Seconds later, liquid seconds in which his motionlessness dissolved without break into smooth motion, he had moved forward, his arm swung back, his arm swung forward, the ball was spinning soundlessly down the alley, it struck the pins with a tremendous crash and the alley was empty.

Ahrlquist turned and walked back. His face was expressionless. A babble of triumph burst from the onlookers. They had been vindicated, their day had been given meaning, their existence had been given a triumph, they lived now, victoriously, on the crest of triumph, justified and alive. Lucas stared at Ahrlquist in amazement and respect.

"Get the idea?" Ahrlquist grinned, pleased, unable to conceal his pleasure.

"Boy!" said Lucas simply.

On the way home Ahrlquist turned to him suddenly.

"I'm gonna warn you again—stay away from those split-tails!"

"Split-tails?"

"The dames. The stupid dikes we got."

"What'll I do? I've got to answer them—I've got to be there—I've got to do what they ask me to—what's the matter with them, anyway?"

"I'm just warning you, lay off. You're either with me or with them."

They walked a while in silence. Ahrlquist cried out suddenly:

"Art, that's what they love, pictures and music and beautiful crap like that. That's what they talk about. To hear them pretend—they could go on for hours if they think you're listening—and as to that awful thing! Oh, my God. Oh, touchmenot. Ohwhatareyouthinking!"

"Did you—ah—did you—try—?"

"I took out the young one, spent two good dollars feeding her. Then she pretended she didn't know what I wanted. All surprise. All amazement. That I would think of such a thing! I should have smacked her right in the puss."

Lucas looked at him expectantly.

"I told her off. I told her just what I thought of her, her and any other split-tail like her. She knew what I meant, all right. Next morning I told them right then and there, I said, 'You do your work and I'll do mine,' I said. 'I don't want anything to do with any goddamned split-tail trash.' That's what I told them. So now they let me alone. Two dollars, feeding her goddamned face, filet mignon she ordered! For nothing! And she knew it all the time."

Lucas shook his head commiseratingly.

"You know something? I've got an idea they're women lovers! Look how they stick together, like man and wife! For two dollars I could have had any nurse in the hospital! Give me a nurse, every time. Give me a girl that knows the score."

"A nurse?"

"Why, boy, a nurse is the best lay you can get. Nurses first, then schoolteachers."

"Don't they get fired, I mean they have to be in by midnight—"

"How long do you think it takes to get a piece? Say, you're not a virgin, are you?"

"Me? Heck, no! I just didn't know about nurses—"

"Fired, hell! They got to catch them first. Wait until you're an intern. You'll see. Hell, they stand 'em up in linen closets, empty rooms, diet kitchens, just whip up their skirts and pour it to them. Those interns get the best. And you know why? Look at the life those nurses lead! Up at five o'clock, mucking in bedpans all day and then what? Squat together reading last month's magazines they stole from some patient. You ever see the food they eat? Just give one of them the chance at a steak and a movie! Schoolteachers and nurses. They're always ready. Boy, you're going to have your eyes opened!"

"I sure didn't know that!"

"What else have they got in life? The only other thing is someday maybe they can marry a doctor. That's what they're all out for."

"She could help him—"

"What does he get he couldn't get free? So he marries her and gets a free nurse and maybe she's got a couple of hundred dollars saved. And all he'd have to do is wait a little and marry a rich girl! Maybe find one that comes to him in trouble. Lots of doctors do that! Plenty!"

He grinned suddenly. "Don't be surprised if I'm a little late tomorrow. If they can afford to hire a helper they can afford to give me a raise."

Next morning Lucas was at work when the two women arrived.

"Here so early?" Miss Dorchester's brows lifted.

"Where's the Ahrlquist?" Miss Jeanette glanced quickly around the laboratory.

"I think he had something he wanted to see the hospital about," Lucas said lamely.

"Well, that's something," Miss Jeanette said, relieved. She carried a paper box. She walked with it to one of the metal-topped tables and from behind a row of tall bottles she brought forth a box of tea, a can of evaporated milk, and a small box of sugar.

Miss Jeanette, who had rinsed and filled a flask, set it on a ring and lit a Bunsen burner.

"So you've been out with the Ahrlquist. Now, you know all about us!"

"Leave him alone, Ann."

"We've heard about his stories," Miss Jeanette said grimly.

"Do you think you'll like laboratory work?" Miss Dorchester asked.

"Oh, yes!" He looked about the room. "Yes! Yes, I—"

"He's got that look in his eye, Ann!" Miss Dorchester cried. Miss Jeanette whirled to see. Lucas reddened, looked from one to the other. "I'm sorry!" Miss Dorchester apologized. "Dr. Aarons told us. We were talking about it. He said whenever you talked about Medicine you got a look in your eye—and you had it, then—"

Miss Jeanette pushed a muffin closer to him. "He filled you up about us, didn't he? What did he say?"

"He can't eat and talk too," Miss Dorchester protested.

"He didn't say much, Miss Jeanette," Lucas began miserably.

"You can't help but be sorry for him," Ruth said.

"I'd as soon feel sorry for a snake!" Ann snorted.

Ruth smiled.

"All right, but even his bowling, the thing he loves, the art in his life, he does it without passion, I know he does, without feeling, without anything, without even wonder. Does it grudgingly, without delight. You've got to feel sorry for him," Ruth sighed. "You can't help it. You can't help him, either."

"I'd just like to stay out of trouble," Lucas said quietly.

"You've got nothing to be afraid of," Ruth said. Lucas stared at his cup. "He can't do anything to you, really. Dr. Aarons has a very high opinion of you."

"And he knows all about Ahrlquist." Ann smiled grimly.

Ruth shrugged. "I've got twenty-two blood counts and a sed rate to do before noon!" she lamented. Lucas leaped up.

"I'll help!"

"You put that dish down!" Ann cried. "If you want to do something go into pathology and get me a clean towel!"

Lucas sped out. The door closed behind him. Ann turned slowly.

"Ruth, that boy was hungry!"

"I know."

"He hasn't eaten!"

"Ann, I don't think that boy had breakfast!"

"He's starved!"

And all the while beneath the words, the looks, the woman looks, speaking rapidly, promising themselves, deciding, feed him, see he gets enough to eat, tactfully help him, draw him out, we're needed, it's done, then, agreed, it's begun, it's begun and he's ours.

"Tomorrow–" Ruth began rapidly, but the door opened and Lucas burst in.

"I couldn't find a towel! I looked and–"

"They're all done, anyway–"

"Aren't you free today?" Ruth asked. "No classes?"

"I thought I'd get a little familiar with the job–it won't do me any harm–" Lucas recollected himself. He had work to do. He went hastily to the mop closet, found a dust rag, began dusting bottles.

"Is *that* what he asked you to do?" Ann demanded.

Before Lucas could answer, Ahrlquist entered. His face was grim. He walked directly to the closet, put on his white coat in the silence that had fallen when he came in, and without a look at the women or Lucas went to his test equipment and began his day's work.

The rest of the morning passed in silence.

At noon Ruth and Ann rose, chatted easily a moment, left to eat lunch in the doctors' and nurses' dining room. When the door closed behind them Ahrlquist picked up a flask and hurled it across the room. It burst against the door. Lucas gaped.

"That bastard!" Ahrlquist turned slowly to Lucas. "That Jew son-of-a-bitch!"

Lucas stared at him, bewildered.

"That Aarons! That kike Jew pisspot!"

"What did *he* do?"

"What do you think a Jew would do?" He grimaced, hunching his shoulders, shoving his open palms forward. "No *gelt!*" he said harshly, "no money, got to save every nickel! So we can eat kosher food and grow a beard and buy a foreskin!" He shoved his hands in his pockets. "No raise! You got to be a Jew to get by around here!"

"A Jew—?"

"You know what a Jew is, for Christ's sake, don't you?"

"Sure—"

"Well, what do you think Aarons is? He's a goddamned Jewboy, that's what he is! You got any Jew blood in you?"

"No, but—"

"Well, that's what you need around here! Jew blood. Don't they have Jews in Milletta, in that jerk town you came from?"

"No! I don't know! I'm sorry you didn't get your raise, but you can't talk about Dr. Aarons like that! I didn't know he was a Jew, I don't know what a Jew is, except it's a religion, he doesn't pay the salaries, he's a nice guy and leave him alone!"

"Who the hell are you, talking to me like that! What are you—a Jew lover?"

"He's my friend!"

"A Jew lover!"

"If that makes me a Jew lover, then I'm a Jew lover!"

"You'll last a long time around here, boy," Ahrlquist promised vengefully. "I'll promise you that! You may last as long as a week. Then we'll see what your Jew friends can do for you."

"Just because a man is a Jew—"

"Just because a man is a Jew! Why you dumb little Jew lover, didn't you know the medical profession hates their guts? Why, he's almost been thrown out of here on his ass a dozen times, all they want is an excuse. And me taking you in— I'll fix you! By God, you'll see! You better quit now, while the quitting's good."

"Listen, Ahrlquist!" Lucas took a step toward him. "I'm not afraid of you. I don't know what you're talking about, but I'm not afraid of you. I need this job. And the day you put me off of it—" His eyes glinted with sudden rage. He balled his fists.

"Why, you Jew-loving son-of-a-bitch!" Ahrlquist seized a heavy pestle, his face swollen, red, contorted.

"Go on," begged Lucas. "Just raise that! Just raise it—"

The laboratory door opened. Dr. Aarons entered, smiling.

"Not at lunch, gentlemen?"

Ahrlquist turned. He sniffed.

"I smell Jews," he cried.

Dr. Aarons reddened. The scene registered slowly, the words last of all.

"I beg your pardon," he said quietly.

"Don't apologize!" Ahrlquist begged elaborately. "I was just telling our Jew-lover friend here how lucky he was to get twelve dollars and a half a week—a fine bargain!"—he leered—"when a skilled technician can't get a five-dollar-a-week raise." He smiled ingratiatingly. "And just at that point you walked in and I said 'I smell Jews!' "

Lucas looked at Dr. Aarons. Tell me to do something, anything, his look begged.

Dr. Aarons stared at Ahrlquist coldly.

"You should be discharged," he said. "You are an excellent worker. Your disappointment was not of my making. I am waiting for your apology."

"Apology! I haven't said anything! What have *I* said? I've just said I didn't like Jews. I wouldn't mean *you*, of course, Dr. Aarons. Not *you!*"

"You shut your mouth!" Lucas cried. His arm shot out, his open hand jarred stiffly against Ahrlquist's bony shoulder, spinning him around. He clenched his other hand, waiting.

"That'll be enough, Marsh!" Dr. Aarons said coldly. And to Ahrlquist, "You're discharged."

"Try and make it stick!" Ahrlquist cried mockingly.

"Come!" said Dr. Aarons to Lucas. He opened the door. Without another look at Ahrlquist he ushered Lucas out, shut the door behind them. They walked down the corridor. He exhaled a pent breath. He turned to Lucas and smiled with his mouth.

"You should have let me sock him!" Lucas said hotly.

"And would that have changed him?" Aarons asked quietly.

"All that stuff!—He must be crazy!"

"Thank you, anyway," Dr. Aarons said gravely. "Now the sooner you forget it, the better."

That was the thing to say. He had said it. And now his eyes were sick with an old pain, his stomach was a dull knot, now it had come again, he had been free, almost free, now it had come again. There was no place on earth, there was no sanctuary, there was no escape, there was a mingling, there was freedom, peace, and one day there was a line, there was a fence, there were Jews. And there were other people. And now, today, this moment, he was a Jew again, wincing, ashamed, and nothing to fight. Nothing to oppose. Nothing to protest. In the earth, in the whole earth, healed and whole, there was this chasm. He stared across it, tiredly.

"Get your lunch," he said. They had come to the end of the corridor.

"I don't feel like eating—"

"Go on. Nothing has happened. Go and eat."

He turned abruptly aside and walked swiftly away down a corridor.

The dining room was almost empty. Lucas sat down, he looked about him fiercely, confused with a vague sense of shame, daring someone to call him Jew lover. No one paid any attention to him. A probationer, a pert brunette, crisp in her striped blue, came in and sat down beside him.

"Nice day." She smiled briskly.

"Yes," said Lucas soberly.

The young girl looked down in mock exasperation.

"Everybody's so sober here! What is this—an operating room?"

Two interns eating silently at the far end of the table paused to eye her loftily. She stared back, unabashed.

"Where do you work?" she asked Lucas.

"I'm in the laboratory," he said in a low voice. Leave me alone, he prayed, go away, leave me alone, let me think.

"Oh, a lab man! My name's Bronson. Dorothy Bronson!"

"I'm glad to meet you," Lucas sighed. "I'm Lucas Marsh."

"Okay, now go ahead and eat your lunch. If you can't be civil—this place is like a morgue. Go on! I won't bother you any more. Go ahead and eat!"

"Yes," said Lucas apologetically. He eyed the forkful of food he had lifted. He put down his fork. He sat a moment longer. Then he pushed away his plate, rose, and left the table.

"Goodbye!" called the pretty Miss Bronson.

But Lucas was gone.

"Goodbye," Miss Bronson said aloud to herself, for Lucas. Then unconcernedly she went on with her lunch.

⁎ CHAPTER 14

Lucas spent a troubled weekend. His conscience goaded him. He was full of disgust for himself. His anger at Ahrlquist was cool now compared to the anger he directed against himself for having cravenly endured Ahrlquist's venom and he regarded himself as partly responsible for the vicious attack on Dr. Aarons, as having tacitly encouraged it by not rebuking Ahrlquist the night before.

I could have prevented it, he told himself bitterly, if I'd shown him he couldn't talk that way the night before.

And now if Dr. Aarons knows we were out together the night before, friendly, probably talking about him—

He went to Dr. Aarons' office early Monday to make a clean breast of his shame and his guilt.

Dr. Aarons was not in his office. Lucas strode to the pathology lab. A group of students, some seated, the majority standing beside a table, were gathered about Dr. Aarons, who bent over a lump of tissue, scalpel in hand.

"I remind you that the two ducts often communicate within the substance of the pancreas. . . . We now open the duodenum by the usual longitudinal incision in the anterior wall of the descending portion and we study the interior. . . ."

He straightened. The students leaned closer. Dr. Aarons looked over their heads, oblivious to them, gazing toward a window.

"I see it!" a student cried.

And now they all crowded closer, peering and exclaiming, and Dr. Aarons slowly ended his stare at nothingness and lowered his head.

"Then an exploratory could include biopsy of the duodenal mucosa adjacent to the pancreas?" a student asked apologetically.

"It must! Carcinoma of the pancreas is frequently an extremely difficult diagnosis to make, it is often impossible to examine all the area involved and all the area must be examined before carcinoma may be excluded. . . . This patient—" he touched the patient, the lump of tissue, the death of the patient—"this patient—" he lifted the patient, the lump of tissue—"died of carcinoma of the pancreas. We have examined the pancreas. Now we have pancreatic tissue at some distance from the pancreas, and this tissue, too, was carcinomatous. Where there are symptoms of cancer of the pancreas, and where examination of the pancreas discloses no carcinoma, the duodenum must be searched for pancreatic tissue."

Dr. Aarons waited. The babble of surgery and diagnosis died.

"This is pathology, gentlemen. This patient died of carcinoma of the pancreas. We have seen here this morning that cancer of the pancreas must be looked for outside the pancreas itself. . . . We will now prepare tissue mounts of the area for study tomorrow—"

He turned to pick up a paper and saw Lucas.

"Yes?" he said, startled.

"It's nothing. I'm sorry, sir . . ." Dr. Aarons turned away. Lucas closed the door humbly. An Ahrlquist could prevail against this.

In the other laboratory, the women looked up.

"Good morning," they chorused, smiling, then turned back to their work. Free of Ahrlquist the laboratory was a friendly place, the wincing terror of the unpleasant was gone, tyranny lifted. He walked toward them genially.

"My gosh!" he said, "I just walked in on Dr. Aarons! He was holding a class—"

He stopped, turning at the sound of movement, turned to see Ahrlquist, the same Ahrlquist, Ahrlquist moving unconcernedly, with studied disregard, among his testing apparatus, stooping, squinting distrustfully at a petcock.

Lucas looked incredulously at the women. Ruth turned. She nodded understandingly, confirmingly, shook her head, turned back to her work.

Ahrlquist said nothing. Lucas walked to the closet, put on his white jacket, went to a sink and began to wash a quantity of waiting flasks.

"Not those," said Ahrlquist mildly. "I'm not done with those yet." Lucas hurriedly left off washing the flasks and busied himself with other glassware. Now what? he asked himself, confused. What's he doing here, still? He's not supposed to be here! What's that tone for, that soft tone?

He dropped a length of glass rod. It smashed noisily. Ahrlquist looked up indifferently. The women did not turn. More confused, Lucas cursed himself, mortified, swept up the fragments, returned to the sink and with exaggerated care resumed washing.

In a short time, noon approaching, the women rose, and still wordless, left for lunch. For a few moments longer Lucas and Ahrlquist worked in silence.

"You're playing it dumb, boy." Ahrlquist ceased work and looked at Lucas compassionately.

"I don't understand," Lucas said stiffly.

"You're a green kid— It's nothing to me—I'm just telling you for your own good."

"Telling me what?"

"I'm still here, ain't I?"

Lucas swallowed.

"I just went to the superintendent. That's all. And here I am."

"Did you tell him what happened?"

"I told him *my* side—hell, who do you think they're going to get for what they pay me? Technicians are scarce. And I'm good. And they know it!"

"Look!" Lucas' face hardened. "I don't give a damn what you told him or didn't tell him. And if you do it again one of us is going out of here feet first! Now you listen to me! Because I'm telling you!"

"You want to get straightened out, boy."

"I'm just telling you, now! That's all!"

"Look! I don't know what Aarons is to you—"

"He's been goddamned nice to me! And you, too, probably!"

"Well, it's your funeral," Ahrlquist shrugged. "I've told you how the rest of the human race feels, how the doctors feel about 'em, if you choose the Jews nobody can stop you. It's a free country."

"You can't tell me that a man like Dr. Aarons—that there's anything wrong with a man like that—a full professor—what would they ever hire him for in the first place? You can't tell me that a man like Dr. Aarons—"

"Go dig your own grave. I've told you. I'm here still, ain't I? He fired me—a full professor!—and I'm still here. So what do *you* think?" He turned away indifferently. "It's all right with me. Just remember what you're sticking up for. It's *your* neck."

"And it's your mouth," said Lucas. "And I'm going to bust it if you ever open your mouth about him again."

Ahrlquist laughed shortly. He shrugged.

In the office of the superintendent Dr. Aarons faced Dr. Bellows.

"I'm afraid I don't quite understand," he said levelly.

"Oh, come on now, Aarons. You know what an ignorant mind is! When you came here I warned you this sort of thing might happen! If we had to discharge an entire hospital on the basis of their prejudices—why, you know about O'Connor! He's a Catholic! And look at the trouble he has, occasionally. Come, man! Look at it professionally! You're a doctor—he's a laboratory technician! Almost a patient! It takes a sick mind to be intolerant—"

"I agree with you. Yes, the boy is really sick. I'm sorry for him. I really am. But he was insolent, unforgivably insulting, publicly, in the presence of—"

"I've told him!" Dr. Bellows said grimly. "Believe me! You'll have no more trouble with *that* young man! He won't forget in a hurry! I told him, I said—"

"If he doesn't owe it to me, he owes it to the dignity of the profession to make as public an apology as he delivered his insult."

"I've got it! I've got it right here!" Dr. Bellows triumphantly pushed a piece of paper across his desk.

"I am sorry if I said anything I shouldn't have. I lost my head. Signed, Joseph Ahrlquist," the note read.

Dr. Aarons looked up, flushing.

"I made him write it out! So he'd remember!"

It's no go, Dr. Bellows knew, scanning Dr. Aarons' face. He doesn't believe it, well, I didn't really think he would, I thought at least he'd take it for face saving, save the situation all around, what makes a Jew so stiff-necked, why do we have to have Jews, why do *I* always have to be the one on the spot! He heard Ahrlquist again, indignantly refusing to make a public apology, offering to leave then and there, he heard himself dealing firmly, cautiously, no love for Ahrlquist, technicians scarce, wages low, Ahrlquist reluctantly signing an apology, an apology that said nothing, half intimidated by a clear threat of being blackballed. And now after all this work, here was Aarons, here was the whole thing toppled, all a mess again, back where he started.

"He's a good man, Doctor," he tried again, controlling his irritation. "You've said so many times. Technicians—" he shrugged, spread his hands to show how scarce technicians were, how low the pay was at this hospital—"I guess you know our fix, Doctor." He smiled ruefully. Help me, you son-of-a-bitch, help me! His face smiled man to man.

"I confess I'm a little amazed, Doctor," Dr. Aarons said quietly. You, too. You, too, Bellows. For the love of God, you too. And I never dreamed it—I never so much as—

"Well!" Dr. Bellows rose with finality. "It's your department, of course. If you say he has to go I'm bound to support you."

"I'd hoped the way you felt—you, yourself—something more than mere protocol would have dictated your answer—"

"Of course! Of course! Don't misunderstand me, Doctor! I beg of you!" He put a hand on Dr. Aarons' shoulder and looked at him earnestly. "We don't tolerate that sort of thing here! This is a state institution—quite apart from my own natural feelings on such matters—which you have reason to know—" I hired you, did you understand that? Yes, you understood— "I'm back of you to the limit!" Hiring a Jew means trouble. Sooner or later it means trouble. It's going to come up and you can't stop it. "So let there be no misunderstanding between *us,* Doctor! I beg of you!"

Dr. Aarons sighed. He's not the worst, and he's not the best. It's not too bad. Really—it's not *too* bad. . . .

"I confess I was more upset than I should have permitted myself to be." He smiled wryly.

Now you've won, have you? Yes, you've won, now. All I have to do is find another technician. Just because of you. Well, you'll bite the bullet a little bit.

"Ahrlquist will be gone by the end of the week."

Dr. Aarons' eyebrows raised. Now what? I fired him Saturday! Lingering on here for a week?

"Have to give them some sort of notice—takes that time to get a new man in—" Next time you won't be so quick, my friend. Next time maybe you'll work it out yourself.

His hand on Dr. Aarons' shoulder he pushed him gently toward the door, walked with him.

"Shall we see what incredibility the diet kitchen has dreamed up today? I must tell you about Williamson—the new orthopod, he came in to see me the other day . . ."

They passed out of the office and walked gravely, decorously, the mantle of the medical profession thick upon their capable shoulders, toward the doctors' dining room. Once, as they walked, Dr. Aarons laughed appreciatively. A passing nurse smiled respectfully.

"I want to tell you about yesterday," Lucas said later that afternoon. "There's something on my mind and I—"

"Yesterday?" Dr. Aarons wrinkled his brows.

"Saturday! I mean Saturday! I wanted to tell you—"

"No need," Dr. Aarons said gently.

"It's about Ahrlquist—"

"Mr. Ahrlquist will be leaving us at the end of the week. Simply do your work . . ."

"Yes, sir," said Lucas. He left Dr. Aarons' office. He walked back to the laboratory. He doesn't want to talk about it, he's too big, it hasn't touched him, did you see him in front of that class? A louse like Ahrlquist couldn't touch a man like that. . . . He's a doctor, he may be a teacher, but by God! he's a doctor! Yes! And Lucas strode into the laboratory.

It was deserted.

He halted, waiting, looking, to be sure. Ruth and Ann had left. Warily, he walked through the laboratory. Ahrlquist was gone.

He looked about exultantly. It was empty. It was his. He was alone in it, free to touch, to handle, to manipulate what he pleased. Like a penniless man, pockets suddenly filled, the fingers of his desire riffled the riches of his opportunity while his eyes crammed greedily the complexity, the glisten, the intoxicating array of equipment.

He walked slowly down an aisle of apparatus, in a forest of glass he touched the glittering branches tenderly, before a blood gas determinator he halted, his eyes raced over glass within glass, tubed, mazed, exact, and with sudden courage he turned at hazard a petcock on a volumetric burette. Measured drops began to fall. He closed the petcock hastily. But he had done it. And he walked on, touching here, handling reverently, touching again, things he had never touched.

In a little while he came to Ruth's chair, her table, her microscope. He looked at it a moment, exultantly. From a tray he picked a stained slide. He considered it a moment. Then he put it back. He breathed quickly. He would make his own slide. As he had covertly observed, as he had memorized, he began the ritual. He took two clean slides. He washed the middle finger of his left hand with alcohol. Uncertainly, a little fearful of the quantity of pain, he pressed a blood lancet to the washed fingertip. He pressed the spring. He felt a sudden sharp jab. He snatched away the lancet. A gout of blood was welling on his finger tip. Excitedly, he touched the drop of blood to one of the slides and the drop was deposited on the glass. With the edge of the other slide he spread the drop as he had seen Ann and Ruth do, a quick movement and, where there had been a drop, a thin, even film. He looked at his slide disappointedly. The smear was irregular, thick here, thin there, wavy, blotched. He waved it impatiently until it was dry. He set it on a tray. Carefully, he poured stain upon it. Step by step he completed the staining process.

Now, shakily, he approached the microscope again. He turned on the microscope light. He inserted the slide in the stage. At the last moment he went to the door, opened it. The corridor was empty. He returned to the microscope. Happily, guiltily, tenderly, he bent over the eyepiece, his fingers touched the focusing knob.

In the things Hominidae has made from the familiar and the commonplace materials about him there are certain items which in their shapes, their color, their implicit function, are to certain men attraction sure as a lodestone; such an item grips him, flies to his hand, triggers an excitement objective, unreasoned, and oblivious, a thunderclap of first love, a hunger which with feeding becomes a stronger hunger, a fulfillment, an added function of the very body it inexorably and imperishably enchants.

In the grip of such a fascination Lucas now strove to glimpse that which he had made with one of the tools he was made for. He could see only a blue blur. Cautiously he turned the focussing knob. He saw nothing. He moved the knob the other way. He saw only a dim blue field. He moved the knob again, unconsciously faster, the blur cleared, he twisted the knob. There was resistance. He turned harder. There was a small, splintering crash.

His scalp prickled with horror. He had broken the slide. He had driven the eyepiece through the glass. He stared at it, unable to move.

"Having trouble?" Ruth's voice came from behind him.

He jumped. He rose, keeping his back to her carefully. His face burned.

"I thought I'd have a look— I guess I wheeled it down too far—"

She bent quickly.

"You didn't use the oil-immersion lens, did you?"

"I—ah—"

"No! You didn't!" She straightened. "No harm done."

He steeled himself.

She saw him brace, hesitated. There's no use telling him no harm done because he won't believe it. If I try to be reassuring he'll only feel worse.

"Watch me!" She sat down.

On a stained slide she deftly dripped a drop of oil, an instant later the slide was in the stage, the nosepiece had flicked over, the oil-immersion lens had contacted the drop, lifted it a microscopic fraction.

"Look!"

Deprecatively he bent to look. His head jerked up.

"Pretty, isn't it?"

He stared at her.

"Now, here's all you have to do . . ."

A half-hour later she rose.

"I'll run along now," she said. The bemusement faded quickly from his eyes.

"I only came to get this." She leaned across him and picked up a novel.

Flustered by her nearness, Lucas scrambled awkwardly to get out of her way.

"I'd be glad to teach you smears and stains, if you'd like to learn—"

"Would I!"

"Yes . . . Well . . ." She turned to go. He watched her forlornly.

She stopped. "Oh! By the way, if you'd care to have supper with us—just a snack, you understand—it just occurred to me that—"

"I'd love it!" He rushed for his coat, he was struggling into it as they left the laboratory.

All his life Lucas Marsh had heard from his mother phrases to frame the life beautiful.

The life beautiful was not the life lived. Upon the common animal necessity for feeding, Ouida embroidered a ritual of gesture, of movement, the fork so, the fingers thus, the napkin a serviette that hid by its grace the fact of food and the filthy doom of necessity.

Often, also, Ouida would describe to him the home of her dreams. But though she panted after beauty, or adornment of evil, which often was to her the same thing, her visions were opulent but indistinct.

"And music—!" she would exclaim. "Great music!" And often as not she would mention a musician, instancing a composer she did not know. "Fritz Kreisler! Ah, darling! There's a great musician!"

And a fine building, oh, a very fine building, her eyes would gleam with the fineness of it, her being lift hungrily. "Gothic," she would murmur, "Romanesque!" and she was not too sure of either. "And books! Rich books! In fine bindings!"

He had heard of fine books but had never held one in his hands. He had heard of music but not the music his mother respected even though she had never heard it. He would have said of painters, Well, Rosa Bonheur is a great painter, and he had seen "The Horse Fair," and Rembrandt is a great painter, and Wagner is a great musician, and he would have said "Rembrant" and "Waggoner," for he was not yet privy to the code his fellows had agreed upon, the phonetics of mode, the decrees of grunt, and the aristocracy of agreed-upon articulation.

He was reverent about art without knowing precisely what it was.

In this town of overstuffed jacquard sofas, an ornate frame containing a chromo of an Italian girl bending for a drink at a wall fountain, and the sober and respectable fumed oak, assassinated mahogany and slit and perforated gum fretwork, the apartment of Ruth Dorchester and Ann Jeanette contained a low English couch, two William and Mary tables, a worn but Khorassan rug, a quantity of excellent, dinted, unmatched pewter, two pictures by Van Gogh, a Pissarro, a Sisley, a Murillo Virgin, and half a dozen English poems printed on strips of fine paper and pinned to the wall. Also, there were books—paperbacks in French and German, books by Coppard, and all the Powys, by Humbert Wolfe and Sassoon and Blake and a set of *The Bibelot, L'Uomo Finito* and *Valle Inclan* cheek-a-jowl with Laurence Sterne and the *Tale of a Tub*.

Into this apartment came Lucas. For a long time he was too shy to notice much. When the strangeness of the apartment was borne in upon him he sat confused, respectful, and startled.

He had no standards by which to judge what he saw or experienced. Even on his second visit, he was uncertain what to praise, whether he was inwardly commending the right thing, what was to be noticed and what was commonplace.

Nevertheless this was a new ingredient, definitely added to his life, giving him new certain standards by which he reacted to the conditions of his living wherever he was to find himself. And his respect for the two women was implemented by awe, by a determination that they think well of him. He absorbed whatever they gave him, tried to see things as they saw them, hear sounds as they heard them, he wanted to be identified with them, to know what they knew.

And for their part they fed him pompano cooked in paper, they sang German lieder and off-the-beaten-path Italian songs, he learned what a villanelle was and that the poems hung on the wall Japanese fashion were called hokkus, he drank wine and did not like it and praised it obediently and hopefully. They opened a world of minor graces to him and caparisoned his thinking with possibility.

And they drew him out, they made him talk of Milletta and Ouida and Job and he was astonished that they both came from small Midwestern towns, he rebelled at this and never accepted it. And they were astonished that he could tell them so little of Milletta.

"Tell us about your mother," said Ann.

"She's dead," he said, and stopped.

"What did she think about your being a doctor?"

"Well, she was against it, at first. She—had a different way of looking at things. She always wanted to be free, free of her body, live as spirit. So she was against me being a doctor. But then one day I told her I had to be."

"And your father?"

Lucas' eyes became wary.

"You'll have to have his help," Ruth said gravely.

He was silent a moment. I'll have trouble with him, all right. He'll never let me. This is all the rope he'll give me. I don't know what I can do. . . . But he's going to have to let me. . . .

"Hey!" he cried suddenly.

He beamed.

"It's a building lot! Mother left me a building lot. It was a couple of them, that's what it was! Two of them!"

"Why, that's wonderful," said Ruth. "And now, with what your father can give you—"

"Tell us about Medicine, Luke," Ann said abruptly.

"What shall I tell you?"

"What does being a doctor mean to you?"

"Mean?"

"Why not a writer, or a lawyer, or—anything?"

He thought a long while. He thought of all the things a doctor was. He thought of the hospital, he thought of the sick, of Medicine, of surgery, of the guardianship of the living, the shining fellowship of the robe. Of another world, another language, another thinking, another people.

He sighed. He shook his head helplessly.

"I don't know . . ." he said.

They looked at him, waiting. But he said no more.

"I'll get the cake," said Ann. She rose. "It's mocha."

Once, later, the talk veered to Dr. Aarons.

"Does he know all this stuff, too?"

"Stuff?"

"What we've been talking about—poems and pictures and music and books . . ."

Ruth shook her head wryly. "Doctors don't have time for books—only for the books that are essential to them."

"Most of them don't have time even for current medical literature," Ann mourned.

The doctors they know, Lucas thought. It must be the doctors they know.

"But when it comes to pathology—!" Ruth cried.

"The university is lucky to have a man like that," Ann said gravely.

"The papers he's written!"

"He could head the pathology department in a university twice this size! I've often wondered what keeps him here."

"Is it because—" Lucas checked himself, floundered. "I mean, has he been in any—trouble?"

"Trouble?" Ann looked at him anxiously.

"What kind of trouble?" demanded Ruth.

"Oh, I don't know—I was just trying to figure out why he stays here—just at random—it just popped into my head." They don't even think of him being a Jew. It never occurs to them. So Ahrlquist is wrong. That was just Ahrlquist.

"He's one of the finest men I've ever met," Ruth said slowly.

"Don't get any Foreign Legion romantic notions in your head," Ann said severely.

"Just to make conversation," Lucas shrugged, embarrassed.

"Of course you know he's Jewish?" Ruth said suddenly.

"Oh, yes!"

"And what, exactly, does that mean to you?" demanded Ann quickly.

"Well, he has a different religion—"

"I don't think Dr. Aarons thinks of religion very often, one way or the other." Ruth shook her head. They looked at Lucas, waiting, expectant.

"I'll tell you the truth," he blurted, "I never ran up against this Jewish business—outside of the Bible I never heard the word Jew, even—until a few days ago."

"Well, it isn't a religion," Ann said noncommittally. "Oh, it's a religion, all right, I don't mean it quite that way. Most people don't know their own, let alone so complicated a business as Judaism. What people judge is a way of life. And the way of life of a person is brought about by the tensions and the restrictions and the opportunities of their past. The history of the Jews has been a very unhappy one and a long time ago, wondering why they were hated and feared I came to the conclusion that it was because they were tense, apprehensive, and insecure. People have a tendency to hate those who have not, even more than they hate those who have. Because those who have not make them uncomfortable, they are reminders of want who disturb the pleasures of the feast, like the poor pressing their noses against the windows where a banquet is eaten."

"I think that's oversimplifying," said Ruth.

"I don't," said Ann. "I think it states the whole case. I think all the rest is just rationalization, case building."

"But what have they *done?*" cried Lucas.

"No," said Ruth, "I think fear is the basis of prejudice. I agree with you there. But I don't think the fears you mention are *all* the fears. There's fear of foreignness, too, fear of the stranger, fear of the human who is unknown . . ."

"Is it anything they *do?* Anything they've *done?*" demanded Lucas.

"It depends on the instance which makes up your mind. If you meet a stranger whose religion is different from yours, whose historical background is different, and who is under different tensions, and you do not like the shape of his nose, or his manner, you will form an opinion and a prejudice and extend this, in your mind, for future reference, to *all* people of the same group, to those you have not met, to the babies, to the dead and the unborn."

"But what sense is there in that?"

"The sense is in reality—not the logic for a reality, but the reality. And that is how things are."

"And that is how I will never be."

"And that is how you must never be."

"It was just Ahrlquist."

"Whatever it was, it was just Ahrlquist."

"There's no problem, none, really none at all."

"Not for you."

"That's right." He sighed, relieved, reason and logic clear, science undefiled.

Next day Ann and Ruth stayed after hours at the laboratory while Ann taught him how to make a Gram stain. Each day thereafter they taught him some new procedure, carefully, patiently, absorbed and fulfilled.

There were other evenings. He embraced them. He absorbed new knowledge, new sensations, made them his own.

"Have you noticed?" Ruth fretted. "He's begun to look at me—you know what I mean—he's so sweet—I wouldn't want him to think—"

"Poppycock!" Ann snorted. "What harm is there? What are you worrying about?"

"But I'm twice his age! And everything's so nice . . ."

Stout, short, dumpy, hair-in-a-bun, doomed and uncomely Ann looked at her levelly.

"I wouldn't worry," she said wearily.

"I suppose not. No, I suppose you're right. It's only that—that I wish . . ."

"Yes," said Ann. "Sure."

A few evenings later, the supper dishes finished, Ann untied her apron, put on her hat and coat.

"Where are you going?" Ruth demanded, astonished.

"Is there something I can get for you?" Lucas rose.

"No, you sit down. Stay just where you are." She opened the door of the apartment and stepped firmly over the threshold. "I've got an errand. I probably won't be back until late."

The door closed behind her.

"Oh, dear!" Ruth looked at Lucas. "Shall we go to a movie?"

He rose to help her with her coat. And then, almost without realizing it, he had put his arms about her, he was kissing her. He was amazed.

When she could free herself a little she put her cheek against his, holding it there, hard, keeping her mouth from him.

"Sit down," she whispered gently. "Sit down, dear . . ." She freed herself. Unsteadily, he sat beside her, he tried to begin again. She held him off, she whispered to him, after a long time he quieted, he sat with his head resting on her shoulder, blood still pounding thickly in his body, her hand gentling him, caressing his forehead, his hair.

"You mustn't, you know," she murmured.

"Why not?"

"Because not. You're a nice boy and we're terribly fond of you, both of us. You just be your own sweet self—"

He reached for her but she turned deftly, she was free, she rose, she bent over, she kissed him quickly on the forehead, she trotted to a mirror.

"My hair!" she cried, she saw him in the mirror, walked to him, put her hands on his shoulders.

"There can't be any more of this," she said soberly and kindly.

"I'm sorry," he said.

"No, I don't want you sorry, either. Just—no more."

He lowered his head.

"Look at me! It's all right, Luke. We're not even going to pretend nothing happened. An hour from now you could be resenting me, being very male and indignant."

"It isn't that—"

"Well, it could be. And it probably would be. But it's not going to be. You haven't done anything to be ashamed of. I just don't want any—anything further—and I'm complimented and I think you're a dear, fine boy and tomorrow when I see you at the lab that's what I'm going to think, looking at you. Do you understand? Is it all right with you? Do you consent?"

"I do. I do. I just wish—"

"And tomorrow night you be here for dinner."

The door closed behind him. He walked down the corridor. In a little while he became conscious that the night air was cool on his face. He looked about. Somewhere on the left the college slept. On the right were a few lights in the town. He hesitated. He walked toward the campus a few steps. He stopped rebelliously. He was wide awake. He turned from the shadowed buildings impatiently. He walked toward the town.

In the town he found an all-night diner. He entered, thinking in another world, the lights, the rattle of crockery, roused him sharply. Guiltily, he avoided the eyes turned toward him, the browsing, half-incurious inspection of a half-dozen men at the counter. He ordered a cup of coffee. When it arrived, when he began to sip it, the other diners turned back to their own, a cycle completed. The scrutiny lifted, the censor gone, Lucas relaxed gratefully. He brooded, trying to think, summoning thought. But his thoughts would not be arranged. They leapfrogged, he could neither order them nor marshal them nor anticipate them. They were of Ruth, they were of himself, they were of the days that had passed, small things, great things, details and whole structures, of newness, of his own newness, of things becoming and things become.

Then memories of the hour just passed quickened his breath. It was the first time. It had come so very close. He finished the last of his coffee, fumbled for a coin. The counterman's back was turned to him. On his left, three stools away, a pair of truck drivers sat motionless staring at their cups.

"What the hell's happened to Eddie?" one asked suddenly, a small man, wiry, big-nosed.

"He got another run." His companion was thickset, rumpled, his stout face deeply lined.

"Yeah?"

"You heard?"

"I heard something was doing. I heard he was fired, company mixup, something."

"No . . . they put him on another run."

"Good!"

"Yeah . . ."

"I heard he was fired."

"No. That's what happened . . . He wouldn't go over the bridge."

"You're kiddin'."

"Nope. One of the bridge guys told me. For months! Eddie'd drive up, the toll guy'd see him, he'd take his toll, close the gate, get into the truck and drive it across. Eddie'd just sit there, shaking. Toll guy used to wait for him. Minute he spotted him he'd close the gate or turn it over to another guy."

"What got into him?"

"Don't know."

"Come on sudden?"

"The way I figure he's had it for years, finally got so he couldn't stand it any more."

"Wouldn't drive over a bridge!"

"Couldn't!"

"*Any* bridge?"

The thickset man nodded, wonderingly. "They give him another run."

"For Christ's sakes I was talking to him, close as you are, just a couple of weeks ago!"

"Trembling like a leaf, the toll guy said. Just sitting there."

"He was just as normal, sitting right across from me—I tell you he didn't *look* wild, he didn't *talk* crazy—"

"He *ain't* crazy!"

"No, huh? Jeeze!"

"He just can't drive over a bridge."

"*Any* bridge, huh?"

"Not none."

"Big ones? High ones? Certain kinds of bridge?"

"Not none."

"I'm a son-of-a-bitch. I gotta tell my old lady."

"Guy comes out to meet him. Eddie just moves over . . ."

The counterman turned, saw Lucas.
"Over here!" he called.
The truck drivers turned, looked at him somberly. Lucas walked to the counterman, paid him for the coffee, eyes followed him as he pocketed his change, as he left, turned away as the door closed behind him.
The streets were empty but now the impression people had made in the empty space, the space they had walked through, were like footprints and he was aware of their passing, of their wake, the streets were people's streets, people who bowled and people who were afraid to cross bridges, they belonged to people, snug in their houses now, waiting to rise, sleeping all about him. He walked briskly home, less alone than he had been in years.
In the morning, his world again, and he progressed from class to class, impatiently. In the laboratory, nothing had changed, he searched their faces but there was nothing there, the night before might not have happened. He was relieved.
"What are you going to do tonight?" he asked casually.
"We're going to get a good night's sleep for a change," Ruth said promptly.
"Oh!" he said, disconcerted. "I was going to— I was going to bring some books back—"
"Some other time," Ruth said.
The door of the laboratory opened and Dr. Aarons entered.
"How about a little tissue mounting?" he smiled.
"Oh, no!" Ann and Ruth groaned in unison.
"I've just got a few— I fell behind yesterday, and—"
"Go on to lunch!" Ann turned to Lucas.
"Aren't you going?"
"We'll be down later."
The door closed behind him.
"How's he doing?" Dr. Aarons asked. "Everything all right?"
"Well," said Ann, "he's doing Gram stains—"
"Him?"
"And Wrights—and a few sed rates—oh, and Pappenheims, of course—"
"And hemoglobins—" said Ruth.
"And blood sugars, of course!" Dr. Aarons snorted. "No, but seriously! Is he keeping the place clean?"
"He *does* those things!" Ann protested.
"Honestly!" cried Ruth.
"I don't believe it!"
"Well, he does."
"Does he know what he's doing?"
"Of course he does! As much as we do—"
"But when does he get time? How did he learn?"
"He comes early and he goes late. That's how he gets time."
"You mean it? You really mean it?" Dr. Aarons' eyes were faraway. "What do I need you to do tissue mounts for? That's pretty nice of you to teach him, give him your time," he said soberly.
"I'll bet you could teach him to do tissue mounts," said Ann.

"It needn't stop there, either!" Ruth said.

"No, it wouldn't stop there. You're right. I'd teach him tissue mounts, then I'd teach him something else, and in a month he'd be teaching pathology and I'd be out of a job!"

"You bet you would!"

Dr. Aarons' face sobered. "Got one of his slides handy?" he asked.

"Here's a sputum," said Ann.

"I'd like to see it." He walked quickly to the microscope. He looked. He raised his head. His eyes were faraway again. "Yes . . . That's all right . . ." What did you expect, he asked himself. Did you expect anything else? Didn't you know? Yes, I knew. Only—only I wish it was me! starting all over again! He turned to the two women.

"Quite a pair of little mothers, aren't you?" He smiled. "Remind me to bring you my socks and buttonholes . . ."

In the dining room Lucas looked about for a seat, saw the brunette probationer-nurse, and a little amazed at his own courage walked to an empty chair beside her and sat down.

"Look who's here!" she said happily.

"What's good today?" He grinned, uncomfortable.

"*You're* good today. Going to take me out tonight?"

His face reddened. Then as he looked at her, groping for an airy return, his heart began to pound. She saw his look.

"Why not?" he said awkwardly, trying to be debonair.

"You going to take me to a movie? And cuddle?"

He looked down so that she could not read his eyes, it was all a joke, he mustn't let on, she mustn't think that he—

"You bet!" he said hoarsely.

"Nurses' Home," she said rapidly. "Seven o'clock." Her face was expressionless. "Seven o'clock—handsome. . . ."

She looked tinier than ever in street clothes, Lucas thought, walking proudly with her from the Nurses' Home that evening. She was very pretty.

"What picture?" she demanded.

"You pick it!"

"I look all right?" She stepped under a street light and turned slowly.

"You look beautiful!"

She took his arm again.

"Know something?"

"What?"

"You do too!"

"Me?—I—"

She turned him unceremoniously, she moved against him, she reached up, she pulled down his head, her lips were on his mouth. Abruptly she released him.

"Now let's go to the movies." She took his arm and turned him again.

"Wait!" protested Lucas. He tried to halt. She walked on.

"First let's go to the movies," she said.

When the darkness was around them, when they had settled themselves in the back row of the balcony to which she directed him, he waited, unsure. At last, the picture begun, she gave a little sigh. Next moment he felt her small hand. It groped toward his lap, found his hand, dragged it back to her lap. She pressed it gently to her body.

Later, eons later, he stumbled after her up the aisle, the lights blinded them, then they were in the dark streets and he lurched beside her, his head clearing only a little, she walked faster and his legs obediently followed, she turned aside, they were on the grass now, walking over grass, he stumbled, they were in a small park, they had come to a flight of steps, he was sitting beside her on the top step, his arms were about her, he was kissing her mouth, her lips opened, she leaned back.

CHAPTER 15

The basement dining room for the hospital staff had once been a pantry. A single long table crammed it, condiments clustered in four precise groups and between these, in a line down the middle of the table, were six small pitchers stuffed with upright knives, forks, and spoons.

Here, visiting physicians came with a jovial air of democracy, dutifully praising the food. Here came the interns, withdrawn, speaking to each other in low, mystic monosyllables full of portent and mutual understanding, eating deliberately, turning expressionless faces to an occasional outburst from one of their less dignified fellows. Here, the nurses sat primly, on their capped heads the curiously designed headdresses, banded in black, that were the symbols of the hospitals from which they had graduated. Here they spoke politely to each other, wary of manners, sitting upright, eating carefully, speaking carefully, knowing their place but allowing no one else in it, either.

Here sat the laboratory workers, eating quickly and silently, vastly outnumbered; here, somberly, ate the resident; the department heads, suddenly vivacious, prating the sacred language when lay executives were among them. Here sat the probationers, the young girls from farms and cities, from high school and department stores, penniless, regimented, rebellious, subdued, forever hungry, their youth bursting from the seams of the blue-and-white-striped cotton that distinguished them from the elite sisterhood, the ladies, the graduate nurses.

Here the language was the common language but each group spoke among themselves in the subsections of it peculiar to their occupations. From the doctors floated such phrases as ". . . caudad? Orad, I would say . . ." and from the interns, ". . . so I knew, once I saw the taeniae coli and the epiploic . . ." and from the nurses, ". . . wasn't it *warm* today, I must get some new handkerchiefs . . ."

To this dining room Lucas came next day near the end of the noon hour. The table was almost deserted. Dorothy was there, dawdling over dessert, plainly waiting for him. Keeping her company another young probationer inspected Lucas steadily as he seated himself next to Dorothy.

"So *this* is the one!" She leaned forward to emphasize her stare.

"Oh, shut up, Jenny! Why so late, Luke?" Under the table Dorothy pressed her thigh against his.

"What I heard about *you!*" Jenny giggled.

"This is my roommate. She's Jenny Ordway."

"Pleased to meet you," Lucas said, bewildered.

"Look at those eyelashes!" said Jenny.

"Quit!" Dorothy glanced sidelong toward the end of the table where two interns ate.

"Oh—oh!" called Jenny.

Lucas looked up.

A nurse was about to take her place opposite them.

"Nuts!" Dorothy muttered, shockingly loud. The newcomer appeared not to have heard. She was a young woman of twenty-two, of medium height, somewhat heavier than the two girls. Her hair was pale blonde, almost tow, her eyes were blue, her face was heavily boned, her chin was cleft.

"Har yu!" She smiled cordially. She spoke with an accent. "And wot's gude?" she demanded. She reached for a bowl of stew and helped herself enthusiastically.

She did not notice that no one had answered her. She looked about the table genially and began to eat. She ate slowly and with relish. She appeared to be completely satisfied with the plain and tasteless fare.

"Skowhegan!" Dorothy snarled under her breath.

"What?" Lucas bent to hear better.

"I'll tell you later."

"What floor you working on, Dorothy?" the nurse asked, amiably, reaching across the table for a piece of bread.

"Third floor," the probationer said sullenly.

"Anyway," Jenny said, "there's a dance the thirteenth, and—"

"Charge nurse is Miss Vinters," the nurse interrupted imperturbably. "That's gude. You be gude to her she treat you gude."

"I got to be getting back." Dorothy rose.

"Me too," said Jenny.

"So! You don't eat dessert, girls? You like to keep your figure, hah?" The nurse grinned amiably and significantly at Lucas. "You new orderly?" she asked Lucas.

"I work in the laboratory," Lucas said.

"New janitor boy, hah? You go to college or just janitor?"

"College."

"You coming?" Dorothy demanded.

"Let him finish!" the nurse protested. "He don't have to watch his figure."

"Come on, Dorothy," Jenny said. "See you later, Luke." They walked stiffly out.

"Nice girls," the nurse said approvingly. "You know them long?"

"Not long, no."

"Nice. Nice girls. Got two more years, then they get their caps. Then maybe marry some nice doctor, settle down, all fixed."

She applied herself again to her stew. Lucas waited uncertainly. No nurse had ever spoken to him sociably before. She continued to eat. He took up his spoon and finished his dessert, pushed his plate away and rose. The nurse looked up.

"Goodbye." She beamed hospitably.

"Goodbye," said Lucas, startled.

"That pest!" Dorothy explained. "That dumb ox!"

"What does she do?"

"She's operating-room nurse. She ought to stay there. Have you ever seen anything dumber? I mean, dumber?"

"She's got kind of an accent–"

"Accent! She's just Swede through and through! One hundred percent dumb Swede! Why, she's the butt of the whole hospital! 'Ay coomb fum Minny-Soe-Duh!' "

"What does she do?"

"What do you mean, 'what does she do'?"

"I mean, what does she do that's wrong? I mean–"

"What does she do that's wrong? Why, she's a Swede, Luke! She's just a big dumb Swede! Where you been, Luke! Don't you know what Swedes are?"

"What's the matter with Swedes?" Luke asked defensively. He asked the question with a shade of belligerence to distract Dorothy from guessing his ignorance.

"Oh, Luke! Oh, I'm not saying *all* Swedes! Some Swedes are some of the finest people I know. But when you get a dumb one–why, they're just like a hog, or a cow or something! No manners, no dignity–just *dumb!* Why, the whole hospital knows her!"

"I don't know her," Lucas explained. "I never saw her before," he added apologetically.

"You must be deef, then! Deef, dumb, and blind!"

"What are you getting so mad about?"

"The whole lunch hour ruined just because she had to butt in–"

"Oh, come on, Dorothy!"

"And you! What are you going to be doing, all the rest of the month! Going around with those la-de-dah art lovers in the laboratory? Sure! I'll bet you sleep with both of them, don't you! Both of them! Right now!"

Lucas recoiled. Dorothy's face was paler.

"Admit it!" she cried, triumphantly and cut to the heart at his flinch.

"You don't know what you're talking about!" he said angrily.

"No, I suppose not. Not *them*! Laboratory technicians!" She minced the words daintily, spitefully. "Much too good for any of us. Keep to themselves and read poetry and look at pictures. The fat lady and the titless wonder!" She stuck out her little finger, "Would you have tea or lemon?" she mimicked Ruth, pursing her lips.

"Cut it out!" Lucas cried. Ruth and Ann receded into another world, a rich, cultured, fine, secure world, and he joined them there without hesitation, looking with revulsion on Dorothy and a thousand Dorothys, on a world beneath.

"You are, aren't you!"

"Listen here–!"

"You're sleeping with her! With the thin one!"

He stared at Dorothy incredulous and furious. He saw in her angry eyes a flash of despair and pleading, grief and helplessness.

"You don't know what you're talking about," he said earnestly. "You just don't know, Dorothy."

"No, they're out of my class. I wouldn't understand, would I! Girls like that never think of a man! Why, they wouldn't know what to do with a man! And you've never kissed her. I suppose you're going to tell me that!"

"What's the matter with you? What's happened?"

"I just don't like to be two-timed!"

"Well, who's two-timing you?"

"No, I suppose you're just going to be sitting in your room with your hands folded the next thirty days—"

"*What* next thirty days?"

"Oh, you! That's what I was trying to tell you at lunch when that—that cow—butted in! I go on night duty tonight. I'll be on night duty"—her voice rose, despairing—"for a whole damn month!"

"No!" He looked at her with real consternation.

"And you on the loose with that too-good-to-pee poetry reader," she said, but his consternation had satisfied her.

"Honestly, Dorothy," Lucas protested, *"honestly,* you're wrong—you're dead wrong—you—"

"Did you like Jenny?"

"Jenny—who's Jenny?"

"My roommate Jenny! The girl who was with me at lunch—you sat right next to her!" she cried irritably.

"Oh! . . . Sure! sure, she's all right—"

Dorothy's face whitened.

"Well, you take *her* out! See? When you want to take somebody out, you take Jenny."

After the movies they walked sedately along the sidewalk, heading automatically, tacitly, toward the park. On this first evening with Jenny, Lucas was self-conscious and polite. Jenny drew him to a halt outside a department-store window.

"That's a pretty dress," she said, staring.

"Yes, it's nice. Not as nice as you've got on," he said hastily.

She drew back, looked down at herself, smoothed her skirt.

"What, this? This old thing? I've had it a million years!" She looked up at him. "You really like this, Luke?"

He eyed her figure guardedly, turned hastily. "It looks swell! It really does!"

She took his arm. She had seen his look, she was satisfied.

"I've got a TL for you," she said presently.

The park was just ahead.

"What's a TL?"

"Oh, you! You know what a TL is!"

"If it's got something to do with that dress—"

"Silly! That's not a TL. I wonder if I'll ever be able to afford dresses like that. Just walk right in and buy it and walk out. I wonder who does it? Just anything they want."

"Wait until you're a nurse. Nurses get good money–"

She looked down at her scuffed shoes. She wriggled her toes idly to see whether she could feel the pavement beneath the thin spot in her right sole. "I'm going to handle only private cases. Nothing but private."

"That's where the money is." Lucas nodded wisely. He fingered the two worn bills in his pocket.

The street lights were dimmer here. The park had begun. At this hour the town was preparing for bed. The sidewalk echoed their steps.

"Don't you honestly know what a TL is?"

"Honest."

"It stands for trade last. When somebody says something nice about someone you tell them, but first they have to tell you something nice somebody said about you."

"Oh, sure! Now I remember!"

"You knew it all the time!"

"I swear–"

"Well, first you have to think of something nice somebody said about me."

He thought a moment. "Well, somebody said you had a pretty figure."

"Oh, you made that up! Who said it? Who?"

They had ventured onto the grass. They walked slowly, aimlessly, always toward the small copse of trees somewhere in the night ahead.

Lucas tried to think of a name.

"One of the interns," he said.

"I'll tell you mine. One of the girls said you had the nicest–"

She broke off and turned her head, listening. They halted. From the darkness, from nearby, came a soft sound.

"It's somebody crying." They looked at each other, then turned and walked in the direction of the sound. Huddled against one end of a park bench sat a small, elderly woman. Her gray hair had loosened wispily. Her feet did not touch the ground. She was weeping quietly and tiredly, her hands over her face.

They looked down at her but she did not notice them.

Lucas cleared his throat.

"Is there anything we can do?"

The old woman started. She cringed. She peered at them fearfully.

"Would you help me?" she begged. "Would you please help me?"

"Of course!"

"Sure, honey!"

"I want to go home. Will you take me home? I'm lost . . ."

"You bet! You just tell us where it is!"

"I just went out for a little walk. I must have got confused. I've walked and walked. I'm sorry. I don't want to be a trouble."

"No trouble at all!"

"Don't you worry, dear–"

"I don't know what happened–I'm just–lost . . ."

Lucas took her arm gently and helped her to her feet. In the dimness she trembled.

"I'll be very glad to pay you," she said. She opened a shabby purse. She felt in it a moment. "Here!" She extended a quarter to Lucas. Her purse dropped. He picked it up, flat, ravelled cloth, quite empty. "I can pay you for your trouble."

He pushed the coin gently away.

She insisted. "I'll be glad to pay—"

Lucas took one arm, Jenny the other, they led her toward the sidewalk.

"Where do you live, dear?" Jenny asked.

"It's that big house . . ." she began. She darted a wary look at them. "It's quite a big house," she said quickly. "Harmon Street. I don't know what happened . . ." She shivered. "I was lost . . ."

She was very small between them and over her head Jenny looked quickly at Lucas.

"Is it the—the Home, dear?"

The old woman lowered her head.

"Yes," she said in a small voice.

"Well, don't you worry, honey! We'll have you there in a jiffy!"

"I just came out for a walk. It's not easy to be cooped up all the time—and I must have walked too far—taken a wrong turn—and all I wanted was a little walk—just to get away by myself—"

As they neared the Home for Aged and Indigent she tried again to give Lucas the quarter.

"Please! I've been such a trouble! Take it for all your trouble."

The door of the Home opened. A tall matron peered at them. The old woman shrank. The matron promptly called over her shoulder:

"Mary!"

She stepped forward and seized the old woman's arm.

"You!" she cried triumphantly.

"I'm sorry, matron—"

"You've had your last chance, Mrs. Duncan. You've been warned and warned—"

"I just went for a walk—"

"What's the trouble?" Lucas flared.

A second matron hurried out.

"You! You, is it? And half the town turned upside down looking for you!"

"That's who it is, all right," the first matron sighed.

"Well, you know what's going to happen to you, now!" the second matron said firmly.

"Please, matron—"

"We've had enough of it and that's all. This is the last straw."

She hustled the old woman inside, she hurried her along a hall, the slender, small woman docile, doing her obedient best to keep up with her, they disappeared. "Please!" The old woman was weeping.

"It'll do you no good! You've been warned enough!" And they were gone.

"Wait a minute!" Lucas found his tongue.

"Yes!" echoed Jenny. "What—"

"What's going to happen to her?" Lucas took a step in the direction in which the old woman had disappeared.

"She's an inmate!" said the matron.

"I know, but—"

"She's been told and told and told," the matron said sadly. "And the minute you turn your back she wanders off and gets lost. Four times. Four times this month!"

"You mean to tell me you're going to punish her?" Lucas breathed faster.

"How would you like to have a house full of them wandering off, and you responsible to the state—"

"She was trembling!" Jenny cried. She glared at the matron indignantly.

"And none of us knowing whether she'd been killed or laying hurt somewhere—the whole place topsy-turvy—she's been warned and warned," the matron said compassionately. "The poor soul knows the rules." She sighed. "Tomorrow morning she's going to Nortonville."

"But that's the insane asylum!"

"They get old. They go wandering around—"

"But she just went for a little walk! She felt cooped up and wanted to be alone and she went for a walk and—and got lost—"

"They'll take care of her at Nortonville. There's nothing the matter with Nortonville."

"But she's not insane!"

"The Home's full, as it is. Pack-jammed—"

She looked at them with sudden interest.

"You relatives?" she asked hopefully.

"We just happened to find her—"

The matron grimaced. "Well, then . . . thanks for bringing her back. We're obliged to you."

"Us? Don't thank us!" Lucas snorted.

"She'll be all right." The matron nodded. She closed the door.

They stood uncertainly. The looked at each other. They dropped their eyes. They looked again at the closed door. They walked into the darkness again and it was cool on their cheeks and it hid them and they were glad of it.

And slowly it became bearable, there was distance between them and the Home, distance and darkness and, a little with each step, they left it behind.

"That poor, poor old thing!" Jenny said at last. She turned to Lucas defensively. It's not my fault, her look said. What could I do? Did I do wrong?

"There must be somebody you can report a thing like that to!" Lucas vowed.

"They get old, you know," Jenny said apologetically.

"But the insane asylum! Why send her there? The last thing in the world that poor old thing wants is to be cooped up! There's no reason to send her there! She's not senile—"

"Yes, Luke. Yes, she was," Jenny said softly.

"Jenny!"

"A little, Luke. A little senile."

"Now, Jenny! My God!"

"Just the least little—when they get old—at first you don't even notice it—my grandmother—"

"I didn't notice," Lucas said, uncertainly.

"Yes, Luke. Honest!"

"You'd know, I guess," he said reluctantly.

"I see them in the wards. Honest! And you were fine, oh, you looked so brave standing there, standing up for the poor old thing—"

"Gosh! When she tried to make me take that quarter—"

"It's all right, Luke. She'll be well taken care of." He turned to her anxiously. "They take awfully good care of them! And think of her wandering around in the cold, in the park all night—"

"That's true . . . that would be terrible . . ."

"No, it's the best thing, Luke. It's really best . . ."

They came again to the park.

"I'm going to take nothing but private cases," Jenny said. "Private, home cases, good homes, twenty-four-hour duty. Where I can eat in peace, all I want, the kind of food rich people have, and dress well and get paid. Convalescents . . ."

"Nurses make a lot of money, sometimes," Luke said.

"When I came into it I never thought of money. I come from a farm."

"Lots of farmers where I come from. You ever heard of Milletta?"

"Farmers!" Jenny shuddered. "At first all I wanted was to get away. But the day we were given our uniforms, when I did my first day—you know something? I *wanted* to be a nurse."

"You'll be a good one."

"But it's forever! It's four whole years! And you're poor, poor, you get up poor and you go to bed poor, your shoes get holes in them, the food is awful and you're always hungry, when I pass a bakery and see those whipped-cream cakes I have to turn my head away, and candy, and a thick juicy steak—just once—and a new dress—or a hat—"

"Students don't have much, either," Lucas said awkwardly.

"Five dollars a month! That's what a probationer gets! You just be a girl and young and—and—healthy—and try five dollars a month."

They came to a small hill. They sat on the grass.

"Tomorrow we'll see if I can scrape up enough for us to have a steak. Maybe a small one. What do you say?"

"It's different with you! You'll be a doctor someday. A doctor! Do you realize that?"

"I know," Lucas said humbly. He put his arm around her shoulder.

"It's late," she said meditatively. "I'll get killed. I'll have to go through a window—"

"In a minute," said Lucas. Her shoulder was soft and firm. Her body was warm against his chest.

"We've got to be true to Dorothy," Jenny warned, smiling.

"We will."

"I promised . . . Otherwise . . ." She snuggled closer. "You're nice, Luke . . . You're not rough and—and grabby—"

"Shhh," he said. And then, " 'You cannot dream things lovelier, than the first love, I had of her.' " His voice was low, he tried to control its awkward shaking. She looked up, surprised. He hugged her closer. " 'Nor air is any, as magic-shaken, as her breath in, the first kiss taken . . .' "

"Why, Luke, darling . . . that's poetry . . . Are you saying poetry to me, Luke?"

"It's Humbert Wolfe," he said. "Listen . . . 'And who in dreaming, understands, her hands, stretched like a blind man's hands . . .' " Jenny sighed. She closed her eyes. " 'Open, trembling, wise they were, you cannot dream things lovelier . . .' " His voice faded. They sat in silence. His heart was beating hard. Against his cheek her cheek was warm, a little moist. Her voice was drowsy.

"That's lovely, Luke. . . . Do you like Edgar Guest? Home we had a whole book—"

He turned her to him. He stopped her mouth with a long kiss. Her hands tightened about him. She held her mouth on his. The night drifted slowly over them. He moved, he moved again. For an instant she wrenched her mouth away.

"No! No, don't! Don't, Luke . . . Luke!" And then, "Oh! . . . Oh! . . . Aaahh . . . That's good . . . That's—that's . . ."

Then she was silent.

Now the days passed, and these were days of youth. It was the first time Lucas had been a youth and he studied hurriedly, he rushed from his morning classes impatiently, he cut classes. He studied little. The hospital enfolded him and he walked the crisp corridors reverently, each day he gained new courage, soon he walked boldly through the wards as if he were on some errand, once or twice he ventured into the maternity section. But best of all he loved to linger unobtrusively outside the wide swinging doors of the operating room. There, the white-clad interns entered, their faces abstracted, sometimes laughing casually, without merriment, conscious of their dangling masks, their other-worldly vestments. And the doctors, advancing to the double doors in clothes which were almost uniforms in themselves, the suits all vaguely similar, of hard, thin cloth, shoes black, round-tipped, and shining, dull ties, spotless linen, the doctors walking measured steps, ignoring the world to confer with mannered, intent smiles, chatting gravely on new instruments, making medical talks, passing obliviously thus through the swinging double doors. And sometimes an orderly and a nurse would swing silently along the corridor, pushing a wheeled stretcher bearing a human figure all silent, staring ceilingward, glancing wide-eyed sidelong, eyes closed, the head wrapped grotesquely in a ritual towel, fastened ritually, the body covered with a ritual blanket, ritually tucked in, and without pause or murmur or sound of any kind except a bump at the swinging doors, the stretcher, the patient, the nurse and the orderly would disappear, the doors would swing behind them.

And sometimes such stretchers would emerge from the swinging doors, and before they swung shut he could glimpse doctors, now robed in white, ritually gloved, masked, talking animatedly, and the patient, ritually swathed, breathing stertorously, would disappear in a twinkling down the corridor, leaving a strong and a delicious wake of ether.

And a few times a strange aura would fill the entryway, a sense of excitement and of boding, of something about to happen, something stern, something that must be punished, something of guilt. And in this oppressive aura Lucas could see as the stretcher passed him that a sheet had been pulled over the patient's face, and that there was no breathing here, and the shape was human but there was nothing for it here, nothing in the hospital, it was without value and there was nothing to be done with it. There was a small ritual provided for it, but that was all. Then in a moment the doctors would emerge slowly, chatting as when he had first seen them, and the ominous aura faded and the life of the hospital, which had paused for a moment, ticked on imperturbably, ordered, serene, act upon act. And Lucas watched the doctors, and worshipped them with his eyes and went back to the laboratory disappointed in the body that had failed them and which now lay below, in the basement, in a basket, waiting silently for their goodness and their wisdom, waiting to be opened, this time utterly, to disclose to their good and other patient fingers how it had failed them.

He heard the cries of newborn babies. In a week he learned through the side-mouthed sotto-voces of the probationers with whom he was becoming fast acquainted the hoarse yells of women in labor and which was hard labor and which was yelling.

Daily he foraged through the hospital, daily he saw new sights, heard new sounds, daily he was intoxicated, and these sounds and these scenes were the weather and windows of the house in which he lived.

In the evenings there was Jenny, there were a furtive half-dozen other probationers, he went often to Ruth's and Ann's apartment.

There were such evenings and long days in the laboratory and the new things learned, and there were the evenings at which he was becoming more and more adept, when he adventured with probationers, and his body belonged to such evenings. Hunger swiftly became appetite. He learned the dark places of the parks, the hallways of apartment houses, the secrecy of cemeteries, the slope of riverbanks, what places were safe and which were thrillingly dangerous.

And these days, these things, all these days and all these things, this mosaic became a pattern of excitement and voracity, and the impact of Medicine, and body and love, and they were willful days, days without a reckoning, studies forgotten, in which he ruled himself and bade himself do as he craved and he kept no account but lived as a body and a mind would live, whichever voice was strongest, oblivious to the order to which he had bound himself.

In this fashion, in the space of a few weeks, the pleasures, the raptures, the new horizons, new conduct, new freedom ripened him, he passed from boy to uncertain man, he gained assurance, he was astounded at the success of duplicity and acquired confidence in it, he discovered that he was personable in the eyes of others and that he could trade heavily upon it and he was somewhat delivered from maternal rule by the discovery that by appealing to the maternal he could rule it. He became an entity. He became a person of his own.

"I understand from Miss Jeanette and Miss Dorchester that you're picking up laboratory technique," Dr. Aarons said to him one day.

"They've been teaching me—"

"So I understand. I may start you on a few tissue identifications."

Lucas stiffened.

"Unless, of course, you haven't time—"

"Oh, I've got plenty of time—really! Plenty!"

"If you're sure you have the time. I don't want to encroach on your recreations—you should have some time for recreation—"

"Honestly!" Lucas protested.

"Because it may involve a little night work."

"Not a thing! I haven't got a thing to do!"

"That's fine, then. Your nights are for study. I'll bet you know."

"Is there anything—anything, say, I could study in the meantime?" Lucas looked in the direction of a microscope.

"Slides, you mean?"

"I've never seen a tissue slide."

Dr. Aarons opened a drawer. "Here's healthy kidney tissue, here's a diseased sample. Here's healthy liver, here's diseased liver. And here's a spleen." He put the glass slides in an envelope and handed it to Lucas.

"I'll be very careful with them," Lucas said reverently.

"Yes. Next time I see you perhaps you'll be able to tell me the differences you observed. Would you like to see something? Tell me what you think of this."

He flipped a light switch, bent briefly over a microscope, straightened, gestured to Lucas to look. Lucas stared through the tube. On a blue plain a host of small whitish circles loomed, and in the areas between the circles streamed a profusion of irregular dots, streaks, a river of small marks whose only plan was irregularity and profusion.

"Well?"

"I think—I think there's some cells there."

"Many cells. What sort of tissue would you say the cells formed?"

"I don't know—not bone . . ."

"No, not bone. Anything else?"

"No, sir."

"Look again. What you see is cancer, carcinoma. And the cells are gastric tissue. You've seen cancer before? Well, now you've seen it again. A particularly beautiful specimen. Cancer of the wall of the stomach. The wild material, the formless stuff, crowding the cells, absorbing some, spreading everywhere, that's the cancer."

"That's the form, then."

"It has no form."

"That's what I mean."

"That's true. But in its aggregate it can take form, very definite form—"

"Like in kidney cancer—"

"What do you know about kidney cancer?"

"I just read somewhere that in certain kinds of kidney cancer, or tumor, or something—"

"That the growth roughly resembles the kidney on which it feeds. That's right. Where did you read that?"

"Do you know what I thought? I mean, I don't know anything about it, of course, but I couldn't help thinking . . ."

"What did you think?"

"Well, you know how Medicine has used the enemies of the body—like vaccines and deliberately giving fever for syphilis, and—burns for some kinds of treatment—well, I thought, I mean the idea just hit me when I saw that about that kind of kidney cancer, maybe someday that's how they'll cure cancer!"

"As a vaccine?"

"No, no sir! I mean deliberately implant cancer. Turn it against itself! Use it! I mean, it's a growth, and the chief enemy of the body is worn-out organs and someday they'll train cancer to do what I'll bet it's trying to do—grow new organs. Because look at the kidney form! It almost seems as if that's what cancer is *trying* to do, it's a kidney cancer and the cancer grows in a kidney shape and it's just like a kidney except that it hasn't any function and maybe it could be taught to have function!"

Dr. Aarons smiled and shook his head to cover his embarrassment.

"I don't see why not!"

"Well—ah—cancer grows wild, you know—"

"But it grows."

"Yes—that's quite true—it grows. . . . Well, cancer is a big subject. You'll understand more about it every year. Yes."

"But it's possible! Isn't it possible, sir?"

"No."

"Absolutely impossible?"

"Absolutely."

"I don't know the mechanics, of course. I don't know how it could be done. But just to train it, say—use its growth potential—make it grow new organs, new bones, whatever you need—"

"I understand."

"And it's not possible?"

"No."

"But I really mean it!"

"You have had civics? Yes. You know what anarchy is? Cancer is anarchy."

"But—"

"It is simply not possible. When you study you will see why. It is not possible even to discuss it with you until you are better grounded. You must know physiology."

"Yes, sir."

Dr. Aarons shrugged. "Take care of those slides. They're excellent mounts. And study—when you have a chance—the fundamentals!"

The clinical laboratory was empty. He put the slides carefully in a desk drawer.

Ruth had bought a book on her way to work. It lay near the microscope, *Three Plays* by Brieux, slim, bound in a tapestried cover. He put his fingers tenderly on her microscope.

He bent closer to her desk. She had left a memorandum to herself.

Ruth and Ann had been dividing the work Ahrlquist used to do. The note said: "Total nitrogen—Kjeldahl."

Now he knew where to look, where to find out what things meant. He riffled pages impatiently. In one of the books lining the far wall he found Kjeldahl's method for determining total nitrogen. It was a complicated formula. He brought the book to the long table and set out those things the test required. One by one he brought the seven chemicals. He inspected the digesting rack with its six curious flasks. Then he set up the distilling apparatus. All of this took time, the materials were unfamiliar to him and the equipment complex and delicate. Now he read the formula again. He had overlooked a pipette and an oxidizing flask. He found the catalogue of a chemical supply house and searched the illustrations for an oxidizing flask. Finding the picture he searched the laboratory until he found the flask, brought it to the long table. He found a hood and a Bunsen burner. He saw the words "Erlenmeyer flask" and he reasoned the size and brought it to the table, then litmus paper—he had overlooked that. The test suggested a Hopkins bulb, and he found a picture, but there were four varieties. He inspected the equipment minutely, traced down the bulb, found it already in place.

The door opened. He fled to another part of the laboratory, exultant.

He heard Ruth cry out:

"He's set up the whole thing!"

"For Heaven's sake!"

"The Kjeldahl I was dreading! He must have seen my memo. Look! The whole thing!"

"Luke!"

"Eh?" He pretended to be absorbed, disturbed in another task. "What do you want?"

"You come out here!"

He came out.

"Luke Marsh!"

"How did you know what to set out?"

"I looked it up."

"You're coming to dinner tonight! And I'm going to make you the best roast chicken this side of Iowa!" Ann cried.

"I really can't," he said wretchedly.

"Oho!" Ann cried.

"I've got to see one of my profs . . ."

"So it's true! You little devil! We *heard* we had a Don Juan in the lab—Luke! You little devil. So it's true!"

"Absolutely not!" he said hotly. "Whoever said it's a damned liar!"

"And you don't know any little dark-haired girl named Dorothy? Little probationer?"

"I never heard of her! Never!"

"Luke!"

"Wait a minute! You mean a little dark-haired probationer sits next to me in the dining room now and then? Is that what you mean? For Heaven's sake! She just sits next to me!"

"But why shouldn't you?"

"It makes me sick!" he said. "Lies! Gossip! What for? Why?" His eyes were desperate.

"It's all right, Luke."

"It's not all right!" He strode out of the room. He walked rapidly down the hall.

"What did you do that for, Ann?" Ruth reproached.

"I thought he'd be pleased. Most men are if you tease them about their love life."

"What's going on here?" Dr. Aarons walked in, looked amiably at the two women.

They looked up, startled.

"Ann here—we were having a little fun."

"I expect you were. Your helper passed me in the hall as if he was walking through a shadow! What did you do to him?"

"Oh, the poor kid! We were teasing him—"

"I was teasing him about girls."

"Ah? You've heard too?"

Ruth shrugged. "You can hear anything at a hospital."

"It's easy enough to say about a boy like Luke," said Ann. "Good-looking and all. We happen to know differently."

"I'm glad to hear it," said Dr. Aarons urbanely.

"He's much too fine," said Ann. "Too withdrawn, too sensitive, too far above such—" She shrugged contemptuously.

"He's a very nice boy," Ruth explained earnestly.

"Ah, yes." You're laboratory workers, he thought irritably. You're a part of science. And you talk like that. What are you turning your back on?

"You can see how he reacted to the very thought," Ann said more quietly.

Can you be moved? he wondered. Has living, your living, rotted the tendrils of all female reaction in you? Is there a gap now, a synapse, a nothingness between the evident and the response? Have you carried past the act of coitus, have you made it not exist and only the child, the result?

"Yes, I can see," he said amiably. "He has reached the ripe, the bursting age. He has reached that period when he is fittest for procreation. Accordingly, the perfect and oblivious knowledge of his cells is bending every effort to see that this organism perform a cardinal function. He is at the age fittest to breed and he burns to breed."

"I suppose you're right." Both women smiled politely.

"Alas, it's a matter of cold science and not philosophy."

"Of course," said Ann, "there are certain community restrictions . . ."

"Oh, yes! The local ground rules. In Africa some communities decree he must first kill and then breed. In America he must first be joined to one woman and then breed. In Melanesia he must first be circumcised and then breed. There are ground rules and ground rules. There are all sorts of community restrictions. These elaborate gambits have become more important than breeding itself. We love our rules more than our purpose. It has nothing to do with reality, however. It is like a savage inventing a legend, and a whole set of laws to go with it, about an airplane engine."

"There is something to be said about a certain amount of community order," Ruth said dryly.

"Order is a woman's institution," said Dr. Aarons. "It was probably invented by the weak. Strength makes its own order." You're leading me off, now, he thought suddenly. That lovely female trick, off the trail, away from the ponderable, into the imponderable, away from sex—away—away—away—

"But that hasn't much to do with our young friend. So far as the law of his cells is concerned he was born for this moment, this age, this time."

"I wonder if he realizes?" Ruth smiled.

"I wonder what he's been taught," Dr. Aarons speculated. "Do you know that in Japan a Japanese woman thinks nothing of bathing nude in public, with a naked man, but she would die of modesty if anyone glimpsed the nape of her neck?"

"So *that's* why they wear those buns covering the nape of their necks!"

"I see you have your Kjeldahl all set up for that nitrogen?"

"Luke did that," Ruth said proudly.

"Luke? Set up a nitrogen determination?"

"Absolutely. He set it up all by himself. When we came back from lunch there it was, waiting!"

"He's full of little things like that," Ann said instantly. "Does them all the time. For both of us."

"You've both been very kind to him," Dr. Aarons said. "He has an excellent mind." He told them Lucas' theory about cancer.

"So reasonable? Yes . . . Not to you, of course." He looked significantly at the microscope. "Apropos," he said, "I had a letter yesterday from Dr. Weinstein—I've mentioned him to you? Yes. He's doing an *arbeit* on steroids."

"Did he get it?" Ruth asked. "The appointment?"

"He's a fool," Dr. Aarons said levelly, his eyes hard. "I told him what to expect. He went ahead and applied anyway."

"But the position was open—he's the senior man—it *belonged* to him—what could they possibly say!"

"He's a Jew."

"Even if they *hated* Jews—you can't tell me they *all* hate them—"

"They turned him down."

"No!"

"Of course!"

Dr. Aarons flushed.

"He brought it on himself. I warned him."

Dr. Aarons compressed his lips to choke back further words. "Well!" he said, and forced a smile. "I mustn't keep you any longer—"

He waved his hand vaguely toward the laboratory racks and left.

Lucas left the laboratory early that evening.

"Do you mind?" he asked anxiously.

"So *that's* why you did the setup for me!" Ruth teased.

"I don't have to go. I can get out of it. I'll stay. We'll have an evening together, the three of us."

"You run on to your professor," said Ruth. "We'll get together later in the week"

"Yes," said Lucas humbly. "I'd better."

He left. He hurried to the dormitory.

What's got into me? He demanded angrily. What have I done? What am I doing? All of a sudden I want every woman I see! It's got to stop! This is the last! This is positively the last! He thought of Jenny Ordway. He tingled suddenly. He bounded upstairs.

He opened the door.

Job sat on the bed, waiting for him.

Lucas stared, his mouth open, rooted.

"Hi!" said Job mildly.

Lucas licked dry lips. "Hello, Father," he said warily.

"Been waiting for you." He rose. "Had supper?"

"No—I wasn't going to—I mean—"

"Well, get your hat, whatever, we'll go out. I want to talk to you."

Lucas thought of Jenny Ordway, waiting. His mouth opened, but he could not say any words.

"Yes, Father," he said humbly.

"Well, let's go, I guess."

"I'm ready."

"Aren't you going to get your hat?"

"Uh, no, I guess I won't." Then as Job hesitated, "Fellows don't wear hats much."

"Ohhh! . . . College stuff, huh?"

"Yes, sir."

"Well!" He nodded his head, took his hat off. "Guess I won't wear one either. Maybe they'll take me for one of those college fellas."

"Yes, sir," Lucas said eagerly.

"I guess there's a little life in the old horse yet."

He was thinner, Lucas saw now, there was a faintly seedy air about the usually sharply creased clothing he wore on trips.

"Nice place, here," Job said soberly as they walked the campus.

"Yes, sir."

"Well," said Job, "that's the way it goes."

"How's—uh—how's Charley?"

"Gonna have to retire him pretty soon. Getting too old. Can't seem to turn it out any more."

"I'm—sorry I missed you. When I came home. Hope you don't mind."

"Some surprised me. One of the things I want to talk to you about."

"Nobody was home. And I looked over the town and I wondered what I'd be doing there all summer."

"Yep."

"I wrote you. When you didn't answer I guessed it was all right."

They entered a modest restaurant. They ordered.

"Now I want to know first of all what's going on," Job said directly.

"I tried to explain in my letter. I told you. I wrote how it would save money and time for me to go to summer school and when you didn't answer—"

"I want to know how you came to forge my name at the bursar's office."

"I didn't forge it. I—"

"If you could do it any better you'd be in the penitentiary. You forged it, all right. You took a pen or something and traced it."

"I watched you write. I wrote it the way I thought you'd write it."

"You did better than that. You forged it, all right. Now, what else did you copy my name to?"

"Nothing! Not one thing! Look, Dad—"

"I want the truth."

"I'm telling you the truth. I just watched you write and I remembered how you sign and when the bursar said I had to have your signature I thought, all right, I'll do it, I didn't know when you'd be back and the way he said it I had to have your signature right then and I couldn't for the life of me see any harm in it, so I just wrote it. The way you'd write Mother's sometimes, when she wasn't handy. Just a convenience, that's all it was."

Job pulled a folded piece of paper from his pocket. He smoothed it out. It was the letter Lucas had signed in the bursar's office. He studied it a moment.

"You traced that." He pushed the paper to Lucas, who looked at it, white-faced. "You traced it, didn't you."

"What do you mean?"

"Didn't you?"

"Well, I wanted it to look right—"

"You put a piece of paper over it and traced it."

Lucas sat silent.

"Don't lie to me, Luke."

"Yes, I did."

"You traced it out and then you ran back with it to the bursar. That's how you managed it."

Lucas said nothing.

"That's forgery. You could be put in prison for that. Your mother'd feel pretty good if she knew that. Didn't you think I'd find out?"

"I *knew* you'd find out. That's why I thought it was all right! That's why I did it!"

"But you didn't write me, saying, 'Dear Dad, I have forged your signature and I got money from it and paid my way through college doing it.' "

"No. And that was wrong, Dad. I'm sorry about that. To tell you the truth, at first I thought you wouldn't mind, then I was afraid you might and got a little ashamed of doing it at all."

"That's what you did, all right."

"Yes, sir."

"That's what you did. What's happened to you? You knew I'd find out. You don't get up early enough to put anything over on me. A dumb kid stunt like that! I thought college would make you smart. Is that all you've learned?"

"No, sir."

A doom grew in Lucas, a fear so terrible he was unable to think at all.

"I'm sorry, Dad." His lips moved thickly.

"Bringing me all the way up here, taking me away from my business, not knowing what I'd find when I got here. You're going to be safer with me. Where I can keep an eye on you."

"Please, Dad! I'll never do it again!"

"No, you'll never do it again. Because I won't give you a chance to."

"I just did it once."

"Another thing—what are you doing around here? What are you up to?"

"Studying! My gosh, Dad, if you could see the stuff I've been studying—night and day!"

"You haven't been studying. Whatever else you came here for, you haven't been studying."

"Dad! Not studying!"

"That's what I said."

"Not studying?"

"No, not studying. They tell me your grades have shot to hell."

"Who said that!"

"The college office."

"They said my grades are low?"

"Your name's Lucas Marsh, isn't it?"

"They must have got me confused. They read off the wrong grades—"

"They showed me. Lucas Marsh. Failing, failing, failing. Good for a month, good for a couple. Then failing right down the line."

"Not me! No, sir! The forgery I'll admit, but when it comes to grades! There's been some mistake. No, sir! I'll go there and see!"

"Been screwing around a little, ain't you?"

Lucas licked his lips.

"No—I—ah . . ." His wits warned him in time, somehow flashed through the panic, the chaos. Don't lie, now. Not about this. He'll like this. He'll approve. It's man stuff. "Well, the fact is, I've got to be honest with you, Dad, there's no use lying to you, I guess I'm a chip off the old block. I mean—"

"Understand you got a job?"

"Janitoring the laboratory at the hospital."

"Pay anything?"

"About ten dollars a week. I thought that way I'd relieve some of the strain—"

"Well, there's strain, all right. To tell you the truth I was going to take you home with me."

"Oh, please, Dad!"

"Then I found out the rest of the term was paid for, anyway. I'll tell you, Lucas, you couldn't have picked a worse time."

"Maybe I could send you some of mine," Lucas said eagerly. "Some of what I earn—I'd be glad to, Dad."

"You know what that would buy me? That wouldn't buy me two round-trip tickets to Meridian. No, you've got your college money, the money I promised your mother I'd set aside. Else you wouldn't be here. Working in a hospital!"

"I've got to go on with it, Dad! I've got to!"

"You don't got to anything. I thought by now college would have straightened you out. I don't see what good it's doing you if all you've learned—"

"I promised Mother!"

"What do you mean you promised Mother?"

"I said I'd go through my pre-med and at least one year of Medicine. I gave her my sacred word. Dad, I'll work nights, I'll do anything, I'll— Dad, Mother left me those two lots, I'll sell them, I'll—"

"Two lots? Where? Oh! . . . I see. . . . No need to do that. Don't want to be foolish, selling when you ought to hang on. These are no times to sell. Why, you couldn't get a fraction of what they're worth. No. Forget it. I'll see what I can do." He shook his head, worried. He clicked his tongue. "I'll raise the cash, some way. They take notes here?"

"I don't know, Dad. I don't think so—"

"Well, we'll see, we'll see."

"If you knew what this means to me . . ."

"Now, I want an end of your foolishness. You buckle down and you study. Quit screwing your head off and stay in nights and study. At least if you're going to stay here—study! And remember—that's a jail offense. You're lucky it was your father."

"Yes, Dad."

"Now I got to get the next train back."

They rose. Job took a step and turned.

"What you doing?"

"I was just going to leave a little tip," Lucas said apologetically.

"Oh!" Job fumbled in his pocket. "Put your quarter back." He dropped seventy-five cents on the table. They walked to the cashier. Job paid the bill. They headed toward the railroad station.

"Good evening!"

Luke looked up, startled. Ann and Ruth were approaching. He managed a small smile.

"Good evening," he said formally. "Evening," Job said mechanically. They slowed a moment, then smiled and walked on.

"Friends of yours?" Job asked.

"Them? Oh, no. Just some people work over at the hospital."

"That blond one looked pretty good, that's the kind of stuff you ought to stick to, older women."

"I guess you're right. I hardly know them."

"If we meet any of your friends introduce me. I'd like to meet them."

"I will! You bet! I want them to meet you too!"

"Might steal one from you if you don't look out."

"From now on—I study!"

"Well, don't go overboard, either. A little now and then never did anyone any harm."

"Not for me!"

At the station they waited awkwardly, talking aimlessly until the train arrived.

"So long, boy. You watch yourself, now. Have a good time."

"I'll be working hard, Dad."

"Need any money?"

"Not a thing!"

"Here—"

"I don't need it!"

"Take it anyway!"

"But I don't want it!"

"Take it."

The five-dollar bill dropped to the platform. Lucas picked it up.

In the train Job settled himself. He inspected his fellow passengers absently. He folded his arms and looked out the window.

Well, it was a bad business. No doubt of it, left a taste in the mouth. Well, it was over. It was a bad trip, altogether, and there wasn't anything else he could have done. A girl in a meadow looked at the train, shading her eyes with her hand. Job smiled. She flashed away. His smile faded. He looked at the passing fields soberly. The boy was a world away. He sighed with pity for him. The ties were loosed, the contact gone, he had dropped behind, dropped away, alien, strange, receding like the field flashing past, like the last field here and then gone.

It was a little sad, it was like a death, somehow. A distance, a far, far departure. Lucas should be himself, Job, a younger Job, a partner, an extension of himself. Well, you can't count on anything in this world. Still, I would have sworn it. Well, you can't lose what you haven't got. I would have sworn it, all the same. Kid stuff! He wants to be a doctor. He still wants to. And before he knows it he'll *be* a doctor. And then it'll be too late. The mind of a child. He'll never grow up. He's lost. It's too late. He's done for. He sighed again. He shook his head.

Well, Ouida!

You've got what you want!

I hope you're satisfied . . .

A field flashed past. It was gone. Another took its place. It was gone. He's ashamed of me, he thought suddenly.

Those two women.

The ones who said hello to him.

Job nodded at the landscape. He nodded on.

Yep!

There was no doubt of it. Lucas had known 'em both. He was scared to death for fear I'd meet 'em.

He pondered this a moment in mild surprise. That was Luke. That's what had happened. He grinned privately. What a world! What a concourse of queerness! A planet swarming with unpredictable and frantic players. He beamed, he chuckled.

And now Luke.

Well . . .

Luke . . .

And how about the mother? He frowned suddenly. He turned from the window, wary. What lots was he talking about? What two lots? Were there two more? The kid was crazy. There couldn't be. It's the same ones. Sure. Only two. He remembered them a moment. Those. Yep. Those were the ones he meant. Wish there *were* two more . . .

He fell to considering where he could get money. He had to have four thousand dollars. He had to have it in a hurry. This time he simply had to have it, talk wouldn't do, persuasion wouldn't do, nothing would do but money.

Charley might have a little more tucked away. Some he hadn't mentioned. Even if he got the four thousand it was staving off, it was a question of time, it was a question of a breathing space, anything could happen if he had it, it didn't make any difference how bad things looked. The next step was four thousand dollars. Charley might have four hundred. Better not fire him until he found out. Who else was there? Was there anybody else? Was there somebody he hadn't borrowed from? There was no one. Not a soul, Job conceded. He had borrowed from everybody. He was right up to the limit. Wait! There was Alexander! He was a doctor. Doctors had plenty of money! Doctors were always investing! He smiled cheerfully. Draw one breath at a time. The tangle of his empire was a single breath. Four thousand dollars. That was the next breath. Take it. There was leather in automobiles, he remembered suddenly. For the shock absorbers. For the springs. For—for—for probably a million things! One breath at a time. That's all. And there you are.

"This seat taken?"

Job looked at the man, exhilarated. He took in the fat figure, the important face, the petulant mouth, the gold chain in a single glance.

"Not at all, brother. Sit right down make yourself to home. Job Marsh's the name." He extended a hearty hand. His fingers closed lovingly over the reluctant fleshy palm offered him.

"Sherman!" the man said heavily.

"Glad to know you, Sherman. Harness is mine."

"Jewelry," Sherman said ponderously.

"Four stores—Meridian, Tyre, Milletta, Wetherly. Just been to see my son at college."

"That so?" Sherman thawed a little, impressed.

"Yes, sir! Fine boy—say, don't have an opening for a good harness store out your way, do you?"

"Don't know. . . . You looking for another one? Seems like four ought to be enough for any man—"

"You might think so." He paused, considering this, then smiled appreciatively. "Fact is," he explained apologetically, "I'm in kind of a spot. Just signed a contract with the Dodge people for twelve thousand dozen sets of spring covers, I've got the cash, I need the place—"

The fat man whistled. He licked his lips covertly, the lovely, furtive, naked licking Job loved so well.

"Sounds good," he said covetously. He pretended caution. "Won't that take a lot of capital?"

"Don't think so." Job frowned. "I mean a name like Dodge—they're good for millions." He spread his palms.

"Of course! Of course! I was just thinking." The fat man licked his lips delicately.

"What did you have in mind?" Job asked benignly.

Lucas watched the train until it disappeared. He looked after it emptily. For a while the cramp of fear still held him, held him automatically, the incident was over, he was safe, his father was gone. But it had been close. It had been a near thing. And the train was gone. But the cramp held on.

Marks low? Marks failing? In so little time? This place turned treacherous, this sanctuary, this he had won?

He tried to remember the past weeks, even the past days, but they eluded him, they were a flow of time without distinction, a sum apart from the time that had preceded them, these days were made separate by his inletting, by belonging, by the feast of the flesh and the ritual of orgasm, by the emptied campus tilting beneath his weight, tilting him into the actual corridors of the hospital, into the communion of adult notice, and these days were a stolen time, they were swollen with guilt and blown with pleasure beyond any resemblance to days, they were time, time past, exploding now in a sudden horror and disappearing as they exploded.

And on the clear plain of time-being fear watched him, waiting, a figure far off, far as the distance to the bursar's office, fear which had no face at this distance and was motionless, but had shouted and was still now, listening to the echoes between them, "you have failed," saying, "failing right down the line, sliding out, going, going—"

"No!" Lucas cried aloud. "No!" he cried again for the sound of his voice, to drown out the echo. And again, "No!"

Only, No was not enough, No was only time to think, and he turned and walked back, walked from the railroad station, through the interrupting streets, onto the empty campus at last, lifeless, empty enough to think in.

And now the immediate past was an unrelated pattern, having no relevance to himself and to the accumulation of characteristics which he had become, and least of all a relevance to Medicine. It was a jumble of days, suspended, diffuse, having no objective nor struggle, a sort of chaos intersecting purpose.

And borne up in this chaos were humans, a taste of all humanity, bowling, reading hokkus, fleeing farms, frantically dedicated to excel, scrabbling for minutiae to king, Faustian, desperate, crying their eminence of the irrelevant, the contemptible, the fantastically useless, as a reason for surviving and for the deference of man and the protection of God, and the gift of life, and of a life's time.

And there was no intersection, here. They were alien to him as he was alien to them, he was of a community complete in himself, wherever he found himself, a part of all the community of Medicine and so he must move and they must find their own, now and forever, and he fought no longer to become a part of anything, he walked rapidly to the administration building to learn the worst, to face it, to conquer it if there were minutes in the hours of the twenty-four in a day.

And when he had seen the worst he was frightened. And there was no time to lose. None. None at all.

None.

He studied all that night.

⋆ CHAPTER 16

Dr. Aarons surveyed him coolly. He leaned back in his chair.

"I've seen this coming," he shrugged. Suddenly he was tired of Lucas, furious at the anxiety in his eyes, angry at the conjuring of old memories, now he wanted to be rid of him, to hurt him, to forget he ever lived.

"So you won't get a scholarship. And you may even flunk out. That's it, isn't it? I'm not blind or deaf. I've heard rumors. And you aren't the first and you aren't the fiftieth—you—I've seen thousands like you—" He waved his hand and dismissed the problem.

"I just thought if you could see your way clear—"

"To let you work half-time? Sure! Where does that leave you?"

"Well, I could—"

"You could spend *half* your time unbuttoning your pants when you should be opening your books."

Lucas flushed.

"I'm sorry, sir—"

"Hang your sorrow! Don't be sorry to me! *I'm* not Medicine! *I'm* not what you came whining to me ready to give your life for. *I'm* not a boy's dream about wanting to be a fireman! I'm a professor. And when the time comes—if you're still here—I'll give you grades. And I'll flunk you if you fail without even wondering what your name is!"

"It was just a few classes! I just cut a couple of—"

"You just cut! What do you think this is, a rah-rah course?"

"I know—"

"Let me tell you something! You don't know anything! This is something you've never imagined! There aren't any rewards. There's not enough money in all the world to buy you through. There isn't any breathing space, there isn't time to sleep, there isn't time to eat, there's eight hours of classes every day and six hours of study every night and every possible spare moment you can cram between. You don't have to learn a lot. You don't have to learn the most of it. You have to learn everything! Everything that's put before you! In a language you never heard before."

He stared at Lucas with a little hatred, waiting for a word, a chance to strike home. Lucas stayed silent, his head down.

"I'll never do it again!"

"I'm afraid that doesn't concern me. It's Medicine you want to apologize to. I can't grant you absolution." He looked at his watch. "Take the job part time if you want to," he said indifferently. He smiled with his mouth, brief and wintry. "I'm sorry—I have work to do."

"I'll make it up—you'll see—"

Dr. Aarons rose, flared, slammed the desk, exasperated.

"Get it through your head! Once and for all! There's no such thing as making up! This is Medicine, now! You're going to have to remember the name of every bone, every nerve, every muscle, the name of every bump on every bone, you're going to have to describe every process—"

"*All* of it?"

"Six subjects at once. Every day, day after day. Get that Cunningham's *Anatomy* from the case behind you. All right? Open it at any page. Got it? What page?"

"Page 1142. It's about—"

"Never mind what it's about. Start at the top of the page." He leaned back and closed his eyes. " 'Two. The helicis minor muscle covers the crus of the helix. Three. The tragicus muscle runs vertically over the greater part of the tragus. Some of its fibers are prolonged upward to the spine of the helix and constitute the pyramidalis muscle. Four. The antitragus muscle covers the antitragus and runs obliquely upward and backwards to the—' "

"But that's exact! You're quoting it verbatim!"

"That's exactly what you're going to have to do. You're going to have to be able to do that to graduate in Medicine. That page—or any other page—in any of thirty-five books—few books with less than a thousand pages."

He drew breath. He looked at Lucas somberly.

"And then, after four years of this, *if* you graduate—then you find that while you were studying new things were discovered they never taught you. And you master these new things. And in the meantime still other new things have been discovered, books full of new things. And you will be in practice by that time and then you will find that unless you read and study constantly each year you will know less and less, Medicine will have progressed and you will have been left farther and farther behind."

He stopped, tiredly. He sat down.

"That's all . . . You'll really have to excuse me. . . . You can thank your Gods you're not in Medicine, yet."

"And yet some fellows manage to work their way through," Lucas said mildly.

"In a city," Dr. Aarons said briefly. "Where there are jobs. This is a small town. There's no pay. And there's no jobs. Is that brutal enough? Does it sink in? No jobs! None!"

He looked away from Lucas to hide a growing contempt. His mind went back to the days of bitterness, the days when he roamed the wilderness waiting for the Promised Land. He thought of being a Jew and the quota against Jews at medical schools, no more than ten percent admitted and the fight for marks to put you among the lucky ten percent and professors marking Jews low. The days of bitterness, the days of knowledge, the days when his life itself was a crippled thing because of his hunger. Work, and he groaned under it. Fatigue, and he fell asleep again in class the moment the lights went off and the slides were flashed on the screen. Hunger, and its acids cramped his belly. And one day, when he could struggle no longer, the high plateau reached at last. And he was a doctor. And the first thing to be seen was a sign, the letters, the burning letters of God. NJA. No Jews Allowed. And there was the wilderness again. That was all. Just a little wilderness. And a little work. And finally, reluctantly, there was this professorship. And now, in this backwater, his dreams clawing at him still, he watched while others soared.

"Yes," he said dully, far away, remote, "it could be done." He was tired. He had been through it all, again; four years of it. He had talked far too long. Actually, it didn't matter. "Well," he said indifferently, "that's how it is. I know you're interested in Medicine. You'd better start the habit of studying. Otherwise I'm afraid you won't get through."

"About the job . . ."

"That's all right. You can work part time."

"Thanks, sir. I really mean it. I—"

"That's all right." He turned back to the papers on his desk. Moments passed. He was aware that Lucas had not moved, did not know what to do next, how to take his leave. Then it left him. The contempt and the wish to escape dropped like a stone and he felt Lucas' fear and uncertainty and misery. And abruptly, coldly, he hated himself. He rose. He looked at his watch.

"I'm late." He looked at Lucas, then quickly away. "Have you ever seen an operation?"

Lucas started, stared at him, swallowed, collected himself.

"I—I've gone out on calls with Dr. Alexander—boils and things."

Dr. Aarons nodded.

"Come along, if you like." He walked toward the door.

His heart pounding with dread and eagerness, Lucas followed him to the very doors of the operating room. Dr. Aarons turned.

"Do exactly as I do," he said slowly.

"Yes, sir," said Lucas, pale.

"You understand?"

"Yes, sir!"

"This is an operation for ovarian cysts, and it will include a pelvic exploration. A former student of mine is operating."

He looked at Lucas again. Lucas licked his lips. Abruptly Dr. Aarons turned.

The double doors swung open.

They were walking through them, they were walking down a short corridor. They entered a room. A nurse, her head turbaned in white gauze, smiled at Dr. Aarons, looked curiously at Lucas, handed each an identically folded bundle of white clothes. Dr. Aarons nodded and walked out. Lucas bobbed his head uncertainly at the nurse and hurried after him.

They entered the next room. Lockers lined the walls. A half-dozen interns lounged in wicker chairs, stripped to their undershirts, gauze masks rakishly and carelessly dangling around their necks, white skull-caps pushed back on their heads.

"Good morning, sir," they said respectfully.

"Good morning, gentlemen."

Then they stared coldly at Lucas. Lucas dropped his eyes. Abashed, he followed Dr. Aarons, found an empty locker, undressed as Dr. Aarons was doing, put his clothes in the locker, put on white ducks, from the corner of his eyes watched Dr. Aarons shake out the bundle, which became an ankle-length robe. The interns, who had been chatting as he and Dr. Aarons entered, were silent now, pretending not to watch. Dr. Aarons, without a glance at Lucas, put his arms through the long sleeves of his gown and turned his back to Lucas. Lucas shook out his own bundle and put his arms through the sleeves. An intern rose, walked to Dr. Aarons, tied the strings of the gown in back. Then he walked back to his chair.

"Thank you," said Dr. Aarons.

Lucas reddened. Dr. Aarons put on his skullcap, and as Lucas copied him Dr. Aarons stepped behind him and tied the strings of Lucas' gown.

"Thank you," Lucas muttered. His voice was loud in his ears. Dr. Aarons picked up his mask, began to tie the top strings.

"Looks like a good one today," one of the interns said politely.

"I thought Williams was going to be a pathologist," said another.

"So did I," said Dr. Aarons dryly, and at his tone the interns laughed politely, obediently.

"Too bad to see a good pathologist spoiled to make another mechanic." Dr. Aarons shook his head.

"He was two classes ahead of me," another intern ventured. "I thought he was going to be a pathologist, sure. One of your pets, wasn't he, sir?"

"One of my best," said Dr. Aarons. He smiled at the group, nodded, walked to the door. Lucas turned, stumbled, and followed him into the corridor.

As they walked Dr. Aarons glanced at him.

"You can wear your mask under your nose or over," he observed mildly. Lucas quickly pulled the top of his mask down under his nose as Dr. Aarons wore his. "It doesn't make much difference. Don't touch anything. Don't let your gown brush anything." At their left a half-dozen men were scrubbing their hands and forearms at a row of sinks. Ahead was a sea of white tile, a wide archway, they were through the archway into a brilliantly lit room; in the center of the room, under a great bank of lights, was an operating table. On the table lay a patient.

Lucas followed Dr. Aarons, close on his heels. They skirted the room, there was a flight of steps, there were banked seats. Dr. Aarons sat down. Lucas sank down beside him.

For a few moments Lucas sat rigidly, seeing nothing.

"Anesthesia," Dr. Aarons muttered.

Cautiously, Lucas turned his head. Wheeled apparatus had been brought to the head of the table.

"Comfortable?" asked the anesthetist.

The patient apparently mumbled an answer.

"I'm going to put this over your face—so. Now just get accustomed to it. No, don't breathe deeply. Just relax. Breathe naturally. . . ."

Lucas became aware of nurses about the table. Amazed, he counted six of them. Two wore probationers' gowns. Of the remainder, one made regular trips to the sterilizing room, bringing instruments and cloth-wrapped bundles. One stood beside the anesthetist. The third arranged instruments and gauze on a wheeled table. The fourth, her back to him, was apparently in charge.

The doctors, who had been scrubbing, now came one by one into the operating room, their shoes covered with white cloth slippers, their arms in front, elbows almost touching, their forearms bent sharply up, their hands dripping. The third nurse quickly picked a gown from a table, held it up, the doctor plunged his arms into the sleeves. She handed him a sterile towel. He wiped his hands. Another nurse tied the gown strings behind him. He walked to the second nurse, who shook powder over his hands. "Seven," he said, and she gingerly uncased rubber gloves, held them while he lunged his hands in.

He walked to the table holding his hands up and stood silently. He was joined by another. Then they were all there, aligned on either side of the table, waiting.

As the last man stepped into place the fourth nurse turned, the third nurse pushed an instrument table over the patient's knees, the fourth nurse removed the sterile towel that covered the instruments.

"Ready?" one of the men asked quietly.

The anesthetist nodded.

The fourth and third nurses had bared the patient's belly and in almost the same movement covered it with a slitted sheet. Now of the draped patient all that was visible was a narrow strip of belly skin. The doctor, looking at the skin, put out his hand. In a movement too deft, too quick to follow, the fourth nurse had placed an instrument in the waiting hand, the doctor held it over a bucket which one of the probationers whisked beside the table, the fourth nurse was pouring antiseptic over gauze gripped in the instrument, still staring at the patch of skin the surgeon swabbed the area, he threw the instrument on another table, as his hand returned empty the fourth nurse had slapped a scalpel in it, another doctor's hand reached and she had slapped a clamp in it, and another hand and another instrument, all wordless, too fast to follow, without falter, without pause, unerring and perfect.

Beneath his mask, Lucas' mouth opened. He peered harder. Her hair was turbaned tightly in sterile gauze. She was gowned as the doctors were. A mask was tight over her face. But there could be no doubt of it. This automaton of perfection was Kristina Hedvigsen. Dorothy's 'dumb Swede'!

Lucas blinked, dumfounded, humble with admiration. He felt an elbow in his side.

"Skin," said Dr. Aarons.

The surgeon had cut through the outer layer of skin. He was waiting. Across the table another doctor clamped small bleeders in the cut area. A third sponged the flesh dry. An instant before their hands had been empty, and in that instant Kristina had put the right instruments in each hand in almost the same movement with which they handed her a discarded one.

"Fat," whispered Dr. Aarons.

Dimly, Lucas saw a layer of yellow in the red wound, then the scalpel cut down, blood followed, welled up as the blade drew the length of the cut, clamps, swabs, retractors, now, Kristina's hands flashed, were never still, moved with a mind of their own, waiting with the right instrument as the doctor reached.

"Fascia—superficial . . ."

And Lucas, straining to see, saw muscle cut, then deeper muscle.

"Peritoneum . . ."

And there was a cut but nothing to see, nothing but more clamps, more swabs, and Kristina tireless, easy, unerring.

"Now they've come to it," whispered Dr. Aarons. "There's the tubes, there's the uterus." But Lucas could see nothing but vague red tissue and the dark, instrument-filled aperture. "Now clamps, these are large vessels, now he's tying off . . ."

A doctor glanced up, turned his head, stared at a clock on the the wall, glanced at the anesthetist, bent over the table again. Time passed.

"Are you seeing all right?" Dr. Aarons whispered.

"Yes, sir." But suddenly Lucas had seen the whole patient, the form beneath the draped sheets, the upright feet beneath the cloth. His stomach heaved. This was not a segment of flesh. This was a whole human being. The impact shattered his objectivity, projected him onto the table. His head swam. He grew dizzy. Desperately he tried to command himself. Desperately he looked away, stared at the tiled wall, stared at the lights.

"Big one!" said Dr. Aarons.

Lucas turned his unwilling head. The surgeon was delivering carefully, cautiously, through the suddenly narrow slit a murky red balloon, large as a grapefruit, on either side his assistants retracted, the balloon was through, it was free, it lay atop the incision, an instant later there were clamps in the surgeon's hands, the pedicle was snipped, the balloon sagged, towels covered it, the third nurse lifted it cautiously to another table.

"All over, now. All over but the shouting," Dr. Aarons muttered. Lucas looked at the clock. It was a moment before the dial conveyed meaning to him. An hour had passed. He looked at Dr. Aarons, startled.

"Now the hard work . . ."

Lucas looked at the table. The human had withdrawn. The patient was once again a slit of flesh seven inches long and five inches wide into which sutures were passed and drawn tight and passed again and drawn tight, over and over.

The anesthetist removed the inhalator, peered at the patient, nodded to a nurse, who altered valve settings on two long cylinders. The inhalator was replaced.

Now for the first time Lucas became conscious of the odor of ether, he sniffed the incense keenly, savoring it, the group about the operating table had relaxed, the pace was slower, the doctors had begun desultorily to talk to each other. Kristina, silent, had relaxed, and the other nurses, observing her covertly, lost their tension.

The surgeon who had been in charge of the operation abruptly halted his stitching, glanced up at the clock, nodded to an assistant across the table, walked away, peeling off his gloves and dropping them. A probationer darted to pick them up. The assistant resumed stitching, the surgeon untied the top string of his mask and walked out of the doorway.

A few moments later it was over. The last stitch was in place. The drapes were whisked away. The instrument tables were pulled back. The skin was covered with a pad, taped, the body was a body again, gowned, blanketed, the inhalator was gone, the anesthetist's hooped shield, the cylinders were being wheeled to a corner, the doctors were strolling from the room, peeling off gloves, untying masks, chatting easily.

And Kristina, Kristina watched as the two probationers cleaned the floor of bloody cloths, dropped instruments, watched the other nurses deftly wheeling equipment away, watched the stretcher wheel soundlessly in, the two probationers help the orderly lift the limp body to the stretcher, watched it start from the room, glanced about again, then slowly stripped her gloves, untied her mask. A probationer swiftly untied the strings of her gown, the bottom string of the mask. It was really Kristina. She glanced at the clock. She glanced at the archway. A new stretcher was being wheeled silently in. The last of the instruments were gone to the sink or the autoclave. The operating table was newly draped. The soiled linen had disappeared. The patient was being lifted on to the table. A new tray of instruments was being carried in. The second nurse followed with fresh linen, new rubber gloves neatly packaged. Kristina looked briefly at the patient, walked to the scrubbing room.

Dr. Aarons rose.

"Coming?"

Lucas looked up at him, started, rose hastily.

Carefully, they skirted the walls again. They were in the corridor.

"He did very well," said Dr. Aarons.

"Yes, sir," said Lucas.

They undressed in silence, put on their street clothes; when they were walking downstairs Dr. Aarons said:

"Time for lunch."

Lucas looked at him blankly.

"Did you like it?"

Lucas nodded.

Next day Lucas arrived at the hospital dining room early. He waited eagerly. He ate slowly, drawing the meal out, interns, nurses came, ate, departed. Lucas sat on. Jenny came in. She took the seat next to him.

"I thought you'd be gone."

"I got here late."

She ate, digesting his abstraction.

"We're not going to have much longer."

He was silent.

"I mean Dorothy's coming back."

"That's right, isn't it."

"I mean she's off night duty."

"Oh."

"Next week."

A nurse came in. Lucas looked up quickly, looked down, disappointed.

"I said she comes back next week."

He looked at her blankly.

"So what are we going to do?"

"Do?"

"What's the matter with you, Luke? Didn't you hear a word I said? I said Dorothy was coming off night duty next week!"

"That's all right."

"Well, what about us! We've got a week left! And then what happens? Are you going to go back with Dorothy? Or how are we going to tell her? What are you keeping looking up for? Who do you expect?"

"I'm not expecting anybody."

"Well you keep looking around and not listening. Honestly, Luke! Isn't this important to you?"

"I can't help it, Jenny. I'm not going to have the time. I won't even be eating here after this week. I've had to give up my lab job except for an hour or so a day. Just clean-up work. My grades fell."

"Your grades fell?"

"Yes, yes! That's right! They fell!"

"Well, don't get mad at *me!*"

"I'm not mad."

"You can't tell me you're going to spend all your time studying!"

"That's just exactly what I'm going to do! Exactly!"

"So you don't want to see me any more."

"I didn't say that—"

"But that's what you mean."

"Look! Jenny! My *grades* are down! I haven't got any choice!"

"I noticed the minute I came in you were different. It's all right with me. If that's the way you want it."

"I don't want *anything!*"

"It's all right with me. You can go back to Dorothy if that's what you want. But why don't you just come out and tell me?"

"Look! . . . Jenny! . . ."

"I know! Your grades!"

"Well that's what it is! Now, goddamn it—!"

"You don't have to be mad with me, Luke."

"I'm sorry, Jenny—honest . . ."

She ate a while, brooding.

"I just bought a new dress. I had six dollars and I took a week of another girl's night duty for two dollars and it cost me eight dollars."

"I bet it's pretty."

"It's blue. It's the one you liked, the one we saw in the window that night. I bet you forgot. You saw it there and you said you liked it."

"I didn't forget, I remember."

"Maybe there'll be time . . . Maybe you'll find one evening, an hour or so . . . We have fun, Luke! Don't we!"

She rose.

"We're awful busy upstairs. I never saw anything like it! Honestly! It's terrible. Maybe some night I'll come around and throw stones at your window. I've got to rush. If you knew what I been through this morning! Well, so long, Luke . . . You'll let me know, won't you? I mean—don't worry . . . I've got to run . . ."

He sat guilty and ashamed. The dining room was deserted. He stared at his empty plate.

It was not that he had loved Jenny. But he had used her and he discovered, a little desolately, that he had no common bond with what he used. This was the last of Jenny, this was the last hospital adventure. He walked on impulse to the women's wards. The charge nurse scanned his uniform and nodded pleasantly.

"I'm from the laboratory," he said deprecatively.

"Oh, yes—" she reached for her book—"we have a specimen for you, do we?"

"Oh, no. No—if you have, I'd be glad to take it back with me. But—yesterday Dr. Aarons took me to see an operation, a cyst—"

"Oh, yes! Dr. Williams' case."

"Yes, ma'am. And—" he shrugged apologetically—"I was just wondering how she was."

"Well, sure! Well, aren't you nice! She's doing fine! Just fine! Would you like to see her? Come on—" she rose—"we'll go see her. She'll be tickled."

This brief contact with yesterday's glory was all Lucas had hoped for. To see the patient was completely unexpected. He followed eagerly.

They entered a large room, the walls lined with beds, in which young women, old women, fat women, thin women, middle-aged women became a community, in which even those who lay motionless followed the nurse and himself with the stare of cows halting their feeding. The nurse stopped beside a bed.

"Here's a young man come to see you, Mrs. Sierker," the nurse said, beaming. "He's one of our laboratory men. He saw your operation and came to find out if you were all right. Now, isn't that nice?"

The woman in the bed managed a weak smile. Lucas looked at her curiously. She had features, now, and an age, hair, a mouth, thin hands, a personality, an entity, where yesterday she had been the scene of an operation, a swathed, prepared, indexed, managed mass surrounding an area of operation seven inches long.

She smiled weakly, and her lips, parting, showed a gap in her teeth, and he looked hurriedly at her eyes.

"You're looking fine," Lucas said, embarrassed at the sound of his own voice.

"Oh, we're doing fine, aren't we," the nurse nodded, beaming. "We had a little soup this noon and our doctor's been to see us and we're doing just fine. And isn't this a nice young man to take time off to come to see you?"

The woman nodded. Her lips moved.

"What?" Lucas leaned closer.

"Did you see it?" she breathed.

"Yes—yes, I saw it." He smiled encouragingly.

"Was—was . . . ?" her words trailed, her eyes questioned.

"It was a beautiful job! Beautiful!" I wish you had been there, Lucas thought. I wish you could have seen it. His mind quickened at the memory, the glitter, the flawless precision, the other world.

"You see?" beamed the nurse.

"It was a miracle," the woman murmured.

Lucas smiled uncertainly.

"I know." She blinked weakly. "I should never have lived . . ."

"Now, who told you that." The nurse beamed imperturbably.

"I was given up for dead." She looked at the ceiling, steadfast. "I've been saved by Almighty God. I know. . . . There must be something He wants me to do. . . . I'll have to try and find out what it is. . . ."

"You go to sleep, now." The nurse smoothed the coverlet, inspected the bedstand expertly. "We'll let you rest and this evening we'll have a nice, big dinner—"

The woman smiled and closed her eyes.

Lucas and the nurse moved off, walked down the aisle of beds, followed by the eyes.

"She's all right," the nurse said. "Be up and about in a few days."

"What did she mean—what she said?"

"Oh, they all say something. For a day or so they're the center of the universe. Then they settle down with the rest of us."

"Maybe she's religious . . ." Lucas nodded.

"Her? Good Lord no! I know all about her. There isn't a religious bone in her body. Her name's Sierker, husband runs a little bakery down on Swiner Street. Hope he brings some pies in. My, isn't the food getting awful?"

"She certainly seemed convinced . . ."

"Yep . . . Oh, they're all like that. My goodness, look at these charts!"

Lucas returned to the laboratory.

"What are you looking so down about?" Ann inquired presently.

He shook his head apologetically.

"Dr. Aarons took me to see an operation yesterday and I went to see the woman and she's convinced that God saved her for some reason and she's going to spend the rest of her life finding out what the reason is." He looked at them defensively. "She believes it just as calmly and purely as she believes she's alive."

"Was it a good operation?" Ruth asked delicately, after a pause.

"Oh, it was a beauty!" He told them all he could remember of it. From time to time during the afternoon he remembered some new detail. Once he returned uneasily to the woman's statement.

"It was like she had seen something completely true, something she could see even though we couldn't, see and live for, look forward to—some reason . . ."

Ann looked at him noncommittally and turned back to her microscope.

They left the laboratory together some hours later. In the corridor they overtook Dr. Aarons.

"Through already?" He frowned playfully.

"Oh, yes," said Ann, "we haven't time to go gallivanting off to see cysts removed and strawberry festivals."

"An old pupil of mine." Dr. Aarons nodded.

"We know! That's all we've been hearing all afternoon." Ruth shook her head.

"Yes," Dr. Aarons ruminated. "Harold Williams. He did quite well, I thought. Huge cyst. Very large. He was quite upset. Run-of-the-mill case. No complications. Patient suddenly began to haemorrhage. Died an hour ago." He sighed. Then he turned to them, smiling. "Well, that's one thing about pathology. None of your patients die on you."

He nodded and turned off.

Ruth and Ann looked at each other, then at Lucas.

"Well," said Ann, "so much for destiny."

"Will we see you tomorrow night?" said Ruth at the door. "We're having your favorite chicken."

"And I've got that book you wanted. The Blake," said Ann.

"I'm sorry," said Luke, "I've got to study."

They waved and sauntered homeward.

Lucas stood, trying to think, a woman big with child pushed past him, jolted he made haste to hold the door open for her, she entered the hospital, the door swung shut, he walked to his dormitory, he tried to think, the dormitory loomed before him.

A postcard from Alfred was waiting for him. "Drifted down past here yesterday. See you soon. Don't study too hard," it said. The other side bore a picture of a river flowing past a German town, a river and a town and the quaint houses of a strange people lining the banks. Lucas studied the postcard absorbedly. This was a German postcard. It had come through German hands. These small figures were German people, those were the windows in German houses. And Alfred was there. He studied the postcard again, alert for strangeness, the foreign, the bizarre, the difference, the something to be grasped.

When he rose he propped the postcard carefully on his bureau. He sat down to study. He remembered the operation again. He remembered the operating-room nurse. He remembered she was the same nurse Jenny and Dorothy spoke of contemptuously. He remembered how this nurse had tried to join their conversation. She would be open, she would be wide open to a little friendship, a little respect, she was a pariah, evidently. She must be lonely, then. And if he was nice to her—*why, she was in charge of the operating room.* Just in charge of the operating room, that's all! Just in charge of that whole magnificent wonderland, glittering and gleaming and sacred and closed.

He shook his head to clear it of visions. He bent to his books. When he looked up it was past midnight. He studied until shortly after two o'clock in the morning, at which time he fell asleep. He was grateful when he wakened that he had fallen asleep over his desk, for if he had gone to bed he knew that he would never have wakened so early. It was half past six, and he had saved the time of dressing, he slapped his face with cold water, towelled his face and the back of his neck vigorously, sat down at the desk and bent over his books again.

He went to his professors and begged for makeup time. It was too late for mercy, the tasks they set him must have shown him immediately that they knew makeup was impossible as the assigned labor.

Sometimes he cleaned the laboratory late at night. Sometimes he whisked through it and fled in half an hour, and then prudently spent two hours next time, reading as he swept, reading as he emptied the cages. He set himself an absolute limit of six hours' sleep every night, three days later changed this to five hours, then settled at four. The last two days he did not sleep at all.

He made up with three days to spare. But one of these was a Saturday. It had been a near thing. It was over now. It would never be nearer. Or as near. The youth part was over.

✶ CHAPTER 17

The term ended. Lucas rode back to Milletta. Before him, like a Carcassonne, rose the towers, the bright sun, the shining rivers, the golden hours of his reverie and his tumult. And as this dreaming became intolerably sweet, inexorably his thoughts swung to Job and the interview that came nearer with each passing field, each revolution of the train's wheels.

Geographically, his world was the known terrain of Milletta and the campus of the university and the shops and streets which surrounded it. The history of this world was his own history and the history of those whom he admired or among whom he had been born and brought up.

He was vaguely aware of the world of the newspapers, but this other world was a flat cosmos of words. His sphere was exterior to this larger sphere, touching the larger sphere, revolving about it, touching it as two circles touch at a single degree.

There had been a world war, but it had come to him as music and uniforms and excitement, his species had evolved certain sequent sounds which thrilled and excited or alarmed many other animals; hearing martial music, the scream of the great apes disciplined to cadence, the chest thump disciplined to drumbeats, Lucas prickled and exulted with the fervor of his heritage. This was war, this and the uniforms, the excitement of those around him. The issues between nations were words. They were not an emotional experience, there was no empathy here, only side taking. War was a jungle noise and the hysteria of those who heard it and the excitement of watching those who marched to it.

It ended Job Marsh's life but not his living, although he did not know it and would have laughed his laughter accepting the proof. It ended the lingerers of this phase in American civilization and history, the overlaps, the carry-overs, the harness shops, the gas-mantle manufacturers, the buggy-whip makers, the stiff-collar and collar-button manufacturers, the Victrolas, the carriage stripers, the waggoners, the hundreds of occupations which had been superseded and now were cut off in the midst of their lingering, even while men went on learning these trades, cut off brusquely and with finality.

Here is Lucas Marsh, now, a part of this tide, loving no one, knowing he is alone and has always been alone, sighing, unnourished, for what his mother offered him as love, wincing at the thought of his father, alternately hating him and mawkish-fond for love hunger.

Here is Lucas Marsh who sees the world he lives in clearly, through his father's eyes and his mother's eyes and his own eyes, and knows that men are the dupes of his father, and potential beasts, the lip-curls of his mother. And that women are for coitus and cooking and home provenance, and sometimes, surprisingly, to teach, but always for use, and it is an agreed convention not to mention this nor the secret thing that is done or dreamed of at night.

There had been a war, and men had fought in it, but "fought" was a word, and men had died in it, but "died" was a word. And there had been issues, but issues were words too. And there had been soldiers, and these had been citizens one day, and uniformed and soldiers and different next day, and then they were citizens again, no longer uniformed, undistinguishable from the mass of humans habitually about him. There was a memory of uniforms, of men marching in formation, of intense popular interest, of unashamed excitement conjured by parades and music.

There had been a depression also. It was not a great depression. Historically, it was a single tear beside the misery of the age when the forests died and the glaciers came down and there was no food, and the shelters were somewhere buried under glacial tilt. It had no place in the company of depressions man had known on the planet before man was nationed. It had no place in the roster of depressions man had catalogued when first he began to write his own history, the great plagues, the great fires, the great floods. It was a small whimper in the awesome wail of even America's depressions, the depressions that had moved the boulders of history as if they were pebbles. It was the shakedown depression, the after-war depression of 1922, it lasted two years, and it was gone, and almost it left no mark.

Here is Lucas Marsh now, charted among these things, adventuring from day to day, led by his vector, come to this time.

In the order of things, he had enrolled for medical school. He had written Job for the money and receiving no answer he had boarded a train and now he rode anxiously homeward.

As the train neared Milletta, Lucas brightened. He blinked at the hills with a glad sense of belonging and to the fields, to a remembered tree, a strip of fence. He grinned at them, happy presentments in a swift-passing throng of home things, impatient for the train to stop, to be among them. But when the train stopped, the moment he descended at the station his joy ended, he was home, the sense of going home, of coming home, the motion toward the adored, had ceased, it was the motion, and now that the kinesis ceased the emotion ceased, and as the train pulled slowly out he stood on the platform, and part of him went with it, yearning, melancholy, saying reluctant goodbye. He watched the train out of sight, then picked up his bag and strode off briskly. The going home was over.

He went directly to the shop. The front room was empty. He stood uncertainly. Then Job stepped into the room.

"Didn't know who you were." He grinned. "Thought you might be a bill collector."

"Nope. Only me." He smiled back at his father, embarrassed, trying, as usual, to pretend a common footing, this time trying to pretend that he, too, dodged bill collectors and knew all about them, he and Job.

"Got to watch the bastards." Job shook his head. "Come on, time to close up anyway. No—this way. We'll go out the back way. Quicker."

He was older. He was thin. His fair hair was long. His clothes were baggy and rumpled. His nails were very long and very dirty.

"Hasn't changed a bit." Lucas spoke loudly to hide his embarrassment, his recoil from his father's appearance. "Same old town," he said. "Same old place."

Job looked briefly at the town, at his familiar instrument.

"Goddamned place'd be the better for a couple sticks of dynamite," Job said disinterestedly.

"I guess you're right."

"Place's worn out. Picked over. Finished years ago."

"How's everything going? I mean in—Tyre, and around?"

" 'Bout the same. Nothing new. School over?"

"Summer school."

"Oh."

"Yup . . . Summer school's over . . ."

"All over, eh?"

"That's right. And say, Dad—"

"Feel like something to eat?"

"Aren't we going home?"

"I been taking my meals out. Over to Whelans."

"The boardinghouse?"

"Not much of a hand for cooking myself. Easier this way."

"Say, that's right."

"What are you figuring to do this winter?"

"That's the point."

"Figure to work in the shop?"

"That's what I came home to see you about—"

"Certainly can use you."

They mounted the steps of the boardinghouse and a few minutes later sat down with the boarders.

"My boy, Luke." Job grinned proudly. "Just got in from college. One of these here college kids."

And in the slow stares, the small babble of talk that followed, centering about Lucas, Lucas when he was a boy, Lucas now that he was grown-up, Job basked, beamed, preened, glanced sidelong at Lucas, and Lucas wished himself invisible, inwardly he grimaced with dislike of everyone about the table, there was something contemptible to him in their vegetable faces, their earnest appraisal of the trivial, the obvious. He saw Job's face, he heard him, with a sick sense of the indecent, a disgust that had to be borne because it was a fixed and immovable thing, a father, like a physical defect.

When the meal was finished they walked slowly toward the house. There was much dust inside. It was not a house Lucas would have been proud to bring his college friends to, it never had been, he realized, and any love he had ever had for it was a private thing, a matter private to a Lucas who was not alive now, a Lucas he understood but had almost forgotten. He had a small yearning to go to the cemetery to see his mother, but it was a yearning to be treasured for its poignancy and not for its performance, it could be put by and thought of and not acted upon.

"Well," said Job, "I guess we better have a talk."

"I'd like to, Father—"

Job nodded and waited.

"Well, it's about college, Father . . ."

"Still college, eh?"

"Yes, sir."

"That's what I thought." Job grinned slyly.

"That's right. About college. That and the money Mother had you set aside for my college education."

"What money?"

"That's what I want to know."

Job's face hardened. He looked at Lucas levelly. Lucas flushed.

"What are you talking about?" Job asked coldly.

Lucas stared at him. Who the hell is this? Job asked himself suddenly. And Lucas' face stared back at him, a stranger, a young fellow sitting there, red-faced, having the effrontery to be angry, a young stranger, a young fellow demanding money. Abruptly he was indifferent, the play was over, the game of having a son, the play palled, it was all over and he was indifferent.

"I have to tell the bursar."

"What do you have to tell him?"

"I have to tell him whether I am going through medical college." Lucas' tone was dogged but softer. His mind raced trying to remember legal possibilities, ways by which his father could be compelled to follow his mother's wishes, to pay his way through, community property, last will and testament, bequest, he tried to remember . . .

"Well, you seem to have made up your mind," said Job. "Why don't you tell him?"

"You mean you don't object any more?"

"That's what you want to do, isn't it?"

"Why, yes, yes—of course—" Lucas stammered.

He's of no use to me, Job thought dispassionately. No use whatever. He's moon-struck like his mother. Obstinate and childish, a complete child, worthless as a six-year-old. I can't go any further. Tomorrow I'm going to have to raise six hundred dollars. That'll keep me going for a week. When the week's up I'll need eighteen hundred. But by then—who knows? Stranger things have happened. Six hundred. Not in Milletta. No more. I'm done here. What the hell does he want? Oh, yes, he wants his college money. *His* college money.

"You wouldn't let your old dad go to the wall, would you? When all you'd have to do is postpone it a year?"

"No," Lucas said slowly. "No, of course not!" he said spiritedly, as the occasion demanded.

"I was just wondering, Luke. Just wondering, that's all. I remember a little boy I used to dandle on my knee, used to come to me for pennies. You're quite a stranger, these days. There's just the two of us left, you know."

"Of course, Dad! I must have sounded—I don't know what I must have sounded like! You know how I feel. You ought to know. I didn't realize—I didn't think things were that bad—"

"Who said they were?" Job grinned.

"You mean they're not?"

"I mean you go on back to college—go be a doctor—be whatever you've made up your mind. Hell, boy! I'll not stand in your way. Go to it."

"But if it cramps you—in any way—if you need it—"

"It's not going to cramp me."

"Oh, Dad, I'm so glad!"

"Because I haven't got it."

"What do you mean?"

"I mean I haven't got it."

"I don't understand."

"It's gone. I needed it. And it's gone."

"You mean my college money?"

"Now, Luke, that wasn't your college money, as you put it. That was just an idea of your mother's. I don't know where you got the idea it was something fixed, some fixed sum that was yours. *I* never told you it was."

"But time after time—"

"Oh, I heard you, all right, I knew you had something in mind, it wasn't doing any harm."

"But it was a fund—a regular sum set aside—just for my college—Mother said so—you said so—"

"Just keep your shirt on. I don't know what wild schemes you and your mother cooked up for the use of my money. All I'm trying to do is set you straight. There isn't any fund and there never was any fund. Now if you want to go to college let's start talking from there."

Lucas stared at Job, fascinated, horrified, stricken, numb, waiting for the next words, not hoping, believing nothing, content to let him speak, content for speech to fill a vacuum.

"Now that we understand each other I don't say I'm not willing to go along with you—for a year—until you get on your feet. A year, mind. And don't be coming to me at the end of the year talking about funds. There's nothing I approve of in this thing. I'm doing what I'm doing mostly because you had a misunderstanding. Someday you'll wish you listened to me." He shrugged. "You've got a year. Do what you please."

"Yes, Dad," said Lucas. Now he wanted only to escape.

"I thought someday I could be proud of you."

"I'm sorry, Dad."

"You just haven't grown up. You never grew up. And now you never will. I'm sorry for you."

In the train back to college Lucas clung to what he had. He refused resolutely to think farther. He had Job's permission to take his first year in medicine. He had Job's promise to pay for it. It wasn't a promise exactly. But it was an agreement. And yet it wasn't an agreement either. Lucas tried desperately to recall what exactly his father had said. "I don't say I'm not willing to go along with you—for a year—until you get on your feet." He had said that. There was no mistake about what he had said. But that wasn't saying, "I *will* go along with you." On the other hand he knew Lucas was going back to college and he hadn't stopped him.

And that's all I have, Lucas thought. It's the best I can do. I'm heading back to college. Every mile takes me farther from the chance that tomorrow he may change his mind. Once I get to college I'll go straight to the bursar. I'll put what he said on record. Then he can't go back on it. He can, of course. He can change his mind and write and countermand the whole thing. But if I keep very still, and do nothing to anger him, and don't even let him know I'm alive—he may forget. He's in trouble, his mind's on other things, he may forget. It's all I can do. There's nothing else I can do.

And the train fled on, the rails clacked past, the fear grew in his breast, long before they reached the college town his body was wet with sweat.

He stepped off the train while it was still in motion, raced to the bursar's office, told the bursar he had just come back from a visit to his father, that his father approved his enrollment in medical school, and that he had instructed Lucas to say that his check would shortly be in the mail. The bursar frowned uncertainly, reluctantly nodded.

Now Lucas escaped from the bursar's office. He went to the sanctuary that was left him, his dormitory room.

He entered, shut the door, leaned against it. Alfred rose from the bed. Lucas started, then stared at him, wordless.

"Hi! What the hell's the matter with you?"

"Alfred!"

"What's happened?"

"Happened? Nothing! I was just surprised—you gave me a start—when did you get back?"

"What are you so relieved about? Anybody after you?"

Lucas hesitated. It would be wonderful to tell him! Pour it all out, get it off my chest, lay bare everything, get free of the weight of it.

Lucas was sorely tempted. It was a great effort to resist. But he knew Alfred. Little by little, over the days ahead, when it didn't count, when he wouldn't need relief so urgently, he could drop a fact here and there, and Alfred would absorb it, and comment on it, and perhaps there would be a word of advice or comfort.

"No," he said slowly, "couple of fellows I been ducking. I just came from the bursar's office, signed up. How about you?"

"Long ago, son, long ago. Well, let's take a look at you, you've grown, son, you've grown. Place agrees with you. I been waiting for you. I've taken rooms downtown, couple of nice rooms in a private home, what do you say?"

"Well, I don't know—you know what I mean, Alfred, I'm thinking of the money—I mean I'm kind of limited—"

"I'm broke myself. Spent next term's allowance on one last bang-ho in New York. This place's cheap. I've taken the best room. Your share will be seven dollars a week."

"I can't do it."

"Five, then."

"What are you going to do, support me?"

"My boy, to a man like me you're a jewel."

"I'll make it up to you, studying."

"Sure you will," said Alfred imperturbably. "That's what I figured."

"Okay, then, that's fine."

Alfred looked at him curiously.

"What's happened to the mild and meek roommate I left behind? Whence all this briskness, clear thinking, and decision?"

"I don't get it. Did I say something—"

"Never mind. I'm glad to see it. You want to see the room or take it sight unseen?"

"I'll take it. It can't be very bad if you picked it." He forced a smile. His anxiety blurted a candidness. "I don't know how long I'm going to be able to keep it, though." Instantly he saw this was a mistake. Alfred's face became expressionless.

"What do you mean?" he demanded.

"Oh, nothing! Nothing! God! I can afford five dollars a week, I hope."

"I was wondering." But Alfred's face was still wary.

"No, I was just thinking, I fell behind once this summer, grades went to hell. That's all."

"You?"

"Me!"

"Fell behind?"

"Right into the cellar. Hell to pay."

"My God. You finally did it. You don't gamble. You don't drink. You're not out for anything. So it was dames. What's her name?"

"Who?"

"The reason you quit studying."

"No, no. It wasn't that. Oh, I picked up with a couple of probationers over at the hospital—"

"Sure. You're not kidding anybody. Wait till I tell you about the *Fräuleins,* chum. Come on! We've got all evening to talk. Let's get you moved." He strode to the bureau. "Where's your suitcase? . . ."

Next day Lucas proudly took Alfred to the laboratory to introduce him to Ruth and Ann. That evening they dined in the women's apartment. Lucas preened, walking homeward.

"Nice girls." Alfred nodded. "Little old for you, son. Little old, aren't they?"

"Maybe so. I wasn't thinking about that. Nice apartment they've got."

"Very nice."

"Did it all themselves."

"I don't go much for that ultra-feminine stuff."

"What do you mean, 'feminine'! I suppose that isn't class!"

"Class, all right. Almost self-conscious, if you get what I mean."

"I don't."

"You don't?"

"No."

"All those whatchacallits—hokkus and stuff—I mean doesn't it strike you as almost self-consciously arty? Sterile, kind of?"

"Those are two tremendously well-read people—"

"Oh, well read! Yes . . ."

"And they have taste—"

"Almost throw it at you."

"And if they were a little younger you'd think they were terrific. You know what, Alfred? They're just no use to you!"

Alfred digested this a moment.

"True," he said equably. "True. But where does that leave *you?* They're nice, nice people, couple of middle-aged girls trying desperately to substitute art and culture, like middle-aged spinsters always do, for a home in the suburbs with four kids and plans to take a trip to Europe once before they die like they always planned to do when they were at Smith, or Radcliffe, or South Scrotum or wherever. You've lived in a small town all your life, all that's big stuff to you. Me, I've seen it."

"You mean you're used to better?"

"I didn't say better—"

"You trying to tell me you move among people like that?"

"Hell, no! Sure, they're well grounded. Everything you say. And they've done a fine job on that apartment. But there are others like them, son. Thousands and thousands of apartments like that one, thousands of people like that. Fine people. Swell people. No need to get sweated up. I'm not low-rating them. All I'm saying is: You've met them, they've given you something, they like you, you like them—now what?"

"What do you mean, 'now what'?"

"I mean just that. Are you going to marry both of them?"

"Oh, come on, Al! Don't be silly!"

"Well, that's what I mean. You've got to learn to take things like this in your stride, son. This isn't the beginning and end of the world. There's a lot more where that came from. It's a big world. And since when did a doctor need culture?"

"Are you kidding?"

"I don't mean the wealthy ones, that suddenly go in for culture like a kid collecting arrowheads. I mean the run-of-the-mill doctor. The guy who probably hasn't read six books in his life, thinks Landseer is hot stuff, and music makes him nervous."

"Boy, what happened to you in Germany!"

"Why, I've always known that. Honestly, Luke! Haven't you?"

"I don't say what you say is true. But even if it is, which I know it isn't, what chance do they get to read? Or go to the opera? Or an art gallery?"

"They don't. And they haven't any natural bent toward those things. Their cultural background is zero. And you might as well face it, son.

They know their trade—we hope—and without their medical knowledge, stripped of it, they're about where they were when they left high school. If there."

Lucas grinned.

"Boy, you've got some surprises coming to you."

"Not me, son! You!"

"How about you? What kind of doctor are you going to be?"

"Me? I'm going to be the most fashionable surgeon in Mamaroneck, Park Avenue, Rye, Newport—"

"Come on!"

"I mean it! Oh, I'm going to know my business! I'm going to be good! But I've got my choice of three classes of people to sell my services to. I've got the poor, the middle class, and the rich. The poor—let's face it—will net me nothing. And I'm no philanthropist. There isn't a philanthropical bone in my body."

"Nobody can accuse you of that, Al!"

"No, that's right. I've got just one life and I'm not throwing it into a slum practice. I'm going to work for the rewards and I want the rewards. It's just as easy to get up at night for a five-thousand-dollar ulcer as a ten-dollar ulcer—and hate yourself for taking the ten dollars. And I don't want the middle class. There's too much of it and you kill yourself taking care of it, and in the end you split fifty percent of your business with a collection agency, and the best it gets you is a Cadillac every year, membership in a good country club, a middle-class wife, and a hobby of photography."

"That's not enough."

"No, you're damned tooting that's not enough. You think you're being sarcastic, but you're not. You're hitting the nail right on the head. I'm aiming for a Rolls-Royce every other year, and the yacht that goes with it. I'm aiming for every one of those wonderful, real things. And I'm aiming for the position and the dignity and the honors that go to the doctor for the rich."

"I hope you get it."

"Not for you, though."

"No."

"You're going to be noble. Among the poor."

"I'm going to practice Medicine."

"So am I."

"You think you've got it all figured out, Alfred. Everybody's made up differently and maybe right now that's right for you. The way you think. But one of these days I think it's going to dawn on you all of a sudden that Medicine is the end itself. You're thinking of it as the means. Well, it isn't."

"How do you know?"

"Because I know it. You've just got an opinion. I *know*. You've got a set of preferences. And I know that there aren't any preferences. Medicine is the end. Becoming a doctor is just the means to that end."

"Oh, for Christ's sake! Now, I see! You're talking about research!"

"No, I'm not talking about research. I'm talking about Medicine."

"Well, don't let God hear you. He might get jealous."

"I can always pick up extra money shining your Rolls-Royce."

"That you can, lad, that you can. And it'll be there for you to shine. Don't worry about that."

"Well, I'm sorry you didn't like Ruth and Ann better. Personally, I want to see all I can of them."

"And more power to you! Gosh! Why not? How about those probationers you were bragging about?"

"How would you like to see an operation?"

"You kidding?"

"No, I might be able to arrange it."

"You—?"

"That's right. Working in the lab this summer I worked up quite an in, here and there. I even know the head operating-room nurse!"

"Well, by God, Luke! You've really taken hold! Politics and everything! I'm proud of you! Do you think you can?"

"Fix it up? Sure! Oh, I'm not *that* sure. But I think so. I think it could be arranged."

"Well, you son of a gun!"

Lucas went to Kristina next day. She was glad to see him. Her eyes brightened and she talked animatedly of a party her friends were giving.

"You bring your friend!"

"I will. But—do you think . . ."

"Sure! I tell them a couple of students want to see an operation. I tell you what! Tonsils tomorrow. All right?"

"How would you like to see a tonsillectomy?" Lucas asked negligently.

"You got it fixed up already?"

"There's a price tag. We've got to go to a party."

Alfred frowned, puzzled.

"This operating-room nurse—I told her about you—she's Swedish and she's got a married girl friend and they're having a party."

"Why do we have to go?"

"She asked me. I said all right."

"I wished you'd asked me too."

"You want to see an operation, don't you?"

"It can wait, you know. I'm going to see plenty."

"I don't see how I can call it off."

"It's all right. I'll tell you what we'll do. So long as we're roommates I won't make any dates for you and you won't make any for me. Not blind. All right?"

"Fine, fine!" Lucas said heartily. He was embarrassed and ashamed. I never could have said that to him, he reflected. Nobody I know talks that way. It's the rich. It's the fabric of his life. It's natural to him.

"You know something. Al? I don't mean to hurt your feelings but deep down I bet the only people you really like are rich people."

"You're wrong. There's nothing I need I can get from the rich."

"I could never have said what you said just now."

"Too brutal?"

"No, you're right. But I never could have said it, all the same."

"But you'd have wanted to."

"Maybe."

"The hell with it."

"Sure."

"We're all made different."

"Maybe I was too anxious to show you an operation. Now I'm worried about the party."

"I'll live . . ."

"I didn't see much," Alfred complained as they walked homeward after the operation.

"There isn't much to see, actually. You have to be assisting, I guess, right on top of them."

He said nothing more. He withdrew into himself and thought intimately of the setting, the panoply, the drama.

"That the girl you meant? The one ordering the others around?"

"That's her."

"Couldn't see much of her. Nice figure."

He's trying to say something nice, Lucas realized.

"She's from Minnesota," he said negligently, "one of those Swedish places, Wisconsin, Minnesota, someplace."

Alfred looked at him. Lucas found his look disturbing.

"Got to be Swedes, I guess," he said lightly.

"Got to be lots of people," Alfred said evenly. "You don't think much of her, do you?"

"She's a swell operating-room nurse!" Lucas protested.

"Sure. Well, just learn this way of the world. You're a big guy now. You don't have to trade with people like that."

"Trade with them?"

"Swop. Go to their parties if they let you come to their operations. You just take what they have to give. That's reward enough for them. Believe me. I know. Nothing pleases a poor person more than giving something to a rich person. Having it accepted. They just can't give them enough."

"You trying to be a cynic? A real old college cynic?"

"It's a rule. I didn't invent it. Remember it. It'll save you trouble."

"Look, Alfred, you don't have to go to this party, you know. The way you feel, it'd be better not. I'll make up some excuse."

"You mean to say you want to go?"

"No, I don't *want* to go. Not particularly. She's nothing to me, God knows." He paused, irresolute. "What the hell's the use of hurting people!" he burst out.

"No use," said Alfred equably. "No use at all. What time we due?"

At the Nurses' Home Kristina was waiting for them. At first Lucas did not recognize her. She sat on one end of the waiting-room sofa, a magazine in her lap, unopened. She sat in an island, isolated, alone, and this was apparent. Through the waiting-room capped and caped nurses walked measuredly, erectly, remotely, clad in the panoply of their corps.

Occasionally a passing nurse would call out to another. No one called out to Kristina. Lucas looked quickly at Alfred. Alfred had not noticed her. He was looking interestedly about him.

"There she is," Lucas jogged him. But even when he turned and saw her, Alfred's face remained imperturbable. Lucas' heart sank.

Without her uniform Kristina had been divested of any possible allure. She seemed to have shrunk, to have grown younger. She looked out of place here, a maid the nurses might have hired. Her dress was dowdy. Her feet, in sensible shoes, looked large and clumsy. She sat like a farm woman, flatly, her knees apart. Her face, which in the hospital had been framed by the white turban of the operating room into a shining visage of science now seemed dull and bovine. They walked toward her and she looked up and seeing them rose instantly.

"Well, good evening!" she said, grinning. She stuck her hand out, there was no evading it, first Lucas then Alfred received a quick shake full of friendliness, neither looked at the other, quickly they steered her out of the room, past the doors, out onto the street.

"I look different, hah?"

"You look nice, though," Luke said quickly. "Swell!"

"You like uniform better." She turned to Alfred. "If I wore my OR turban he would be very happy. What do you think of a boy so stuck on Medicine?"

"I think he's nuts," said Alfred succinctly.

"Hides everything, the uniform. Every girl looks like every other girl. When I was little girl I cut pictures out of papers, nurses' pictures. Then I think nurse's uniform most beautiful dress possible."

"He's a nice boy," said Alfred, "but he's got no taste for the finer things. He wouldn't appreciate the kind of dress you're wearing."

Lucas swallowed. He held his breath, frightened.

"Is good material." Kristina looked at her skirt complacently. "I make it myself."

"You did?" Lucas struck in swiftly. "Why, that's beautiful! And you made it yourself? Really?"

"That's the scientist in him coming out," said Alfred. "He wants an affidavit."

"Sure," said Kristina, imperturbably, "I sew, I cook, I keep house since I was little girl. All good Swedish girls do this."

"Now, Kristina! I hope you're not *too* good!"

"Why?" she asked directly.

"He means too good to go out with a couple of medical students," Lucas said desperately.

She laughed.

"Why should I look down on you? Soon you will be doctors and I will just be another OR. You boys hungry? Got big appetite? You Luke—you need put on a little fat!" She poked his ribs. Lucas winced.

"He gets thin thinking about struggling humanity," Alfred said, delighted. "You going to feed him up, Kristina?"

"We going to have fine Swedish meal. Jesus! That Oley, that husband of hers, he's lucky man! My girl friend. Bruni. You never eat Swedish food you gonna have a surprise!"

Over her head Alfred looked at him. Well, the look said, there it is, you can see for yourself, it's no malice of mine, I'm not making it up, you see what she is and this is what you're getting yourself into. And me, too.

"I had no idea you were so—so nationalistic," he said to Kristina, as severely as he dared and yet with that in his tone which provided an instant retreat.

But she looked merely puzzled.

"So—so fond of Swedish things," he said lamely.

"But I am a Swede! I get lonely! Swedish people are friendly people, not like people here, nice people but not friendly."

"You should see her in the operating room—when there's a big one on!" he said strenuously to Alfred.

"She looked fine the other day," Alfred said politely.

"No, but you should see her when there's, say, an ovarian cyst—"

"You see that?" Kristina asked.

"You bet I did. Dr. Aarons took me. Why, half the time I forgot to watch the operation, just watched her!"

"Just movements you learn after a while, isn't it?" Alfred asked.

"That's right. Just movements. Like a drill, like a soldier. To him everything in Medicine is wonderful. Show him the label on a bottle, he thinks it's wonderful."

"She's got you pat!" Alfred cried, delighted.

"I was that way myself," Kristina said quickly to Lucas. "You get over it. It's all right."

"We're talking about three different things," Lucas said angrily. "Alfred's thinking about money to be made from a trade, you're talking about escaping from a Minnesota farm to a nurse's profession—and I'm talking about Medicine!"

"Which Medicine?" said Alfred coolly. "The art? The science? The profession? The what?"

"We here now," Kristina said mildly.

They turned to face a small frame house, crowded by small frame houses on either side. Kristina knocked.

"Hey, Bruni!" she called out simultaneously.

The door flew open. A blond, stocky woman of about thirty confronted them grinning happily, exposing two gold front teeth.

Kristi and Bruni threw themselves into each other's arms, then fell to belaboring each other's backs in an access of good fellowship.

"Kristi!"

"Bruni!"

They spoke rapidly in Swedish, laughed uproariously.

"We late?"

"You chust in time!"

"Shake hands with friends of mine!"

"My name is Marsh, Mrs. Swenson. And this is my roommate, Alfred—"

"I know! I know all about you! Come in! Come in!" She pulled the door shut behind them. "Oley! *Oley!*" she bawled into the depths of the house.

So the evening began. It progressed through an excellent Swedish meal, through a period of digestion, through gusts of explosive talk, long pauses, the long, dull, incredibly boring evening ticked away its interminable minutes. In the early part of the evening, Lucas' nerves were raw with embarrassment. From time to time he stared helplessly at Alfred, but Alfred stared back blandly, turned away to listen attentively to Oley, a painstaking and detailed account, punctuated with slow pauses, on the quality of modern pencils and the distaste for work of the city worker. Oley was a bookkeeper. And once Alfred caught Lucas' eye to whistle appreciatively at ten small cups and saucers, fair souvenirs Bruni was collecting.

"I got more, even—back in Minnesota!" Kristina protested.

The embarrassment became a dull ache. Then Lucas joined defiantly with the laughter of Kristina and Bruni and Oley, slapping his thighs as Oley did, but always Alfred was imperturbable. And after a while defiance faded, too, and dullness succeeded it, it became an effort to smile, to hide a yawn, and finally the evening dragged to an end.

They were on their way home, Alfred talked animatedly with Kristina, occasionally they turned to Lucas, and Lucas plodded step after step, counting the blocks, and at last they were in front of the nurses' quarters and then there was a wait while the evening was discussed again and then there was a great outpouring of good nights and Kristina was gone and the evening was ended and they turned homeward.

"You don't have to say it," Lucas said dully.

"You've got to learn sometime."

"I'm sorry."

"I wouldn't have sat there if I didn't think it was reaching you."

"I see what you mean, now."

"Yup. And if I hadn't been there you'd have put up with it, somehow. No one would have known. And somehow you'd have put up with it. And maybe you'd have gone back."

"I'd have gone back."

"Sure. The operating room would have taken you back."

"I know it."

"And if you had to, if you kept at it long enough, if there wasn't any other way of getting it, you'd have made yourself like it. You'd have let down. You'd have fashioned yourself a little like them. So you could take it. And then more like them. Just so you could get what you want."

"But why? Actually, what's the matter with them? There's nothing the matter with them. You're a good guy, Alfred. You're not like that, either. What is it?"

"You're an awful kid about some things, Luke. I'm an awful kid too. Only I've been up against it and you haven't. It's a rule, boy. It's a law. I don't know a thing about it. About what makes it tick. All I know is, there it is. It's the way the world goes."

"You can't just dismiss it like that."

"Sometimes you have to. You've seen it work. I could have talked to you until I was blue in the face. It took an evening like this to make you see it. Now you've seen it. Now you know."

"But there's nothing wrong with them. They didn't kill anybody. They laid themselves out to be nice to us, fed us, put out their best—"

"And you can't just kick them in the teeth. And you hate yourself for the way you feel about them. I know. I've been through it. Once, a long time ago. We had a stableman. Nicest guy you ever saw. Smart, too. Well, what? He didn't come to college with me. He didn't go to prep school when I went. What are you going to do? You can't take them with you."

"But you can't hurt them."

"No, you can't hurt them. You just stay away from them. Be polite to them, be kind, even. But stay away from them."

"Take what you want from them—"

"That's right. And they're always glad to give it. I don't know why. So don't ask me. You don't have to be bitter about it. It's the way the world's set up. I didn't make it that way. This world's made up of people who want a great deal and people who settle for anything. You know how it is, boy. If you want a thing so you can't stop you're going to get a piece of it. Maybe the others get a kick out of helping you, identifying themselves with someone who wants something that bad. All I know is you've got to travel with your own kind of people. That's the only way you'll ever get anywhere. Nothing else ever works. Take what you want and say thank you and keep going. Don't get mixed up. Make it clear you're not going to. Because once you do, you're nothing. Nothing at all. Just tangled up."

And Lucas thought of Kristina, and he thought of the operating room and how knowing her meant almost magic access to it.

"My God!" he blurted angrily. "What kind of a world is this! Isn't there any kindness in it? Is everything cut and dried and take what you can get?"

"She can't read your mind." Alfred grinned. "If she's your passport to the operating room, use it. Or, if you want to lay her—"

"My God, no!"

"Well," Alfred shrugged. "You know what the score is. You know what she is, you know what you are, you know what you want, at least you've got things straight. And it only took one evening."

"You're a lot like my dad in some ways," Lucas said resentfully.

Alfred looked at him levelly.

"I don't know him. But so are you. Now forget it."

"I know—but I don't want to be—"

"That's how it is, though. Now let's drop it. Let's go from here. . . ."

The first days of Medicine left no room for any kind of thinking, any speculation, any philosophy, anything but the first days of Medicine.

It began very briskly. He saw his first corpse and before he could assimilate the impact, the integrity of a dead unit, the ways in which it was his image, but differed from him, being dead before he was even sure that it was really dead and not apt to sit up and talk to him, he had been assigned a part of it. He drew a slip of paper and drew a lower left leg, he and Alfred, and they looked at it, confused and frightened and full of despair and behind them an instructor loomed suddenly and said:

"The first thing you've got to do is study the surface landmarks. Don't use your knife until you've studied it. Notice that the broad, flat medial surface of the tibia is subcutaneous throughout its length and is continuous below with the medial malleolus, which is also subcutaneous."

And he waited impatiently while they grabbed for their new notebooks and began scribbling furiously.

"If you'll listen to what I'm trying to tell you you'll see what I'm talking about and not have to take notes every time I open my mouth. Just look and understand." But they took notes just the same, if only to keep themselves from looking.

It began with the very first day, there was no preamble, there was just a vast beginning and an hour after it began all of them were hopelessly behind, scrambling desperately to remain in school. It began without preamble, with an armload of books, with eight hours of classes, with words which were an entire new system of communication, with memorizing the incomprehensible, with despair, with panic, with resignation to the impossible.

There were no exceptions. The sons of doctors, previously confident and superior, stared with stupefaction at the stupidest and saw the same stupefaction reflected back at them. They were all in it together, this became apparent in the fourth hour, they must cling to their mutual ignorance or perish, they must cling to each other, each must somehow help the other.

In the anatomy class, when the first dissection began, when these young humans began cutting these dead humans, there was the sound of retching from a part of the room and Lucas and Alfred saw a student vomit on a cadaver, saw an instructor walk to him with a cloth extended in his hand, look at him coldly, stand over him coldly while he cleaned up his spew, warm on the cold but infinitely valuable cadaver, shared with him his insignificance, plain in the instructor's look, beside that precious book, the cadaver. A little later one fainted, and then two more, and when they came to, one left. And this one was not heard from again.

"Don't faint!" whispered Alfred. "Whatever you do, don't faint. They say if you faint it's curtains for you."

They stared at each other, white and sick.

But they cut all the same, they cut, they all cut, they did what they had to do to lay bare the mystery of what was inside, and what was beneath that, and that, they cut and they hurried out when the hour ended, escaped to the corridors and the next class, knowing miserably that tomorrow their leg, their lower left leg, would be waiting for them, waiting for them to take up where they left off, to pry, to disclose, to note down, detail by infinite detail, structure by structure, muscle by muscle and nerve by nerve and bone by bone and day after day, until there was nothing more to be noted, and then the foot and then the upper leg and on and on until there was nothing left, until they had seen it all, felt it, traced it, noted it, found why it worked and how it worked.

And in three days, shakily, with bravado, they were calling the leg Joe, their Joe. Their boy. And in a week they found to their unbounded amazement they had actually remembered a few things, remembered them with their reason, and then the morass of things that could never be learned by reason, never until months or years after, overwhelmed them and they learned by rote, hearing each other, coaching each other, committing sentences, then paragraphs, and one day whole pages. For there was no other way.

"What do you think of it now?" Alfred asked bitterly, a man cheated, a man who hadn't expected anything else.

"I'll make it!" Lucas said, almost happily.

"Sure you'll make it! We'll all get through it, somehow. But what do you think of Medicine, boy? Medicine with a capital M and a halo?"

Lucas grinned fiercely, exultantly.

He was embarked at last.

Shortly before the middle of the term the bursar sent for him.

Job had paid no bills.

Job had paid nothing.

There was no word from Job.

There was no answer to any letters.

"I will have to have the money," said the bursar.

"Yes, sir," said Lucas dully.

"Or you will have to leave school."

He stood, waiting.

"Do you think you can have it tomorrow?"

"This is Tuesday. Can you give me to the end of the week?"

"You've put me in a very difficult position. You understand you are now indebted to the university. You owe more than two hundred dollars right now. Two hundred and fourteen dollars and eighty-seven cents. I have trusted you. You are surely not asking for more time."

"I know exactly how you feel. Everything you say is true. This is ridiculous."

"We have written your father and have received not even the courtesy of a reply. The board has instructed me—"

"That's exactly where I'm going. I'm going straight home. And when I come back I'm coming back with the money. In my hand."

"We've acted in good faith—"

"There's no excuse. Absolutely none. You can imagine how I feel. So by Saturday this will be over—one way or the other—and as to the two hundred dollars I want to assure you—you've been so nice to me—you don't have to worry—"

"Until Saturday, then. . . ."

In Milletta the harness shop was closed.

The house was closed.

On the streets townspeople he knew spoke to him guardedly, reluctantly, their faces a little averted, as if there had been a death in the family.

At the bank he learned that Job was bankrupt.

"We'd like to contact him ourselves."

"But you don't know where he's gone?"

"There's a lot of people around here'd like to know that."

"Thanks for your trouble."

"Mean to say *you* don't know where he is?"

"No, I don't! What do you think I'd be asking you for?"

"Don't know. Just seems strange, is all."

"Well, I don't."

"Can't blame folks for being a mite upset. Took in an awful lot, he did. We're holding his notes for nearly seven thousand. Did a lot for him. Can't understand that fellow. Never any notice, even. Just packed up one night and the next morning there wasn't hide nor hair of him. Just vanished. Even took in that old fellow Charley, worked for him. Took his life savings. Knew there wasn't a chance of pulling out. Took them just the same, poured 'em down the rathole along with the rest. Poor old Charley's on the town now. If you hear where he is, if he writes you or anything I'd appreciate—"

"I'll let you know."

"Just drop us a line."

"I'll do it. Don't worry. The minute I hear from him."

"Don't think we hold it against you. It's not your fault. Hope I didn't put it that way, make you feel—"

"I know. You don't know what he's let me in for."

"No! Here, now!"

"Oh, I'm in it, along with the rest. I may be his son, but I'm in it too. He's got me stuck too. Supposed to have paid my college tuition. Bursar called me this morning. He never even answered any of *his* letters—told me I'd have to leave college—and all with never a word, never a syllable, never a thing to warn me, let me know."

"Well, I'm sure sorry."

"I suppose the house—"

"Nothing there. Mortgaged up to the hilt."

"And the shop?"

"Boy, that man didn't leave anything. It's all picked over, bone-clean. There's nothing. Not a penny. Funny, your own dad to do you that way. He's a nice fellow, Job. I'd never have thought it of him. Knew your mother too. Fine, upstanding woman. Knew her when she was a little girl. Don't know what got into him."

"He wanted to own the earth, that's what got into him. He wanted to own every harness store in the entire world, and every iron mine and the steel mills to run 'em, and every tannery and all the cattle. If you want to know. That's what got into him. Mother had him pegged right. Mother knew. He took everything she had, too. Blew it down the drain. Even her jewelry . . ."

"You never know. I'm sure sorry. If there's any way we can help you—"

"Well, that's what got into him."

"Well, you let us know."

"And here I am broke with him. You don't make college loans, do you? I mean, to help a fellow through college? I'd pay it back! Believe me, I'm not like him—!"

"Well, now I don't see how—I'm afraid we don't. Course I know you'd be good for it. It's just we have to have certain forms, the way we do business we got to have collateral—"

"No chance?"

"I'm afraid not. Like to oblige you. But it's not my money. The depositors—"

"Maybe a personal loan? I could work, this summer! I'd find work somewhere! Maybe he'll be back, maybe there's something still left—"

"Well, I'm afraid not. Things are pretty short, nowadays. Little depression, you know, little shakedown. What was it you wanted it for, to go on through college? Yes. Well, the way things are—"

"Thanks just the same."

"Like to help you."

"I know."

"Got my hands tied. If there's anything I can do, though—"

"I know. And I'll let you know the minute I hear from him!"

"Sure would appreciate that—"

"The minute I hear! That you can be sure of!"

He left the bank, mortified, embarrassed but a little self-respect salvaged having stood on the side of the law, angry, heart-whipped, feeling the furtive looks of passing townsfolk like ants on his skin, desperate for a hole to swallow him, a darkness to cover him.

Like a child in trouble he returned to the empty house. He stood before it, walked around it, paced the porch, tried the locked doors, peered through the locked windows. But nothing happened, there was no help here, no hope, only emptiness and a feeling of strangers, of a house no longer his, of trespass. He went to the cemetery, to his mother's grave, to the one spot truly his, the place where he had a right to be, the plot of ground beneath which she lay buried. And there he stayed a half-hour, pretending to arrange a rusted can that once had held flowers and into which he now thrust awkwardly a bit of branch he had broken off. But it was getting darker, he could not stay there forever, there was at last no help here either, and he knew this, despaired, went reluctantly with many a backward look, turned his back and walked to the station and boarded a train back to the university.

⋆ CHAPTER 18

As the train bore him back to the university he sat in a kind of stupor. Panic froze him. All his short life there had been problems, no day was pre-solved, he awoke to enigmas that might that day be settled by the decrees of chance or the solutions of the counsel life had appointed for him or his defiant will would somehow outface the problem or, the day passing, a new day's problems would bury the old. And always there was hope, time and experience had taught him hope, taught him that even though the solution might be beyond his undertaking a solution existed, an answer for every problem.

For this problem there appeared no answer.

Job was gone, Ouida was gone, money was gone, the shops were gone, his home was gone, the house in which he had lived. He might have mourned the loss of these sincerely at another time; at another time he might have felt the collective loss as a crushing disaster. His fear was too great now. His mind was an empty well into which he shouted frantically do something, do something, hurry and do it. And from the emptiness echoed: Do what? What? What is there to do?

He rubbed his damp palms together between his knees. Well, he said to himself, let's be calm, let's think a moment, let's be reasonable. How am I going to do it? How am I going to stay in med school? Now who is there? Who have I got? Who might help me?

Aarons?

All right.

Now there's Aarons. How the hell can I go to Aarons for money?

Listen! he snarled at himself, do you want to go to med school? You'll go to Aarons! And you'll like it! And he knew he would go. His belly dwindled in shame, visioning it. And he knew how little hope was there. But he forced himself to think of Aarons.

He was saving his best hopes for last. Aarons, he thought scornfully, still holding off thought of the good ones, the possibles, not tested yet, still a chance until they were analyzed. Aarons . . .

All right, then, Ruth. Ruth and Ann. Ruth or Ann.

It could all be private, no one need ever know, just a little loan, just enough to tide him over. There was something horrible, something frightening about asking for money, he pictured the scene, he saw himself advancing: "There's something I want to ask you about . . ." And then—

What did you say next? "I want to borrow some money from you. My father has skipped out, he promised to pay the bursar and he never paid a cent, they're going to throw me out. Can you possibly loan me just enough—I mean, I'll pay you back this summer—" And now he turned to them. He waited, for the expression on their faces, the sign of win or lose. He waited, he looked at them, waiting, he saw himself standing there. And there was no expression on their faces. It was as if they were waiting for him to finish. Try as he would he could not imagine an expression on their faces, the picture stayed agonizingly still.

He closed his eyes.

All right.

Then the kingpin. Then the ace in the hole.

Now, let's go.

All right: "Alfred, I'm sorry, I know you hate this sort of thing but I haven't got any choice. Wait a minute and listen to me, hear me out, here's what happened and you'll see what I mean."

And the second thing—

And the second thing was they all said no.

The world stood still for a moment.

Then he smiled. He leaned back in the dusty coach seat.

And that was silly. Because they aren't all going to say no, he told himself fiercely. What's the matter with you, you fool. You're in a jam, that's all. Other people have been in jams before. It isn't as though you're asking somebody to give up every cent they have in the world. All you need is a couple of hundred lousy dollars. And everybody knows you have to keep going. You know, they know, they all know it.

When he got off the train his heart was thumping with fear. He went directly to Dr. Aarons.

"I'm in a jam, sir," he said.

"I can help you with anything but money," Dr. Aarons said lightly.

"Yes, sir." He smiled tightly. "Only the thing is it *is* about money, sir."

Dr. Aarons heard him through.

"I wish I could help you," he said.

My God! thought Lucas. I've forgotten the doctors back in Milletta! He hardly heard Dr. Aarons for the flood of relief that filled him.

"I'm in the same spot as our mutual friends back in Milletta," said Dr. Aarons. "Personally we have no funds. I suppose I have as much as three hundred dollars in the bank against this month's bills. I suppose you've already heard, just having come from Milletta, that your father also managed to borrow a sizable sum from Dr. Alexander and Dr. Kellogg? No, Lucas, I'm sorry, I could borrow and lend you what I borrowed. But I already have obligations. And I wouldn't really be helping you. I'd just be helping you, at best, through a single term. And then you'd be right back where you started. It's a hard fact, you might as well face it, you'll just have to lay your career aside for a year."

"For a year!"

"Or as long as it takes you to earn enough money—"

"And then quit another year to earn more for the next—"

"That's right. It's not too bright a picture, is it? I wish I could help you. If you were further along there might be a chance for a scholarship, if your grades were good—have you exhausted all your resources? All of them?"

"No, sir." Lucas rose. He sighed and smiled confidently at Dr. Aarons. "It was very good of you to hear my troubles," he said, trying to sound grateful, "and I really had a nerve coming here—"

"Not at all! Not at all! I only wish—"

"I know. You don't have to say it, sir."

"I'll be interested to hear what you finally decide—"

Lucas had reached the door.

"Yes, sir."

"Don't leave here without telling me—"

"I've just thought of something," Lucas said confidentially.

Lucas summoned the echo of that speech, made himself hear it over and over again as he walked up and down in front of the apartment house where Ann and Ruth lived. His mouth was dry. And when he entered to say what he must say, Good luck! he said, Good luck! Good luck, boy! over and over. And then he turned and made his swift walk to the door.

"Would twenty-five dollars help?" Ruth asked, when he had finished. She rose and walked to the desk, took three bills from an envelope and held them out to him. "Would this tide you over?"

He looked at the money blankly.

"It's all I've got," she apologized. "We both have to send money home every week—and the way we live . . ."

"We can't even sign a note for you," Ann said despairingly. "She's already signed a note for me. Isn't there anybody—?"

"Sure!" said Lucas. "It's all right! I hate myself for even troubling you." Now he wanted only to escape, he lowered his eyes to hide the resentment there, all his agony, all this for nothing.

"Anyway take this!" And Ruth bent and thrust the money into his coat pocket as he rose.

"No, no—it's no good to me—"

"You take it! Take it anyway! I wish it were a million!"

"It's a start." Ann nodded.

"Thanks," he mumbled. "Well . . ." he walked to the door.

"Where are you going? Stay and have dinner! What are you going to do?"

"It's all right."

"Yes, but how?"

"I just thought of something," he mumbled. He managed a smile. "I'll see you later . . . and thanks!" And before they could say more he had closed the door behind him.

Now there was Alfred.

He headed away from the dormitories. He walked in the park, trying to think, trying laboriously to put one thought ahead of another. His legs tired finally and he sank gratefully onto a bench. He made himself stop remembering the look on Dr. Aarons' face, he made himself stop hearing himself talking to Dr. Aarons, stop hearing the doom in Dr. Aarons' answers. He had not expected his quest here to be successful but he was staggered by the meagerness of an adult's, a full professor's, resources. While he thought of Dr. Aarons he could stave off the memory of the interview he had just fled. And yet after a while, after he had grovelled in the shame and the futility and the defeat and the lost self-respect of that scene, of the unforgettable, as long as he lived the unforgettable, he heard the campus clock toll, a pang of fear kicked him, time it was tolling, time, and he had so little time left, Alfred, he thought of Alfred, now it was time to think of Alfred.

He imagined a scene.

All right, Alfred, you've got the money. First of all, let's get that straight. You've got it. You don't need it, it's just laying there. And they're going to kick me out and all I need is small change. Just a couple of hundred dollars. How about it, Alfred? Just three hundred! Say four —and I can pay you back this summer!

All right, how about it?

What do you say, boy! If I had it you know you wouldn't even have to ask!

What was there to say?

What could any man say?

It was going to be rough. Alfred was funny about money. He wasn't stingy—Lucas cudgelled his memory—no, he wasn't stingy. It was just—well, there was something nameless, something you couldn't put your finger on, something about Alfred and money—

He was rich. He was probably wary about being victimized. Probably brought up that way.

Still . . .

It was going to be very, very difficult. It was going to be terrible.

But whatever it was he would have to bend his neck, take his beating.

And get the money.

There was no question about it—there was something . . .

I don't care what it is. No matter what it is. He's not going to just sit there and see you thrown out of school. Not his own roommate. Not when he's got it. Not when all I need is just four hundred dollars. Three hundred. I can get by on two hundred—I'll give them half. I'll tell them I'll give them the other half in a month. That'll give me a month. Thirty whole days. Four weeks. Anything can happen in four weeks!

He rose almost jubilant.

Alfred was dressing to go out.

Lucas sat on his bed, watched him a moment.

"I'm in trouble," he blurted abruptly.

"*You're* in trouble!" Alfred laughed shortly.

Lucas waited.

"Six shirts not back from the laundry and this goddamned thing two sizes too small and a roommate who doesn't even wear the same size diapers—! And *you've* got trouble!"

"I need four hundred dollars. They're going to kick me out."

Now it was said. He had said it quite calmly. He relaxed, he had a sudden fierce happiness in their companionship, the two of them together.

"You what?" Alfred had turned. He was staring at him. Around the edges of his eyes and his mouth were those lines again, the remembered lines, the money.

But he wasn't fooling anybody this time. Those lines were just on the surface along with the attitude. Everybody had an attitude about this or that, and this was Alfred's. But he wasn't fooling anybody. Lucas smiled at him confidently.

"Come on, Luke," Alfred said, irritated at the smile, "what'd you say?"

"Dough, Alfred," said Lucas gaily, even enjoying the pain the word must cause Alfred and the dutiful battle it meant Alfred was going to put up, was putting up right now, because they were brothers, after all, they were alone in their room together, outside was the world and here they were together.

"What do you mean, 'dough,' " said Alfred quietly.

"I mean money. I'm not kidding, Alfred. I really mean it."

Alfred looked at him carefully.

"Are you sure you know what you're doing?" he asked awkwardly.

"What do you mean?"

"All right," Alfred conceded, but now the money look was on his face strongly, his whole face was the money look. "Tell me about it."

"I need four hundred dollars or I'll have to leave school." He said it defiantly, aggressively, he heard himself, abashed. "They've got me, Alfred," he said in a low voice, "I'm afraid they've really got me."

"I'd still like to hear about it," Alfred said coolly.

And suddenly Lucas felt very tired and he was looking at the world, Alfred, the room and all, through the wrong end of a pair of binoculars and it was receding, drawing far off, getting smaller.

"My father's gone," he said slowly. Somehow that seemed the place to begin.

Alfred finished tying his tie. He smoothed down the front of his coat, inspected himself in the mirror. Then he turned to a chair and sat down facing Lucas.

"All right," he said, "let's have it."

"That's the size of it," Lucas said. "Except here I am and you know what it means to me and that's what I need."

"You mean he skipped right out? Disappeared?"

"Nobody knows where he is. And I don't care."

"There isn't any way you can track him down?"

"They've tried. The bank's tried. Nobody knows. The only problem I've got is what I'm going to tell the bursar Saturday."

"Nobody disappears without leaving even a trace! You can depend upon it! He had to go off somewhere, somewhere in a hurry. You're getting all worked up for nothing. He's probably back right now. I've seen these things happen before.

"Have you tried your relatives?" Alfred asked suddenly. "All your relatives? One of them ought to know. That's it. That's where he'd be, all right!"

"There wouldn't be any. He wouldn't go to his sister—she hates him. I don't even know where she lives, any more. He had some brothers, too, I swear I don't even remember all their names, where they live I don't know at all. Mother," he said carefully—"Mother's folks are dead, Mother had some friends in Cleveland . . ."

"Christ! If *my* father disappeared—we're not a big family—but my God!—really, Luke!"

"Would you know their addresses? The ones you hadn't seen in years or maybe only heard of? If your father was gone and your mother wasn't there to ask, and when you went home the house was empty, and his friends were looking for him, and the bank was looking for him?"

"Christ!" said Alfred. And then in a lower tone, this time embarrassed, "Christ!" again.

"Well, that's what's happened," Lucas said, tired. "That's what I'm trying to tell you. Will you help me, Alfred?"

"Didn't he even pay your tuition?"

"I owe them two hundred dollars. I owe this term. He never paid a cent. Right now I owe them two hundred dollars."

"My God, Luke!"

"I know."

"Wait a minute. What do you need *four* hundred for?"

It was at this point that Lucas knew definitely that it was no use, that he was not going to get it, that Alfred was not going to give it to him. And even as this truth, this heavy truth plummeted to the bottom of his soul and made a sickening pain in the softness there with its weight and its foreign body, even so he knew he would have to ignore it and keep on fighting stubbornly, even though Alfred knew he knew it and everything said from now on was just said above the roar of the other, determined sentences, obstinately put together, because you had to keep on fighting, fighting and ignoring, there wasn't anything else to do.

"What do you need *four* hundred for?" Alfred was repeating stubbornly.

"I have to go on, Al," he said mildly.

"Oh," said Alfred reluctantly.

"I already owe them two hundred. Naturally, after this experience, they'll be worried about the rest. So if I give them two hundred more . . ."

"Okay . . . But that'll only bring you to around April somewhere. What then?"

"By then I'll have more."

"How?"

"I don't know. But I'll have it."

"You'll have it?"

"That's right. I don't know how. But I'll have it."

"That's the trouble with you, Luke. You're a nice kid but you've got your head up in the stars. You don't know how but you'll have it. How do you know you'll have it?"

"I *don't* know. But at least I won't be taken by surprise—I'll be able to plan ahead, to do something—to have a chance—"

"And what'll you live on, in the meantime?"

"I'll make out."

"Off me?"

Lucas started, he straightened, his face reddened.

"Now don't go off half-cocked. I'm trying to make you see things realistically for once."

"What do you mean, off you?"

"Who else? Am I going to be treated to the spectacle of a roommate starving while I eat plenty, keeping a brave smile on his mouth and a look of endurance and resolution in his eyes, ignoring the plenty, grateful for crumbs—"

"What the hell's the matter with you, Alfred!"

"Nothing's the matter with me. *I'm* not in trouble."

"Well, I am. I'm in trouble and I'm in bad trouble. I'm about to be thrown out of school. Because I need a few hundred dollars. And the money doesn't mean any more to you than—what do you think I feel like, sitting here, having to ask you?"

"That's the point, my friend. What do you think *I* feel like, being asked? Don't you think I have to account for my money? Do you think it's limitless, a sort of pool I stick my hand into and pull out whatever I want? Where do you think I'm going to get four hundred dollars from?"

"You?"

"Sure! Me! I know what you're thinking. All I have to do is write home for it. In the first place I feel rotten doing that, because I know how I've been brought up about money. We don't lend money. Not to friends. Not to anybody. It's a rule. And it's a damned good rule. Poor people buy approval. They loan money, all right. The poor help the poor. And they give to the rich. Nobody wants the poor. And they want to be wanted. So they loan money. Free and easy. Generous as hell. Maybe, like I said before, it buys them approval. Maybe it's all they can afford. But we've got money. We don't need approval. And there isn't money enough in the whole world to buy everybody's approval. You know I heard my Dad say a damned smart thing once. My sister came in and she said she'd overheard an acquaintance say something horrible about him, about Dad. It was quite a shock. All of us just sat there. And Dad thought a moment. And then he said, mildly, 'I don't know why. I've never done anything for *him*.' I've never forgotten it."

"Look, Alfred—"

"I know. You still need four hundred dollars. You need it to stay in college. And now I'm supposed to write home for four hundred dollars. What for? Why, to loan it to my roommate. And suppose I do? Suppose I were to sit right down this minute and start the letter? Could I start it knowing I was doing something wrong but everybody can do something wrong once in a while and stretch a point, give me the money and that's that? You know damned well I couldn't. That would be just the beginning. Aside from the way I feel about it myself, don't you think I know my own father? What do we do come April? My roommate needs another two hundred dollars. Same reason. What have you let me in for, Alfred? Also, from time to time I'll need a few bucks extra to pay my roommate's room rent, buy him a meal."

Lucas said nothing. He looked at the floor. There must be something to be said. He could not think of it. He just stared at the floor dully. All he knew was, now he had nobody. And now there wasn't any peril any more. Now the suspense was over. Now he had nothing.

"You've got to be realistic," Alfred said sympathetically. "That's all I'm trying to tell you, boy. You've got to face things. You've got to see them as they are. You see, don't you? You see how it is?"

"It's all right," said Lucas.

"I've got to go. I'm late." He rose. Lucas nodded. "Listen, boy! You're a swell roommate! Inch for inch you're the best cock I've met on the campus. I like you, Luke! I really like you! I don't want anything to happen! I want you right here in this room! I want to keep an eye on you and help you! And don't think you don't help me! And don't worry. People have had blacker jams than this. He'll turn up. I've got to go. Bunch down at the Nu Sig house. I've been telling them all about you."

He looked guiltily at his desk. "I know I shouldn't be taking the time out—"

"Alfred." Lucas' face was white.

Alfred's face became wary again.

"Alfred, can you loan me *two* hundred dollars?"

Alfred looked at him steadily and impersonally.

"I told you, Luke. I'm sorry. It's a rule. That's how it is—"

But Alfred didn't matter now.

"Could you loan me *one* hundred dollars?"

Alfred looked at him steadily. He was silent a moment.

"Luke, old sport, I'll tell you what I'll do. I'm going to loan you fifty dollars. I'm not going to loan it to you. I'm going to give it to you. That's this month's allowance. That's all I have."

Lucas nodded humbly.

"Thanks, Al."

"I said that's *all,*" Alfred said significantly. He looked hard at Lucas to see that he understood.

"I understand."

Alfred took out his wallet, extracted some bills, held them out. Lucas walked to him and took them.

Alfred watched, standing there, the bills in his hand. The anger faded from his eyes. He dropped a hand on Lucas' shoulder. He shook him affectionately.

"So long, kid. Make an extra set of notes for me on histology, will you? With those nice drawings of yours?"

Lucas nodded, not looking up.

"I'll be in late," Alfred said. He turned, the door closed upon him, he was gone.

Lucas sat on the edge of his bed a long time. He put all the money he had in a neat pile beside him and he counted it carefully as if every move counted. He had ninety-three dollars and he counted the bills again, then he sorted them by ones, fives, and tens, then he arranged them all face up, the faces on the bills all looking the same way, straight up, then he put the ones first, the fives second, and the tens last.

It was still Tuesday.

He put all the bills carefully into his billfold. They made quite a wad. Ninety-three dollars.

Tomorrow would be Wednesday. Wednesday, Thursday, Friday, Saturday. Four days. He went over them again, forcing himself, naming them.

Then he tried to think. His mind rebelled. No! There wasn't anything more to think about. There wasn't anything to remember. The thing to do was to keep from thinking. The thing was to keep the mind a perfect blank. Just for a minute. Just to rest. He rose quickly. To get out of this room. This still bloody, still quivering place. To get out in the air, to get outside, to be swallowed in the dark, the darkness, the biggest cave of all.

For nearly an hour the darkness was healing. The night was cold on his face. Then, like a tide receding from a shore and leaving naked those things it had covered, the covering darkness was open night, full of eyes, unwinking, watching and accusing.

And they were watching his shame, the shame of a man in a place in which he did not belong, a man who had promised to pay and had not paid, who had no right here. Look at him, his father has run away, bankrupt, half a county looking for him—the fellow who didn't have a home, even, and no longer friends, not friends now, but people who knew him, alerted, wary, guarding what they had.

His head down, dreading encounter, he stole across the campus. He avoided buildings. He came to the street leading to the hospital and as he walked along it he defied his censor, the tears fell, his cheeks were wet with them. He heard a distant shout from a dormitory. He dashed his tears quickly away. He swallowed. He bit his lip. He halted.

"Please help me," he said. He said it with his heart, a total appeal, to a god unknown.

"Help me," he said again, waiting.

He walked on.

Outside the hospital he stared through the darkness at the dim outlines of the building, his eyes fondling the bricks. He looked intently at the lighted windows, hoping to see something, for a keepsake. His eyes roved the building, imaging it, to remember.

He walked on. As he passed the hospital he said goodbye to it. He paused occasionally to look back. He resumed walking, walking aimlessly. In a building ahead the doors swung open and a dozen chattering nurses emerged. He averted his head, put one foot ahead of the other, thought of nothing. The nurses' voices grew fainter. He was safe again. The darkness was with him. He was jarred suddenly from behind. The blow made him stumble. He ducked, looking back, frightened.

"Oh, excuse me!" cried a girl's voice, mocking.

"Oh, we're so sorry!" cried another.

"Why, it's Luke!" said the first in mock surprise.

"Oh, did we bump into you?"

"*We* saw you skulking by!"

"Hello Dorothy, hello Jenny," he said, trying to smile.

"What's the matter? Gotten too high-hat for your friends?"

"He's keeping company with a head operating-room nurse! The OR! What does he want to go bothering with a couple of probationers!"

He walked on.

"I could report you to the superintendent!" she yelled. "You and your dumb Swede!"

"Come on," pleaded Jenny.

He walked on. He turned a corner. After a while he turned his head slowly. They were not following. The street was empty.

And as he walked away the echo of their voices in his mind, as he walked away the memory of the encounter, as it dimmed, sank into the welter of numbness, his mind nudged him, his intelligence was trying to say something, he stopped.

Kristina.

Kristina is a nurse.

The quick and the dead.

The quick, now.

I'll say, Kristina, I'll say, I don't know whether I ought to tell you this or not . . . Kristina . . . I wonder if you could see your way clear . . . I wonder . . . well, it's this way . . .

No . . . No! . . .

He walked faster, fearful of losing her when he had just found her, just discovered, just embraced the fact of her, the chance.

He licked his lips.

We could be engaged. Just engaged. And I'll say to her, when people are engaged, I'll say to her, I'll say, Look, Kristina!

"What's the score?" Alfred asked next morning.

"I don't know. I don't know yet."

"It'll be all right. You mark my words, boy. I know."

"Alfred—what would you think if—"

"Got a plan?"

"No—I mean if I didn't hear from him—"

"Look, Luke. Let's be sensible. Medicine isn't the only way to make a living. Oh, I know you like it. But face it."

They dressed in silence.

On the way to classes Alfred smote his head.

"I knew I'd been trying to remember something! It was in Germany this summer! Fulboating! English fellow wandered into the same thing as you! Didn't hear from home over a month! He was all ready to go to the English consul, work his way home, blow his brains out! And the next morning there was his letter."

"Sure."

"I'm not kidding!"

"Okay . . . Thanks . . ."

Dr. Aarons met him in a corridor between classes.

"Any news?'

"No, sir. Not a thing."

"Wait a day or so. You're bound to hear something."

"I've got until Saturday."

"I think you'll hear before then."

"I'd do anything to go on."

"Yes."

"I mean that, sir."

"I know."

"Anything."

"Are you trying to tell me something?"

"No, no! What I meant to say was—"

"I understand. Believe me. Nothing dishonorable."

"No, sir. Nothing dishonorable."

"Yes. Your confreres in the laboratory send word by me that they want to see you."

"Could you tell them, sir? That there's nothing new?"

"I think perhaps they want to see you in person."

"I wish I had something to tell you. If you could just say—"

"No. I think you'd best go yourself. They've been very kind to you."
"I know. It's just that—"
"Fine girls. Very high standards."
"Yes, sir."

"Have you got any money? Any money at all?" cried Ann.
"I've got ninety-three dollars."
"Why, that's wonderful!" said Ruth.
"Certainly," said Ann. "That's something to work with!"
"But I need—"
"You go see the bursar! You tell him that—"
"It's no use. He's already told me—"
"No matter what he's told you! If you go see him—and you show him ninety-three dollars in good faith—"
"It's something, after all! Look at it from his side!"
"Don't you see? The university would have *some*thing!"
"All right . . ."
"Don't be reluctant! After all, next month maybe Ann or I can help. Just go right in! What else is there to do?"
"Do you mean you've thought of something? Lucas!"
"No, no! It's nothing. No. I was just thinking how to go about it . . ."
"Well, you just go right down there this noon and walk right up to him and you say—"

"I'm sorry, Mr. Marsh," the bursar said. "Our rules are very emphatic on this point. I'd like to help you, but the university is run on very definite rules. I made a mistake in the first place, one I'm afraid I'll have to answer for—"
"Mr. Johnson," said Lucas, cold now and uncaring and vengeful, "would you rather the university lost two hundred dollars or one hundred and seven dollars?"
"Mr. Marsh, it's your duty, your plain and evident duty, to turn in whatever funds you have against this bill, this debt. I was accommodating, I went beyond the rules and now—"
"You'll have to answer for it, won't you. Well, I'm offering to reduce the bill by half. Practically half. I'm showing good faith. It's not so bad to make a mistake for a hundred dollars as two hundred, is it?"
"Mr. Marsh, I don't think your attitude does you credit. I want to tell you frankly that—"
"Look, Mr. Johnson, this isn't my fault. All I'm trying to do is go to college. That's not a terrible thing, is it?"
"But if I let you go on what assurance have I got—"
"You haven't got any. And neither have I. This isn't my doing. But I will cut the debt in half. And all I want is thirty days. If I don't hear in thirty days you're no worse off than you are now. And you've got ninety-three dollars to show the powers that be some reason why you let me continue. What have you got to lose?"
"It's not a question of what I have to lose. It's a question of method. All this is highly irregular. Highly."

"Will you do it?"
"I don't see that you leave me much choice."
"I'm doing the best I can."
"You're sure that's all you have?"
"I don't even know what I'm going to eat on, Mr. Johnson."
"Ah, yes! Well . . . These things are very unfortunate . . . I'm sorry, of course . . . You understand . . . Ninety-three. Correct . . ."
"Yes, sir," said Lucas. "Yes, sir. I understand."
He knew what he had to do now.
And if it failed he must steal.

⁎ CHAPTER 19

He had a month now.
And that was all he possessed.
But he was rich in it.
And he hardened very swiftly, the catastrophe cupped him, bled him of abasement. The heat of his shame cooled and he viewed disgrace coldly and discredit, humiliation, and unrespectability with irritation. He appraised the rules in which he had clothed his outlook, the straps and belts, cinctures, bridles, knots, ties, clasps, reins, latchets, which, all fastened, all tied, laced and woven, made conscience and moral sense, ethics and conduct. And he appraised them coldly and the names left them and they were knots and bindings, a miscellany, accumulated, intricate, agreements with chaos.
He put them by. He stepped out of them, clad only in his necessity.
He appraised life as if he were a stranger to it, seeing it alertly, life being what he must have and what he must be, and the people in it.
He saw them in terms of his need. He assayed them against his need, measured them, saw them clearly in relation to himself, saw them clearly, what they had, what they thought, what they summed.
There were no longer any rules.
There was only necessity.
He sold a suitcase, a few books, a pair of cufflinks. Richer and poorer by eight dollars he went to the hospital dining room next day and waited for Kristina.
"Hallo, there!" she greeted him, and laughed.
"What's the matter?" he asked, frightened.
She put a hand on his arm.
"Excuse me. I'm not laughing at you. No, no. Would you like to see something? Come! I will show you a hero!"
He smiled obediently, trailed her down the corridor.
"What is it, Kristina? What's up?"
"I show you something you never see again in a million years!"
"But tell me!"
"If I tell you, you will never believe me! Come on!"
They entered a men's ward. The probationer at the desk rose quickly, seeing Kristina.

"Could we see Mr. Carter, please?" her lips twitched. The probationer smiled.

"Certainly!" She walked down the aisle of beds. Kristina, with the composure of a graduate nurse and the head of a department and the diffidence of an official in another official's bailiwick, followed close behind her.

The probationer turned briskly between two beds.

"Hello there, Mr. Carter," she said

Lucas, at the foot of the bed with Kristina, tried to smile ingratiatingly.

"Hello, hello, hello, hello, hello!"

The man in the bed was a somewhat undernourished white male, single, aged seventy-three, well developed but showing obvious weight loss, chronic illness. His hair was jet-black, without any gray whatever, his face was wrinkled in a grin, he had small black eyes, set deeply in his skull, and an enormous, sweeping gray mustache, yellowed about the mouth. His hands rested quietly on the counterpane, they were pallid, streaked with blotches, and the fingers were clubbed.

"Hallo, yourself!" cried Kristina.

"I've brought you some visitors," said the probationer brightly.

"You remember me?" asked Kristina.

"Sure, sure, sure, sure!"

The old man grinned at Lucas. Between him and the two nurses there was an air of expectancy which seemed to be focussed on Lucas, and Lucas smiled anxiously, trying to evince what was expected of him.

"This is a medical student," said Kristina.

The old man nodded and grinned, waiting.

"He came to see you."

The old man squeezed his eyes shut as if he could no longer bear the exquisite, the secret, his grinning jaws writhed and beneath the mustache a great hole opened, his toothless mouth.

The two nurses looked at each other and laughed happily.

"Now come on, Mr. Carter!" the probationer coaxed.

"This man was a great fighter!" Kristina said solemnly to Lucas and the old man watched to see the effect of this on Lucas.

"Is that so!"

The old man nodded blissfully.

"Fit Injins all m'life." He nodded, and winked portentously. "Fit 'em in Albuquerque, fit 'em in Californy, fit the piss out of 'em!"

He tried to struggle to a sitting position, turned midway toward his nightstand.

"I'll get it!" the probationer cried and pushed him back and opened the stand drawer. She took from it a faded and a yellowed sheet of thick paper and handed it to Lucas.

"Albert Eddler Carter," the document said in flowing script. And above it, "The United States of America." And beneath these, "For services above and beyond the call to duty, and for heroism which mirrors the finest tradition of the Army Scout Corps . . ."

Lucas read swiftly. The man in the bed was a hero. At the bottom of the paper was the award, the ribbon of the Congressional Medal of

Honor. He examined this detail curiously. Then he looked up, looked at the old man with respect.

The old man cackled, gratified.

He tried to sit up, his breath came harsh and quick, he coughed a little blood, he never stopped grinning delightedly. The probationer pushed him back on the pillow, seized his hands.

"Now, now! We mustn't get excited!"

"We have to leave you, now," Kristina said.

"No, no!" the old man wheezed, looking from one to the other of the two women, his eyes hurt.

"All right," said the probationer. "You can show him. But just once!"

The old man relaxed, grinning happily.

"Mr. Carter has something he wants to show you," the probationer said.

Lucas leaned forward a little. The old man looked at him reflectively. When he was sure he had Lucas' entire and devoted attention he raised one of his hands slowly, his eyes never leaving Lucas', he put his hand slowly on top of his head, his mouth opened, he lifted his hand.

Lucas cried out.

For a moment he thought the man had lifted his head off.

In the lifted hand the old man held his hair, all of it. The skull beneath was dead white, crisscrossed with a patchwork of scars.

"It's his own hair!" Kristina cried. The probationer beamed. The old man's eyes never left Lucas'. He did not move. The orifice that was his mouth gaped in its widest grin.

"Scalped me!" he chortled at last. "Sons of bitches scalped me!"

"The Indians took his scalp right off!" Kristina explained.

"Waited till he turned his back to sculp another one, reached up and got him through the balls, belly and backbone. One shot."

"Then he got his scalp back—"

"Had it tanned—"

"Worn it ever since!" The old man let his scalp fall back on his skull, where it hung askew.

"Isn't he wonderful?" cried the probationer, straightening the hair lovingly. "Now, that's enough. Thank you, Mr. Carter—"

The old man began to cough again. Kristina and Lucas walked from the ward.

The happy cackle followed them from the room.

"Look, Kristina—"

"So now! What do you think of that? Every day something else. My God! A hospital! I tell you! You ate dinner yet?"

"Dinner . . ."

"What I say, dinner? I always forget! Back in Minnesota at noon we eat dinner. At night eat supper. You eat *lunch?*"

"Yes, I have—"

"What you eat?"

"I had a sandwich—I have to get back to classes—"

"You're watching your figure, hah?"

"Oh, no—say, Kristina, I had an idea—"

"Maybe I got to take off a few pounds. I think I'm too fat."

Down this new avenue Lucas followed eagerly.

"You? Don't you dare take off an ounce! You hear? Not one ounce!"

"Oh, no! I think I'm too fat!"

"Where! You just show me! Where?"

"You don't see? My God! Pretty soon my clothes don't fit me!" She slapped her thighs hard.

"There? You're worrying about your hips?"

"Oh, no, no! You wrong! *Much* too fat!"

"Kristina! Will you believe me? Don't you take off a single ounce!"

"I like to eat. I think I eat too much."

"You know something, Kristina? I never noticed girls' figures before—"

"Hoo! You never notice!"

"Oh, I don't mean that! But there's something about *your* figure—I mean, the way *you* look—I mean, so far as *I'm* concerned—"

"A girl shouldn't let herself go—"

"You just let yourself alone!"

"What does a man know! How's your classes? Why don't you come around to see any more operations?"

"I haven't had time! *You* know what those hours are! Every day, now! I've *wanted* to . . ." Now! Now if he could break in! "Look, Kristina . . ."

"I thought maybe too many girls, eh? I hear all about you! Oh, my!"

"What'd you hear!"

"Never mind!"

"No, tell me! What?"

"I hear!"

"It's not true!"

"Hoo—hooo!"

"Kristina!"

"I hear about a certain young probationer—and another—and another—"

"But it's not true, don't you see? It's just not true—"

"Those girls know what they're doing! They catch a nice young doctor, pretty soon they got a doctor for a husband—why not?"

"Because I wouldn't have them! That's why not!" he cried angrily.

"You better be careful, then!"

"Don't worry! Even if I had a chance when would I get to take a girl out, now! Eight hours' study every day. Four hours, five, six, every night!"

"No, that's right. You got to study. You got nothing left but Sundays. Sometimes Saturday night."

Unaccountably his chance had come again.

"I guess you stay pretty close to home too?" he said warily.

"Me? Oh, is always something to do. I sew—I go see Bruni—I walk—is always something."

He drew breath and plunged.

"Would you mind if I went along?"

"Sure! Why not? It's a free country—"

"Come on, now! You know what I mean!"

"Who? Me, you're thinking of taking out? Oh! Now *I* got to be careful!"

"What do you say, Kristina? Sunday? Is this Sunday all right?"

"Let me see . . . Yes, I think all right, Sunday. What time?"

"What time for you?"

"We go in the morning, eh? We have dinner at Bruni's! This time *I* cook!"

They grinned and parted. He rushed away, full of relief.

"You hear something?" Alfred asked that night.

"Not yet, no."

"Well, what are you so happy about? I thought you'd heard something."

"No," he sighed, "not a word . . . not a single, goddamned word . . ."

"Well, you will. Don't worry."

Lucas nodded.

Thereafter he was careful not to smile.

"So, Kristi, what you think?"

"What I *think*?"

"All right, all right! Is nice-looking poike. Is snels poike. But what you know about him? What you *know*?"

"Trude! You have seen him! You don't like him?"

"Na, na! Of course he's nice! But—I yoost *say*, that's all."

"We see . . ."

"Is anyway somebody to go out with . . ."

"You ask me, is some somebody."

"I don't ask you."

Kristi grinned.

"So what is like where you live?" Kristi asked as they walked home from Bruni's.

And Lucas told her earnestly about Milletta, that small place, that quiet place, miles away.

"You got girl there?"

"Girl? No. No girl." And he looked at her saying, You see I am free, will you have me? "You got a fellow, Kristi?"

"Nobody will have me!" she said archly.

"We ought to get together."

"Ah, no. You like probationers."

"Now, look! Kristi—!"

"You never talk about your people!"

"My mother?"

"You mother and father, you sisters and brothers. You family."

"My mother's dead."

"I'm sorry . . ."

"Yes . . . Someplace I guess I got a couple of uncles and aunts. I don't know them. I never saw them. You know something? I don't even know where they live! Could you believe that?"

"What happened?"

"It sounds funny to you, doesn't it? Swedish people are great on family, aren't they. I don't know. My father's people, these are. He never talked about them much. I guess they weren't too close as a family. That's the way it is, I guess. Some families are close, some not. Well, now you know all about me."

"And your father?"

He gave her a long look.

"Kristi, I'm going to tell you something . . ."

And he told her about Job.

"So now you got nobody," she said in a low voice, when he had finished.

He said nothing.

He drew a little away. He walked in silence.

She joined him. She put her arm through his. They walked in silence.

At the door of the Nurses' Home they said only good night, there was nothing left to say, there had been too much said, they said simply good night, they looked at each other, they parted.

At noon next day he was waiting for her. He smiled at her shyly.

"Hello, Luke," she said softly.

He put his hand swiftly under his coat, drew out a small box of candy, thrust it at her.

"Here!" he whispered.

She looked at it, her mouth open. He moved off.

"Luke—" she called after him. But he waved and was gone.

He was too much for her. He knew what he was doing. He knew what he had to do. He knew what he must have. He knew she liked him. He knew all about her. And he did not dislike her. She was, after all, the head operating-room nurse. That was not nothing in the social scale of the world in which he moved, not to a medical student, a mere student. She was not ugly, after all. She was downright attractive when you bothered to really look at her. She *could* be. When you came right down to it, what was the matter with her? She was damned nice, when you came right down to it! Too good for most of them around there. That's what.

A fellow could do a hell of a lot worse.

Next day he waited for her and they had lunch together. During the meal he looked meaningly at her, saying, You and I, Kristi. You and I, eh? And her eyes softened and they looked quickly about to see if they had been observed.

"He's got nobody, Bruni!"

"What do you mean, 'he's got nobody'?"

"Nobody!"

"Nobody?"

"No mother, no father, nobody!"

They looked at each other, silent.

"Kristi!" And Bruni put her hand on her friend's hand.

Kristi nodded.

"Ah, ah, ah, ah, ah!" Bruni shook her head in pity.

Kristi nodded.

"Oh, Kristi! . . . Such a nice young feller . . . So good-looking . . . So polite . . ."

"He brought me candy," Kristi said in a low voice.

"No, no, no . . ." That one who had so little should even then give.

"How much money has he got and he brings me candy. Not polite. But because he likes me. Yes, it's true. He likes me, Bruni." And she raised her head and nodded, saying, looking Bruni in the eye. "And I like him too."

And Bruni digested this, and accepted it, and said simply,

"What you do, Kristi? What you do?"

And Kristi looked at her, the two women met in their eyes, in their looking, repeating, hearing again, affirming, accepting, saying everything.

"I don't know, Bruni," said Kristi, saying, I'm afraid so, Bruni. Yes, I know, yes, yes, it's begun . . .

There was still something. There was still a way to bind her fast.

He was excited. He would have this, too. He had not thought of this. He had not even thought of it.

And he began to think of her kindly and lovingly, Kristina, for all the things she had, all she would give him.

He did not think of anyone else, he did not think of Ruth and Ann, nor of Alfred, nor of Dr. Aarons, he would not permit it, when the thought came to him he thrust it off, he recoiled, he struck the thought from his mind. He and Kristina. And he withdrew with her from all of them, into an uncensored world of their own, empty except for them, living their own life, dead and blind to all others.

And it would have to be soon.

"Are you taking a night off?" Alfred was startled.

"There's something I've got to do."

"In the middle of the week?"

"I'll make up Saturday night."

"I don't get it."

"I'll just work Saturday."

"But what in the name of God—is it a girl?"

"Do you think I'd take a night off for a girl?"

"No, but what in the name of God—what's come over you?"

"I'll tell you sometime . . ."

"It's your life, boy . . ." And he had returned to studying as Lucas left the room, he was gone, buried in his books.

And as Lucas hurried into the night, hurried toward the nurses' quarters, he passed the lights of the rooms, the rooms where medical students studied, he did not know them, he could not distinguish them from the others where lights burned, too, but they were there, they would be burning long after the others, long, long after the lights for other courses were out. They had fallen into a pattern, all of them, all the eighty-eight of the first year's group. And in this pattern the day began at 8:30 in the morning with the first class. And it proceeded through anatomy, histology, embryology, biochemistry and physical chemistry, through physiology, neuro-anatomy, radiology and psychiatry and an hour of clinic, of correlation lectures, and there was an hour for lunch and then it was 5:30 and classes were over for the day. And then there was a quick meal and then study. And study began during the meal, an open book propped beside the plate. And study ended at midnight. And it was all strange, it was all new, even the language was different, a new language had to be learned, and for every waking hour there was despair and fear, alternating, and insecurity and desperate competition and hopelessness and hopelessness and hopelessness.

And that was the pattern for each day of the week. Each day except Saturday. On Saturday classes ended at one o'clock. In the afternoon there was sleep. In the evening some studied, some walked for an hour or so, one or two of the bravest or the most foolish went to the movies. Sunday there was study again. And that was the pattern.

And this was Tuesday.

It was eight o'clock.

And Lucas was on his way to the nurses' quarters.

They walked for a while and then Lucas led Kristina into the park. It was always the park for there was no place else.

He led her to a bench and he put his arm on the back of the bench so that it fell upon her back and shoulders. And for a while he sat quietly. Kristina said nothing.

His heart was hammering.

"I'm glad I got you," he said, looking straight ahead.

"How you know you got me?"

"You know what I mean, Kristina."

"It's nice here. You come here with plenty other girls, I bet."

He turned to her and said sternly,

"You've got to stop talking that way, darling. You hear?"

It was the first time he had ever called her darling, he put the word in his mouth and his ears heard the sound of it. And Kristina, hearing the word, was elated and confused and her eyes tried to look at him searchingly.

"Hoo-HOO! So, it's darling now!"

"Kristina!" He bit his lip. He forced the anger from him. He let his shoulders slump. "All right. All right if you want to make fun of me . . ." He made himself smile at her, Punish me, the smile said, go ahead, it's all right, I'll take it . . .

"Now you're mad."

"No. I'm not mad. Why should I be mad? Kristina, don't you like me? Don't you like me at all?"

"Sure I like you! You're a nice boy—"

"Because the way you treat me—the way you're always laughing at me—"

"I don't laugh at you," she said in a low voice.

"But you are! You were laughing just then—"
"I just say first thing comes into my head. What shall I say?"
"Because I like you, Kristina, you know that, don't you?"
"I hope so—"
"You mustn't hope so! You must know it! You must! Do you hear, Kristina?"
"I hear."
"Because it's important. Even if you don't like me."
"I didn't say that . . ."
"You do like me, don't you, Kristina? A little?"
"You're a nice boy—"
"I don't mean that. I don't mean that way . . . Do you, Kristina?"
"Yes . . ." Her voice was almost inaudible. She looked intently at her hands in her lap, thumbing one finger.
He took her hand. He turned toward her.
"All I know is, I love you. Don't laugh. Don't make fun. That's all. Now I've said it. Now you know. I love you, Kristina. I can't help it. I love you." He stared at her, waiting.
"Kristina . . ."
"I like you too," she said shyly.
"Oh!" He dropped her hand. He turned from her and looked straight ahead. He slumped dejectedly.
"You're young," she said anxiously.
"That's it! You're right! I'm young . . ."
"My grandmother was married when she was sixteen. My grandfather was eighteen . . ."
"You see? You see? Ah, please, Kristina—"
"But what I got, tell me! What you see in me? I don't speak good, I don't know nice things, you read books, you go with different kind of people, what you want with a dumb Swede?"
"Kristina! You must never say that again, do you hear me? Never! I love you, Kristina. And it's like a knife in me! You wouldn't even *think* it!"
"But—"
"Never! Understand me? Why, you're lovely, Kristina! And do you think it's nothing to be head operating-room nurse? Nothing? Do you know what I'd give to know what you know? What you think is nothing?"
"That! Luke! You don't ever think I'm—pretty!"
"Have you seen yourself, Kristina? Tell me that. Have you ever really, truly looked at yourself?"
"Oh, Luke . . ."
"It's true! You don't know! Why, we have everything in common! Everything! You're everything I want!"
"Someday you'll be a doctor. Then what!"
"No, Kristina . . . No . . . You're wrong . . ."
"What's happened! You are going to stop? You are not going to be a doctor?"
"I'm afraid not . . . No . . . I'm afraid all that's over . . ."
"*You* fail? Is not possible! Luke!"

"Of course I haven't failed! I'd never fail!"
"Then what–?"
"It's something– No! I guess I'd better not talk about it. Especially to you . . ."
"You got to tell me."
"No, Kristina . . ."
"You got to!"
"You'll hate me–"
"Why should I hate you? You did something?"
"No . . . That's the trouble! I didn't do anything! It's–it was done to me–I can't tell you. No! I'm sorry! No! No, Kristina! No . . . It has to do with my father . . ."
"Your father!"
"Yes."
"Your father! You told me he's gone! He's left you! What–"
"He's left me, all right! He's left me ruined!"
"Ruined!" She echoed the word. Comprehension came. Her shoulders sagged. She laughed with relief.
"It's money," she cried. "I thought–I didn't know what–I don't laugh at you, darling–"
"I should never have told you!" He turned his hot face away.
"But *I* have money!"
"You?"
"Of course! You think I spend my money like the other girls? I save my money! Sure! How much you think I spend? I get fifty dollars every week, I pay my room, I get my laundry, I get my meals, how much you think I spend?"
"I don't know. But that's yours, Kristina! That's not me!"
"But that's my job! That's only natural! Of course I help!"
"I couldn't! Don't talk about it! No, don't!" He shook his head angrily. "I wanted to ask you something. Now, this spoils it."
She was silent. She looked at him sidelong, as he brooded, she tried to think of something to say, she could not. She waited helplessly.
"Kristina! If I was to ask you, 'Kristina, will you marry me'–"
She looked at him, pale.
"If I had asked you–tell me! Tell me honestly! What would you have said?"
"I don't know," she said in a low voice, for she was thinking of the need, now, and of how it had changed everything, and of the two suitors now, Lucas and his need, of everything that had changed and become serious, deadly serious, and no play, now, no gambits, not even lightness of boy and girl but something that was becoming irrevocable.
But in his ears it was a knell.
"Will you think, Kristina? Not now! Will you tell me?"
"I will think," she said gravely.
"Because I love you, Kristina. It means the world to me." He drew her to him roughly. "You've never even kissed me," he said desperately. He tilted her chin. Her lips were surprisingly soft beneath his. He felt her arms about him, her lips parted, and now she twisted away, he felt her hand on his arm.

"No," she said huskily. "No, darling . . ."

"I want you . . ." And he kissed her again, strained her to him. But her hand stayed on his arm.

"Are you afraid," he whispered.

"Kanske," she said shyly.

"What does it mean? Tell me?"

"Maybe," she said.

"Tell me!"

"That's what it means. Maybe . . ."

"Tell me, Kristina—!"

"We see . . ."

There was, finally, a letter from Job.

It was waiting for him next morning.

He ripped it open. There was only a folded sheet of notepaper. There was no check. He tore the envelope apart. There was nothing. There was only the folded sheet of notepaper and Job's writing upon it.

Dear son,

No doubt you will be surprised to learn I have decided to settle here for a while, in this town. No doubt you have heard by this time a lot of stories, most of which are bound to be exaggerated, one way or the other and everything would have been fine if Kumper in South Wetherly hadn't decided to be a hog and try for 90 cents on the dollar and if they'd let me alone I could have paid a hundred cents and now they'll get nothing. That's the whole story no matter what they tell you so of course there was nothing else for me to do they left me no choice. I am on here as manager [Lucas glanced at the letterhead: "Acme Reliable Harness and Leather Goods, Trusses for Male and Female."] *and am now thinking of buying an interest in this place as I feel something really could be done with it. So take care of yourself and drop me a line from time to time and if you need anything why just let me know.*

With love, your father,
Job Marsh. Please burn this.

The envelope was postmarked Chillicothe, Ohio.

He waited for Alfred to comment. But Alfred behaved as if he had not seen a letter handed to Lucas. Was it politeness? Was he waiting tactfully for Lucas to mention it? He's afraid! Lucas thought suddenly. He's going to ignore the whole thing. If it's bad news he thinks I'm going to ask him for money again. He was safe, now, he was safe from Alfred, safe from them all. And a spasm of hatred for Alfred, for all of them, twisted his viscera.

Worried, are you? he said, he almost said it aloud.

"Here, look at this," he said roughly. He forced the letter on Alfred.

Alfred read it without change of expression.

"He'll have something before long," he nodded.

"Sure!" said Lucas, as if the matter no longer interested him.

"That's the way to look at it!" Alfred said uncertainly.
"Why not?"
"Just like I told you."
Lucas shrugged.
"He'd better!" Alfred said, nettled at Lucas' calm.
"That's right! That's absolutely right!"
"What's up?"
"What do you mean, 'what's up'?"
"You're not worried, or anything."
"Do I have to act worried, old boy? What is it you want me to do, grow pale and faint and grovel on the floor and kiss your ass and beg for fifty more nervous dollars?"
"Don't get smart."
"Oh, I'm not smart. I know that. Just smart enough so you'd flunk without me." He looked aside elaborately, inwardly trembling, almost over the brink of rage, waiting for the next word.
But Alfred at that moment saw the letter again, he lowered his eyes, and gathering his books walked from the room. Lucas followed. They walked in silence toward the School of Medicine.

In Chillicothe, in the small harness store that had reluctantly taken him on as a substitute clerk during the illness of a regular employee, Job Marsh, unscarred, unshaken, unperturbed, keen on the scent as any hunting animal in a new place, among familiar quarry, evaluated his locale with bright and steadfast eyes, ready for man.

When they were still some distance from the medical-school buildings Lucas' anger left him. He was indifferent to Alfred, walking at his side. With each stride he could see the buildings more clearly, at last he was able to distinguish the memorial stones from the brick about them and a few steps later he could read the nearest names, Sydenham, Galen, Hippocrates, and then Vesalius and Koch and Pasteur and Paré, and then they were at the steps of the building and he lowered his eyes humbly and contrived to brush against the stone entry.
He walked down the corridors with Alfred on the way to the cadaver and the leg they had now christened Zebedee. They passed a student oblivious to them, murmuring aloud, over and over to himself, "Never Lower Tillie's Pants, Mother Might Come Home," and responding automatically Lucas silently told the rosary of the wrist bones, navicular, lunate, triquetrum, pisiform, multangulum majus, multangulum minus, capitate, hamate. As they approached Zebedee they passed the cadaver of a middle-aged woman on which four students were already working. They stripped the cloth from Zebedee, all but his face, and as they bared the muscle, its body, its origin, its insertion, and all the time Zebedee's face carefully covered like the faces of all the cadavers in the large room, Lucas unaccountably saw himself in this place, the middle-aged woman had made him think of Ouida, he remembered who he was and what he was. It was a bad moment for him, a spasm of envying every boy his boyhood, coveting the family, their togetherness, and himself alone, himself about to be more than ever alone in this marriage and in

what he had become. He wondered what he could have done to make things different, to keep the rules of which he had divested himself, the pattern which united the others, what he could have done not to be alien, knowing he had met each circumstance as it arose and that he had done the only things he could have done and the only things no boy here would have done. Recollecting, he drifted farther from them. He did not hate them. He knew the separation was irrevocable. He hoped merely not to be found out. He hoped to be as much part of other humans as they now permitted him to be, not to lose what he had, knowing what chap it was they accepted, knowing it was not the Lucas Marsh he slept with.

An instructor approached. He bent hurriedly to work on Zebedee. He cut lovingly. There, Zebedee, he said, silently, there, there. It's all right, old fellow.

A great fondness for Zebedee welled in him. He felt a bond between them, the more real for its silence, for this matter in the shape of a human which was familiar and known and stable and forgiving and tolerant and kindly.

There, Zebedee, he said silently. There you are, old fellow. It's me. It's Lucas.

And he cut tenderly. And with love.

This friend.

⋆ CHAPTER 20

Alfred and Lucas found a truce zone in their study, they fashioned of study a whole new social structure and their talk was of their books and resolutely ignored all else. In this truce they managed well. In a few days they were able to smile again over careful jokes, to protect each other in the unending warfare of classwork and to share again their common fears.

For the class had by now resolved into a daily battleground of competition. A ruthlessness, born of panic, nourished by fright, jostled by despair, was the daily classroom pattern. When one man was able to describe a muscle or a process the class had not studied there was a frantic scramble to discover how he had come by this information. There was the constant fear that in the next class, or on the next day, someone would offer information not common to all of them. There was unending, ruthless competition.

In this battle of the students against the apparently invincible jungles of the new language in which was written the towering complex of material they were required to compass every day, untangle, map and absorb totally and never forget a detail travelled a month before, there were arrayed eighty-eight determined to become doctors, and these noosed eighty-eight, despairing on their trapfall at day's end, each day their last, waited resignedly for the signal they had been dropped from the course. Nakedly vying, stripped of all niceties and all pretense, they competed openly not to be the first to be dropped, not to be noticed, if possible, but not to be first, fought a delaying action, always exhausted, always speared on by the panic nearness of execution.

There was also a paradoxical convention of self-defense in which all members of the class were somehow bound to help the falling or the about-to-fall. Outside of class the strongest helped the weakest, groups of three or four, neglecting their own study for an hour or so, would surround some helpless member and pound at him, swear and curse and scream at him, drill into him what he had not memorized, what he could not understand. A brisk trade in books sprang up, books supposed to cover questions in some future examination; magic lists of questions went secretly from hand to hand. Outside of class it became an inviolable rule to give help when asked.

But the group was never entirely stable. Pressure produced sudden exceptions. The class had its marked failure, its sealed, walking doom, his name was Erskine and from the first Erskine was the obvious choice to be dropped, he was avoided in class, his very presence brought fear. He was the first to be helped. The group discovered group aid with Erskine as its first exemplar. Everyone had helped Erskine by the end of the first month. An examination was posted. It became known that Erskine had a list of questions and answers.

Jubilantly, three of the class cornered him.

And then, amazingly,

"No sir!" he cried. "No! You're not going to see these questions!"

And while they looked at him, stupefied, he hid the list under his coat and ran to a corner, cowering defiantly.

And with Erskine were three members of the class who were always looking for nuggets, items of boiled-down information, three who quickly gave up, ignored the prodigy of study and memorizing, and devoted themselves to sidling up to other students and furtively begging for the fragments, for the essence of books digested endlessly by the others, for the few words that really mattered, the magic words that would pass examinations.

There was always fear. Unending fear.

There was the day during the first fortnight when Lucas and Alfred and the two other students assigned to Zebedee, looking at Zebedee dubiously, about to start a fresh exploration, were surprised by a silent, feared instructor who appeared suddenly beside them. He looked at their frightened faces gravely, he bent over Zebedee, he straightened.

"Gentlemen," he said slowly, "next year one of you will not be here."

They were always in panic, panic for an intonation, panic for a fancied look, panic for everything. Now they stared at him, stupefied.

He watched them a moment, expressionless. Then he pointed a bony finger at Zebedee.

"Him," he said quietly, and walked on.

On the fifth day it came to Lucas that the course appeared impossible because it was designed to appear impossible, that no one actually expected them to learn all that was set before them but only as much as possible, that those who learned most would continue and those who were unable to accumulate a predetermined minimum would be dropped.

"I've got it figured out," he told Alfred, his excitement and relief expunging the last reserve lingering from their estrangement. "Alfred, old boy, the light has finally dawned."

He cried out his conclusions.

"Maybe so," said Alfred. Then, because he, too, wished to believe, "You're probably right. By God, you are!"

Three days later there was a minor examination.

"I am going to discuss these results with you informally," the instructor said next day. "Hereafter, the only discussion you may expect will be the official notifications of your failure. The results of this test may be called fair. There is some evidence that the majority of this class is attempting to assimilate about seventy percent of what we are studying. There may be some who feel that is all we require. Those who do so will fail. You will learn everything that is set before you. This is your first and your final warning. Not half of it—not seventy percent of it—not most of it—but all of it! In other scholastic halls"—he waved vaguely toward the rest of the university—"college is a contest—a contest for good marks, a contest to outwit instructors, a game. Here, there is no contest. Here, we deal with something that cannot be talked of in the same breath with scores, diplomas, and marks. We are dealing with human life, with the lives of those who will put themselves at the mercy of your judgment and knowledge. We have no alternative but to insist that you learn everything set before you—not a commendable percentage, but everything. You will need everything. Everything, everything we know, everything is little enough."

Here and there in the classroom shoulders slumped, despairing. Some were frightened, some stared at him incredulous. Abruptly, perversely. Lucas' ambition was nothing less than the impossibility just demanded. Now there were no more doubts, now the demands of the course were clear, unequivocal, bracingly perilous. In a seat beside him Alfred rallied from the shock, considered a moment, glanced sidelong at Lucas, leaned imperceptibly closer.

"You need money, now?" Kristina asked when they met at noon.

"No, no," said Lucas, knowing he needed it, savoring his new security, putting off the inevitable. "Not now, Kristi. Probably hear from Dad any day. Might hear tomorrow."

"You seen the bursar? They let you go on like this?"

"It's all right. Don't let's talk about it."

"You feel better paid up. You got enough to worry you."

"Let's talk about us."

"I got plenty. What do you say? Only take a minute to get it—"

"Not now," he said, confused, "someday, maybe, thanks, though, thanks a lot, Kristi, I'll be all right, but thanks, I'll go see him, don't worry, it'll be all right." He put his hand on her wrist. "You know what happened in class today? Fellow fainted for the third time, nobody knows what's the matter with him, he ought to be used to it by this time, they sent him to the dean's office. We think he's through."

"Poor feller," Kristina said, wondering at the satisfaction in Lucas' voice, studying his face.

"Yes," said Lucas vehemently and without pity, "it's a damned shame. Yes," he said, with relief that the hand of death had passed over him for another victim but might return if he sided with the victim, "yes," he said carefully, "a damned nice fellow, too. . . ."

"He's ashamed to take my money," Kristina told Bruni.

"That's *good*!" Bruni nodded vigorously.

"I know!" They looked at each other triumphantly.

"That's the way it should be."

"But I got to make him, though. He hasn't paid his tuition. That father of his! He's got enough to worry about without tuition. Leaving a feller like that right in the middle!"

"Maybe if you loan him—"

"He won't take it."

They sat brooding the same thought, each waiting for the other to speak it.

"I guess I got to marry him right away!" Kristina smiled as if the thought were a pleasant joke between them.

"I guess so." Bruni smiled an appreciative return.

"Well, I guess that's what I'll do."

"That's right."

"You think it's all right, Bruni?"

"All right? What else?"

"Sooner or later—"

"Certainly—"

"One time's the same as another—"

"What you even talk about it for?" Bruni asked severely.

Kristina looked at her with love.

"Where you go? Why don't we see you? Why you don't come here?"

"We walk."

"Just walk?"

"Sometimes we walk in the park."

"You should come here! You could sit here!"

Kristina smoothed her skirt.

"You know something?" she asked shyly. "Sometimes that man of mine—sometimes he's pretty fresh . . ."

Bruni looked at Kristina's downcast head, narrowed her eyes. Abruptly, she rose.

"I think you get married right away!" she said firmly.

Kristina pleated her skirt with a slow thumb and forefinger.

"I think so," she said in a low voice.

"I give you a big party. We have Jussi and Sven and Marta—maybe Oley's boss—everybody!"

"What you think—my man is like yours? Can take a day off for a party to get married? We got no time, Bruni. Like Luke says, the class goes right on without him. He can't lose a day. Not even one day!"

"But you got to have a party! Kristi!"

"Sure! Someday we have a party. Someday we have a honeymoon, too. Trudi! We don't even have time to look for a place to live!"

"That I can do."

"Will you look, Trudi?"

"Who else? I buy you a ring, even."

"I got my mother's—"

"But a girl's got to shop—she got to get things—!"

"What I need! I got to work, too, Bruni!"

Bruni looked at Kristina for a long moment. Her friend was alone, they had been together, their thoughts were simple, intersecting patterns, they were one with each other, their odors, colors, garments, their hopes and their pasts, intermingled, a common fund, fluid, diffusing through the tissues of communication. Now Kristina was alone. She was another person. She was Kristina about to be married. It would always be good. It would never be the same.

She looked at the different Kristina, she sighed imperceptibly, she wove her thoughts to the new thinking. Lucas was a nice boy. He was good-looking, he was quiet, he worked hard, and someday he would be a doctor. And Kristina was crazy about him. Kristina had found her man. This had come to her friend, her fellow, her fellow female. A girl must be married. Now it had come to her Kristina.

"What does he say?" she asked. "Does he want to get married right away?" And her look said, I tell you, Kristi, men are funny, first they can't wait, then they hold back, remember Oley, remember my own Oley.

"This one will not wait at all! *Snabt! Genast! Igår!* Yesterday! That's when he wants to get married! And he's right. My feller's right, Bruni. What are we waiting for?" And her look had suddenly remembered Oley, Oley incomprehensibly holding back. And Lucas. This prize.

Two days later Lucas walked with Kristina and Bruni, walked quickly, wasting no time, for this was the noon hour and there were two apartments to look at. They were to be married Saturday. They were to be married in four days.

Kristina walked sedately, a sereneness, almost a complacency on her features. On the other side of Lucas walked the friend of the bride, the almost bride, and Bruni this day was circumspect, deferential, for this man was unknown and now, at this point, a careless word might rob her friend of her man.

"I think it's very nice of Bruni," Kristina said after a while.

"It certainly is! It's darned nice of you, Bruni," Lucas said quickly.

"I got lots of time. It ain't like I had a house full of kids," Bruni shrugged.

"That's one thing *I'm* not going to have!" Kristina said firmly.

"Who said anything about kids!" Lucas cried.

They looked at him quickly.

"Kristi didn't mean anything." Bruni smiled disarmingly. "She just meant—"

"What I say? I only said—"

"All right, all right!"

"What's the matter, Luke? What you so jumpy about?"

"We're getting close?" Bruni exclaimed. Lucas looked up.

They were very near the street in which Ruth and Ann lived.

"Not here, surely!" Lucas protested. "This is too expensive," he exclaimed.

"One of them's around here," Bruni said uncertainly.

"Let's look, after all," said Kristina.

"No, I know this neighborhood—"

"You do?"

"One of the fellows told me. Told me all about it. Very expensive."

"Not so very. Not really."

"Let's see, anyway," said Kristina.

Each step was bringing them closer and as they drew nearer the perilous place, perilous with the possibility of exposure to Ruth and Ann, to the awful chance of this is my wife, I'm married now, the surprise, the shock, the sizing-up, the contempt, the pity, the accusation, the inevitable meeting if they lived nearby—

"Wait!" said Lucas. And he stopped. He made them stop too. But it was too late.

Around a corner came Ann. She was walking directly at them.

"Let's go this way," Lucas cried and would have pulled them away. But Ann had seen them. And even then he pulled them anew.

"Hi!" she called out and walked faster. And now there was no escape, now she was here, and he looked up guiltily,

"Hi! Hi, there!" he cried and tried to smile, tried to make a smile of understanding, he and Ann, they two, the rest not counting.

Now Kristina and Bruni put on their company faces. And back of these faces was the wary female face, wary of a possible adversary, wary of a possible adverse comparison.

"Where have you been?" Ann demanded. "What in the world's happened to you?" She turned to the two girls where they stood a little aside, decorously, blankly smiling. "We haven't seen hide nor hair of him!" she said aggrievedly.

"I haven't had a second!" he cried before they could speak. "Not one earthly second! We're just out right now, just in the lunch period—just came out—you can imagine—"

"That's all very well, but you've got a minute! You could stop by for a second—just to let us know—" She recollected herself, turned to Kristina and Bruni. They shifted uncertainly, still smiling. "How do you do," she laughed apologetically. "Pleased I'm sure," said Kristina, said Bruni, there was the hesitant shadow of a bow, Lucas winced at the Swedishness, the accent, the clumsiness.

But Ann did not seem to have noticed. She hesitated.

"Are you all right?" she asked anxiously.

"Oh, fine, fine!" he said, trying to head her off.

"They haven't—they aren't going to—"

"No, no! Everything's all right! Something's happened! I'll tell you later! It's nothing—I've got to run, now—"

"Well for Heaven's sakes, drop in! Let a person know! We thought you'd—"

"No, no! You'll see—you'll see—very unexpected—you know—"

"You be there Saturday!" Ann ordered. "Now be there! We're expecting you!" She turned to Bruni. "This boy! You see that he gets there!"

"Right! Right!" Lucas retreated. "Saturday, sure!"

"Saturday!" Ann warned. She smiled cordially at the girls again. "Bring your friends."

"Okay," said Lucas. "We'll see you—"

Kristina smiled friendlily, stood firm.

"What do you think of my feller?" she asked casually.

Lucas shuddered, quickly managed a begging grin at Ann. You and I, the grin said, that's the way they are, you understand, don't you? Nice girls, that's the way they are, real characters, I just happened to be out with them, you know the type . . .

"I think he's very nice," Ann smiled back, ignoring Lucas after a brief look. "But I won't think he's very nice if he isn't there Saturday—"

"Don't worry—I'll be there. Well, I'll see you, then—"

"We can't Saturday," Kristina shook her head, always smiling.

"Not Saturday—" Bruni cut in, archly.

"Saturday we gonna be—"

"We're going to be out on a date!" Lucas said loudly, desperately.

"Well, then—"

"Monday!" Lucas shouted, drawing the girls off forcibly. "See you Monday!" he called over his shoulder, nodding his head vigorously, walking hard, drawing the girls with him.

"Monday!" Ann admonished, waved, a little puzzled, and walked on.

And then, before questions, before the barrage he knew was coming.

"Thank God!" he said. "Thank God, *that's* over!"

"What was the matter?" Kristina asked blankly.

"Matter? Why, she'd just stand there and talk your arm off! That's all that's the matter! Where is this place, Bruni? We haven't got much time left."

"She spoke like a friend of yours," Kristina said.

"We're almost there," Bruni said meekly.

"Friend of mine—!"

"I thought you were going to introduce us."

"Introduce you!"

They both looked at him, waiting.

"Why, she works in the hospital! She works in the lab, there! Why, I thought you knew her sure! Why you know *her*—"

"I don't think so," Kristina said uncertainly.

"Sure you do! She works in the lab! I thought all you people knew each other! She lives right around here! Why—if I'd known that . . . !" He looked angrily over his shoulder, stopping, turning to face the street he knew would be empty, as if to say that if Ann were there he would repair the oversight instantly, it was ridiculous. . . .

"I'll bet you've told every nurse in the hospital!"

"No, no!"

"Sure you have!"

"Luke! I said I wouldn't! I haven't!" She turned to Bruni. "You never know how they're gonna be about first-year students getting married," she explained.

"That's what some of the fellows say," Luke defended.

"So when he told me that—"

"Sure!" said Bruni. "Why take a chance? What business is it of theirs?"

"Only when I saw she was a friend of yours—"

"Hey!" cried Bruni. "We here. You can see from here! The third house! Upstairs!"

"Upstairs?" Lucas echoed. "Upstairs?"

"How about the other place?" Kristina asked quietly.

"We're here!" Bruni said, startled. "We're here, Kristi!"

"I don't know," Kristina said slowly. They had halted now and Kristina stared at the house, her face expressionless.

And Bruni, slowly sensing something was wrong, that within her Kristina was revolving some slow thought, some negation, Bruni stood with her friend, her fellow woman, said, nodding,

"Well, maybe it would be expensive here—come on! I think you like the other place much better!"

"Wait a minute!" Lucas protested, feeling no protest, anxious to go on. "What's the matter with *this* place? We're here, at least—"

But the girls had already begun to walk on.

Something I done, Kristina said to herself. Something I said. He's ashamed of me. Maybe Bruni—maybe Bruni said something . . . Such an educated woman, that friend of his . . . all his friends, I think . . . And me! A dumb Swede! . . . The poor boy . . . Trying to be so nice . . . But I'll learn! You bet! He'll be proud of me!

And Bruni thought,

Kristi knows. That woman looked old, but Kristi knows. She knows what I don't know. There's something here. Something between them. Is not good to live so close, then. Kristi knows.

"What are you so quiet about all of a sudden?" Lucas smiled at them affectionately, safe now, altogether safe.

"Quiet?" echoed Kristina. "What's the matter with you, Bruni! You worse than Oley!" She hugged Lucas' arm fondly. "That's the Swede!" she cried. "I guess you stuck, Lukey! I guess you got a dumb, sit-in-the-corner Swede! *Det tror jag!*"

"Hah!" Bruni giggled.

"What's that! Tell me! That was Swedish, wasn't it?"

"Lordag . . ." Kristina said softly. And instantly Bruni swept into gales of laughter. *"Lordag!"* she echoed helplessly.

"What is it? What's Lerr-da? Tell me!"

But they were convulsed, they turned blushing faces from him, *Lordag,* Saturday, and they would not, could not, tell him,

And laughing helplessly, ignoring his protests, ignoring him until, protestingly, he laughed too, they came to the other apartment Bruni had found, and still laughing found it good, the landlord smiling at them, puzzled, a little wary of their laughter, their quick acceptance, and Lucas bounced on the bed to try the mattress and asked,

"Lerr-da?"

And at this they fell helplessly into each other's arms, the landlord laughed with them, not knowing why,

"Does it mean bed? Is that what it means? Is that why you're laughing—?"

"No, no, no!"

"Yes!" screamed Bruni, nodding at Kristina, "that, too—!"

And while they screamed louder, coupling Saturday with bed, Lucas shrugged, smiling, told the landlord the place would do, the man waited, smiling . . .

"Kristi," Lucas said deprecatively.

"We take it?" she asked, trying to master her laughter.

He nodded.

"Excuse me!" Suddenly she understood. She fumbled in her pocketbook. The landlord, still smiling, looked discreetly away.

The secret was almost too much to contain. He longed for someone in whom to confide, someone to talk to, talk to about everything, the world, the state of a man, of marriage, of women, of what to know, what was known, what to do, to receive envy, to bask, to be elated.

"What's wrong with you?" Alfred asked once, catching him staring into space.

"It's this—this anconeus business—"

"But you're studying physiology!" Alfred peered closer at the open book before Lucas.

"I know it! It's this damned electricity stuff! I'll never get it!"

"What!" Alfred looked at Lucas, startled.

"Oh, I'll get it, all right! Don't mind me! It's just—Alfred! Can I tell you something?"

"It's your business, understand. Only if what they say is right we're going to have a test Friday and—"

"I'll get it! Don't worry!"

"Is there anything I can help you with? I mean, sure, you know it better than I do, hell! You explained it to *me*! But maybe if you say aloud what's got you stumped, sometimes just saying it aloud will—"

"I got it! I got it, now!"

"Sure?"

"Absolutely!"

Alfred watched him. But Lucas was now reading steadily. The thought of the possible test released him, redirected him, now absorbed him completely. He read, he stored, grimly, lovingly, exultant,

". . . the resting heat production rate of frog nerve in oxygen at 20° C. is 4.14 times 10^{-3} cal. per gm. per min . . ."

Read it three times, happily, fiercely, committed it,

"When oxygen is replaced by nitrogen . . ."

"I'll tell you how it is," he said. "This is what it means. The nerve's got an oxygen reserve. See?"

"No."

"I'll show you . . ."

On the next day he passed Dr. Aarons in a corridor.

"Hello," he said filtering his voice of all expression. "Good afternoon, Doctor."

"What? Oh, hello there!" Dr. Aarons nodded absently, smiled amiably, walked on.

If you knew, Lucas thought, bursting, if you only knew. I'm safe! I'm safe from all of you!

Next day, when evening came, Lucas could bear it no longer. He must speak to Alfred, he must tell him, the past was pardoned, he looked at him fondly, he would ask him to be his best man!

"Alfred," he said, trying to restrain his voice, and Alfred looked slowly up from his book, "Alfred, I've got to tell you something!"

"What's up?"

"All right, now . . . Prepare yourself . . ."

Alfred looked at him patiently.

"I'm going to get married!"

Alfred eyed him blankly.

"That's right!"

"Married?" Alfred drew away.

"Tomorrow."

"But you can't—!"

"We're going across the line. To Elkham."

"Who's 'we'? What are you talking about, Luke? Start again!"

And Lucas, who had been refuging in syllables, in the grudged necessities of speech-answers, who had been breathlessly enjoying Alfred's consternation, wincing at it, grinning the while, savoring the burst gates, the relief, now anxiously, now faced the necessity of presenting Kristina as winningly as possible.

"You know her."

"Who?"

"Kristina." The word was out now.

"Who in the world is Kristina! Are you kidding me, Luke?"

"You know! Think!"

"I'm sorry. I don't know any Kristina."

"That girl in the operating room! My God! You were over to her house!"

"*That* girl! That's Kristina?"

"Certainly! The head operating-room nurse."

He looked at Alfred eagerly. Alfred tried to orient himself.

"You're crazy!"

Lucas winced. He continued to smile.

"Why?"

"Why, you can't, that's all!"

"Why do you say that?"

"Because you can't! I don't know what jam you've gotten yourself into—"

"There's no jam—"

"You mean that—that Swedish girl—?"

"That's the one." They looked at each other without smiling now. "I'll tell you what, Al. I was kind of hoping you'd be best man . . ."

"Me?"

Lucas lowered his head. Disappointment sickened him, his viscera coiled with it. Rejection and shame sagged his shoulders, he turned away.

"That's all right, Alfred," he said thickly. "I just thought I'd ask. Forget it."

"You've got your whole life ahead of you."

"That's all right."

"You can't get married now! Why do you have to get married so quick for? Why tomorrow?"

"We've been planning it for some time. Don't worry about it. It's all right."

"Have you any idea what you're letting yourself in for?"

"What do you think I'm letting myself in for? What's this terrible doom you seem to think is about to fall on me?"

"She's older than you! She's—why, she's a nurse, Luke! She'll always be a nurse. You'll be a doctor."

"Oh, come on, now, Al!"

Under his contemptuous look Alfred flushed.

"You think I'm a snob, don't you! Maybe I am. All right, say I am."

"Look, Al, I don't need any lecture—and no matter what you're thinking of saying you'd better keep it to yourself."

"I don't know what you've done—I don't know what's happened—all I know is you can't get married. We've had our differences. But this is something else. Forget the fact that she's on a lower social level. Forget that she can't speak a simple sentence, that there's not one thing in common between you, that year after year the difference is going to widen, that you're doing something on the spur of the moment, throwing yourself away—"

"I know what you're going to say—"

"You haven't got a dime. You've got all you can handle, right now! You don't know where your next month's food or rent is coming from! You only want one thing in the world, really, and that's to become a doctor! And you don't even know whether you can do that! And you're taking on a wife! Have you gone crazy? Are you nuts, or what?"

"Look, Alfred! Just skip it, will you? Don't start playing my guardian all of a sudden. Just skip it. Don't say any more."

But Alfred was staring at him. There was sudden comprehension in his eyes.

"You're marrying her for her money!"

"I said skip it, Alfred!"

"That's what you're up to! You couldn't get dough any other way! And she's probably got money saved up! And she gets a regular salary!" His voice hushed, awed. "You'd do that! You'd actually marry that—that—"

"It's none of your business! Just remember that!" He rose. "You're full of help, now, aren't you! Now you're full of help. All ready to save your poor roommate from a terrible mistake!"

"That's what it is, isn't it! That's what you're doing!"

"You know right from wrong all of a sudden and let's be suave, let's be men of the world, we'll laugh at all of this someday, put him straight, manage him easy—"

"It's true! Isn't it!"

"Good old Al! But you weren't so calm and collected when I came to you desperate for just enough to keep going and you knew what it meant to me—"

"I told you how I felt about money—"

"Sure! You weren't calm and collected then! No sir, I touched you right where you lived, didn't I! *Money!* It means that much to you, doesn't it! You and the rest! Money's different! It's better than human beings. It's metal and it's paper and you've got more than you'll ever spend as long as you live and you could have helped me and never felt it as much as a paper clip—"

"Nasty money, isn't it! Look who's marrying for it—"

"You dirty bastard—"

"I don't have to take that—"

"You know why I'm doing this! You know whether I'm marrying for money or not! You know—nobody better—"

"Just watch your mouth. I know you're in a jam. But *this* girl—all I'm trying to show you is—"

"They don't marry for money your side of the tracks, eh? And you're just trying to help me! I'm about to marry a Swede! God forbid, eh, Al? The one human being who'll help me!"

"Feel better?"

"You're goddamned right I feel better!"

"Forget me—"

"I can't get over it! Not one son-of-a-bitch will raise a finger to help me and this girl comes along and all of a sudden everybody's full of pious noises! All of a sudden everybody knows right from wrong!"

"Will you wait?"

"Don't bother—"

"Somebody's got to tell you—"

"Doesn't cost you a dime, does it?"

"She's a bohunk! She's a dumb Swede that's got her claws hooked onto you and my mother wouldn't hire her as a maid—"

"You no-good son-of-a-bitch!"

"But if you want to throw yourself away on a servant—"

"You're a whore! You and your whole family! You do what you do for money—"

"At least my father's not bankrupt—"

"You and your father can kiss my ass—"

"Remind me of that next time you come begging for some of his money!"

"You're cheap, Al. You've got a price. I'll take Kristina to the lot of you—"

"You have her! You can take your two-bit Swede and pimp your head off—"

Lucas knocked him down. Swiftly he seized a lamp and threw himself on Alfred smashing at him with the lamp base. They rolled about the floor, floundering, kicking, slamming their fists at each other, Lucas' straining fingers found Alfred's throat, exultantly he began to strangle him. He had known no such physical joy since he was born. Suddenly aware, suddenly frightened, Alfred wrestled desperately, cleared his body an instant, raised his knee, shot it upward, slammed it into Lucas' abdomen. Stunned, Lucas relaxed his grip. Alfred rolled sidewise. Quickly he pulled himself erect, stood warily, panting.

"I'll kill you," Lucas promised between heaves. "I'm going to kill you!"

"You're going to get the hell out of here! Right now! Tonight!"

"I'll go when I please. But I'm going to kill you first! You and all you've ever meant to me! The whole world of people like you!"

He struggled to his feet and sat on the edge of his bed, hunched over, fighting for breath, waiting.

Alfred watched him, saying nothing, breathing hard. He picked up the lamp, put it on the desk, picked up the scattered books.

He studied Lucas' bent head.

"I put it wrong," he said rustily. "I'm not begging your pardon. I don't like you any more. But I said it wrong. I'm sorry about that."

"You stay with your kind—you and your kids' games! Just stay away from me. Just keep to yourself! Because if you ever say one more word about her—about the one human who's making this possible—"

He rose and peered at Alfred, murder again in his eyes, the insanity of the cornered.

Alfred backed away.

"That's the way you want it—"

"That's the way I want it!"

"I've said all I'm going to say."

"You'd better."

"We're stuck through this course. Alphabetically, we're stuck together. That's something we can't change. We're stuck together in classrooms, anyway, for at least four years. You've paid your rent on the room and we're stuck here too. I could move out—"

"Don't worry, I'm not going to be here long!"

"That's right, isn't it. You'll be moving."

"Monday."

"Well, I'll go it alone . . . I'm sorry this had to happen . . ."

"So am I."

"You hear what I'm trying to tell you? I'm sorry it happened."

Lucas went to the mirror and examined his cut face. Suddenly it was as if he was alone in the room. He had a desire to seek Kristina, to be alone with her. For Alfred he felt only a dull hate, a hate uncovered, but their potentials were reversed now, he was dominant, the authority, the value of Alfred was gone, he was a familiar stranger, coped with and past. There was no longer peril here. There was no longer anxiety. He felt Alfred waiting for him, waiting for the next word. He felt relief. He felt the initiative.

He turned from the mirror, averting his eyes, walked to the desk, sat down, and picked up a book.

"That's the way it goes, I guess," he said. Determinedly he began to read, read the first sentence again and again, finally found it, read on, read the second.

Alfred waited a moment. Then, seeing there was no more, he sat down, looked up once at Lucas, then gave up, pulled a book toward him, began to study.

* CHAPTER 21

They were married in Elkham, next day, over the border, in the next state. There was a great rush to be there before the license bureau closed and Lucas cut his last class and with Kristina, heavily powdered, stiff, even her shoes new, with Bruni who was her bridesmaid, with Oley, her husband, who would give the bride away and act as best man, they arrived at the Elkham City Hall with only minutes to spare.

Lucas was wholly surrendered to the adventure. This was a game of the world about him, and he enjoyed its novelty, enjoyed himself as chief actor, enjoyed the garments of estate, maturity, and role, was fascinated by these things and puffed up by them. Of Kristina and her nearness he was ponderously conscious, the bride symbol, waiting the rites. The women shifted nervously, spoke in high-pitched voices, babbled, shrieked, rebuked themselves to prim gravity, broke anew into laughter that drew the eyes of their fellow passengers. Oley grinned at Lucas and his eyes apologized for them. Lucas did not care. Determinedly, he was one of them.

As they neared Elkham the women became grave and decorous again.

"It's a shame—your mother at least—" Kristina said.

"Yes," said Lucas, frowning obediently, "Mother would have loved this."

"She look like you?" Bruni asked respectfully.

"She look yoost like him," Kristina answered promptly.

Oley clucked his tongue in the noise humans make when grief is new. Lucas tried to accept it becomingly. Uncomfortably he explored himself for an appropriate emotion.

Kristina was staring at him.

"Don't look so bad," she said.

Lucas fingered the bruises on his cheek, a cut beside one eye.

"They think *you* did it! They think you beat him up already!" Bruni laughed helplessly.

"A bad thing—a fall!" Oley clucked again.

"I ought to have known better! I know those stairs! I know every inch of them!" Lucas protested.

"If I didn't know better I would say you been fighting," Kristina marvelled.

"You could say you were fighting for Kris," Bruni giggled. "You could say you were protecting her—" She hit Kristina violently in the side with her elbow. "You need protection, eh, Kris? Tonight I bet you need protection!"

"Bruni!"

"You never have to fight for Swedish girls." Oley nodded sagely, passing on momentous advice. "They take care of themselves . . ."

"Would you fight for me, Lukey?" Kristina asked, prodding his embarrassment, "tell me, Lukey! You fight for me someday?"

"I might," he said airily. "You never can tell."

When the train stopped they rushed straight for the license bureau.

But outside, for a moment, on the threshold of the office, standing in the corridor, halting a moment, letting Oley and Bruni through first,

"Are you all right, Luke?" She asked it in a low voice, urgent.

"Sure," he said gruffly, and his heart swelled, offering him freedom even at the last, waiting his word.

"Luke?"

"I love you, Kristina!" he whispered fiercely. Her face softened, her eyes lowered submissively, he had a sudden presentiment that she knew him, knew everything, consented, accepted what there was.

"Come on!" he said, mock-fiercely, and drew her into the room up to the long counter where the clerk waited, Bruni and Oley grinning at them. They walked to the counter, to the waiting forms, he reached for a pen, dipped it, they gathered about him, pressing on him, to watch.

He wrote the date. He wrote his name. Place of birth. . . . Date of birth. . . . Mother's name. . . . Father's name. . . . He came to the bride's name. He stopped. His stomach lumped. The name of the bride. He could not move. He dared not raise his eyes.

"What's the matter?" Bruni cried suddenly. They stirred beside him.

"Kristi!" he begged.

"What, dear? What's the matter?"

He licked dry lips.

"Your name," he managed, not remembering, thick with embarrassment.

"Here!" she said, relieved, she shouldered him aside, took up the pen, "here, let me—!"

"Kristina! You know how to spell *that*! And then H and E and D, V and I and G—S-E-N!" she scrawled triumphantly.

Hedvigsen! Kristina Hedvigsen, he must have known it once, all this Kristina, Kristina all the time—

"Only a Svede can spell Svede names!" Oley assured him portentously.

It was done.

The form was filled. The arms were raised. The oath taken. The fee paid.

"I pay it," said Oley, pushing them aside. "This is my pleasure!" he announced formally.

"I keep the paper," Kristina folded the license carefully, the ink still damp, held it in her hand.

They rushed out into the streets of Elkham to find a man to marry them.

There was no lack of these. In this town there were more marriers than merchants, the chief wealth and industry rising from laws permitting quick and uncomplicated unions of humans. On almost any street in Elkham, as they soon found, there were from two to a dozen signs advertising justices of the peace or ministers prepared for a small fee to recite the ritual of union according to the whim or belief of the union seekers.

They wandered among these signs hilariously for a time, wealthy with choice. Kristina watched Lucas for a sign of preference. When Lucas at length began to look questioningly at her she knew the time had come to end the sightseeing.

"Well, come on," she said, "I guess we get it over."

They stopped on the sidewalk and in the nearest houses curtains drew unobtrusively back and watchers waited. Lucas, Bruni, and Oley looked to Kristina.

"Does it matter to you, Luke?" she asked diffidently.

"What do you mean? Matter which one? No, I don't care."

"You got some church, eh?"

"I was raised Methodist Episcopal. You pick the one you want."

"You don't care?"

"Not a bit," he said loudly.

Kristina turned uncertainly to Bruni.

"Well, then I guess—I guess Lutheran, eh?"

"Sure! Lutheran!" Bruni said stoutly.

They found a Lutheran minister. The service was brief. They were married in less time than it had taken to obtain a license. The words were spoken, the ritual completed as Lucas was trying vainly to feel it all, all that should be felt, this high moment, as Kristina sought to draw it out, to dwell in the process of change a while longer.

The minister smiled at them and put his book down, watching them. They stirred uneasily, they realized the rite was ended. They waited, there was nothing more. They turned to Bruni and Oley.

"Kiss her!" cried Bruni. And as Lucas awkwardly leaned to Kristina and she blushed and obediently leaned to him, *"Lycka Till!"* shouted Oley, "Good luck!"

So they began, there was nothing more, really, when they went over it in their minds later, to recapture it, to relive it, to remember entirely, to recall details overlooked, insisting that there must have been more, there must have been, this could not have been all, but it was all, there was nothing more.

No trumpets blew. In their persons there was no change. They tested and felt no closer to each other. They had the legal and the religious assurance of union, all that society could give them it had given, and this was the assurance that their union was socially perfect.

They spent their first night in their recently rented apartment. And Lucas, still gripping the fact of marriage, recalling the rite, the formula, the setting, hearing the clerk again, watching Kristina fold the license, climbing the steps of the minister's house, reliving the tension, the impending, the about-to-be, stubbornly holding it, waiting for more, began at last to see that the great, the dreaded, the waited, the pondered, the infinite moment had passed, and that like crossing a longitude, a date line, a boundary, nothing had perceptibly changed. Magic had been invoked. Rite had been carefully articulated. Heaven had been supplicated. Now they were married. Now he was married. Now the moment and the humans passed as two streams merging and where they had merged there was no sign, there was only the evidence of slowly onward passing, of time.

It had grown dark, Bruni and Oley had gone shouting homeward. He was alone with Kristina. They were married. And he was alone with her.

"You kind of quiet," she said shyly.

He sat down near the window, holding this moment, seeking a new self in it.

"It's funny," he brooded. "Do you feel married, Kris?" He waved an arm helplessly.

She considered this, he was her man and he wanted something and she tried to imagine what he wanted so that she could give it to him.

"How did you think you'd feel?" she smiled, cautiously.

He looked up quickly.

"Do you feel married?"

"Sure, I feel married!"

She began to bustle about the apartment, opening drawers, smoothing clothing already smooth, rearranging toilet articles. He watched her, envying, trying to feel what she felt.

"What are you thinking about?"

"I'm thinking, well, now it's done. I'm trying to feel what it feels like."

"Now it's done," she echoed, testing this, continuing to arrange their clothing, absently making near-surgical supply bundles of them. "Yes . . . For a man this comes after marriage. For a woman it comes before."

"Before?"

"That's the difference. When a woman decides, when she thinks if he asks her she'll say all right, when she thinks that, then it's over, then she's married, it's done, all the rest is just a celebration, parties, laughing, whatever."

"Then you knew long before, didn't you? That we were going to be married?" He smiled, disbelieving.

"Maybe."

"Oh, come on, now, Kris!"

"I don't know . . . I think so. What are we talking about? Is everything all right?"

"No, no! It's all right, Kris. I was just trying to feel how it was, it was all over so quickly, I ought to feel different, changed—"

"You think too much. Wait a while."

"Anyway, we're married!" He rose, excited suddenly by the realization, by the implications that followed, he was alone in this room, with this woman. "I'm tired," he said, stretching elaborately.

"Yes," said Kristina without looking up, without looking at him, and she stopped immediately fussing with the clothes, she brushed past him to the window and drew the shade down, he looked past her and saw that she had put his pajamas, folded carefully, on the bed. Her head lowered she took up her nightgown and walked to the bathroom. The door closed behind her.

Lucas undressed rapidly, racing to get into his pajamas before she came out. He was in bed in a twinkling. And there he lay, waiting for her. After a long time she came out. She looked quite different. She was smaller, curiously fragile. She was in her nightgown. She got quickly into bed. They averted their eyes from each other, each overwhelmed by this novelty, neither moving.

"Well," he said to the waiting room, "well, we're married."

She turned, awkwardly she threw an arm over him, put her face in his neck.

"Hello, Lukey," she breathed in his ear.

And instantly he felt the warmth of her body, he was swallowed up, she lay passive, breathing fast, waiting. His hands found her, he caressed her exultantly, she hesitated, resisting, then remembering, no longer resisting, she cried out once, then she was still.

Later, spent, as she nestled softly against him, exploring, sifting, seeking the essence of union.

"Did you . . . ?" he asked suddenly.

"What?" she parried.

"You know . . ."

"Sure!"

"I mean—did you have fun?"

"Sure!"

"It was wonderful, wasn't it!"

"Shhhh . . ."

"What's it like? For a girl?"

"Like for you!" She moved restlessly.

"Tell me, Kris!"

"I don't know . . ."

"Come on!"

"I don't know how to tell you—it feels all nice, and—and—"

"Did I hurt you?" he asked anxiously.

"No," she lied. "Hey! I'm cold!" For he had pulled the covers down.

"I want to see you!" She huddled, stiffening against his eyes, grudging, and then abruptly his eyes were like a feeling on her, she breathed faster watching him, feeling the shamelessness, feeling him look, her eyes were half closed, her mouth was open, she felt his body.

And a moment later,

"Now!" she cried out.

He lay thereafter, thinking, brooding. She was his, now. This was what it would be like. Had he done something wrong? Had he failed? He winced, sensing half-surrender, ministration. Forever? Forever and ever? He moved his head to look at her. She was nearly asleep.

"Did you then, Kris . . . ?" he murmured.

"Shhhh . . . Go sleep . . ." And she turned and threw her arm around him. He lay still, feeling the weight of her arm. After a while, when she began to breathe evenly, he drew reluctantly away. He turned on his side. He slept to himself.

In the morning they dressed, and for both it was an adventure, it was elating to dress with a man, with a woman, it was a newness to be savored and they went out smiling, the day was sunny, the air was crisp on their cheeks.

"Like Sunday!" Kristina exclaimed.

"It *is* Sunday!" he cried, laughing at her.

"Say! Maybe we go to church, hey?"

"What for? On a nice day like this?"

"Lukey!"

"Do you always go to church, Sunday?"

She looked up at him guiltily, bashfully.

"We just married, Lukey . . ."

"You! A girl that's seen as many human beings opened as you have!"

"What's that got to do with it! You believe in God, don't you, Lukey?"

"Sure, I believe in God! Kristina, I'm going to ask you something. Don't be hurt, now. But I wish you'd stop calling me Lukey!"

"I'm sorry—"

"It's nothing. I don't know why. I just don't like it."

"What do they call you? Your mama and papa—what do the boys call you?"

"Just Luke."

"Nothing else?"

"That's all. It's just something—just the sound of the other—"

"Maybe I call you Mister. That's what my mother called my father."

"Always?"

"Always. And he called her Missus."

He laughed.

"All right, Missus!" he mocked. "No, I believe in God, all right—"

She looked at him intently and saw this was so. She was reassured. Inside, this made her at peace and serene and already much, much more married.

"We don't have to go to church."

"I'll go if you want to. If you really want to."

"We don't have to. I'm happy yoost like this." She hugged his arm hard. Her eyes were fierce with delight. "I'm hungry!"

And promptly Lucas' stomach clamored. They walked eagerly toward town. In the clear air the sound of church bells, that unlooked-for music, startled them. They laughed, delighted.

"It's a good thing my mother didn't hear you say church," he chuckled.

"She was against church, Luke?"

"She sure was! Oh, she was religious, all right! She believed in God and all! But she thought services were empty forms, some kind of hypocrisy—she could explain it all to you—"

"Not mine! Mine went to church every Sunday, rain or shine, storm, snow, no matter what! Once they went, they took me, too, I was little girl, and it was such a blizzard! And they got there, they were all alone, there was nobody in the church, not even the minister!"

"What did they do?"

"Oh, they yoost sat there. By and by the minister came, by and by a couple more." She sighed. "They never missed. Never!"

"I don't do that," she ventured, noting his silence.

"I think God's there if you need Him," he said hesitantly.

"There's a restaurant!" she cried, to end it. "I'm dying!"

They ate hugely, they watched each other select, they found in what ways they were different there and in what ways the same, they watched each other eat. And after, they walked. And when they were tired they sat in the park a while and Kristina lifted a foot and massaged it, grimacing, and he watched like a husband, indulgently.

"You're on them all day," he nodded.

"It's the worst of it," she confided. "It's a good job—but it's the worst of it!"

"Which is the worst of them all?"

"Thoracoplasty—anything on the chest—!"

"How about brain?"

"Ah, that we don't see much. Once in a long, long while. That's bad, too. Takes forever. But the chest . . . !"

"You've got them all figured out by how hard it is on the feet."

"After a while you get used to them," she said uncertainly, defensively.

"One thing puzzles me. I always wanted to ask it. Here you are, you like Medicine, you're the head operating-room nurse—tell me! Why haven't you ever tried to go farther?"

"What else?"

"Well, you could study, you know! You could try to become a doctor! With your background—with what you already know—"

"I've got no head to study—"

"You've got money—you could do it little by little—it's a funny damned thing! The people with money never seem to want to do anything—"

"They already done it. That's how they got the money."

"Anything worth while. Anything that counts. And the people who *want* to do something never have the money."

"Because people who want money make it and then there's not enough to go round."

"Being around it so much—haven't you ever wanted to go on?"

"You go on for me, Luke."

"But you don't want to go on? You don't want to? For yourself?"

"You think everybody's like you? I like my job, I do my job, that's all I want."

"But why weren't you a clerk, then? Any of a thousand things?"

"You mean why did I go for a nurse?"

"Why did you pick Medicine? It must have pulled you somehow. Why did you pick it?"

"You know what it is like in Minnesota? You been there? No? Well, it's a good place but not for a girl. Maybe for a wife. Not many people, the farms far apart. And there is nothing but farmers. When you talk you talk always the same thing, something about the farm. Well, that's all right, and to tell the truth I didn't mind it so much, and then one day a girl two farms away comes home in white uniform, white cap, white cape. Comes home from graduating. Oh! That cape! I'll never forget it!

From that time on nothing will do. I must be a nurse. And finally one day my father says all right, he gives me some money—" She shrugged.

"And that's all? You saw a pretty cape."

"That's it. Oh, I'm not sorry—"

"And once you saw that cape—"

"That's it."

"I like to know what pulls people on. I like to know what makes them tick. What they want, where they're going."

"Maybe you want too much from people—"

"I don't want *anything* from them!"

"I mean you give them too much, you think they've got more than they have. You think everybody's like you?"

"Everybody's got *some*thing that's pulling them!"

"Ahh, I don't know, I don't know—*you,* maybe. You got it so strong you think everybody's got it."

"No," he said automatically. "No, you're wrong—"

"When I first met you I thought I never saw such a lonely boy. So lonely. So wrapped up—"

"I'm not lonely—!"

"Doesn't know other people live—the world goes on around him and he goes his own way. And he's so lonely. And he doesn't know why."

"That's how it seems to you?" He smiled tolerantly. But he was confused, a terror that was always there rose grinning for a moment before he could thrust it back.

"Yes," she said gently, "that's how it seems. You don't know whether is spring, autumn, or summer. All you know is what you want. All you see is what you need. Everybody is a little lonely. It is not new to be homesick. But you are homesick for where you are."

"Sometimes I don't understand, Kris. It's true. Sometimes I just don't understand. I want to be like other people, I want to *want* to be with them, to be of them—"

"Yes," Kristina nodded sagely. "That I know. Why should you try, after all? You're the way you are, we'll work it out together, you and me. You got something they haven't got. You got what you got. Not everybody's got that. You can't have everything."

"It's got me. Do you know that, Kris? That's what the trouble is. That's all I think about. That's all I *can* think about!"

"Yes," she said gravely, "it's got you. Now it's got me, too."

"There it is, it's the greatest thing a human can know. It's the best knowledge there is, it's all by itself. As long as I can remember I've known that."

"I know . . . even when you were a little boy . . ."

"That's right!" He looked at her, startled, pleased.

"And how about doctors?"

"That's what I want to be, Kris. All the doctors I've ever seen."

Her smile faded.

"You're going to be the best of them all!" she cried. "Wait until they see *you,* Luke! Just wait! Tell me, Luke: has he asked you anything? The bursar? Don't you have to—"

"I wish you didn't have to help me, Kris. I wish I could do this myself —I feel rotten—nothing can make me feel good about it!"

"What you think! You married a poor girl? A husband's got a right to a dowry! What kind of a wife doesn't help her husband! What you think I am?"

"You're wonderful, Kris," he said uncomfortably.

"How much you need? Don't tell me! I know how much you need! You need six hundred fifty-four dollars, eighty-one cents! You want it now?"

"You've got it? You've got that much?"

"I got more, even! I get it for you first thing Monday. We get it tonight. You pay him Monday!"

"All of it," he said, awed.

"All of it! Then you don't have to worry! We give them every penny!"

"Oh, Kris! Oh, my God, Kris!"

"You see what it's like to have a wife? Now you're not alone any more, eh? Now you know I'm with you!"

Now peace filled him. It was perhaps the first peace he had ever known. In the living, in the world in which he moved, a stranger even to himself, lonely not knowing himself, lonely not knowing others, moving alone, and thinking alone, peering anxiously at the people around him as through the windows of houses and himself outside, this woman had come to his portion, this fellow human, this Kristina who was not alien, who was as others were, and who knew him, and wanted him, and was even proud of him, and who was unalterably his, married a thousand years in this one day.

And she had brought him what he needed, this great thing, this money which he must have, naked of it, hopeless for it, a stranger to it except through fear. And now life was easy, it was all over, the nightmare was gone, he was safe, he looked at her, yearning to give her what he felt, this greatness, this gratitude.

This is my wife! he cried to himself, swelling, look at her! She knows me! She knows my innerness, and I'm not afraid. See her! That nurse's walk. If a probationer came along how her face would become serious with respect, Good afternoon, Miss Hedvigsen, and she would nod her head pleasantly, just so. And the woman part of her, the body, the blond hair, the blue eyes, the pretty Swedish face, the trim figure, ah, but I know what those swellings are where the dress, the material, peaks, those are breasts, my breasts. We will be together, apart, away from everyone. And he winced, thinking of Alfred—let them think what they want. We will keep to ourselves. Away from them. Away from them all. Safe.

The day was bright. He looked at it with joy. He noticed things he had never seen before.

For he was safe, now. It was safe to look.

They returned to the furnished rooms late in the afternoon. Unfamiliar with each other, with their new roles, a little shy, they walked homeward.

"I'm way behind," Lucas fretted. "Two whole days."

"Tonight you can study."

"No, I've lost it. I'll have to get it from the others. The gist of it, anyway. There's no time to memorize it all."

But when they came into their own rooms again it was strange and exciting to both of them how quickly this place had become home. They looked about them with satisfaction, they smiled at each other broadly, swelling at what they possessed. I have a man of my own. Kristina grinned and her bosom raised, this is our place, I'm sorry for the girls at the nurses' quarters, all girls, no man to look out for, no place to be a wife. And Lucas fondly smiled as he picked up a lanky, overdressed doll figure Kristina had brought from her former room, the only thing really she had brought except her clothes and the only other home possessions she had accumulated.

"This looks like a whore," he said, amazed. "Look at the painted cheeks, this hair–"

"That's real hair!" Kristina protested.

She took the doll from Lucas, smoothed its dress, patted it fondly, propped it against the mirror on the oak bureau.

"I got to write home," she said proudly. "I got lovely stuff there from my mother! We fix this place up, eh? Don't you got anything you can bring?"

"I don't know." The memory of the house sobered him. "Last time I was there the door was locked."

"Your mother's picture, anyhow. You want I should come with you?"

"No, no! Maybe we'll write. I don't want to go back. Not now. Maybe later."

"It's a nice place." He leaned against the bureau admiring the sad wallpaper, the thin carpet, the five framed chromos, the bed, the bureau, the two chairs, the table.

"It's got a good kitchen," she said sagely. They walked eagerly into the next room. "We save a lot of money here."

He opened a drawer and his fingers played curiously and possessively among the knives and forks, the six knives, the six forks, the apple corer, the can opener, the bread knife, the strainer.

"Sure got a lot of stuff here."

"Furnished so-so. I get lots more." But she beamed proudly.

"Our place!" He looked about him, grinning.

She walked to him and took his arm, viewing it with him, standing at his side.

"We pretty lucky," she said soberly.

In almost any other academic course the sudden marriage of a classmate would have been a week-long diversion, an occasion for chattering, examination, speculation, gaping observation. And for weeks afterward Lucas would have been notable, for all his academic years he would have been the fellow who married in the first semester of his freshman year. Kristina's fellow nurses buzzed about the happening for a week, the routine, the progress of hospital work buried the sudden marriage and all that could be discussed about it as inexorably as death is forgotten in a hospital, for in a week in a hospital there are many deaths and many recoveries and many births and many sudden emergencies to contend for attention with the infrequent breaks in living pattern of those who, ministering, absorb each hour's pressing problems. Among the members of his class Lucas was pointed out for a single day. In that day many students he did not know took a few minutes to wish him well and under cover of the perfunctory and customary noises of well-wishing prescribed for this happening hopefully listened for some new gift, some detail which would add to the bizarre fact that he had married. And when there was none they returned to routine without complaint and without further interest.

His instructors severely made no mention of it with the exception of Professor Fletcher, who observed during an anatomy lecture that he understood one of his students had progressed rather further in blunt dissection than he had expected at this time. This information was gratefully received by the students after he had paused long enough to allow them to dissect it, and their gratitude was further augmented by the fact that seven members of the class were discovered automatically taking his words down in their anatomy notes, verbatim, as matter for study.

"What sort of a chap is this?" Professor Fletcher asked Dr. Aarons at luncheon. "I understand he's one of your protégés."

"Oh, not exactly a protégé," Dr. Aarons protested. "He came to me for advice once or twice and during his pre-med I used him as laboratory janitor. I rather wish he'd come to me for this."

"Oh, I don't know what difference it makes, really. Have we an official attitude toward it?"

"No, no, no! I do think he has enough to worry about without—"

'She's a nurse, after all. She knows what the score is. I dare say she'll help."

"We have a lot of nurses. I'm rather surprised to see him pick this one."

"That means you regarded him rather more than most."

"I'm not altogether sure whether it's a boyish dream, a fixation on an ideal, like wanting to be a fireman or a cowboy, carried on past puberty, or whether he's that very rare thing, that solecism, an organism born with a single purpose, a single avenue of organic expression."

"I think you could say that of any of them. Nobody studies Medicine unless they want to. He seems a nice enough chap, quiet, studies well, seems to be keeping up. I should say," he said, surprised, "he's keeping up rather better than most."

"Do you find him outstanding?"

"No, I think he might be if he didn't try so hard to understand all he studies. He wastes too much time on that. None of them know—you can't teach them—that it's a waste of time, right now, trying to understand everything. Simply to possess it is enough, one day understanding dawns and then they have it. No, if he spent all his time just possessing, memorizing, getting it any way he could so that he'd have it examination time why then—"

He shrugged.

"He's an odd fish." Dr. Aarons nodded. "His mother's dead, his father was against his studying Medicine, went bankrupt a few weeks ago and skipped out, the boy hasn't any money, he came to me to borrow some to go on with—"

"And now he gets married!"

"And he married a nurse. . . ."

"Proper conduct for any young medical man. That's been done before."

"And for the same reason. Not quite—but the same reason, basically the same."

"Well, he's settled now. He didn't flounder, he didn't wander off to try something else, he knew what he wanted, evidently, and he did what apparently had to be done. Quite a ruthless character, your young man."

"Or maybe driven. I don't think he reasons quite so cold-bloodedly. Humans are the sum of their drives. Some of these drives are basic. Some are artificial, responses to culture, environment, or history."

"And you don't really know whether his is basic or artificial. And if it's basic, whether Medicine is basically a drive of his—"

"Or something he's made into a drive. And in the final analysis that's our basis of judging conduct, isn't it. If it's a basic drive, and it's opposed, the human is going to survive at any price and there aren't any ethics and there aren't any laws. And we understand, and understanding of course is pardon."

"Well, in any case, you can't help him and I can't help him. It's nice to have something happen out of the ordinary, though, isn't it. Something to talk about. Something to break this numbered page, on a numbered day, numbered faces, numbered hours, year after year . . ."

And he rose from luncheon, walked down the corridor toward his classroom, his one o'clock classroom, and on the way, spying an anxious student walking to class, oblivious, desperately cramming from a book, he went to him, took the book from him, saying, "What have you got there?" and before the student could close his mouth to answer began ripping pages out of the book, saying severely, "You don't want to read that! That's crap! He's all wrong there!" and passed on, the pages fluttering to the floor behind him.

"A fifteen-dollar book!" the student murmured, awed, to the group that quickly and anxiously collected about him. And they all trooped to class, adoring Professor Fletcher, bound to know what *should* have been written on those ripped pages.

I have all I can do to teach pathology, Dr. Aarons frowned. I've helped him. I've done what I could. I happened to take a fancy. I wonder what you'd have done, Fletcher—if he'd come to you—if he was a Jewish boy! Hah! You don't have to tell me! I know where I am. I know how I got here. Well, and it's not forever. And he went back to himself, lonely and a little angry on this island. And that evening he thought again that if he wanted he could always go to Vienna, and in any case he owed it to himself. And right up to the day of his death he might go, that was his story, that was freedom, that was tomorrow.

Miss Samuels, the probationer, saw her first.

"She's coming!" She ran into the main operating theater, her blue uniform belling about her.

The instrument nurse, the first dirty surgical, the two assistants crowded to the operating-room entrance.

Kristina, turbaned and ready for the day, grinned broadly.

"Miss Hedvigsen!" gasped Miss O'Neill, first dirty surgical, "we just heard!"

Miss Moore and Mrs. Brady, the two assistants, smiled, waited. Mrs. Ames, instrument nurse, put her hands on her hips.

"Well! Why didn't you tell us!"

"Nothing to tell you."

"Oh, listen to her! 'Nothing to tell you.' Never saying a word. What do we call you now?"

"Just Miss Hedvigsen," said Kristina serenely. She began to scrub.

"Isn't it wonderful?" sighed Miss Samuels.

"Do we know him?" asked Miss Moore.

"His name is Marsh," said Kristina. "Lucas Marsh. He's a medical student. I guess you saw him."

"When?"

"What does he look like"

"How did it happen?"

"All right," Kristina smiled. "What's first this morning, Miss Moore?"

"Ovariotomy—then amputation of the cervix—"

"Are we ready?"

The first and second dirty surgicals dashed off.

"Ready, Miss Hedvigsen," said Mrs. Ames.

"Get the extra-size retractors for Dr. Paine, get plenty of Allises, in case they want it, get that new kit for Dr. Romberg—"

"Yes, Miss Hedvigsen—"

The first intern came in, a second followed almost immediately. They began silently to scrub. Kristina, scrubbed, ready, walked slowly through her domain, took up her station.

"Lunch," she said briefly through her mask. "Plenty time to talk at lunch . . ."

"Yes, Miss Hedvigsen."

"Put that bucket farther under the table—"

The operating-room crew fell silent. The first doctor had arrived.

But in the laboratory words floundered in the debris of dismay and in this debris they saw the shards of broken faith and half-shaped designs now gone for nothing, and shock and horror and protest and hurt dried their mouths and moistened their eyes and made a death for them, a sigh, a headshake and a lost sheep's death.

"But if he'd come to us . . . !"

"If he'd *told* us, at least . . . !"

"If he'd just given us a chance . . ."

"We'd have found *some* way—we could have done *some*thing—"

"Not even to say a word—"

"If we hadn't helped him it'd be one thing—"

"Just for a handful of silver he left us . . ."

"Just for a ribbon to wear in his coat."

"Well, one thing, we'll have to have them over—"

"We'll wait for *them!* Let *him* make the first move!"

"Luke! Our Luke! I—I just can't get over it!"

"I never will. . . ."

And his classmates said,

"Hear you got married, Buster?"

"That's right!"

"That's what we heard. Well, what do you know!"

"The head operating-room nurse, at that!"

"Kind of sudden, wasn't it?"

"How the hell do you get time! Say, what did you do about the mechanism of referred pain? What did you get on that?"

"I just memorized it—"

"So did I! I met a sophomore yesterday said it didn't matter a goddam whether you understand it or not just so you could answer it exam time—"

"A lot of this stuff—"

"Hey! Didja hear what Fletcher did? Did you see that apparatus with string and wax and the skeleton—"

"Here he comes!"

"Yeah, well good luck, fella—"

"Yeah, good luck—"

In a week Lucas and Alfred addressed each other with restraint. In two weeks, irreconcilable, they had bridged the past dividing them and they sat together and studied together in classrooms, neither more nor less than they were before, now knowing it; and in a month Lucas had begun to go to Alfred's room to study there with Alfred and another student who now slept in Lucas' bed.

Besides Professor Fletcher there were Professor Rautner and Professor Willie, these three in anatomy. Where Fletcher was brilliant, Professor Rautner was precise, was indefatigable, was purest science. He was a perfectionist. What he knew he recited diffidently and remotely, thinking aloud, and they made their notes hastily and silent. Their awe of him began the day he launched a lecture on the pharynx. The class moved restlessly. There were murmurs at last and Professor Rautner paused, astonished.

"It's not the pharynx—it's the eye, today!" cried Alfred.

And Professor Rautner, who had been lecturing without notes, taking them ever deeper into details of anatomy not in their textbooks, stared at them unbelievingly, then rushed into the hallway to the bulletin board, sure enough today's lecture was on the eye, they had filed out behind him silently, he looked at them open-mouthed, he shook his head, dropped his eyes, walked quickly back into the classroom, followed by the class, and, as the last man reached his seat, began immediately to lecture without notes or text upon the eye, taking them even deeper than he had with the pharynx.

They were very proud of Professor Rautner, they were very proud of Professor Fletcher, when they cried admiringly of these men and others Lucas dropped his eyes modestly as if he, too, were being praised, so proud he was of them all, so reverent, so worshipful.

But in this year there was also Professor Willie who drew nasal septums laterally, fat Professor Willie who sometimes came to class in suspenders, shirtless, who brooded at them, picking his nose, who must, Lucas was very sure in the beginning, be gifted rarely in some undisclosed stratum, who would one day startle them all.

He and Alfred were working on a fat cadaver one day trying to find in the gross, lumpish buttocks the fine, white posterior gluteal nerve. They were working nervously and carefully. In their textbook, plainly printed, consulted by both that morning, burned the sentence, *"The careless dissector will soon reveal himself by cutting the posterior gluteal nerve."* They explored slowly. Finally they paused, helpless, defeated.

"What's the matter?"

They turned apprehensively. Professor Willie stood there, rolling a toothpick in his mouth.

"We're having a little trouble, sir," Lucas said humbly.

"Can't find it, eh? Gimme that!" He snatched Lucas' scalpel. He bent over the cadaver and slashed through the fat buttock. He deepened the slash. Then he slashed again. He dropped the scalpel, fumbled in the gashes, spread them to show the ends of the white nerve, cut through. "There it is!" he shrugged, sucked his teeth reflectively and walked away.

Lucas avoided Alfred's eyes.

He looked at Professor Willie unwillingly, at this stranger in this cosmos, this freak, despicable and alien.

And thus he came in time to regard Professor Wallace, whose histology lectures were finally, one had to admit, worthless. And thus he looked at Professor Dietrick, that pompous man, that instructor of the young in the mysteries of the ancients, that man who kept the company of Professor Rautner and Professor Fletcher and the other great wardens of the faith, Professor Dietrick of the thin mouth, the thin hair, the yellow teeth, who crunched a dog's tail with an ordinary pliers to demonstrate in the animal's agony that it was not completely anesthetized, who used a wrench to kill laboratory rabbits, smashing them with thinly concealed pleasure.

They did not disillusion, these interlopers. They removed themselves, automatically, from the true, the ineffably good, the nobility whose patent they ludicrously wore. The ranks closed. And Lucas stood in the ranks, disdaining them.

In that first year twenty-two were dropped and one committed suicide. Marvellously, two of the nuggeteers were not dropped, continued with the class.

It was in that first year, when the load was so great that after a week's despair he crept one day to Professor Rautner's office to beg for time, even to resign and begin the year again, Professor Rautner uncurtained the solidarity of Medicine.

"Look about you at the class, think of your fellows," he said somberly. Then, after a pause to let Lucas think,

"Have you done that?"

"Yes, sir."

"Now pick ten men who are dumber than yourself. Think! . . . Pick ten."

Lucas pondered.

"Yes, sir."

Professor Rautner studied Lucas. He paused dramatically, then,

"Those ten are passing," he said quietly.

The year ended.

Lucas had passed. Of the eighty-eight only twenty-two were dropped.

"It was the same in nursing," Kristina said imperturbably. Lucas smiled. And this night, for once, he forbore to be rude to Bruni, to deride Oley, to estrange, to corrode implacably and consciously the bonds of their loyalty to Kristina.

And that night, elated with victory, he seized Kristina, she hid her face in his neck, he carried her to the bed.

"My clothes, my dress, Lucas—wait—" He ripped her underclothing, and uncontrollably, "Now!" he cried, *"NOW!"*

"Yes, Lucas."

And even through the near-deafness of his frenzy he heard that dimly, heard speech and not exclamation, heard a word and not a cry.

When she returned from the bathroom, ready for bed, she spoke to him happily. He answered shortly.

"What's the matter?" she asked, dismayed.

"You don't feel a thing!"

"I do! I do! I feel what you do!"

"All right, tell me! Tell me what you feel!"

"Oh, Lucas—"

"Tell me!" He pushed her away. "Tell me what you feel!"

"Lucas, what do you want of me? What is it? I'm trying! I'm trying so hard—"

"I don't want your trying! I want—I want—" he looked at her helplessly.

She looked back at him, yearning, speechless.

"Oh, come on," he said, sad for her, guilty, moved, "the hell with it, Kristina. I guess we're stuck with each other." And he put his arms around her and he felt her flesh beneath the thin nightgown, slowly, deliberately, he caressed her, her breath came quickly, he continued on and on, his hands never still, artful, gentle, secret, her eyes grew blind, he moved backward, slowly sat in a straight chair, holding her, stumbling to follow him, he pulled her on his lap, gentling her awkwardness, his hands moving her, her body inert, slack to his will, mindless with desire, she moaned softly,

"Now?"

"Now," she whispered. A flutter trembled through her muscles. And again, "Now," she whispered, and there was another flutter, and "Now," she said again,

And this time, caught up involuntarily, his senses exploded, he cried out, he soared above her, transported beyond her whisper, her body and her being.

That night he comforted her. She snuggled to him gratefully. She slept peacefully in a little while. He lay awake, thinking.

"I feel as much as I can," he heard her say again. That is as much as she can feel, he sighed. He heard her whisper again, "Now," he felt again the tremor of her muscles. "Now." And it was shallow, it was deep for her, it was all she had. And I'm stuck with her, he said, and his heart sank, he fell asleep.

And for the rest they had the law's permission to tenant jointly. There was time for almost nothing more. In the morning Kristina, waking, would often find Lucas already at his books. She would make a hurried breakfast for them and while they ate he would read on, or he would hand her the book and recite to her what he had memorized. Leaving their rooms they would walk a short way together, soon their paths separated and she would walk on taking with her the fragments unsaid of her days past or her day ahead with which she had been making contact with him. And he, having heard little, as little as he could, walked quickly on, the lighter for her absence, free now to think, to frown, and to remember.

Occasionally at noon they would eat hurriedly together in the hospital dining room; she looked forward eagerly to these occasions for a chance to be a wife contacting her husband, nourished more by the meeting than by the food. But Lucas knew that his presence was permitted because his wife was a hospital functionary, he was ill at ease and he came only when the prospects of free food, hot food, dulled his embarrassment. The meal ended he rushed back, anxious to cram before the first class of the afternoon began.

When the day ended she might come home to find him already studying. Then she made dinner unobtrusively and while they ate he studied. Sometimes, rarely, he would put by studying, interrupted by his own excitement over some happening in class. At such a time she might manage to bring to him a happening in her world; they were always the same, a new nurse had turned out badly or well, a new doctor, the obsolescence of instruments, the occasional inefficiency of the autoclave. After a time he listened without hearing, and she listened without hearing, also, for his talk was of people she did not know but whose lives and habits and thoughts she knew completely, knowing Lucas'.

When the meal was over he began to study almost before she had the table cleared. And for the rest of the evening, until midnight, he studied on and on and on. Then she would perform the offices of womankind, as she had performed them at the Nurses' Home, she would wash her hair, wash her underwear, attend her nails, repair her clothing; there was this change that now she washed and mended Lucas' few clothes also. At times she would leave quietly and walk to Bruni's, but after an hour or two she would rise guiltily, apprehensive lest he needed her while she was gone. But when she let herself in, a little breathless, he would be where she had left him, reading on, he would look up without interest and, if she entered quietly enough, he would not notice.

This was the pattern of their joint tenantry of these rooms, broken only by the occasions when he left immediately after dinner to go to Alfred's or some other student's rooms and study there, or around examination times when he looked at her or at his books unseeingly, haggard and distrait. Or on such Sundays as could be extorted, perhaps once a month, when he might walk out with her nervously and reluctantly, walk a while, talk aimlessly, look in the windows of an instrument supply house, sit in the park; and what they had to tell each other was soon told, there was nothing new to talk about except once, Professor Aarons' new car, bought through investments everyone was making in this era so opulent that times and not history were measured by it and even professors in small towns were fearlessly and exultantly winding and setting their lives to its golden hours.

But it meant little to them, except incurious, surface wonder, for Kristina's salary was unchanged and their lives were limited, era or no era, by what she earned and what his tuition took of it, and what their living took of what remained. Sometimes, when Lucas bought few books, Kristina managed to save in that month as much as twenty dollars.

After Sunday dinner Lucas usually slept the entire afternoon. But he always woke in time to study for an hour before supper as preparation for the evening's study that followed.

Monday, there were classes again.

In the first year there was insecurity and competition and these were the rule of the pack, and outside the classroom desperate buttressing of the weak, as if the weak, failing, might blood the faculty and make them thirst for more.

In the second year there were seventy-two in the class, six dropped sophomores winning a chance to take the course again. And here the insecurity eased and some of the competition also. For they had passed the first year, those survivors, they had passed, they had done their utmost and knew they had failed and incredibly their best had been enough, they had not been dropped, after all. No year could be as bad as that first. There was still competition, but now there was also competition among the faculty. For when a momentous examination in chemistry impended, physiology professors then jumped in jealously, stiffening their demands, promising an even more searching examination in physiology. And they observed this. The survivors had become battle-hardened. They were able to lift their heads and observe it.

There was as much and more to study. But the language was mastered now. The habit of assailing the impossible was a firm and fixed habit. Where they had despaired they were sardonic. They attacked pharmacology, parasitology, pathology, clinical pathology, public health, neuro-anatomy, ward medicine, physical diagnosis, these new names. And in the last quarter, unperturbed but groaning, they went also to lectures in surgery, medicine, pediatrics, obstetrics, gynecology, psychiatry, urology, anesthesiology, even onchology, neurology, and twice, thoracic surgery.

They were a group now. They stood together. They had learned something they were to carry through Medicine and all through their lives as doctors. They had learned what was not known and this ignorance they shared that with each other and with their masters. They had learned each other's weaknesses and they had learned that others knew theirs too. And they were a group. They were in the fold. They had a secret. And little by little it became borne in on them that they, and only they, members of this craft, this art, this science, this profession, knew this secret. Amazingly, this ignorance was not apparent to the world. It was apparent only to those who had studied what they had studied, who knew what they knew. And when the realization that this was known only to themselves, that they were protected from the outside world by the outside world's not knowing or caring, when this wonder became conviction, then fact, then the bonds which united them became lifelong. And in a little while what they did know and what the lay world did not know was a factor too, and in time, for the sake of their faith, this superiority became as strong and secure a bond as their shared ignorance.

It was in the second year that Lucas as an official acolyte of Medicine saw his first patient. He ventured to the edge of the gulf that separated them, prepared to retreat the instant the patient discovered that this was all a game of the professors, that Lucas was just a human like himself.

But the patient, an old man, humble with the anxious humility of a lifetime in which one did not go to doctors but to clinics, stoic in well-learned clinic patience, lowered his faded eyes and answered the form questions so meekly that Lucas rallied.

"Married?" Lucas demanded finally.

The old man hesitated. Lucas looked up impatiently.

"Yes, married," the old man decided.

"Wife living?"

"She just died . . ."

"I see! What did she die of?"

The old man gazed across a lifetime, considering.

"I said—what did she die of!"

The old man looked at him anxiously.

"Nothing serious," he said apologetically.

Lucas lowered his eyes.

"I see," he said gently. And that night, brooding on this, he perceived humanity, saw the silent mass waiting outside the hospital, uncomplaining, humble, waiting for the awful absolute of eyes that knew, dumbly waiting for relief, that chance, that indifferent chance. Thereafter, for a week, he kept his eyes averted, feeling the censor, feeling exposed, knowing what he did not know.

"There's an awful lot here we'll never use," Alfred said one day. He shrugged.

"But we've learned an awful lot, Al."

"Knowledge we'll never use."

"Oh, I don't know—" But Lucas did know. He knew that he would use everything he had ever learned.

"I was talking to a senior. He said the same thing. Memory, he said.

Memory's the thing. Sometimes I wonder—what is a doctor? Is a doctor a man who remembers?"

"I don't get it." Lucas tried to imagine what Alfred meant.

"You'll wind up in a lab! That's where you're headed. Some goddamned research institute."

"Why? Why do you say that, Al? What is there about me makes you say that?"

"Well, it isn't envy, boy. That I can tell you."

"You're still going ahead the way you planned? I mean a good practice and—and—"

"Don't worry! You won't hurt my feelings—"

"You know what I mean? What we used to talk about?"

"No. Not quite. Now my ideas are bigger . . ."

"Bigger?"

"Bigger and better. Say, I been meaning to ask you: Hear from your father, ever?"

"Just the second letter. He wanted money. Kristina sent it to him." He looked up guiltily. The name had slipped out.

"And how is your wife?" Alfred asked formally.

"Fine, just fine. You'll have to come over sometime."

"Yes, I will. When this damned work lets up a little—"

"That's right."

"Well, what do you say we hit this radiology crap—"

The chairs grated over the floor.

During the first summer he had worked in the laboratory again.

He greeted Ruth and Ann and they greeted him as if they had just met, or met after a single, long past introduction. Once, Kristina and he went to the women's apartment, they chatted stiffly, anxiously. And once, dutifully, they came to his home and there Kristina cooked a dinner and behaved as anxiously as they had behaved.

Intimacy had long since died. Lucas forgot them and did his work. After the visit to Ruth and Ann's house there were few visits to Bruni. Kristina went occasionally, but Lucas seldom knew.

When the second year ended they celebrated again. A week later Lucas came home jubilantly.

"It's true!" he shouted. "Everything they told us is true! The main worry's over!" Kristina waited, smiling, bewildered, delighted he was kind again.

"You're on your own," he cried. "Don't you see? It's terrific! You don't have to sit in lectures! You don't have to sit in labs—we had our first exam and it wasn't paralyzing—it's great! All they told us is true!"

"I'm glad!" she grinned. "I'm so glad for you!"

"You're glad? What do you mean, you're glad?"

"I'm glad, Luke. I'm awful glad—"

"Now you can help me! Now, you can really help me! Come on! We're going out and celebrate . . ."

"We don't have so much money," she began dubiously, then seeing the look on his face, "No, no! Come on! We got plenty! I—I just remember!"

"Now you can tell me about the operating room."

"What will I tell you?"

"The mechanics, this time! How you put on a gown, how you scrub, every detail. Let's start at the door . . ."

And though she told him all she could think of, though she answered a hundred questions and then a hundred more, talking all through dinner, all the way home, far into the night until at last he let her go to sleep, he forgot it all the moment he walked through the wide swinging doors to scrub for the first time.

He looked about in panic. Four doctors and two seniors were scrubbing at a line of sinks, paying no attention to each other. Hesitantly, Lucas went to a vacant sink. From a shelf he took a mask and cap and donned them. And there he stood. He was paralyzed with horror. There were no faucets. A passing probationer tapped him on the back, pointed beneath the sink. Lucas looked, saw a pedal, stepped on it. Water flowed into the sink. He looked about. Not a head had turned. They were oblivious to him. He picked up a brush and soap. Carefully he washed his hands, his forearms, scrubbing until the skin reddened, then he did the ritual of fingers, inside each, then the other side, then front, then back, then the whole hand again. He left the sink with his hands dripping, his forearms dripping, held stiffly in front of him, his hands on a level with his eyes, and went to the basins, dipped hands and forearms in the first, dipped hands and forearms in the second, passed dripping into the operating room. And there was Kristina. Their eyes met only for an instant. Then she turned briskly away, she would have helped him if she could, but here protocol dictated what she should do, what she should say, even, and the head operating-room nurse nodded, gestured, almost never spoke. Of the four nurses subordinate to Kristina, one held out a square cloth bundle to Lucas as she had held it out to each of the others. They were all gowned. They ignored him. He opened the gown, holding one end. It fell, upside down, the sleeves nearly touching the floor.

"Drop it!" A voice cried sharply.

Lucas dropped the gown instantly, frightened, bewildered.

The gowned and masked figure which had spoken from beside the operating table nodded almost imperceptibly. A nurse bent swiftly and the gown was gone from the floor. Another nurse held out a second package, held it so that it opened, he put his hands through the sleeves, she tied the strings behind him, motioned with her head for him to walk to the wall at the foot of the operating table. If there was expression on any face it was hidden by the masks. He passed Kristina, standing impassively beside a tray of instruments. Against the wall stood a nurse beside an array of cloth packets.

"What size?" she demanded, she looked at his hands.

He tried frantically to remember what size gloves he wore.

"Nine!" he blurted, finally.

She hesitated.

"Are you sure?"

"Well, he should know!" came the sharp voice from the table.

Promptly, the nurse unpinned a packet labelled "Nine," she reached for a can of talc, he held out his hands, she sprinkled them, held up a glove. His hand plunged in. It was two sizes too large. Then the second hand.

Praying they would not fall off, he walked to the table. One of the white figures moved slightly, and he stood obediently beside him.

"Are we ready finally?" the sharp voice asked. And without waiting for a reply he stuck out his hand. Kristina slapped an instrument into it. He bent. The instrument cut. The operation had begun.

Sometime during the operation, he was never sure when, someone handed Lucas a retractor, guided his hand over the incision, dipped the retractor in, pulled his hand to show the pressure he was to exert. Sometime later he was told to pull the instrument out. The rest was a haze, a blind prayer not to do the wrong thing, not to move, not to be noticed.

Then it was over.

"Well!" said the sharp voice, and untied his mask, "Well, well!" He said it pleasantly, smiling. He smiled at all of them. Then he turned and walked out, untying himself as he went, a nurse fluttering near him, helping with the strings, catching what dropped.

Now the other masks were untied, the faces were smiling soberly over work accomplished, the patient was being lifted onto a stretcher, the operating table was suddenly empty, Lucas looked at Kristina. She nodded once, shortly. She winked. He walked out of the operating room drawing and expelling a deep, deep breath.

"What did you think?" she asked that night, securely and a little proudly.

"He was warm!" Lucas said. "That's the first shock I got. That guy was warm!"

"It wasn't a he," Kristina laughed. "That was a she!"

"Well, she was warm," Lucas said stubbornly, "that's all I know. That's what gave me a shock. I was sure surprised! You've got no idea how cold a corpse can be!"

There was surgery the first twelve weeks including all the specialties, there was public health, medicine, obstetrics, gynecology, pediatrics, there were all the secondary courses, there were no more clinics, it was ward work now, the work still began at 8:30 every morning and ended at 5:30 that night, but there were afternoons off occasionally, spent, invariably spent, in sleep, Lucas, all of them, went straight home to sleep, even if only for an hour. There was never enough sleep. But now in this third year it was possible to go out on Sundays, to work sometimes only five nights a week until midnight and one night until nine and the other night perhaps not at all. But in the third year, with the wards, there was weekend duty that came to all of them in turn, and this was not bad, except that you could not sleep.

In this year they had a professor who asked, as he asked every class, "Which would you rather have—syphilis or TB?"

They pondered, grave and anxious.

"Syphilis!" said Lucas at last. And waited, fearful.

"That's right!" he cried happily as he cried to every class. "It's easier to cure—and you have more fun getting it!"

The class laughed obediently.

In this year there was a lecturer in a high purple collar, a stickpin, pointed shoes, a man of destiny, a man who had once in the arc of a lifetime grazed immortality. He had discovered a strange substance, he was excitedly at work on it, a few more experiments and he would publish, then in Canada Banting published, the world exploded, the man looked up, dazed. He had almost discovered insulin.

He spent one lecture a year telling a class about it, he relived each agonized step, he looked at them, unbelieving still, and always, at the end, as he mounted the cross, his eyes filled, he turned away abruptly, strode from the room, his cheeks wet with what remained in the squeezed and nearly dry fruit of his life.

In this year there were jubilant and expansive discussions in odd corners: "How about prostigmine and physostigmine—sympathomimetic or sympatholytic?" And they swelled happily, challenging, arguing, disputing, sure in the answer, propounding for the sheer luxury of foreknown answer. "Ah, but how about epinephrine—look at epinephrine! In large doses it's vasoconstrictor!"

And again,

"Yes, but if a woman claims on her deathbed—on her deathbed, mind!—that some MD did an abortion on her—her evidence is acceptable! Don't forget that! She can be lying, just to kill the guy! And the court'll take her word!"

"And you're full of shit, you know that, don't you?"

"Am I? I am, eh? Well, just ask Professor Knox!"

"You've got fecaliths in the circle of Willis—"

"All right! Just ask him!"

In this year the fear of failure was almost gone. The harshness almost disappeared. There were no more sudden drops, no seats emptied wordlessly overnight, no unaccountably missing faces. There would be, instead, decorously, silently, secretly in the mailbox, in a student's personal mailbox, a blank, white envelope. And within there would be a card: "The Department of Pharmacology regrets to inform you that you have failed to meet the department's standards in the last exam."

In this year one of the three nugget men was caught and dropped.

He was on obstetric duty, he was required to sit at the bedside. He nuggeted a staff man for procedural information, confidently wrote his name on a likely case, went to dinner and left the patient in labor.

Twenty minutes after he left the patient went into hard labor. The resident was summoned.

"Didn't he *know*?" he snarled, shocked.

"I thought he was all right, I just left him here," the staff man stammered, "he asked enough questions—"

He was gone next day. This was Erskine, the man to whom the class supplied notes all the freshman year, who somehow obtained a neuro-anatomy nugget book on the eve of a neuro-anatomy examination and when they came to him, excited, refused flatly to loan it.

"Remember?" Alfred nodded. "We told him next day no more notes—"

"And he came to us begging, one after the other of us—'Please! Please take the book—' Can you imagine? Leaving her in labor like that? Not even *knowing*?"

"Well, there's still two left," Alfred said significantly.

"Yes, but *they'd* know! *They'd* know at least . . ."

In this year it was discovered to the amazement and joy of the class that one member, aged twenty-three years, had never seen a naked, living girl and had absolutely never kissed one.

"A medical student?"

"Yes, by God, a medical student!"

"What's he gonna specialize—gynecology?"

"Brester! You ought to know him!"

"By God, I sit right next to him and never dreamed!"

"Let's go find him. Maybe we can take him to a whorehouse! Come on!"

In this year Lucas, taking the history of a sixty-five-year-old patient, asked her gently how often she had relations with her husband and whether she enjoyed congress.

The nurses howled with delight.

"Sixty-five years old, mind you!"

But the patient smiled happily. And thereafter, though he smiled sheepishly when his question was echoed at him, Lucas made it a point, remembering the look in the old woman's eyes, to ask all elderly females the same question. And when he came into their ward they could not have enough of him, they mothered him, one began to crochet him a sweater with fingers that would never finish a sleeve, they loved him, he was their doctor, their young man.

In this year it was said to him for the first time,

"You're a doctor now. Go over to that patient and find out what's wrong with him." It was a queer feeling and unforgettable, he would always remember it.

In this year he knew that Medicine was really all that he had ever studied.

Then it was magically the fourth year, so remote a distance lay suddenly behind him the mind could not bridge it, it was the fourth year and the load was like the third year, except that now ophthalmology and otolaryngology were added, and now he made his own decisions, now in surgery he sutured, in medicine he prescribed, the staff man signing the prescription.

"Now," said the staff, "now you practice Medicine as you would in your own office!"

Now, amazingly, no patients died, not from malpractice, no stitches gave suddenly in the middle of the night, deep, internal stitches to bring the resident running, the operating room hastily crewed and lit; now in the challenge confidence was slowly born, nourished by repetition, made secure by example, and they were closer than before, the group was solid now, they smiled at each other easily, the end was in sight. They had done the impossible. They had done it together. They knew their worth now; they knew what they knew. And they knew best of all that flesh was not fragile but would endure many mistakes, yes, and perhaps, unaccountably, be the better for it. And that there was a force beyond that which they brought to the bedside—"Medicine is the application of physical forces to the alleviation of disease"—a force in the patient himself, something incredibly durable, something—you could only call it Life.

And that fought on your side, too.

Every time.

Almost every time.

And now there was more talk of specialties.

"I think GYN," said Alfred. "But there's pediatrics too—"

"People always pay for their kids," another said sagely.

"What's that old crap about Skin? Your patients never die, they never get well, and they never get you up at night—"

"I want Ob!"

"You're a chump! You'll never sleep!"

"What are you going to do, Luke?" asked Alfred.

"GP," said Lucas. And there was no doubt in his voice.

There was more time this year.

Saturday afternoons, while Kristina worked in the operating room, he could go to movies. Sometimes he could go out with her Friday evening. And there was all day Sunday. Now, there was always Sunday. Alfred was absent every other weekend, home with his parents or taking long trips to football games or parties.

And one weekend, Kristina working late, Lucas met Dorothy again, met her at the movies. And suddenly, looking at her, speaking to her awkwardly, he was surprised by a great hunger. It was a hunger to hear someone cry in passion as loudly as he cried, a hunger for fellowship in passion, and for confirmation in his maleness and his ardor.

"I've got a place by myself now," Dorothy said. "Oh, but you wouldn't know! Yup! I live all by myself now."

And on the way there: If she asks me to come up I'll say I have to meet Kristina, I'll say I've got to be on duty, I'll tell her frankly, Look, Dorothy, I like you and all that, but the fact is I haven't been well, lately, I'll say . . .

She struggled a little at first, pretended outrage. Then abruptly it began, she bit a pillow to keep from crying out, she cried out anyway. And then it was over.

He rose, dazed. He was empty. And into the emptiness guilt rushed, filled him, distended him, he could not wait to escape. He left her mumbling indignantly, crying out angrily to him as he stumbled down the stairs. He felt the night air on his face. He walked until he was tired.

When he reached home Kristina was there, waiting.

"Hello there," he said awkwardly, wincing for the blow, sure she must read his day written on him.

"I'm sorry I'm late," she turned from the stove. "They held me up—a girl got sick—"

"It's all right. I just took a walk."

"That's what I figure. I bet you're hungry."

"Maybe," he said hesitantly, "maybe you'd like to go over and see Bruni tonight—I mean you and me?"

"Why, Luke!"

"Come on! We'll eat and go. Bruni's all right, when you come right down to it. And so's Oley. I—I guess I just got tired of them . . ."

"They like *you,* Luke."

"I know. What do you say? You'd like that, wouldn't you?"

She came to him and put her hands on his shoulders.

"I got the best husband in the whole world!" she said solemnly.

"I stink!" he cried angrily.

"No, you don't stink! You're good! You belong to me!" He lowered his eyes. She gave him a push and went back to cooking.

He stood uncertainly in the doorway.

"I got you something today," she said casually, squinting at a skillet.

"Good," he said mechanically.

"It's on the dresser . . ."

And he went obediently to the dresser. There was a package there, long and narrow, flat. He opened it idly. It lay bare. For a moment he looked at it almost without seeing it, his eyes seeing, his mind refusing to interpret. He put his fingers on its surface, slowly, against illusion. It was real. His fingers stroked it, shaking. His eyes filled.

It was a wooden sign. There were two hooks by which it might swing. On it, in regulation letters, it read,

LUCAS MARSH, M.D.

CHAPTER 22

The sign stayed upon his dresser throughout his internship.

His existence now divided; like an amoeba his entity drew out, divided, became two, and he inhabited either demesne with the ease of use.

By day he was an intern. He was a student and he was treated as a student. "Doctor" was a word used to describe his status, a word to differentiate between student and the revered beings to whom had been entrusted Medicine's full responsibility, it was a staff word, an adjective, a classification, an epithet of convenience. He was a supernurse, regarded by registered nurses with barely concealed contempt because he did not know how to give an enema, administer a ward, or care for the sick with practice and ease, reluctantly deferred to because of hospital protocol. And the doctor absent, he was the doctor, the young man left in charge, instructed, rigidly limited, chiefly a watchman, chiefly expected to surrender his charge no worse than it was given to him.

In this part of his divided existence the essence was never-ending indoctrination. He learned hourly. The hospital was a giant classroom. The books he had studied came to life. The humans were paragraphs or pages or whole chapters, made animate. He and his fellows could be taught methods of reasoning, but not reason. They could be furnished with examples of judgment, but not judgment. Their memories had been trained so that this function was now a prodigy.

It was about four months after his internship began that he learned about time. He learned that it was part of every prescription and the basic sum of any prognosis. Willy-nilly, time was dispensed while the physician stood by.

Time was an ally. Or, when it was measurable, it could be an antagonist, a limit, which, since it was beyond control, had to be opposed with what drugs, measures or knowledge could be summoned; in such a circumstance time was most significant.

Time was a function. Time was an essence. Time was a measured interval, a pulse record, a respiration chart, a sedimentation rate.

And then time was a medicine in itself, fighting usually on the patient's side, another doctor, another nurse, a sort of lesser God.

And then one day time came to him as life itself, part of life, seen that way, all of life, seen another way, time as tenure, time as essence, time as the representation of being, time as the living, death as the dead.

He learned to fight for time. And one day, out of habit, fighting automatically for time, he began to fight for life. On that day life became immutably the one thing to fight for, to fight all out for and time became an assistant in that fight or occasionally an antagonist. The phase when success was a well-graded paper, success in curing a disease, success in carrying out that which had been taught him, that phase was ended. Now the only goal of life was Medicine and the only goal of Medicine was the fight for time, for life.

And in this new world centuries remote from the boy he had been, although he moved in a world of Medicine, moved among doctors, was called doctor himself, it was not complete. It was a time of waiting. He was not yet a doctor.

The remaining part of his existence was his home. It had acquired new power, and this had happened since the sign LUCAS MARSH, M.D., first appeared on his bureau. Home was a place to dream, now home contained that sign. It was apparent to Kristina how much he valued it, when she touched it to dust it she lifted it self-consciously, handled it with conscious care. But she was unaware that around this symbol Lucas had built a cave and that this was for him the whole symbol of home. Home was an address where there was a room where the sign stood. Beside this sign he dreamed his dreams, hoped his hopes; he sat in the amphitheater of his own life, clutching the sign which was his ticket, dreaming his dreams of the game to come, waiting for the game to begin.

The fortunate in his class had obtained the internships they coveted. Their reasons for yearning for the hospitals of their choice were as varied as the men themselves and they were based upon the opinions fixed by talking among themselves or heard from their seniors. The majority sought appointments to large city hospitals, and for the most part they were indifferent to the city or its location.

One of the most authoritative at such senior sessions had been Brundage, one of the two nuggeteers who succeeded in graduating. He was listened to with respect for in his role as a nuggeteer he had time to gather information when others were studying and because it was tacitly agreed that anyone who could get through Medicine on his wits had proved the validity of his wits and was accordingly a person to heed.

"Everybody's going to the cities," he nodded sagely.

"Everybody's been going to the city for twenty years," said Avery, the class rebel.

"Yeah, but the stuff we're taught today is so high-standard that you've got to have hospitals to practice it. And the cities are where the hospitals are."

"It wouldn't be the dough in it," Avery deprecated.

"Sure, the dough's there."

"What's the matter with money?" demanded Alfred.

"If you like money that much what's the matter with banking?" asked Avery. "Although I suppose I shouldn't ask you—a real poor fellow like you—"

"You're all damned smart and full of holy crap when the word 'money' is mentioned. I'd just like to know one thing—where's the money coming from to support this high grade of Medicine? Where are we going to get our high-standard equipment? How about the upkeep of those high standards? Who's going to pay that little thing called the bill?"

"Why, we're going to get a cushy practice, Al, like you."

"Sure, we're going to make the patient pay for what we buy, whether he needs it or not!"

"How do you know when he'll need it? I'm not so sure Al's wrong."

"Every doctor his own hospital—"

"That's right! We're taught the finest! We deserve every gadget, every toy, everything we want! And the public's got to pay for it—"

"I didn't say that. I just want to know where you're going to get the money from to run your office the way you'd want to after what you've been taught—"

"And anyway," said Avery with finality, "the practice Al wants—well, so far as his patients' pocketbooks are concerned they just won't care!"

"Well, what of it? The rich get sick too, don't they?"

"A man can do clinic work," Lucas offered.

"Silent Sam! Look who's come to!"

"Where you gonna practice, Luke?"

"Who said he's gonna practice! Nothing so sordid as patients—or money—eh, Luke?"

"That's the trouble with you guys," said Brundage. "You start an intelligent discussion, first thing you know you're arguing like a bunch of kids."

"Will you for Christ's sake listen to who's talking," said Avery, awed. "God help your patients, Brundage!"

"Oh, they'll get by," Brundage said imperturbably.

"What are you going to do—nugget them?"

"You want to listen to what I got—or do you want to play!"

The room fell silent.

"I got it cold. I got it taped—right from the source. And here it is—here's your bread and butter! The national average is about 750 patients per doctor. In the South they got 900 to every doctor. In the West, 650. In the Northeast they got 700 and in the Central States they got 750."

"All right," said Avery after a moment, "break it down."

"The South pays least. The best pay is the West. Next comes the East. That's for towns of 2,500 or less."

"What's 'South' mean?"

"Where's the North?"

Brundage consulted a notebook.

" 'South' means all the South Atlantic, East-South-Central and West-South-Central States," he recited. "And 'East' means New England, Middle Atlantic and East-North-Central. And 'West' means West-North-Central, Mountain and Pacific."

He paused impressively.

"That's for small towns. Remember this, men: the small town is out! It's getting worse every year. You work in a small town—I don't care where—and your average gross income is gonna be $6,500 tops—and it can go as low as $4,000. That's gross."

"That's for fellows just beginning practice?" asked Alfred.

"I got it all subdivided. Wait—yeah! That's for fellows just beginning—that's for fellows in practice less than 13 years. The next group, 13 to 27 years in practice, they make the highest—at least a thousand a year more. The lowest group is the grandpappies, guys in practice more than 27 years. They make a thousand a year less than the beginners."

"So how about cities?"

"So now we come to towns from 2,500 to 100,000. The South grosses $7,000, the West $8,000 and the East $6,800. But the big cities, the ones with over 100,000 population, every one of them except in the South they make less than the small towns! You know why?"

"Sure—everybody rushing off to practice in the big cities!"

"Exactly!"

"What's the over-all average for the whole country—the net, now, not the gross?"

"Wait a minute—you got to take in specialists too—here it is!—$4,270."

"That's not bad," one said soberly.

"And times are getting better all the time—"

"I got more! I even got the kind of calls!"

They leaned forward, admiring.

"By God, Brundage, where'd you get it all?"

"You just keep nuggeting me. I knew there'd be a time when I'd nugget back. You protect me, by God I've been protecting you! Got it all out of official statistics!" He looked around the room challengingly. There was no challenge. He flipped the pages of his notebook. He looked up.

"What kind of case you think you'll get most?"

There was no answer. They looked at him expectantly.

"Go on—guess!"

"Heart—"

"No, female probably—"

"Accident—"

"You're wrong. You're all wrong." He leaned forward impressively. "It's minor respiratory!"

The room buzzed with interest.

"One third of all your cases and one fifth of all your calls—minor respiratory! Accidents are ten percent. Communicable diseases, ten percent. Say you make $4,500 a year, $1,500 is going to come from minor respiratory!"

"What about GYN—"

"Way down the list! Six percent! Including OB!"

"How about digestive—"

"Minor's seven, major's four—and you Skin guys: four and a half percent—and you Otos: two!"

"And those are facts, Brundage?" said Alfred.

Brundage thumped his notebook.

"Those, by God, are facts!"

"And there you are," said Alfred. "Whether you like it or not, gentlemen, you'll pay for your X-ray machines, you'll pay for your equipment, you'll function as doctors on the broad base of the cough and the common cold."

"And we mustn't forget," said Avery quietly, "that, as Dr. Fletcher says, of 100 patients 80 would have gotten well without any medical assistance whatever—and of the remaining 20 the illness of 10 will be psychosomatic."

"To hell with all that," said Brundage. "At least now you know where your bread's buttered."

"Where you going, Al?" Lucas asked, troubled, when the gathering broke up.

"Me? Same place I always was—New York, the Cabot Hospital. Oldest, richest, most genteel in the city. The biggest city in the world."

"You really mean it?" Lucas asked uncertainly.

"Of course I mean it! Why? Where you going?"

"I don't know—wherever I can get in, I guess—"

"Why don't you try for a big one? You've got the grades—"

"I don't know—"

"What don't you know? I'm not talking about money—I'm talking about internationally famous places—Boston, Maryland, Illinois—where you can learn something—where you can specialize—"

"I guess so," said Lucas.

"You better be making up your mind. You're going to need drag, for one thing. . . ."

"What's the matter with you?" Kristina asked.

"Nothing," he said automatically.

She looked at him uncertainly, then went on to the kitchen.

In a little while she returned.

"Something happened today?"

He looked at her irritably.

"What's the matter?"

"You just sit there so quiet," she said apologetically.

He jerked his hand in a gesture of dismissal.

"Maybe I could help."

"It's nothing for you."

She stood a moment longer, watching him, hopeful he would say something else. He sat, thinking. She returned to the kitchen.

She came to him again. He had not moved.

She cleared her throat.

"Is it the microscope?" she asked timidly.

He sighed. He frowned up at her.

"What is it? What is it, Kristina?"

"It will only be a couple of months! Then—you'll see!—we can maybe pick up a good one!"

"Oh, Kristina!"

"Used. Good as new. But right now—well, the bag, the emergency kit, the ophthalmoscope, the blood pressure, the stethoscope—you know yourself—cost one hundred eighteen dollars—"

"Oh, Kris! Go away, will you? Will you please go away?"

"Don't be mad—"

"I'm not mad—"

"I can't help it—"

"I know you can't help it—"

"I only want to help you—"

"You can't help me!" he shouted. "Will you understand that, Kris?"

"Maybe if you told me—"

"This is something you don't know anything about."

"I might know—"

"You don't know. What you know you know well. This is completely outside your experience."

"I only try to help."

"Kris! Will you leave me alone? Will you?"

"You don't live by yourself, you know, Luke. I live here too. I married you. I come home, I see you sitting there, I think maybe I can help. Why do you shut me out?"

"It's just that—all right! All right, goddamn it! I'll tell you!"

"Don't be mad—"

"Will you for Christ's sake let me tell you?"

"Just don't be mad—"

"Well, shut up and listen, then."

"I shut up."

He rose and looked out the window.

"A group of the fellows was talking—"

"I don't see you, all day—when you got night duty I don't see you at all—weeks at a time—"

"Do you want to hear this, Kris? Or don't you?"

"It's only natural—it's my own husband—we should talk together—sure, I don't know so much as you—still—"

He sat down resignedly.

"All right, Kris. You have it your own way."

"I heard you. When I get a chance to talk? Tell me? When I get a chance to tell you the home I want, where you going to practice, what plans we got for us? I heard you. A bunch of the fellas was talking—"

"Never mind—"

"No, no—"

"Forget it–"

"Please, Luke–I shut up–you was talking–"

"We were talking about Medicine . . ."

Kristina nodded sagely.

"Well, not about Medicine, exactly–about where to practice. And, and–how much income–"

"That's good!"

"What's good about it? That's the whole point! This damned Brundage we nuggeted all through school, damned if he hasn't got statistics somewhere to show exactly where to go and what to practice to make the most money–"

"That's too bad," Kristina said insincerely. "Still–"

"Still, hell! That's all right for fellows like Alfred. He thinks that way automatically. But the rest of the fellows, by God they listened too! I tell you they listened damned seriously. They didn't miss a word!"

"Maybe you practice in Minnesota, hey? You like Minnesota, once you see it! I gots lots of friends there–"

"Minnesota! I don't even know where I'm going to intern yet! You ought to hear them! They'd got it all mapped out!"

"Why not, Luke?"

"Why not? Haven't you heard a word I've been saying? Is Minnesota all you can think of?"

"It's pretty cold in the winter. People there pretty healthy. I got to admit that."

"Oh, goddamn it, Kristina, don't you ever understand anything? Anything I try to tell you? You want me to talk to you, you want to know all my problems, I try to tell you–"

"I'm listening! I heard every word–"

"You don't hear a goddamned thing–"

"Don't shout, Luke–"

"I might as well be talking to a bedpost–"

"What are you so mad about? It's only natural they should talk about how to make a living. When Bruni and Oley were married and Oley wanted to be a bookkeeper they asked lots of people–"

"Kris!"

"It's only natural–"

"Kris! I said–Kris!"

"What did I do now?"

"Just shut up! Will you do that? Just shut up!"

"Maybe I don't understand."

"I'm talking about Medicine. Not bookkeeping! And what do you know about either! Why will I never learn! Why do I open my mouth, even! Go away, Kris! Leave me alone! Go out in the kitchen and do your dishes!"

"We haven't even had supper yet–"

"Fine!"

"Where you going?"

"I'm going out."

"But you haven't eaten–"

"I'm not hungry–"

"Look, Luke—I'm sorry—I didn't mean to make you mad—"

"Just leave me alone, Kris—"

"A cup of coffee, only—"

"Will you leave me alone?"

"Let me go with you—"

"I don't want you with me. I want to think. And if you lived a million years you'd never know what I'm thinking about. I know that, now. I guess I've always known it. You're dumb, Kristina. You're dumber than hell. How you ever got to be head operating-room nurse I'll never know. You talk about being alone. How the hell do you think I like living alone?"

"I'm sorry, Luke. Maybe I try too hard. I'll be quiet, now—I'll listen—Luke! You coming back?"

"Oh, sure . . . Sure . . . I'll be back . . ."

He was gone.

She waited at the open door. When she was sure he would not return she waited longer. Then she closed the door. She leaned against it a while. Bethinking herself she ran to the window to glimpse him. But he was gone, out of sight. She sighed. She went to the kitchen. She turned off the flame. She put the dinner dishes away. And when that was done, when her kitchen was ordered, she went methodically over the small rooms tidying them. Every so often she licked her lips nervously.

When there was at last no more to do she looked at the clock. It was past ten. She sat in the chair by the window where he had been sitting. She tried to imagine where he was. She went over their talk, trying to see what had angered him, what he had been brooding about, what he had tried to tell her. She shook her head at her obtuseness. Still puzzled, she let her thoughts slide to the house they would one day own, her linens, her silver, her dishes, the closet space, the kitchen. She looked up guiltily. It was nearly eleven. She rose, went to the bureau, took out all his socks, examined them minutely, put them carefully back. She inspected her face in the mirror. She frowned at a small blemish on her cheek. She squeezed it tentatively. She looked at it again. Her eyes fell to the sign, LUCAS MARSH, M.D. She picked it up gingerly. She brushed it on her sleeve. She put it softly down. She stared at it a long moment. She went back to the chair. She sat down. She waited.

"You are always disturbed about something," Dr. Aarons said. "One would think you had invented Medicine."

"I've come to you for advice."

"Yes, but what you want is reassurance. That's what you really want. You want me to tell you they were wrong to discuss Medicine on such a basis. That the Medicine you idealize is the right Medicine, the true, the good. You've had a shock and you want me to tell you it isn't so, it was just a bunch of foolish seniors—"

"I know what's right and wrong."

"I'm sure you do. You know as much as Aristotle, then, and more than Pontius Pilate. I didn't know you had time to study more than Medicine."

"I would like to know your opinion of where I should serve my internship."

"Have you got a previously formed opinion you want me to confirm?"

"I haven't got any opinion whatever."

"Where do you want to practice?"

"I haven't any idea."

"Find out. Whatever state you want to practice in, look up the hospitals there. That's your first step. Then select the hospital you think you'd be happiest at—and apply."

Lucas hesitated.

"I don't know what state I'd be happiest in." He tried not to think of Brundage.

"A man usually establishes practice in some community where he is known. Unless he can buy a practice or is known to some doctor who will take him on as an assistant."

"There are already three doctors in Milletta—"

"There won't always be. Doctors, you will find, die as briskly as less sacred folk."

"I'd prefer not to go back to Milletta."

"Oh, yes! There's the affair of your father . . ."

Lucas waited.

"I don't know what state you'd rather practice in! How do you expect me to know that?"

"I wanted you to tell me what kind of a hospital I'd learn most at, have most opportunities to learn. That's all I want."

"Do you know what specialty you want?"

"No, I don't."

"You don't know whether you'll practice a specialty, you don't have any geographical preferences, you are nauseated by what we may call the yardstick of Brundage. It is very clear that what you want is a shrine, some great and famous Lourdes where you can worship, tended by priests world-known for their piety, their integrity, and their glory." That is what I want, he told himself savagely, and that is what he must want too. God kill us both.

"I am sorry to have taken up your time—"

"No, no! Wait. If you know right from wrong you know I am speaking the truth. You are not looking for flesh and blood but for the representatives of flesh and blood. You want the wafer and not the sweating apostle. Well, there's Johns Hopkins, and I don't have to tell you who's there. And there's Rush and Massachusetts General and Adams and Cushing and Cleveland and Crile and Minnesota, and the Mayo brothers, and Presbyterian—"

"I'm sorry, sir. I've provoked you in some way and I don't know how and I'm sorry for it. But there's no use going on. You've been my professor and you've been kind to me. I thought, knowing me, you could sum up my fitness and direct me to some place where I could extend what I know and remedy my weaknesses—some place you'd know where I'd fit—I wanted advice."

"You want advice about a Medicine that doesn't exist. I can't grope through the maps of your dreamworld."

"All I want to do is practice Medicine. I just want to know where to go so I can practice the best Medicine I know how, where I can learn the most of what I love the best."

"Some place where Medicine is practiced for the sake of Medicine—"

"All right—"

"Where you can drink in vast draughts of it at the feet of the mighty—"

"All right. Put it that way."

"And from whence you can sally forth to—oh, what's the use! Medicine . . . ! You haven't even met the human race, yet! You haven't—I can't begin! There's no place to start. What does it matter where you intern? Go to Presbyterian! You've got everything there!"

"Thank you very much. I'm very grateful—"

Dr. Aarons waved wearily.

Lucas escaped.

"Unless you're going to practice some specialty," Dr. Fletcher said dubiously.

"I'm not. I'm sure I'm not. What I want is general practice."

"Yes . . . Well—if you haven't got your heart set anywhere—"

"No, sir!"

"You know, all over the country fine doctors-to-be are interning at small hospitals—"

Lucas relaxed, nodded gratefully.

"The mighty in Medicine are a passing lot. Yesterday's great names, most of them, the names I wanted to study under, those are names you've never heard of."

"Yes, sir."

"And you want to practice in a city?"

"I don't think so. No, sir."

"I'll tell you something. There are still frontiers of Medicine. I don't mean research. That's only a field of Medicine. I mean areas where medical care is scanty. Areas where there aren't any doctors at all. Areas where a man can practice all Medicine—"

"Away from specialists—"

"That's right. We're in an age of specialization. There's not much doubt about that. From the patient's point of view that's either a blessing or a curse. When I was graduated a patient complaining of indigestion would go to a GP and be diagnosed and treated in two visits. Today, he gets a gastro-intestinal X-ray series, a chemical analysis of his gastric secretions, and probably a couple of gall-bladder series. And that's money. And the more diagnostic tests, the more specialists are called in. And that's more money. Do you know the greatest disease a man can have? The most frequent? The one you'll be called on to treat most often?"

"Well sir, Brundage said respiratory tract made up thirty percent—"

"Well, it's not. It's not respiratory tract and it isn't heart and it isn't cancer. It's poverty. That's your enemy. That's your disease. That's your prime foe. Poverty. That's where the stress is. That's the enemy humanity's battling against every conscious moment. That's the stress that's stacked against every cell. The pressure never lets up. And the weakest cells give. There's your enemy—and you'll run back and forth along the levee, shoring here, shoveling there, and you'll never stop, from morning to night, you'll never stop. And you'll never do more than check—'Take it easy,' you'll tell the patient. 'Doc, I can't take it easy. I got to work. My family'll starve . . .' 'Well, then take this medicine . . .' 'Will it help, Doc?' . . . 'It won't take the place of what you need—you've got to rest—you've got to take it easy . . .' 'Doc, a man's got to live!'

"Or else: 'What you need is an operation. Understand? . . .' 'And how long will I be in the hospital? . . .' 'About three weeks . . .' 'And—how much?' 'About three hundred ought to cover it—my fee, well you can owe me, we can arrange payments . . .' 'I can't afford it, Doc . . .' 'But you've got to have it! . . .' 'I can't—I can't afford it.' And you know it. You know now he or she can't afford it. And there isn't any medicine in the world to help him. Nothing but money. I tell you eighty percent of the sick today, eighty percent could be cured in sixty days with paper. Paper and metal. Money.

"And they'll bring their kids in. And it'll be a girl, maybe, with a harelip, strabismic, bowlegged, a girl needing plastic surgery. And you'll know, looking at her, watching her trying to hide herself behind her mother, that someday that kid's growing up to a twisted, maladjusted human. You know the stress from that. And you know that when it comes to earning a living, surviving, the handicap's going to wring its terrible toll there also. And you will see her, if you put your mind to it, you'll hear her in a doctor's office thirty years later, twenty years later. 'I'm sick,' she's saying, 'I don't know what's the matter with me,' and the weakest organ, the weakest aggregate of cells has broken down. 'You've got to have the kidney fixed, those lungs, that stomach, whatever. And most of all you need a plastic . . .' 'How much will it cost?' 'Well, it may run five hundred . . .' 'I can't. I haven't got the money . . .' That's what you're going to see when you look at that ten-year-old kid."

"I'm going into small-town practice. That's where I'm going. I've made up my mind."

"Intern where you want. Pick some place with big names. See if you can get in. You've got the grades."

And within Lucas a warning knelled, it was the first warning. A name was only the man back of it. And the dream was better. It was better to worship from afar. Better—

"I wonder if it would be possible—I wonder if you'd say a word for me—"

"Yes? You've got some place picked out?"

"I wonder if I could intern here—"

"It's as good as done." He rose and extended his hand. "I think you've made a very sensible choice!"

•

"It's the only thing for a chap like him," Dr. Fletcher told Dr. Aarons. "Even if he isn't the chap he seems to be."

"It sticks out all over him."

"Well, it worked."

"Yes, it worked. I feel as if I'd deliberately condemned him to poverty."

"Well, don't. It's what he had to have. We just saved him five years finding out. And we got a doctor out of it."

"Thanks to Brundage—"

"Thanks to Brundage."

"They're right, too, in their way. There's nothing wrong with earning a living. Brundage aside, the rest have got their illusions—"

"That's something I didn't tell him. Poverty's the sickness of doctors, too. . . ."

"You're a fool to stick here," Alfred said. "You've always been a fool. But this caps it."

"I'll be all right. How's your appointment coming?"

"It's all but fixed. I got a letter from Dad just yesterday. We've got Sturmdorff himself in our corner. I'm just waiting for the letter . . . It took some drag, I'll tell you that . . ."

"God! It must have. Three vacancies!"

"It did. It took all we had."

That afternoon, flushed with security, swollen with success, feeling this small place smaller, seeing it already from an eminence, Alfred quarrelled with Professor Dietrick, the pompous man, the cruel one,

". . . due to pathological amyloid substances in venules of the kidney," he concluded firmly.

"There are no such things as venules, there," Professor Dietrick announced.

"Would you like to see a textbook on the subject?"

"How dare you!"

"Because I'll be glad to read it to you."

"Let it lay, let it lay," Masters hissed, tugging at Alfred's sleeve. Lucas listened open-mouthed, paralyzed.

"Your reading requires an interpreter, I see. I don't know what Medicine you intend to practice but I should like to inform the rest of the class that the interpretations of this, ah, gentleman, will find short shrift in either oral or written examinations conducted by me."

"We've all had to listen to you. And we've kept our mouths shut. You teach your own particular brand of Medicine. Which are we going to believe—you, or any textbook you can name? There are venules in the kidney. It states so plainly. It doesn't even take a lecturer to know that! You want me to read it?"

The class was absolutely silent. Most kept their eyes down.

Professor Dietrick stared icily at Alfred. Then without a word he left the room.

The letter of appointment was not in the evening's mail nor the next. A week passed. Alfred called his father. The next day brought the answer.

Alfred made his apology before the class.

Professor Dietrick listened in silence. At the end, he nodded his head slightly. Alfred sat down. Professor Dietrick proceeded with the lecture.

A week later the confirming letter arrived.

"But a pompous, ignorant ass like Dietrick—a nothing stuck away in a little jerkwater school!" raged Brundage.

Alfred sighed, smiled wryly.

"The long, long arm of Medicine," said Avery. "A voice in the wilderness calls—the ranks close—Medicine, my boys—Medicine—!"

"I'll tell you something," Alfred said soberly. "He was right."

"The side of the angels," said Avery. "If you can't lick 'em, join 'em!"

Alfred flushed.

"Lay off," said Lucas.

"He doesn't bother me," Alfred said serenely.

But when Avery left, Lucas left with him.

"It's a long arm, all right," he said tentatively, after they had walked a while in silence.

"It's Medicine, boy! It's the old closed corporation! The ranks close. The old guard stands firm. Even for a swine like Dietrick!"

"For you and me too!"

"Yes, even for you and me. Well, tell me, Luke! How do you like it?"

Lucas said nothing. He would have said, "It doesn't have to be true, it's just an interpretation." And then they would have talked, dissected, restated, analyzed, talked, talked endlessly. And all the same, the feeling wouldn't have gone. It would still be there. Still frowning. Not proven. He said nothing.

"I'm going to intern right here," he told Kristina.

"Yes?" Kristina sparred.

"Right here!"

"You talk it over? You talk to the professors?"

"Why? What's the matter?"

"I don't know. I just ask you."

"What have you got against here?"

"Nothing—"

"Then why did you ask me like that?"

"I didn't ask you like anything. I just—"

"You just talk too goddamned much!"

"I'm sorry."

"If you've got something to say—say it. If you haven't, just keep your mouth shut."

"What's the matter, Luke? What's the matter?"

"Oh, for Christ's dear sake!"

"I'm your wife—"

"You don't have to remind me—"

"I just wanted to know—I don't know how to talk to you—I didn't mean anything—"

"You never do!" And he stalked angrily out, hunted in vain for Avery, walked to the park, sat there, brooding.

When he got home the room was in darkness. He stumbled over an object in the middle of the floor. He turned on the lights. Kristina was in bed, her back to him, her head partly covered.

Shamming, he decided.

He bent angrily to pick up the object over which he had stumbled. The light revealed a sizable package. He lifted it. Something rattled inside. It was quite heavy. He stripped away the wrapping paper. He uncovered a mahogany box. His breath came faster. He opened the gleaming box. Gently, slowly, he drew out the microscope, new, glorious with three stages, complex and beautiful, with an adjustable field, three eyepieces, a thirty power,

He gazed at it. His eyes filled.

"Kris," he breathed.

There was no answer.

He turned. He walked to the bed. He sat down and shook her shoulder, gently.

"Kris—"

She turned hesitantly. She had not been sleeping.

"Oh, Kris!" And he threw his arms about her, hugging her, kissing her—"

"What you want?"

"Oh, Kris—"

"Zeiss, like you said?"

"Kris, darling—"

"Is a good one!"

"I'm sorry, darling. I'm so sorry. I'm so ashamed. I talk to you like you were a dog, or something. And then you do something like that . . ."

"You got lots of strain. I know. It's hard for you, too. You're a good man, Lucas. I don't worry. I know it's hard—"

"And all the time I was talking to you like that it was right here—why didn't you stop me—oh, Kris—Kris—"

"I borrowed on my salary—"

"Oh, no! You're my girl, Kris! You're my girl!"

"You need a light. A light I couldn't get—"

"Never mind—what's a light!"

"Next month, maybe—"

But his mouth stopped hers, he cradled her, her lips warmed, in a moment he stripped the covers back, he drew her to him,

"It's been so long," she sighed.

Then he stopped her mouth again. The room was alive with them. They were heavy with hunger.

He began his internship a month later.

Avery was one of the few members of his class who stayed on and Lucas gravitated to him.

"Sometimes," he said one day, "it sounds like you were almost sorry you ever started Medicine. Sorry to be in it!"

They were waiting to make rounds.

"I talk a lot, don't I."

"The same thing, over and over."

"I wonder if you ever hear me?"

"I see the same things you do—"

"No, you don't. You see and you hear. But you—"

"I wince at the same things you wince at—Brundage—all the rest—"

"No, it's just the behavior you see. And that's what you wince at. To you they're just naughty boys, profaning solemn moments. So far as you're concerned they'll come around in time and be part of the greatness, decorous, dedicated, and unearthly. To you any other eventuality is incomprehensible. You've never even thought of it, have you?"

"Why does it always come back to me? What have I got to do with it?"

"What you don't seem to realize is that they are exactly what they are, they'll never be any different. That's all the concept they have. They're Medicine as it really is. They're ninety percent of all doctors."

"You know you don't really think that way. No one goes into Medicine unless he really wants to—"

"They're merchants of service. They have a service to sell. They've learned how to take care of people. They're licensed. For a fee they'll help people who never learned how to help themselves. They've paid their money and their time to learn all there is to know of the human body and the medicines for it. They'll sell that knowledge at a price. So many dollars per problem."

"You're talking about Brundage now. Brundage and the few fellows like him—"

"And do you know what holds us together? Our union? It's fear and ignorance. To the average human his body is a great and a sacred mystery. And the man who knows the riddle of the mystery is a god. That's what we are—gods. And the thing that holds us together as a group is our realization of this. We know how the public feels about us. And we know what *we don't know*. We know a lot. But we don't know the simple, basic things. We've got a rough idea but we still don't know positively where blood is manufactured. We don't know how the kidney secretes urine. We don't know why we wake up. We don't know why we sleep. We don't know why the heart beats. We don't know what triggers cells to regenerate. What we don't know about a cell itself, the very basis of life, would fill more volumes than all the theories we've ever studied. We don't know why a woman menstruates. We don't know how the fertilized ovum crosses the space between ovary and tube. We don't know why a child is born—what triggers birth—what shock is—"

"We don't know anything, do we?"

"Oh, yes! We know a hell of a lot more than the people who pay us to take care of them! That we do! We know eight medicines—eight specifics out of all the tens of thousands known to man—which medicines will specifically cure the disease for which they are administered. Eight—and only eight! We can set bones. Mechanically, we get better all the time."

"Why blame Medicine? It's not our fault that laymen think of us as witch doctors!"

"Because we trade on it! And you know goddamned well we trade on it!"

"You're thinking of Brundage, again—"

"Thinking of Brundage? My God Almighty! What happens when any of us makes a mistake? We're a solid front! Nobody can make a mistake in Medicine, don't you know that? Who the hell can testify but another doctor? And who's going to testify for *him* when *he* makes a mistake? What do you think those lines mean on your diploma—'privileges and immunities'! What do you think immunity means! The right not to be prosecuted when a patient dies! That's what it means! The right to get away with murder. Do you think privileges means only the right to park overtime because you're tending to a patient?"

"And just exactly how would you practice Medicine if the law were a gun aimed at your head while you cut or dosed? How would you like to be McDowell doing the first ovariotomy without anesthetic and without antiseptic while a mob howled outside waiting to lynch you if the patient died?"

"He was quite a guy, wasn't he!"

"You're damned right he was! And that woman would have died if he hadn't had the guts to go ahead!"

"I know it. The best of us have guts. That's true. The best of us are unselfish, dedicated, kind of. The best of us know what we know, all the worst of it, and go ahead, anyway. But there aren't many. And the thing that gets me is the closed-corporation business. The way humans look at us. And the way we trade on it. Not the fact that they think we're reverend witch doctors. That's terrible enough. But the way we encourage them to think that way. The tacit knowledge, when we look at each other over a patient, of what we don't know—the trusting ignorance of the poor slob—"

"It's time to go look at the poor slobs."

"Goddamn it! I guess it is!"

"You're all right, Avery. I know that—"

"I still haven't touched you, have I!"

"Sure! I understand what you mean—"

"But you think it'll all pass, don't you! It'll all smooth out. Because the Lord our God is one God. And it'll all come out in the wash. And all I've said is just stuff on the surface—a nice guy talking a little wild—good old Avery—"

Lucas shrugged and smiled. They walked down the corridor to the first ward.

"Here they are!" Avery said in a low voice. Lucas smiled absently. His eyes lighted in anticipation. "You know what they are, don't you, Luke? They're not human beings. To you they're just one of the materials of Medicine."

The smile faded from Lucas' eyes. He looked at Avery uncertainly, startled.

"Just reagents, boy," Avery smiled happily. "Let's see how they've reacted. . . ."

In the first ward they went from bed to bed, checking charts, checking dressings. As when he had first entered a ward Lucas was aware of the eyes of the patients, watching him. Avery's last remark had done this, Lucas discovered resentfully. The flesh beneath the dressings now belonged to people, the dressings were on people and not on wounds, and the detachment of procedure vanished. There was in the ward room a sense of waiting, the room was furnished with it, it canopied each bed with an aura evident as the bed itself.

Lucas, familiar with the injury, was surprised to see that the fracture case in the first bed was quite young. He had treated him, he had seen him on rounds for more than a week. He looked at the chart. They were almost the same age.

"How'm I doing, Doc?"

"You're doing fine," Lucas smiled automatically.

"Harness bothering you?" asked Avery.

"My foot goes to sleep. Hung up that way—it kinda goes to sleep—"

"Well, well, let's take a look—"

Avoiding Avery's eyes Lucas checked the suspending harness gravely, made an infinite minor adjustment, frowning, then stepped back.

"You'll be all right now," he said cheerily.

"Thanks, Doc. I'll be out of here soon?"

"Absolutely."

"In a week?"

"We'll see . . ."

They passed on to the next bed.

" 'I dressed the wound and God healed him,' " Avery said, expressionless.

Lucas flushed. At the next bed he stood back, deliberately.

"Well," said Avery going forward, "and how are we, today?"

"I don't know how you are, but I'm in pain!"

"Gas troubling you?"

"You're goddamned right it's troubling me! Or whatever it is!"

There was hate and fear in the man's eyes. Clarence Jones, aged thirty-nine, mechanic, appendectomy, third day. No fever, pulse, respiration normal, medication delivered, no bowel movement.

"Let's have a look!" Avery's voice was cold, his features set. "Miss Berkley—" The nurse pushed the dressing tray close.

"Son-of-a-bitch!" the man yelled suddenly.

"It's not necessary to yell—" Avery straightened.

"It isn't hurting *you*!"

"Nor use profanity!"

"You just take it easy!"

The three tending him settled into a chilly silence.

"Ow!"

"It's all over, now—"

"God damn it!"

"I'm going to have to ask you again, Mr. Jones—"

"If I was rich you wouldn't be yanking me like that!"

"Now, that's hardly the attitude for a sick man we've just done our best to help—"

"I got gas pain enough without you monkeying where I was cut—"

Avery wrote "prostigmine" on the chart. The nurse deftly filled a syringe, Avery bared the man's thigh, slipped the needle home.

"You'll feel better now," he said coldly.

The ward listened, watched, waited.

"By God, I'd better!"

Avery nodded. They walked to the next bed.

" 'The physician is practitioner as well as scientist,' " Lucas murmured " 'A bedside manner is the way doctors handle their patients as personalities and has an important effect on the functioning of their physiological systems.' "

"Snotty bastard!"

Lucas looked at him blandly.

"Give you much trouble, Miss Berkley?"

"I don't know what got into him, Dr. Avery–"

There was an old man in the next bed. He looked up at them placative, apologetic.

"How are we doing today, Mr. Barnes?"

"Oh, fine, never better, Doctor. You fellas are whizzes–"

The kidney basin beneath the covers was partly full of pus. A length of rubber catheter meandered through a maze of tape and safety pins to a hole in the abdomen over the bladder.

Lucas picked up the chart. It was the same as it had been yesterday, the same as it had been a month ago.

"You're doing fine, Mr. Barnes–"

"I'm sure grateful. I sure am." He lifted his head, glanced fearfully at the next bed. "Fellas like that shouldn't ought to be allowed in a hospital!" he wheezed vehemently. "The way he talked to you fellas! Doctors and all! Swearing right out in front of a nurse!"

"Don't you worry about those things!" Lucas smiled cheerily. "You just take care of yourself." He nodded. They walked to the next bed.

People were the noises they made. People were faces and expressions on them. People were personalities but the personalities were ailments too. There was no norm. There was just an arbitrary line, marks on paper. People were their illnesses, their adjustments to living, to illness.

The sixth bed was interesting. It was Thomas Bretton, truck driver, thirty-four, colored, accident, observation. Miss Berkley looked at them significantly as she drew back the sheet.

"Well, well," said Avery. "What have we here?" He smiled reassuringly at Thomas Bretton, colored.

"Probably Dr. Swander will want to look at this," Lucas nodded brightly.

Miss Berkley left immediately to call the resident.

Thomas Bretton, colored, had a ruptured bladder. The urine which normally filled it had emptied under the skin and now swelled in a long blister eight inches down the inside of his left thigh.

"Give you much trouble?" Lucas smiled noncommittally, making conversation until Dr. Swander arrived.

"Don't feel a thing," the Negro answered apprehensively. "What's wrong?"

"What Dr. Marsh means is, do you have much pain from your accident?" Avery cut in.

"Pain? Sure I got pain! I got plenty pain! I can't piss, for one thing–"

"We'll take care of your urination problems–"

"Sure funny when a man can't piss—"

Dr. Swander arrived at the bedside, close behind him Miss Berkley.

"Well, well! What have we got here?"

"Patient complains of difficulty urinating." Lucas pressed the sac of urine. The patient raised his head to look. "Now, now," said Miss Berkley, "you lie back, now. This doesn't concern you—"

The three looked at each other swiftly. This man has a ruptured bladder, said Dr. Swander's look. I know, said Avery's look. I concur, said Lucas' look.

"Aspirating needle," said Dr. Swander, straightening. Miss Berkley departed.

"Hit him right head on, did you?" Lucas asked, to cover the waiting.

"God, man! He hit me! Right on the corner of Currant and Oxford —I was comin' round the corner and—"

"I don't know what gets into people driving these days," Avery commiserated.

"Seems like everybody's got a car," Dr. Swander complained.

"Good times like these people driving ain't no business driving, man gets a hundred dollars first thing he got to have a car—ain't nothin' wrong with me, is there, Doc? Nothin' serious, I ain't hurt bad'm I, Doc, it's all right, ain't it—?"

"Now, now—" said Dr. Swander. Miss Berkley handed him the aspirating syringe, he turned his body to hide it.

"You'll be right as rain in no time!" Lucas said cheerily.

The patient glimpsed the long needle and rose upright.

"Whatcha gonna do! Man, you ain't gonna stick that thing into me? Doc, you wouldn't do that—?"

"Lie down!" ordered Dr. Swander.

Avery, who was nearest, helped Miss Berkley force his shoulders back to the pillow. "For God's sake, Doc!" Then he screamed.

The sac was empty, at last, a catheter inserted, a basin to catch the flow. They moved on to the next bed. Midway they stopped.

"Schedule him tomorrow," Dr. Swander ordered. "Keep him quiet." He walked on. Thomas Bretton, colored, next day would be opened, his torn bladder repaired. They considered whether to go and watch. They walked on to the next bed.

"You figuring to practice around here?" Lucas asked, as they slumped in the dressing room, rounds over.

"I don't know. I don't know whether I'll practice at all."

"What?" Lucas sat upright.

"I mean it."

"You mean just stick here? Stay at the hospital?"

"Maybe. Here or someplace else. Maybe I'll even—teach . . ."

"Oh, no!"

"Why not?"

"Nothing, I guess. I mean there's nothing wrong with it. I guess—I guess I was just surprised."

"Oh, if you want money—sure! A fellow that starts practice today is lucky. His practice is all made for him. Everybody's rich—everybody's rolling in money—there's a fortune to be made—a doctor I know put four thousand into stock a year ago and he's worth over a hundred thousand today—"

"It's not that, altogether. All I meant was, if that's what was worrying you—"

"You practice for me. Where you going to set up shop?"

"I don't know, yet. Some small place. But Avery—"

"Oh, don't worry, don't worry, I haven't made up my mind yet . . ."

But both knew he had.

And Lucas, walking home, was sad.

"He'll probably end up a teacher," he told Kristina.

"Too bad for his wife." Kristina shook her head, commiserating.

"His wife! Doesn't it occur to you he's doing what he wants to do?"

"How does he know? Young fella like that?"

"Christ, Kristina! How does anybody know? But you can't judge everything on the basis of how it's going to turn out for his wife!"

"Got to have teachers. Sure. Got to have them. Only when I think what the poor woman's got to go through—"

"He isn't even married yet!"

"Don't get mad—"

"I'm not mad! But just once I'd like to discuss even the least, the most trivial thing with you—"

"You think like a fella thinks. That's all. A woman thinks like a woman."

"She *thinks*! She thinks with her uterus!"

"Maybe—maybe that's the way things are—she thinks different—that don't make her wrong, Luke—somebody's got to think of such things—"

But Lucas was no longer listening. He walked to the bureau and picked up a letter there.

"When'd this come?"

"It was already here." She walked from the room carefully. The letter was from Job. It was postmarked Chillicothe.

"He hasn't moved, then," Lucas said sourly. He tore off the envelope and read warily.

Dear son,

Hope this finds you well and everything going all right and studying hard etc. Well, I must say things turned out on schedule as it was easy to see this place was a gold mine if worked right and the former owner I tried to tell him but he wouldn't listen to what he had. Anyway I am all set, now, as you can see

Lucas glanced swiftly at the letterhead. "Job Marsh," it read, "Finest Harness, Repairs."

and the fact is this is better than Milletta, Tyre, and all the rest no matter what would have happened. Maybe your mother was right when she used to say everything happened for a reason because if those fellows hadn't been so greedy would never have come here and never have known. Have my eye on a place just about to go out of business, can be picked up for a song, couple of places, matter of fact, all run like this fellow used to run this one which I'm glad to say I now own, lock, stock, and barrel as the saying goes and things have just begun. Hope you are all right as things are fine here but money is tight at present although just temporary because of expansion making funds tied up to some extent, but if you should need anything let me know and maybe I can do something although not convenient right now.

Write when you get the chance.

And his sprawling signature followed with a flourish.
Beneath,

P.S. Doctors ought to be making a mint these days, what with wages out of sight, etc., we're off to the races as the saying goes, so if you want a chance to double and triple your money I'll be glad to cut you in for a slice, or if you know any rich doctor friends would like an investment guaranteed to triple in a year would appreciate letting me know.

He sat with the letter in his lap. Kristina returned. She ignored the letter elaborately.

"You want to eat?" she asked gently.

"Come on! I'll take you out—"

"I got it all fixed—"

"I want to go out." He rose. She took her apron off. "He's done it again. He's got another shop! God knows how he swindled the poor chump—but he's got it. Went to work for him and took the shop away! He's off again!"

"He's all right?"

"Him? He's made of the leather he sells! You couldn't kill him with dynamite."

"He's started business again—"

"Yes, by God, he has! I got to give him that!"

"He'll be all right. Nowadays everybody makes money. Even Oley. You couldn't lose money if you tried."

"I'm just tickled to death he didn't ask me to send him some!"

"Lucas! Your father—!"

"The son-of-a-bitch! And I wrote him we were married. And he didn't say a word about it. Not even God bless you. Come on! Come on, Kris! Let's get out of here!"

Out of it,

Out!

Out of the room where he'd opened the letter.

And the letter was dead now, paper, the true memento, a link with the room, not what it was at all, but paper, and he tore it as he walked, ripped it and tore it, mazing the shame into meaningless shredded words.

good to no one, unconnected, and dropped them little by little into the gutter.

"Maybe he meant to. Maybe he thought he did," Kristina said when the last of the paper had fluttered from his hand, when they had walked a while in silence.

"The hell with him."

"It's your father, that's all," she said deprecatively.

"Even your folks wrote us—corny cards, sure—but something, at least!"

There was nothing she could say. And looking covertly at his face, stormy and disillusioned and hurt, his eyes rolling as if he were looking for a stick to bite at, she knew it was a time to be very carefully silent.

His own father, she thought, it's not right. He could have written, at least. I'm his daughter, now. That's not right. And she tried to understand what kind of people these were, the mother and father who had raised her man, they were foreigners, speaking another language, having different aims, thinking different thoughts. They were outside her experience. Her heart ached suddenly for Lucas, for the shame he must be feeling. For the twilit loneliness his vague youth must have been. But one thing was clear, her duty was clear, it was not a pleasant duty, nor, as far as she could see, even fair, but it was her duty not to let Lucas hate his father, and somehow, somehow gently, to prevent his speaking disparagingly of him. It was tribal duty which one did not analyze, an instinct and an obligation.

"Everybody's different, Luke. Everybody shows their love a different way," she murmured at last.

He looked at her, hurt and astonished.

"Whose side are you on?"

"I'm on your side, Luke! It wasn't the right thing to do! I don't say it was! You got a right to be mad! Only—it's your father."

"Father, mother, what are you trying to do—sanctify them? Those are words, not people. They're not sacred and they haven't haloes and they're just the people you see all around you. They're biological partners and they do it to each other because they like to do it and a child comes of it, and they don't even know which time they did it makes the child and then they raise the child because the community requires them to and they'd be arrested if they didn't, and maybe they even like children. That's what a father and mother is!"

"Oh, Luke!"

" 'Oh, Luke!' You going to tell me about love? How sacred and unvarying is the love of a parent for a child? How about that six-year-old in Ward J—with a fractured skull and a broken right humerus where its loving father beat it with a poker—for nothing?"

"He was drunk, Luke! He was an animal—"

"All right, how about the little girl with the burnt hands her mother held on the hot stove—she'll lose one hand, you know—how about the dozen that come in every month, the thousands who don't use a poker or a hot stove and cripple them for life just the same, the tens of thousands we never see—"

"Not all parents are good parents—"

"You're damned right they're not—and none of them are holy or sacred because they took care of a helpless young thing and did what they were expected to do!"

"There's a lot of parents, Luke, you don't know anything about, men and women who sacrifice, who go without, just to make a kid happy, parents like mine who worried all the time about raising me right, did without lots of times—"

"They did it because they wanted to. It made them happy."

"Parents have died for their children—"

"Two years ago there was a flood—and mothers were throwing their own kids in so there'd be room for themselves, in the boats—"

"I know, Luke . . . You got to try to see the whole picture . . ."

"I don't think you've heard a word I've said!"

"I have. I know. I know what's going through your mind. I know. Wherever you look you're going to see something to prove your point. Wherever I look I'm going to see something to prove mine. And when I see it, I'll be happy. And when you see—what you see—how about you?"

He looked at her sharply, surprised.

"At least I won't be disappointed, I won't have the rug pulled from under me . . ."

And there was another thing. Papa's getting pretty old, she thought. She thought of it often, nowadays. I should be back there, somebody's going to have to take care of him, tend the house. If I could just get Luke to go to Minnesota, if we could live nearby, if I could drop in every day . . . If I could say it right . . . If I knew how . . . So he wouldn't be mad . . .

"What are you thinking about?" Lucas asked irritably.

"I was thinking about Minnesota," she said a little desperately, seeing his lips tighten.

"We've gone all over that—"

"I was thinking about my father—"

"Well? What about him?"

"He's getting old, Luke— Somebody's got to look out for him."

"You've got folks! You've got aunts and uncles! He's got brothers and sisters!"

But I'm his daughter! she wanted to say. *I'm* the one! You don't understand! And she knew he did not understand and that there was no use at all, no use floundering further, going deeper, more helplessly, more hopelessly into the morass of individual experiences. Maybe there would be a time, maybe he would mellow, maybe she could work on him, maybe he would soften, maybe there would be a time . . . later . . . soon . . .

"I guess so," she said quietly.

"They're bound to look out for him . . . Look, Kris! I won't go to Minnesota, understand? Now get that clear! Get it straight! Because I'm not going! Ever!"

"I didn't say anything about Minnesota. Did I? You don't have to get all excited. I don't know what's so terrible about Minnesota. You've never even been there. You've got a down on it. You must have heard something—"

"Kris!"

His face was whitening with anger, in his eyes, behind the rage, there was the faint look of pain and betrayal, she saw this with fear, then a pang of loneliness, of protest, then the embarrassment of love.

"No more!" she cried. "I stop! Come on, Luke. We eat . . ."

They found a workingman's diner. They sat in a booth.

"Ham hocks and lima beans," he read the soiled menu. "That's for me!"

She looked automatically at the price. She read the top item.

"Why don't you try the steak, Luke?" The steak cost much more.

"No, no." For he had seen the price too.

"A good piece of meat will make you feel better–"

"I like it! I like ham hocks and lima beans!"

"I think I have the omelet–"

"Why don't *you* have the steak!"

"I'm not hungry. Not for steak–"

"The stew, then?"

"Ah, no! You never know what they put in a stew! I take the omelet." The omelet cost less than ham hocks.

She picked up her empty glass and looked intently at it. She picked up a fork, squinted at it, began to rub it with a napkin. From the corner of his eye he could see the waiter approaching.

"What's the matter, Kris? Quit it!" he said urgently, his voice low.

"These places—they never wash anything clean–"

The waiter stood beside their table. Lucas looked up at him, hoping to catch his eyes, to divert it from Kris, smiling friendlily to hide his embarrassment, to mollify the waiter.

"I'm going to have the ham hocks!" he said loudly.

And when the waiter had taken their orders and gone on,

"What did I do!" Kris was confused.

"For Christ's sake! When you go to a restaurant do you have to pick up everything on the table and inspect it? How do you think they feel when they see you do that!"

"I don't want to eat with a dirty fork–"

"Well, look at it. Just glance at it. If it's not clean—tell him so—quietly."

Her face reddened.

"I'm sorry."

"For Christ's sake, Kris!" He was angry now for having to tell her, for pitying her because he had embarrassed her, because she had embarrassed him, because the waiter might have been–

"I heard a TL about you today," she forestalled the remainder of the outburst, made a smile. "Something upstairs."

"What?" he asked, still frowning.

"Something nice. Something one of the surgeons said—Dr. Lawrence. You know Dr. Lawrence?" She smiled at him significantly. Dr. Lawrence's least words were not heard lightly.

"He doesn't even know me."

"Yes, he does. Oh, yes."

"I've never said two words to him," he said hopefully.

"Oh, yes! But he knows you, all the same. He said to Dr. Turner he'd rather have you as first assistant than anybody at the hospital!"

"No! No fooling, Kris?"

"That's what he said. Resident and all."

"No kidding!"

"Well, why not? It's true. They know who's good, Luke. I see them all. And I tell you this, there isn't one can hold a candle to you! No, sir! When you're good, I got to tell you! And Dr. Turner said you better be careful that's his wife right there, and he looked around, and Dr. Turner said, 'Kris! You know Kris!' And his mouth opened, and then he remembered and he said, 'That's right! By God, I forgot! How are you, Kris? How's marriage?' And I said, 'I'll tell him, it'll make him feel good you bet to hear Dr. Lawrence said that,' and he said, 'You tell him, Kris, he deserves it, just don't give him a swelled head—' "

"How did he happen to say it? Which one was it—"

"It was a hernia. A repeat. Gordon botched it. One of Gordon's jobs—"

"He just had hard luck," Lucas said automatically.

And Kristina, about to contradict, knowing she was right, recalled herself in time, remembering her man.

"You think we don't know—we nurses?—me, who's seen so many—"

"You ought to—if anybody does—"

"I know, all right. I'm not only head operating-room nurse. Once, I was ward nurse and took care of them after they'd been operated on. I know. Believe me."

"That's the truth. What you know you really know, Kris. You work like clockwork."

She flushed.

"Sure! Just last week a doctor came in—I'm not saying who—he's a big man—he's no fool—abscessed appendix. All right. First thing he makes a big, long incision—"

"He had to because—"

"Sure. I know. He wants to make it long enough so he can pack around with gauze to keep the pus from getting on the peritoneum!"

"That's right."

"Then he blunt-dissects a big mass of blackish, swollen omentum, here and there spotted with lymph fluid. So what does he do? 'Looks gangrenous,' he says. And he cuts it out."

Lucas frowned, thinking.

"Maybe it was gangrenous . . ."

"It was protection. It was swollen with what it was working on, because it was working. What he cut out was full, loaded with protective material. Not only that—he spent time taking it out. More shock for the patient. And naturally where he cut left a long, raw surface—just asking for post-op bowel adhesions. Then he took out the abscess and the appendix. And then he inverted the stump of the appendix—"

"But you're supposed to—"

"I don't know, Luke," she leaned back, reflecting. "I don't know . . . Where you sew, there—"

"The caecum—"

"Yes—it's pretty frail—it's swollen—the stitches are almost certain to tear out if the caecum balloons and then the least you get is a secondary abscess—"

"But, Kris! You're all wrong! Everybody does it that way," he said mechanically, thinking hard meanwhile, seeing a grain of wisdom, hearing the faint tone of truth, remembering precedent at last. "You ever see anybody do it any other way?"

"Few fellers," she remembered. "They just tied it off. Didn't invert it. Never had any trouble. But anyway! Next he cleans out the abscess cavity, rubbing and swashing around—this, that, the other. And finally he doesn't suture all the muscle planes separately. Just asking for a hernia!"

"Who was it?"

"No, I won't tell you. Fellow from out of state," she lied. "But there—aseptically everything okay! Operating style—beautiful!"

"And what happened?"

"I don't know," she lied again. The patient had died a week later, it had been the whole point, having reached that point she knew that telling him would only hurt him.

"Probably got along all right," Lucas frowned. "But you fellows really watch, don't you?"

"We don't miss much."

And you understand what you're seeing, too, he thought. By God, Kris, I didn't know that about you. I really didn't. My God, how many operations have you seen! And we just take you for granted. You're a hand. That's always there with an instrument. He looked at her, analyzing, thinking on a new plane, with new ingredients. You've been a nurse. That's all you've ever been. That's what you know and that's all the detail of life you know. Except when you were a girl. You learned how to keep house. You never learned to handle a knife and fork, you don't know how to dress, your voice gets too loud, in everything else you're rudimentary. But you sure know nursing. And when you see something—nobody's fooling you! But there's a touch of treason in what you say. I've got to set you right, there . . .

"An omentum will fool you," he said gently. "Fool the best of us."

"If you'd seen it—"

"You may have a point about the damage, though." She was right and he knew she was right. "About the appendicial stump—"

"What do you think, Luke?"

"I—don't know."

"Stands to reason."

"I'd like to try it, sometime . . ."

"Hey! Look at me! I keep on talking! Eat, Luke! Eat your dinner!"

"Yes . . . So Lawrence said that . . ."

"They all say it! They know all about you! You ought to hear them . . . Steady . . . Smart as a whip . . . Good man . . . Damned good man . . . Ought to go far . . . And their faces say even more! Eat, Luke! Eat!"

He bent to his food, absent-mindedly. He looked up, surprised.

"Say! This is good!"

Quickly she took a forkful from his plate. He looked around to make sure no one had seen her. She tasted the food and looked at him, expressionless.

"You like that?"

"It's wonderful!"

She tried what was left on her fork again, to make sure. It was bad. It was tasteless, the texture was stringy, it was bad.

"It's terrific!" he said, trying more.

He doesn't know good food from bad, she sighed. All this time I've been making him the best I know, I'm a good cook, making fine food out of twenty cents, and all this time it hasn't meant anything to him.

"What did he do about the transversus abdominis?" he asked suddenly.

"About what? Oh, about the– I didn't see that, I had to turn away for something and–"

"Kris!"

"No, I just had my head turned." She spoke rapidly. "Sometimes I'll make you ham hocks and lima beans! When I make them–!"

"Kris!"

"What is it?" She smiled brightly, defensively.

"You don't know the transversus abdominis?"

"Sure–"

"You don't, Kris! You haven't got the least idea! With all you know!"

"But Luke! It's so many years ago–"

"By God! And for a minute–"

"It's years, Luke! When I was a student! You forget, Luke. My goodness, the anesthesiologist stands just three feet from me–I can't give anesthetic. Sure! I know how! I could make out! But you only remember what you have to. I've got my four or five girls, I've got to see that every doctor has laid out for him what he wants–one wants this instrument, the other something different–all for the same operation, I got to know what each one wants, remember it. Some like to have an instrument slapped hard in their hand. Some curse at you unless you just hand it to them, gentle. Some like to tell you, some like never to say a word. You have to have spare trays in case of accident, you got to be sure there's plenty of dressings, that the autoclave's right, enough gloves, the right sizes, check every suture, check every needle–my God, Luke!"

"But the transversus abdominis–!"

"And Luke, how many doctors you think can name the nerves of the leg? Anatomy of the liver? Do you think Lawrence himself can do it as well as a first-year, a second-year student? New equipment, new methods, new operations–it's all I can do to keep up with operating-room technique!"

He shook his head.

"I guess it's possible," he conceded. He thought a moment longer. "You're probably right. But this–God, Kris! Don't ever let anybody know you don't know where the transversus abdominis is! Look! The first muscle cut through–"

"That's the external oblique!"

"That's right! That's what I mean! You see them every day, after all! And under that is the internal oblique—"

"Aha! And *then* comes the transversus!"

"See?"

"I forgot."

"But Kris—!"

"I'll remember! Eat now! You want dessert? Pie?"

Waiting for Kristina to finish, he looked about him. Kristina was the only woman present. All the men were workingmen, dressed in the jackets and caps that were a workingman's uniform, that dressed them all alike, plumber, carpenter, mason, truck driver, that made this place their place, with whom the counterman was interchangeable, let him drop his apron, put on a jacket and cap.

And he was Dr. Marsh, he was a doctor, eating with them, if they only knew, he inspected them hurriedly, but they were all eating, placidly eating, their eyes would never see a white coat on him, a stethoscope dangling from the pocket, a white uniform on Kristina, a doctor and the head operating-room nurse.

Kristina had finished and was looking at him curiously.

"Going to have dessert?"

"Maybe I try the pie," she said decorously. "We see how the pie is. You looking at those men? Look how many are eating steak!"

"Shhh!"

"Count 'em!" She lowered her voice. "Can you imagine? That's how much money a workman makes nowadays. All of them eating steak. And the poor doctor has ham hocks and lima beans."

"They were good, though." He would not have ordered the steaks, anyway. They were thin and overcooked, poor-grade meat. But he would have liked the choice.

"First fellow on the left, far end—heart."

"How do you know?"

"Blue lips—third fellow sebaceous cyst—"

"How—"

"Look at it! Under his ear—and the fifth one's nephritis, see how puffy his face is—"

"It's wonderful!"

"You can tell when a patient's cyanotic, can't you? You do it often enough. Well, these are just some of the rest of the signs. People are books if you can read them. I do it all the time." He shrugged. "I wonder how often I'm right."

Suddenly the small diner oppressed him, the faces, the crowded stools, the food congealing on the plates. He wanted to be at the hospital, feeling the white, the shining, the order, he thought of the familiar interior sensually, he longed to be there, he rejected the thought of going there at this time of night, off duty, he frowned, balked, irritated.

"Come on. Let's go."

Kristina rose obediently.

"Oh, I'm sorry! Finish your pie—"

"No, I'm done. It's all right. Not so good, anyway."

And they walked out. And in the night, walking, they were alone together. Their concerns were their own. The world's life moved about them, these two small figures were adrift in that dry sea, particles incurious of other incurious particles, animate, purposeful and purposeless. And in the vast bulk of the happenings of this world, among the myriad happenings time would classify, underline, pass over, mark for a moment, mark for an hour, mark for an era, funnelling upward in a twisting time-wind bearing millions of pages and millions of words and voices bearing words, Domegk was beginning the experiments which would produce the sulfa drugs from the trash pile of German dye factories, setting down the day precisely in his notebook.

The world was shouting exultantly the greatest wealth that Hominidae had ever accumulated, the greatest number of things he had ever owned. Trotsky, Kamenev, Zinoviev, Rakovsky and Radek were exiled. The screams of 124 dying went upward from the Cleveland Clinic Hospital of Dr. George W. Crile, where fire, explosion, and chemical fumes from X-ray films bathed the vowels of this discovery for them,

And the Papal state was revived, and a revolution began in Mexico, and President Hoover proclaimed the Kellogg-Briand anti-war treaty under which sixty-two leading powers pledged themselves to renounce war as an instrument of national policy,

And all about them the affairs of men as nations locked and interlocked, in a timeless pavane, a grave and endless dance, full of the music of treaties, crackling with paper, smiling with wax, smiling and jubilant with function, merry with peace, dancing a new dance, old as Hominidae, over and over.

And in the nations, in the cities, in the towns, this generation and this genus resolved into units, busy with gain, delighted with hope, gained and set by, praised its proverbs, thanked its God for those things it had resolved were thankworthy, asked for more, praised its God for the rules of life it had determined God had given it, set out upon the full course of the year of man's presence nineteen hundred and twenty-nine,

A penny saved is a penny earned,
Put your money in the bank and you'll always have it,
The old folks knew best,
Man is essentially decent and well-meaning,
Thrift is the bulwark of the wise and the protection of the weak,
Step on a crack,
And you break your mother's back.
Secure.

They moved off into the night toward their home, their small rooms, lonely in themselves, lonely among all others, part of the whole, separate as different species. They saw the people about them incuriously, they were the well-worn, well-noted furniture of their home, the place where they abode. They found their home and went up to it and slept with those who slept.

He rode the ambulance the next afternoon, he and Avery, and they had just come in from a call. In the accident ward a nurse waved to them frantically. They ran to her. On the bed lay a four-year-old boy. His face was white. His clothing was bloody.

"His penis!" the nurse cried.

Lucas bent quickly, opened the boy's clothes, straightened, stared, startled.

"Clamps!"

He noticed the woman standing at the bedside.

"His penis's gone! Cut off!" he said to Avery.

"For the love of God!"

They felt for pulse.

"Transfusion—"

And Avery sped off. Lucas grasped the small stump of penis, squeezed tight, there was little blood left to flow.

"He cut it off," the woman said dully. She spoke like a sleepwalker.

"How did that happen!"

The woman was about twenty-eight. Her face was gray. She was dressed in a cheap housedress. She wore a wet apron, bloodstained. In her right hand she held a washrag.

"I was bathing the baby," she said. She recited it, listening. "I had the little girl in the bathtub. I was kneeling down, I was bathing her, all of a sudden I didn't hear him, I tiptoed into the living room, he was sitting there, playing with himself, I scolded him I said, 'I told you what I'd do, I'll get your daddy's razor and cut it off,' he cried and said he wouldn't, I gave him a cookie and went back to the baby,"

The nurse rushed up with clamps.

The child's breathing was very slow.

"Adrenalin, quick!" And she sped away again.

"I was washing her and all of a sudden I heard behind me, 'Look, Mama!' and I turned around and there he was. He was sitting in the corner. All over the tiles, all over everything. Blood. Blood everywhere. And between his knees his daddy's razor . . ."

Avery rushed in with the transfusion equipment and a donor. Lucas hurriedly, frantically assembled the tubing, fitted on the needle, bent over the boy.

"It's too late," said Avery. He dropped the child's wrist. Lucas stared at him stupidly. Avery shook his head. "No use," said Avery. Lucas felt a lifeless wrist. He turned to the mother. Through the hospital windows a sunny morning streamed. The warm and friendly light blinded her and her eyes blinked.

"I'm sorry," he said.

"I tried to get them to stop," she recited. "I ran out in the road carrying him. They wouldn't stop—"

The nurse covered the child with a sheet. Avery put away the apparatus. Lucas stepped to the woman and put a hand on her shoulder.

"If you'd got him here just a few minutes earlier—"

"Now he's gone. He's gone, hasn't he? He's gone."

"Yes . . . He's gone . . . You must try to—"

"Little Tommy. I took him, I ran with him, I tried to get them to stop—"

"It's not your fault. Try to pull yourself together. Remember, you're young, you've got another child—"

"My baby!" the woman whispered. "My baby!" she screamed suddenly. "My little baby! In the bathtub! In the water!"

And she ran from the room, slipping over the polished floor, falling as she reached the door, Lucas scrambling to help her up, fighting free from him—

"We'll go in the ambulance," he cried to her, following. "I'll take it, Avery," he called back over his shoulder. His words vanished, far below there was the quick sound of the ambulance gone, in the silence of the room Avery and the nurse looked at the small sheeted body. They drew a long breath.

"You won't need me, Doc?" the donor asked awkwardly.

"No, no you can go." Avery turned, surprised.

The man lumbered off the bed and walked out. The nurse pushed the wheeled tray down the aisle between the beds.

Avery was in the dressing room waiting when Lucas returned. He looked up inquiringly.

Lucas shook his head.

"No kidding!"

"Gone," said Lucas. "Dead a half-hour. Eighteen months old. Little girl. In a bathtub half full of water."

There was nothing to say and their silence said it. The silence grew longer and each was thinking but no thoughts came.

"How in the hell!" Avery said angrily.

"Nice little home, husband's an electrician, everything clean, bright morning, peaceful, everything okay, she did the house, she was washing the baby . . ."

"And out of nowhere . . . !"

"Out of nowhere . . ."

"Now, she's got to tell the husband . . ."

Lucas shook his head, trying to think.

"Just in a twinkling—the home emptied—both kids gone—for nothing! For nothing! Just like that!" Avery raged.

"I hope the man's not the ugly kind—the poor thing's had all she can take. She was just dazed. She couldn't even cry. I gave her a shot. I called him . . ."

"He'll come home—she'll tell him what happened—they'll sit there—meat! —just meat the cleaver's landed on. . . . And they should be up on a mountain!" Avery cried suddenly. He rose. "They should be on a mountain, on a high mountain, casting a shadow long as the steeple of a church! That's tragedy! That's the perfect *tragos* of the Greeks! . . . They should be gods to fit such tragedy! And he'll come home. And she'll tell him. And they'll call the undertaker. And after a while they'll eat, because they have to eat, and they'll go to the toilet because they have to go to the toilet and there's nothing, there's nothing they can do . . . nothing. . . ."

"They've got to go on," said Lucas mechanically.

"Two little figures. Two specks in the cosmos—"

An intern burst in excitedly.

"Hey! Hear some little kid cut his pecker off!"

Down the hall a bell clanged.

Lucas and Avery rushed out to answer it.

⁎ CHAPTER 23

The weeks passed, the months passed, and their passage was the slow addition of techniques, of things learned, of learned things practiced and repracticed. And through these days, these weeks, these months marched the faceless, the aggregate cells having human shape and function, colloids responding to electrical stimulation, the human race. They had voices, they had histories, they were cases, they were the material each day furnished for application of the learning Lucas accumulated.

And he was third assistant, and then second assistant and in the end senior house surgeon.

And as the weeks passed, as repetition grooved the gyri of memory deeper, as his senses and his hands behaved automatically, his conscious brain was little by little freed from the burden of remembering. He began to think, to observe independently. The humans became people, distant entities, removed from him by a wide gulf, for their living was not his living, their thinking was not his thinking, the link between himself and them was their pain and what he could summon to relieve that pain.

But they became people, all the same, and no longer aggregations of tissue. And for some of them, either because they represented a triumph, or because being chronic cases he became accustomed to their faces he acquired a fondness not unlike that attachment he once cherished for the leg of the cadaver, for old Zebedee.

And as Time made memory deeper, held memory fast, as he became a compendium of things learned, of movements performed automatically, he acquired the leisure for pride and for independent thought.

The hospital staff regarded him with respect. Of this he was only vaguely conscious, knowing in himself how much he knew and how much was known that he did not know and how much was unknown and perhaps unknowable.

"He knows more than he'll ever have any use for," a young intern said authoritatively.

The other interns shifted uneasily, pondering this.

"He goes around in a dream," the young intern added.

"What makes him tick, Avery?" asked another. "Doesn't he ever have any fun? Was he like that when he was a student?"

"What do you mean?" Avery fenced.

"Doesn't he ever think about anything but Medicine?"

"He's been on his own a long time," said Avery. "You fellows have got homes, all sorts of attachments. Old Luke's only got Medicine. Why? What's the harm?"

"Old! We've all got so we think he's old. He's no older than you, Avery. He's no old man. He's just an old young man."

"He's married, after all—"

"To that doughhead Kris! How the hell did he ever happen to marry her? And he never talks to her, when he's in the operating room she might be any other nurse, I've watched him, even when they meet, when they're ready to go home or something—he barely talks to her, not cold or anything but not like a wife at all, like a thing—"

"That's his business. And as to doughhead, she knows more operating-room technique than you'll learn in ten years—"

"I'm not saying that—"

"You're talking about things you don't know anything about. I don't know anything about."

"What good's it going to do him to know all he knows—all he keeps on learning?" the young intern asked warily. Then as the other sighed, or smiled condescendingly, "All right! But will he ever use it? That's what I want to know!"

"And he treats patients the same as he treats his wife," said another. "The same damned way. They're not people at all. They're just things. Just—material."

"Why don't you ask him?" said Avery irritably.

"Christ! I've worked with him two years now! And I hardly know him!" the third assistant burst out. "I know him just about long enough to ask him the time of day!"

"He's following a line," said Avery slowly. His forehead wrinkled. He tried to shape words about a formlessness he barely saw but saw definitely for all it was dim. "He's—he's a doctor—"

"Well, what the hell do you think we are?"

"He's a doctor. You're doctors too. We all are. But he was born one."

"Were his grades especially high?"

"They would have been higher if he hadn't been a born doctor. Because then all he would have to do would be to remember, like Ergenbright, who remembered everything and was top man in the class. It's like Keats not being top man in English. The trouble with Luke was he had to understand why and then when he understood he had to drive a little farther and all the time the rest of us were just remembering and going on to the next thing and there were some fellows, like Ergenbright, who had memories, who were all memory, and of course they got the grades . . . But Ergenbright now, right now, wherever he is—"

"He went to Johns Hopkins—"

"That's right. But whatever he's doing he doesn't know one-fifth what Luke knows about the same thing. And he never will. And that's what he is. It's all he knows. He's a functioning organism that rises each day to a world which is a world of Medicine. That's what he is. And that's what he's stuck with. He's not a bad fellow. He really isn't."

"But what good's it all going to do?" the young intern persisted.

They looked at him gravely.

Lucas entered. He looked about the room.

"Perkins," he said quietly. The young intern stood up. "You removed a growth from the foot of a patient in Ward B."

"Just a wart," said Perkins. "I noticed it, making rounds, and I told the old fellow I'd snip it off for him." He reddened. "I charted it. Why?"

"The charge nurse kept it. You removed an epithelioma."

The room stilled.

"It was bothering the old guy. He said he'd had it for years. I just cut it out and—"

"It was an epithelioma. When you cut it you liberated malignant cells and they are now adrift in his bloodstream."

"It looked just like a wart—"

"It was an epithelioma."

Lucas stared at Perkins helplessly. What can I tell him? What is there to say? He looked about the room.

"Saunders?" he challenged the third assistant.

"I was in charge," Saunders assented. "I saw it on the chart." He turned to Perkins. "Don't you know the difference between a wart and an epithelioma?"

"Sure, but—"

"Describe an epithelioma."

Now the room ringed Perkins and he became an enclave, a substance surrounded by a foreign tissue, and he stammered through a description of epithelioma.

"You know, then, what an epithelioma is?" asked Avery.

"Yes."

"Then how do you justify the removal of an epithelioma under the circumstances in which you charted it?" asked Saunders impersonally.

"It seemed to me—"

"You have described an epithelioma. Are you able to recognize one?"

"Sure, but—"

"Then if you are familiar with epitheliomas how do you account for the fact that you cut into this one?"

"I thought—"

"Describe the operation for the removal of an epithelioma," Avery cut in.

Perkins began. The room listened silently.

"Did you perform this operation?"

"No."

"What are the consequences of the removal of an epithelioma in the manner in which you removed it?"

"Malignant cells are liberated into the general circulation."

"Is there the possibility that the patient may now die of cancer?"

"But—"

"Is there that possibility?"

"There is."

"How strong would you say that possibility is?" asked Saunders.

"Quite strong."

"In your judgment is the removal of a growth without first conferring with your seniors consonant with sound medical practice?"

"No. But it looked just like—"

"You are familiar with epitheliomas?"

"I am."

"Describe an epithelioma, please."

"Again?"

"Please."

And when he had finished,

"Now describe in what manner a wart, as you call it, differs from an epithelioma . . ."

And through it all Lucas stood by the door through which he had entered, coming no farther into the room, looked and listened anxiously, spoke only at the end, when Saunders turned inquiringly to him, and Perkins stared humbly at the floor and the rest stared at Perkins or stared elsewhere,

"I will have to report this," said Lucas uncomfortably. "As you know, I will be blamed for it. They will be quite right. In future no growths will be removed without conference, no surgery attempted without conference."

"I'm sorry," said Perkins.

"I'm sorry too," said Lucas. "We all make mistakes," he said mechanically. He turned to the door.

"Going to eat?" Avery rose.

"Might as well," said Lucas.

They walked out together.

"Reminds me of your little girl with the blank cartridge," Avery smiled.

"I wish they didn't have to be so hard on him," Lucas assented. "I don't know what else they could do, though. I hate to see it. It's not a patch on what I'll get, though. And Saunders. And you too!"

"He'll learn. I can see that kid just like it was yesterday. You putting the ointment on her palm and old McCrea coming by and taking over and giving the kid gas and making a long cut in the palm and out pops a big felt wad—"

"And never saying a word—"

"No, not a word. All he asked you was one question: 'Under your dressing would the patient have developed septicemia? Or lockjaw?' "

"Then he walked on . . . But it wasn't an epithelioma . . ."

Not with you, thought Avery. Not with you. Your mistakes were always with the little things of life, the things you could always have controlled, mistake or not. No—not an epithelioma. . . .

"Anything up today?"

"I'm dissecting."

"Dissecting!"

"I've got kind of an idea. . . . I'll be down in the morgue. You've got that gall bladder—"

"Three o'clock. And then an amputation of the cervix—"

"I loosened that splint on your fracture case, that elbow, Ward C," Lucas said apologetically.

"It was loose when he came in. I tightened it—"

"I know. A splint that long," Lucas said deprecatively—"it's so long—pressing on the elbow that way, almost sure to cause ischemic paralysis—"

Avery flushed.

"No kidding!"

"I just loosened it a little—"

"Thanks! Thanks a lot!"

"Sure," said Lucas gently.

As they entered the dining hall the noisy room quieted.

Dr. Aarons sat at a desk in a corner of the morgue. He looked up absently as Lucas entered.

"Good afternoon, sir," said Lucas.

Dr. Aarons nodded briefly and returned to his notebook. Lucas passed the cadaver on which Dr. Aarons had been working. His eyes summed the opened figure, the hemisphere of skull removed, a complete post-mortem, his eyes reported, he had a moment's curiosity, in the next instant he saw the sheeted figure beyond and moved forward, oblivious.

He reached the sheeted cadaver. He removed the sheet. The body, which, living, had been a woman of middle age, spare, white, pauper, coronary thrombosis, and now was dead, not white, not pauper, not thrombosis but tissue, pattern, inanimate, all these things, and, as he looked, treasure, treasure belonging to him, rare treasure, for the time his instruments penetrated and questioned and disclosed, his property, rare property, and his.

He arranged his instruments with scrupulous precision. He made an incision in the abdomen. Slowly, carefully, he began to work. He closed his eyes. He worked on, his eyes closed.

"Working without gloves?" a voice said suddenly.

He opened his eyes. He looked confusedly at Dr. Aarons.

"I said: Are you working without gloves?"

"Yes, sir," said Lucas. He looked at Dr. Aarons resentfully.

"Yes—well, that's a good way to go like Kolletschka."

"I'm using a scissors."

"What are you working like that for? With your eyes shut? With a scissors? If I may be allowed to ask? And without gloves?"

"I can feel better, sir."

"What difference does it make what you feel? If you know your anatomical landmarks? Or is that really what you're brushing up on?"

"No, sir."

"Well, then what do you feel?"

"I'll tell you what I feel!" He thrust his hand deeper into the abdominal cavity. "Right now I feel adhesions! And I'd never feel them with a rubber glove! And right now I feel rebound from a buried ovary that I'm nowheres near! That's what I feel!"

"So you're thinking of doing away with rubber gloves?"

"No, sir. I didn't say that!"

"What are you going to do if you get a hernia case?"

"I'm going to use rubber gloves. Because if I don't I run the risk of infection—the area's that much bigger. But when it comes to an appendectomy, or any other incision that ought to be small—"

"Ah, so! And now I see you're going to use small incisions, eh? You're going to limit your view as much as possible—"

"I don't have to see if I can feel—"

"You don't have to see, eh?"

"The sense of touch is far more accurate than the sense of sight—"

"So you're going to revolutionize surgery by making small incisions and operating barehanded!"

"I didn't say that—"

"Then what are you wasting your time for?"

"I don't agree with you that I'm wasting my time. It's my time, I'm on my own time and—"

"And now that science has finally discovered asepsis and rubber gloves you're determined to discover how to go back twenty years."

Lucas shrugged. He drew a deep breath. He looked away, his lips hard, shut tight against the anger pushing against them.

"Well, maybe you're right . . . Let's see . . ." Dr. Aarons' tone was abruptly mild. "Have you an appendix there?"

"Yes, sir. Buried in adhesions."

"I see." He took out his watch. "Suppose you take it out."

"Now?"

"Right now!"

Lucas' fingers promptly plunged into the small incision. He felt the end of the large intestine, he tugged the mass upward, his fingers gripped the tangle of tissues. He felt the appendicial finger, he stripped the adhesions, his scissors snipped, his fingers emerged, he laid the appendix, cleanly stripped, on the table.

Dr. Aarons looked at his watch. He looked up.

"Forty-five seconds," he said, expressionless. "Not bad . . ."

"And if I was working by sight I would have run the risk of damaging a ureter or an iliac vein—and all the time I could feel them easily with my bare hand!"

"And if your appendix was adherent to the posterior surface—?"

"Then I'd have to make a larger incision. But as to infection, no sir!"

"Why do you say 'no sir'?"

"Because I've seen it! I've taken culture after culture of pus from the peritoneum and with the exception of saprophytes and an occasional pus cell they were sterile!"

"So you've found something out?"

"I've found out this! That the patient is nine times out of ten his best antiseptic. That the fluids you get out of the peritoneum smell like hell but the smell only means sulphur alcohols or sulphurated hydrogen caused by microbes most of which are saprophytes. I've watched it happen time after time! The careless operators who don't take the trouble to mop up the peritoneum thoroughly get the best results. And now I know why! They don't damage the peritoneum with rubbing and sponging. And Daw's proved that you can't get all the fluid out of a peritoneum anyway! He took some milk and poured it into an open cadaver and no matter how much he sponged—"

"I'm familiar with Dr. Daw's work."

"And once or twice when I inadvertently spread purulent fluid—trying to separate adhesions—spread it right onto healthy peritoneal tissue—I saw that I hadn't started a new peritonitis at all."

"Do you know what happened?"

"Yes, sir. The purulent material excited the peritoneum it touched to a sort of hyper-leucocytosis—thousands more white cells marched in and took over."

"And to whom have you spoken about all this?"

"No one, sir."

"And how much dissecting have you been doing."

"All I can, sir."

"Roughly . . ."

"About—about a hundred and fifty—"

"A hundred and fifty, eh?"

"All told . . ."

"I see . . . And your conclusions are?"

"That the best surgery is to get in and get out. That modern asepsis and other aids have made the surgeon's detail work more important than the patient's physiology. That's one thing. Before anesthesia and antiseptics they'd take minutes to do what we take half-hours to do—"

"And look at their mortality records—"

"Yes, but those who lived, lived because they took minutes—"

"It's possible," Dr. Aarons said serenely. "And what else? What about the gloves?"

"That ties in with the time sequence. You can work faster and more accurately without gloves. You can feel better than you can see. So wherever it's possible *not* to use gloves—don't use them!"

"That's all?"

"That's all. Except leave the peritoneum alone. Handle it gingerly. Don't pack, because the pack damages tissue that's already well prepared to take care of almost any abscess. And in the worst cases use a small drain instead."

"And how about haemorrhage?"

"Isn't that practically blood in circulation, sir?"

"Free blood—in the peritoneal cavity?"

"Well, don't the tissues start absorbing lymph from it the moment it's free? In that sense, isn't it circulating? And for the rest—"

"And you haven't spoken of this to anyone."

"No, sir."

"Why not?"

"Well, I did mention it to Dr. Eddleston one day and he looked at me as if he thought I was crazy—"

"I see. You don't, of course, practice it here."

"I do what I'm told. But when I get out—when I'm in practice for myself—"

He looked away. He looked at the far wall, thinking.

Dr. Aarons put his watch back in his pocket. One hundred and fifty dissections, one hundred and fifty and not a word said! Working it out himself! And he's right. He's just as right as they are! But—by himself! All to himself! Well, it was true, then. It was all true. It was true when I first saw him.

He cleared his throat.

"There's a point I'd like you to remember," he said mildly. Lucas started.

"When you work blind, when you separate an adherent mesentery, you may make a small hole in it. You must always close that hole. Your eyes will serve your fingers, there. That's one danger. The patient comes out of ether, coughs and explodes a loop of bowel into the hole and you've got a bowel obstruction. Nobody knows what's happened until the patient comes to me. And when the patient comes to the pathologist the question is academic."

Lucas nodded, listened intently.

"That's about all. I find nothing grossly erroneous in what you have discovered. Unless you are under the impression that the discovery is yours alone—"

"No, sir. I'm sure others must have found this too. I haven't read of any, but I'm sure—"

"Yes . . . Well," he looked at the cadaver, "have you done what you came for?"

"I thought—I half intended to do a little more—"

"You go ahead." He walked away a few steps then halted abruptly. "Tell me! Is it possible you intend to specialize in surgery?"

"Oh, no, sir! No indeed! General practice!"

"That's what I understood."

"Yes, sir!"

"Yes . . . Well . . ." He waved vaguely and walked on. Lucas returned to work exuberantly. At the door Dr. Aarons looked back. But Lucas had forgotten him. His fingers were at work in a new incision. His eyes were closed. His hands were bare. He was frowning. Dr. Aarons walked on. He sighed. He was lonely. Vienna, he thought. Just give me six months . . . Just six. . . .

As he left the hospital that evening Avery fell in step with him.

"Some day," said Avery briefly.

"We haven't got many left."

"Today makes up for all of them. One gall bladder through eight inches of fat, a frank breech, two T and A's, they had to call me in on that amputation of the cervix, what do you make of Saunders?"

"What did he do?"

"I swear I don't believe he knows his landmarks. I came in, there were five of them sweating it out, Saunders had taken over, they had the cervix half dissected out, they were holding up the operating room, standing there, milling around, Saunders was dabbing around getting nowhere, the minute he saw me he started throwing instruments around —'Why the hell don't they give us some decent clamps? These goddamned superannuated things!'—and he pitched four of them against the wall, one after the other. I just stood there and he picked up a scalpel and the next thing I knew he was within an ace of the bladder!"

"What did you do?"

"I said there was a D and C in the other OR and would he mind . . . He was tickled to death. Went right out. The cervix wasn't much. He had it just about right. He didn't seem to know how to go on . . . Funny! You work right alongside of a guy, he sees everything you see, and you never know how much he knows . . ."

"He's going in for GYN, too . . ."

"Then that damned breech—"

"Freedman was handling that—"

"What are you going to do? He's going to specialize in ophthalmology. What the hell does he care about OB? I wouldn't care myself! What good's it going to do him?"

"That's so . . . Only thing, they give a degree in Medicine. Not ophthalmology. And they've got to stamp him fit—for Medicine, not ophthalmology. He ought to know that—"

"He does. But he *still* knows he's going to be an ophthalmologist. And he keeps right on asking himself what the hell he's doing delivering babies."

"I'm going to catch hell for Perkins—"

"You sure are. You know something? It couldn't have happened in a private room."

"What do you mean?"

"It couldn't even have happened in a double room—or a room for four!"

"I'm afraid I don't understand you."

"You understand, all right. I'm just chipping away at the citadel and you're reconnoitering, scenting a possible attack right from inside the lines. Look at you! Look at your face!"

"Well, I can't do that very well, can I, Avery?"

"Aha! Now you've decided to be tolerant. Now you'll deal with this as with Avery the radical. Let's listen with good humor to what the fellow has to say. He's a nice guy, Avery. Just a little radical sometimes. Doesn't mean anything, though. Basically sound. One of the team."

Lucas tried to think of something to say. He grinned helplessly.

"Nobody's touching your citadel. You can live in it. It's not going to be demolished. Just see it as it is. It couldn't have happened in a private room because Perkins wouldn't have dared to operate on a private-room patient without direct orders."

"I don't see your point—"

"You mean you hadn't thought of it before—"

"No, honestly—"

"Would Perkins have taken the responsibility of removing a growth from a private-room patient? Just walked in and said, 'Here! That growth's got to come out!' and removed it—just on a whim?"

There was no way out.

"No, he wouldn't."

"Well, why didn't you say so in the first place? You knew what I meant! Why stall around so I have to pull it out of you shred by shred!"

"I just—"

"You're so goddamned afraid somebody's going to say something to deface this holy church you've built up inside yourself—worship all you want to, Luke! But don't go blind!"

"Why do you have to always be looking for crevices to chip at and enlarge and find something wrong?"

"It's a defect of my character. It's called being able to see with your eyes wide open. Maybe I want it to be perfect as much as you do. Maybe that's why I fret at it. You ever happen to think of that? Maybe I love it for what it can be—not because I haven't anything else to love."

"It isn't altogether that."

"The point is—some patients are protected. What protects them?"

He waited.

"I suppose it's money," Lucas grudged at last.

"Of course it's money. You don't have to be afraid to say it. It isn't our fault. We didn't make things that way. But the more I thought of it, the more I thought of other things. Do you know what? If two patients—if X and Y were both down with the same illness, identical patients, identical illness—and one was rich and one was charity we'd regard the rich man's illness as far more grave than the charity case's. We'd look at each other more soberly, we'd think more slowly, the man's illness somehow would get to be as important as the man!"

"They'd both get the same care," Lucas said mechanically.

"They'd shit get the same care! Poor man would have appendicitis. Rich man would have Appendicitis. With a capital A."

"Whatever the frailties of human attitude, the specifications of Medicine are exact. They'd be treated alike."

"Maybe."

"There's no maybe to it!"

"Oh, come on, now, Luke! You've made rounds! How does a doctor act in a private room and how does he act in a charity ward?"

"Successful men have a right to a certain amount of respect! Whose money keeps the hospital going? Who pays for the charity patient's bed? What difference does it make how two patients are treated so far as approach is concerned—so long as they both get the same Medicine?"

"Are you going to treat rich and poor alike, Luke?"

"You're damned right I am!"

"How are you going to keep an office going? An office is just like a hospital, you know. The rich pay for the poor."

"I treat disease—not people!"

"That's right. That's your answer, Luke. That's what protects you. You don't even think of people as people. You don't know anything about them. The only person whose problems you know is yourself. All the rest is a vague blur, with voices."

"Oh—it's me, now!"

"And never get the idea that they both get the same Medicine. Never get the idea that a poor man's treated—as a man, as a whole organ—like a rich man. Just remember Perkins."

"To you apparently all Medicine is venal, just a service that's bought and paid for, so much an ounce—"

"No . . . I don't say that . . . But there's a thing that flaws a man, makes the ape peep through pure science—a thing that comes between a man's best hope and what he is . . ."

They walked a while in silence.

"Not for me and you, boy," Lucas said awkwardly, at last.

"No." Avery stopped. The trouble faded from his eyes. "Not for me and you. You, because you're what you are—and me, because I'm going to teach!" He smiled, friendlily.

"You're kidding!"

"That's how I'm going to hold on to what *I* have!"

"But don't you want to—"

"I want to hang on to what I have. I don't want to be diluted by compromise, by clear thinking, by sick seeing, by adjustment to reality. Let's put it that way. So the way to do it is to teach. And the goose hangs high. I've already spoken for it. I've got a place right here. Now—what are you going to do?"

"General practice—"

"I know—but where?"

"I haven't figured it out—"

"You going to set up your own office?"

"I—I don't know." Because if you don't think about it, if you know how much it takes and you haven't got it, and you just don't think about it—it might happen, anyway. But once you face it—

"What are you doing tonight?"

"Look, Avery! Will you help me figure it out? Will you?"

"You got a copy of the A.M.A. home?"

"Dozens of them! Come on! We'll all eat—"

"We'll eat on me!" He felt in his pockets. "God! We can't do that, either!"

"Kris'll have enough! She's always got some tucked away!"

"Ten dollars a month! Boy! It doesn't go very far!"

They walked on, talking animatedly.

"I wanted to get some place in the country—"

"You'd better pick some spot with a hospital—"

"That's right! Some place with a hospital—town of about five thousand—"

"Your own empire. Five thousand patients and just practice Medicine."

"General Medicine!"

"All the Medicine there is!"

They were seized by an identical thought. They looked at each other, startled. Then Avery slowly shook his head.

"You know something, if I had the money I'd go in with you—"

"We could set up an office together—!"

"We haven't got the money. We'd need seven, ten thousand dollars. You haven't got it. I haven't got it either."

"We could start small—"

"We'd need instruments—we'd need equipment, we'd need X-ray, lab, a million things. The kind of Medicine we practice that's the equipment we'd need . . . We couldn't practice with less. Not and give the patient what we know he has to have . . . And the first year or two—with maybe no patients at all—"

"How much money—no kidding, now!—what's the barest minimum!"

"Five thousand!"

"All right, five thousand!"

"You say it like it was a nickel—" but Avery looked at Lucas behind a hard-leashed hope.

"How much can you lay your hands on?"

Avery reddened. He hesitated.

"I've got eight hundred dollars," he blurted. "Eight hundred dollars in a lot my father left me!"

"That's almost a fifth! And I've got—wait a minute! What about that lot! Man! You've made me think of something!" He turned slowly to Avery. His mouth hung a little open. "Why—I've got lots, too!" He remembered Job. "I think." He blinked. "My mother left them. . . . Sure! Sure, she did!" He lifted his eyes, his mouth still a little open. "Hey!"

"I suppose we could get credit from instrument and supply houses. That's one thing, Luke. Everybody else does—"

"Those vultures!"

"They still give credit! And nowadays everybody's rich!"

"Just get what we absolutely need—"

"I don't mind eating light—"

"I'll go back to Milletta tomorrow! I'll find out about lots—at today's prices—why, they might bring—a thousand dollars—"

"It isn't as if we had anyone depending on us—whoa!"

"What's the matter?"

"You're married!"

"What of it?"

Lucas looked at Avery, bewildered. Then he understood.

"My God, boy! I'd never have got through med school if Kris hadn't worked! Kris is no liability! Christ! She can be our office nurse! Save us fifteen hundred, two thousand dollars a year!"

"But if there's no money coming in—a wife's got to eat—"

"Why, she could even get a job! If there's a hospital she could be head OR—"

"And if they've already got one—"

"She could be a nurse—anything—!"

Avery was silent.

"What's the matter?"

"For a minute there you talked as if she was a chattel or something—this where you live?"

"Come on up. It's not that. Maybe I do get to thinking of her— I guess it sounded funny, at that—"

He opened the door and stood aside.

"Hey! This is all right!"

Lucas beamed.

"You got a lot of room—Boy! Look at that!"

"I salvaged that test-tube rack—"

"Look at the mike, though!"

"Kris gave me that!"

"The hell!"

"Yep! And those slides—I guess you know where they came from—"

"But you got a whole miniature lab laid out here!"

"I tried to use the oven for an incubator—come on, I'll show you the kitchen, see what we got—"

"This is a swell layout!" Avery looked about the tiny kitchen. Lucas opened the icebox. There was a large cake of ice and two small packages, a bottle of milk.

"I guess we got to go out," he said.

They heard the door shut.

"Hey! Kris!" Lucas walked into the living-room-bedroom, Avery following him. He looked at Kristina, beaming. Kristina smiled.

"You know Avery—"

"Hi, Kris!"

"Good evening, Doctor—"

"Avery, Avery!"

"We got an idea, Kris! We're going to have dinner and the three of us are going to talk over the biggest thing since iodine.—Hey, Kris! There's nothing in the icebox!"

"I know! I'm sorry! I got to shop—"

"Let's go out! We got enough money?"

"I'm right between paydays—" Avery apologized.

"Sure! Sure!" Kristina said heartily. "Sure! We got enough! I guess we don't starve, do we?"

"That's right! Kris has always got it! I don't know how she does it, but when you need it—"

Kristina grinned. "I'll get some money!" She walked hastily to the closet.

"That the bank in there?" grinned Avery as Kristina bent and began to rummage in the closet.

"That's Kris' bank."

"It's safe place—" Kristina's voice came out muffled.

"Sure!" Avery snorted. "No robber would ever dream of looking in a closet for money!"

"Not where Kris keeps it! It's safe as the Bank of England!" Lucas paused, watched Avery's face. "You know where she keeps it? She hides it in a box of Kotex!"

"No!" Avery roared delight.

"Right between the napkins!"

Kristina emerged, red-faced.

"Don't you, Kris!"

"That's right," she smiled, blushing.

"Can you imagine a thief—?" Lucas demanded.

"No!"

"We go?" grinned Kristina.

"We'll find some little place—"

"Take along a couple of copies of the A.M.A.," Avery reminded.

"What for? What do we need them now for?"

"Look! Let's cover all bets! Take 'em along!"

Lucas shrugged. He walked to the bureau, opened a drawer, picked out three copies of the *Journal of the American Medical Association.* Avery picked up the wooden sign from the bureau top.

"Got it all set up and ready, eh?"

"Kris bought it," Lucas said hurriedly.

"It's a beauty! You get everything for this boy, don't you?" He put the sign down and looked around. "Nice home, you keep everything spotless, Kris—by God! To look at you in the operating room nobody'd ever know you ran a love nest like this—"

"You never been here before." Kris made this as a sound, it had no meaning, she knew he had never been here before, it was the first time Lucas had ever brought any guest home. She was overwhelmed by this. And in addition an outsider's admiration and praise were a joyous din in her brain stirring all thought into confusion.

"You can't beat her!" Lucas said proudly.

"I see you every day and I'd never have guessed it!" Avery shook his head.

"Oh, I'm a good Swedish girl! When a Swedish girl takes care of her man—you know any Swedish girls, Avery?"

"Come on," said Lucas. "We can talk on the way! Kris, listen! We've got an idea, Avery and I, just an idea, mind, but when I tell you what it is . . ."

They walked downstairs and out into the street. Kris' head turned from one to the other, trying to absorb, to sort out, to examine what they had to say. From time to time she thought of something. But she was not quick enough, and the tide rolled on. It was only after they had eaten and had begun to riffle through the pages of the medical journal that Kristina managed to get their attention.

"You know for sure, Luke, you remember right, you sure your mama leaves you lots? You never mention it, maybe something's changed, something's happened—"

"Oh, for God's sake, Kris!"

"No, she's got a point there, Luke—"

"The both of you! I tell you I'm sure!"

"Because—I hate to tell you—"

"Well, don't tell me, then."

"Don't be mad, Luke . . ."

"I'm not mad. I know we haven't got anything—I know where it went, you don't have to remind me—I know Mother left me that lot. That's all. And I'm going back to sell it and—"

"She just doesn't want you to get your hopes too high."

"Both of you," amended Kristina.

"But it might work out, Kris," said Avery.

"We could go to Minnesota," Kristina said daringly, reopening a long-dead issue, feeling safe before company. "I got lots of friends in that place. Where I live is many know me—I would bring you plenty patients! You bet!"

"For the love of Christ! Are we going into that again?"

"Is a nice place, Minnesota." She turned to Avery. "You would like it, I bet. You would like it fine! Plenty of pretty Swedish girls, plenty of money, plenty of farms—"

"I've heard a lot about Minnesota. Nice state . . ."

"Do you realize I'd have to take state boards to practice there? Both of us?"

"Don't they have reciprocity?" asked Avery mildly.

"I don't think so. Anyway—" he reddened, pausing—"anyway, just get this straight! Get it straight—and forget it! I'm—not—going—to—

Minnesota! Understand? Now—or ever! Understand?" Not where you come from, not ever, a million miles away from you, from everybody like you, from the essence of you, from people who talk like you, think like you, admire what you admire.

And he looked this at her, directly.

"Here's one!" cried Avery. They turned to him. He read from the medical journal:

" 'General practitioner—no major surgery; to work with a group of three men doing general practice; large city in Iowa; must work hard; good salary to begin, associateship later.' "

"Big city." Lucas shook his head.

"Maybe you'd like Maryland? 'Young physician, full-time assistant general practice; Baltimore, Maryland; willing to work, contract, guarantee and percentage. Excellent opportunity. Enclose photograph, age, education, references.' "

"But that's for one. And a big city, too. Get one for both of us—"

"Let's just see what they are. If I find one for both of us I'll read it—here's one near you, Kris! 'Practice for sale—Michigan; in rural, virtually unopposed, essential location, modern, completely equipped; gross approximately $40,000; price $65,000. Low down payment if references satisfactory.' "

Avery and Lucas looked at each other.

"It's right here! I read it word for word!"

Lucas bent to look.

"You see?" Kristina exclaimed. "There's money there! Like I say! Plenty money! Rich farmers!"

"Just like a business, isn't it!" Avery and Lucas ignored Kristina, looked at each other. Avery dipped his head. "Here's another," he said implacably. "Here's one for both of us: 'Opening for two young doctors who wish to do general practice together; in New England country town; yearly combined income $20,000 net: $35,000.' "

"New England people are poor," said Kristina.

"That's right, Kris," said Avery. "But listen to this: 'Here is your opportunity to have a large and rich clientele; in one of Cleveland's largest suburbs on a main road with ample parking. We can consider those who care to make an investment of $10,000 for an office; the investment will make you part owner and draw a dividend and it may be paid off by a sinking fund if desired.' How's that, Kris?"

She looked at them, bewildered.

"Well, Kris, what do you say? What's the matter?"

"That's in the magazine?" she asked doubtfully.

"Right here in the official journal of the American Medical Association. One right after another!" Lucas said tightly.

"Doctors advertise like that?" she asked dubiously.

"Show it to her!" Lucas urged.

"Here you are, Kris—" Avery handed her the open journal. And as she began to read, "You've been married to Luke too long. He must have infected you. Why should you be surprised?"

But his eyes were a little sick behind the raillery.

"Didn't you ever read these, Luke?"

"Have you?"

"Why, it's just putting Hippocrates on a business basis, that's all. No harm in that, is there? Why? Did you think it was a sacred calling, or something? What was it Brundage used to say? 'Doctors got to live, too, boys, don't forget that!' "

"But right out in the open like this—" Kristina looked up, shocked.

"Nobody sees that! The public doesn't see that! That's a medical journal," Avery expostulated.

"It isn't the jobs so much, it's the practices for sale," Lucas had opened another copy of the *Journal.* "My God, listen to this: 'Colorado; established growing practice grosses over $20,000 and can be doubled.' 'Georgia; Lucrative unopposed general practice.' 'Michigan; will make money the first month.' 'Florida; practice for rent.' 'Kansas; practice averages over $1,000 a month—' "

" 'New York—upstate,' " interrupted Avery, reading from another copy, " 'lucrative, unopposed, $15,000. Will introduce. Has to be seen to be appreciated. Should net $12,500 first year—' "

"One right after the other," Lucas threw down his copy.

"What do they ask you to send photographs for?" Kristina looked up from her copy.

"So they can see whether you're a Jew or a Negro," Avery said quietly. "Science doesn't distinguish. Only scientists."

Lucas swept the journals aside.

"What good is it? What did you want me to bring these for?"

"Don't get sore at me. I just thought there might be something to give us an idea . . ."

"That's the way it is," Kristina said pacifically. "You can't change it—"

"That's not the way it is, at all! I'm surprised they take such advertisements! A reputable journal like this—"

"*The* reputable journal—" said Avery.

"There's others here, though, don't forget! There's column after column of ads with jobs that pay $3,000 and $4,000 a year, serious jobs, where a man can practice Medicine—"

"In hospitals. That's right. And mostly specialties. But that isn't all, Luke."

"It's awful! Seeing it in cold print that way—"

"There's agencies, boy. Here's one, old established, reputable—we can write them, find out what we want—"

"First you sell your lot. Find out how much you can put up." Kristina folded her arms and nodded.

"How about it, Kris? What do you think!" Avery looked at her gravely.

"I think it's fine."

"How does it strike you, being our nurse?"

"She'll do it—" Lucas protested.

"I'll be glad."

"Swell!"

"But first we find out . . ."

Lucas looked nervously at Avery. To him the speech sounded too flat, too much like cold water, too much as if Kristina was making a noise to say that she and he belonged together, they were in one group and Avery hadn't been admitted to it yet.

"It'll be all right," he pronounced harshly, "and Avery and I are going in this together."

"We hope—"

"No, we don't hope. It's what we're going to do."

He looked at Kristina with dislike. He resented having to wince every time she spoke in front of someone else, he never knew what she would say, but it was always something that made him anxious how the other person was going to take it, or else it was something stupid that made him ashamed. Now she was throwing cold water on this.

"Put your foot in it, didn't you, Kris?" Avery grinned.

"That's something nurses get used to. A nurse is always putting her foot in it," Kristina smiled philosophically.

Now she was calling attention to the fact that she was a nurse. Lucas' shoulders slumped.

"Especially an operating-room nurse—"

"Oh, my God, yes!" Kristina nodded.

"Doctors never notice the head operating-room nurse. When he's brought off a rough one he's generous, he's enthusiastic about her, she's terrific. When he hasn't brought it off her cut-and-dried efficiency is a reproach to him."

Kristina nodded.

"You fellows'd be good together. You'd make a good team."

"That's right. I'd handle the people and Luke'd handle their bodies."

"I suppose that's meant for me," Luke said. "Sometimes I wonder how you people ever put up with such an eccentric."

Avery looked quickly at Lucas. Then he looked at Kristina.

"You're a very lucky eccentric, Luke," Avery said. "Not every eccentric has a girl like Kris."

Lucas' head lifted sharply. But Avery was smiling at him steadily, with his mouth, and there was no derision in his eyes, and he meant what he was saying.

"Well," he said awkwardly, "I guess tomorrow we'll know one way or the other . . ."

"We'll do it!" Avery prophesied confidently.

On a sudden impulse the three shook hands across the table.

The rule of Brundage, Lucas thought in the train going toward Milletta, the rule of Brundage, the rule of Perkins, the rule of Saunders. Things acquired perspective when you were travelling, when you were in motion. Now the hospital was a stage and he was receding from it and all the figures on it were clear and took their proper size. And Brundage and Perkins and Saunders and Alfred, who was somewhere in New York making the moments count and the contacts and the money, and Avery, who wanted to be a teacher just because a handful of students in a little college town weren't Medicine as he saw it, why all these weren't Medicine at all, they were just people who didn't really have anything to do with Medicine when they turned out like that, they were just fellows who had been given every advantage and passed their tests and hadn't fallen in line yet.

They weren't doctors. When it came to doctors there was Aarons; all right, say what you wanted about Aarons but there was a man who was a doctor, who knew, who was implicit with knowledge. And there was Townsend and Graves and Turner and Gordon, and when you came right down to it these were the settled men, these were what Medicine really was, these and the rest. These were the Elder Statesmen, the true representatives, and if it was courage you were looking for, why there it was, just taken for granted, look at any one of them. And if it was honor, the same, and if it was purity and ethics and science and all that was best and purest and most singingly high in this otherwise expendable world, why there it was, like a rock, like a cathedral, like all that he was living for.

All you had to do was look at it.

He sniffed contemptuously, turning his thoughts from the university world, from the figures who didn't matter.

The man across the aisle almost certainly had an intracranial disorder. Probably a tumor. He had a tic, his left eye twitched. When his eye twitched he scratched the base of his left thumb. It was the—the palmo-mental reflex. Down the aisle a man walked draggingly, syphilis without much question, there was a woman at the end of the car with myasthenia gravis. All about him there were walking, sitting signs of this or that, the car was peopled with animate clinical evidence, walking symptoms, living evidence of disease, wearing their frailties plain to the initiate, hid from each other.

Avery was a fool to think he was distant from humanity. He was never unaware of it for a moment. He knew humanity as Avery would never know it. Knowing humanity wasn't some damned attitude or other. It was really knowing it, what made it tick, what ailed it, diagnosing it, knowing how it could be cured, always being polite, trying to make them feel you were one of them. Helping them, never letting them down, making them live whether they wanted to or not.

Was it healing? It wasn't, exactly. Healing was just one of the things that happened. Relieving pain? Relieving suffering? Well, that was important too. But that wasn't it either. Those were just incidents. Repair? Well, that was another item. What it all boiled down to was life, when you came right down to it, there was really nothing else, just life. That was the main thing, the thing that summed them all. To fight for life even though the man's last breath was fading and you knew it. To keep right on fighting. And when he was dead to keep right on fighting still. Until he was really dead. And there wasn't any use fighting any longer. And then to the next one. Fiercer than ever.

Yes sir, it answered all the questions. All you could bring up was answered right there. All you had to do was apply it. The fact that out of a hundred patients eighty would get well without ever going to the doctor was just typical cynicism, somebody trying to be bright. A doctor's concern wasn't with people who didn't need him, no matter what the people thought. His concern was with their life. And if they got well anyway, well, good luck to them. That was all a doctor was after. To keep them living. He couldn't live their lives for them. The mistakes they made were their own mistakes. It hadn't anything to do with keeping people living. And it certainly wasn't any appraisal of Medicine. Healing was an incident, and repair was an incident, and cure was an incident, and relief was an incident. The main thing was to keep them living. Because life was the most precious thing on earth. It was the most precious thing on the planet. The other items were a silly race for specialists, furniture to sharpen their claws on. But life was the house of Medicine itself.

The train stopped. The porter was calling Milletta. He rose, his thoughts dispersed, his heart beating oddly fast, feeling a little fright, a great apprehension, as he always had when he was a boy returning to this place, there was always something riding, something about to be decided, something he had his heart set on and knew he wasn't going to get.

"He seems to have made a clean sweep," Mr. Benjamin said. He shook his head. He looked at Lucas.

"But—but do you mean he signed *my* name to this—to these papers?"

"That's what he seems to have done," the banker said.

"There's nothing here? Nothing at all?"

"He signed your name, and he put it up for collateral and borrowed money on it and went broke. And the money's gone. That's what he's done, all right."

He looked at Lucas a little eagerly. Do you want us to nab him? the look said, we can do that, you know, here it is, his signature in plain sight, I wouldn't mind doing it, he's got it coming to him, say the word—

"Here's your name—right here—"

"But I didn't sign it—"

"I know. It's a very serious offense. Would you like us to—" He let the sentence dangle.

"No, no." Lucas roused himself. "No, never mind. Let it go. There's nothing left? Nothing at all?"

"Nothing."

"The house? The furniture?"

"Nothing."

"Nothing left over from the sale? The shop—the shops in Tyre, in Meridian, in—"

"Nothing. Not a cent. Not a dime. As a matter of fact if you could give us his whereabouts—there's quite a good sum left unpaid—"

"Nothing," Lucas echoed.

"Absolutely nothing. . . . Some new people have bought the house, if you'd care to go over and look at it—they'll understand—people name of Evans, right nice, got three children—"

"Oh, no!"

"They'd be glad to let you see it, I'm sure, if you told them—I could give them a ring—"

"No. No! That's all right. That's fine. Thanks very much for your trouble, the inconvenience, and all . . ."

"Well, good luck to you—"

"Thanks very much. Ah—I've got to get back. Well, goodbye, then—"

"Any time we can help you—"

"Thanks again . . ."

He escaped to the street. He walked quickly around a corner. His train would not be in for an hour. He thought of Dr. Alexander, he walked swiftly to the old, remembered house, he mounted the steps where he used to sit waiting to carry the bag from the door to the carriage.

Dr. Alexander's office was much smaller than he remembered it. The consulting room was dowdy, jumbled, the instruments were scant, the examining table shabby with long use.

"You going to the city?" Dr. Alexander asked at last.

"No, sir. General practice. Just like you."

"That's the spirit. Glad to hear it. Ever look up my old classmate, Aarons?"

"Yes, sir. I attended all his lectures."

"Quite a fellow, Aarons . . ."

"Yes, sir. Yes, sir, he really is."

"Wasted there—"

"I don't know, sir. You're a pretty big man yourself. I wouldn't say you were wasted here—"

"No, no. Not in a class with Aarons." He shook his head. "Had to take what he could get, you know. He was a whiz, Aarons. And when you got to know him, a really fine fellow. I was surprised, myself. He was damned nice to me. Had to take what he could get."

"Too bad."

"He's a Jew, you know. That never bothered me any. Three or four Jew families have moved here since you left. Seem to be all right."

"I never could understand what all the fuss was about, myself."

"Yes. Well, there it is. . . . Going to practice—ah—somewhere near? I don't say Milletta, already got a young fellow setting up. Makes four of us—glad to have you, of course—"

"No. No, I thought I'd try the northern part of the state—if I could. I wanted to set up with a classmate, fellow named Avery. . . . Yes, well! I've written to Aznoes—"

"It's a fine service. They'll find something for you! Down here just for a visit?"

"Business," Lucas laughed wryly.

"Well . . ." Dr. Alexander rose. "Stop in again, when you're around here. Anything I can do to help . . ."

"It was good to see you again." Lucas looked at the years of service on the man's face, the quiet, controlled eyes.

"Come in anytime, Luke. The other fellows'd be glad to see you . . ."

"I wish I could. I've got to get back—"

"Yes . . . well . . . You ever hear from your father?"

"Not often." Lucas flushed.

"Well if he should happen to write you—" Dr. Alexander saw Lucas' face stricken, broke off instantly. "Never mind," he said. "Send him my regards."

Lucas stumbled down the steps, fled the steps he used to sit on, dreaming, waiting, fled the street he knew by heart, fled toward the station.

Dr. Alexander too. He'd gotten into Dr. Alexander. He'd taken some of Dr. Alexander's few poor dollars. Even Dr. Alexander. To take a doctor's money. Even a doctor . . .

For a moment, waiting for his train in the depot, Lucas was tempted to go to the cemetery where his mother lay. But there was a chance he might be seen, recognized, there was every chance. His mind recoiled from the prospect. He made himself as small as possible. He waited for the train. He did not look out the window until they were long, long past Milletta. Until three stations had gone by.

"So that's the story. That's the whole of it."

"You didn't have to tell me all that," said Avery.

"I wanted you to know. I wanted you to understand."

"Things like that could happen to anybody. He might have been under pressure. Nobody knows what kind of a crack he was in at the time. You can't be bitter about it."

"It was all set. I was so sure about it—"

"Well, what the hell." Avery leaned back. "It was a pretty dream—"

"If there was only some way—some way—"

"I was going to teach, anyway."

"We would have made a swell team."

"What are you going to do? What's the next step?"

Lucas lowered his eyes guiltily. He drew a letter from his coat pocket, passed it wordlessly to Avery.

"Aznoes?" Avery looked up from the letter, surprised.

"Kris gave it to me last night."

"But this is for you!" Avery looked up. "This is right down your alley! Dr. Runkleman—sounds German. This is just what you wanted!"

"Or you! How about the other one—Dr. Pond?"

"I'm going to teach."

"But the two places are practically next door—I looked it up on the map—Greenville and Lepton—ten miles apart—we'd practically be practicing together—in no time we could set up our own office—"

"Nope. I'm going to teach. I've made up my mind. I'll tell you something—I'm just as glad, in a way, things turned out as they did—no, don't look hurt, it's nothing to do with you. I'd just rather teach. I honestly would. What does Kris say?"

"She wants me to write to Aznoes to see if they could place me in Minnesota."

"Are you going to?"

"Man, I wouldn't go to Minnesota unless it was the last state on earth!"

Avery looked at him carefully.

"She's a fine girl, Kris. You know that, of course. She loves you, Luke. She really loves you."

"You bet. Oh, I know—"

"I wouldn't let the fact she's not so quick on the social trigger blind me to what you got there, I mean the way she holds her fork, and all . . ."

Lucas shook his head ruefully, smiling. "A doctor's wife—"

"I know. But don't let it get you."

"I won't. She's a grand girl. She's really stuck through thick and thin."

"I'm going to miss you . . ."

"You old radical, you—"

"Where you going to set up your altar? Greenville or Lepton?"

"What do you think?"

"I'd say Greenville."

"It's got a hospital. County seat. Got a small private hospital, too."

"You look up Runkleman?"

"He's all right. Creighton Medical College, Nebraska, 1889, GP, member of the American Medical Association, born Decatur, Nebraska 1864—"

"Whew! Sixty-six?"

"Chief surgeon, Greenville County Hospital—"

"Three hundred a month. And arrangement. Well, it's what you wanted. Maybe in a few years he'll want to retire."

"I wouldn't be surprised."

"And you can buy him out."

Lucas laughed.

"With what?"

"Well, you've got your hospital, you've got your town of five thousand, you've got general practice and probably all the county surgery you want to keep you brushed up. You're all set."

"I wish we could have had it our way . . ."

"Forget it! I'm tickled to death, Luke! . . . Well, you've got a month, yet. Better hurry and write—"

"See you tomorrow, Avery—"

"Bright and early—"

"You understand about that other?"

"Forget it! I mean it!"

"Well—"

"Say hello to Kris for me—"

On the way home Lucas passed a jewelry store. He stopped. He looked for a long time at a heavy silver bracelet. It was set with one large turquoise. After a while he made up his mind and went in.

The clerk went to the window.

"It's fourteen dollars, sir."

"I see." Lucas knew to a penny that he had six dollars left from the money Kristina had given him to go to Milletta. Six dollars and forty-two cents.

"Something less expensive, sir?"

"No, no thanks. I was just passing . . ." Maybe they sold such things on time. Everybody was buying on time, nowadays.

"We can extend liberal credit arrangements—"

But not for fourteen dollars! My God! If a fellow didn't have fourteen dollars, if you had to go on the installment plan to get something that cost fourteen dollars!

"No," Lucas smiled tolerantly. "I guess I don't have to buy anything on installment that costs fourteen dollars. Not yet! Not yet, that is."

"Drop in again, sir."

But he had started, he looked in other windows now, he began to hunt, in a department store, in the midst of a display of novelty jewelry he saw a pair of earrings.

"Five dollars," said the salesgirl.

"I'll take them," he said instantly.

When he gave them to her, Kristina opened the package self-consciously. When she saw them, when they lay in her hand winking up at her, earrings that she never wore, earrings she wouldn't dream of buying, first because they were too expensive, she bit her lip. Her eyes brimmed with tears.

"Thanks," she said. She nodded her head hard.

"It's nothing. Hope you like them, Kris." He turned awkwardly away.

"I love them," she said simply.

He nodded. He walked to the table and picked a test tube from the rack, looked at it intently as if it were something he had suddenly remembered.

She took the package to the kitchen. When she was out of sight she put up her hands to her face and cried. She cried silently. In a moment she brushed the tears away. She began to fold the wrappings the present had come in, she folded the paper carefully, she put the earrings in one apron pocket, the wrappings in another. It was the first present he had ever given her.

CHAPTER 24

The train to Greenville bore Lucas Marsh through space and time, behind him the years of his youth dissolved, the years of study, of living feinted with desperation, stratagems, machinations, the places in which he had struggled dissolved, discarded themselves, the train was an instrument, a process, a plucking up, a bearing onward, and before him the fields gleamed, stainless, a new land, boundless with newness, racing beside the train, shouting what lay ahead, and behind him slipped the past, into shadow, into darkness, into oblivion.

All his living had anticipated this moment, had moved inexorably toward this moment, had fashioned of him, oblivious to him, the embodiment of the force which had come into his beginning, an entity strong as existence, growing equally with flesh, a life of itself growing besides life, complete, apart, having its own needs, seizing what it would, directing his soul as life directed his body, implacable, inexorable, a force having magnitude and direction, undeviating and unconquerable.

He was a child again, he was a small boy standing on a dusty street in the place where he had occurred, waiting for the greatest man, to be near him, to be fulfilled in his aura, to put his small presence to suckle and be nourished by it, standing reverent, intoxicated, grateful, waiting to carry his bag, waiting to look into his eyes, to serve him, to be one with him.

All this was his again. It rose in him clean and fresh, newborn, as if the weeping, anxious, stained and hampered intervening years had never been.

Before him waited the demesne of his soul, the realm of his vector, the infinity in which his mind and soul would stride, hungering and fed and never filled, and his body follow, he had won to what his life willed, he had come into his own. The dream was made flesh, the force was made man. The hope rose and drew breath and looked wondering and smiled and was made life. The child who knew no other hope, whose world had no other meaning, stood now, fulfilled, on the threshold of Heaven.

Ahead was Greenville.

Lucas Marsh had become a doctor.

Now he looked upon its environs, on the countryside, committing it to memory, seeing the rolling hillsides where feldspar had once been discovered, the scars of old mines, the timbered hills, the peaks crossing endlessly into the distance over dense forest, craning excitedly with Kristina to glimpse the town where it lay cupped in a rolling valley, buttered with farms, striped with fields, yellow and green and black, gliding beside them, racing to meet them, waiting.

And beside him, Kristina, in her own world, dimly but nonetheless powerfully aware of the force within Lucas, that was greater than her husband, that moved him irresistibly, that shaped and presented him, knew of her own knowing, living with it, that this force was greater than the humans on whom it would be expended and that the hour of this knowledge would yawn one day before Lucas. Fended the thought, thrust it away, buried it, stood upon it, a fortress to protect her Lucas.

The train stopped.

They alighted, dazed, smiling endlessly.

Dr. Runkleman was waiting for them. He beamed down at them, a tall man, broad, burly, his hat set squarely on his head, his stiffly pressed mail-order clothes bulging a little beneath his weight, his brown eyes delighted, his bushy brows frowning with pleasure, the unmistakable bathed, laundered, pressed, shined, neat, plain look of a doctor on him. They liked him instantly. They glanced at one another happily. He saw with satisfaction a young doctor, soberly dressed, his eyes saw the careful mend on the coat's breast pocket, the anxious, eager eyes, the thin, handsome, serious face, the student's look, the shy, boyish smile, the look of pleasure for himself. And he saw his wife, this well-looking, sturdy, slim, blond young woman with the look of a Swede about her, saw her simple clothes, saw her easy, competent hands, saw the respect and pleasure in her eyes. And he smiled again. He was delighted. He was amazed at his good fortune. He was content.

"Well, I expect you're tired after your trip, want to wash up a bit before I take you around, I thought I'd take you around a bit, show you the town when you're ready—"

"Not a bit, Doctor," cried Lucas. "I mean—you're all right, aren't you, Kris? The trip was nothing, we just sat there and enjoyed ourselves—"

"I'm fine, Doctor," said Kristina. "You do just what you want!"

"Well . . . If you're sure, Doctor—"

"Absolutely," said Lucas, tingling.

"We can see it as we go." The car left the station behind, headed away from the town into the countryside. "You saw the mines I expect—"

"That's what they were, then! Mines!"

"Old feldspar mines. Yes. This is one of those towns. Just another piece of the earth, all woods and trees, and then one day some feller, just wandering along, kicked up a piece of this feldspar stuff and you know how it is, it glittered and there was a little mica with it, too, and first thing you know it's worth a little and there's a regular rush."

He beamed at them. They were listening intently.

"Well, that's about how it was. That was about eighty years ago and pretty soon the deposits gave out or the demand got thin, probably a little of both and the something-for-nothing boys moved on and the stores that came in stayed on, and the land was pretty good and that's your Greenville. Quite a bit of lumbering, got one factory, a tile plant on the edge of town that makes vitreous pipe and they're starting to try out a line of dishes, pottery and stuff. Outside of that the rest of town makes a living taking in each other's washing. They work in the stores—we're a crossroads town and Greenville's the county seat, back in the hills there's little villages do all their trading here, come for miles—and there's quite a few wealthy farms scattered around. But in the town the man who sells tires takes his money and buys groceries and the grocery man buys hardware with the tire man's money and the hardware man buys tires—and they all come to the doctor." He laughed and a moment later they joined him.

"There, now! How's that for a chamber of commerce?"

"Perfect!" said Lucas.

"They should hire you!" Kristina cried.

Lucas looked apprehensively at Dr. Runkleman, but he was beaming happily and undisturbed at Kristina.

"And there's two hospitals, Doctor—"

"That's right, Doctor. We got the County and the Valley. The Valley's a little private place, nothing like you been used to, started about five years ago in an old private house, an old mansion, really, they've got it fixed pretty good, I do quite a bit of work there. And the county keeps up the other one—I'm the chief surgeon, you'll be my assistant."

"Fine!"

"You like surgery?"

"Indeed I do!"

"He likes everything!" Kristina cried. "Whatever there is—he likes it—so long as it's Medicine!"

Lucas smiled and licked his lips.

"Well," he shrugged, "I guess that's as good a reason as any for being a doctor . . ."

"You're right!" said Dr. Runkleman heartily. "Well, you'll get plenty

Medicine here. We're snowed under. We got four other doctors—you'll meet them—" He looked at the watch on his thick, hairy wrist, then quickly at a spot in the countryside.

"Call?" Lucas interpreted eagerly.

"You go right ahead!" protested Kristina. "Don't let us stop you—you got work to do, why, you forget us—"

"Well . . . If you don't mind . . ."

"Not a bit!"

"That's Oakum over there . . . I might just make a call here, long as we're passing—just for a minute . . ."

The car turned off the macadam, bumped along a dirt road past a tiny, ramshackle store, a clot of five weather-beaten houses. Before the last house the car stopped.

"Here we are," he said apologetically. "I won't be but a minute." He opened the door, got out, pulled his bag from the rear seat.

"Oakum!" echoed Kristina. She looked about her, settling herself.

Lucas swallowed.

"Mind if I come with you?"

"Come right ahead! Glad to have you! Not that you have to start right in today, you know . . ."

"They're sick today as well as any other day! I'm glad to start, Doctor. I don't mind it a bit. You just lead the way."

"Want me to come, too? Need a nurse?" Kristina called hopefully.

"Well, I guess we better not overwhelm them. I tell you what—we'll be right out, how'll that be?"

"You're the doctor."

They turned and walked toward the house.

"This is a little girl," Dr. Runkleman said in an undertone. "They asked me to stop in if I was going by—"

"If you were going by!"

"Yes, they always say if I am going by. Well, one of the neighbors called in, she's got a bad cut, they say, ripped her scalp on a nail."

Two hounds materialized, snarling. Dr. Runkleman glanced at them absently, hefted his bag. He knocked at the door.

An old woman, toothless, a few sparse hairs blown whitely over her pink scalp, opened the door, gestured them in with a knotted stick of a forearm.

They entered.

"Well, now," said Dr. Runkleman, "hear you've had a little trouble."

The old woman gestured to a murky corner.

"Danged nigh sculp h'self," she reported.

Lucas stumbled over a broken chair. The room had a foul, sour odor, in a corner he made out a wood stove; one side legless, propped with a chunk of wood, there was a dirty table, a cupboard, three chairs offering burst springs and ripped entrails of hair and rotted burlap webbing. On the floor was a soiled straw mattress. On a drunken bed he made out a tiny form.

"This is Dr. Marsh," Dr. Runkleman said.

The old woman looked at Lucas, nodded awkwardly.

"How do," she creaked.

Dr. Runkleman looked down at the bed. A small and very dirty four-year-old girl stared up silently. Her head was wrapped in a soiled rag.

"Yes," said Dr. Runkleman. "Well, now. Let's see, what have we here . . ."

"How did it happen?" Lucas asked the old woman.

"Playin' round, three o'clock in the mornin', ripped it on a nail."

"Three o'clock!" echoed Lucas.

"Oh, some of the kids stay up pretty late around here," Dr. Runkleman said impersonally.

Lucas, who had looked away for a moment, looked back at the little girl. He started. The five stitches were in, Dr. Runkleman was fishing in his bag with his free hand for dressings. Lucas blinked.

"Now you'll be all right," Dr. Runkleman smiled down. "I tell you what. Next time you come by my place, I'll tell you what! I'll give you—an apple! How's that! Would you like an apple?"

The old woman fumbled beneath the slack of her dress bosom, from a tobacco sack brought out two coins, looked up at him warily.

"Se'nty-fi' cents?"

"That's right," Dr. Runkleman said heartily.

It was good to be in the air again.

"Kind of close in there," Dr. Runkleman said apologetically. Lucas grinned amiably.

"Didn't take you long," Kristina called from the car.

"Just a cut—a little tear," Dr. Runkleman wedged heavily in the driver's seat.

"I turned my head for a moment—and he had five stitches in," Lucas announced.

Dr. Runkleman gave Lucas a grateful, shy look.

"Thirty-five years— I guess I've done enough stitches," he deprecated.

They drove back to his office on Greenville's main street. They entered the office, at one side he unlocked a door. He stood aside. They walked through.

"What do you think, eh?"

"There's five rooms!" Kristina said, surprised.

"That's right. You like it?"

Lucas saw a pipe protruding from the floor. He turned inquiringly.

"A dentist used to have this," Dr. Runkleman said. "Yes . . . he hasn't been here for a year. I tell you what! I can let you have this place for fifteen dollars a month!"

"But that's wonderful!"

"Five rooms!"

"That's right," Dr. Runkleman chuckled. "You can fix yourselves up right here—"

"Right next to the office!" Lucas exulted.

"Of course we take it!" Kristina cried. She looked greedily about the five rooms.

"I'll bet you make it look all real nice and pretty. I'll bet you're just the girl can do it!"

Lucas and Kristina looked at each other.

"We haven't got much furniture just now," Lucas admitted.

"We got nothing!" said Kristina. "But in Minnesota—"

"We figured on staying at the hotel until we could pick some up, or rent a place furnished—"

"You did? Well now, look here! You come with me. I got an idea." He crooked his finger archly, they walked through the office corridors, out the back door. A few feet away loomed a huge house.

"That yours?" Lucas asked, awed.

Dr. Runkleman, smiling, unlocked the door and they followed him in.

"My goodness," Kristina breathed.

They were in a large living room. It was crammed with mail-order furniture, the most expensive in the catalogues. Lucas winced.

"It's beautiful!" he said stoutly.

"Doctor! Doctor!" murmured Kristina. "A beautiful home like this and you never married!"

"It's comfortable," Dr. Runkleman nodded, delighted.

"Comfortable!" Kristina echoed.

"I should think so," Lucas mumbled.

Upstairs Dr. Runkleman stood in the doorway while Kristina admired a new, unused bedroom, its new oak bureau, its new oak bed, its new mail-order rug, its curtains.

"This will be your room until you move into your own place. In the meantime I got plenty of furniture out back—stored away"—he waved his arm vaguely. "Maybe I can help out, piece what you've got, you don't have to buy so much. Anyway—no good staying at a hotel, spending money. Now that's the way we'll do it." He looked at his worn wrist watch again. "My housekeeper's off today. . . . How do you like fried chicken with French-fried potatoes? Then we'll drive around a little more."

"It's a shame to use up your Sunday like this," Kristina grimaced. "The one day you got off."

"We've got to see about getting you a car."

Lucas looked quickly at Kristina. They had one hundred and twelve dollars.

"I've got an old one—" Dr. Runkleman locked the front door carefully behind them—"you won't like it much, it's pretty bad, I use it sometimes when this one is laid up. You can use it until you get one of your own."

"I learned a little on the ambulance—"

"Oh, yes. Got to have a car here. Long distance between places. That's the Catholic church."

"I was wondering—"

"Yes. We're neighbors." He looked at the low stone wall separating his driveway from the church. "They stay on their side of the fence and I stay on mine. You Catholic, by any chance?"

"Oh, no. Mrs. Marsh is Lutheran. I guess I'm Methodist Episcopal."

"I don't get much time for church. No. Now over there," and he pointed to his neighbor on the other side, "is Ben Cosgrove. He's a lawyer. Now, I wonder what you're going to think of him."

"I don't know many lawyers."

"We got two, three of them. And afterward I want you to meet Dr. Castle, Dr. Henry Castle. And then maybe, later this evening, if you feel like it, we'll go over to the County."

In a dozen blocks the sidewalks ended, the houses were farther apart, a dozen more and they were on the highway and the town was behind them folded from sight in the hills.

"This Dr. Castle—we do quite a bit of work together. He's a Canadian. Getting old—like I am. I help him out with surgery, now and then."

"In Minnesota," Kristina said politely, "there's quite a few Canadians. They're French, aren't they?"

"Well, now, this one, I'm pretty sure he's English. Yes. English descent. He's a very well-educated man. Then we've got Dr. Kauffman, and Dr. Binyon and Dr. Blake, they run an office together, sort of clinic."

"The three of them?"

"No," said Dr. Runkleman carefully. "Dr. Kauffman is a Jew."

When they had finished eating the waitress who had served them, a thin, blond girl not quite thirty, held a five-dollar bill toward Dr. Runkleman.

"What? What's this for?"

"It's on account, Doctor. I've already paid ten dollars. Now I owe fifteen more. I'd have paid in sooner, only—"

"Do you owe me money?"

"Dr. Snider said it would be thirty dollars."

"When did he tell you that?"

"When I was leaving the County. I paid in ten."

"He did? I see . . . Well, now you just keep that and I'll see if I can't straighten it out . . ." His eyes were hard. Carefully, he put down a ten-cent tip.

He managed a smile as they got back in the car.

"I don't know what they're doing over in the County. That's Dr. Snider—you'll meet him tomorrow, he's in charge of the County—somebody over there must have got things mixed up. I took out her appendix and I guess somebody got things mixed up."

"It's free at the County, isn't it?"

"That's right." He was silent.

They were in bed at nine o'clock.

"What do you think?" Lucas whispered, "living right next to the office—! You can't beat that. I can just roll out of bed in the morning and open the door and I'm there. Kris! Did you see that old woman where we stopped for that call? Do you know what she paid him? Seventy-five cents! That's what he charges for a call!"

"Maybe just poor people."

"Everybody. Seventy-five cents to a dollar and a half. Thirty dollars for an appendectomy, fifteen dollars for tonsils and adenoids, seventy-five dollars for a delivery and six months postnatal care—"

"And he's got all this! That seven-room office, all that equipment, that brand new X-ray, the five-room wing we're going to have, this big house, two cars, all that furniture—"

"And sixty office calls a day! Sixty! Sixty calls between one o'clock and six-thirty! Is it possible? In the mornings he operates at the County from eight until eleven—then the Valley, that's the private hospital, if he's got any scheduled there—then back to the office—then there's his rounds—and the calls in between—and the night calls—"

"He's a nice man. You like him, Luke?"

"There's a man who's practicing Medicine! And to hell with the money!"

"Giving us this room until we get settled . . ."

"You should have seen him! He picked up that needle, I turned my head for a minute, I turned back—and he had five stitches in and reaching for the dressings!"

"What was it?"

"Little girl, four-year-old, big gash in her scalp, caught it on a nail. At three o'clock in the morning! Playing!"

"We gonna have a nice house, Luke. I'm gonna fix it up real good. Do you think maybe he might take me on?"

"I don't know. Let's see his staff," Lucas twisted uncomfortably. "He knows you're a nurse. He didn't say anything. He's probably got all the help he wants."

"We could use the money. Tomorrow I clean that place from top to bottom. . . . Was it a pretty little girl, Luke?"

"I wonder what happened to the dentist."

"I'm going to put up curtains—"

"We've got to get a stove—"

"I'll look in the stores. Second hand is just as good—"

"Now remember, Kris, you're a doctor's wife—"

"They don't know me—"

"Maybe you better get it in Lepton, somewheres down the line—anything second hand like that—it'll reflect on him, too . . ."

"Oh, Luke! A place of our own. Our first place! Our first home! . . . And you've been on your first case, already! . . . That poor little girl! . . . Do you like children, Luke?"

"You bet I do. Cute little thing. Never said a word. Big black eyes watching— Now, wait a minute, Kris! You're not getting any ideas, are you?"

"About what? I didn't say anything—"

"About kids! That's what!"

"Someday we're going to have kids—"

"Someday!"

"I was just thinking—"

"But this isn't someday! Understand? Now get it straight! And don't get any ideas in your head! Now, you listen to me, Kris!"

"All right, all right—"

"I'm deadly serious!"

"We be all right."

"Well, just don't forget!"

In the night the phone rang and Lucas, rousing groggily, dressed and stumbled downstairs and found Dr. Runkleman with his hand on the knob and his bag in his other hand, ready to go out.

Dr. Runkleman grinned friendlily, surprised and pleased.

"You don't have to get up."

Lucas smiled. He picked up his bag. "I hope I've got what we'll need, here. I didn't know what to pack—I've just got the straight run-of-the-mill hospital kit—"

"I got plenty here. Everything. Hope Mrs. Marsh didn't get waked up—"

"She's used to it."

"If she wants to we can use an operating-room nurse at the County now and then. Think she'd mind?"

"She was head OR when she married me—just quit to come up here—"

"Wonderful! She'll show us up!"

They drove a long way into the dark countryside, through the farm country, past the far-apart farms.

When they stopped Lucas sensed rather than saw a house set some distance back from the road.

"They might at least have left a light on," he protested.

"Yes," said Dr. Runkleman.

At their footsteps dogs came roaring. They tripped and stumbled toward the house. The din grew. Still no light appeared. Finally they reached the front door. Dr. Runkleman pounded. They waited. There was no answer.

"And this is the house which called a doctor up in the middle of the night?" Lucas cried incredulously.

"I'll just try the back door," said Dr. Runkleman.

He pounded at the back door. The dogs roared louder. He pounded again and again. Finally a light came on. A moment later the door opened.

The sleep-swollen face of a hulking farmer peered at them resentfully, he saw their bags, pointed wordlessly to a bedroom, carried his kerosene lamp ahead. A woman lay sleeping. They roused her. This was the patient.

"You called us, didn't you?" Lucas asked the farmer uncertainly.

"Had a bad spell a while back." He grunted.

"Something's the matter'th my chest," she said soberly.

Dr. Runkleman shook some pills out of a vial.

"You're all right," he said.

The woman nodded. The farmer lit their way to the door. They stumbled back toward their car. When they were halfway there the lights were extinguished in the house. They reached the car in darkness. They drove off.

"Seventy-five cents?" Lucas asked tonelessly.

"That's a dollar," Dr. Runkleman said apologetically. "Night call."

"And they called you up in the middle of the night—got you all the way out here—for a mild cold?"

"They don't know. They know she's got cancer, carcinoma of the spleen, already metastasized. So any symptom she gets—"

"But not even to have a light on for you!"

"Yes . . . That's the way they are," Dr. Runkleman said cheerily.

He smiled at Lucas reassuringly. I know why you're saying that, you're saying it because you're indignant for my sake, I appreciate it, it warms me, I like you; but don't get mad, it's a waste of time, you'll see after a while, that's how they are, it doesn't matter, I'm not insulted, that's what I treat.

Lucas' heart ached suddenly with affection for this burly, shy man, trying awkwardly with the punctilio of a grandee to be kind, to give him ease. A wave of fierce protectiveness for him, for his battered bag, his expensive cheap shoes, his mail-order clothes.

They returned to the house. They went to bed, they fell asleep again. It was a good night. They were awakened twice more before dawn. At the second awakening Lucas' body, incredulous and outraged as it always had been on night duty, stumbled to the waiting car, his numb mind rousing last. At the next call he rose resignedly, rose from habit, moved and thought more easily.

And at the last awakening the rebellion, ripped untimely from the womb of slumber, the wrench, the maimed upswimming, threshing climb to consciousness, this normal mechanism of man was tamed, led docilely by discipline, and abruptly the abnormal became normal, he awakened undazed, his mind began to function almost instantly, and then, its work done, the alarm met, function performed, he fell lightly and thoroughly and easily asleep again, unresenting and controlled. The groundwork for this transition had been prepared during his internship. Now the structure in a single night became absolute and permanent and the fixed future of his days.

Before he fell asleep after the last call he mused drowsily on this community which was his, now, his laboratory, his hospital, his field. He explored the data of the day, the details, the faint notes, the signs, and he sighed happily for the man's, David Runkleman's, skill, his grasp and his silent knowledge. He would work with him obliviously, hand to hand, these two knowing what they knew, intent, forever ready, impersonal units of the great game, the greatest force that man possessed, that possessed man, these two, lonely and together. He gave a fierce sigh of happiness and fell asleep.

⋆ CHAPTER 25

In the morning sunlight the County Hospital's low, rigid lines elated Lucas with anticipation, he did not notice the countryside in which it was set, he alighted from the car with Dr. Runkleman and holding his gaze on the squat structure he walked to it, savoring the moment, savoring this first sight of it, possessing it.

Shaped in a square U, the wings at the rear, the length of the building was divided by a corridor, on either side of which were the wards. In one wing was the X-ray room, the operating room, the emergency room, and a surgeon's dressing room. In the other wing was kept the county's poor and those too infirm for work but not yet sick enough for hospitalization.

Dr. Runkleman was showing Lucas the hospital's seldom used laboratory when the door opened and a short, thin, elderly, tousled figure precipitated itself into the room.

"Told me you were here!" the man cried, accusingly. "God damn 'em! Never get 'em to tell you anything!"

Startled, Lucas looked at Dr. Runkleman.

"This is Dr. Snider," said Dr. Runkleman.

Lucas took his limp hand and surveyed the man thus lifted into brotherhood by the mention of the single word "doctor." There was a stain of tobacco juice at the corner of his thin lips.

"Dr. Marsh," said Dr. Runkleman. "He's going to help us out."

"Pleased to make your acquaintance," said Dr. Snider. He swallowed and his bony Adam's apple bobbed beneath a patent bow tie. "See you found the lab, all right—"

"I've been showing him around."

"Like to fool around in the lab?"

"A sort of sentimental attachment. I worked my way through school doing lab work," Lucas confided.

"Anything you want, you just sing out. That right, Dave? We're kind of shorthanded here, I guess Dave's told you, sort of use this place for a supply room—"

"Well," said Dr. Runkleman, walking to the door, "I guess we got a little job this morning—"

"Need me?"

Dr. Runkleman nodded. The three walked down the corridor toward the operating room.

"Well, you won't find us much," said Dr. Snider. "Just a little old backwoods hospital after what you been accustomed to. Used to have a hospital of my own over the state line—"

"I told him," said Dr. Runkleman.

"Guess you got enough OB to keep him busy, anyway, eh, Dave?" Dr. Snider asked slyly.

"That's what I'm here for," Lucas said promptly. "All the work I can get."

"Oh, you'll get enough work, all right. Dave'll find work enough for you. He'll keep you busy. Eh, Dave?"

"Yes," said Dr. Runkleman evenly. "There's plenty of work."

As they entered through the wide swinging doors of the operating room three nurses looked up quickly, curiously and nervously.

"Good morning, girls! Brought you a nice, new doctor! A young one!" Dr. Snider announced loudly.

Lucas flushed. The nurses smiled uncertainly.

"This is Dr. Marsh," said Dr. Runkleman. "Miss Adams, Mrs. Pomfret, Miss Punce."

"New man!" cried Dr. Snider. "Came straight from the state university! Now you girls get the lead out of your ass this morning! Don't disgrace us!" He turned to Dr. Runkleman. "I'll be right with you." He turned and walked out.

"I guess we're about ready," Dr. Runkleman smiled amiably at the nurses. "Sorry to be a little late this morning—"

They walked toward the dressing room. Speech means nothing, Lucas told himself sternly. Neither speech, nor chewing tobacco, nor small, mean eyes, nor all the marks of a bumpkin. Beneath these things which do not count is a doctor. Deal with the doctor. Forget the rest.

"What do you think of him?" Dr. Runkleman asked impersonally. In the tiny dressing room he had pulled off his shirt, his undershirt, revealing a great hairy chest, a hairy belly, he folded his clothes carefully.

"Must be quite a job handling this whole hospital," Lucas said evenly.

"The girls do all the work!" Dr. Runkleman snorted. "Old Al's got a good thing just being administrator. Used to have a small sanitarium, I guess it got too much for him. He's getting old. I don't use him any more than I have to. Now—those girls—I don't know whether you noticed—only one of them's an RN, we have to do the best we can—Miss Otis, for instance, she'll be the operating-room nurse this morning, she comes when she can, she's got a crippled husband to take care of—"

"Can't they afford a regular OR?"

"Well, you see, old Al keeps bills down to a minimum. That way he stays on the good side of the board. I don't think we've got three RN's on the whole staff."

They dressed, scrubbed, took their places.

The patient was wheeled in.

"Meat on the table!" Dr. Snider sang out happily, following the stretcher. He had removed his coat and now wore a short white jacket.

Dr. Runkleman glanced at the patient, a slim girl of fifteen, her dark eyes wide with fright.

"This will be an appendectomy," he told Lucas. "And I think we might have something else." And then, in a louder voice, smiling at the girl, "Well! How are you this morning! Next time you see me your troubles are going to be all over."

The girl stared up at their masked faces and tried to smile. Dr. Snider sat down at the head of the table, by his side a tray with a mask and a can of ether. He reached forward abruptly and jerked the girl's chin up.

"All right, now," he said irritably, "don't try to take it all, just start breathing. Breathe easy." And he clapped the mask over her greased face and immediately saturated the mask. The girl jerked her head.

"Hey!" Dr. Snider protested indignantly. "What are you trying to do, there? Lay quiet! Now just take it easy!" He looked up at them, injured.

Lucas looked quickly away. Dr. Runkleman said nothing. He looked once at the ether mask, then steadily down at the table. The room fell silent. The girl began to breathe stertorously.

"All right, I guess," Dr. Snider said at last.

Dr. Runkleman took a step to the head of the table. Dr. Snider removed the mask and looked up at him. Dr. Runkleman jerked his head. Dr. Snider obediently opened one of the girl's eyelids, Dr. Runkleman peered at it briefly, nodded, took his place again. The girl was swiftly draped. As they uncovered her shaven mons veneris Dr. Runkleman quickly pulled the laparatomy sheet back in place, quickly and almost roughly. She breathed deeply and slowly now. All that could be seen of her was her umbilicus and the skin over her appendicial region.

Lucas thrust out his hand, Dr. Runkleman thrust out his hand. Miss Otis turned her head from one to the other uncertainly, ready with the long forceps holding the wad of gauze.

"That's right!" Dr. Runkleman said loudly. "That's *your* job!" He withdrew his hand.

"However you want to do it," Lucas said humbly.

"No, no! You're right! Absolutely!"

Miss Otis slapped the forceps gently into Lucas' palm. He held the gauze over a pail. One of the other nurses poured antiseptic over it, soaking it. He swabbed the bared skin. He threw the forceps on the waiting tray. Dr. Runkleman put out his hand. Miss Otis slapped a scalpel gently into the palm. Lucas put out his hand. Miss Otis put a square of gauze in it.

"Harder," said Lucas.

Miss Otis nodded.

Dr. Runkleman looked up at the clock.

Dr. Runkleman cut down on the skin. He made a small incision. Lucas mopped, put out his hand for haemostats. The clamps slapped hard into his hand. He nodded. Dr. Runkleman had already cut through the first layer of muscle. Two small arteries began to spurt. Lucas clamped them. Dr. Runkleman was cutting through the second layer. He waited while Lucas clamped again. Waited a moment after Lucas mopped, waited to be sure. Then he was cutting again, now he was pushing muscle out of his way, Lucas was retracting, clamping, mopping, Dr. Runkleman's fingers disappeared, they emerged, delivering the appendix, he seemed to be working slowly, carefully, hand out, instrument, cut, inspect, wait, put down the used instrument, look, hand out, instrument . . .

The appendix, and the clamp holding one end of it, dropped with a clink into a waiting kidney basin. Lucas looked involuntarily at the clock. Eight minutes. He looked at Dr. Runkleman, incredulous. Dr. Runkleman was everting the stump. Lucas glanced at Dr. Snider. Dr. Snider peered at him, a sardonic smile on his face. Surprised, are you? Figured you might be. That's the way we do it here.

"You assist fine, just fine!" Dr. Runkleman said cordially, holding the tied suture while Lucas snipped.

Lucas shook his head.

"Eight minutes!" he murmured.

Dr. Runkleman looked at the clock. The nurses shifted, pleased.

"That's what it was, wasn't it!" Dr. Runkleman said, as if surprised. If you're going to be surprised, I am, too. You and I. What one does, the other one does. We stand together.

Lucas swallowed.

"I think—we'll just take a look at those ovaries while we're here. Might as well have a look at them. Long as we've got her open. What do you think? I guess we better look." He turned to Dr. Snider. "Is she all right?" Dr. Snider removed the mask a moment, glanced at the still face carelessly, clapped the mask back on. He nodded, indifferently.

Dr. Runkleman's fingers disappeared into the incision, stuffing the end of intestine with it, he groped a moment, his fingers emerged delivering the right ovary, part of the tube, slender in a young girl, slender as childhood, angry-red.

"Yes sir!" said Dr. Runkleman.

"Chocolate cysts!"

"Pretty young, isn't she?" Dr. Runkleman agreed.

"What do you think?"

"Been hittin' it up," offered Dr. Snider from the head of the table. "Probably had a little more'n her belly'n she was born with!"

Lucas looked at Dr. Runkleman. Dr. Runkleman looked steadfastly at the tissue he was clamping off. GC, thought Lucas. It was the face that had fooled him. He would have to stop paying any attention to faces. Fifteen. And wearing that scapular medal. And gonorrhea. Long-standing enough to get to the tubes.

When he reached for a retractor, when he turned back, the area was cleaned of cysts, Dr. Runkleman had found a single small cyst on the left ovary. He called for sutures. He began to sew. He seemed to work slowly. His heavy hands moved deliberately, his thick, stubby fingers closed and opened ponderously. He worked without any perceptible change of rhythm. And Lucas, who from the beginning had concentrated with every nerve on having ready whatever Dr. Runkleman wanted, on being beforehand at every step, on mopping up the blood which obscured the field where Dr. Runkleman was working, and clamping and retracting, and snipping and holding sutures tight, Lucas suddenly followed the rhythm of Dr. Runkleman, adjusted to it like a dancer following a new partner's steps, watched it rigidly, and at the end they were working in unison, in that smooth, flowing move and countermove of partners, a complete, fierce, happy joy to both of them. They looked up and smiled boyishly at each other. They looked at the clock.

"Eighteen minutes!" cried Lucas. He spoke louder than he intended.

"So it is!" Dr. Runkleman nodded, as if he were surprised too.

"In and out in eighteen minutes! Ovarian cysts and an appendix!" No, his tone said stubbornly. No! You're not going to pretend surprise as if this was the first time you did it! This is incredible!

"About the way they did it down at State?" Dr. Runkleman asked diffidently.

"Oh, yes!" Lucas said fiercely, mockingly. "Oh, yes! That's the way they did it!" You know better! You know how fast that was! You know what you did—neat, strong, perfect, hardly a wineglass of blood spilled, you know—you know . . .

This was a craftsman.

Here in these backwoods, this bulky man, apologetic, clumsy-looking, dressed in mail-order clothes, this was a Doctor. This, this was Medicine. He grinned exultantly.

"Seems to be having trouble with her breathing," Dr. Snider said irritably.

Dr. Runkleman moved swiftly to the girl's head. Lucas moved with him. Her lips were blue. She was breathing very slowly.

Dr. Runkleman moved to the space occupied by Dr. Snider as if Dr. Snider weren't there. He put his bulk there and Dr. Snider got out of the way, knocking over his stool as he moved backward.

"Oxygen!" said Lucas.

He looked at the nurses. They looked back at him helplessly. He walked quickly to the tank.

"Where's the mask?"

"Where's the mask?" Dr. Runkleman echoed, his voice hard. The nurses bumped into each other scurrying to find the oxygen mask. They pawed through the instrument case.

"Hurry!" called Dr. Runkleman in the same voice.

A nurse dashed back with a mask. The oxygen began to hiss.

"Epinephrine?" Lucas queried.

Dr. Runkleman nodded.

The head operating-room nurse already had the syringe filled, needled, waiting. The oxygen hissed. The girl's breathing quickened a little.

"Eight . . ." called Lucas. Dr. Runkleman nodded. "Ten . . ." Dr. Runkleman nodded.

"Got blue all of a sudden," Dr. Snider said equably.

There was silence a moment.

"It didn't just happen," Dr. Runkleman said coldly.

"Looked down and damned if she wasn't blue!"

The girl breathed normally at length.

Lucas turned off the oxygen.

"Well," said Dr. Snider, "looks like she's all right, now."

Dr. Runkleman said nothing. He watched the girl a moment longer. Then he nodded, turned on his heel, and stripping off his gloves and mask walked to the dressing room. Lucas followed. Dr. Snider paid no attention to either of them. The door closed behind them.

They undressed. The silence was awkward.

"I've told him a million times," Dr. Runkleman said.

"He could have told us long before," said Lucas, he said it carefully, Dr. Snider was his senior.

"He's a goddamned old fool!" Dr. Runkleman burst out.

"Does he ever operate?"

"He hasn't operated in years. Every so often I use ether. Mostly I give spinals."

So there was a whole story there, plain to be read, a vista clear and unalterable behind the plain, the unextended, the simple words, the embarrassed tone.

"We'll look in at the Valley a minute, got a hernia there, Dr. Castle's patient, I said I'd help him."

And they showered, they dressed, they walked through the wards quickly.

"This is Dr. Marsh," and the faces of the indigent looking up expressionless, wary a little, "What do you think of this, Doctor?" Or, "I'd like you to look at this, Doctor." And a blur of nurses' faces, a blur of patients, some very young, most very old, a small sea of human life. "This is Dr. Marsh. Would you care to look at this, Doctor?" All with the deference, the intentness, most of all the deference as if a great surgeon, a great doctor were visiting and he, Dr. Runkleman, valued and studied his opinion, valued his stature. So that afterward, and Lucas knew it well, this would be Dr. Marsh, the new doctor, Dr. Marsh, young perhaps but of whom Dr. Runkleman asked things, whom he listened to intently, Dr. Marsh whom their own Dr. Runkleman treated as an equal. Or better.

On the way out they passed the X-ray room, which lay in the operating-room corridor. Outside the door there were two beds. They were occupied by two old men. Lucas turned to Dr. Runkleman inquiringly.

"That's the X-ray room," Dr. Runkleman said. "Yes. I guess they're kind of crowded." Lucas looked at him again. His tone had changed slightly. There was some significance here. But Dr. Runkleman said nothing further. They left the County, they drove on to the Valley.

"Wonder what Kris is doing," Lucas speculated.

"Would you like to stop? Shall I drive by? Won't take a minute—"

"Oh, Heavens no! No, no!"

"I could stop just as easy as not—"

"She's housecleaning. She's all right."

"That's a nice little woman. Yes. Very nice. I'll tell you what, I think we'll stop by there . . ."

"No, no, Doctor! Really!"

"Sure?"

"She'll be all right. She'll be fine."

"Well, I've got a couple of T and A's to do—might as well get them over, I guess. Then we'll help Castle . . ."

An hour later Lucas and Dr. Runkleman had removed three sets of tonsils and adenoids, a trained crew moving swiftly and surely with them.

They disrobed in the dressing room. Dr. Runkleman sat down on a cot there and leaned back against the wall, lacing his hands behind his head for a moment. Dr. Castle stooped his head automatically, coming through the doorway, a man in his sixties, his thin hair brown and gray, his face square, his eyes slow and intent, his mouth deeply carved, his nose jutting sharply, a heavy man, a man who looked like an old athlete, dressed indefinably better than Dr. Runkleman, not dressed fastidiously, but beside him Dr. Runkleman looked a little rustic.

"Ah," he said, "you got here early. You beat me."

"Yes," said Dr. Runkleman. He pulled himself up, smiling. "Yes. Now, this is Dr. Marsh."

"Glad to meet you, sir," said Lucas. And after a time Dr. Castle let go his hand.

"What do you think of us here?" Dr. Castle lit a cigarette. There were spots on his vest. Lucas looked up at his face swiftly. Hardening of the arteries. Essential hypertension.

"I think I'm pretty lucky!" Lucas said evenly.

"Oh ho! You've seen him work! What do you think of it?"

"I think I'm pretty lucky," Lucas said simply. There was nothing else to say.

"Now—" said Dr. Runkleman.

"It's the truth," Dr. Castle nodded. "He's all right, old Dave . . ."

"I guess I've seen a few," said Lucas.

"I'll have to buy you lunch," said Dr. Runkleman. "Yes. That's what you're after. All right. I'll have to buy you lunch."

The operation began.

Dr. Castle made the first incision. Dr. Runkleman, watching intently, stood politely by. He clamped. The OR mopped. Lucas stood by.

"Time for you in a minute," Dr. Castle said. He cut slowly, very slowly. His cuts were uneven. He cut badly.

"Getting old," he said, not looking up. And unobtrusively, little by little, Lucas could not say when, Dr. Runkleman took over, Dr. Castle was somehow assisting, Lucas was holding the large retractors in place, the repair was beginning.

Toward the end, the repair completed, closure begun,

"I'll do it," said Dr. Castle gruffly.

And Dr. Runkleman instantly doffed the invisible robe of charge, Dr. Castle began his slow, laborious, repeated moves again, Dr. Runkleman assisting, Lucas assisting both, the OR watching Lucas jealously.

Dr. Castle stopped.

"No," he said. He looked at what he had done. "No. I should have—"

"It's just right," said Dr. Runkleman, "I don't know—maybe if we—" and his hands moved in deftly, apologetically he snipped a few stitches, restitched, it was all done swiftly—"maybe like that—although your way —no difference. Just as good."

"No," said Dr. Castle watching as Lucas began to sew, "No, I did it wrong," he said it quietly and with dignity.

And in the dressing room before he left,

"Come around and see me when you get settled."

"I'll bring him around," Dr. Runkleman promised.

And Dr. Castle nodded and was gone.

"He's getting a little old now," Dr. Runkleman said carefully, knotting his tie. "That arthritis bothered him."

"I noticed. His hands. He's got a touch of hypertension, hasn't he?"

"Henry? He shouldn't be practicing, at all. He's got a presystolic murmur sounds like a waterfall—"

"Mitral—"

"Yes. Notice the flush? Pretty bad."

"He knows, of course."

"Oh, I've told him! You'll see. Knocks him out. He won't quit, though. Just as well. He's all right, Henry. He knows what he's doing. He knows enough to call for help—he was a damned fine man, once. Not so long ago. Made me look silly."

"He knows what he's doing, all right—"

"Just old. That's all."

You're not so young yourself, Lucas mused, troubled, as they drove back to the office. I've got to spare you, I've got to help you all I can. I've got to hold on to myself. Not go rushing in. These people do things delicately. I've got to keep quiet. Be restrained. Like him. Like he is. Be like him.

They ate quickly. When they had finished, Dr. Runkleman looked at his watch. "Well," he said elaborately, "guess it's about time to be getting to work."

And in the office, after he had met Miss Snow, who was the nurse, and Miss Ables, who kept the books and took X-rays, and found the rooms next door washed from ceiling to floor and empty, Kristina having gone out shopping,

"You sit over here," Dr. Runkleman gently indicated a chair beside his desk. And when Lucas was seated, Miss Snow handed Dr. Runkleman two clipped sheets, a case report, he looked at it, handed it to Lucas.

"All right," he said, "might as well start sending them in."

Miss Snow opened the door.

A woman of forty entered. And he sat in an office, a doctor in a doctor's office, and as she came through the door, as his eyes summed her, read the book of her face, scanned the shape of her, studied her motion, roamed her for signs, Lucas' self-consciousness vanished, he was all that he had learned, he was an instrument.

"Well, how are you today, Mrs. Funston?" Dr. Runkleman was heavily cordial, stilted. It was a polite manner, his notion of a social gambit, and in the question there was only the studied and self-conscious sound with which David Runkleman, who began life on a farm, now greeted his kind, as a doctor, and Lucas heard this in spite of himself, as a forever analyzing part of himself heard everything.

Mrs. Funston shook her head, troubled.

"Now—this is my assistant—Dr. Marsh. Yes . . . Now, how's the pain in your belly? Mrs. Funston's the wife of one of our cashiers, Dr. Marsh."

A fat woman, she was too fat, her complexion and conjunctivae had the muddiness of chronic gastritis,

"I still got it." The woman sat down stolidly.

And as she did so she smoothed her dress, she looked at them defensively and with the moment, with the look, Lucas expertly stripped the speaker of personality, clothing, status in the tribe. His eyes saw only the gesturings of the flesh, the mute language of a thousand tiny tissue fingers shaping a wrinkle here, pulling a line taut there, pitting a surface, smoothing it, roughing it, heaping it, gesturing endlessly. His ears heard only the dumb tongues of the body, the unworded sounds, the rustle of breath, the flub-dup of heart, the dull sound, the sharp sound, the hollow sound, the grating, creaking, crackling, blowing infinity of messages clearly spoken by these dumb tongues.

He looked at Addie Funston, his ears heard Dr. Runkleman unobtrusively drawing her out for his benefit, he sifted these things for the sounds and signs of neurosis, he explored her clothing for telltale disorder, stains, apathy.

Here was simply a woman who was eating too much. Now he ceased to analyze, the problem was over, and he reverted to the social noises indispensable between physician and patient, the polite, the tactful, the gambit.

The door closed behind Addie Funston. They walked out of a private door down a corridor lined with eight rooms. In each of these rooms Miss Snow had by now established a waiting patient.

"Seemed to show a little gastritis," Lucas said, his tone politely serious.

"She's in every week." Dr. Runkleman smiled. "There was a sort of puffiness to her skin—a little muddy . . ."

"Yes, and the conjunctivae—"

"She'll be in again next week. . . . Now, let's see." He looked down the corridor, picked a door at random. He opened it. A thin blond girl rose uncertainly in the narrow cubicle. Miss Snow came to them swiftly, handed him a card.

"Oh, yes! Miss Peterson, isn't it?" Dr. Runkleman smiled. Miss Snow closed the door quietly and hurried off. "This is Dr. Marsh, Miss Peterson. Miss Peterson is a bookkeeper—" he consulted the card—"down at the Acme Garage. Now, what seems to be your chief complaint?"

Miss Peterson flushed. She licked her lips, her lips opened, but she closed them again. She was a willowy, long-legged young woman of twenty-four, her skin slightly erupted, eyelids reddened, hands cold and somewhat moist. She looked hesitantly at Lucas.

"Well," she said reluctantly, "it's—well—it's my flowers."

Lucas blinked.

Dr. Runkleman nodded.

"When you have your flowers—when your period comes—do you flow a lot more than you used to?"

"No, sir. I—ah—well, I'm always just miserable, the pains come on so bad, I use hot water bags but it doesn't help, somebody told me a hot bag of salt but nobody can swallow a whole bag of salt—every month it's the same thing, four days gone, two days in bed, I just can't stand it any longer."

"Yes. Well—you can't stop, you know."

"Sometimes I think I'd be better off dead. And all those men in the shop, every time my flowers comes around they know, I can see them snickering, they pass remarks—"

Nothing here. Lucas had stopped analyzing two minutes after the girl began to speak. He heard the rest with his hearing faculties, he did not need his reason, he stood patiently until it was over. Here was just another human being, granted life, given the miracle of function, of potential, granted life and function and potential and the mechanism to express these things. There was nothing gravely wrong with the mechanism.

A thought, which had first come to him during his last year at the hospital, seeing hundreds of such humans, came again to him unresolved and vague and persistent. He put it away.

Dr. Runkleman looked at his watch. Miss Snow materialized, handed Dr. Runkleman a card, disappeared to tidy the room they had just quitted.

In the room they entered there were two people, the man was fifty years old and looked seventy, he was emaciated, a carpenter angular as his folding rule. He looked at them, spoke only when questioned, his wife volubly rattled off her husband's symptoms. Her features wrinkled with distaste as she described the taste of the last medicine Dr. Runkleman had prescribed. Dr. Runkleman prescribed a new medicine.

The door closed behind them. They walked down the corridor to the next room.

"He's never going to get well if she keeps on taking his medicine," Dr. Runkleman chuckled helplessly. "Whatever I prescribe for him—she takes it. Well . . ."

As they entered, Miss Snow winked at them knowingly.

"Well, hello there, boy!" Dr. Runkleman said heartily. "How are you? How would you like a nice apple, eh? I tell you what, the minute they're ripe you come by and I'll give you a nice apple, how would you like that? Now, let's see how we're coming along . . ."

The six-year-old stared at them silently.

"Said it hurt last time," his eighteen-year-old brother grinned.

"Well, this won't hurt, just drop your pants, now, this won't hurt a bit . . ."

Lucas looked and automatically moved to help set up the apparatus.

The six-year-old silently submitted to treatment, and, his brother leading the way, silently marched out again. He walked spraddled. The injection burned raw tissues in a urethra inflamed by gonorrhea contracted from his twelve-year-old sister.

The door opened.

The door closed.

They moved to the next room.

A new face, a new body, a new shape, a man, a woman, old, young, middle-aged, a baby, a heart, a stomach, a splinter, a boil, a bowel, a growth, a liver, a kidney, all hidden by the clothes, hidden behind the face, behind the expression, behind the voice, behind the speech and what was said every day and what was replied, and what was worn, and what was pretended, all stripped here, startlingly bare, looked at, viewed, listened to, treated, prescribed for, then robed, dressed, hidden again, walking to the door, gone, mingling with the mass as before entered.

Room after room, case after case, the quick look, the quick question, the rip of the prescription pad, the corridor, the next room, the next case.

And in an hour they had completed the circuit twice, they were back in the office, a little guiltily Lucas had adapted himself to the pace, missing a great deal, knowing he was missing a great deal, shrugging inwardly, guiltily, trusting Dr. Runkleman.

"Getting the hang of it."

"Going pretty fast," Lucas admitted.

"You'll get used to it. There's nothing wrong with most of them—you found that out at the hospital, I expect—I tell you what I do, if they can sleep nights, if the pain doesn't wake them up—I just like to make them comfortable till it gets better or we can see what we're dealing with—if it gets worse—they'll be back!"

"Sort of keep them at bay," Lucas murmured, his voice impersonal.

"About all we can do— Yes, Miss Snow? Oh! I wonder if you'd mind taking this one, Doctor—"

"The second door on your left," Miss Snow called. She ushered a new patient into the office. She hurried after Lucas. "I'll introduce you . . ."

But this was his own. This was his first in private practice. He looked at the young woman keenly. He resolved to miss nothing. He checked her silently, he listened as he looked, as his fingers probed. Miss Snow hovered a moment uncertainly, saw him absorbed, was gone.

The pelvis was normal.

He listened to her heart sounds. He moved to her chest. He palpated her abdomen.

". . . and my roommate, she teaches phys ed, she thought I'd better drop in, we room together, you know, and being as she teaches phys ed—but even so, one day last week I could hardly correct my English papers—yes, that's it! Right there! Right over the stomach!"

"And it pains you before breakfast?"

"Ever so badly! And I feel much worse after I eat—"

"But it doesn't wake you at night—"

"No, not the pain—"

"What does wake you?"

"It's been a nightmare . . . I've got to tell somebody or go crazy! I don't know where to turn. There's something I've got to know—my roommate . . . Doctor, listen! I'm almost sure she's having—relations—with a man! Tell me! Have I got syphilis? We both use the same toilet seat—I touch whatever she touches—I can't stand it! For God's sake, Doctor! Tell me!"

She pressed her hand against her abdomen as a sudden spasm knifed her. Her eyes never left his face.

"There's absolutely no sign of syphilis," Lucas said evenly. "I'm sure you've nothing to worry about. But we'll do a blood check just to make sure—and I'd like to do an X-ray on your stomach—"

"Oh, please, Doctor! Anything! Anything!"

He took a syringe of blood. He made an appointment with her for X-rays. He walked out of the room with her. He smiled pleasantly, leisurely, confidently, wishing her goodbye. Miss Snow hurried past him, tidying a freed wisp of hair. Dr. Runkleman opened the door of an examining room, walked quickly to the next door, saw Lucas and stopped.

"Everything all right?"

"Fine," said Lucas. They paused a moment in the corridor. Lucas told him the story. Dr. Runkleman nodded through a half-smile.

"Have to send that blood to the city," he said, consideringly. "We send all our Wassermanns there—what we send."

"I'm sure it'll be negative—"

"Negative as yours or mine—yes . . . same as the X-rays . . ."

"I thought we'd better be sure—"

"Oh, absolutely . . . yes . . . of course she's going to kick like a steer when she gets the bill . . ."

"But it's just routine, I—"

"Oh, you're right! Absolutely! . . . Eight dollars for the Wassermann, ten dollars for the X-rays, say a dollar for the visit, that's more than half a week's salary for her . . . and everything negative . . . nothing to show for it . . ."

"But I don't see how she can complain—"

"Oh, she won't say anything to us! Not a word. But after a while, when the fear's all gone, little stories'll trickle back—'They certainly overcharge you for nothing—they certainly don't care how they get their money . . .' "

"Oh, I'm sorry! I guess I thought I was still at the hospital—routine—"

"Don't you worry about it!" Dr. Runkleman clapped him on the shoulder. "I guess we can stand it—you and I . . ."

Crestfallen, swelling with new affection for Dr. Runkleman, sternly bidding his training to be silent, to think as Dr. Runkleman thought, straightening his shoulders a little from fatigue, he followed Dr. Runkleman into the next room. A pregnant woman awaited them stolidly, she got up on the table without being told, they worked in silence, she got down again, they smiled at her cheerfully, spoke to her briefly, she was gone, they were in the corridor again. Miss Snow was before them, she handed them a card, she walked to the next door.

"That was fast," Dr. Runkleman beamed four cases later. "I don't know how I managed without you! That's what I call teamwork!"

And Lucas glowed, he grinned self-consciously, he resolved to work even faster. All else was forgotten. The doors opened. The doors closed. New faces appeared, became known, in a twinkling became intimate, disappeared. Strangers took their place. They walked from room to room, up and down the corridor, in and out of the rooms, back to the office, into the corridor again, room to room, four doors down, cross over, four doors up, the office, the corridor, begin the circuit again.

And always Miss Snow was before them, tidying a room with a few pats, a fresh towel, filling the rooms as quickly as they were emptied, filling them from her apparently endless stock in her endlessly crowded waiting room.

And the door opened. And a new face, impatient:

"I've been waiting a long time—"

And, smoothly,

"I'm sorry. A little rushed today. What seems to be the trouble? . . ."

And the door closed,

And the next one waiting apathetically,

The next one impatiently,

The next one impatiently,

After a while Lucas automatically took one side of the hall while Dr. Runkleman took the other. When they met they smiled briefly, passed quickly on. They met in the office again and Lucas was sure the day was over. He relaxed, slumped.

Dr. Runkleman looked at his watch.

"Three o'clock . . . Still coming, Miss Snow?"

"Still coming."

The door opened.

The door closed.

The faces blurred.

Occasionally a face sharpened.

The two men, the deacon saying worriedly they'd all be a lot happier if Dr. Runkleman would just have a look, and the reverend smiled gently, and the deacon flushing, well, for one thing right in the middle of the sermon, just up and leaving the pulpit! There's nothing to be ashamed of, if a man's sick—that's what doctors are for . . .

And then, quietly, Dr. Runkleman told them, they looked at him in astonishment, he told them again, they left finally, the deacon went out stricken, the minister gently dazed, they would let him know, they would tell him what they wanted to do about the small brain tumor next day or so,

And they were glad to have met Dr. Marsh—very glad to have met him. . . .

The doors opened.

The doors closed.

"Still coming," said Miss Snow . . .

Seven respiratory complaints, three more prenatals, a gall bladder, a postnatal, two boils, a splinter, a mending rib, a soft mass in the breast, an itching scalp, four infants, a diet, an impetigo,

The doors opened and closed.

"Still coming," said Miss Snow.

. . . and all the woman wanted to know was if she did it. She was her mother and she had a right to know. She'd worried as long as she was going to, you tried to bring them up right—and look at her. Won't open her mouth.

"Did you do it, Betty? What your mother says?"

The girl sat, stubbornly silent.

Dr. Runkleman rose. The mother pulled the girl to her feet, pushed her ahead of her, stumbling from the push, toward the examining room.

No, she had not done it. Lucas straightened. She was still intact. Virgo intacta. He looked at the mother coldly.

"Three dollars," Dr. Runkleman smiled with his mouth.

"But you usually charge—! You! You just wait till your father comes home," the mother fumbled angrily in her pocketbook. The girl was silent. She hid the hatred in her eyes by staring resolutely at the floor.

The door opened. The door closed. Miss Snow ushered in the foreign body in the eye, ushered out the tongue ulcer, ushered in the heart, the sinus, the kidney, the bone marrow, the migraine,

. . . and she thanked him kindly, she smoothed her ragged dress, her shoes were gaping strips of rotting leather, her watery blue eyes brimmed, she laid on his desk two dead chickens, she just stopped by to thank him kindly. No, she had plenty of medicine, plenty still left, her old, bony, blotched, veined hands trembled, she looked at the chickens, she licked her thin blue lips, she tore her eyes away, she looked up at him happily.

"They're just fine! Aren't they beautiful, Dr. Marsh?"

She stumbled out. She looked around the waiting-room proudly. The door closed behind her.

"You know she's stolen them!" cried Miss Snow. "You know perfectly well, Doctor. Can you imagine, Dr. Marsh? At her age?"

"Well," Lucas said evenly, "when you come right down to it I guess there aren't many patients who'd steal to pay their doctor bills . . ."

Dr. Runkleman looked at him admiringly.

"Feeling tired?"

"No, no!" lied Lucas. "I'm right at home. This is just a busy day at the hospital."

"Still coming, Miss Snow?"

"Still coming."

It was like the hospital, really. But not so many. Not so many that you couldn't keep track. Not so many that you could hardly remember the last, the one before, too fast to store away,

And the thought came again. It was not so vague, now . . . It was not clear but it was becoming stronger. There was pity in it. And a curious terror.

What a man wanted . . . what his life was for. . . .

And what he spent it on.

And the faces, the blurred faces, the bodies, rose as at a window, heaped up, immobile, staring, seeing nothing, and between himself and them a sense of waiting, wary waiting . . .

The unshaped thought weighed more heavily, more demandingly, eluded him. He was tired, he brushed it aside impatiently. He walked quickly down the corridor. Miss Snow beckoned.

The door opened.

The door closed.

Patient after patient after patient . . .

The young man's face had the anxious lines of the hopelessly ill, his eyes were dull, his look was blank, in the wheelchair his frame was bare and sharp, the lineaments of his face giving way sullenly to the Hippocratic facies, tissue outlining the Presence. Dr. Runkleman leaned over him and smelled the smell, the breath of the dying. Dr. Runkleman patted his shoulder noncommittally. He was wheeled out, incurious, uncaring, barely noticing them, remote, gone deep into himself, a pebble sinking in the soft ooze of his corrupting cells, finding no bottom, out of sight, out of hearing, finding nothing.

"I don't think I've seen you around here, have I?" Dr. Runkleman asked politely.

She said no.

She was twenty-six. Her clothes, her hair, expensively groomed, her voice was cultured.

"I heard about you," she said carefully. "I live in Amelot. I was just driving by—"

"Anybody recommend you?"

"No . . . I heard some friends talk about you . . . I was just driving by."

"I see . . . Well, now, what seems to be the trouble?"

"I don't know, Doctor. It's in my genital area. An itching, a sort of burning itching—and I keep staining—"

"Have to wear a pad all the time—"

"That's right! What is it? Do you know what it is?"

The young woman lay on the table, draped, her knees arched apart, her heels in the table stirrups.

"Now, let's just see," said Dr. Runkleman. Her genitals were clean. At the bottom of her vulva there was a small whitish-yellow leakage.

"Everybody always wears their very best underwear when they go to the doctors," the woman said mock-tragically, her voice tight, trying to make talk. "And the doctor tells them to undress and leaves the room and he never sees it."

"That's right," Dr. Runkleman said genially. He slipped a speculum in the vagina gently, turned it, opened its jaws, the vaginal tract was reddened, at the end the cervix looked tender, swollen, a trickle of yellow-white was oozing from the cervical opening. The woman winced.

"Might as well come in a barrel," said Lucas.

"That's right," the woman said gratefully. "It would be a lot easier."

Lucas swabbed some of the yellow-white material from the cervix. He rolled the swab expertly over the glass slide. He walked toward the door.

"I often wonder why women bother to wear any underwear at all when they come to the doctor," he said.

"Oh, Doctor! A woman has to wear underwear! Especially then!"

"Morale," Dr. Runkleman grinned. "That's it, isn't it? I'll bet that's it! Morale!"

"You men! You'd never know the difference!"

"That's the truth!" Lucas laughed.

"Is it tender here?" Dr. Runkleman probed gently. The woman winced. The door closed behind Lucas. He took the slide into the small laboratory room, started the first stain, reached for the second solution, washed, dried, waited, reached for the counterstain.

Under the oil-immersion lens the field glowed color, blurred a moment, leaped up, spread out clear and sharp. Inside the white cells were pink, coffee-bean-shaped organisms, plants, plants without chlorophyll, plants growing in the tender soil of human tissue. And these healthy plants were round, clumped in pairs, and from their shape and their disposition their name was as plain as the shape and disposition of an oak or a rose, and the name of these plants was gonococcus.

Lucas returned, laid a slip of paper before Dr. Runkleman.

They looked up at him.

Dr. Runkleman glanced at the paper. "Yes . . . Well . . ." The woman's face was strained.

"What's the bad news, precisely?" she asked carelessly, smiling, her eyes anxious above the curve of her mouth, her fine white teeth.

"I'm afraid we've got a little bad news here," Dr. Runkleman fingered the paper gently.

"I've heard my friends talk about it," the woman said, as if the three of them had heard the same thing. "What do they call it? Luke—Luke something . . ."

"Leucorrhea? Yes, that's right. That's what they probably call it."

"I take douches for it, don't I? Some kind of douches?"

"Yes . . . Now, what you have here—I'm afraid you have gonorrhea . . ."

The woman looked at him woodenly, ignoring the dropped spoon, the butler's clumsiness, the passed wind, the accidentally dropped cup.

"Gonorrhea?" she said. And they were talking about someone else.

"I'm afraid so . . . I thought when I first examined you—"

"But that's impossible," the woman smiled evenly.

"Yes, I know how you feel, and I wish it were, but that's how it is, don't worry about it, it's just an organism."

"But—wait a minute! How do you—how do you pick up such things—I've heard of toilet seats! That would probably be it, wouldn't it! Toilet seats! I was in a department store about two weeks ago and—it was very careless of me, I really know better, but—"

"When did you last have relations with a man?"

"Relations! With a man? Never! I've never had relations with a man in my life!"

"Intercourse. Sexual intercourse—"

"I know what you mean—"

"I don't know how that toilet-seat business got spread around. . . . You don't get it there."

"I never had relations with a man in my entire life!"

"Yes . . . Well . . . we'll treat you for it, but that's how you get it. Maybe you know the man. Better stay away from him. And be careful of your discharges. It doesn't matter to us. It's all right. We're doctors. That's what we're for—to take care of you—"

"You're very insulting to say the least!" The woman had risen.

"I'll tell you what. So you'll know," Dr. Runkleman said diffidently. "Dr. Marsh can tell you. Those little devils, those bugs are mighty hard to keep alive. Even under the best conditions, even in a laboratory where you try to keep them alive. So on a toilet seat—they die in a few minutes. And they won't live just anywhere, they won't live on the skin, that's not their medium. No. . . . We're not judges, it's nothing to us, there's only one way to get it, you're an intelligent woman—"

"My bill, please," said the woman steadily.

Dr. Runkleman nodded. He began to write.

"I tell you now, as I told you before! I have never had relations with any man in my entire life. I'm sorry that isn't enough for you. That, and my word of honor!"

"Here you are," said Dr. Runkleman. She took the bill, opened her expensive purse, put a bill with his statement, placed them on the corner of his desk.

"Just a moment! This is too much! I'll get you change!"

She looked at him contemptuously.

"I should have known better than to come to an ignorant hick doctor!" She shut the door quietly behind her. For a moment they did not look at each other. Miss Snow opened the door. Dr. Runkleman nodded. The door closed behind her.

"She didn't get it off any fence paling!" Dr. Runkleman chuckled.

"Why do they do it? Why do they just stand there and tell you black is white?"

"Didn't go to any doctor in Amelot. No. Drove clear out here. Wonder if that's her name? Cultured woman, wasn't she?"

"'I never had relations with any man in my entire life.'" Lucas echoed.

"Stood right there and looked us right in the eye—"

The door opened.

The little boy had an earache. His neck was thin, like his mother's.

Their tissues, mother and son tissues, were thin, needy, half-good at their best. They were never at their best. They were average. The little boy screamed thinly. Dr. Runkleman injected some warm oil. The door closed behind them.

The door opened.

"Four o'clock," Dr. Runkleman smiled.

The man was forty-five, appeared fifty, his grayish-brown face was deeply lined, he was short, poorly dressed, he fumbled his thick, callused, scarred hands, the dirt ingrained in their cuts and creases under the short, curved, broken nails.

"And this is Oscar Glaimer, you've seen his shoemaking shop—the one next to the bank—"

"Oh, yes," said Lucas. "Oh, yes! Nice little shop."

"Yes . . . Well, now . . . What can we do for you?"

"I got—" The man squirmed.

"Got a pain? Got a pain somewhere?"

"I got a pain in my ass," the man said humbly.

"That so! Well, now! Well let's have a look at it. How long have you had it," and they were on the way to the examining room, "bleed much?"

And when the man was upended, kneeling, his face resting on the table,

"Feel that prostate," Dr. Runkleman said interestedly, he looked significantly at Lucas, he withdrew his finger, Lucas donned a glove.

As his middle finger probed upward Lucas was aware that something was badly wrong, it was as if his finger had thrust into a cavern, there was slack, relaxation, the walls did not clasp closely as in a normal rectum. There was mass. There was almost certainly cancer here.

He withdrew his finger and their eyes met above the kneeling man.

"You've got some bad piles there, did you know that?" Dr. Runkleman asked mildly.

"Got something wrong." The man's voice was muffled.

"Yes—" Dr. Runkleman began assembling the long tube of the proctoscope—"well, let's just have a little look, let's see . . ."

Then they were back in the office. The seated man looked at them, Oscar Glaimer who had run the shoe-repair shop in Greenville for twenty-two years. And he was a stranger, now. There was a secret that was no longer a secret, a thing between the dead and the living, a barrier, a reclassification.

"You've got a trouble there," Dr. Runkleman said, and he spoke to Glaimer through a presence between them, "I've got some bad news for you."

The man looked from Dr. Runkleman to Lucas, then back to Dr. Runkleman.

"Oscar," said Dr. Runkleman, "I'm sorry to tell you this, but I'm afraid you've got cancer."

"Cancer!" And now the man had the secret, and now they were not three men discussing illness but two, two against one, two telling, one hearing, now the barrier was complete.

"You sure?" Now he struggled, now he tried to come toward them, back to the world of the living.

"I'm going to fix you up at the County," Dr. Runkleman said. "No use your wasting a lot of money." He wrote in his book.

"Got to operate?" The man licked his lips. He was adjusting himself to the feel of his bell, listening to the bell tinkle, feeling the bell around his neck, the belled man, the dying-living, a few moments before a man, now a man with cancer.

"Yes," said Dr. Runkleman. "Yes, it's your only chance, Oscar. I think it's gone pretty far."

"What do you think?"

"I don't know. I honestly don't know. The biopsy'll tell us. But there isn't much doubt. We'll have to go in and see."

"Am I going to die?" There were three choices in the question, am I going to die, am I going to live, am I going to live and be man-cancer, tubed and cut and rotting and wary.

"Wouldn't do any harm to get your affairs in order. Like the rest of us. Yes. I'd do that, Oscar. I've got you down—I've got you down for the middle of next week."

"Well . . ." The man rose. He twisted his hat gently. "Well. I guess that's that . . ." He waited hopefully.

"I'll tell you something, Oscar. I'm not going to get your hopes up. But you can't tell. Not till you see. I've seen some pretty bad ones get well. . . . Now, you just take these—for pain . . . I'll have Miss Snow tell you what to bring to the County . . ."

The door closed behind him.

"They wait and they wait!" Dr. Runkleman cried indignantly. "What does he expect me to do about it?"

Lucas shook his head. His mind pictured again what the proctoscope had revealed.

"You going to operate?"

"We'll see!" Dr. Runkleman said shortly. "Come to me at the last minute! This isn't the first he's felt something wrong! What do they expect *me* to do?"

Lucas peered up, startled. Dr. Runkleman's face was red with anger, resentment. Lucas looked quickly away.

The door opened.

. . . forty-two, thin, her face wrinkled with suffering, her eyes dull, her thin hair hanging lankly and lifeless.

"Got to do something," she said. "I'm goin' out of my mind. Got to do somethin', Doc."

"Don't feel any better, eh?"

"Worse. Jist—jist—worse . . ."

Her fingers twitched nervously. One eye had developed a heavy tic. Dr. Runkleman sifted the papers of her case record. He studied them silently.

"Figure it's my lungs? I get to gasping, sometimes, I don't know whether it's my last breath—then my gut hurts, I keep throwin' up, nothin' sets, nothin'! Seems like all day I'm afire, my nerves janglin', an' the pain in my bowels, my joints is afire—"

"Your lungs came out all right," Dr. Runkleman laid down an X-ray.

"Nothin' wrong?" the woman was incredulous. "Worked all my life, worked myself to the bone, worked night and day, never sick a minute—"

"We've checked everything," Dr. Runkleman nodded. "Now here's what I think. Shall I tell you what I think? I'll tell you. I think your nerves are gone. I think you're a nervous wreck."

"You mean all these pains I got—you trying to tell me ain't nothin' but nerves? You tryin' to tell me that?"

"I'll tell you this. I'd rather have a broken leg. Because in two months I'd mend."

The woman looked at the prescription distrustfully. She stood a moment, digesting this slowly, telling her body what she had heard, hearking inwardly for an answer.

The door closed behind her.

The door opened.

"Ain't gonna be deformed, is he?" the woman asked anxiously.

"It's almost impossible to set this break without deformity. The amazing thing is that he'll have so little," Lucas said.

"I did want him to play the violin. We just bought him a violin."

She stared at the boy malevolently.

"Come on, you!" She pushed him out.

The aged Chinese had an ulcer covering his right ankle. The bones could be seen clearly. There was little suppuration. His young son and daughter removed the bandages, the gauze packs which covered it. They looked quietly at Dr. Runkleman. The father beamed jovially.

"I'm afraid this is going to hurt again, Sing," Dr. Runkleman said in a low voice. The old man nodded agreeably.

With a scissors Dr. Runkleman debrided the dead tissue, snipped the edges raw, with forceps he picked at the crater, plucking up chunks of dead and living flesh until reluctantly the gaping tissues bled. The Chinese, his head bent forward, watched intently.

"Hurts, doesn't it!" Dr. Runkleman jerked his head commiserating. Lucas' lips drew back over his set teeth.

"Oh, yes! Yes!" The old man grinned, nodded in quick agreement.

And then it was finished, the ankle wrapped again, the son and daughter had lifted their father and held him, his arms about their shoulders, his good foot on the floor, they thanked Dr. Runkleman gratefully, they were gone. Next time they would cut deeper. Next year there would be no foot, no ankle. Sing would smile.

The young high-school girl and her mother entered smiling and Dr. Runkleman rose to meet them.

"Worked, did it?" He beamed.

"Worked fine!" said the mother. "Look at her!"

The girl tilted her chin, offering her face. Dr. Runkleman peered at the face closely.

"You should have seen her a month ago!" the mother cried to Lucas.

"Glasses all right?" Dr. Runkleman asked.

"Fine!" said the girl. "Just fine, Doctor!"

The door closed behind them.

"Well," said Dr. Runkleman happily. "There's one! There's one for the book!"

"What was it?"

"Well, sir, that girl, her whole face was just covered with little abscesses, yes sir, abscesses and acne and pimples and I don't know what all. She was a mess. I tried everything. Her stomach was always upset and nothing worked, I even sent her to a skin man. No good. Finally—what do you think I did?"

"Hormones?"

"I sent her to get her eyes checked! She needed glasses. That's what! Whatever it was set up a whole train of phenomena. Put on a pair of glasses. There went the stomach trouble! There went the skin trouble! My goodness! Look at the time!"

"Thinning out, now," said Miss Snow. "Starting to dwindle down."

Two haemorrhoids. A gashed knee. A black vomit. An appendix. A measles. An X-ray. Four hearts. Lucas plodded on.

The door—

"Are you the doctor?"

"That's right. Have you got any pains?"

"I went to Dr. Binyon, Dr. Binyon put me on a soft diet."

"I see. And when do your pains come?"

"Sometimes I get running at the bowels."

"Suppose you tell us all about it. First about the pains. Do you have pains?"

"I get specks floating before my eyes. Then my skin breaks out in little brown spots. Sometimes little blisters between my fingers—"

"Do you have a pain now?"

"My tongue gets coated. My ankles swell."

She looked at him anxiously.

The door closed behind her.

The door opened.

A fat, blond sixteen-year-old boy came in hesitantly, behind him waddled his mother, pink-cheeked, obese, her eyes hard and wary.

"Show the doctor!"

"Aw, mom—!"

"Drop your pants. Hurry up! This is costing money!"

The boy's trousers came down reluctantly. Dr. Runkleman walked to him. As he crossed the room Lucas could see the sac in which the boy's testicles hung swollen grotesquely. Dr. Runkleman put a finger tip in the boy's inguinal ring.

"Cough, please. Cough for me, son . . ."

Dr. Runkleman withdrew his finger and stood aside for Lucas. As Lucas put out his hand, the woman laid a fat hand on his forearm, turning to Dr. Runkleman.

"Does he have to do it, too?"

"Why, yes. I'd like him to."

"Same price?"

"That's right!"

"All right. I just didn't want any double examination charges. I don't mind him learning, only not at my expense."

Dr. Runkleman ignored her. He looked at Lucas, waiting, his lips tightened. Lucas withdrew his finger and nodded.

"Give you much trouble?" Lucas asked sympathetically.

"Some," the boy admitted. He looked guiltily at his mother.

"Some!" she echoed contemptuously. "If you didn't try to run around like a wild man with the rest of those wild kids you'd be perfectly comfortable! Some! You go on out, go on, now! Go on outside and wait for me!"

And when the boy had gone silently out of the room:

"What's he got?"

"Hernia and hydrocele."

"What's that?"

"Rupture. His gut's ruptured and his testicles—you saw his testicles."

"What do you have to do?"

"You have to operate, madam. That's what you have to do. You have to operate."

"How much?"

"Depends on what we find. Somewheres around seventy-five dollars."

"I never heard of such a thing! Forty, now—forty's my best price. That's all!"

Dr. Runkleman rose and walked to the door.

"What harm will it do? What's the danger in it? He's walking around healthy as the next—eats enough, God knows!"

"A rupture may gangrene. People die of gangrene. The hydrocele may permanently injure him sexually."

She thought a moment.

"I guess he's all right," she decided. "We'll let it go awhile. Maybe he can earn some to pay it off."

The door closed behind her.

"Is she poor? Does it mean that much to her?"

"Her? Poor? They've got a farm—why that farm of theirs is one of the best in the whole county! And the father's worse than she is! You ought to see the daughter! Kid goes to school in rags! Ashamed to lift her head."

The door opened. Miss Snow pursed her lips.

A woman in her forties, gay, nervous, her hair a little disordered, a tiny tear in her dress, her skin the velvety skin of an alcoholic.

"I've got no patience with them," said Dr. Runkleman. "None whatsoever. Her father went the same way."

"Who have you got no patience with, Dave?"

They looked up, startled. Dr. Runkleman jumped up, he walked to the tall, burly man behind whom Miss Snow stood beaming in the open doorway.

"Henry!" he cried, and began to pump the big man's hand vigorously. "What are you doing here? Henry, I want you to meet my new assistant, Dr. Marsh, just came here!"

Lucas, who had risen with Dr. Runkleman, now came tiredly forward. The man held his hand in a firm grip, looked at him keenly.

"Well, well!" He smiled cordially.

"Yep! Got myself an assistant!"

"Business gets any better we'll have to raise your taxes!"

"Henry's the mayor!" Dr. Runkleman explained. "A vote for Henry

Granite is a vote for Henry Granite! Watch out for him, Dr. Marsh. What brings you here, Henry? What's on your mind?"

"Oh, I just thought I'd come in for a little check-over—if you've got the time . . ."

"Time! We've got nothing but time!" Dr. Runkleman winked broadly at Lucas.

"I should have made an appointment—I told Miss Snow no need to shove me in ahead of all those good folks out there waiting—"

"Oh, we've always got time for the mayor, I guess," said Dr. Runkleman. "That right, Dr. Marsh?"

"Absolutely!" Lucas exclaimed dutifully.

"Well, I don't like to ask for any special privileges—"

"Come on in here! Let's have a look at you!"

In the examination room Henry Granite hung up his expensive suit carelessly, draped his handmade shirt over a treatment table.

"Don't bother to take your shoes and socks off," said Dr. Runkleman. "Where do you get such clothes, Henry?"

"I've been trying to wean him away from the mail-order catalogue for ten years," the mayor said to Lucas. "He just doesn't seem to understand that a tailor-made suit lasts longer, takes more abuse—to say nothing of the looks of it."

He took off his underwear and stood before them naked.

"Haven't got the time. My Lord, in the time it takes a tailor to measure me and fit me I could make six calls and a breech delivery—let's see you, Henry. Let's take a look at you . . ."

The body before them, now that the clothes had been removed, was anonymous, it revealed nothing of its wearer, it might have been worn by a logger, a miner, or an athlete. It was a well-muscled body, carried erect, and now that the clothes had been removed it was not so impressive and it stooped a little.

"Hold still, Henry," said Dr. Runkleman.

"You know I often wonder what goes through you fellows' minds when you look at a person—I mean beyond the cardinal signs you study—"

"I've tried over and over and I never can tell," Lucas said. "In the hospital, in the clinics, coming into a room full of stripped humans I've looked at them, I've singled them out, I've tried to guess—this one's rich, this one's poor, this one's mean, this one's proud, this one's skilled, this one's smart—you just can't tell. When they're naked they're just the living. The survivors. It'll fool you, every time."

" 'When Adam delved and Eve span, who was then the gentleman?' . . ."

"That's right. But it's more than just social status—"

"So that the true and false reside not in things but in the intellect—and we mustn't judge a thing by what is in it accidentally but by what is in it essentially—and a man is false not because he knows false opinions but because he loves them—"

Lucas stared at the naked man, startled.

"Say 'ninety-nine,' Henry," said Dr. Runkleman. . . . "Again . . . again . . . breathe through your mouth . . ."

The examination ended.

"I guess you'll do. You ought to be good for another fifty years. You've got a good body, there, Henry. You take care of it."

"It's the best I've got. I guess I have been given a little more than most. I like to take care of it. I guess you know why I came . . ."

"Kicking up again?"

"Just a little . . ."

"Sure! I figured it was about time for another little finger wave—"

He donned a rubber glove, anointed the index finger with lubricant.

The mayor grimaced. Lucas looked sympathetically aside.

"What do you think of our village? What you've seen?"

"Over here, Henry . . ."

"It's a wonderful little place, it seems to be run so well, so orderly—"

"Just bend over the table . . . That's right . . . Bend way over . . ."

"It's coming along. It's come a long way—"

"We've got about as solid a town as you'll find in the state," said Dr. Runkleman. "You're doing a fine job, Henry. Really fine." He inserted his finger in the mayor's rectum. He began to massage the mayor's prostate with his finger tip.

The mayor grunted, twitched.

"I'm doing my best," he said, his voice muffled. "I don't always know what 'best' is. Sometimes I have to remember that every man pursues good without knowing the nature of it—I try to be— *Oh!*" he cried, wincing.

"Sorry, Henry—it won't be much longer—you'll feel a lot better . . ."

He withdrew his finger. He peeled off the rubber glove. The mayor straightened. He grinned at Lucas.

"Isn't that typical? Plato coming out of one end and a doctor's finger coming out of the other!"

"There's going to be more than a doctor's finger coming out of a lot of people again this year," Dr. Runkleman said meaningly.

"It'll come, Dave," the mayor smiled indulgently, "it'll come—in time. Just be patient—"

"I'm really serious, Henry."

"I know you are, Dave." The mayor dressed leisurely. "But you know how much money it'll take, too. Overhauling the whole water system—" He shook his head.

"Typhoid?" Lucas asked, incredulous.

Dr. Runkleman looked steadily at the mayor.

"Oh, we get a little of it," the mayor shrugged. "Most of the town's wells are shallow, I guess they could have been better placed, and those open ditches leading in—"

"It's going to be worse this year, Henry. We've got money enough to build a new fair grounds—"

"I know, I know. But look at it my way. I'm a doctor too. I treat the body politic. And like you, I wait in my office, when I'm being mayor and not running my lumber yard, for people to come to me and tell me their troubles and when they present their ills I make sure the ill isn't imaginary. And then I try to cure it. But like you—I've got to wait until they come to me . . ."

"It's a shame, Henry. It's really a disgrace!"

"I've pointed it out, Dave. You know that. Once a year, regular as clockwork—I can't change people and the way they think, I can't make them prefer clean water to a fair grounds—it's the way people are, bread and the circus—"

"I thought typhoid was just about nonexistent," Lucas interrupted. "The only case I've ever seen was in a textbook!"

"Seventy died of it last year," Dr. Runkleman said without inflection. "Right here in Greenville. I'm just waiting for that school well, Henry. I'm just waiting for it to explode."

"Dave, you know these people as well as I do. It just isn't possible to sell them on a new water system when it would mean going without a fair grounds—"

"They'll think of it when their kids get hit! When that school well starts—"

"I'll probably try again, Dave. You're going to make me a mighty unpopular man. . . . I'm glad to have met you, Dr. Marsh. Glad to welcome you to Greenville. Drop by some night, when you find time . . ."

"I will," said Lucas gratefully, "and perhaps when you tell them about the children—"

The mayor paused. He thought a moment and smiled sadly. He looked up at them.

"It isn't children that reaches them, you know . . . not children . . . It's dead children . . ."

The door closed behind him.

"Well . . ." Dr. Runkleman shrugged. He picked up the rubber glove, its finger still glistening with lubricant, and dropped it in the sink.

"How long?" Lucas demanded.

"Ten years, now. I've been telling them ten years." He looked at his watch. "My goodness!" he said, startled. "Miss Snow will have a fit!"

They walked quickly out. The four rooms swallowed them, the procession began again.

a gray-haired man, expressionless, slow speech, tardy moves, lethargic,

and Lucas' mind, peering through the grime of fatigue, considering, remembering, demanding, and then sight, clear and positive, item, item, and answer: the lethargy of the postencephalitic,

two feeding schedules, two teethings, and he plodded conscientiously, trying to neglect nothing, trying to be fast and to be perfect, seeing in the nick of time the unbalanced facial movements, the signs of a recent stroke,

then an eye, an itch, a burn, a cut, a burn, a dropsy, a menopause, a cold, a cold but,

and his intelligence rang a warning, his senses extended, the hand was hot, the eyes frightened, he saw the sweat stains at the armpits, through his fatigue he tensed a little with excitement, he might have missed this, he must be careful, he peered closer at her neck, there it was, small, unmistakable, beginning exophthalmic goiter,

The doors opened.

The doors closed.

He rubbed the back of his neck covertly, wearily. A doubt furrowed his brows. He considered worriedly. He tried to think. Had he missed anything? Had one gotten away from him? He tried irritably to think. He could not think. He looked at the man warily. His clothes hung loosely. Therefore he had lost weight. The two top buttons of his trousers were unbuttoned.

Think, now.

Think . . .

Remember . . .

Gallstones?

Cirrhosis of the liver?

Cancer of the peritoneum?

Talk to him . . . Listen carefully . . . Feel . . . Prod . . . Speak to me, disease, speak to me, feel, fingers, look, eyes, listen, ears,

one of you knows,

one of you speaks its language,

Be ready, mind. Be ready!

The door opened.

The door closed.

The silent, voluble, noisy, frightened, greedy, guilty, venal, wary, cunning, wily, stupid, apathetic, uncaring, insane, trembling in agony, going deaf, going blind, just born and doomed, screaming for no pain, wincing, cowardly, stoic, shabby, shameless, overpowered with modesty, hating, tangled, hysterical, smiling, dishonest, thieving, lying, helpless, filthy, shambling, racing, young, old, middle-aged, always the eyes, the eyes frightened and waiting, dissimulating, begging, secret and naked, the stream, the shuffling stream passed into the office, showed their tissues, exhibited their sores, voice after voice, face after face, body after body, cavity and cavity, lump and hollow, body and soul,

And then the day ended.

It was dark.

The first day was over.

The door shut upon this day for the last time.

"Go home, Miss Snow."

"Some day, eh Doctor?"

"That's right. What have we got tomorrow?"

"County called. Gall bladder and appendix. Eight and nine. You've got an inquest at 1:30. Two new OB cases. Miss Doherty ought to deliver tonight—and Mrs. Swanson."

"Well," he turned to Lucas, "how do you feel? How did you like it?"

The day was ended. Dr. Runkleman did not appear particularly tired.

"Fine! Just fine, sir!" Lucas said carefully.

His weary mind considered uneasily. He's not tired. They had passed over Dr. Runkleman like water.

R-r-rip! And a prescription.

"What's your complaint?"

The flash of an instrument.

A quick look.

R-r-rip! And a prescription.

He tried to emphasize. He tried to see what Dr. Runkleman saw, to feel for his attitude, for what he had learned, for his truth.

The human sea rose before him.

He caught his breath. His eyes darkened. He felt very old. He had sensed a thing. He sensed the vague, black edges of it, of a cave, of a darkness, of the cave's end. He shivered. His mind fled from it in panic.

"Somebody walk over your grave?" Dr. Runkleman smiled.

"Sixty-two cases!" Lucas said rapidly, flustered. "I was just thinking of what we did today. I can see where I can take a lot of it off your shoulders—"

"That's right. Believe me, I'm glad to have you. This will work out just fine. Yes, sir! Just fine! Say! I wonder what that wife of yours is doing?"

"Kris!"

They laughed.

"I'd forgotten her!"

They walked quickly to the door separating his wing from the offices.

Kristina, on her hands and knees on the floor, looked up tiredly, pushed hair back from her forehead, tried to scramble to her feet.

"Here, here!" Dr. Runkleman seized her elbow, helped her.

"Oh, that's all right, Doctor!"

"What you been doing, Kris?" Lucas smiled through his frown, looked about the rooms curiously. "What did you do? Don't tell me you scrubbed them all over again!"

"She likes things clean! You can see that!"

"How did it go, Luke? Was he all right, Doctor?"

"I never saw so many patients in my life—"

"We hit him pretty hard, today. It was just one of those days. I don't like to handle more than sixty patients—"

"You must be dead!" She looked at Lucas, pitying.

"Me! How about Dr. Runkleman!"

"Don't worry about me! Say! I think we ought to celebrate! What do you say—how about a real Chinese dinner?"

He frowned, seeing something in a corner.

"What's this? Have you bought something already?"

"I got a refrigerator!" Kristina beamed.

"I see. Well, well! Now, that's a beauty, isn't it! Where did you get it?"

"A little store—Claring's, up by the post office, you know where you turn right to go to—"

"I know Claring. Sure. Let me see, now. How much did you say you paid for it?"

"Thirty dollars!" Kristina cried proudly.

"That seems cheap enough," Lucas said sagely.

"That's right. That's right. It's a good piece. Well, now. I'll tell you. Suppose I just give him a ring—"

They followed him, wondering.

"Hello, Claring? Hello. This is Dr. Runkleman. How are you? That's fine. Say, now, I've got Mrs. Marsh here with me, you know Mrs. Marsh, the wife of my new assistant . . . Yes . . . About that refrigerator she bought . . . Yes, it's a dandy . . . I wonder if you could come by and pick it up tomorrow? . . . Oh, no! It's fine. I just think she can maybe do a little better . . . No, Claring, I think you'd better pick it up. . . . I see. Well, I'll tell her and see what she says. . . ." He covered the mouthpiece. "He says twenty dollars. I think that's all right. I think you better get it, as long as he says that— Hello, Claring? Mrs. Marsh says it's all right, then. . . . Sure. . . . sure, I'll tell her. . . . Well, if you don't take it, you know, it won't do you any good. . . . That's right. . . . You take it and let me know when the bottle's gone. . . ."

He hung up.

"There, now! Now let's go and eat!"

"How did you do it?"

"What did he say?"

"Oh, Claring's all right. He just didn't know you. He thought you were new. He's a patient of mine. Luetic."

They ate in the small Chinese restaurant next to the pool hall. And neither Lucas nor Kristina had ever eaten Chinese food before, even pseudo-Chinese food, and Dr. Runkleman beamed happily at their surprise and pleasure.

They had almost finished when the call came.

"It's for you, Doc," said the counterman. "Somebody from the County they brought to your office."

They entered the darkened office, a nurse from the County was there, on a bench in the reception room lolled a big man, breathing whiskey, his torn clothes soiled, one foot on a stool.

"Broken leg, I think, Doctor," said the nurse. "I'd like to stay. I have to get back. They just brought him in. Dumped him here and called the County."

"What happened," Dr. Runkleman chewed the last morsels of his unfinished meal, bent, took one of the man's arms, put it about his shoulder. He straightened. The man came up effortlessly.

"Driving," the nurse said. "Somewhere on the Wood Hill Road. Went over the edge. Clear down to the bottom."

"Anybody else?"

"No. He was all alone."

"What are you doing?" the big man said thickly.

"You go ahead," Kristina said to the nurse. "I'll help."

"You run along," said Dr. Runkleman.

Lucas took the man's other arm around his shoulder. They moved him into the examining room.

The bright lights flicked on. The glare hurt.

"Well, now, let's see. What happened to *you*?"

"Come on, come on!" said the man.

"Had a little to drink, didn't you?"

"Fix my leg!"

"Well, let's see now." Dr. Runkleman kneeled. Lucas gently peeled the torn, wet shirt from the man's torso. The heavy muscles leaped out, moist with sweat. The huge chest panted. Dr. Runkleman turned the foot slightly.

"Hey!" the man shouted. "Hey! Goddamn you!"

"Yes," said Dr. Runkleman. "I think it's broken. We'll have an X-ray."

"You do that again, Goddamn you—!"

Dr. Runkleman pressed the man's knee.

"Does it hurt here?"

The man's face contorted in pain.

"You son-of-a-bitch—" He drew back a heavy forearm—"you do that again, you bastard, I'll smash your face in."

Lucas tensed, ready to lock his arms around him.

Dr. Runkleman looked up coldly.

"You just try it!" he said. His eyes warmed to anger. "You just go ahead and try it!"

The room was silent.

"You just raise your hand!" Dr. Runkleman said. The room was vibrant with inarticulate menace. "Just try it!"

"That hurt," the man said sullenly.

"Anytime you feel like trying something you just try it!" The heavy hand, the powerful chunky arm that had hauled the man so easily to his feet lifted Dr. Runkleman erect.

"Goddamn leg's broken!" the man said heavily.

"Take him into the X-ray room!— You just keep a civil tongue in your head! When you feel like trying something you just let me know! I've had about enough out of you!"

In the X-ray room, moving him on the table, the man bellowed again, he drew his arm back. Dr. Runkleman leaned over him quickly, his ponderous fist ready.

"Hurts," the man subsided.

They worked on him silently.

When the films were developed there were two easily seen fractures.

"Want me to give him a shot?" Lucas murmured.

"Him? No, not him! Big fellow like that doesn't need a shot! Little pain won't hurt him. We'll get him out of here. Get him over to the County. I'll take care of him tomorrow."

The man eased himself to a sitting position, waiting for the ambulance.

"How much I owe you, Doc?"

Dr. Runkleman ignored him.

He fumbled in his pockets and after a time drew out a crumpled bill. He tendered it.

"Here."

"You'll need that for whiskey. You'll need more than money before you're through with this."

"I didn't mean to—I was just talkin' rough. Goddamn that hurt me. How'd you like to have a car fall on toppa you down fifty feet!"

There was no answer. After a time he put the bill sullenly in his pocket. The ambulance lights flicked outside. An attendant came in. The man got gingerly off the table. The attendant moved quickly toward him.

"No, no!" said Dr. Runkleman. "He's a big, strong man. He's very strong, this fellow. Let him help himself."

The attendant swept their faces inquiringly.

"All right," he nodded at the man, "let's go. Let's get moving."

The man took a step, started to pitch forward. Lucas moved involuntarily, reached him in time, helped him into the corridor. He was surprised to see Kristina beside him. He looked apologetically at Dr. Runkleman.

"If I hear one word of you causing any disturbance," Dr. Runkleman said coldly, "one word, mind—!" He turned to the attendant. "Just call the police. Understand? Tell them Dr. Runkleman said to call them!"

"I'm sorry, Doc," the man mumbled. "I apologize."

Dr. Runkleman walked out of the room. Lucas and Kristina followed. "Can't say no more'n that, can I?" the man demanded.

"C'mon!" said the attendant. "Get movin'—"

"Look, Jack! I got a broken leg—!"

"My heart bleeds, Mac! My heart just bleeds . . ."

The man shambled after him, groping down the dark corridor, limping heavily, helping himself by leaning a heavy hand caressingly along the wall.

"I said I was sorry, didn't I? I said . . ." His voice trailed back, then the door closed, the ambulance doors slammed, he was gone.

In their bedroom they whispered a long time.

"That feller ought to be ashamed of himself," Kristina said indignantly, loyally. "Coming to a doctor for help and then—"

"I'd just as soon not have seen it," said Lucas finally. And then, "What a day! Oh, Kris, Kris! What a day!"

And he told her of the day.

And she told him of the town, of the people in it, of the furniture she had seen, of how Dr. Runkleman was liked, of what they said about Dr. Castle, of Dr. Binyon, of Dr. Kauffman, of how expensive sheets were, of the home they were going to have, and he listened drowsily, thinking, half hearing.

"You know who had the place before we did? It was a dentist. He used to drink all the time. He killed himself. Right in that room where the pipes are. They came in and found him one day. Shot himself during the night."

"Who? In our place? Where we're going to live?"

"That's right. He was always drinking, it was vacant six, seven months, Dr. Runkleman wouldn't rent it, maybe he couldn't—"

"He didn't tell us. I wonder why? I wonder why he didn't tell us?"

"Oh, he will, Luke. He'll get around to it. Maybe he thought—well, maybe he wanted us to have it and maybe he was afraid if we knew we wouldn't—"

"Probably . . . I don't care . . ."

"I don't care, either. . . . You happy, Luke?"

"Happy!"

"I'm so happy . . . It's hard to imagine—a home of our own . . ."

"Not our own. Not yet. We've got the use of it. And no tools of my own. I'm using somebody else's home—and somebody else's tools. . . .

My God! So many cases . . . so many . . . how he does it . . . I hope I didn't miss anything, that's all. I just hope I didn't miss anything . . ."

"How were the girls? What kind of help you got? You got a good OR?"

"Someone temporary. She can't always come. Used to work at a big hospital, somewhere. Got a crippled husband. She's quite good. But the rest of them! Most of them aren't even RN's!"

"I'd like to see . . . Get me in sometime, Luke . . . When I get finished with the house . . ."

"Operating—I don't know what I expected . . . I guess just to look at him you wouldn't think . . . you'd have to see it, Kris . . . You'd just have to see it . . . Kris?"

"Uhhh? . . . I'm awake. I'm awake . . ." Drowsily she moved her hand, resting it on his bare thigh. For a moment her warmth enticed him from the edge of blurring consciousness. He half opened his eyes.

"You want to, Kris?" he whispered thickly. And then, mustering the effort, "Kris?"

Her deep, even breathing answered him, was the only sound in the dark room. He closed his eyes. Almost instantly the sweet drug of sleep numbed him, ended his thoughts, surrendered his being, he was unconscious. The grateful darkness was complete. The house slept.

An hour passed.

The phone rang.

Jangling and startled, up from the depths, half upright, groggy, listening, half hearing.

Miss Doherty was having pains. They were now coming at nine-minute intervals.

And Dr. Runkleman's voice, far away, the sound of the receiver put back.

"I'll go, Doctor!" Lucas called out.

"Luke? Wah—what is it?" Kristina summoned by his shout, groping bewildered.

"No, no! You go back to sleep!"

"No, Doctor! Please! Wait! I'm coming!"

Lucas struggled heavily into his clothes.

"Go back to sleep, Kris,"

He grabbed his bag on a stumbling run, the stairs clumped beneath him, the front door opened, slammed shut, they were gone.

⋆ CHAPTER 26

A week passed. The days repeated themselves. The people he had seen on the first day by now had passed through the offices again. Throughout these long days he was seldom aware of Greenville, that it was a strange place, that it had trees, forests, streams, a variety of roads, of farmlands, that the days were pleasant or unpleasant, all this rushed by him without perspective, in fragments, and so rapidly that he contacted of this place and its mechanisms, its living pace, its savor, its reactions, only what was put before him by patients.

The long days, the broken nights, equipped him with the fierce and masochistic satisfaction with which a professional soldier gloats over a difficult campaign. In his student days there had always been some time off. Here in the arena of reality there was simply no choice. He was on duty twenty-four hours of every day. There were in each day fourteen hundred and forty minutes. Each minute he was sleeping he might be called, and every minute he was awake he was practicing Medicine.

The demands of the day were inflexible, exterior, and this situation freed him from any nudge of guilt for doing what he most desired to the exclusion of every other human activity and the expense of any other human who might be emotionally involved in his life actions.

He absorbed a little more about Miss Snow. She lived by herself in a staid, small home on the outskirts of town and apparently had no social life and she awaited the congregation of the town's sick each day with anticipation and satisfaction, and quickly accepted Lucas as a deaconess might welcome into the executive hierarchic structure a new junior pastor.

He still had difficulty remembering the name of the woman who kept Dr. Runkleman's books, but he now knew vaguely that she was paying for professional services to herself and her nebulous family.

He was uneasy about the head nurse at the County. He wondered about her honesty, her connection with Dr. Snider; from hints and wordy glances he had intercepted he was positive that she was a tyrant to the small staff, she was an old registered nurse, he had never seen her in action but he knew that she was limited, professionally, and he felt that her fabric was shabby and cruel and glumly evil.

Dr. Snider simply made him wince. He saw little of him after that first day, for Dr. Runkleman would not use him in the operating room except to give ether. Usually Dr. Runkleman gave spinal anesthesia, which eliminated Dr. Snider from the operating room almost entirely. He was nominal head of the hospital, but Dr. Runkleman was chief surgeon there, the only other doctor at the County, except Lucas. Dr. Snider ran the hospital thriftily, always mindful of the budget, he worked on a small salary, he had a vague and very small outside practice, there was no real reason for the board to replace him. And Dr. Runkleman was always there to protect him. Dr. Runkleman was the County's real head.

Kristina had not planned a day of her own for many years and when she had done rearranging furniture and walking uncertainly from room to room, knowing no one in the town but the two nurses in the forbidden territory beyond the door which connected their home to the office, she finished her survey by recleaning one of the already spotless rooms. She did not feel it was respectable for a woman to be abroad in the town before noon unless she was on a specific and obvious errand. A woman in the streets was not taking care of her house. Shopping released her once a day. There was just so much market dallying she could dare and still not be suspected of dallying, after which she had to come home. If she shopped in the morning the whole afternoon and the rest of the morning gaped empty and lonely before her. She therefore made work for herself in the mornings, restraining herself sternly until noon when she would know Lucas' pleasure, whether this day permitted him to gulp what she set before him or whether, more likely, he would be eating at one of the hospitals or somewhere in the town with Dr. Runkleman.

But so soon as the hour of lunch ended, Kristina flung open the door and after a hasty, careful glance at buttons and hair sallied out into the town, past house after house, until, after three blocks, she was in the town, the market place, the rows of shops, stores, garages, pool halls, groceries, which were the exterior life of Greenville.

Obedient to her image of a woman who had the best professional interests of her husband at heart and who wished to be beyond the reproach of her fellow women, Kristina each day bought her groceries at a different store. She was carefully polite so that the town, through the grocer, might obtain the best cultural impression of her husband, and she was virtuously on her guard to fend and parry the veiled probings, the greedy curiosity of all in the town with whom she came in contact.

As she walked to each new store she looked sidelong to see what lay beyond. When she had finished her shopping she stood a moment, affecting concentration. Then, with a start, as if remembering, she walked in the direction down which her glance had speculated. After a long look at each store window, she would reach the end of the block, explore the next reach, turn again, and thus return to the direction from which she had started.

She was entitled to walk home leisurely and she walked home leisurely, gazing about her at the small homes and their straggling lawns as much as she liked, as she had a right to do. Occasionally she passed a fellow woman who fell silent at the sight of her and who examined her from head to foot in silence, studying every smallest detail of her dress and her person, unsmiling, as she herself, at such encounters, studied them. It was the same in the stores, or on the main streets, it had always been the same, here and elsewhere.

"You eye each other like strange dogs. You look as if you hate each other. As if you were walking along warm and friendly and all of a sudden ran unexpectedly into an enemy," Lucas had grinned contemptuously, one day as they walked together during his internship.

Kristina was surprised.

"Hate each other? I don't feel anything."

"Well, you look as if you hate each other. Your faces get all cold and looking for dirt or concealed weapons or—"

"A woman has to know all she can about another woman," Kristina had explained simply. "Quick. She has to know it quick."

"What for?" Lucas had cried, amazed.

And she had just looked at him. She tried to think of what to tell him, that the bitterest enemy of one's own kind was one's own kind and that all women went about in armed truce watchful for transgression of the rules, of the thousand, of the myriad, rules, of appearance, of conduct, of posture, of look, of grooming, cleanliness, fashion, attitude, bearing, tone, moral index, quality, rigid pattern of action, movement, byplay, which composed the great rule, the rule of being a woman. A woman among other women.

She shrugged, she sighed helplessly.

Now on her trips, the novelty becoming threadbare, as she neared home, no longer noticing houses or people, she speculated whether Lucas would be home for dinner and whether he would like what she would prepare and whether he would notice it. She began to think of things to tell him, remembering carefully all she had seen of the town and its people, mentally listing these details, arranging and rearranging them in the order in which she would finally present them to him.

If he came home cross with weariness she planned what to say and how she would behave, moving slowly, speaking little, speaking quietly, gently, turning his irritation. If he came home grinning she planned how she would stretch that gift as far as possible, trying not to let him become too hilarious but making the mood stretch, watching every word, thinking before she spoke, alert for anything that might end the relaxed and happy mood. If he came home and behaved in a certain way, touching her unexpectedly, looking at her a certain way, talking to her a certain way, then she would know he wanted her, and she planned each detail of how he would take her easily and afterward how she would pet him, and stroke his head, and lie in the night, thinking long thoughts of nothing, feeling only great content and fulfillment and possession and home and need and rule.

This night Lucas called to her from the bathroom as she poured soup into the plates on the carefully set card table in the living room.

"What's this stuff?"

He had come home smiling. Kristina hurried to the bathroom.

He was holding a fancy shaving mug in the bottom of which was imbedded a cake of fragrant shaving soap.

"That? Oh, that's a little surprise. People ought to give each other surprises, it's nothing, I got it at one of the drugstores. Is it all right? Is anything wrong?"

"Pretty fancy. I don't need stuff like this, Kris. Thanks, though. There's just stuff I need more . . ."

"It didn't cost much! You'd be surprised—"

"I've seen them. I know how much they cost." He came out, sat down. "What you got tonight? Soup? That smells good, Kris!"

"No, really! He gave me thirty percent off!"

"You're kidding! Was it a sale or something?"

"I had to buy some toothpaste, and I just happened to see this and I asked offhand how much and he said, 'To you—' and then he said a third off. 'You're the new doctor's wife, aren't you?' he asked. And I said I was. And he said that's how it was, to tell you it would always be at least a third off, whatever he had. He said he was glad to have your business."

"What business?"

"The prescription business."

He looked at her steadily. She looked back anxiously. He reddened.

"You know what this means, don't you—"

"I didn't see any harm in it—he said all the other doctors—"

"It's just a kickback, that's all! It's just the kickback system! You know what fee splitting is? Well, this is fee splitting. Do you know any reason why he should give us something for nothing?"

"He said in return for your business—"

"I'm not in business. I'm practicing a profession."

"He said all the doctors—"

"I don't care what he said. He's lying."

"That's terrible. I'm awfully sorry, Luke. I won't let it happen again—"

"Don't even go in there any more!"

"I won't! The nerve of him!" Kristina said eagerly. "Your soup's getting all cold, Luke. I'll take it back first thing in the morning."

"Tell him what I said—"

"I will. Are you going to tell Dr. Runkleman?"

"I'll tell him tomorrow. He'll be glad to hear of it. What did you do today?"

"Oh, I went shopping—I cleaned house—"

"I know, I know! But what did you do? What else?"

"Why . . . nothing. Was there something you wanted me to do? Something you told me?"

"No, no! That's all right. I just thought—you're not bored, are you? You must miss your job—your life—"

"Oh, but I love this! I wouldn't trade for anything—"

"Oh, come on now—"

"Why, Luke, there isn't a girl living I'd trade with!"

"You mean to tell me you don't even miss doing what you spent years doing? What you spent all your life training for?"

"I wouldn't go back for anything! Sure, time hangs a little heavy sometimes. But I've got a home, I'm married, this is my home . . ."

"And you're content with that?"

He believed her but it was incredible all the same. He felt a pang of rebellion for her, thinking of the years, the career, the life flung aside and not missed, stepped over as one would step over a dropped garment, dressing.

And she looked at him troubled, trying to empathize— What is it you want, what do you want me to feel, what shall I say, don't you know about people, do you think everyone is like you, will I always disappoint you?

And Lucas, who had been about to begin a long, intimate monologue on his flight into practice, on his exultation to be practicing at last, on all his reactions to everything, which is to say what he had learned and what he was learning and his adjustment to the real, the actual, the living practice of Medicine, Lucas stopped with an effort, checked himself, knowing it was hopeless to discuss it with anyone who could turn life on and off like a spigot, he longed for Avery, he could not talk to her, she would never know what he was talking about.

"I wonder what old Avery's doing . . . I ought to drop him a line . . ."

So this was the way it was to be. This was being married. This was how it was, at last, now they were in their own home, now the years stretched ahead, this was how she was, this is how it would always be. He looked at her curiously. She was half smiling at him, a little anxiety in her eyes, he felt suddenly guilty, she was so anxious to please, she was what she was, this is what had happened to him, he must be tender with her and patient, try to meet her on her own terms, speak what she understood.

"Did you write your father yet?"

"No—no, not yet—"

"But you should. You sit right down and write him a letter, Kris. You've got to do that."

"He's a nice old man, really Luke, I think you'd like him . . ."

"Tell him when we're set up in a home of our own we'd like to have him come on."

"Luke!"

"What's the matter?"

She jumped up and kissed him, hugging his head hard.

"Well, you write him." He swelled with her gratitude. Unaccountably he wished the old man were coming tomorrow so that her joy would be double. "How are the people, Kris? Get to meet anybody?"

"The people—here? . . . Oh, yes! . . . Just stick in the mud, Luke! Just like in Minnesota. Little town—everybody the same. . . . You think it's a good town, Luke?"

"I think so . . ."

"This is where you want to practice? This is what you want?"

"It's going to be all right." And he was thinking ahead, thinking of the time when he would have an office of his own, that dim, that distant day.

"Pretty soon we'll get to know people. Then you won't be so lonely."

"I'm not lonely, Luke. I got you, I got my home, I'm not lonely at all."

She stacked the dishes rapidly, she moved quickly, happily anxious to be through, to begin writing her letter. He watched her, reading her easily, a man sitting in a chair watching a woman, he was lonely, the world swept away from him, he was in a void, watching, alone.

He picked up a medical journal, he began to read, in a moment he was farther alone than ever. He was himself, isolate, a human bound upon a single errand, moving among errandless humans. He sighed consent, one of a fraternity apart from the rest of man.

It was raining next morning as he drove to the County Hospital in the car Dr. Runkleman had lent him. He was abroad early and very happy, he walked impatiently from the doctors' parking space to the side door, eager to begin.

He walked into the men's ward, surprising the nurses, supping with pleasure the concern and respect with which they greeted him, the flurry he occasioned. He walked from bed to bed among the patients, smiling at them affectionately, old friends he and they, beings he had explored, whom he held in his protecting hands now. There was his friend Chapman, on whom he and Dr. Runkleman had worked for four full hours, using every trick of science they could remember or study to repair, to stitch, to mend, to patch an abdomen, a diaphragm, and a lung shattered by police bullets after he had held up and robbed a filling-station proprietor, and Chapman, whom they had pulled through somehow and who would recover, and stand trial and be executed for murder, smiled at him wanly in this hospital, this life serenely beyond life, immured from it, this world in which only life was important, and saving life, and all reality was only this.

Bed by bed he passed them by, his friends, his creatures, moving confidently, dispensing smiles, a pat from the master, a keen look at the charts, reassuring by feigned absorption, a prized murmur, an awkward joke prized as the highest wit, the doctor making his rounds.

Through the men's wards, through the old men's ward, the senilities—"Cunningham over there's been a bad boy again, Doctor. He stuffed another magazine down the toilet!"

"Now, now, Cunningham! I'm surprised! And I thought we were such good friends!"

And Cunningham gaping at him vacantly, a slow tear gathering in the corners of his wrinkled eyes, and on either side Jorgenson, vacantly tearing strips of paper, Pacello staring mindless at the ceiling, Jales and Rodriguez and Bannerman watching him intently.

And out of there, out of the thin smell of age, and incontinent urine and the indol and skatol of never entirely absent feces, into the women's ward to speak a long while to thin Miss Robinson who still couldn't resolve to allow them to remove her diseased kidney and who was sinking lower each day, Mrs. Chancellor peering around the huge abdominal mound of her dropsy, the old women impatient for his attention guarding their sole claims to humanity's attention, the wounds in flesh which would never heal. The girl he and Dr. Runkleman had operated on his first day, and who was now nearly ready to go home and subdued in the presence of her elders all around her. And Miss Wanders, silent and alone and withdrawn, near the terminal stage of tuberculosis, and in a room all by herself, near the delivery room, Mrs. Randolph, smug and vain in the knowledge of her rarity, her skin rubied with the jewels of her consequence, a rare case of erysipelas.

Was there a world outside this? They lived within these walls and it was all their world until the day of their reluctant exodus, that curious day of mixed eagerness and sadness. And ever after, from the outside they would look at the hospital walls with an exile's look of intimacy and affection and loneliness. But this was Lucas' world whether he was in it or out of it, all other living was interstitial, a suspended space, a marking time. They would leave. But this was his, forever.

The delivery room was empty. There were two expectant mothers in the maternity ward, a solitary infant in the nursery. He looked at the newly born tissue which would soon do all the things its kind could do, subject to the limitations of the cells rostral to its motor and premotor areas, which it had been born with and which had already decided the infant's potential, its cry was healthy, he looked at the chart to learn its sex, left the nursery and met Dr. Runkleman in the corridor outside.

"Made rounds already?" Dr. Runkleman was pleased.

"Just the men's and women's wards—"

"I don't know what I ever did without you!" Dr. Runkleman shook his head admiringly, grateful. "Looks like I might even have time on my hands today!"

There was only one case waiting in the operating room, a woman who had attempted an abortion on herself with a wire coat hanger.

"She didn't do that all by herself," Dr. Runkleman said darkly after the dilatation and curettage. "That cervix was already dilated. There's a chiropractor and his wife over in Lepton, we're going to catch them someday—that's what they do, they know just enough to dilate the canal and charge fifty dollars, then they sit back and wait for nature to take its course. I've scraped seven of them already this year!"

"Will she talk?" Lucas demanded. "Can we make her talk?"

"Why should she? She's had what she came for."

"She paid fifty dollars. And it didn't work. Maybe she'd talk if she thought she could get her money back."

"They don't. They never do. Almost never."

And Lucas remembered his hospital experience, plucked a volume of abortions from the library of memory, knew from the first page this was so.

They looked at each other, sworn enemies of what had been done, implacable enemies of the doer. Here they were inseparable, in this terrain of man considering the absolute and bound by that of it which he could understand they viewed this act with a single mind, with automatic abhorrence and implacable enmity.

They were doctors and in becoming doctors their subject which was life had made the law implicit. The stuff of life was infinitely more precious than those who possessed it could ever understand.

It was neither fear nor tribal taboo which made this act of abortion detestable. It had nothing to do with statute. It was not ethics, ethics of the race or of the profession, it was not social disapproval or professional reproach which said no, which deterred, for none of these things were as strong as the repugnance, nor as absolute as the barrier.

It was the deed against life. And in all living there is no sin like the sin against life. And these were doctors and to them the final value was life, and this ultimate material was as inexplicable as it was precious, and there was no sin comparable to that of those who destroyed it, who destroyed this stuff, this miracle, this which their lives were spent blindly and doggedly preserving.

"We'll get them one of these days," Dr. Runkleman promised.

"Yes," said Lucas, for this was inevitable too. "But even chiropractors —how can they do it?"

"It's not always chiropractors, you know. It just happens in this case, this particular case—why, we had a man here when I first came here, a doctor—"

"I know," said Lucas hurriedly, the words swam off into the darkness, into the void of sound, willed to be meaningless. "What I mean is, even a chiropractor—"

"Part of it's the law. If the laws were changed—"

"No matter what the law said, I'd never do it. Never!"

"No," Dr. Runkleman said slowly, "no, it can't be done. Not really . . ."

"Any more than a judge can sit on the bench and deliberately hand down wrong law—"

"And yet, you know, I was sorry for that fellow, that one we caught, I mean sitting there, no hope from anywhere, from anybody, the very ones he helped turning against him—"

"He knew what he was in for. He knew patients. And he knew what he was doing. Every one of us, chiropractor, midwife, or doctor, nurse, orderly, or student—there's one *knowing* in all of us. And when a man goes against that he becomes a whore."

"If he does it as a general thing. If he makes a practice of it—"

"No—not even that! Just once! Then he's all whore. The most he can get is forgiveness. But he's still a whore. He's a forgiven whore. And he can kill himself for it. And then he's a dead whore. And that's all there is to it. There's no undoing it. It hasn't anything to do with people at all."

Dr. Runkleman sighed. He nodded.

While they were completing rounds they came to Oscar Glaimer again. The biopsy had confirmed carcinoma of the rectum. Each day Dr. Runkleman entered his room reluctantly, examined him halfheartedly, left uncommitted.

"Well, how are you today, Oscar?"

"You going to operate on me pretty quick?"

"Maybe we better build you up a little first. Don't you think?"

"You're the doctor . . ."

"That's right!" the nurse said. There was a certain hostility in her tone. They both looked up, surprised. The nurse and the patient exchanged glances. Then she walked with them into the corridor.

"Are you going to operate, Dr. Runkleman?" she asked.

"We'll see . . . we'll see . . ." Dr. Runkleman studied her.

She was about to say something, she choked it back, her lips tightened, she walked abruptly away.

"What's the matter with her?" Lucas demanded.

The head nurse enlightened them. Miss Paget had fallen in love with the patient, she was in love with Oscar Glaimer.

"Of course she isn't an RN," the head nurse said contemptuously. "Did you ever hear of such a thing? They're going to get married—and him with inoperable carcinoma of the rectum!"

"You see everything," Dr. Runkleman shrugged as they walked down the corridor.

"How can they get married?" Lucas protested.

Dr. Runkleman shrugged.

"Are we going to operate?"

"Well . . . I don't know, now . . . What's your opinion?"

"Pretty far gone . . . But there's a chance, of course . . ."

"You think so?" And Dr. Runkleman's tone said that he did not think so, that if they operated the patient would die, that against this almost certain failure there was dubious credit for a success, and a death, a black mark for failure.

"Why, I don't know . . . I think so . . . You never can tell, of course . . ." Lucas said dutifully. But protest writhed within him, and he was a little sick, because it was suddenly plain that Dr. Runkleman had a horror of the doomed, that he turned from them, that he would have none of them.

As they left the building Lucas noticed a single bed outside the door of the X-ray room, an old, old man lying peacefully in it, gazing endlessly at the ceiling.

In the past week, on his way in or out of the X-ray room he had more than once squeezed by a bed placed against one wall.

"Taking a lot of X-rays nowadays, aren't they?" he asked.

Dr. Runkleman looked quickly at him. He laughed appreciatively. "That's right! Certainly taking a lot of X-rays!"

Lucas looked at him, puzzled. There was evidently something here which Dr. Runkleman assumed he knew. Perhaps Dr. Snider was processing his private patients with County equipment. He said nothing.

That evening there was an emergency call to the County and he rushed from dinner to attend a man stabbed in the liver.

It was soon over. There was little to do. He prolonged it as long as he could. He saw the man safely bedded in the men's ward. He lingered a moment, the ward and the humans in it settling quietly for the time of darkness, readying for the small overnight voyage, there was nothing for him here, he walked reluctantly into the corridor.

The bed he had seen that afternoon was still standing outside the door of the X-ray room. The old man in it lay as he had seen him last, peering intently and unwinking at the ceiling.

Lucas frowned.

Now what on earth is this! he demanded of himself. Why is that man left out here in the corridor, somebody has forgotten and left him there, this is a fine piece of carelessness . . .

And he passed behind the head of the bed to look into the X-ray room. He started. Another bed stood there. And in the bed was another old man. His lips tightened angrily. This was outrageous. County or no County, this was really going too far. He walked quickly down the corridor, looking for a nurse. As he passed Oscar Glaimer's room the door opened, Miss Paget came out.

She looked at Lucas guiltily, startled.

"Come with me, please," he ordered shortly.

"It's on my own time," she said defensively. "I was just sitting with him for a few minutes—"

Lucas ignored her. He stopped before the bed standing outside the X-ray room.

"I want to know what's the meaning of this."

"Of what, Doctor? If you mean— I didn't know it was against the rules just to sit with him. Somebody has to give these poor devils a little time now and then—he may be just a charity patient but if he had money I bet they'd be operating on him soon enough—"

"I want to know why this man, brought here for X-rays, has simply been abandoned here, left here overnight. Why isn't he back in the ward, where he belongs? What's he doing out here? And him—" his voice rose angrily as he pointed inside the X-ray room—"brought here for X-rays, simply left there. He's been there all afternoon. I know. I was here. I saw him. I want to know who's responsible."

"It's not my ward," she said automatically.

"I want to know who's responsible."

"But Doctor—"

"Why their pictures weren't taken—why they weren't returned to the ward!"

Now she understood. She stared at him, amazed. Then, slowly, a small, vindictive smile relaxed her features.

"Why, Doctor!" she said mockingly, "surely you know why these patients are here!"

"I don't understand your tone and I have no idea why two old men are left here untended—simply wheeled into a corridor and left there—simply pushed into an X-ray room and forgotten—" he stepped through the doorway—"in an unheated room!" he cried indignantly. "Without blankets! Have you ever heard of pneumonia? Do you see how cold it is in here?"

She listened to every word intently, she listened greedily, enjoying his anger, full of satisfaction. She brushed the lank brown hair from the sides of her plain face.

"That's it, Doctor. What is it they say? Pneumonia! Enemy of the young—friend of the aged!"

"What are you talking about. Just exactly what does—"

"That's how we kill 'em, Doctor! Didn't you know! That's what we do with them—here at the County! Of course!"

Lucas, about to burst out at what was patently gibberish, and disrespectful gibberish at that, restrained himself. There was triumph in her tone, and she was secure, secure in the truth. She was delighted to be opening his eyes to something.

"What are you talking about!"

"That's why they put them in there," she said patiently. "Pneumonia! Friend of the aged! Oh, yes! That's how we do at the County! They don't really feel it, you know. No, they're too old. They're senile. Childish. Even if you gave them blankets they wouldn't keep them on."

Lucas listened now in a vacuum, his thinking had stopped, his mind now received only sound, heard what Miss Paget was saying, heard it dully, beyond shock.

"And so . . . they lie still . . . because they're old . . . and that way they're almost sure to get pneumonia, lying still . . . and just to make sure . . . why, the X-ray room's always cold . . . and the cold further diminishes their resistance . . . and so . . ."

"Miss Paget, you are making very serious charges. I want to warn you that—"

"But I'm not making any charges, Doctor! No charges at all. You asked me and I'm telling you. You see we haven't got all the room in the world here at the County. There's always someone waiting for the beds, especially the old men's and the old women's beds. Have to keep them moving, you know. And when they get *very* old, so old that you can be sure the end is only a matter of a day at the outside—why then—why then, we just speed it up a little. It's not my fault, Doctor! I assure you I didn't make the rule."

"Who made it?"

"That's not for me to say, Doctor. I'm not running this place. Why, look at that poor Mr. Glaimer, lying there, knowing he has cancer, waiting for an operation, he has a *right* to an operation—"

"Get me some blankets!"

"I'm sorry, Doctor. I'm not on duty now."

"I didn't ask you whether you were on duty. Get me some blankets. Now."

He walked to the old man's bedside. He looked at the chart. Carlile Emmons. Eighty-four. The skin which covered his skull and the bones of his face circled among many wrinkles, a bony nose, the sinking eyes had made an infinity of ripples around the deep caverns where they fell and these rippling wrinkles stayed frozen, immobile, arrested, not flowing out and on into smoothness as they spread over the fluid tissues of youth, and his eyes, those two dropped stones, stared unseeingly at the ceiling. About the corners of his thin and bloodless lips a small, meaningless smile was fixed. He held a bedpan in his arms and he cradled this as if it were a child and occasionally and unexpectedly he crooned to it.

"Well, how are you tonight, Mr. Emmons," Lucas said in the voice for patients, it was not a question, it was a reassuring sound, a vocal pattern of comfort. He took a thin wrist, felt for the thin and rapid pulse. The skin was hot. The patient did not answer.

Mr. Emmons had sunk very low.

Behind him Miss Paget came up.

"I didn't think he'd last till now," she said. She spread two blankets on top of the sheet and coverlet which had been all the old man's covers. "There now, Mr. Emmons! How does that feel?"

Behind her the night nurse came bustling, apprehensive.

"I want hot water bottles—set up a hypodermoclysis—get me some adrenalin—more blankets—some oil—"

"Yes, sir," said the new nurse, frightened.

"This is Miss Boston, Doctor," said Miss Paget. "I guess I can go now—"

But Lucas had already begun to work on Carlile Emmons. His stethoscope carried to his ears the liquid sounds emitted in the bases of the lungs, the waves of a sea of death come in the tide of his age to drown him. Pneumonia had already begun.

There was not much the mechanism of Carlile Emmons could do to assist him. The tissues had lost their response. The sensitivity to pain which age administered deftly to dull the approach of siege and death had long lulled the mechanism. The face which Carlile Emmons wore was serene to unfelt pain which a few years before would have made him groan and gasp. Within him the tide rose inexorably and he lay indifferent, he clasped the bedpan in his thin arms and he crooned to it lovingly, his friend and his company.

Lucas did what he could. And then pausing to consider the old man he remembered the other patient waiting in the corridor outside the door. He began to push the bed down the corridor. Miss Boston ran to him.

"No, no, Doctor!" She was aghast. "Let me do that!"

"Get him back in the ward!"

"I will! I will, Doctor!" And she pushed the bed down the corridor.

"What's going on here?" Dr. Snider grinned.

Lucas turned.

"Didn't mean to startle you. Somebody told me you'd come in and was upset about something. Anybody giving you any trouble?"

Lucas paused a moment.

"I was called to an accident case," he said carefully. "A man was stabbed in the liver. I was about to leave. I noticed a bed standing in the corridor outside the X-ray room. There was a man in it. I went into the X-ray room. There was another bed there. I found a patient in this bed, left without covers, aged, obviously suffering from pneumonia—"

"Didn't Dave tell you?" Dr. Snider gave him a comradely, guilty grin.

"I'm afraid I don't understand."

"Sho! He ought to've told you! Didn't you ever notice before? I thought you knew . . . I'll tell you what it is, let's walk down this way, we can sit in my office . . ."

"I've got to take care of the patient!" And Lucas walked ahead of Dr. Snider into the X-ray room, he went to Carlile Emmons' bedside and felt for his pulse.

"Hey, hey!" Dr. Snider cried. "What's all this? What've we got here!" He gestured, surprised, at the equipment Lucas had ordered brought in.

"This patient has pneumonia," Lucas said flatly. He spoke carefully. He spoke to his superior, the head of the County Hospital, of a matter which was superior to both of them, they being doctors.

"Figured he'd have," Dr. Snider smiled, nodded quietly. "I'll tell you something. You don't want to get all excited. This man is eighty-four years old. We've got just so many beds. Old Carlile here, he's reached the end of his ways. I looked at him yesterday. I said to myself, Well, old Carlile, you've got about twenty-four, forty-eight, seventy-two hours at the outside."

"I see."

"Got to have the room, you know."

Lucas said nothing.

"We've got room for just so many. Got a dozen waiting for this bed. . . . So when the time comes, when you can see it's just a question of hours or days . . ." He shrugged. "They don't feel anything, they're just as happy here as they would be in the ward. . . . So that's how it is. Don't worry. I look 'em over first."

It had been said, now. Lucas considered this dazedly. This skinny, untidy, tobacco-chewing old man had said what he had said. He was a doctor. And he had said it. There was no blinking it, there was no misunderstanding, he had said what he had said. This old man, this Carlile Emmons, had been put here to die. He had been deliberately put here, in the cold of the X-ray room, and those who had put him here knew why he had been put here. They knew that without blankets he would almost surely develop pneumonia in this cold room. And they knew that pneumonia would kill him. That was why they put him here.

"Just so you understand," said Dr. Snider. "I thought Dave sure told you."

And Dr. Runkleman knew it too. Shame dropped his eyes as he remembered Dr. Runkleman's puzzling nods and smiles, his air of sharing a secret. Was it possible? Was it really possible?

Carlile Emmons began to babble again to his bedpan, caressing it, and Lucas turned to him.

"Do the damnedest things, don't they?" Dr. Snider nodded. "Been hugging that bedpan four days. First day he started I said to myself. Here he goes, watch him, now! I got so I can smell it a week away!"

"If you'll excuse me, now, I've got to attend to the patient," Lucas said as evenly as he could.

"Tend to him? Why, you're wasting your time. You're not going to do anything for him! He's gone, man! He's gone!"

"Not yet," said Lucas. "And until he does I guess you know my duty as well as I do."

"You do as you want. If you want to waste your time staying up all night with old Carlile that's between you and Dave. I'm just trying to tell you something. I'm just trying to keep you from wasting your time. It's the way we do things—"

"It's not the way I was taught to do them."

"I know all about that. I was young once, myself, full of piss and vinegar, fresh out of school, carried the whole world on my shoulders. Now I tell you this! That man's going to die. There isn't anything you or I or anybody else can do to prevent it. He's going to die and he's going to die before morning—"

"We'll see about that!"

"Oh, you'll see, all right. He'll be dead by morning! Comes six o'clock old Carlile'll be deader'n a mackerel. I'll stake everything I know on that! You can't save him and nobody else can. He's just going a little quicker'n he figured and saving us a lot of time and trouble. And you've got healthy patients who need you. Just think it over."

He turned in the doorway. He looked a moment into Lucas' eyes, burning at him. He shrugged.

"Stay all night if you're a mind to," he said, mildly contemptuous. "If I was you I'd have a little talk with Dave."

He left, and with his departure the shame went with him, most of it, that of it which made speech and thought impossible. His unkempt presence was gone, his voice was gone with it, and his words, speaking the unspeakable. Lucas turned quickly to Carlile Emmons. He put his palm anxiously on the old man's forehead. He listened to his heartbeat. He drew adrenalin into a syringe, the needle went into the arm and Carlile Emmons did not even wince.

"You're all right, old boy," Lucas said thickly. "Don't you worry. Don't you worry a bit. Don't you worry about those sons of bitches, *I've* got you, now! . . ."

During the first hour he transferred the old man's bed back to the ward. He had curtains set up. He roved the hospital restlessly, levying any equipment that could possibly be used. He moved all this within the screened space surrounding Carlile Emmons' bed, oxygen, hypodermoclysis, syringes, solutions, hot water bottles. The small space became a hospital within a hospital.

Carlile Emmons slept, now. He breathed more easily. The rattling sounds from his chest, the bubbling of air through water-filled sacs, had diminished. Some small nuance of waxy yellow had given reluctant way in his tissues to the sluggish faint violet of returning blood.

He slept, his arms cradling his bedpan, his stubbled mouth was open and the air snored from that toothless cavern, then air was drawn greedily in, the process went on, and as all living men breathed on the planet that night, Carlile Emmons breathed, his heart pumped; as they were alive he was alive.

"Want m'wife!" the sleeping figure croaked suddenly.

Lucas jumped.

Carlile Emmons' eyes had opened, he stared ruminatively at the ceiling.

"Want m'wife," he repeated peevishly.

"How are you, Mr. Emmons?" Lucas bent tenderly over the old man.

"Lucy! Where air ye! I'm a callin' you! You hear, wife?"

"That's right! You use your lungs! You call out all you please! I'll be right here! I'll get her for you . . ."

But Carlile Emmons' eyes had closed. He was snoring again.

Lucas watched him anxiously. But he breathed as before. His fluttering pulse pounded doggedly on, a little slower now, a little slower, Lucas sighed, a little slower, thank God. He tiptoed to the bedside table. He picked up the old man's chart.

Carlile Emmons had presented himself to the hospital a month before. He had come in off the highway, the broad state highway that ran just beyond the hospital. He had been only a week among the ambulant old people. Then he had been put to bed with a cold. After that he remained in bed. He was eighty-four. He was single. He had never married. He had once been a farmer. His occupation was laborer. He had been a child and had had the diseases of childhood. He had been a man and had had his appendix removed. He had labored. And he still breathed, his heart still pumped. And these facts were his links to the humans about him. Lucas looked again. No, he had never married.

None? No living relations?

Lucas gingerly opened the drawer of the bedside table, the patient's cache, sacred and personal. In the drawer was a rusty apple core and six dried orange pips, a dime, a piece of string, a thumbed, ruled, folded piece of paper.

No relations?

Carlile Emmons was writing to someone. Or someone was writing to him.

Lucas opened the folded sheet.

"Der Lusy I been at this plase it is alrite but I want you shud be with me. I will close now hopeing you come soon if so be you can come as I have wated long enuf. Sinserely your husbin Carlile Emmons."

"He thinks he's married," Miss Boston whispered.

Lucas turned. She stood at his elbow, her eyes on the letter.

"He isn't?" Lucas looked at the letter uncertainly.

"I suppose she's very real to *him,*" Miss Boston said defensively.

"But you're sure! He hasn't got a wife—not even somebody he calls 'wife'?"

"It's only in the last week. Before that he used to boast about being single all his life. Oh, no. We looked, he even babbled out a crazy address, and we looked—oh, no! there wasn't anybody. Not even any such address."

Lucas folded the letter, reluctantly shut the drawer upon it, looked uneasily at Carlile Emmons.

"How is he, Doctor?"

"He's all right," he whispered absently. He gestured to her with his head. They walked out of the ward, into the corridor.

"He's pretty old," she said in the corridor. "You know, Doctor, when they get pretty old—Dr. Snider says he won't live past six o'clock—"

"Has he ever been wrong?"

"I don't think so, sir. I don't think—ever."

"I happen to disagree with him. Does this sort of thing really go on—is this standard practice here?"

"They don't really know, you see—I don't mean to be telling you, Doctor, but an old person—"

"That's true. An old person doesn't feel pain which might be unbearable to a younger patient—"

"And we're always so crowded—and as Dr. Snider says, they don't even know they're here, it's just a question of hours, really, it doesn't really make any difference to them, just an hour more or less—"

"I'll tell you the difference. A doctor's job and a nurse's job is to save life. Understand? To prolong it as long as possible. And then to go on fighting to bring it back. Understand? Never forget that. You're not just a glorified waitress and chambermaid. You're a nurse. And that's your job. *Life!* And all the rest is just incidental."

"I only work here, Doctor—"

"I know you only work here. And so long as I work here that's what I expect of you—on every case I attend. And now I'll tell you something. I'm going to save this man."

Miss Boston looked at him apprehensively. Involuntarily she looked at the clock in the corridor. It was ten o'clock.

"Yes, sir," she said dutifully. "Is there anything else you want, Doctor? Anything else I can get you?"

"No." Lucas thought intently. "No—not right now—you tend to the rest of your patients . . ."

They walked down the darkened corridor silently, they stopped a moment by the front door, by the admission room, they looked out at the moonlit world outside. The big state road rolled carelessly and broad past the County Hospital, smooth and reaching, the wind in its face. Lucas looked at it somberly. Miss Boston watched it sigh into the unknown and she yearned forth on it, borne away, rushing away, past the bend that hid the County Hospital forever.

"That's where they come from," she sighed. "More than half the old folks we got here. Right off that highway. They've got no folks. And they're too old to work. And they just keep going. On and on and on. Till they stop . . ." She was silent, thinking. "They must walk by a lot of hospitals," she mused, wonderingly. She sighed. "But finally—they stop. . . ."

Lucas shook his head sadly.

"Nobody knows whether they're unhappy or lonely. Remember that. We say that of senile people—we say they can't feel and don't know and don't care. But nobody knows. Just remember. It's probably true. But nobody knows . . ."

She nodded thoughtfully.

"Poor Mr. Emmons. He's in bad shape, isn't he?"

"Yes. He's in bad shape."

"Calling out for his wife. Poor soul. I suppose he's always wanted a wife, secretly, maybe. And now—you're sure there's nothing I can get for you, Doctor?"

"I'd better go back and have a look—I won't need you for a while—"

"I'd watch him awfully carefully, Doctor. The minute he showed anything I could call you—I mean you could go home—"

"Go home?"

He walked down the corridor, frowning, he tiptoed to Carlile Emmons' bedside. The old man slept as he had left him. There was no perceptible change. He looked at his watch. It was ten-thirty. He put a chair by the bedside. He sat down. He folded his arms.

And now his mind ticked off his armamentarium, the weapons he could assemble against death. Dextrose and saline dripped slowly into the old man, feeding his tissues. The bed was warm. His head and shoulders had been elevated to make breathing easier. Oxygen. Not needed yet. Adrenalin. Not needed yet. Himself. And he sat there, ready.

Not much. . . .

No . . . Not much. . . . Wasn't there something else? Something else you could do? There was nothing to cut, nothing to treat, nothing to dose . . . There was—well, there was just tissue, old, very old, eighty-four years old, threescore and ten, fourteen years past, an old, old man—senile—every tissue worn, fragile, worn out, slipping, tired, old, old, old,

"Lucy!" Carlile Emmons cried warningly. His eyes were wide open again.

He was alive.

"It's all right, old-timer." Lucas rose instantly.

"You *git* here!"

His eyes closed. He slept again. Lucas gently drew a withered calf from beneath the covers, anointed his hands with oil, gently and tirelessly massaged upward, upward, helping the blood to creep in the flaccid veins, gently kneaded, squeezed the blood upward, the foot was icy cold except where the hot water bottle had warmed the skin, warmed the outside, only. And he rubbed the old foot gently, slowly. . . .

And after a long while he went noiselessly to the other side, to the other leg, and commenced again, gently, slowly, endlessly. . . .

He must have dozed. He must have gone back to his chair and sat down and dozed off. He was dreaming that old Carlile and his wife were in bed together, that he was caring for them both, their heads were side by side on the pillow.

The cry wakened him.

He hasn't got a wife, he said automatically, his eyes opened, the next moment he realized where he was, he was standing, Carlile Emmons was sitting upright, his face was wattled red, he was gasping, he was starving for breath.

Lucas fumbled for his stethoscope. Gently, hurriedly, he pried Carlile Emmons' fingers from the bedpan he clutched to his chest. He put the bell of the stethoscope against the old man's chest. The rustling sounds racketed back to his ears. The râles. He dropped his stethoscope and tapped against his fingers on the chest wall. The sound came back dull, markedly dull, the dullness of a full cask.

"Help!" croaked Carlile Emmons, gasping. And his voice had the tone, the odd pectoral tone. He fell back on his pillows. His pulse was thready, compressible. The body was telling him, it was telling him something had happened, Carlile Emmons who had gone to sleep barely in the first stage of pneumonia, arrested there, sluggishly on his way out of it, had passed with shocking speed into the second stage, into the second stage of pneumonia.

And now heedless of noise, Lucas worked as quickly as his mind and hands could fly, he stumbled over the chair, he was adjusting the oxygen mask as Miss Boston hurried through the screens to his side.

Carlile Emmons' face had become markedly blue. He began to cough as he fell back and Miss Boston wiped from his lips the prune-juice-colored, the red-brown sputum of haemoptysis, of lung haemorrhage. His body was cold, now. The fever had suddenly gone.

The oxygen began to hiss from the sides of the rubber face plate. Lucas spread his fingers over its edges, jammed it tighter to the old man's face. Miss Boston uncovered the limp shanks, parted them, forced a catheter into the rectum, dropped the free end into a kidney basin. She refilled the hot water bottles.

They waited.

Lucas stared at the coverlet over the old man's chest. Beneath the coverlet his eyes, the eyes back of his eyes, the eyes of association and memory, saw the thin chest wall, plunged abruptly beneath the skin and bone, saw the lungs dilated fully, expanding for air, gasping for it, the sacs that should be empty full of blood and fluid and mucus. He saw the lungs, their brown-red, liverish color, his fingers felt the soft surface, once rubbery, now easily broken. And he knew that hardly any trace of the functioning substance of the lungs remained except the bronchial tubes and the larger vessels.

He looked up, out of the chest, into the room, his eyes met Miss Boston's. She was staring at him with pity. As their looks met, she dropped her eyes.

Lucas forced a smile.

"He's not dead yet," he whispered.

She looked at him, startled. All she had ever learned or observed told her in the barest glance that Carlile Emmons was almost gone. He would go any minute. Involuntarily, she looked at her watch, caught herself, looked at Lucas guiltily.

"What time is it?" he asked harshly.

"Five minutes after four." She said it apologetically.

He peered quickly at the oxygen apparatus, adjusted the flow minutely, strode to the foot of the bed. He threw back the covers.

"Take one leg! I'll take the other!"

And without waiting for her he began a slow, rhythmic, upward massage. They worked in silence.

You won't die . . . you're not . . . going to . . . die . . . you're not . . . going to . . . die . . . He cadenced the strokes. His arms moved. His mind messaged. Listen, flesh! Hear me! . . . You're not . . . you're not . . . not . . .

He felt her eyes on him, she was looking at him uncertainly, her movements had begun to flag. He glared at her. Hurriedly she increased her efforts.

"If there was only something—something to give them—there's nothing for pneumonia, is there—nothing . . ."

"Save your breath . . . There's nothing . . ."

But his mind stormed, protested, sent its thoughts battering against the easy-yielding blackness, the void of the unknown.

"Slack up," he said suddenly. And she stopped promptly, gratefully. "We're tiring him out."

He studied Carlile Emmons, his eyes red with fatigue, begging for a sign. Carlile Emmons lay motionless.

"Sponge him. Sponge him with warm alcohol."

Sponge him, his thought echoed, sponge him with warm alcohol, the echo resounded bitterly. A sponge, a sponge and warm alcohol against this mighty antagonist, wet the skin, sop gently, and all the while, inside the man a merciless and very powerful enemy moved easily from cell to cell—give him a manicure, cut his hair, trim his toenails—

He turned desperately to the treatment table.

"Digitalis—" he cried.

"It's in the dispensary—"

"I'll get it—"

"The second shelf on the right as you go in—"

He raced to the dispensary. In the corridor the clock said fifteen minutes to five. Seeing it he ran faster.

He found the shelf.

Digitalis.

I don't think much of digitalis. I never have. Not here. I don't see what good it can do. But everybody gives it . . .

He snatched the bottle. Two grains . . . No, a grain and a half . . .

His eyes roved the shelf of bottles His eyes begged them to speak, plumbed his memory, speculated frantically.

Strychnine. Of course! Desperate but—

And caffeine . . . Caffeine . . . Why not?

Aconite—no, no! Wait! Certainly, aconite! One-half to two grains—better go easy . . .

That's all—

Wait!

Gelsemium!

Now, what the hell was that doing here! Must be fifty years old. Whoever used gelsemium now? But in the old days—in the old days—a thread of memory tantalized him, his mind clawed at it—

Try it!

Try anything!

He rushed back to the ward.

It was five minutes to five.

Carlile Emmons was still alive.

"I think he's slipping," Miss Boston hesitated. "He's trying to groan—"

Lucas jumped to the head of the bed, gently removed the oxygen mask. His heart gave a great bound of relief. The old man's face was not so blue. His breathing was shallow. It was deeper, though. He listened hard. It was ever so little deeper.

"We've got him! I think we've got him!"

His shaking fingers fumbled a needle on a syringe, drew up digitalis, injected. He stood, then, looking at the old and almost vacant face.

Looking at him, seeing his intent face, the small agony of desperation in his eyes, his rumpled clothes, his hands hanging helpless, his desperate, unwinking intentness, Miss Boston shut her eyes with pity.

It was past five.

It was nearly six.

And Dr. Snider was never wrong.

He was a dirty old man, if he had ever learned anything he had forgotten it, he was a doctor only by title. But on this one thing he was never wrong. He knew death. He knew it when he saw it. It was the last thing he possessed to be proud of. He was unerring.

It was after five.

And Dr. Snider said six.

Don't you know you can't save him, she cried inwardly. Don't you know it's impossible? You're just breaking your heart? He's old! He's eighty-four! He's got pneumonia! Boy! Boy! Boy! You're fine, boy. You're wonderful. I love you. But give up, boy. Let him die . . .

Lucas looked up at her. He grinned tiredly.

"I think we've got him! I think we've got a chance!"

He felt the pulse, felt the stimulated heart beat faster with digitalis. And as they looked Carlile Emmons' eyes opened in his gray face, he grunted, his bony hands groped weakly seeking the bedpan. Lucas lifted it to his chest, put the bony arms gently around it. Carlile Emmons nestled it and hung on.

They watched him.

"I've got to go—" Miss Boston hesitated.

"Yes, you go—"

"Can't I bring you some coffee?"

"No, no! You take care of your patients."

Carlile Emmons' eyes were closed. He breathed delicately, laboring.

"Come on, Carlile," Lucas whispered. "Hang on. Just hang on. I've got you. You're going to sit outside in the sun and—and fish, maybe. Do you like to fish, Carlile? I bet you can fish! I bet you can fish swell! Would you like to fish, Carlile? You and I?"

It was life. It was Carlile Emmons' life, it was a piece of all the life there was. It was the tiniest spark. But it was a spark. And the living in him hungered to go into Carlile Emmons, to give him of his living, to link heart to heart, lung to lung, essence to essence.

Live, Carlile Emmons!

Live!

It was five-thirty.

The minutes ticked on.

Lucas leaned closer. He listened. He opened his mouth to hear better. He strained closer. The hair at the back of his neck raised, the skin tingled with shock and fear. Carlile Emmons had begun to gurgle.

Aconite!

Lucas' fingers flew to try aconite. Digitalis—no more digitalis—caffeine—give him caffeine!

"Carlile! Hang on, old boy!"

And his cheeks—was there a patch of red there? Was his face getting livid?

"Carlile!"

The pulse was weak and thready. The old man shivered slightly. The fever was back. The aconite—

He forced himself to wait.

The thermometer read one hundred and four and four-tenths degrees.

It was rapid, it was so rapid, it was all so rapid—

"Carlile! Do you hear me? Fight, boy! Fight! Fight for Luke! Fight for your old friend, Luke!—"

He threw back the coverlet. He began to sponge the wasted body, he sponged on and on— Life, go from my fingers, go into his body, take it from me, channel, pour through, feed, go into him, feel me, go into him . . .

Carlile Emmons breathed. Then his breath stopped.

He breathed again.

His breath stopped.

Slow.

Slower—

Gone!

A shudder.

Stillness.

Then slow . . .

Imperceptible—

Definite . . .

Movement—

A breath . . . a long, long pause . . . a wait . . . stopped . . . a breath—

And Lucas released his own pent breath.

Strychnine.

It couldn't go on like this.

Each breath was his last.

Any breath now, it would stop.
So strychnine.
Almost sure to bring on a coronary–
Give it!
But–
Give it!
Now!
His reluctant, shaking fingers filled the syringe, drew up one-hundredth of a grain, the needle plunged home. He hesitated. Then he pressed the plunger.
He trembled. He stood waiting.
The pulse beneath his fingers beat stronger, it was small, it was weak, it was dying. But it was stronger.
He had stopped thinking now. He could no longer reckon or reason or plan. He could only move, countermove, desperate and blind.
Carlile Emmons was drowning. His lungs were full of fluid. The tide was almost at his throat. His tissues were worn out. There was no strength left in them. There was only life. His wasted body had shrunk smaller.
A great weight of fatigue and dullness crushed Lucas into apathy. For minutes he simply stood, motionless, silent, seeing nothing, watching.
His eyes received a sensation. He blinked irritably. Then the message importuned, became clearer. He blinked again and looked up. He stared incredulously.
There was light.
The windows were no longer black.
He stared at the faint blue-gray. He began to tremble. It was dawn.
Carlile Emmons was still breathing.
There was a clangor in the corridor.
He looked up angrily.
Miss Boston came in.
She looked at Carlile Emmons.
It was twenty minutes past six.
She gaped at Lucas.
He stared back at her, haggard, fierce, protective.
"He's alive!" she whispered.
"You bet he's alive!"
Breath sighed out of her.
"You did it!"
"We're running out of dextrose–"
And she flew to get more, electrified, part of the victory.
In his bed Carlile Emmons breathed small breaths, jerkily, gurgling a little, breathed more strongly. His pulse was thready but no weaker. The lividity had left his cheeks. In the strengthening dawn light his sunken cheeks clung to the bones of his jaws, in the depths of his sockets his eyes opened, his fingers twitched.
"It's all right, boy. It's day, boy. It's day. It's all right . . ."
Lucas drew his hand tenderly over the stubbled jaws, he found the

bedpan, he laid it on the old man's chest, he put his arms around it. One bony arm slipped lifelessly off.

Miss Boston rushed back with the dextrose. Behind her came two of the day staff. They walked up diffidently, their eyes boring at Carlile Emmons. They saw him breathe. They looked at each other. It was true.

And even as they looked, he began to breathe better. His pulse was stronger. The life that had fled deep down in him, hiding, burying itself, lest it be found, plucked out, sent unheard, wailing out of the lips, out in the world, the hidden life crept timidly, slowly, peeped from the eyes again.

They smiled. All of them standing about the bed saw that and smiled. They knew that light. It was life. This body was a human, again.

Then the lids closed. And Carlile Emmons slept.

At seven-thirty Dr. Runkleman came in.

He stared at Lucas, amazed. His mouth opened.

"Hey! What—what—"

"Pneumonia," Lucas croaked. He cleared his throat. "Pneumonia," he said clearly.

Dr. Runkleman glanced at the still figure in the bed. He saw an old man, saw that he was breathing, saw the apparatus, stared again at the gray face of his assistant, remembered the long day before.

"My God!" he cried. "You been up all night?"

Lucas smiled tiredly.

"Never felt better in my life."

They looked up. Dr. Snider had come in. Lucas stiffened. Dr. Runkleman watched his eyes fill with hate and loathing. Dr. Snider bent over Carlile Emmons.

"Morning, Dave . . ." He straightened. "Pulled him through, did you?" He looked at Lucas, saw his eyes, looked quickly away. He cleared his throat. He looked at Dr. Runkleman. "Minds me of an old feller we had in here once," he began deprecatively—" 'member old Charley Fears? Swore to God he wouldn't last the night and by Jesus—"

He stopped. His voice trailed.

Lucas had walked away, he was walking out of the ward.

Dr. Runkleman looked at Dr. Snider impersonally.

"I warned you," he shrugged.

"Now, Dave—you know how we're fixed here—you know good and well this old devil didn't have a day in him—"

But Dr. Runkleman had followed Lucas out of the ward. He found him in the dressing room. They undressed silently. Lucas walked toward the shower.

"Why don't you go home and sleep—"

"Me?"

"Go ahead! Go home and get some rest!"

"My gosh, Doctor! I'm all right! I'm used to—"

"You're reeling. That's how all right you are. Go on! I don't need you this morning, anyway—just an appendix—the rest'll keep."

"There's just one thing I want to know—"

"I've told him! I've warned him!"

"What are we going to do about him?"

"He's old. He won't be long, now. I thought he'd quit last year. I'll keep an eye on him."

"He's not a doctor."

"He'll watch his step now."

"He's not a doctor."

"I'll keep an eye on him."

"Are we going to report him?"

"I thought you knew! When you said the other day—'taking a lot of X-ray pictures'—I thought you knew."

"Knew? Knew a thing like that was going on? Knew a doctor—a doctor of Medicine—was deliberately killing patients?"

"You have to be reasonable. I know how you feel. You've been up all night, all this is new to you, he's almost always right, it's only a question of hours, I don't like it any better than you do, he's got to make a good showing, they don't give him money enough—"

"And he's taking money from patients, isn't he! He's milking charity patients. On the sly."

"I don't know . . . I don't know . . ."

"He's dangerous. You see that, don't you? He can do anything—anything—"

"I'll see it doesn't happen again. That's the last of it! I promise you! I should have stopped him long ago. I'm just as guilty as he is. Now, go home. Please. Get some sleep. A couple of hours, even—"

"You're not! That's his job—you can't be every place—you can't do everything—he's the head of the hospital—no, really, Doctor! I'm all right—a shower'll fix me up."

And he stepped into the shower.

"By God, you saved him!" Dr. Runkleman shouted above the noise of the water. "You pulled him through!"

"I thought he was gone a dozen times!" Lucas shouted back.

"I wouldn't have given him a chance! Not one! Eighty-four!"

"And lobar pneumonia!" Lucas grinned happily, stepped out of the shower, his eyes tired but alight. He nodded gleefully. "He's living, by God!"

"I don't see how you did it . . . No . . . No, sir . . . Never . . ."

"He's got his bedpan, and we're going fishing someday and by God, he's alive!"

They robed, they operated swiftly, Lucas felt the nurses' respectful glances, Dr. Runkleman beamed, Lucas reluctantly smiled, then Dr. Runkleman winked at him and Lucas grinned openly.

Nothing he had ever done in life had pleased him so much. Not even his diploma had rocked him with such fierce joy. And as the moments passed the magnitude of what he had done accumulated, detail by detail, the whole fact filled him, swelled, passed from him, towered above him, greater, larger than he was, leaving him humble, an instrument, a living instrument, now truly part of the great game. He had saved a life.

He tiptoed with Dr. Runkleman to Carlile Emmons' bedside, saw him sleeping, breathing, his pulse stronger, watched him, nodded, gave the nurse jealous, careful instructions, waited to be sure she understood, left reluctantly, walked with Dr. Runkleman down the corridor.

As they passed the X-ray room he looked instinctively for a bed. The corridor was empty. The X-ray room was empty.

"There'll be no more of that." Dr. Runkleman's face was granite. "Now, there's nothing at the Valley—not a single thing. Nothing but rounds. Go home! Now go on—"

"The office calls—"

"I'll wake you! I promise!"

Lucas drove home.

Kristina was out shopping.

He took off his shirt. He looked at himself in the mirror. He grinned at himself happily. He walked to the bed. He considered it a moment. He sat down on the edge. He put his feet up. He sank back slowly. He looked at the ceiling. He began to think. Broth. He must remember to order broth. Broth? Why broth? He frowned. He shut his eyes to concentrate.

Kristina was shaking him.

"Wha—wha's matter?" Almost instantly he was sitting upright. He blinked at her. "Wha—what time is it?"

"It's almost two o'clock."

"Two o'clock?"

"You poor kid! I'm so sorry, Lucas! It's the County—Dr. Runkleman said I'd better wake you—first he thought we shouldn't, then he thought—"

But Lucas had already flung himself into his shirt, he grabbed his coat, he was tying his tie on the way out.

Minutes later he was at the County Hospital. He went straight to the ward. He walked through the screens. Oblivious to the hovering nurse he bent over Carlile Emmons.

The old man's breath was very shallow. His pulse could hardly be felt. His heart sound was faint, grudging, tired, listless, doomed.

"Hey!" Lucas cried. His heart beat fast with panic. "Hey! Carlile!—*Strychnine!*—Hey!"—she slipped the syringe into his hand—"Hey, wait!" —the needle entered the tired flesh. The plunger shot home.

"Carlile!"

His breathing stopped. After an infinity it resumed again. For an instant the pulse came stronger. There was a faint sound. It came again. It was there. It was unmistakable. Carlile Emmons' old mouth hung open. His eyes stared sightless at the ceiling. And with the breath, with the last breath, with the one before it, with the one beginning now—

There was a rustling sound,

There was the sound of dry leaves,

There was a rattle.

It grew louder.

His tortured chest strained for another breath. His heart pumped once more, uncaring. On his glazing eyes the cornea puckered. His body shivered. The rattle came again, this time loud and shocking.

Then there was silence.

The silence was complete.

There was no more breath.

Carlile Emmons was gone. The body with that name lay in the bed. The chest was silent, the heart had stopped, the sightless eyes were blank forever.

The nurse stirred.

Lucas expelled a long-held breath.

The old man's jaw slid slowly open. Mechanically Lucas shut it, hid the indecent naked cavern of his mouth. Slowly, gently, he disengaged the stiff fingers cuddling the bedpan to the dead chest.

The nurse began to bind up the lower jaw, which had fallen open again.

Heartsick, Lucas turned away. He passed the useless litter on the bedside table. In the glass tube of the hypodermoclysis outfit the fluid still drip-dripped methodically. He put out his hand to turn off the flow, put it down again, walked from that last sign of life out of the ward, into the corridor.

A little knot of nurses gave way before him, looked at him, dropped their eyes.

"Too bad, Doctor," one murmured.

There was a murmur of sympathy.

"Well!" cried a voice defiantly, he looked up, it was Miss Paget, "you saved him, anyway! You put old Snider's nose out of joint! You saved him!"

"Saved him?"

"Sure you did! He would have died at six o'clock, wouldn't he? You're damned right! And you held him on till two!"

The nurses murmured.

"We're proud of you, Doctor!"

"Six to two!" a nurse cried loyally. "That's eight whole hours!"

Lucas nodded numbly.

He walked through them, down the corridor, out of the hospital.

He shook his head dazedly. He looked at the state highway. He looked at his hands. Carefully he got into his car, he started it, he put it in gear, he released the clutch, he drove back to the office.

"Died?" Dr. Runkleman asked gently.

Lucas nodded.

Dr. Runkleman shook his head.

"Too bad . . ."

CHAPTER 27

The discovery that it is not possible to reveal a mind to another comes early and unprotested to the majority of humans. They are reassured and protected by it.

There are others to whom this discovery gives anguish. They struggle all their lives to disclose themselves.

But there can arise to either group crises, punishment, wounds, shocks, which make the impossibility of complete communication suddenly intolerable, which make the effort to communicate imperative, as if, in communicating, the crisis, the punishment, the wound, the shock would by mutual pain be made bearable or opposed or annihilated.

Lucas, having no one else, told all that had happened to Kristina. He rushed to her, he who was usually apart from her, to tell her what had happened, to show her what he was and what this had done to him. He told her everything, he went over it step by step, doggedly, not knowing which detail would communicate, omitting none. He sat by, as he told it, listening carefully, quick to remind himself, carefully correcting himself once or twice, silent at last, looking to her, betrayed, incredulous, demanding, demanding he knew not what.

And Kristina groped through his vehemence, harpooned by his need, desperate to solace, to solve, to set all aright.

"They'll get in trouble," she said darkly. "Someday they'll get in trouble, sure!"

Lucas stared at her, stunned.

"Trouble!" he echoed.

"Wait, Lucas! Wait! Don't be mad. I know what you mean. I don't talk so good as you. But I know you. I know what such a thing is to you—a crime," she cried indignantly, trying to feel it as he felt it, "a terrible, terrible thing—"

"I don't mean behavior, I don't mean public morals—"

Kristina searched desperately within herself for something to comfort him.

"I remember the first time I saw it," she said in a low voice.

"You saw it!"

"Not old men, of course. I was very new to the OR. It was a woman, she had cancer, they opened her up it was all over her, everywhere—hardly any liver, hardly anything. I remember how the doctors looked at each other. Then they began to close her up. She was a rich woman, it was a big doctor. He didn't sew her up altogether. He left three, four little arteries, left them open—I was new then, almost I was about to tell them, I opened my mouth, the doctor happened to look up, he saw my eyes, he waited a minute, looking at me cold, then I looked away. When you're a nurse, Luke—" she said apologetically.

"I know—they wouldn't have got away with it! Not if I was there!"

"Afterwards—I saw this many times. Some doctors, yes. Some doctors, no."

They were silent.

"What can you do, Luke?" she asked at last, miserable. "When it's hopeless—when they can't live—when you can't help them—I asked myself many times, isn't that helping them?—the doctors weren't bad men—some of them were great surgeons—"

He sighed. He began patiently, simply, a long way back. Perhaps at the end of it, when she understood, she would tell him.

"When you're born it's hopeless, Kris. That's when it begins. It's hopeless and no doctor can help you. You're going to die. You die a little every year. But this is the one thing a doctor does not know. Not for sure.

He does not know it is hopeless. He may be afraid it is hopeless. He may be honestly convinced it is hopeless. But he does not *know* it is hopeless."

"But when they get so old—"

"He doesn't know what age is. It's relative. And he doesn't know what death is. What will absolutely kill. He doesn't even know what life is. But he knows it's there. And he knows which side he's on. He believes in life. He knows the enemies of life. And he never joins them."

"That's wonderful, Luke. . . . That's what *you* believe."

"Me? That's what all doctors believe!"

She looked away. He flushed.

"There may be one or two like Snider," he conceded.

"What did Dr. Runkleman say?"

"I just don't understand. He knew what was going on. He knew it all the time. And he's been letting him get away with it."

"But he doesn't like it—any better'n you do."

"He could have stopped it."

"Are you going to talk to him any more about it?"

"I'll tell you the truth, I'm embarrassed to. I keep waiting for him to bring it up. I know we ought to do something about it. Letting it die like this is just about the same as letting the old man die. And Snider—" He shook his head violently, as if to clear it. "How many has he killed, do you suppose? How many?"

Kristina nodded soberly.

"I got used to it. But I always felt guilty-like when I saw it. I never felt that—well, it was just—of course the people were goners, there wasn't any doubt about that, there wasn't anything you could do—"

"Nobody's a goner, Kris. Not ever. Not even when they're drawing their last breath. You never can tell. So long as you've got a country you go on fighting. No matter how bad it is you go on fighting. When it's hopeless you go on fighting. You don't ever stop. You never switch to the other side. Well, a doctor's country is life. In a way he hasn't got any nationality. His country is all life, everywhere. That's his country."

"I'm not saying, you understand. What's wrong is wrong. But we've all got to go sometime—that old man was eighty-four, after all."

"What are you trying to say?"

"I don't know . . . I don't know, Luke! I feel the way you do!"

"Do you think nobody's lived past eighty-four? Do you think we're supposed to set the time when people die? That it's up to us to say this man lives and it's time for this man to die?"

"I know . . . I know . . ."

"You fight for life, Kris. There isn't anything else worth fighting for on this whole planet. It's all that belongs to a man. The noblest thing about him is the fact that he's living, just living. Whatever else he is or ever may be stems from that."

She saw that talking had helped him. He had accumulated words to girdle the unsayable, they bound it loosely, a word, a syllable, a tone, an inflection rebounded, echoes of what was immured in his vector, of what there were no human words for. But he was eased a little, he was weary, he had talked, the rage was out of him, it was not over, it would never be over, he was sick now, sick with it. And he had come to her.

She trembled for fear of saying anything that would spoil it. She trembled in desperation to say something that would bind him to her, bind him for next time, make them closer, make them one.

And he waited, waited hopefully, sharing with her, offering all he was.

"I tell you what I think," she said desperately at last, "I think a man like that—somebody should put *him* in the X-ray room!"

He opened his mouth to answer irritably, he checked himself, he sighed and fell silent. She was distasteful to him, he realized abruptly. She was a world away. He should never have told her. Now she, too, knew. What does she think about? he wondered. What goes on inside her? And he looked at her curiously, a blank wall behind which lived a stranger. He smiled wearily, he nodded and went to bed.

There were no operations scheduled at the County next morning and rounds there were quickly over. The patients seen the day before had not in the intervening time changed materially, their eyes, Lucas noticed, had still the expression of fear and amazement, the surprise of those amazed by life, that commonplace, as a thing that had been overlooked.

They looked at the two doctors making their rounds, hoping to discover some secret that was being withheld from them, something the doctors knew of their lives which they themselves did not know. It was the young doctor's face they watched particularly for the older man was a fixture, him they knew well, his face would reveal nothing. The young man's face was tired and stern and otherwise expressionless as the older man's, but he was not so well known and with the unknown there is always a chance.

They presented their anxious eyes at which the two doctors glanced briefly, then, having glanced at the charts, the two doctors broke off communications with the body and with practiced voices communicated briefly and meaninglessly with the persons and passed on to the next bed.

Those who were in bed wore eyes precocious with pain, and they shared a common knowledge. When they emerged into the world again they would carry a startled awareness. They would know fearfully that all living was spent in a prison and that this prison was their own body and that the wardens were chance and accident and there was no mercy to be expected in this prison and that punishments, tortures, barbarities could come senselessly and without warning, now they saw their life for what it was and knew there was no possible escape from it but death. And this prison without fixed laws, without any philosophy of justice as their kind had conceived justice, had as its cardinal rule that life was to be treasured and clung to in the face of all its agonies, and that in the end they must die anyway.

They looked at Lucas and Dr. Runkleman, alert for a sign, an inflection, a word, a turn in their fate. And seeing none the anxiety receded in their eyes, drained back to that inner pool of the mind from which it had flooded, and they lay back and looked at the ceiling where Time was written and where they traced letters so large that the words were meaningless and this they would do, suspended, until evening rounds.

Dr. Runkleman and Lucas were not due at the other hospital for an hour. They returned to the office.

"You know, this might be as good a time as any to make your calls," Dr. Runkleman suggested mildly.

Lucas smiled, puzzled.

"Your courtesy calls. It's always a good thing to make courtesy calls on the other doctors, I think, doesn't do any harm—anyway, that's what the book says."

"Fine," said Lucas heartily. He felt older. He noticed with surprise that he was at ease with Dr. Runkleman for the first time since his arrival, he no longer felt any urge to ingratiate himself.

"I've got a few prescriptions we'll get filled on the way," Dr. Runkleman nodded.

The word made Lucas remember.

"That's something I've been meaning to talk to you about," he said, frowning. "Mrs. Marsh went shopping the other day and one of the druggists tried to take thirty percent off her bill. Claimed it was professional courtesy. Told her the prescriptions we'd send along would make up for it. Said it was usual here."

"Who was that?"

Lucas told him.

"Did she take it?"

"No, she didn't. I sent her back with her purchase."

"Good for you! I'm glad to hear it!"

Lucas relaxed.

"He's got no business talking that way." Dr. Runkleman's face was flushed.

"It's absolutely unethical."

"Well, it's common practice enough . . ."

"Sooner or later some patient is going to end up paying for my shaving cream."

"I wouldn't pay any attention to him, if I were you. I'll have to have a word with him."

Dr. Runkleman sighed resignedly and absently worked a pencil back and forth in his fingers. Lucas watched, waiting. He looked at the pencil. Dr. Runkleman continued to twirl it. It was stamped with gold lettering. For a moment it ceased to twirl. Lucas read the legend on it. "Compliments of Usherwood and Heep, Morticians, a Friendly Service, A Friendly Cost."

Lucas looked quickly away.

"Have to take people the way they are, I guess," Dr. Runkleman decided at last.

"I guess you're right," Lucas said. He eyed the pencil. An undertaker's pencil, a souvenir, a reminder, Doctor, don't forget us, it *will* come, death's bound to, don't forget us. And the thirty percent—I don't know how much you buy, probably not much, razor blades, maybe, little stuff like that—but you've been getting it. Maybe now you won't any more. But you've been getting it. Live your life, Lucas. Live your own life. Leave him alone. He's a fine fellow. And you're making him unhappy. He noticed for the first time the imitation leather engagement pad on

Dr. Runkleman's desk. It was discreetly stamped "Flather & Trocar, Morticians, Ambulance Service, Day or Night."

Well, what? What, then?

There's nothing new here. You've heard it all before, you've heard it as a student, fee splitting, gratuities, a little something extra, Doctor—what are you after? What are you looking for? He asked this angrily.

"You know, Doctor, I've been wondering, I wonder if you shouldn't raise your fees a little." Suddenly he heard himself saying this. He listened, surprised.

"I'm pretty low," Dr. Runkleman agreed.

"You could double them and still be low."

"I'm lower than the rest. I know that."

"We might lose a few. But they don't pay, anyway!"

"That's right. . . . I'm low, all right. . . . No . . . I think we'd better leave it alone . . ."

"But seventy-five cents! A dollar—"

"They're used to it. That's what I've always charged. They'd begin to wonder how I'd improved, why my services were worth more, all of a sudden." He laughed. "Why, I like white sidewall tires! I'd just love to have them on my car!"

"Why don't you?"

"That's all I'd have to do! The minute they saw them they'd say: 'Look at him! Riding around in white sidewalls that I paid for! There's where my money went! Into white sidewall tires for him!' "

"But seventy-five cents . . . !"

Dr. Runkleman looked at Lucas, smiling, saying nothing. He looked at him as if he were trying to make up his mind about something. His expression did not change. He rose.

"Let's take a little drive," he said.

They did not visit the other doctors at once.

"I'm from farming stock," Dr. Runkleman said.

"You must know all about these farms," Lucas waved at the passing countryside.

"I got up at four o'clock every morning. It was in the north. Very cold. Short summers. All I can remember is work." He seemed to be reciting this without reminiscing, as if this were a prelude to something, as if he knew something and was on the point of telling it to Lucas, a secret, a secret that dredged up unwillingly, on which he tugged and would not let go.

"There were nine of us. We got up to work, we hardly talked, we never stopped, there were nine of us and we never stopped, and we had nothing. No sir," he smiled, "nothing." He nodded, remembering, smiling without any mirth. "Some years I put by twenty dollars. That was my share. And then my father died, I sold to my brothers, I went to North Dakota, I said I would never farm again as long as I lived, and I had four hundred dollars and I started Medicine."

"And you worked your way through? You did, didn't you!"

"You could do it, then. Oh, I knew the value of a dollar. That part was easy. And after the farm the work was even easy. And then I came here. And that's what I charged."

"But you travel so far—there's a new way of computing fees, by mileage—"

"I've got up in the dead of winter—you haven't seen one of our winters, yet—and the snow up to the horse's belly and flagged down a freight train, they all used to know me and my bag, and ride into the mountains and they'd let me off and I'd make it through the snow, right up the side of the mountain, a mile to the top. And deliver a baby. And charge five dollars. And then flounder home again. And maybe one day get half of it."

And that's where the practice comes from, Lucas nodded, that, and the seventy-five-cent calls, the dollar calls, the mail-order suits.

"I was only thinking of you, Doctor," he said quietly.

Dr. Runkleman's eyes twinkled. He stopped the car. Lucas looked out. Dr. Runkleman waved at a woman working in the garden of a trim, almost new home.

"That's mine," he said. "I rent it out. Got three more houses in Greenville." He smiled slyly. "All from seventy-five-cent calls . . . and not buying every new gadget the supply houses send around . . ." And Lucas recollected the worn instruments, the plain furniture of the office, the linoleum shabby here and there.

They drove on. In nearby Madison Dr. Runkleman stopped outside a four-storey apartment house.

"Got to see my janitor a minute," he said elaborately, enjoying Lucas' stupefaction. He was back quickly. They returned to Greenville.

Dr. Runkleman owned also two livery stables, a thriving roadside restaurant many miles away, property here, land there, Lucas stared at him, wide-eyed.

"Wouldn't do to let people know," he said soberly, still smiling. And Lucas sensed there was no one else in the world to whom David Runkleman had ever told these things.

"You've earned it!" he said fiercely.

"Wouldn't do to raise fees."

Lucas shook his head, still dumfounded.

"I'll tell you a little secret. There's two boys I'm putting through medical school—farm boys, boys who know the value of a dollar—one's in the second year, I thought the other was going to help me out here, he's going to be a medical missionary."

"By God!" It was all Lucas could manage.

"One of these days now, maybe just a year or so if all goes well, you'll have time to learn the ropes by then, I'm going to quit. I'm tired. The way the market's going it won't be long. All I want is a guaranteed income, a thousand dollars a month, a thousand for life. I'm pretty close. I'm getting closer. And I'll lease you the shop—what do you say to that? Or sell—and you can pay me out of what you take in. Any way—any way that's easy for you. And then I'm off. Have you ever wanted to go to Australia? I don't know why . . . that's where I've wanted to go all my life. Fish and hunt . . . Just hunt, hunt, hunt." He laughed at himself. "I've never owned a gun . . ."

He was silent. Lucas tried to arrange his stunned thoughts. Above all he had seen, all he had learned in the incredible past hour, hammered the words: "I'll lease you the shop . . . or sell . . . you can pay me out of what you take in . . . in a year . . . maybe two—"

"Well, this is all between us." And he looked at Lucas as a father might look at a son.

"Oh, God, Doctor!" Lucas protested, struggling for words.

Dr. Runkleman patted his knee.

"I know, I know." He nodded. He stopped the car. "Well," he stretched, he smiled brightly as if they were just awakening from a nap, "here we are—might as well stop here, first!"

Dr. Binyon and Dr. Blake could almost have been brothers. In their dress each faithfully copied the other, they wore light, tweedy clothes, they each smoked pipes, they wore heavy brogues, the hair of each was cropped short, they wore horn-rimmed glasses.

"Had an hour off today so I thought I'd bring around my new assistant. Meet Doctor Marsh," said Dr. Runkleman, a senior doctor, following ritual.

"Glad to welcome you," said Dr. Binyon without enthusiasm.

"Any relation to the Boston Marshes?" Dr. Blake asked hopefully.

"I don't think so," said Lucas.

"Jordan, Marsh, you know. Big department store—"

"No—no, I'm sure not . . ."

"Well, what do you think of our fair town?" sighed Dr. Binyon. And without waiting for an answer, "I was wondering when you were going to hire an assistant, Dr. Runkleman. With all the business you handle—"

"Well," said Dr. Runkleman, rising, "I just thought I'd bring him around and make you acquainted—"

"Like to see our shop before you go?"

"Thank you," said Lucas.

They showed their offices and equipment with confident pride. Room after room glittered with new equipment.

Dr. Binyon looked at his watch.

"We'd better be going," said Dr. Runkleman. "Got to drop in on Dr. Kauffman . . ."

"No hurry," said Dr. Blake, walking them to the door.

"Glad to welcome you, Marsh," said Dr. Binyon.

The door closed behind them. They drove toward Dr. Kauffman's office.

"Trying to start a clinic," explained Dr. Runkleman. "That means they handle everything a GP does only at fancy prices."

"How are they?"

"Oh, all right, I guess. When there's an operation both of them operate. Often as not call in Dr. Gordon from Lepton. Four of them were doing an appendix three weeks ago, busy as beavers."

They smiled at each other, amused, a little smug.

"Took four of them, eh?"

"That's right. Got to pay for that new equipment some way. Been here four years, now, and I swear they get new gadgets every year. Had four X-rays so far, each one bigger than the one before. They're all right—got their own ideas on how to run a practice—maybe they're right . . .

Keep to themselves . . . Give you kind of the idea they're missionaries and the rest of us are barbarians."

"They looked at each other kind of funny when you said we were going to see Dr. Kauffman."

Dr. Runkleman flushed.

"I've heard talk," he said slowly, "they call him a Jew, I hear they sneer at him in front of patients . . . They're always knocking somebody, though . . . I've never heard about them saying a good word about any of us. . . . They'd better keep their own house clean! I've never had much respect for a doctor who won't take night calls."

"Not take night calls!"

"That's what the patients tell me. That's another thing they've started. They say if the patient is so sick he needs a doctor then the best place for him's at the hospital—and they tell whoever calls to call the ambulance."

"You don't mean that!"

"That's what they do! They tell them to come to the clinic. And if whoever calls says they're too sick to come—then they tell them to take him to the hospital!"

"My God! And that's Medicine?"

"That's the kind they practice."

"But not to answer a call!"

They had stopped before a modest cottage.

"This Dr. Kauffman, now—he's kind of sensitive . . ."

"I know," Lucas nodded understanding. "I had a professor Aarons—"

"You know, then. Good man. Doesn't have much practice . . . Well, I guess those people have a pretty hard time . . ."

Dr. Kauffman, a short, stout man as old as Dr. Runkleman, greeted them politely and warily.

He inspected Lucas carefully.

"Good to welcome you, Doctor."

"Dr. Marsh is from State."

"State?" Dr. Kauffman wrinkled his brows, thinking. His face cleared. "Oh, yes! Then you must know Dr. Aarons!" His tone guarded, on his face the expression of a man who may hear of a kinsman.

"He was my pathology professor. A fine man! A great man, really! He was very kind to me."

Dr. Kauffman beamed.

"I've never met him, of course."

"Everyone says he's too good for State."

"Yes . . . Well . . ." The animation vanished from Dr. Kauffman's smile. "I expect he's tried elsewhere," he said dryly.

"We've just come from the Clinic," Dr. Runkleman broke in.

"Oh," said Dr. Kauffman. "The Clinic!" And he and Dr. Runkleman looked at each other without expression.

"What did you think of it?" said Dr. Kauffman politely. "All that modern science can offer, eh?"

"Except night calls," said Lucas.

Dr. Kauffman nodded.

"I don't know—we were taught different—maybe it's the new approach . . ."

"I've never turned down a call—night or day—for thirty-five years," Dr. Runkleman said quietly.

"I thought that's what we were for," nodded Dr. Kauffman.

"But are you sure?" Lucas begged. "Are you really sure?"

"Doctor," said Dr. Kauffman gravely, "I'm sorry to have to inform you but doctors are people. We belong to the human race. We have our saints and we have our sinners. It is a gray world. I have been trying to separate black from white for twenty years and the only place I have been successful is in my photographs." He waved to the walls of his office. They were lined with expensive frames, deeply matted pictures.

"You do these?" Lucas asked, surprised.

"Just a hobby. What you might call—you speak German?—Art for *Arzt's* sake."

"I'm sorry. I don't speak German."

"Oh? Too bad! That was a lovely pun. I must remember to tell Martha—my wife—*Arzt* is German for doctor—I think we all need a hobby, preferably something in the arts, we're apt to be so deficient there—"

"Dr. Kauffman won two prizes last year at the county fair," Dr. Runkleman said proudly.

"Ah, that! That! County fairs! No . . . I try . . . I think we should all try . . ."

"I wish I had the time."

"Oh, you! You and that monstrous practice of yours!"

Dr. Runkleman grinned self-consciously.

"Dr. Kauffman and his wife are the art center of Greenville."

"You must meet her sometime—she's out painting now."

"She does beautiful flowers—better than real—"

"No, no! No longer flowers! Now it's trees! She does well, I think. Very well. I see you like art, Doctor? You seem to enjoy looking at my poor efforts. Do *you*, perhaps—"

"Oh, no," said Lucas. "But I was wondering—could you take pictures with your camera—through a microscope?"

Dr. Kauffman stared at him.

"I don't think so."

"He really means it," Dr. Runkleman said significantly.

Dr. Kauffman's face relaxed.

"Oh!" he cried, understanding, he beamed at Lucas, "Ah, my boy! That will wear off! Believe me! We all had it! The dust of the lecture halls will leave your shoulders—the things that seem so important now—you will have time on your hands—I know you! You are a reader! You will turn to culture, you will be welcome in our little group, Mrs. Kauffman will take you under her wing, once a fortnight she has a tea, there's Ames from the lumber yard, you must see some of the things he does in copper! And a new young man, a plumber's helper, remarkable! He was very shy at first, he blows glass, little figurines—and the girls, it's very exciting, you will be surprised—I will tell Mrs. Kauffman you read! I assure you—she'll be much interested!"

"I wish I had the time—"

"Oh, time! Dr. Runkleman will let you off—"

"Anytime!" Dr. Runkleman promised heartily. "Did I tell you? We have a case of erysipelas at the County!"

"Not really!"

"I never thought I'd see one!" Lucas affirmed. "It's as rare as typhoid—"

"A good deal rarer. I think you'll see a case of typhoid before the year is out!"

"I talked to the mayor again," Dr. Runkleman said tonelessly.

Dr. Kauffman shrugged.

"The tenth time? Or the fiftieth? Ah, well! Someday it will strike the school. Until then—"

"Well," said Dr. Runkleman. He rose.

"Come in anytime, Doctor," Dr. Kauffman said warmly. "Our wives must meet! Perhaps Mrs. Marsh paints? Perhaps she would like to paint? Or she has some other outlet? Mrs. Kauffman will take her under her wing—will you tell her?"

"Mrs. Marsh has never had much time for that—she was head operating-room nurse at State Hospital—"

"Ah! I see! Lucky man! Well—if she should change her mind—or you—"

As they drove away Dr. Runkleman shook his head, commiserating.

"He had a tough time when he first came here," he sighed. "Being a Jew and all. Even today—I try to send patients to him, half of them never go, they don't want to go to a Jew, you'd think being a Jew was infectious, or something. He's a good man. Reliable, honest, pretty skillful, not bad at all. I've never heard a word against him. Only—that he's a Jew." He shrugged. "Well—we can't change the world, I guess . . ."

"No . . . But we don't have to join it . . ."

Dr. Runkleman looked at him startled. Lucas said no more. This day he had met two doctors in business, two doctors who did not take night calls and for whom the town of Greenville was a livelihood. And he had seen the secret empire of a man grown rich from seventy-five-cent calls, a man whose secret ambition was to quit his trade and go to play in Australia.

He thought sickly of Avery.

If he had gone with Avery, if he had taught, he would never have found these things out at all. And they were unblinkable, they were plain, they were facts. These were doctors. These wore the red robe. These were the high priests of man's mightiest mystery: himself.

They were out for money. Their worlds revolved around it. They were out for every cent they could get.

Four of them operating, sweating, over a single uncomplicated appendectomy!

"That's the first time I've seen Binyon and Blake since they came to Greenville," Dr. Runkleman said quietly. "Outside of once or twice at the hospital."

"I hope I'm even luckier," Lucas said bitterly.

"You won't see much of any of them," Dr. Runkleman comforted.

"Just Dr. Castle—occasionally Dr. Rankin over in Lepton. We help him out, now and then." He smiled reminiscently.

Lucas asked no questions.

He could not prevent memory but he denied his thoughts to it. He crammed the pathways of his mind with blocking data, with details doggedly stowed, inspected, until the traffic of his mind was jammed with prescriptions, injuries, symptoms, and all the argosies of Medicine he could dispatch. And in the safety of this barricade he spent his days.

In a week his vigilance warily abated. He became slowly aware that the hurt and confusion within him had never been visible to anyone. There were no onlookers to what had happened.

He watched Kristina but Kristina was aware of nothing untoward, to her the incident of Dr. Snider had been a regrettable new instance of something she had known all along, which she regarded with a certain shrugging distaste but which no longer shocked her.

"Once I saw a doctor kick a nurse right in the behind! She made a mistake and he turned around from the patient and grabbed her by the shoulders and pushed her toward the door and ran after her and just as she got to the door he gave her such a kick in the behind!"

He looked at her sullenly, exasperated.

"Then he went right on operating. He was a very good operator. . . . You should have seen him, Luke."

"Yes," he said ironically, "yes, I'm sure—it would have been very interesting." His face hardened. "I suppose nobody reported him?"

"I don't know," she said, troubled. She was not thinking of this at all, now. She was wondering how things stood between Lucas and Dr. Runkleman. That was the important thing, the only thing that mattered. Lucas was like a girl in some ways, but he would live through what he had to live through, there was no use butting your head against a stone wall, you shrugged and stepped over it and went on with your work and it wasn't there.

"Dr. Runkleman thinks a lot of you," she said shyly.

"I think a lot of him," he responded mechanically.

"It's not his fault if things go wrong—he's a big man here, but he has to take the world as he finds it—"

"And he likes me. He has to take the world as he finds it and he likes me. Isn't that what you're trying to say?"

"I just know how you are when you get yourself worked up about something," she answered humbly.

"You like it here, don't you, Kris . . ."

"Yes, I do . . . It's the first home we've ever had . . . You're doing well. In a few years we'll have enough saved—" She broke off.

"To start a practice of my own?"

"Well—why not? Something like that . . ."

"But then I'd have to compete with Dr. Runkleman."

"He's got so many patients—he doesn't know what to do with all he has—it's only natural, he wouldn't expect anything else—it wouldn't be as if you were competing with him, really—"

He stared at her, smiling fixedly, remote from her by the room's distance, by the world that lay between; she reddened and he gazed at her with cruelty.

"He's going to give up here in a year or two," he said gently. "He's going to retire, sell out to me, give me the practice on my own terms."

"No, no!"

He watched exultation rise in her eyes, watched it detachedly, fanned it higher.

"It's all true. He's told me."

"And you never told me—!" But it was joy, not reproach.

"No," he said agreeably.

"And when—?"

"He wants to kill things in Australia. He wants to hunt. That's what he's always wanted. And he's saved his money. And he's made a fortune out of those seventy-five-cent calls. He's sending two boys through med school on the quiet. He owns property all over the place. He's got investments. The market's going up, up, up. When it reaches the place where he's got a thousand dollars a month—a thousand a month for life—he's going to step out. . . . That's when. Whenever that is—six months, a year—at the outside, two."

"Oh, Luke." She rushed into his arms. He felt her mouth on his. Her lips were hot. He remembered a tag from psychiatry, the lecturer's earnest sentence: "You have to buy your woman . . ."

It was true, then. The woman of her was hottest of all for security.

And brutally he took her, thus, took her on the carpet, the floor, a stranger.

When she returned from caring for herself he was reading, there was a wall about him as if a few moments before they had not been threshing, convulsed, whispering and groaning on the floor. He was reading, in his hands was the latest copy of a medical journal, she knew better than to disturb him, she tiptoed away, part of the house. And in the medical journal, immured, he read the articles of his faith.

The month of June was sultry and there were many showers. The fields and orchards were orderly jungles of green. And overnight in the pale green, the deep green, blooms appeared, pink and foam-white and scarlet, the blossoms and the flowers. The colors excited Lucas for a day, then he drove his rounds obliviously. The burgeoning was a circus poster, soon read, delightful with newness, quickly unremarkable.

"They're going to have a hell of a harvest," Dr. Runkleman predicted gravely. "Every farmer in the county will be driving Cadillacs. Maybe," he said wryly, without any real hope, "I can get some of my accounts paid."

"Isn't this a little bit out of our route?" Lucas asked politely.

"I want you to see this. I think it'll interest you. I've got a couple of old girls up here I drop in on occasionally. Two nurses. Came here after the war. I'm afraid one of them's going to lose her foot."

"Two women?" The car had left the macadam and was bumping cautiously around the constant turns of a rough country road, winding through brush and forest.

"I guess that's what they want. They live here all by themselves, must be five miles to the nearest house—" The car stopped before an old weather-beaten house. They waded through weeds hip high, peered through the windows.

"Must be somebody home," Dr. Runkleman said uncertainly. "They make bread, once a week Agnes—she's the well one—drives their old rattletrap into town and sells it—" He knocked on the back door. "Dr. Castle and I take turns making sure they're all right." They waited. They were about to turn away when the door opened suddenly.

A small, birdlike woman in her late fifties, her face lined, her eyes merry, smoothed a faded cotton dress, stood aside.

"Come in! It's you, is it? Come in, come in! Who've you got with you?"

"This is Dr. Marsh—I brought him out to meet you—he's my new assistant."

"My! He's good-looking, isn't he!" She felt Lucas' biceps as he passed through the door.

He blinked at her, pleased and friendly. There was a curious independence about her, an aura of activity and a total unconcern for any attitude or emotion which humans had agreed were important. She seemed to have left them a long time ago.

They walked through the kitchen. Lucas saw a large professional dough mixer, a large stove with two ovens.

"So this is where the bread is baked," he said, trying to open the gambits of neutrality.

She stood by patiently while he inspected the apparatus by which each week she turned out enough home-baked bread to take to Greenville to sell, to buy tobacco and cigarette papers and flour, and yeast, and canned milk and medicine.

"Pretty good, eh?" asked Dr. Runkleman.

"Wonderful! I hope I'm here someday when you're baking. I love the smell of fresh baked bread."

"I've got used to it," she said impersonally, and walked ahead of them into the bedroom.

On the face of the woman who lay in bed there was a resemblance, they might easily have been sisters. And this was odd, Lucas mused, because their faces were not at all alike.

"Gloria," said the first woman, "I brought you a present. Here's another doctor."

In the barely furnished home, its wallpaper peeling here and there, the worn wooden floors almost without cover, the sickroom was startling. There were two beds here, a dresser, one small ailing mirror, half a dozen pictorial calendars, four wooden chairs, four small tables. These tables were arranged around the sick woman's bed. And this bed was as faithful a representation of the function of a hospital bed as backwoods material and nurses' ingenuity could muster. A framework of ordinary pipe stood about it and hanging from the overhead pipes were various slings and pulleys. At the head of the bed a naked bulb dangled from a cord tied to the overhead pipe. Hanging from the wall beside the bed was a heavy iron skillet, and the rope from which it dangled was in turn fastened to a large nail. From this nail, fastened with heavy cord, hung a large iron mixing spoon.

"You curious?" Gloria promptly seized the spoon and hoisting herself by an overhead pulley belabored the skillet. The room rang with the din. She grinned happily.

"That's how she calls me," Agnes smiled.

"We were both nurses long enough to know better than to depend on the decorous light, the decorous buzzer. What are you doing out here, Doc? Dr. Castle was here just a few days ago."

"I wanted you to meet my new assistant. How's the foot?"

"I think we're going to need some more pain pills," Agnes said brightly.

"Yep," said Gloria. "Running low again. You want to see my foot?" And she started slowly to wriggle her foot from beneath the covers. Neither Agnes nor Dr. Runkleman moved to help her. Lucas quickly drew the covers back. "I generally do that by myself," Gloria said quietly.

"I'm sorry," Lucas said, flushing.

"It's all right. It's just that I like to do everything I can by myself. While I still can."

The foot was bluish. The toes were missing. Where the flap had been stitched there were three crater-shaped holes, there was marked erosion.

"Looks like the rats been at it," Gloria said interestedly.

Dr. Castle painted the stump with antiseptic, replaced the loose pads which covered it.

"What do you think?" Gloria asked.

"You're both nurses—what do you think?" Dr. Runkleman smiled.

"Looks like that foot'll have to come off before long." Gloria nodded casually.

"Well, we'll save it a while yet."

"Might take some of the meanness out of her," said Agnes.

"Might make me more attractive to the men," said Gloria. "Boys love one-legged women. Can't run so fast."

"There was a one-legged sailor in the base hospital—remember, Gloria? He was a terror. Pinching every nurse in the place."

"He didn't pinch you! He pinched me!"

"He pinched me black and blue!"

"We were nurses together during the war. Doctor tell you? She's English and I'm American. We met at this base hospital during the war and when it was over we decided what with one thing and another we'd come back here—any place where it was wooded, where there weren't any people. I guess we've seen enough people, eh Agnes?"

"We saw enough of them as nurses. Then the war came and that finished it."

"That capped it. They're brave and they're lousy, they're good and they're bad, and the hell with them. We've seen enough."

"We had when we came here."

"Would you say we're any different now?"

"No, but we can take 'em or leave 'em. Now we can do that. Eight, nine years in this sanitarium and we can take 'em or leave 'em."

"Listen to the damn Britisher!"

"Listen to the crummy Yank!"

"Now you know all about us. Look at him, Agnes! Listen to the gears mesh!"

"I was just thinking—" Lucas protested.

"Two old biddies living all by themselves way out in the wilderness. Two old Lesbians, which one's the man, which one's the woman—"

"We don't really care much for men," Agnes admonished.

"Nor women, either—"

"It's something we got out of the war. Well—when are you coming out again?"

"We'll be along one of these days," Dr. Runkleman grinned, shutting his bag.

"Bring handsome with you. Don't mind me, Doctor, it's such a wonderful pleasure not to have to say 'yes, sir,' 'no, sir' to a doctor any more."

"She's kind, really," said Agnes, "she's got a heart big as a radish. Her heart's all mouth."

Gloria waved gaily to them from the bed.

As they walked back into the kitchen Lucas was about to speak and at the sight of his serious face Agnes shook her head warningly.

"You finished your baking for this week?" Dr. Runkleman asked loudly.

"All done till next week."

They walked outside. She shut the door carefully. She looked up at Dr. Runkleman, her face was a nurse's face now, expressionless, waiting to be told about her patient.

"She's going to lose that foot sooner than she expects," Dr. Runkleman said reluctantly.

"What do you think?" she turned to Lucas.

He shook his head. "I'd take it off now."

She looked back to Dr. Runkleman.

"Maybe we can save it for a week or so, maybe a month longer . . ."

"She needs more pills. She's eating them up."

Dr. Runkleman wrote out a prescription.

"I don't want to make an addict out of her . . ."

"Not yet," Agnes nodded. "Drop in anytime, Doctor." She turned to Lucas. "Gloria likes you. Doc here'll tell you the tongue means nothing."

"What are you going to do without her?" Dr. Runkleman asked.

"We'll face that when we come to it."

"Going to move back to town?"

"I don't think so. I don't see why . . ."

He nodded. "Don't run out of morphine—"

"This'll be enough."

They drove off.

"You see?" asked Dr. Runkleman admiringly. "Have you ever seen anything like that?"

"They've got guts," Lucas nodded soberly.

"They don't need much. They've got each other. And that's their private world. They make a few dollars now and then and grow the rest. But can you imagine anything unlikelier? Two nurses—burying themselves like that!"

"She's going to lose that foot. The whole foot, this time."

"I know. And so does she. You ought to hear her sometimes. She talks to it like it was a human being."

"Thromboangiitis obliterans—Buerger's disease . . ."

"Endarteritis, I'd say . . ."

"Oh? Endarteritis? Really?"

"Yes—I think endarteritis, all right . . ."

"Not Buerger's?"

"No . . . No, I don't think so . . . Let's see. Endarteritis you have inflammation of the interior coat of an artery and replacement tissue obliterating the lumen—"

"And you didn't find veins and arteries breaking down—all the coats affected?"

"I think you can say endarteritis, all right."

"I'm sorry!" Lucas bit his lip, mortified. "I could have sworn—"

"Doesn't matter, really. The blood vessels are breaking down faster and faster. Her foot's rotting away. She's got a sewing scissors. She snips the gangrenous tissue away herself. What she can't reach Agnes snips for her."

"I wonder if we can save the leg . . ."

"I wouldn't say so . . . No . . ."

"The other foot's a little puffy, little blue at the toe tips . . ."

"That'll be next."

He shook his head.

"But what a pair," he smiled, admiringly.

"Amazing!" Lucas echoed obediently. But how had he slipped on endarteritis? With Buerger's she would have lost her foot a long time ago. How had he ever slipped there? It was the first diagnostic error he had made in three years. Really the first? The first to come up! That was sure! And in front of Dr. Runkleman. He compressed his lips angrily.

"Your PU died yesterday afternoon," said Dr. Runkleman.

"No! It was a perforating ulcer, all right?"

"I don't think there's much doubt of it. You hit it right on the nose."

By God, I did! I hit it right on the nose! Lucas marvelled slowly over the uncanny accuracy of his diagnostic hits. He saw the man again, lying on a stretcher outside the operating room, waiting to be wheeled in. He heard Dr. Runkleman ask him to have a look at him. He saw himself approach the man, look at his blue face, his sunk cheeks, his fingers moved as he felt the abdomen again, watched the pain plod across the stubbled face. He saw himself turning away, heard the words "perforating ulcer" blurt out of his mouth, saw the astonishment on Dr. Runkleman's face.

It was a daring thing to say, to say so quickly, to say so positively. He held his breath, Dr. Runkleman was considering this. The nurses wheeled the man in. And after they had robed, when they stood on either side of the operating table, after he had been given a spinal, as they were about to begin, to open him up—

Dr. Runkleman had paused, uncertainly. He looked at the man's blue face.

"Don't cut me," the man said desperately. "Don't cut me," he groaned.

The usual preoperative noise.

"Don't cut you?" Dr. Runkleman was actually answering. Lucas looked up, startled. "Don't cut you?" And Dr. Runkleman, staring hard at the blue face began to draw off his gloves. "All right. All right, if you don't want to be cut—I'll tell you what we'll do . . . We won't cut you!"

He turned and Lucas followed him back to the dressing room. The amazed nurses were beginning the task of taking the man from the operating table, putting him back on the stretcher to wheel him back to bed.

"He did look pretty blue," Lucas said obediently.

"I think he's a goner."

"Cyanotic, all right."

"He'd have died on the table. No use having a death on the surgical record. For nothing."

They dressed silently. Dr. Runkleman was a little indignant at the trick the man had almost pulled on them. They had stopped in the nick of time.

Dr. Runkleman did not like the doomed. He wanted no part of them. He did not want to see them and he did not want to be associated with them. Lucas recollected this dully. Every man had his flaws. His medical flaws. And this was Dr. Runkleman's. And in all else he was a wonderful man. A wonderful, wonderful man. The investments, the involvement with money—well, he was like a happy child, there, it hadn't really become part of him, just a game, a hobby, a conditioning, even, of his hard childhood . . . And someday Lucas would gently show him that you had to face the doomed, that being doomed was just a condition like any other condition . . . Someday he would work it, working gently, infinitely cautious, tactful . . .

But it was PU, after all!

And Dr. Runkleman was right. The man had died that afternoon, brought back to his bed, lay there a while, and died. He would have died on the table.

But PU!

That's what it was!

He'd been right!

"I shouldn't have been so fast," he apologized. "I knew I shouldn't have the minute I said it. It just popped out."

"You know something? I hadn't even been thinking PU."

"Just a hunch, I guess. I know I didn't have time to think."

"You just keep on having hunches like that! Yes—and the debility fellow whose wife kept taking his medicine, who'd ever have thought of malaria? At this level? Three thousand feet up? I never even thought to ask him if he'd been living in the swamps before he came here. And the woman with the melanoma—and the kid with epilepsy that wasn't epilepsy . . ."

He grinned at Lucas admiringly.

"You just keep it up!"

"I won't be that fast again, though. Not on endarteritis, anyway . . ."

"Well, now you've seen my two old girls!"

"Wonderful," said Lucas dutifully. "Just wonderful . . ."

"The human race!" Dr. Runkleman grinned. He shook his head.

Lucas sighed.

"Quite a show," he nodded.

He needed a form that afternoon, Dr. Runkleman was busy, he searched his desk. In a bottom drawer was a large stainless-steel instrument tray. It was heaped high with coins and bills.

Lucas called Miss Snow.

"What's this?" He pointed to the open drawer.

She looked where he pointed, puzzled. Suddenly she saw the money, drew in her breath.

"My God! He's at it again!"

She lifted out the tray, thumped it, exasperated, on the desk.

"For a prudent, thrifty man, he sometimes does the darndest kid things!"

"There must be six or seven hundred dollars there!" Lucas marvelled.

"All of that! And he'll keep it right there and never tells me and I'll send the bills out—"

"But what for?"

She firmed her lips. She shrugged.

"It's just a little trick of his. I don't know whether you've noticed it or not," she said dryly, "but Doctor doesn't exactly hate money. By the way, where were you two this afternoon when the sheriff called?"

"We went out to see the two nurses, the two old nurses—the ones that live by themselves—"

"I might have known. Well—I handled it all right. He doesn't have to appear. He's such a little boy—he knew the sheriff was coming today—"

"What for? What happened?"

"You didn't hear? Why, they caught that chiropractor—caught him red-handed—he was right in the middle of an abortion when they walked in—I think they said the girl's mother tipped them off—anyway, they got him! And Doctor won't have to testify—"

"Won't have to? But he'll *want* to!"

"That's not what he told me," she smiled kindly. "No, and he's right! What in the world would he want to get mixed up in a thing like that for?"

"Miss Snow, I'm sure you're making a mistake—" Lucas struggled to keep his voice even. "Dr. Runkleman's just been waiting for that man to be caught! I know he'll be tickled to death to give evidence—"

"Then you don't know Dr. Runkleman," she laughed. "Why, I believe he'd take a trip out of the state before he'd give evidence in a thing like that! And I'd be the last person to say he's wrong. What do they need him for? They caught him, didn't they? That's what I told the sheriff. Not that I had to work too hard." She winked broadly. "You know what we're treating the sheriff for! I did just what Dr. Runkleman said, I said, 'Sheriff, Dr. Runkleman said to be sure and ask you if those pills are working.' " She chuckled. "He shut up like a clam. He said it was an open and shut case, probably, and if it wasn't he'd be back. I told him he'd better not. He nodded, and swallowed, and went on out. So *that's* taken care of!"

She picked up the tray of money.

"Now, all I have to do is find out who he got this from—and *that's* taken care of!" She sighed in mock despair and walked to the door.

Lucas stood, gazing after her.

"It's all right, Doctor," she said earnestly. "Don't worry about it . . ."

"No," said Lucas. "No, I won't worry about it. . . . Thank you, Miss Snow."

"After you've been here a while . . ." She nodded reassuringly. She winked at him and was gone.

And now it was too much for him. It was altogether too much. It was too much to be sensible about, and he had never known what being sensible about anything meant, anyway. It had something to do with behaving as everybody else was behaving in the place where he found himself, and not being too upset by anything no matter how terrible it might be, and not wanting too much and not thinking too much and not caring too much. And when it all boiled down it meant going along with everybody else and not making anybody uncomfortable by being different. That's what sensible meant. It had to do with the senses, with the emotions. It was a reflex, a reactor. It had nothing to do with the production of thought or the function of mind.

There was nothing to be sensible about.

He sat in the empty operating room at the County, sat on the table, swinging his legs slowly, secure in the dimness of the dark room, part of his surroundings.

No one would think of looking for him here. There was little chance anyone would come to the operating room at this hour. It was night, and the patients were asleep, and the case he had just stitched up had been wheeled off to bed, and for all anybody knew the doctor had gone home too. He was alone. It was healing to be alone, it was like a sedative. And the darkness was ineffably kind. It was possible to think in darkness as it was possible under no other condition of man's living, to be able to see the darkness; and to think.

There was nothing to think about, either.

It was all remembering.

But when the remembering was done it made a sum of things, it made a sum and the sum was a world, his world, everything that had happened to him, everything he wanted, everything, everybody, and not only here but everywhere.

And it was wrong.

What was happening was wrong. It was sweeping him along with it, and if he was sensible it would go right on carrying him, farther and farther until he was remote from what he was, remote from where he was, where he had won to, one with the rest, indistinguishable from that which he fled.

And there was something to do. There must be something to do before it was too late. Because it must never be too late. Because life, what had been given him and what had shaped him, could be detestable. Could be so detestable that there was no point continuing with it.

There was only one thing he really wanted to do. There was only one life he wanted to live.

And there had to be a way. There had to.

And there had to be an answer. An answer to everything that was going on around him, something that would jibe, that would make sense, that would prove that what he was seeing wasn't true at all, that it hadn't happened, even.

Yes, that was a way of thinking about it. But was it true?

Because now he had to know.

Now there wasn't any going on any longer. Not this way.

He slid off the operating table. He hated to leave the darkened room, he knew as he walked toward the door that in a few more inexorable steps he would be in the light again, back in the world, but there was nothing else to do, he passed a nurse, she was startled, she thought he had gone home hours ago, he smiled, nodded briefly.

"I wonder if you'll be needing me tomorrow," he said next morning.

"Tomorrow?" Dr. Runkleman asked surprised.

"It's Sunday."

"That's right! By George, it is! Why sure! Go ahead! What are you going to do? Take the missus out on a picnic?"

"Well, no," said Lucas. "I thought I'd drop back and spend the day with some of the boys back at State."

"Nothing wrong is there? I mean, nothing's troubling you I could straighten out—"

"Wrong? You mean here? Oh, Heavens no!"

"Anytime, you know— I may not notice it—don't hold it in—"

"You bet!" said Lucas affectionately. He shook the older man's hand.

"I won't be back till late tomorrow night, might come in early Monday morning," he told Kristina at dinner.

"Where you going? What's happened?"

"Nothing's happened. I've just told you I might not be home tomorrow until late or early Monday morning. Does something have to have happened?"

"You just tell me out of a blue sky—"

"I'm going back to State. I'm going to take a trip. I'm going to get on a train and I'm going back to State. Then when I'm through, I'm going to get on the train again. And I'm going to get off at Greenville—"

And all the time he was being cruel he knew he was being cruel and he could not help himself.

"Good! It'll do you good! The way you been working—"

"All right," he said. "Now you know."

He picked up a medical journal.

"Maybe you'll see Avery. Give him my regards . . ."

He nodded.

For a while, after she had done the dishes, she simply sat and watched him read. She thought of where he was going and the thought of the hospital came into her mind, and she remembered that for a while and she remembered her days at the hospital and it was comforting to remember suddenly her own bailiwick, and the doctors nodding to her, for she was head operating-room nurse, and the gauze wound around her head like a badge, and the respectful eyes as she passed. She smiled, she sighed, she looked about her home, her own home, it had been a great change, but here she was. She thought of her cape hanging in the closet and a little pang of sympathy for it touched her heart, the cape of which she was still so proud hanging there in the closet, waiting for her whenever she wanted. On an impulse she got up quietly, tiptoed warily past Lucas. In the other room she walked more freely, she went to the closet, the cape was there, hanging straight and dignified and patient. She touched it lovingly a moment, making it hers again, telling it she was there. Then she took it briskly from its hanger and carried it into the kitchen. She set up the ironing board. She plugged in the iron.

She was lost in her ironing, concentrating, when she heard Lucas behind her.

"What in the name of God are you doing?"

"I just thought I'd iron this—I was sitting there and you were reading and I just thought—I didn't think you'd hear me."

"You were singing—"

"Oh, Luke! I'm sorry! My God, I didn't know—"

"That's your cape, isn't it? What the hell are you pressing that for, this time of night?"

"I just thought I'd—you can't tell! I might be using it, sometime!"

"Use it?" He tried to unravel that for a moment, tried to enter her thinking processes, gave it up.

"Jesus Christ!" he said. "I give up!"

He went into the bedroom, he undressed quickly, he lay carefully on his own side, turned his back. He thought of the train, a wave of happiness drowned his irritation. He shut his eyes. When Kristina came in he was asleep.

He had a moment's terror next day, advancing to Avery's doorstep, that Avery might not be home, might have gone away. On the train, on the way down, he had doggedly tried to read, tried to look at passing scenery, at the faces of fellow passengers, to think of nothing, to keep his mind a blank. Now all that he was bursting to say inundated his mind, and he rang the bell in a panic. There was no answer. He gaped at the door incredulously. Then in an access, part terror, part rage, he rang it again and again and again.

The door opened.

Avery looked at him in astonishment.

An hour later, the fervor of reunion over, a little silence fell. Lucas tried to think of a way to begin. Avery looked at him sympathetically.

"You haven't changed much," Lucas blurted lamely.

"And you didn't come all this way to discuss my looks."

"I've got a lot to talk to you about . . ."

"That's all right. Want to take a drive?"

"Sure! Hey! Wait a minute! You mean you've got a car?"

"Haven't you heard, my boy? There's a boom on. Even poor professors have their Daimlers, nowadays. Mine's a Ford. I put two hundred dollars into something called U.S. Carbon—"

"Who told you?"

"I took a financial page and got a pin and stuck it in—"

"My God," said Lucas, as they walked to the car, "can you imagine how all this must be affecting Alfred?"

"Alfred didn't have such a good time of it, at first. Little stories kept drifting back. While he was here he represented the whole world of riches. He was the rich boy. He was riches itself."

"Well, you know what he wanted. New York should have been like turning him loose in the Treasury."

"No—it wasn't that way. New York—why in New York rich boys are no novelties. He had to fight any number of rich boys, an army of them, many of them richer than he, for that Park Avenue practice. And since riches didn't count in the field he was competing in—" Avery paused. He sighed—"why he had to fall back on knowledge and skill . . ."

They thought about this.

"Are you doing all right, Avery? Do you like teaching?"

Avery thought a moment.

"It's all right," he decided finally. "Sometimes it's—" he waved his hand helplessly— "sometimes it would make even *you* happy!"

"What do you think about it—for me?"

"You want to teach?"

"I don't know . . ."

"Oh, come on, Luke!"

"This is not for me!" He sat up straighter. "I can't go on with it any longer. I've had enough. I've had all I can take. I know it's not going to get better. It's like a doom. I know it's going to get worse. I'm sick of wincing. I'm sick of going on, wooden, pretending nothing has happened. I'm sick of what's happening. I can't go on any longer . . . You don't know . . . I'm sick . . ."

"Hell, Luke. We used to talk about it. Bull sessions when you weren't around. What you were in for. Feeling the way you do. What makes you think I don't know?"

"You couldn't possibly know. You think it's some vague thing of ideals, don't you? Some boyish-girlish idealism? Some shock to the delicate sensibilities!"

"It's a problem of adjustment, all right—"

"And that's just where you're wrong. God Almighty! If I ever have to adjust to that! To what I've seen! To what I know! Adjust? I'll never adjust! I can't! I wouldn't know how! Adjust to murder, maybe? Because, by God, I've seen murder—not mistakes, not error in judgment, not bad luck! Plain, unadulterated, premeditated murder! By a doctor! A doctor of Medicine!"

"Take it easy, Luke!"

"Shall I?" You don't believe it? You don't know Snider. I'll tell you something about Dr. Snider. He's an old man. He chews tobacco. He's forgotten most of the Medicine he ever knew. He never knew much. And he's in charge of a county hospital. He comes cheap. This is a doctor I'm talking about. Remember that. And he kills patients. I don't know how many he's killed by mistake. God only knows that! There's a cold X-ray room at the County. They keep it cold. And when the senile patients—he has them wheeled in, he takes their blankets away—pneumonia—enemy of the young, friend of the aged—he kills them! He plans their death. And he executes them. To make room for more."

"The son-of-a-bitch! Why don't you report him?"

"Because he's an old man. Because Dr. Runkleman doesn't want me to. Because they die anyway. What's the answer, Avery? Is he right, after all? That's the intolerable thing! That's the horror! Is *he* right?"

"Christ! You don't expect me to answer that, do you?"

And Lucas told the story of Carlile Emmons.

"I won eight hours. And then he died, anyway."

"What's happened to you? It isn't up to you or me to say when a man's to die. This time you won eight hours. Christ! Next time you may win a day! What's Runkleman say?"

"He says Snider's an old man. In a way he says what Snider says. He says pretty soon Snider'll be too old and have to quit. And until he does —well, he's an old man. He can't go on much longer. And I like Runkleman. He's been swell to me. He's a really superb operator. I liked him from the minute I set eyes on him. And after I saw him operate the first time—well, you'd have to see him. Then you'd know how I feel about him. How you'd feel about him yourself."

"But he knows what's going on. And he won't report him . . ."

"Oh, there's been some wild rows between them. I've heard stories. Once he threw him bodily out of the operating room. I tell you it's fantastic how bad that Snider is! He can't even give an anesthetic."

"And Runkleman—"

"I don't know, Ave . . . I can't take it any more . . . He's all I've said, kind and wise and skilled." He looked miserably away. He swallowed. "And little by little it comes out—he hates death—he hates the dying—when a case is hopeless he runs, he can't even look the patient in the eye, he doesn't want to see them—he's got a kind of horror—it goes in the record, a doomed man is just a black mark, a sure black mark—he gets a little mad, even, when they wheel one in . . . It's—it's embarrassing—it makes you sick in the pride you feel for him . . ."

Avery looked down.

"But otherwise?"

"All right, that's a foible. He's a fighter. He fights hard. He's got a million dollars. If he's got a cent, he's got a million dollars. He was a poor boy, and he's scared of poverty, and he won't charge people more than seventy-five cents, a dollar, two dollars a call."

Avery whistled.

"That's all he charges. That's all he's ever charged. For thirty years. And out of that he owns apartment houses, he owns property, he's got stocks and bonds, he's almost ready to retire. That's what he's working for. He's honest, and he's able, and he works his head off—so he can retire on an income of a thousand dollars a month—and go hunt animals in Australia!"

"We're not all the same, Luke. You know that— I'm not saying it's right—I'm just saying—"

"Sixty patients an afternoon! That's what we handle! Sixty! Two or three operations every morning. Calls at night. And sixty patients an afternoon."

"Sixty! But you can't—"

"No, you can't possibly do them justice. That's right. All you can do is treat their symptoms. The ones you don't miss. A pill here, a prod there, adhesive tape, tonic, soothing lotions, keep 'em going. Just dab a little on and keep 'em going. That's not Medicine, Ave. That's not Medicine. And every patient I handle I know it's wrong, it's dead wrong, and I'm doing it, and my guts turn over."

"He'll cut down—he's bound to—"

"No, he won't cut down. Because the money keeps rolling in. And nothing happens. The patients muddle along. There's no reason why he should cut down. Not from his viewpoint. And what are you going to do? Are you going to turn a man away when he asks help? Are you going to do that?"

"If you've got too many to handle, you can tell them so. Jesus, Luke! You can't treat them all! There must be other doctors there—"

"There's Binyon and Blake. They operate a clinic. My God, they've got every shiny gadget known to man, they charge two and three and four times his rates—and on top of that they have to call in two more doctors to take out a simple appendix! Are you going to send a fellow man to them to be fleeced? And probably bungled? You can't do that. He's too kind for that. And there's Castle, a fine, decent, wise man. Only he's old, too old, bad heart, got all he can handle. And there's Kauffman. And he's a Jew. And if you recommend to one of these peasants that he go to a Jew he's insulted."

"There's not enough doctors. Anywhere! That's sure."

"You get to thinking about that. You can't help it. Why aren't there enough doctors? Who's controlling the volume so that everybody shares the wealth, so there's five to ten thousand a year to go around for everybody? Who's responsible for this planned scarcity, this guaranteed income, this rigged deal so everybody will stay fairly honorable and not start a fee-cutting scramble? So that we'll be scarce and people will stay humble and respectful against their hour of need? Who's responsible for the state rules, the reciprocities? Why can't a doctor practice wherever he wants to? Any grade A college teaches the same thing, the same Medicine, the graduates are all alike. Who set up the laws, who lobbied them through, the laws that regulate the number of doctors in a state? It's like a fair-trade act. Who did it?"

Avery shook his head.

"I—I can't answer you . . ."

"Oh, yes you can! You can answer me, all right! This is Medicine! This is my Medicine! This is what I believe in! This is my God! This is what I dreamed of when I was a kid, my first dream, the only dream I know. Nobody can tell me it's right. Because I know it's wrong. I know! I know what Medicine is."

"Well, Luke, when you come right down to it, it's what I teach. It's the application of physical forces to end or alleviate disease and suffering and to prolong life."

"It's that. And to a doctor Medicine is a way of living. Money is the force of life for a businessman. Honors are the goal of soldiers and statesmen. Life is the grail of a doctor. Mix his purpose, divert it, dilute it, change his prime objective and he's not a doctor any more. He's practicing honor, or money, or social position. No! He has courage, because he's careless of reward. He has honor because it is not his purpose. He has standing because his days confer it. And money is not his measure, nor his hope. And don't tell me I'm a crackpot. Don't tell me I'm an idealist. I knew that about Medicine before I ever came here. And when I came here that's what I was taught. And that's what you were taught. And that's what you're teaching!"

"That's what I'm teaching, Luke. That's what we both learned. No matter what people do, that's what Medicine really is. That's what *you've* got to remember. Nothing's been changed."

"I know what's happening to me. I know what I'm becoming. It's happening little by little. I'm conforming. I'm going along with the bunch. I'm surrendering. I'm doing it with my eyes open. And someday—"

"You're wrong."

"I'm scared. I'm thinking about ten years from now."

"I knew a priest once and he told me the only reasonable prayer for a doctor was: 'Please God, help me to answer my own prayers.' —Isn't Kris any help to you?"

"Kris!"

"Don't underrate Kris, boy. Don't ever!"

"You know what I did, don't you? She put me through Medicine."

"I know—I know all about it—"

"But you don't have to live with her. You don't have to worry every minute what she's going to say next, you don't have to wince at 'ain't' and 'didn't ought to done' and that laugh and that complete, fantastic, utter lack of understanding of anything that's going on—"

"What a bunch of drawing-room tricks stacked against the girl who put you through Medicine."

"It's not for me. I'm stuck with everything she is and everything she can never be, I don't love, I don't even like her."

"You did her a dirty trick, Luke."

"And I'm paying for it. And don't you forget it."

"How the hell do you figure to pay for it! What good does your suffering do her? Christ, a girl like that'd give you her skeleton if you asked for it!"

"You don't know what it's like. How could you? All you ever have seen was how quaint she was—for a few minutes . . ."

"She was the best operating-room nurse I've ever seen in my life. She knew her job as well as I'll ever know mine. She's honest, she's self-respecting, whether you know it or not she knows you inside out, she's your woman, there's nothing you can ever ask her she won't do. Because she knows that. She knew what she was doing when she married you. And it didn't stop her. She knew what you loved best. She knew what you were already married to. I've always liked her, Luke. I think she's a swell dame. I think she could help you."

"How help me? Change Medicine? Change things as they are? You're not going to tell me it'd be a comfort to talk things over, are you? Get it off my chest? Even if she had the remotest idea what I was talking about?"

"What's the answer? What's in your mind, Luke?"

"How's teaching, Avery?"

"Why, it's all right. It's pretty surprising. You get a couple of hungry students and you'd be surprised how good teaching is! And you know part of you is going out with them, part of you is healing a patient, somewhere—it's fine, Luke! It makes up for a lot!"

Lucas nodded. His face was paler.

"You mean you want to teach?"

"Can you get me on?"

Avery looked at him open-mouthed.

Lucas nodded.

"I've made up my mind. Now I know."

"I'm going to tell you what teaching is. There's a Snider in every class. And there's nothing you can do about it. There's anywhere from three to a dozen nuggeteers—and there's nothing you can do about it. There's a large group of tradesmen, and a large group who'll get through because it's what their parents want them to do. There's a handful of pride-drunkards. And there's a handful of doctors. Fellows who like Medicine, or fellows who love Medicine—and once in a great while fellows who can't imagine anything else. And there's the same pompous asses on the platforms. You sit there raging, while they propound something that went out with the Ark or even something downright false. But there's nothing you can do about it. You have to sit there and smile and take it. And you can't get away from it. It comes to you concentrated, every day. It's all there, all concentrated in four walls. And that's a side of teaching, too. Remember that."

He paused a moment, watching this digested, watching Lucas' face, watching the protest change to fear, to hopelessness.

⁎ CHAPTER 28

July had almost gone. July was a month of burns, of penetrating wounds from hayforks, of wrenched shoulders— "My God! Is it broken, Doc?"—and the pale face, the eyes seeing the hayfield only half mowed; July was a month of bloody vomit from chemical-spray poisoning, of heat prostration, near-drownings, hay fever.

And the people bearing these injuries crowded the office, their eyes amazed, their eyes frightened, their beings brought stock-still with alarm, presenting their persons open-mouthed, a familiar body suddenly become alien and bizarre.

And the injuries were processed, treated, the bleeding stanched, cuts stitched, bones set, bodies physicked, dosed, repaired, released, set upon their mended ways in a world in which the same mischance would maim them again, or mischances not dreamed of, a mischance for any action.

Each day Lucas saw this repeated, saw the grim struggle of man for survival through objectives most of which assured his destruction, and, powerless to check the trampling rush toward safety shut his lips and mended the trampled and the trapped, the trampling and those they trampled upon.

Of the people who bore their injuries to the office he knew little. There were some whose personalities were for a moment arresting before his concentration on their illness obliterated their pattern and made him unconscious of them as persons. There were others who were for a moment or so irritating. But in the end, in the sum of all his contacts with them, these people were injuries. Their faces and their names linked them to the disease to which he addressed himself. Mrs. Jones was the hip cancer. Mr. Smith the broken arm, Miss Lawrence the adjustment problem, Baby Johnson the summer diarrhea with otitis media.

Dr. Runkleman, who had acquired ease and habit in the day's program, who performed instinctively and mechanically and without waste motion or thought, actually had leisure of a sort during the crowded days, leisure for small talk with patients. For Lucas, to know a man's aim was enough. If he was a farmer it was all-important that his injured arm be made to function in the movements of farming, to pitch hay, to milk, to plow. His job was the restoration of function and the relief of pain and he worked at this exuberantly and he felt toward his patients the pride, love, delight which an architect feels passing a building he planned, which an engineer feels watching traffic pass over a bridge he has mended.

But if he treated people as bodies he was nevertheless sensible of them as entities, he had acquired an empathy which amazed him with its accuracy. He was able, in an instant, to see the world as they saw it, he could gauge their honesty to a nicety, he knew clearly, in that first instant of appraisal, to what lengths they might go and of how much evil they were capable, and even the reasoning by which they might explain themselves. He was thus seldom amazed and almost always protected.

He did not, however, view people with the delight and amusement of Job, his father. Each new revelation was a disillusionment even though he expected the disillusionment and was confident of it and he hated the disillusionment, and was hurt by it. He wanted to live more and more alone. His illusions were all in Medicine. He had always been secure there. It was his one sanctuary. And now he was full of fear when he thought about this sanctuary, and determinedly, he thought about it almost never.

Dr. Runkleman noticed in Lucas signs of fatigue, and they made him uneasy for he had a deepening affection for Lucas and he tried uncomfortably to think of a way to tell Lucas not to work so hard, not to invest so much of himself in the daily cases, not to take it all so seriously. It was very difficult to tell that to a young man who had so obviously no other interest but Medicine and who loved it each day more intensely and without any sign of a letup, a tapering off, at all. A man desiring an assistant might be prepared to accept philosophically in an otherwise acceptable assistant interests, outside interests, which would decrease the amount of time he could potentially give his job. But Lucas had not even the suspicion of an outside interest, nothing interested him, nothing but Medicine. You could not, in fairness, step up to such a young man and say to him: "You are giving me more than I bargained for, more than I was prepared to accept—and, for your sake—more than I want."

But there came a day, inevitably, when Lucas paused for a moment between cases, and sighed.

"You're doing too much," Dr. Runkleman said promptly.

Lucas put down a spasm of irritation.

"You think we're handling too many cases?"

"It's the way you go on. They're not going to thank you when you're dead."

"You think I'm devoting too much time to any one case?"

"I don't mean that—"

"I'm not tired, really. If you could handle all this alone before you got me I guess I can't say we're handling too many cases, can I?"

"You know in a way I kind of have to answer to Mrs. Marsh—she'll be in here one day climbing all over me—what are you doing to my husband!"

"Kris?" For a moment Lucas forgot Dr. Runkleman's swerve from the challenge of discussing the number of daily cases.

"Women worry, my boy. We've got to think of the women. You ought to take her out, now and then. Have a little fun. A doctor's wife—it can be plenty lonesome . . ."

"You think Kris is lonesome?"

"Well," said Dr. Runkleman uncomfortably, "one minute a full day as head operating-room nurse—next minute dropped in a small town, cooped up in five rooms, nothing to do all day—"

"But she never did anything else! When she was through for the day she'd go home to the nurses' quarters, or go to a show, or go for a walk, or more likely go over and visit a Swedish friend of hers—"

"Most women like to gad a little . . ."

"Why, she's got the whole town to gad in! The whole day to herself!"

"Do the both of you good. There's some nice people here in town, people you haven't had time to meet yet, real nice, cultured people you wouldn't believe lived here . . ."

"We're pretty plain folks," Lucas said levelly.

Why, he's ashamed of her, Dr. Runkleman thought, astonished. And he tried to imagine what it was in Kristina that Lucas could be ashamed of.

"Well," he sparred, "don't get me in Dutch for working you too hard."

"I love it," said Lucas. "I love every minute of it. But now that you've brought it up—I've been wondering—I don't know quite how to put it—"

"A raise? I've been thinking about a raise—"

"For me? Good God, no! I've never even thought—"

"You've earned it, by George! I was saying to Castle just yesterday—"

"No, no! Really, Doctor! Don't even think of it! What I had in mind—"

"A vacation! That's it! We both need one! We'll start figuring right away—two weeks for you—two weeks for me—you haven't even seen our lake region!"

"I just can't help but feel we're handling too many cases. For them, I mean. So many, we can't do justice to any of them. That Mr. Norris, for instance. There's a case in point. How can you handle sixty patients a day and not miss ones like Mr. Norris—"

"You can't hit them all. The X-ray plainly showed a tumor of the third cervical—we were absolutely justified—"

"And yet if we'd had the time, sir—if I'd only read the history a little more carefully—"

"I missed whatever you missed—the man comes to us with a simple pain at the tip of his left shoulder—the X-ray shows a tumor of the third cervical—"

"That's just it. But the history showed his shoulder pain followed the perforation of a gastric ulcer."

"That's all right. But after the X-ray showed—even if the tumor *did* turn out to be in his thyroid—"

Lucas shook his head grimly.

"I should have taken the time to think. If his history showed a perforating gastric ulcer I should automatically have ruled out probable formation of an abscess under the left leaf of the diaphragm—"

Dr. Runkleman's brows drew together.

"So that was the shoulder pain—up the phrenic nerve and out along the branch that runs to the tip of the shoulder . . . ?" He looked at Lucas admiringly. Then he shrugged. "Well, we were absolutely justified . . . and the tumor's out anyway!"

He sighed.

"You can't hit 'em all. The man's walking around, good as new—"

"I know . . . I wish we'd pulled the left phrenic nerve, too. Because that's what we should have done. While we were at it. Because sooner or later—"

Dr. Runkleman grinned. The anxious look left his face.

"You're a perfectionist, my boy—"

"No, no! That would only be sound Medicine. Sooner or later he's going to—"

"You can't practice Medicine that way. You can try. I don't say you shouldn't try. But it can't be done. You can't work up a complete case on anybody. Ever. A lifetime's too short. And even if you ever got finished—a whole bunch of new stuff would have been discovered and you'd have to start evaluating all over again. So don't torture yourself. Believe me!"

"Perhaps you're right."

"But you don't believe it."

"Sixty cases a day—sixty cases to handle in one afternoon—even if we didn't operate in the mornings, have emergency operations in the afternoons, didn't have to go out on calls—"

"You think we're handling too many . . ."

"I do! I honestly do! It isn't only the Norris case—it's wondering how many others I've missed—how much I've given to those I haven't missed."

"You see, there's one thing you're missing. They're getting what they want. They're getting all they're prepared to buy. That's in time as well as money. People get suspicious when you start spending time with them. They know it's going to cost them money. They won't stand still for tests. All they want is to be patched up and sent on their way. And if you try to give them any more—believe me!—they'll just go to another doctor. They don't want the ultimate resources of medical science. Not if they have to pay for it. And if you gave it to them free it would cost them money anyway, in the time spent when they could be earning."

He shook his head, he paused, he stared at the wall. And the ghostly faces of tens of thousands were there, full of pain and suspicion and desperation and cautious hope and apprehension and cupidity, figures with one hand on the pain, the other on the purse.

"No," he resumed gently, "they come here, they've got a pain, I treat the pain, I treat the cause, if there's anything badly wrong I operate. And for the rest, I keep them going. Just take away the immediate problem and send them on their way. I keep their fees to a minimum. That's what they want. In the end it comes to this: you can't practice Medicine. You've got to treat people. It's people who shape and direct the Medicine you practice. They're the ones who make the rules."

"But surely there's a compromise—"

"You don't believe that, do you? What I just said?"

"I—I'd like to . . . I haven't been through what you have . . ."

"Because if you could you'd see you were just bucking a stone wall. Sooner or later you'll have to come around to giving them what they want. Or else you won't have any patients." He shrugged delicately. "It's their bodies, after all. We don't own them. All we've got is a license to practice on them."

"But isn't there a point when you have so many you can't give them even the minimum they're paying for—whether they know it or not?"

"I don't know," said Dr. Runkleman honestly. "I don't know what the minimum is. I've never really had any bad luck—not enough to scare any number away—and they keep coming, I know how much money means so I don't charge them much, and they know that, and I give them the best I've got and they seem to get along all right—and they keep coming."

He shook his head.

"I know about your thyroid friend. He's coming back. We'll have to treat him for that other thing. I know that. But it can't be helped. We just don't have the time. You've got to keep them going. You can keep twenty going in the time you'd spend running down one case history like the thyroid man. I don't know how you feel about it—maybe twenty people have twenty times as much right to life as one. You can't neglect your twenty while you're running down your one."

"I don't mean turn them away, exactly—"

"No, you won't turn them away. You'll do what I do. You'll see all that come, you'll do the best you can, you'll spread your time out to cover them all. You'll make mistakes. Some will die on you that you know shouldn't have. And some will get well you didn't have any right to expect. And it won't make any difference. They'll keep right on coming."

He sighed, tiredly.

Lucas was silent. He knew Dr. Runkleman's way was wrong. It was not Medicine. It had nothing to do with a sacred obligation. It was Dr. Runkleman's practice. It was Dr. Runkleman's problem. It would never be his. He knew the right way too well. There was only one right way. There were not two Medicines. There was only one.

Miss Snow knocked.

"It's Mr. Cosgrove," she said apologetically.

A slim man, short, dark, in his early thirties, slipped into the room. Behind heavy horn-rimmed glasses his eyes flicked over them while his mouth grimaced a smile.

"Hold the ambulance," he protested. "I'm not sick, put down that knife—"

"This is Ben Cosgrove—" Dr. Runkleman grinned as a mastiff might grin at the barking of a terrier—"the town lawyer. Ben, I'd like for you to meet my new assistant—"

"You're Marsh, aren't you? Don't let this bargain-basement floorwalker give you any wrong ideas. I'm not the only lawyer in town. There's a couple of other shysters here."

"I'm amazed and taken aback!"

"Don't let it spoil your day."

"I'll work on it," Lucas promised. He rose. "Will you be needing me, Dr. Runkleman?"

"Well," said Dr. Runkleman judiciously, "not unless Ben here has finished being the Bad Man of Greenville. What about it, Ben? Is the performance over?"

"Performance is over," Cosgrove said, unruffled. "I've got an idea how we can get Granite to come out for a water system. You're the last on my list. We're going to meet tonight. At Granite's house."

"Ben's been right with us all along," Dr. Runkleman admitted.

"Nothing to puzzle over, Marsh. So far as I'm concerned it's a contest. That's my sole interest. I'm a troublemaker. You and Runkleman—and Castle and Kauffman—you're noble knights out to slay the dragon Typhoid. Me, I'm in it purely for the hell raising. So far we've tried a variety of pressures. We've had committees who tried to sell civic pride. A committee of ministers tried to sell him on the sanctity of public service. We hit him with a committee of doctors who tried to scare him with the danger to public health. We even rounded up schoolteachers who tried to get a tear out of him for the poor, poor children. So far Granite is granite. We haven't made a dent."

He leaned back and made an arch of his finger tips.

"What's your brainstorm, Ben?"

"It's been wide open all this time. And none of us ever noticed it."

He turned to Lucas.

"You ever hear of the Trojan horse?"

"I remember it very well."

"Well, don't forget it. Don't forget anything that has to do with

Greece. Because that's where we've got our sucker. The way to hit Granite is with Granite himself."

"I don't understand, Ben."

"There's a silly sucker in every human. If you want to lick a human don't try reason, don't appeal to nobility, common sense, or law. Find his sucker point. And Granite's sucker point is culture. He's an intellectual snob. And his intellectual hobby is six pages of Plato he once read, two paragraphs of Aristotle, and a short guide to the history of Greece."

Dr. Runkleman sighed. Then he leaned back and smiled.

"No dice, eh?" Cosgrove shrugged imperturbably. "You don't see how a grown man, the mayor of a whole community, can fall for anything so silly. What about you, Doc?"

"I hardly know the man," Lucas temporized.

"I'll get you a silver basin so you can wash your hands and ask me what is truth. You know men, don't you? Both of you? You've treated a few ministers for a dose of clap, haven't you?"

"What's on your mind, Ben? What do you propose to do exactly?" Dr. Runkleman frowned.

"I'm going to try to use Granite against himself. I've gathered the intellectuals of this backhouse. Those whose good opinion of him Granite is most likely to value. You two are included."

Dr. Runkleman shrugged.

"Well, there's nothing wrong in it that I can see—"

"I don't care whether you see anything wrong in it or not. You want the water system. We've tried everything else." He rose. "You coming?"

"All right, Ben," Dr. Runkleman sighed. "Who else did you say—"

"The cream of the town. Castle, Kauffman and his art-mad wife—Harriet Lang, representing practical culture—Bemis Shedd, representing literature and our esteemed local bladder—me, representing law and philosophy—and you two, representing science, young and old. Bring your wife, Marsh. Favors for the ladies, popcorn for the kids."

"Okay, Ben," Dr. Runkleman nodded. Then he frowned. "Did you ask Binyon and Blake?"

"They won't come. No typhoid—no business."

"They're probably busy." Dr. Runkleman's tone was cool.

Cosgrove snorted. He shrugged.

"See you tonight," he said wearily. The door closed behind him.

Lucas and Dr. Runkleman looked at each other.

"What do you think?" Dr. Runkleman said finally.

"Of him?"

"No. Not Ben. Everybody knows Ben. He thinks he's a communist. Wait till you hear him on Medicine. Not Ben. What do you think of his proposition?"

Lucas shrugged.

"You know the mayor. You know him better than I do. He seemed to be a man who wanted approval, all right. He kept quoting stuff—"

"Maybe . . . Maybe so . . . I was thinking of everybody being a sucker . . . I'd never admit it to Ben . . . I guess it's true, all right—in a way, maybe—in a limited way . . ."

"I don't think it's got a chance," said Lucas. "I think he's just set up a situation which he hopes will humiliate Granite, pay him back for opposition, get in some licks. I think that's all he's really after. But—I guess we've got to go, all the same."

"I guess so," Dr. Runkleman said reluctantly. Then he brightened. "Say! This is a good chance for Mrs. Marsh to get out."

"She doesn't mind staying home, you know. She really likes it. She may not even want to go—"

"Well, you try. Tell her she's going to meet some of the nicest people in town. Wait! I'll go with you!"

Kristina's mouth opened when she heard the news. She swallowed. Her face became radiant.

"I get ready right now!"

"Kris! It's not till eight-thirty! Take it easy!"

"Sting him good, Mrs. Marsh. Buy yourself a new hat!"

"I don't need no hat. I just got to get a few things.—Luke! You be home early for dinner?"

"I'll try," Lucas said shortly. He edged out the door.

"You could go just as you are and put them all to shame, Mrs. Marsh," Dr. Runkleman said admiringly.

"Ah, you! What you ought to do is get married yourself. I know lots of fine Swedish girls you could buy hats for, eh Luke?"

"You sure you want to go?" Lucas said uncertainly.

"Go! Sure I go!"

"We'll take you, between us. A rose between two thorns." Dr. Runkleman beamed.

"You're pretty lucky," he said admiringly as they walked back to the office.

"She knows her way around an operating room. I'll say that for her. I just hope these people tonight aren't too—brainy," Lucas said uneasily.

"Don't you worry about her. A nice girl like that—they'll be lucky to know her!"

The phone rang.

"John Roamer," Miss Snow announced.

Dr. Runkleman's face darkened.

"Tell him to go to the Clinic. Tell him I said so."

"The old fool!" Miss Snow snorted.

"Binyon and Blake'll handle him!"

They walked to the car.

Dr. Runkleman smiled with an effort.

"Sometimes," he said apologetically, "I see all I want to of the human race. I guess you found out in your internship . . ."

"We certainly don't seem to see them at their best."

"Not all of them, of course . . . Though I must say—now and then you see a lot of courage wrapped up in one package—there's a kind of cheerful endurance—real bravery . . ."

"I wish I could accept it. Personally, I never know whether I'm looking at courage—or just a high threshold."

"Oh, there's cases, all right. Money's where the trouble starts. Now, that John Roamer, he's a feed merchant here in town, got all kinds of money, I usually respect people with money, they're apt to be more interesting, they've got somewhere. But this man called me in the middle of the night—his daughter—acute appendicitis—peritonitis. Anyway, I saved her. End of the month came, I sent him a bill for one hundred and fifty dollars. You know we usually charge fifty dollars, but I figured he could afford it. He no sooner got the bill than in he comes. He tells me that if it was a question of gratitude he'd pay me fifteen hundred dollars. But the bill just happened to come when he was hard pressed for cash.

"I just looked at him. I've been at it thirty years but I've never got used to it. And I knew what he had in the bank.

" 'All right,' I said, 'just give me half, then. I don't want to let business enter a situation where my only thought was to save your daughter.'

"He looked me right in the eye. 'Well,' he said, 'I'll tell you. The way things are it might take me some time to even pay that bill. You know it didn't take you all told more'n an hour. Now I got thirty-five dollars cash in my pocket. What do you say you take that and we call it square?' "

"My God!" Lucas said softly.

"That's not all. I took the thirty-five dollars. An hour later Castle called me and said Roamer'd asked him to use his influence to get me to cut my bill down."

"What a swine!"

"Six months later he gave the church five thousand dollars."

He shook his head, smiling wryly.

"My Lord, if I was to remember all the John Roamers I've had in thirty years of practice—" he said huskily.

Kristina had put on her best dress. Her blond hair, fine, shining a little, was drawn carefully back, braided, and the braids coiled irreproachably in two flat discs covering her ears. There was a clean, a scrubbed, look about her like a nimbus.

Lucas smiled involuntarily. She watched his face anxiously.

"You think I look all right?"

"You look fine, Kris," he said heartily. He had come in apprehensive, prepared for the worst. But she sat like a child, she had done everything she knew, the look she gave him staked everything she was, everything she had done, on his approval. For a moment he hated himself.

"You look great!" he said fiercely.

Her eyes dropped. It was too unexpected. It was too kind. She understood all that went on in his heart and his mind at this moment. And a part of her winced that he was defending her. She was helpless before the pain of this, and lonely and apart from her man, for his pity meant a gulf between them and it was not new, this gulf, she had stared at him across it longingly and hopefully, a stranger, almost from the first. And the kindness of what he was feeling, this too smote her, for it was very unexpected, and it brought tears to her eyes.

"I don't want to disgrace you," she said humbly.

"How could you disgrace me?" he demanded loudly.

"I know I don't know—I'm not so fancy—I don't dress like you like." She shrugged. "Just a squarehead, just a dumb Swede you got." She raised her eyes, she looked at him steadily, compassionately.

She smiled resignedly.

"That was one good thing about a nurse's uniform," she grimaced. "Everybody looked the same. You couldn't tell."

"I'll tell you what, one of these days I'll have a little time, we'll go down to the city, we'll look in the shop windows you and I, maybe we can both learn something."

"Oh, Luke! Would you?"

"Of course I will," he said roughly. He began to dress. She watched him. She said in a small voice:

"Luke–"

"Yes, Kris," he was taking out a fresh shirt.

"You're not sorry you married me?"

She bowed her head.

He walked to her.

"I think we do all right. You know what Medicine means to me. You know what comes first. And you, Kris–why I couldn't have gone through Medicine without you! Don't you think I know that? I do, Kris! Believe me! I do!"

"It wasn't me," she shook her head. "It was money."

"What?"

"It was money, Luke. It was paper, paper that belongs to anybody. Just paper. That's who you got to thank."

"That's a pretty frail link between two people. Paper . . ."

"I don't complain," she said low, steadfast. "Paper's all right to start with. It's got to be something."

"You're getting to be quite a philosopher," he said uneasily.

"I see a lot of things I didn't see before. You got a right to complain. A fellow like you, he could have a lot better wife than me, smart, fancy, I don't complain, Luke."

"Is something bothering you, Kris? Have you got something on your mind?"

And there was nothing she could say to that. There was absolutely nothing. There was time. There was only time. There was tomorrow. Maybe there would be something. She looked at him, dressing. A pang of pity wrinkled her eyes.

"You look tired, Luke. Nowadays you always look so tired. Not even when you were studying hardest did you look this tired."

"They keep me busy, Kris . . ."

"You like it, Luke? It's what you finally want?"

He turned. He looked at her a moment.

"No," he said bluntly. "No, it's not what I want."

She nodded.

"Sometimes I think it's like a factory! I look at you two. I wonder how in the world can you treat so many people? How can you know what you're doing?"

He shook his head. "You can't turn them away."

"You can't do that–"

"The damnedest part is they're satisfied."

"After all–you're helping people–they're satisfied . . ."

"But not me! I don't ever want to fall into this pattern."

"You'll fix it . . . You'll have a practice of your own. You'll see. When he goes away, you'll do what you please."

"I've thought of that . . . But what will change? Will I turn patients away?" He looked at her helplessly, his tie dangling from his hand.

"You'll work it out," she said confidently. "You're a great man, Lukey."

"No, I'm not. I know what I am. Without Medicine I'm nothing. I know that . . ."

He looked down at his tie absently.

"Without what they are, nobody is anything," she said sadly. "Even a nurse." She looked toward the closet where her cape hung. She saw the clock.

"What are you talking about?"

"Luke! We'll be late! Look at the time . . . !"

"I still can't see why the same principle wouldn't work on the moneyed crowd," Dr. Runkleman said uneasily, as they neared the mayor's home. "They're the ones who have to pay the bill."

"They'd never vote for it!" Kristina warned gaily.

"Now why do you say that!" Lucas demanded.

"She's right," protested Dr. Runkleman.

"Sure," said Kristina. "They never do."

"They're taking the same chance as everyone else."

"No, no! They got money and they don't like to lose any of it. Once it goes, it goes. Only if it buys them something."

"If you will be good enough to explain to me what it is in the organism of a rich person which protects him against the bacillus typhosus I would be very grateful," Lucas said.

They looked at him apologetically.

"There's something about money that makes a person secure," Dr. Runkleman ventured.

"Epidemically secure?"

Dr. Runkleman patted Lucas' knee. "Don't let it bother you. It's the way of the world."

"Oh, but they pay bigger fees," Kristina said gently. "And that pays for the poor people."

Henry Granite received them happily. He was elated. Here were three more delegates to a feast of reason in which he was to be the central figure.

"You're late!" he cried. "They're all here! We've been waiting for you! And this is Mrs. Marsh! Mrs. Marsh, I've heard so much about you—so many of the fair ladies of our town have asked me about you, you're quite a figure of mystery. I must tell them how you look. Mrs. Granite made me promise to tell her all about you."

"I'm very pleased to meet you," Kristina said shyly. "You're the second mayor I ever met. Once when I was a nurse a gallstone patient—"

"Doctors' wives have to stay in the background, you know," Dr. Runkleman said heartily. He spoke hoarsely. He cleared his throat.

"Don't you believe it!" said Henry Granite. "You sit by me this evening. You'll be my protection against these people who've come to attack me!"

On the sofa, the jacquard, overstuffed sofa, a brownish purple richly tasselled, sat Dr. Castle, Ben Cosgrove, and a third man.

"Dr. Castle you know," said the mayor. "Ben Cosgrove—the thorn in the flesh of Greenville, the Devil's Advocate, the voice of doubt—the community conscience—"

"We've met," Lucas nodded.

"And this is Bemis Shedd—the Fourth Estate—the recorder in our midst—"

A stout, tall man heaved himself up a little from the cushions and extended a fat, freckled hand, a grin long in the tooth and discolored, a bald head around the edges of which fair hair spiked and two huge ears hung pendulous as his red and large-pored nose.

"Glad t'meetcha," he said diffidently. "Shoulda been in to see you long ago."

"And he would have, too," the mayor said cordially, "only doctors don't advertise. Eh, Beam?"

The mayor turned, almost pirouetted, alive, gay, exhilarated.

"Dr. Kauffman you know? Yes. And Mrs. Kauffman?"

Mrs. Kauffman was a little disconcerting. She studied them intently, later Lucas saw she did this deliberately for effect, a dark-haired, thin woman, her hair banged across the forehead, hanging straight at the sides, around her neck a heavy string of sealing-wax beads, her face was triangular, her cheekbones high, her nose thin and aquiline.

"It is a pleasure, Doctor Marsh," she said, frowning earnestly. "And Mrs. Marsh—how good of you to come—I have been meaning to call—such long fingers, my dear! Are you an artist?"

"A nurse," Kristina said simply.

"Oh, a nurse! And how fortunate for the good doctor! A nurse!"

"She was head operating-room nurse at State," Lucas said.

"Don't get much chance for art in the operating room," Kristina said.

"That's for you!" Granite wheeled on Dr. Runkleman. "And you, too, Kauffman, all of you! Not much chance for art in the operating room!"

"Someday I'd like to see you in tights, Henry," Cosgrove said meditatively. "Up on top of a white horse, a book of *Bartlett's Quotations* in one hand and a baton in the other, and all the time the band playing and the horse dipping and wheeling."

"Would you tell them it was all an illusion, Ben? Including yourself?"

"I'm Harriet Lang." A woman rose beside the Kauffmans.

"I was saving you for last!" protested the mayor.

"Dr. Runkleman I know. And this is Mrs. Marsh—and our new doctor?"

Lucas held Harriet Lang's hand. Her dress was a soft, silky material which outlined her figure, her hips boyishly slim, her breasts small, her arms slender. Her neck was long, she was brown with sun, her gray eyes huge, her mouth generous, her fine dark hair, waving, framed her oval face.

She gave her hand a little tug and Lucas released it, stepped back, confused.

"Welcome to Greenville, Mrs. Marsh," she said friendlily, and her voice, low, confused Lucas anew. He stared at her fascinated, then looked guiltily away.

"Pleased to make your acquaintance," said Kristina. She looked at Harriet Lang intently. She had observed Lucas' reaction.

"Our woman of tomorrow," Henry Granite said genially. "Our woman of—"

"Miss Lang," said Ben Cosgrove, "runs the dishmaking department of the Greenville Tile Company. How's business, Harriet?"

"It couldn't be better," she said gravely.

"And that's taken care of. Now, Henry, suppose you get off the stage and let these people sit down and we get down to business."

Dr. Runkleman, who had said nothing and who had contented himself with smiling dutifully, gratefully sat down.

"You sit next to Miss Lang, Doctor," Granite decided. "And Mrs. Marsh will sit next to me. Mrs. Marsh is going to be my bodyguard."

"Doctor—" Cosgrove turned to Dr. Castle and then to the others—"notice I say 'Doctor,' and not 'Henry,' this is official—what's our chances of an outbreak of typhoid this year?"

"Better than last, I should say," Dr. Castle said quietly.

"And you, Doctor?"

"I agree with Dr. Castle."

"Dr. Runkleman?"

Dr. Runkleman nodded.

"Dr. Marsh's opinion I won't ask. He's too new here. He doesn't know anything about the town. Only the sickness he's treated." He moved to a more comfortable position. The smiles disappeared. The faces became serious. Lucas looked at Harriet Lang, warmth grew in him, he looked quickly away.

"We lost seventy-odd last year. We'll probably lose more this year. You heard that, Henry. The water system's contaminated. We need a new water system. If we don't get a new water system we're going to have an epidemic. What are you going to do about it?"

"Now, Ben. Let's not talk about epidemics. A rise in the death rate isn't quite an epidemic. Let's not go scaring people. You know all this is off the record, Beam—?"

Bemis Shedd nodded importantly.

"What's the chance of an epidemic, Doctors?"

Harriet Lang, at Lucas' side, spoke unexpectedly. He was startled. He looked about, ready to protect her.

"It's always good," Dr. Castle sighed.

"I don't for the life of me see how we've missed it so far," said Dr. Kauffman.

"Then we could have one this year?"

"We certainly could!" Dr. Runkleman said loudly.

"You heard 'em!" Cosgrove said grimly.

Henry Granite sighed.

"We've been through all this before, haven't we? You're establishing prior knowledge, aren't you, Ben? Yes—I heard. Also, I heard them last year. And the year before. And, thank God, we've had no epidemic, yet."

"You can't be serious!" Lucas cried abruptly.

"Typhoid's very bad," said Kristina. She shook her head. "Once, in Minnesota—"

Lucas glared at her.

"Of course he's serious," said Cosgrove. "You are now peering into the recesses of the mind of a mayor. That's exactly how he thinks."

"That's not all there is to think about," Bemis Shedd said heavily.

"There's a little matter of money," said Granite.

Bemis Shedd nodded.

"How do we get money for anything?" demanded Mrs. Kauffman. "How do we get schools—government—"

"Surely you can appeal to the people, Henry? Surely Bemis, here, through his paper—?" Harriet Lang asked quietly.

"Let's not go too fast," Shedd said hastily. "Let's not go scaring everybody half to death—"

"Just what is it, Henry?" asked Dr. Castle.

"What's keeping you from it?" asked Dr. Kauffman.

Henry Granite hesitated.

"Now, Henry—" Shedd said warningly.

"The interests, Henry?" Cosgrove asked ironically.

"All right. Call them the interests, Ben. Call them whatever you please. . . . Let's look at this plainly—"

"You're just the mayor," said Cosgrove. "If it was up to you we'd have a new water system. But you're just one man—you have the city council to consider—they're the ones who vote the money—"

"You really have said that before," said Harriet Lang.

"I believe you told me once that even so great a people as the Athenians had to confront that," said Dr. Castle. "Something from Plato, wasn't it?"

Granite's face softened. "I think so," he said shyly.

"Why Henry Granite!" cried Harriet Lang. "I had no idea—!"

"Oh, I read a little," Granite said diffidently. "Just a little. Plato, Aristotle—"

"God, Henry!" Cosgrove said, "you've gone up a notch with me—that's pretty deep stuff! Where do you get the time?"

"I'll tell you something." Granite flushed. "However modern we think ourselves there's extremely little we face today the Greeks haven't made part of history."

"Including a situation like this, sir!" Lucas said humbly.

"That's it—" Granite said eagerly.

"And the powers that be—the Argives—have already intimated to you that they are against this expenditure at this time—"

"That's right—"

Lucas turned to the others.

"History shows that to oppose would be political suicide."

The mayor pursed his lips. He cleared his throat.

"Well," he said reluctantly, "not quite so bald, perhaps–"

"We all know who it is," said Cosgrove. "Lennox, the hardware man, Benning at the bank, Rankin, the feed dealer–those are the boys you listen to, aren't they, Henry?"

"And those are the people you must work with. You must allow their approval to dominate your thinking," Lucas nodded sympathetically. "You want to please everybody. And that's very difficult . . ."

"That's about right. I make no secret of enjoying being mayor–it takes my time, I could be making money in the time it takes–but I like it. And I think I'm fitted for it. There's no reason why I shouldn't admit I want your respect, the respect of this group here–"

"And you've got courage. I think we can all see that."

"It takes courage to make the admission you've just made," Dr. Castle seconded, watching Lucas.

"That's right," chorused Dr. Kauffman and Dr. Runkleman.

"I think from the little I've seen of this town that it's a small republic, a republic all to itself." Lucas' eyes never left Granite's face.

"I've tried to keep it that way."

"I'm sure of it. There's traces here–rather amazing–of that fine republic of Plato's–"

"There never was a finer people than the Greeks!"

"That's right. And I respect–we all respect your ideals. The Athenians were great because they had something to fight for. I must say, as a stranger here, I am more than a little impressed to find a mayor so conversant with the noblest pages of human history."

"I may kid a lot," Cosgrove said, "but I've always respected you, Henry. I want you to know that."

Kristina, who had been gaping at Lucas, turned to Cosgrove.

"I was wondering, Henry," said Dr. Castle, "in your reading about the Athenians–"

Lucas' eyes narrowed. His face suddenly brightened.

"Go on!" Harriet Lang whispered, seeing the look.

"That's true!" Lucas pondered. "The point to remember is–for this republic as well as Greece–what happened to Athens."

He stopped. He looked at Henry Granite.

"What happened?" Mrs. Kauffman said at last. "I'm sorry we're not all so well versed as you and Henry, Doctor!"

"You tell us, Henry!" Cosgrove said respectfully.

Henry Granite smiled happily.

"Doctor Marsh has the floor," he said. "He will tell you."

"The Athenians," said Lucas, "the best thinkers the world has ever known, were content with the most rudimentary sanitary provisions. They fought the Spartans. They lost a battle. They retreated to their fortress, Athens. The whole countryside flocked there. And there was no sanitation. What Sparta could not conquer, pestilence conquered. Athens fell. The Golden Age was over."

Dr. Castle watched the mayor. The others looked down.

"He's right." Granite rose. He had been given something to fight for, an ideal great as the mayorship itself, he had been given it publicly, an occasion and an audience.

"Now, Henry," Shedd said warningly.

"He's right, Bemis. He's absolutely right!"

Shedd looked at the mayor's flushed face, shrugged and was silent.

"You'll do it, then," said Cosgrove intently.

"You'll lead the way," said Dr. Castle.

"Solon himself couldn't do more!" Harriet Lang protested.

They watched him, waiting.

"I'll do it!" he cried. "I'm with you! I'm with you a hundred percent!"

He rose, strode to Lucas.

"And I want to shake your hand! It's a pleasure, Doctor!" He pumped Lucas' hand, struggling with his own vehemence, "A real pleasure. An honor!"

"That go for you, Bemis?" demanded Cosgrove. And all eyes now turned to the newspaper owner.

"I won't say how strong," he said uncomfortably. "I'll go along—I'll do what I can—"

"But you're a newspaper!" cried Mrs. Kauffman.

"Take it easy, dear," protested Dr. Kauffman.

"I won't take it easy! A newspaper is an organ of public opinion, it's more than that! It's the molder of a community, it's responsible to the people—"

"It's responsible to the advertisers," Shedd said shortly.

"You can sit there and say that?"

"I'm the one that's running it. And maybe I ought to know. You've got a newspaper because I've got advertisers. And when they don't like what runs in my newspaper they don't advertise. And what do I use for money, then? How do I print this fine organ of public opinion and community molding—you gonna pay for it?"

"Well!" said Mrs. Kauffman, calling the others with her eyes to witness what had been said.

"But you'll go along, Bemis?"

"I'll print both sides," Shedd said doggedly. "And that's sticking my neck out all the way. The mayor here, if he don't get re-elected—he's got a business to fall back on."

"That's good enough," Granite said magnanimously. "I know Bemis' problems, folks. He's in our corner. That's enough for me."

He sighed.

"I'm glad it's over," he confessed. He frowned. "Have to start making calls tomorrow, see how much all this is going to cost. . . . How many councilmen do you think we can count on?"

"You know what you're doing, don't you?" Shedd persisted.

Cosgrove, Shedd, and Dr. Kauffman gathered swiftly around Granite.

Dr. Runkleman straightened slowly in his chair. He had been staring studiously at his clasped hands throughout Lucas' intervention. He had sat thus because he was embarrassed, to him what Lucas had been saying was as little likely to produce a change in a political fact as a pep talk to a bacillus.

Now he looked at Granite confounded and incredulous, he looked at Lucas and his eyes said everything and his mouth said nothing, and his eyes were a little sick.

Kristina gave Lucas one awed and frightened look, looked at a superior being whose superiority she had just seen demonstrated. Then she looked timidly at the others and slowly pride crowded out awe and she preened, happy for him, happy for herself, raised by association.

Mrs. Kauffman rose with decision. She seated herself by Kristina.

"It is inexcusable our not coming to call," she said earnestly. "But you know what the life of a doctor's wife is—"

"I guess I am lucky, I have nothing to do all day. Almost nothing at all."

"Is that so? Then perhaps you'll think about joining our little art group—you'll laugh at us, I'm sure, just a few in this charming hole who read a book now and then and want some outlet for our humble artistic expressions—we'd be so glad to have you—"

"It gets pretty lonesome, sometimes. But I don't know how to paint. Those things I never learned. Only nursing."

"I expect you spend your time reading. We have a small study group—just now we're doing *Remembrance of Things Past*—don't you adore Proust? So intricate—so almost Teutonic—"

"I don't read much. Now and then I look at the pictures, magazines. I guess I never got the habit."

"Oh? Well, you should come around, anyway. Any Thursday evening. Sometimes people who have never tried are quite amazed at the things they produce in some medium they never thought of."

"It's pretty lonely in the evenings. Maybe some night—if I didn't have to paint, or anything, maybe just watch—sometime I'm sure Lucas doesn't need me—"

"I know what loneliness is. Believe me! You don't have my problem! When we first came to this town—you know we're Jewish, don't you?"

"No! Oh, sure! From the name Kauffman! Sure! I don't know what's the matter with people! They treated you bad? Jews are fine people! We had a Dr. Aarons at the hospital—he was a fine man! He was a Jew. Don't you worry. It's the same with Swedes—"

"I hardly think it's quite the same—"

"Oh, sure. It's the same. The same thing. When I was a little girl I grew up in Minnesota, everybody was Swedes. And one day I saw a nurse, she was wearing a cape, from that minute I wanted to be a nurse, to wear that cape, to be treated nice like everybody treated her, proud to know her."

Kristina shrugged.

"So I got my cape," and her eyes saw the graduating class, saw the cape. "And all through nursing everybody makes fun of me, I had no girl friend, they were ashamed because I was a Swede. All right, so I work harder, one day, I think, you will not be ashamed of me, work, work, work, that's all I did, that's what a Swede knows how to do, work, and that's what I did. And one day soon they make me head operating-room nurse."

And now her eyes saw the nurses' quarters, saw the looks bypassing her, saw the lonely room in the nurses' quarters, saw the evenings and the long walks alone.

"Nothing happened," she shrugged. "I was still a Swede. So I know." She looked at Mrs. Kauffman, she nodded sagely. "So I know. I don't know what's the matter. What's the matter with a Swede? My father always taught me, 'Kristina, you treat everybody alike!' And that's what I always do. All except Norwegians, of course. And maybe there's some good in them, some of them—you know any Norwegians? Maybe I say the wrong thing! My God!"

"No, no," said Mrs. Kauffman. "I know exactly what you mean. Although I assure you—the problem is *not* the same!"

"Maybe over in Sweden they don't like Americans?"

"I see that your acquaintance with the Jewish problem has been somewhat limited. But I assure you, we fare worse than ever any of your nationality could dream of. And for longer, longer than there has been an America, I assure you! You must take my word for it!"

"Don't get mad," Kristina said in a low voice, "I only wanted to be friends, I didn't mean—"

"I'm not angry. It's a sore subject with me, that's all. It's one I never bring up. But when you said—"

"I'm sorry," Kristina said humbly.

"Oh, it's the world! I hate it, I hate it so!" Mrs. Kauffman said passionately.

"You think maybe there's some country where nobody hates anybody for being anything?" Kristina asked timidly.

"Never!" Mrs. Kauffman said passionately. "Never, never! I'm glad I have no children! I couldn't curse them so. I couldn't bear them into a world so rotten with intolerance!"

"I know . . . I used to cry at night. Once I got mad. You know what? I'll tell you something! I got so mad once I said to a girl, 'What's the matter! Don't you like Swedes?' Then later I was ashamed. You know what? Kristina, I said to myself, if you don't like int—intolerance—who's intolerant? What are you so intolerant about?"

Mrs. Kauffman blinked.

"Well, for Heaven's sakes!"

Kristina darted a frightened look across the room at Lucas.

"What's the matter? Did I say something? I didn't mean—"

"Don't be intolerant of intolerance—that's what you said, didn't you?"

"What's all this?" Dr. Kauffman asked pleasantly.

"Abe! Oh, Abe! She just said the most wonderful thing! Listen, Abe. If you hate intolerance, don't be intolerant yourself. Don't even be intolerant of intolerance!"

And she stared at her husband, Kristina forgotten, between them the bond of Jewishness, of rejection and disapproval and unlove, testing the new key, testing the words for magic, for the buckler, the always despairingly sought buckler, for the Messiah of phrases, the Saviour among attitudes, was this it? Was it? She stared at him with mighty hope.

Dr. Kauffman pursed his lips.

"Quite a thought! You've got quite a thought there!"

"She's got it, Abe! I feel it! I know it!"

"Maybe so," he nodded thoughtfully, smiling, "maybe so. You and your husband seem to have things pretty well solved, Mrs. Marsh."

"Wasn't he wonderful, Abe?"

"I must say frankly I never expected the mayor would come around to jeopardizing his precious classical, political neck for anything. Well—it's not over yet. Not by a long shot . . ."

"And Mrs. Marsh is coming to the very first Thursday evening she can make it! Isn't that fine, Abe? You must get her to tell you sometime how they treat Swedish people in this part of the world!"

"Not so bad as they treat Jews, I guess," Kristina said loyally, obediently.

"No, but you must hear her, Abe! You really must!"

The group around the mayor had dwindled to Bemis Shedd and Cosgrove.

With a sort of prescience Kristina looked around the room for Lucas, whose chair was now vacant. He was in a corner of the room. He was talking earnestly to Harriet Lang. As she watched him he smiled winningly and Miss Lang lifted her face and slowly smiled back. Kristina became conscious of her dowdy dress, of her hands, of her hair. Almost simultaneously she had a sense of sickness, a visceral feeling of fear. And look away she could not.

"Dr. Kauffman's been telling me some amazing things about you," Dr. Castle said.

She started, she looked up at him guiltily.

"You seem to have won both the Kauffmans," Dr. Castle said gently. "Do you mind if I sit down?"

"No, no! Please! Plenty room!"

"Maybe you can even win me." His eyes watched her, kindness in them, assurance. He looked in the direction of Lucas and Harriet Lang. "She's a very remarkable young woman. Would you like to hear about her?"

"Oh, yes, please!" And the sickness came back, now, stronger.

⁎ CHAPTER 29

"She's a very remarkable young woman," Dr. Castle said. "She came to this town without a nickel—as I understand it she was just driving through. She was born someplace in New England and studied art and went on to New York and studied more. She saw she wasn't going to be a painter, not a real, topnotch painter such as she'd set her heart on, so she turned to sculpture. But it was the same story there."

Dr. Castle shook his head, admiring the way people set their hearts on things.

"She's a real nice-looking girl." Kristina watched her steadily.

"Oh, half the men in town have been after her. She isn't interested in men, a home. She wants something else. . . . The day she saw that tile plant she stopped her car, she went in to see Bill Dodd. They make pipe up there, sewer pipe, water pipe, all kinds of clay pipe, I'll have to take you up there some time, show you around . . ."

"Thank you very much," Kristina watched Lucas and Harriet Lang, talking animatedly.

"What do you think she did?" Dr. Castle paused.

Kristina turned to him, confused.

"Excuse me—"

"That's all right. She got Bill Dodd to start a little clay-crockery division! She rented a room and she stayed here a month and finally he let her turn out a couple of platters and cups and things, and use a kiln, and she brought them in to him all decorated up—and that was the start of it. And today Bill Dodd tells me half their output is cheap decorated pottery!"

"She must be very smart," Kristina said wistfully. She turned involuntarily to watch them again.

"Tell me—you don't have any children, Mrs. Marsh?"

"Oh, I like kids!" Kristina turned quickly to him. "I would have a million of them!"

"Nothing like children to make a home, sort of the cement, you might say. That's one thing any woman can do—"

"It's true! I know it! Only—only Luke gets awful mad . . . even if I only mention it . . ."

Kristina turned away again to look at Lucas and there was such naked love in her look, such submissiveness in her pose, she was like a poor child peering at a rich child's party, adoring what she saw, never doubting her place, that Dr. Castle looked to Lucas also. And when he saw him, oblivious to his wife, a world away from her, completely happy, Dr. Castle, instead of talking, simply took Kristina's hand, she turned to him, flustered and surprised, he looked in her eyes and smiled.

"I tell you what you do," he said conspiratorially. "While he's out all day why don't you go to the County? You know your way around hospitals, just go on up there and fool around the baby ward!"

"Yes?" Kristina considered this hopefully. "You think nobody will mind?"

"Of course they won't mind! They always have more babies than nurses to take care of them! Why half those babies—don't—even—have—parents!"

"Oh, my!" Kristina whispered.

"You've got a fine man there—"

"Oh, Luke is wonderful—I know. I'm very lucky. Such a man to be tied to somebody who knows only how to be an operating-room nurse. I know . . . A doctor's wife, she should make her husband look good . . . She should dress good . . . I don't even speak good English . . ."

"I've been a doctor more than thirty years and I can count on the fingers of one hand the people I've met who didn't want to be something else."

"Now, what do they want to be?" demanded Dr. Runkleman.

"Hello, Dave. I was telling Mrs. Marsh here, long as I've been a doctor I've never had a patient who was happy being what he was."

"By George, that's the truth!"

"They all keep looking at the other fellow, they want to be what *he* is. When it comes right down to it, nobody wants to be a human being. That's the *real* trouble! They won't compete with themselves!"

He looked meaningly and affectionately at Kristina. She looked back at him earnestly, waiting for more.

"He's got the right idea," Dr. Runkleman grinned. He yawned. "Not so young as I used to be," he apologized. "Had quite a day."

Dr. Castle's eyes became impersonal a moment, he scanned Dr. Runkleman's face swiftly. Then his impersonality vanished and he turned to Kristina, smiling.

"We've been cooking up a little mischief, Dave. Mrs. Marsh here, what with you working her husband to death, is all alone all day. I told her to go on up to the County and maybe they'll let her look in on the babies, when she has the time."

"Why, say! That's a good idea! Would you like that, Mrs. Marsh?"

"I'd love it," Kristina said simply.

"I'll talk to them tomorrow. You just go up anytime you please! You bet!"

"I'll have to speak to Luke—"

"And don't you worry about Dr. Marsh. I'll take care of him!"

"I've been telling her about Miss Lang—"

"Now, there's a fine girl!"

"Dr. Castle told me," Kristina said steadily.

"Yes," said Dr. Castle, "I've been telling her . . ."

The conversation Lucas and Harriet Lang were drinking so thirstily was about themselves. They were oblivious to the rest of the room because they were concentrating, each, upon what to tell the other. And they absorbed this information thirstily because it provided contact and this type of contact was permitted.

They informed each other earnestly how they had happened to come to this place, they sketched their backgrounds for each other. And always, whatever they happened to be saying at the moment, they observed each other with satisfaction, with open pleasure, with hope.

"But do you *like* it here?" Lucas was saying.

"I *live* here. Actually, where I live doesn't make much difference."

"Except New England," Lucas reminded her.

"No. I wouldn't want to go back there. I'd be identifying myself with what I was and automatically accepting its limits. And mine."

"I'm the same as you! I feel the same way! We both have something we mean to do—"

And they looked at each other excitedly. The texture of her skin was almost painfully clear to him. Her mouth was somewhat wide. Her eyes were gray and there were times when he was certain there was encouragement in them. At first he had felt the time she would spend talking to him was limited and that at any instant she would smile brightly and walk away to distribute her presence elsewhere. He talked desperately trying to think of things to say which would detain her.

I'd like to touch him, she thought. I'd like to feel his coat and run my hand up the collar, on to his neck, over his lovely cheeks. He's got eyelashes like a girl's. I'd like to lie down, right this minute . . .

And that's his wife, that dull Swedish-looking one over there. How in the world did he ever marry her! Just how! Why? What's there that I don't see? And there's nothing there, nothing between them, it's all old-hat, it's nothing. If it ever was . . . But why? Why, in the first place? She's looking this way. Be careful . . .

"I don't know about you but when I was young I think we were the poorest family in New England. If an aunt of mine hadn't died I don't think I ever would have finished high school—let alone college."

"You think *you* were poor!"

"Now don't tell me you worked your way through Medicine!"

He flushed suddenly.

"No, I didn't," he said reluctantly. "But pre-med . . ."

So that was it, then. She'd put him through Medicine. She must have. That's how it happened. Maybe had a little money saved up, kept on working, and he was desperate and he married her and she put him through. She looked at him with new appraisal. So it wasn't just words, then. That's how much Medicine meant to him. He'd do anything. And because she knew how infinitely and contemptibly little anything the world treasured or legislated amounted to beside what a person really wanted, was born wanting, was made for, she had a rush of intimacy with him, of consanguinity that pushed days aside and weeks and months, gave her a footing of familiarity with anything he might say or do, a sense of things established and known and accepted, a sense of brotherhood, a pleasant, incestuous speculation.

She glanced at Kristina again, this time looked at her with understanding and a certain restrained pity. Women were not a part of her world unless they were women with impulse, women who were going somewhere, women with aim. These were very few. And all the rest were a forlornly stupid mass, a sisterhood, a herd with rules. And most of these rules were fantastic, incredible in their complexity and emptiness, as incredible as the fantasy of devotion each member of the herd devoted to them, each vigilant for her neighbor, each fearful, forever mindful, forever fearful. Without the trappings and the rules of this great game they would have to face the fact that they simply composed a giant servant class, bred in season, serving tirelessly and continuously, serving aimlessly, dying aimlessly, waiting on men.

And men were as pretentious and as empty.

Except there was something more dynamic about even the dullest man, dynamic at least in potential, they had their rules, too, a pattern which kept their attention from their stark uselessness, their appalling mediocrity, the childishness of whatever they were doing. They had all the seriousness of a child at play and not one in a million was ever occupied with anything more important than whatever it was to which a child gave such absorption.

It was a little eerie meeting another person with perspective and aim, total perspective and total aim. And then meeting him in such a town, in such a parlor, at such a meeting. She had a desire to cling to him, to hold fast, to keep company. She saw Kristina rise. Harriet looked at Lucas with satisfaction. He would do anything to serve his aim, do it automatically and without twinge, and also he was young, and he was handsome and there were textures about his person, his clothes, his skin, his hair, that made her fingers quiver.

He was looking at her helplessly. He wanted her, that was obvious, there was no mistaking that. But it was something that would have to be drawn out a bit, nothing sudden and stupid and quick, but lingering, agonized, perilously prolonged . . .

And meantime there was that look on his face. And his wife was coming over—

"How do you like working with Dr. Runkleman? He must be tired, he walks so bent—"

Lucas looked quickly away, he almost hid a guilty start seeing Dr. Castle, Dr. Runkleman, and Kristina advancing on them.

"Your wife's having a fine time," Dr. Runkleman said happily.

"Do her good to get out once in a while," Lucas nodded. "Everything all right, Kris?"

"I can't think why anyone would want to be a doctor's wife," Harriet Lang shook her head sympathetically.

"It's not so bad," said Kristina. "You get used to it. I hear all about you, though! My goodness! You must be smart! I never met many artists, but—"

"But once, in Minnesota, I knew a girl who painted on china!" said Lucas.

"That's right!" Kristina marvelled. "Who told you, Luke? Did I ever tell you?"

"No, but I knew Minnesota was bound to come into it, somewhere," Lucas sighed.

"My husband makes fun of me," Kristina confided. "I guess that's all I am. Just a squarehead from Minnesota."

"I guess that's all anybody is," said Dr. Castle. "Just a something, from some place."

"I've always wanted to go to Minnesota," said Harriet Lang. "I hear it's beautiful—full of lakes—"

"Oh, lots of lakes," Kristina said eagerly.

"I hope you tell me about it, sometime. I'd like to see more of you and your interesting husband—"

"You're not leaving?" Dr. Runkleman protested.

"I'm afraid I must. I'm a working gal, you know. The tile plant calls me." She looked impersonally away from the protest in Lucas' eyes.

"I'll drive you," said Dr. Runkleman. Lucas looked at him in surprise. He rallied.

"It is getting late," he said. "We'll go, too."

"No, no. It's early. It isn't late at all. You stay here. Enjoy yourself. This is the first chance Mrs. Marsh has been out—don't pay any attention to me. I've just had a hard day—"

"Are you all right?" Lucas asked anxiously.

"Fine! Never finer! I'm just tired. You stay right here! Come on, Miss Lang, tonight an old buck will take you home, for once."

And while they looked at each other uncertainly, he took Harriet Lang's arm, and then it was too late to protest any longer and they were gone.

"Been working pretty hard, lately?" Dr. Castle asked.

"No harder than usual," Lucas said, and as his words died away he was aware that Dr. Castle had not asked a social question. He looked at Dr. Castle, alert.

"A little hoarse tonight," Dr. Castle said mildly.

Hoarse . . . hoarse . . . cough, dysphagia, pain . . .

"No cough," said Lucas.

"Not lately–"

"What's the matter?" asked Kristina.

"I was just saying what a load your husband's taken off Dr. Runkleman's shoulders," Dr. Castle smiled. "Why, he was getting positively run down before you came, he even had a cough, thought we'd have to chain him up and take him to a sanitarium for a rest–"

"He works terrible hard." Kristina shook her head indignantly. "Someone should tell him!"

"Tell him!" echoed Dr. Castle.

Lucas pondered. He had noticed nothing. Hoarseness . . . Yes, hoarseness–that, and a cough–that's what Dr. Castle had just said, he knew what he was saying–hoarseness and cough . . .

"You can't tell a man like Runkleman to stop working!" Dr. Castle snorted. "You ought to know that, Mrs. Marsh. Look at your own man!"

Kristina looked at Lucas anxiously.

"They have to work awful hard," she said fearfully.

"I guess I haven't lost any weight," Lucas said casually.

"He eats good," offered Kristina.

"I don't have any trouble swallowing," Lucas paused. "Swallow whatever's put before me," he concluded.

"Well, I guess that's the answer," Dr. Castle said mildly. "Now, I've seen Dr. Runkleman eat like he hated it–as if it was actually painful for him to swallow–I'm not much of an eater myself–"

"But you got to keep your strength up," adjured Kristina.

"That's the truth," said Dr. Castle. "And I'll bet you're the girl that can do it!"

Hoarseness, cough, dysphagia. . . . Pain? Probably pain. He'd hide it. . . . Lucas' heart beat faster with alarm. And he'd never said a word. Not a syllable. Then those pauses–during an operation. He wasn't thinking. He was resting. Or waiting–waiting for it to pass. And there it was–right out of the blue. He looked at Dr. Castle. He'd known all the time. And Runkleman was worried about Castle. And all the time–

"I guess I'd better listen," he said deliberately, "before it's too late. Kris is always trying to get me to eat more."

"He won't listen," Kristina nodded.

"Now," said Lucas, and he looked at Dr. Castle, "now I'll listen."

"Won't do any harm to listen," Dr. Castle agreed. He turned to Kristina. "Some people are awfully clever," he said. "Ever notice, Mrs. Marsh? They know how to get around people. Even real smart people. Now you take your husband here—I'll bet nobody in town's ever gotten around anybody like that before . . ."

"He sure surprised *me*!" Kristina cried. "Where did you ever know so much, Luke?"

"I opened a book once, at the right place," Lucas grinned.

So Castle had already tried to examine Dr. Runkleman. And Dr. Runkleman had laughed him off. And it was going to take real ingenuity to get a stethoscope on that broad, hairy chest. Real ingenuity. . . . And Runkleman probably suspected—maybe knew—probably knew—and didn't want it confirmed—wanted to go on—just keep on going . . .

Aneurysm of the arch of the aorta—hoarseness, cough, dysphagia, pain—and his mind assembled the sounds the stethoscope would hear, they arrayed themselves from the association centers of his memory, flawless, all present and accounted for, heaving pulsation, diastolic shock, heavy second aortic, tracheal tug, thrill, transverse dullness at the second interspace, unequal radial pulses . . .

"You better loan me that book you opened," said Dr. Castle. "I've been trying to get a stop sign put up on my street for two years."

"Well," said Lucas. "I guess it's about time—"

"No, no!" said Cosgrove. "You don't get off that easily! You started all this."

"You won't need us?" inquired Dr. Kauffman.

"Not now. You run along, if you want to—"

"I'd like to talk to you, Dr. Marsh," Granite said, "if you don't mind. You, too, Dr. Castle."

They seated themselves. Kristina sat uncertainly beside Lucas on the couch. Cosgrove straddled a chair. The mayor laced his fingers and leaned forward from the depths of his chair.

"I don't mind," said Dr. Castle. "I don't mind a bit."

"I know that," nodded Henry Granite. "That's why I want to talk to you two."

"And even if you do mind," Cosgrove told Lucas, "it doesn't make any difference because the way things have turned out you're going to have to take some of the responsibility for this move."

"What Ben means is, that having committed ourselves, so to speak, we're faced with the necessity of selecting a representative."

"A goat," said Cosgrove.

"Someone," explained Dr. Castle, "who can formally and officially present the mayor with a request for action. Someone of consequence who doesn't care what the town thinks. That leaves you and me. Because I don't care what the town thinks. And you're so new here a lot of folks would forgive you for asking them to put up the money for anything so harebrained as a new water system."

"Kauffman, I'm afraid, wouldn't quite do—" said Granite.

"Binyon and Blake know better than to stick their necks out."

Cosgrove ruminated. "When you come right down to it—what's in it for them?"

Lucas flushed. This was a layman speaking.

"What's the matter? Didn't you like the way I put it?" demanded Cosgrove.

"Not particularly," said Lucas. He looked at Cosgrove with cold anger. The disillusionments of the past months had conditioned him to unexpected enemies.

"What didn't you like about it?" Cosgrove asked.

"I don't know what right you have to assume knowledge of Dr. Binyon's or Dr. Blake's motives," Lucas said frigidly.

"Why, everybody knows what those quacks' motives are," said Cosgove lazily.

"Now, gentlemen. Ben! Behave yourself," bade Granite.

Dr. Castle sank deeper into his chair. Kristina looked to him, frightened. He winked at her broadly. She looked away uncertainly.

"All of a sudden our young newcomer pops up as spokesman for the medical profession," Cosgrove protested. "If you can call Binyon and Blake the medical profession."

"I understand," said Lucas, "that you're a professional man yourself. I don't know what the law's ethics are—"

"Oh, yes you do," said Cosgrove serenely. "They stink and I'm only another lousy ambulance chaser—"

"That, of course, is something you are in a better position to decide than any of us—"

"And I'm well aware of the low esteem in which the exalted followers of Hippocrates hold us. We'll take any side, won't we, Doctor. That's what galls you boys most. But what pains my ass—excuse me, Mrs. Marsh, I'm just a common lawyer fellow and you've got to expect such things of me—we'll use the sacred, secret password language—what gives me rectalgia—is the way all too many of you boys regard us lesser humans who didn't study Medicine and haven't got a mutual-protection tong."

Kristina watched Cosgrove, stupefied. Dr. Castle listened placidly, his eyes never leaving Cosgrove's face.

"I don't know why you have to do things like this, Ben," Granite said indignantly. "We know you, here. We're used to it." He turned to Lucas. "He doesn't mean anything, Doctor. Believe me! It's just Ben's way of showing off—"

"I'm a terrible fellow," nodded Cosgrove. "I do an awful thing. I come right out and tell the truth. Bang! Just like that. Just as if I was saying good morning."

"I don't entirely understand your—feeling—about Medicine," Lucas said, containing himself, savoring the luxury of virtuous containment, "but it seems to me that coming from a member of a profession your remarks about Doctors Binyon and Blake savor a little of the irresponsible."

"They overcharge you, Ben?" Granite grinned.

"Me? I've got nothing against Binyon and Blake. Marsh here seems to feel he has to defend them on some noble grounds or other. You'd do that, wouldn't you, Marsh? No matter what you might personally know about another doctor—if you'd just come from seeing him kill a person—you'd feel called on to defend him, wouldn't you? Because he was another doctor? You might not even know his name, he could be totally unfit to practice Medicine and you'd cover him someway. That's true, isn't it?"

"And just exactly who would be the judge of whether he was fit or unfit?"

"Aha! There we have it! Where the blind are leading the blind let's have no criticism of a stumble. What is a mistake, anyway? We're all in this together, none of us really knows much for sure, let's present a united front. Because the day we lose public confidence—the day the public finds out how little we really know—we lose our standing, we lose our income, we lose our privileges. We might even lose our immunities—the immunity that lets a doctor kill a man and not be tried for manslaughter."

"You couldn't very well practice Medicine without those immunities, Ben," Dr. Castle said quietly. "A doctor's bound to make mistakes—I know I have, dozens of them—I bet I've made enough mistakes to fill a graveyard. But if I'd been serving time for all I've killed I couldn't have saved all the ones I've saved, either. And I bet that's enough for a small city."

"That's you," Cosgrove frowned.

"I can't speak for other doctors," Lucas began acidly.

"Doctor, you're living in a dreamworld," Cosgrove said compassionately.

"You ought to know what hours a doctor keeps. How he works and slaves and studies—what he has to go through!" Kristina said angrily.

"He gets well paid for it," said Cosgrove softly. "He enjoys every minute of it. And anytime it stops being fun he can quit."

"A lot do, you know," observed Dr. Castle. "They go off and do other things, sell insurance, work in laboratories, maybe some of them even go in for law . . ."

"Sure," said Cosgrove. "It's just a trade like any other trade. One of the best there is. In fact it's not a trade, it's an industry. There's nothing wrong with that. Just so they don't take themselves seriously—"

"Do you know anything more serious than life or death?" Lucas demanded hotly.

"And exactly what do you think you know about life and death?"

"Are you serious?"

"I'm very serious. You've studied four years, you've interned two years, you're out in practice. You've memorized everything man's discovered about the body, the gist of it, anyway, and what do you really know?"

Granite laughed.

"Now you're being silly, Ben."

"Am I? Am I really?"

"I think so," said Lucas.

"Well, let's get down to what's really basic, then. The major things, the stuff of life itself."

"All right," said Lucas, "let's do that."

"I'm not going to ask you questions because the sound of you repeating 'I don't know' would bore me. I'm just going to tell you what you don't know. You don't know why the heart beats. You don't know why it stops beating. You don't know why bone regenerates, where blood is manufactured, why the lungs work, where the mind is, what appetite is, why the nerves feel, why a woman comes to term in nine months instead of six or twelve, what starts the birth, you know almost nothing about the entire endocrine system, not even the essential trigger mechanism of death."

He paused. He looked at Lucas expectantly.

"Now, just a moment!"

"Do you know the answers to these things?"

"We know quite a bit about them—"

"But you don't know. You don't know how many senses there are, or just what constitutes a separate sense. You don't know how an anesthetic anesthetizes. Your whole so-called science is full of it-is-probables about these things. But not one of them do you actually, really know. And these aren't little details that don't matter much and are just laying around waiting to be solved. These are the very basic facts of life itself. The simplicities. The facts of life."

Lucas' throat was dry. He looked at Cosgrove with hate. He tried desperately to think, to confound him utterly.

"You've got it all figured out, haven't you?" he managed at last. "No use calling a doctor in next time you're sick. They wouldn't know anything, anyway—"

"Oh, yes. They know quite a bit. I'm talking about what they *don't* know."

"Why?" asked Dr. Castle gently.

"Why? Because every so often I get fed up with the omniscience-mutual-protection idea. It sticks in my craw. I hate the way a doctor will get on the stand and defend a doctor he's certain has killed or maimed or robbed somebody. I hate the way the guilty in Medicine get off scot-free. I hate the way the innocent protect the guilty."

"We none of us really know—" said Dr. Castle.

"You said so yourself," said Granite.

" 'What is truth?' asked Pontius Pilate. And he washed his hands. Do you think the public knows what you don't know? And I haven't even begun. I could go on and on. I could go organ by organ not just little mysteries—"

"The difference between us is that I could make a longer list than you," said Dr. Castle. "And so could Dr. Marsh. But it isn't what we don't know that bothers you, Ben. What we *do* know takes pretty good care of you."

"That's all right. But let's not trade on it. And don't tell me you don't! You're a mystic order, you do everything you can to keep it that way. You robe like Ku-Klux Klanners. You've got your sacred rituals, you've got a code of ethics that hasn't anything to do with ethics unless self-aggrandizement is ethics. You compose your features in an awesome mien, you parade inscrutably before the patient, you take pains to learn and speak a strange and incomprehensible language, you're intoxicated with the joy of speaking it to each other, you're witch doctors, you've got everything but the high sign and the grip. You trade on human ignorance. You own the human body. The patient doesn't own it. You do. It's your property. And he'd better keep his mouth shut or you deny him the relief he's crawled to you for. Sternly, too. Oh, you're very stern about it. You've built up a big business. You regulate the number you'll allow in. All you want is plenty of business for all. And protection. Complete protection. Otherwise you won't play. You foster the delusion of omniscience. Sometimes you say you're scientists and sometimes you say you're artists. You've never made up your mind which front you want to offer for the public's respect. You don't dare lay it on the line. You know better. You've got the will to obscure. You've made millions out of it. You've come to occupy dread, and high, and respected positions in the community. And Jesus Christ help you when the public finds you out. When the time comes when you run out of new discoveries to keep their minds off what you really are, what you've really done—"

The room was silent. Lucas' anger long ago had been drowned in amazement at Cosgrove's vehemence, at the intensity of his conviction, the dedication of his assault.

"Well, Ben," said Granite, "you've made your speech on Medicine for this year. Feel better?"

"I haven't even started," Cosgrove said grimly.

"Yes, you have, Ben," said Dr. Castle. "Everything but prescriptions. Everything you had last year, at least—unless you've got something new?"

"What's the prescriptions?" Lucas forced himself to be amiable, to talk like Dr. Castle.

"He wants to do away with prescriptions," said Dr. Castle.

"You mean just go into a drugstore and order anything you want?" Kristina gulped.

"Asking for trouble, aren't you?" Lucas smiled coldly. "You think people are equipped to prescribe for themselves?"

"I don't know whether you realize it, Doctor, but prescriptions—the laws, that is—haven't been in force very long. Not too long ago the citizen hadn't been stripped of that liberty. He had a right to go to hell in a bucket however he wanted. He had a right to go into any drugstore and buy just about everything he wanted. And you know something? He didn't wipe himself out. The human race didn't disappear. It wasn't even affected much, one way or the other. But that was before the doctors protected him from himself. For his own good, of course. Have you ever heard of kickbacks for prescriptions, Doctor? Well, I have. Right here in this town. Would it amaze you that so noble a creature as a doctor would charge a patient for a prescription, pocket the money, then get a kickback from the drugstore in the form of cash or a trade discount? Do you know why the public drug bill is so high? Why a package of aspirin costs almost as much as the actual cost of half a barrel of aspirin tablets? And do you know that you've had laws lobbied and enacted by a group you maintain in Washington and pay well? And do you know that you've had laws passed so that if you complained to me of a pain in the head and I said you had a headache and prescribed an aspirin I'd be liable to jail for practicing Medicine without a license?"

"I also know that these laws have given you pure drugs, protection from quacks and charlatans, protection from—"

"But who asked you to protect us? Who in the name of God ever assigned you the function of protecting the human body? By what right do you arrogate to yourselves the divine decision that you are the protectors of humanity? Who said the human body belonged to you? Who gave you the right to pass laws giving yourselves sole power over it?"

"Why, the people, wouldn't you say?" asked Dr. Castle gently. "The people pass the laws."

"Like prohibition? And the right to shoot quail from a moving streetcar? Their elected representatives, you mean. The people don't pass laws. Pressure groups pass laws. Lobbyists pass laws. Privilege passes laws. Doctors pass laws. Everybody passes laws but the people. Any little group with an ax to grind passes a law and gets rich from its operation and tells the people it's respectable or for their own good."

"And isn't that something very like what we're doing here tonight, Ben? A little group of us getting together and deciding what's best for the town?"

"It's the truth." Ben shrugged suddenly. "It's the absolute truth."

"People aren't noble," said Lucas. "They can't be governed by inborn nobility and responsibility. It isn't automatic. Nobody's noble. I don't feel particularly noble myself any more," he said wryly. "If there's anything noble about us—and maybe it's vanity and not nobility—it's people who know protecting those who don't know. Maybe the missionary in us—"

"There's nothing personal in all this, Doc. It wasn't aimed at you. It's not your fault. It's the system."

"And if aspirin tablets cost so much," said Granite earnestly, "think of the research, the new drugs that come out of the profits."

"Spare me," Cosgrove groaned. "For God's sake, Henry! At your age! If you're going to hand out that old crap why not include how much a drug house makes over and above its research?"

"They're entitled to make a dollar, Ben—"

"Well, just keep it on a dollar basis, then. Don't run in any of that benefactors-of-mankind crap on me. No—it's the system. And that includes the drug houses who gift doctors with company stock . . ."

Granite rose. He threw up his hands. Dr. Castle stretched.

"Oh, God! The system! Here we go on communism!"

"I've read *The Manifesto*—Marx—I'm familiar with its principles, perhaps I'm not as well versed as I might be—"

"Well, it's the answer," Cosgrove said simply. "It's the only answer. It's the one answer to all man's problems on earth." He nodded, staring at the carpet. Lucas smiled uncertainly.

"You talk it over with him some other time, Ben." Dr. Castle rose.

"That's right," said Granite. "Sometime when AT&T isn't nearly three hundred on the big board, when every workman hasn't got a chicken in every pot and a car in the garage, when the country hasn't reached the highest peak of prosperity of any nation in the world's history—"

"It's going to bust right in your face," Cosgrove said somberly. "You wait. You'll see . . ."

"You predicating that on anything, Ben? Anything except hope, that is?"

Cosgrove shrugged. He rose.

"Nope," he admitted. "I've got more money in the bank than I ever had in my life. I don't know what keeps things up. All I know is, if this is right—communism's wrong. And I know communism isn't wrong. Not Marx. Not Engels. Not Lenin. It'll come. Just wait. It'll bust right in our faces."

He turned to Lucas. He put out his hand.

"No hard feelings. I'll be around to see you one of these days—now that we've got all that out of the way—"

"Watch him, Doc!" Granite grinned. "Now he's going to try to convert you."

"Not me!" said Lucas. "I haven't even got the time to be an American."

"It's all decided, then," Granite said. "You're the goat, Dr. Marsh? You're going to send me a formal request for action? You sure you don't mind sticking your neck out? That's fine, then! We'll have a new water system in by fall or my name's not Henry Granite. . . . Didn't know what you'd let yourself in for, did you, Mrs. Marsh? Don't mind old Ben, here. His bark is worse than his bite. We're all used to it . . ."

And Kristina, smiling uncertainly, shook Cosgrove's hand stiffly, they made small sounds of departure, the door closed behind them, they stood on the sidewalk, Lucas, Kristina, Dr. Castle.

Lucas let out his breath.

"Whew!" he sighed.

"Quite an earful," Dr. Castle assented.

"What's the matter with him? A doctor bite him once?"

"I never heard such a thing in my life," Kristina said indignantly. "The nerve of such a man!"

"Does you good to listen to him," Dr. Castle said mildly.

"You think he *believes* all that?"

"Oh, yes. He believes it, all right." He looked at Lucas consideringly. His eyes twinkled. "And oddly enough some of what he says—is true!"

"Oh, I suppose in a broad, general sense—"

"No, in a definite, particular sense!"

Lucas shrugged. Inside, he hid panic.

"There's bound to be a certain amount of bombast in any profession," he conceded. "I suppose now and then a certain type will get impressed with his own importance—on the other hand—"

"Do *you* know anything?" Dr. Castle interrupted. He looked at Lucas, his eyes troubled, earnest. "Anything for certain?"

Lucas stared at him, speechless.

Dr. Castle sighed.

"Well, so long," he said tiredly. "Go home, children." He wrinkled his nose wryly. "I've got to operate in the morning."

The phone rang as they opened the door after a silent ride home.

Kristina drooped.

"Go to bed." He picked up his bag.

"It's you I'm thinking of."

"Well," he said dully, "it's my job."

And the door closed behind him.

Kristina stood as he had left her. Her eyes were on the door which had just closed. Her eyes kept the memory of Lucas' eyes. Her ears heard the tone of his voice. She stood, still, listening.

At the hospital the lights were on in the emergency room. A policeman on night duty stood at the door importantly.

"She's right in here, Doc, we brought her up."

The woman was about fifty, gray-haired, she wore a bathrobe over her nightdress, her feet were in slippers. She sat quietly in a chair, her hands folded, and at his entrance she looked up intently, her eyes gray and intelligent.

The night nurse came to his side.

"Swallowed a pin," she whispered.

Lucas put on a smile.

"Now, what sort of pin was this?"

"It was a safety pin, Doctor," the woman said calmly. "My name is Sylvia Phelps, I think I should tell you I'm a Christian Scientist. I was restless, I got up to boil myself some milk, I was about to pin my bathrobe, I put the pin in my mouth, a mouse ran across my feet, I gasped—I swallowed the pin."

"Yes," said Lucas. "Well, that's all right. Lots of people swallow pins. Do you feel it? Can you show me where?"

"Here," the woman gingerly put her hand at the juncture of neck and chest. "I'm a Christian Scientist, Doctor—"

"I know. And you don't believe in me. Let's go into the X-ray, shall we?"

She followed him obediently.

"But in a case like this—"

"I understand. It's perfectly all right. But I don't want you to talk any more. All right?"

The woman nodded. She smiled at him gratefully and serenely.

The pin showed clearly under the fluoroscope. It had become fixed a short distance in the ascending branch of the right bronchus.

"We'll use the small operating room," Lucas ordered briefly.

"Yes, sir," said the nurse. She lingered at the door. Lucas walked to her.

"What is it?" he asked in a low tone.

"I don't know much about this," she whispered miserably. "I'm not an RN—"

For a moment Lucas thought of getting Dr. Runkleman. It was the logical, orderly thing to do. Then the knowledge of his own abilities gave him angry security. I'll do it myself, he decided. I'll do it myself. It was a small satisfaction, beside the uncertainty the world had become, to marshal thus his knowledge of his own skill, but it was a valid knowledge and he smiled grimly and pridefully for it. Here, at least, was something he could rely on.

"Is there an RN on duty?"

"There's only Miss Paget. She's not on duty. She sits up with Oscar

Glaimer—that cancer of the rectum patient. I'm sorry, Doctor—if I only knew how to help I'd be glad to—it's not my fault, really—"

"You get Miss Paget."

While she was gone he wheeled the elderly Miss Phelps into the smaller operating room, switched on the lights, connected the portable fluoroscope. Miss Paget came in in time to help him transfer Miss Phelps onto the table.

"We've got a swallowed pin here," he said to her easily. "And I know you're not on duty but we're both mighty glad to have your help."

"Shall I scrub?" she asked coldly.

"Well, I think we'll set this screen just where we want it—" and he adjusted the fluoroscope— "there! Do you see it?"

"Yes, sir." Their bent heads touched.

"Well, now we'll go have a quick wash and look for a few tools and while we're washing Miss Phelps will lie right here, perfectly still, so—and I'll tell you what we'll do."

He grinned reassuringly at Miss Phelps, who smiled back at him untroubled and serene.

"You going to do that yourself, Doctor?" Miss Paget asked as they scrubbed. "Don't you want Dr. Runkleman?"

"I think we'll manage. Now here's what we're going to do. Have you got a long alligator forceps? A real long one?"

"We've got a special one—the last time Dr. Snider had trouble giving anesthetic, he let the patient swallow—"

"Never mind," said Lucas easily. "We're that much ahead, anyway. Now, we'll get this forceps and we'll use a local. I'm going to make a buttonhole an inch above the breastbone, into the windpipe. And then I'll want cocaine to spray the bronchi. Then I'm going to reach in with the forceps. You keep your eyes on the screen. When the jaws are right there, when they're open over the pin, you say 'Now!' Understand?"

"Yes, sir. But my God, Doctor. What if she coughs?"

"She's a Christian Scientist."

"I don't care what she is, she's almost bound to cough—!"

"Miss Paget, tonight you're going to see Faith in action. There's no better patient than a Christian Scientist. She's a Christian Scientist. And she won't cough."

Miss Paget shrugged. She left to prepare the tray.

Lucas walked smiling into the operating room. Miss Phelps smiled back at him politely.

"We're going to get that pin out," Lucas nodded. He took one of her thin hands. "And now we're going to have to depend on your cooperation. Will you give me that?"

She nodded.

Miss Paget entered. She held out a pair of rubber gloves and he shook his head. She uncovered the tray.

"It's not going to hurt much—a little discomfort, perhaps—"

Miss Phelps winked at him, grimaced her contempt of pain.

He swabbed the area at the base of her thin neck. He took a fold of skin and injected it.

"I'm going to make an opening here. I'm going to reach in with an instrument. I'm going to grasp the pin."

He looked at her searchingly, hoping she understood.

She nodded, closing her eyes slowly, opening them with composure.

"As the instrument enters you will feel an intense desire to cough. I don't know how you will master it." He paused. "But I know that you will. If you cough when the instrument goes in, it may puncture a bronchus. And then we'll have trouble." He smiled at her, his friendliest smile.

Her mouth opened.

"I shall not cough," she said.

He put his finger quickly before his lips. She nodded. She looked at the ceiling a moment.

"Ready?" he asked quietly.

She nodded and closed her eyes.

Miss Paget put a scalpel into his extended hand. Slowly, he made a small incision. He cut again. The trachea was open. He looked at Miss Paget. She nodded. She handed him the long forceps. He glanced at Miss Phelps, her eyes remained closed, her face serene. He opened the forceps. Miss Paget pressed the fluoroscope. He opened the incision. The forceps entered the trachea. Miss Phelps lay motionless. Slowly, intently, he passed the forceps down. Now he kept his eyes on the fluoroscopic screen, watching it as infinitely, cautiously, the forceps advanced. The forceps were his hands, were long fingers, slowly the slim fingers moved, slowly, down, down, down—a trifle more right—to the back—

"Now!" said Miss Paget.

He closed the forceps. He felt metal clamp on metal. He held the jaws tighter. Slowly he began the long upward retreat. Slowly the pin hooked on tissue—infinitely slowly he turned the forceps, turned an infinite fraction—it was free, again. Then on, again—upward—slowly . . . Below Miss Phelps' back-tilted chin six inches of the forceps had emerged—then seven,

Then it was out.

It clanked.

It lay there, bloody, in the tray, the forceps opened, there was a small tinkle as the pin struck the tray's metal, Miss Phelps lazily opened her eyes.

"All done." He smiled at her. "All over but the shouting."

Miss Paget passed him a needle. She stared at him.

"I'll just put a stitch or two here—not as good as I'll bet you could hem—and—first thing you know—what with one thing and another—we'll have you—as good as new!" He knotted the last stitch, clapped on a dressing and stepped back.

Miss Phelps put a finger questioningly to her mouth.

"Talk? Can't do you any harm, really. I'd just as soon you rested—"

"I didn't move, did I?" said Miss Phelps.

"No," said Lucas, "you didn't move." He squeezed her hand. "I didn't think you would."

The night nurse appeared in the doorway, looking at them apprehensively.

"You just take Miss Phelps here, and put her in a nice comfortable bed and take good care of her. And Miss Phelps—I'll see you in the morning."

She smiled and the nurse wheeled her out.

"That was some job, Doctor," Miss Paget said.

"You did just fine," he said happily. "And just remember this! If you can ever make your choice of patients—take mothers with little children—or Christian Scientists!"

He felt fine. In an obscure but logical way he had refuted Ben Cosgrove.

He walked to the basins and began to wash. She hesitated.

"Dr. Marsh—about Mr. Glaimer . . ."

"Oh, yes. Cancer of the rectum—"

"Dr. Marsh, no one knows this yet—" she brushed her straight, lank hair from her plain face— "but we're going to be married."

"Married!"

"That's right—"

"But you know—you must know—the patient—why, you know what the picture is!"

"We've talked it all over. And we've made up our minds. We don't know how much time there is left, but whatever there is— Doctor! Please! Couldn't you say something? To Dr. Runkleman? To get him to operate, at least? Mr. Glaimer's been here almost three months and he just comes in, he looks at him, and he goes out—"

"Are you asking me to question Dr. Runkleman's judgment? You're a nurse, Miss Paget. You ought to know better than that! If Dr. Runkleman feels Mr. Glaimer can be operated on—"

"Oh, I knew you'd say that! I knew it!"

"What else can I say? Oh, come now! You've let your emotions get the better of you. You've let yourself get involved with a patient—"

"Will you do it? We trust you! We know you can do it! If there's a chance, we know you're the one that can do it!"

Her eyes filled, her mouth awry, imploring.

Lucas shook his head.

"I'm sorry," he said. "You know how impossible that is. Even if I disagreed with Dr. Runkleman . . ." He dried his hands. He looked away.

"Thank you, Doctor," she said dully.

"You did a bang-up job tonight," he said earnestly. "And—think a bit! Think things over!— Is Mr. Glaimer comfortable? Is he in any pain?"

"No," she said, her head bowed, "no," her voice was muffled, "he's all right . . . he's in no pain . . ."

"I'll see you tomorrow, then." He nodded, he walked briskly into the corridor, he started toward the door, relieved.

The night nurse met him at the door.

"Miss Phelps?" he halted quickly.

"No, it's a Mr. Gunnis—stomach pains—call came here—"

"Gunnis?"

"Here's the address. Must be one of Dr. Runkleman's . . ."

Even in the darkness the Gunnis house stood out from its neat fellows on either side. Lucas swished through the weeds to the doorway, he stumbled once over a tin can, the door opened and the light revealed a woman in her thirties who peered at him fearfully, managed a cringing smile, and stuttering, led him to a bedroom.

"All right, you! Get the hell out," snarled Mr. Gunnis from the bed. His face was unshaven. From a corner of his mouth trailed a thin brown streak of tobacco juice. Mrs. Gunnis left hurriedly.

"Well, now," said Lucas pleasantly, opening his bag, "just what seems to be the trouble, Mr. Gunnis?"

"Got a gut ache," Mr. Gunnis said briefly, showing yellow-and-black teeth. "Didn't they tell ya?"

"That's right," said Lucas. He put his hand to the coverlet to draw it back and repressed a start of aversion at the filth of it. He unbuttoned the long underwear over Mr. Gunnis' stomach. As he began his examination he heard a splatting sound. He looked up quickly. On the wall a liquid smear of spat tobacco juice flowed down slowly. He looked at Mr. Gunnis. Mr. Gunnis looked back at him imperturbably.

Lucas frowned. He bent again. His fingers investigated the flesh beneath them. Mr. Gunnis grunted. He winced.

"Hurt you there?"

Mr. Gunnis spat on the wall beside his head again. The spittle ran down.

"Some," he said. And spit again.

"Stop that!" Lucas said sharply.

"Stop whut?"

"Stop spitting on that wall!"

Mr. Gunnis gathered a mouthful. He raised his head. He spat a stream of tobacco juice and mucus over the wall again.

"My house, ain't it?"

"It's your house and if you do it again I'll rub your goddamned nose in it!" Suddenly Lucas trembled with fury. "Go ahead! Just do it again! Just you do! Go on! I'm waiting for you!" He bent over the man, aching with fury, blind with rage, waiting.

Mr. Gunnis stared back at him. But he did not spit again.

Reluctantly, Lucas moved away, finished his examination. He shook out a handful of pills.

"Take these," he said coldly. "And if you're no better call another doctor! That'll be three dollars."

Mr. Gunnis looked at him malevolently. He reached beneath his pillow. He counted three limp bills from a worn wallet. He laid them silently on the bed. He made no move to button his underwear or draw up the sheet. Lucas picked up the money distastefully, he nodded briefly and walked out. As the front door closed behind him he heard clearly a contemptuous splat! He breathed the fresh night air gratefully, he walked quickly to his car. Automatically, he looked at his watch. Less than an hour had passed. With luck he'd be asleep by midnight.

The town slept. The dark streets stretched before him. The small night winds prowled the trees and the leaves rustled decorously, there was a sense of space and of quiet possession, of moist coolness and unhurried time. He was drowsy. His home, its neatness, its cleanness, surprised him as he let himself in. He had not noticed it before. There was a light in the kitchen. On the immaculate stove simmered a coffeepot. On the shining white enamel table gleamed a cup, a saucer, a spoon.

He poured a cup of coffee. He turned off the stove. He sat down. He sighed wearily. He sat and thought.

After a time he rose, the coffee untasted, he turned off the light, he tiptoed into the bedroom. He undressed in the darkness. He slid carefully in beside Kristina. She moved drowsily. He lay perfectly still. She slept on. The warmth of her body came to him. He began to think of Harriet Lang.

He did not think guiltily now. His world had changed. It had never been his world, at all. It had been a world he imagined. The world that was, the real world, was a world he detested. It was a world in which the sounds were pious noises and the sights were schooled actions and beneath the pious noises were the screams of the dying and the frightened and the punished and behind the schooled actions and the smiling gravity with which people misdirected attention from their intentions and their maneuvers was the naked ape of the jungle, cruel, implacable, and responsible to nothing but survival.

This was the real world, beside which all aberrant kindness and mercy and dignity and skill and civilization itself were a handful of occasionally encountered virtues, interesting for their presence, remarkable for their presence in the overshadowing face of things as they really were.

It was necessary to face facts. It was finally necessary to face any fact, to admit it, to be angry but not hurt, to be coldly angry, to be angry with contempt and to spare himself nothing of it, not even the contempt.

That was the world. Well, he could shine in it, he could shine in his own eyes, he could do what he wanted, still. And he could have what he wanted, now. He could work for it without conscience and without pity, he was free, he was bound by nothing, now, nothing but his own life, his own rules for it, his own needs, his own desires.

He thought of Harriet Lang again. He thought of her without guilt, freely, liberated, exhilarated by freedom. She was his and he would make her his. That was to start with. He would do what he wanted. And he wanted her. And he would have her. As soon as could be. He wanted her. He wanted her badly.

And the Medicine he practiced would be his Medicine.

He was full of anger. He fell asleep.

⋆ CHAPTER 30

"You got in early," Kristina said at breakfast. She said it tentatively, there was a great deal she wanted to talk about. There was little time. In a few minutes he would be due at the office, he would open the connecting door, the ocean of Medicine would swallow him, he would be gone without trace, their home would be empty of him as if he had never been there.

"Lucas," she said, "do you ever smoke a pipe?"

He stared at her, astonished.

"I don't smoke—" he began, exasperated. He checked himself. He looked at her keenly. "I believe they're right!" he exclaimed. "You're lonely! First Runkleman—then Castle!"

She said nothing.

"But you've got the whole day to yourself! All to yourself! All that time! You can do whatever you want to do! You can read—you lucky devil, you can read and read and read—"

She shook her head deprecatively.

"I never was a reader."

"I know! But don't you see? This is your chance! Oh, Kris, just try it! You can't imagine what it's like, what you're missing, what I wouldn't give just to read and study and read—"

"It's not for me like it is for you," she said reluctantly.

"All right—all right!" he said impatiently. He looked at her, balked, resentful. "You don't like books—you don't like music—you don't like art—you've never played games, not and like it—what's the matter with people, then? The town's full of people! Go out and meet some people!"

"I'll tell you what it is, Luke . . ." Then she halted uncertainly. She tried to think of words. Her inner self reached out to him across the table, trying to communicate, to touch him, to make him aware of her. I don't know much, I don't want the things you want, I'm glad you want them, I'm proud of you. Give me a baby, Luke. Then I'll be happy. Then I'll leave you alone. Just give me a baby, that's what my inside cries for, then there'll be a home, then, little by little, you'll change, you'll give up flying into the sun, you'll live with me, with the rest of us. And you'll be happy, Luke. I know it. You'll laugh and be happy.

"Go on," he said irritably. "You started—go ahead, Kris!" He looked at his watch. "I haven't got all day. What is it?"

"Some people—" she said hurriedly, prodded. "I don't know the things you know—I'm just a girl, Luke. Not everybody was given the same things. I want a home, and a man, and a—" She stopped in time. His eyes were glinting dangerously. "I want you to be proud of me," she said miserably. "Like I'm proud of you . . ."

A pang of pity knuckled his viscera. He swallowed.

"The desire for deference," he collected himself, "is normal, Kris. All humans have it. But you just don't get deference. You have to earn it."

She nodded dumbly. Just go on talking, just say something to me, now you're kind, keep talking, you'll let something fall, leave me with something . . .

"Now, you met some nice people, last night. They'll do for a starter. Get out among them—you don't have to sit by yourself here all day—"

"You know how I am," she said humbly. "I don't want to disgrace you—"

"But how will you ever learn! How? How?"

"I'll try," she said forlornly.

"Didn't Mrs. Kauffman ask you to join their whatever-it-is art class?"

"She's scared like me," Kris said unexpectedly. "Could I go up to the County now and then, Luke?"

"The County? Haven't you been listening to a word I've been saying? God! Can't I ever contact you at all?"

"I heard, Luke. Every word! When you said 'kids' it reminded me—"

"Kristina!"

"I don't mean us! Not us, Luke! I mean up at the County—those kids up there—maybe I could help out—fill up my time—I know they couldn't pay anything—"

"You'd just get in the way," he said, trying to think.

"No, no! You know yourself I'm an RN. My God, Luke! One thing I know, I know hospitals! Dr. Castle was the one who said it."

"Dr. Castle?"

"And Dr. Runkleman said it would be fine."

"Dr. Runkleman said that?"

"Honest! Honest, Luke!"

She stared at him, her mouth opened, her breath held.

Lucas shrugged.

"If Dr. Runkleman said it would be all right . . ." he conceded reluctantly.

"Oh, Luke!" She jumped from her chair and hugged him.

"Don't make so much fuss," he said uncomfortably.

She sat down again promptly.

"You think I can go up to the County today?"

"Sure," he said indifferently, struggling into his coat. "Just stay in the background—"

"I know.— That was a nice party last night, eh Luke?"

"It was all right."

"And you were the one that's going to give them a new water system! My, Luke! I was proud of you! Talking like that!"

"That was a big victory, that was! An intellectual small-town snob who faces Greece once a day, a small-town publisher who deals in paper and ink—and Cosgrove! That was some victory! A hick mayor, a hick publisher, and a hick lawyer!"

"You were wonderful, Luke!"

He studied her, he smiled, he shook his head.

"You didn't hear a word I said!"

"Yes I did, Luke. Yes! Honest! And that girl—" He was walking toward the door, "wasn't she smart, Luke? That Lang girl? The one about the pottery? I thought she was pretty, Luke. Did you notice? Didn't you think she was pretty?"

Lucas shrugged.

"Oh, yes . . ." She watched him.

"Is there anything else?"

"Well, let me think . . ."

But the door had closed behind him.

She looked uncomplainingly at the shut door, testing his words, his tone, his expression, she let her mind become blank, offering it to receive a verdict, before she could read the answer she wrenched her mind vigorously from such thinking as being its own penalty and in the recoil confronted herself on her way to the County Hospital, to the children there.

She stood still an uplifted, ecstatic moment. Then she whirled and flung herself at her housework with fury.

Dr. Runkleman was at his desk, idle, reading a medical journal. He looked up, glad to see Lucas, closed the magazine.

"I've kept you waiting," Lucas winced.

"No, no. I got up early." He sighed. Lucas glanced at him swiftly.

"Rested?" he asked carelessly.

"Oh, fine," said Dr. Runkleman. "Just fine . . . yes . . . I've just been reading of the death of an old classmate."

Lucas nodded politely.

"Heart trouble?"

"Yes," said Dr. Runkleman, "another heart. Don't doctors ever die of anything but heart trouble?"

"It's not a bad way to go."

"It's just such a waste." He rose. "I don't care about the other. It's just the waste."

"I guess we'd all be better off if we stopped long enough to have a checkup now and then," Lucas shrugged. "Practice what we preach—"

"Here's a man spent a lifetime learning, storing his brain full. And here he's dead and all he ever learned is rotting and gone. He can't give it to anyone, it just rots right along with the rest of him. That's what I mean. That's the wasted."

Lucas sighed. "You know—" he looked up suddenly— "if you have time this week I wish you'd give me a little checking over."

Dr. Runkleman clapped a hand on Lucas' shoulder.

"You?" he cried. "You're sound as a horse!"

Miss Snow stopped them at the door. Dr. Runkleman took the phone.

"Agnes!" He smiled after a moment. "What's on your mind?" He listened, he grinned. Then his face sobered. "Bring her down, then . . . Might as well . . . This morning . . . That's right. Get it over . . ."

He hung up.

"Remember those two old nurses?"

"The endarteritis—"

"I guess today's the day."

"She's kept her leg longer than she had any right to expect—"

"I know. I just hate to see things like that happen to nice people."

Lucas smiled mechanically. They got into the car.

"I've always had a kind of sneaking fondness for them," Dr. Runkleman said. "They're not—not the usual patient—"

"Has it ever seemed to you that patients all seem the same?" Lucas asked abruptly.

"Of course I guess you could say they're all individuals."

"Yes, they approach the pattern differently. That's true. And yet all the differences are minute."

"I guess that's the important point—"

"Not to me. To me the important point is that the differences are so minute that they aren't of any clinical significance. If you try to work a prognosis out of it the differences are meaningless."

"I'll tell you one thing, Doctor. So far as patients are concerned you've got to live your own life," Dr. Runkleman said energetically. "They don't give a damn about you one way or the other. You just make up your own life and go along that way and say nothing to anybody. You just remember that. I don't say you won't find nice people. But you just remember that. And another thing: there's one friend who'll never leave you." He stopped the car, got out, patted his hip pocket significantly.

"Your money," Lucas laughed.

"That's right! And don't you forget it!"

"You can lose your money," Lucas objected. "They can't take your mind away—and what you want to do."

"You still need money," Dr. Runkleman said confidently.

"I don't believe it," Lucas said honestly.

Dr. Runkleman looked at him uneasily. His face cleared and he grinned appreciatively.

"You're a great kidder." He shook his head admiringly.

They walked into the County Hospital. Dr. Snider intercepted them.

"Got your wife here, this morning!" he cried. "Nice lady! Came in, said you said for her to see if there wasn't something she could do in the baby ward." He shifted his quid of tobacco to the other cheek. "Hell, we don't have but one kid—little Italian, or something—she's a nurse, ain't she?"

"Yes," said Lucas shortly. "She's a nurse."

"That's what she said."

"It was my suggestion," said Dr. Runkleman.

"Of course! Of course! Glad to have her!"

"Thank you," Lucas said reluctantly.

"Well, she's down there right now, playing with it—"

"Did a Miss Mason come in?" Dr. Runkleman interrupted.

"Somebody or other came in a while ago. Two of 'em. They put 'em in with the women, I think."

Dr. Runkleman nodded and walked away, followed by Lucas.

"You gonna need me?" Dr. Snider called after them.

"No," said Dr. Runkleman, without turning, "no, I think we'll make out all right."

As if she had sensed their coming Agnes met them in the corridor.

"She's all ready," she said. She was pale. "Empty stomach. And everything. Gave her an enema myself, this morning. And she urinated. You may want to catheterize her—"

"Now, take it easy," Dr. Runkleman put his hand on her shoulder.

"She's all I've got. She's been so damned—"

"Want to help?" Dr. Runkleman asked gravely.

"I don't think so. I don't think I could stand it."

Dr. Runkleman looked down.

"We all knew it was coming off . . ."

She closed her eyes. She shook her head.

"There's no doubt of it, now," she said.

They walked into the ward.

From her bed Gloria greeted them as if they were all at her house.

"Going to take it off this morning?"
Dr. Runkleman replaced the coverlet.
"Looks like it," he said gently.
"It won't be bad," said Lucas.
"Hell, I'm not worrying about losing it! Hell! I haven't *had* it so long it's no good to me!"
"That's the spirit," Lucas grinned.
"Spirit hell! That's the way it is!"
"Don't swear so much," said Agnes.
"Long as I'm here I'm going to corrupt every patient who can hear me."
"Gloria," said Agnes timidly, "you want me to assist?"
"You damned well keep out of this! I want somebody who knows what he's doing!"
She put out her hand and took Agnes'.
"General?" she asked.
"Spinal," said Dr. Runkleman.
"Let's go. Let's get it over."

There was never much question that the foot would have to go.
But as they looked down at the purple, red, and yellow-white foot, the purplish ankle above, Dr. Runkleman hesitated. He looked up. Lucas looked back at him. Then with his gloved finger he pointed to the knee. He nodded his head firmly. Dr. Runkleman thought. Then he nodded back.
He walked to the head of the table.
"How you feeling?"
"Feeling fine," Gloria said drowsily. "Feeling nothing . . ."
"Good . . . Just may have to take off a little more than we planned . . ."
"Leave me a little," she murmured.
Dr. Runkleman took his place again. He nodded to the nurse.
"Shall I—?" Lucas asked.
"No-o-o. I've known this foot so long . . ."
The scalpel slapped into his palm and they began to work.
"Wasn't it Diffenbach—something like that—used to do this in ninety seconds?" Lucas murmured through his mask.
"Hip," said Dr. Runkleman. "I guess he'd do this in forty seconds . . ."
The room was silent then.
"Done?" Gloria murmured unexpectedly. Her voice was low, fuzzy, came startlingly loud in the silence.
"Almost," Lucas said reassuringly.
The room was silent again.
And then,
"All right," Dr. Runkleman looked up inquiringly.
"Right," said Lucas.
There was the sound of a saw.
It ended suddenly.
There was a small thump.

"Okay?" Gloria murmured sleepily.

"All done," said Dr. Runkleman.

The nurse took the severed leg. She put it foot first in the bucket beneath the table. The bucket was narrow at the bottom, the toes curled up the edge, the bucket toppled over.

The din was shocking. The leg rolled on the white tile. The nurse upended the bucket, stuffed the leg quickly back in again.

"Leave it on its side," Dr. Runkleman said coldly.

"Drop your watch?" Gloria murmured.

"All done," said Lucas cheerily.

"Home, James," Gloria sighed.

Dr. Runkleman walked to the head of the table.

"It's fine, Gloria." He nodded down at her. "Can you hear me?"

"I hear you—I heard everything . . ."

"It's just fine."

They wheeled her down the corridor, back to her bed.

Agnes questioned them with her eyes, ignored their reassurance, turned to bend over Gloria.

"All right, darling?" she whispered.

Gloria snored.

"She's fast asleep," Lucas sighed. "She's fine. She did beautifully."

"The foot—"

"Just fine," said Dr. Runkleman gravely.

"I—it's—she wanted to save it—you know how she is—she wanted to keep it—"

"Well, I tell you . . . we had to go a little higher . . . we had to take it off at the knee . . ."

"The knee!" Agnes swallowed.

"Don't think we've got a bottle big enough," Lucas said apologetically.

"No," said Dr. Runkleman. "Well, she wouldn't want that . . ."

"The knee!"

"She'll be all right . . ."

"For a while . . ."

"That's right . . . For a while . . ."

"Take care of her," said Lucas.

The nurse wheeled the stretcher away. They walked out into the corridor.

They walked in silence.

They left the hospital and got into the car.

"What do you think?" Dr. Runkleman asked gruffly.

"She's really something," Lucas admitted.

"If only ten percent of them were like her—ah, it's too bad!" he cried helplessly. "It makes me sick."

And part of that cry was pity, pity for the patient, indignation for the way things go, protest for the lost leg. But the greater part was anger for the sly, the lying, the pretending, the mean, the cruel, the cowardly . . . full-legged . . .

And hearing it, savoring its meanings, Lucas tried to feel what Dr. Runkleman felt about Gloria, he tried conscientiously. He could not empathize. His failure confused him. He felt guilty. Well, let's see now, he thought rapidly. First of all the pain—the months, the years of it. The amputation climax. And there were people who fainted, screamed, at an injection. All right—but did she have a high threshold? Maybe that made her so indifferent to pain. Maybe she just didn't feel what other people felt. Or—maybe she'd just gotten so used to it . . .

Maybe . . .

And her composure—her attitude—

Well, she was a nurse, wasn't she? Only, doctors and nurses weren't very good patients. But a nurse, though . . .

He shook his head irritably.

No, no! You never could tell about people. The only thing you could tell about them was that you could expect cowardice, calculation, a furtive, shabby inner husk. You could tell that, all right. It was there. You could rely on it. The thing you could never tell was whether they were really good, the few that seemed to be—

Or just acting! Just putting up a convincing show that sooner or later was going to let you down. Or whether you were kidding yourself, wanting them to be good, blinding yourself, and then one day here it came! and you were dropped with a sickening, scarring, shattering fall.

That's probably what she was doing. She probably didn't feel much pain, to begin with. No real reason why she should, no sure-fire, positive reason.

And she was a nurse. She wouldn't be afraid like the average person, she knew what was happening, she'd seen it often enough. To her it wasn't mysterious and it wasn't unfamiliar.

And for the rest, she'd probably been putting on that act all her life, talking gruff and rough, a real he-girl. She probably enjoyed the dramatic setting, probably enjoyed putting on her act in it—a little life—a small horizon—inside it all, in the core of her, beneath the acting, the posturing life in the woods, there was probably a very dull and unremarkable person . . . He winced at the thought of finding it out . . . having it confirmed.

"Yes, sir," said Dr. Runkleman, "you've got to take your hat off to a pair like that! She took it like I knew she would!"

Lucas shook his head admiringly.

"You don't often see them like that," he said obediently.

The day wore on. The procession of patients began. In mid-afternoon, as they dealt swiftly with an infant's rash, Dr. Runkleman looked up suddenly at Lucas.

"We forgot to look in on Mrs. Marsh!"

For a moment Lucas looked at him puzzled. Then he remembered that Kristina was not home, that she was at the hospital. He shrugged.

"She'll be all right," he said indifferently.

"I clean forgot!"

"Well, if I know Kris—she has, too."

"Well, I guess you'll be having some of your own someday and give her something to really keep busy."

"Maybe," said Lucas levelly. "Maybe someday. Plenty of time for that . . ."

"Don't wait too long," Dr. Runkleman warned playfully. "If I were you—" And then he broke off. He frowned. He cleared his throat. He turned a little aside.

Lucas watched him, alert, helpless.

The moment passed. They returned to their labors.

The day ended.

"How'd you make out, Kris?" he asked that night.

"You know, I'm sorry for you! If that's what you have to work in all day—I'm sorry for you!"

He looked at her, startled. She walked, she talked, she moved about with energy, with force.

"What's the matter? What happened?"

"So that's the County!" she said scornfully. "That's the famous County! They call that a hospital?"

"What did you expect? Bellevue?"

"I've seen small hospitals! Believe me!"

"There isn't enough money budgeted to staff RN's."

She looked at him speculatively.

"You think not, Lucas?"

"I know not."

"You think Dr. Snider's poor, maybe? Him and that head nurse?"

"What are you talking about, Kris? Do you know?"

"Me? I don't know anything. All I know is that everybody at the hospital knows. I was only there one day and everybody rushes to tell me—"

"Tell you what! What gossip, now?"

She shrugged.

"Maybe it's gossip."

"Tell me!"

"Dr. Snider and Mrs. Gaunt have been in cahoots for years—"

"Just exactly what does that mean?"

"It's not my business," Kristina said primly, untouched by the ominous note in Lucas' voice, "only when the whole hospital knows they have been taking money from charity patients for years, now, when everybody says the same thing, when it's common knowledge—when the hospital's run like a pigpen—when every nurse plays politics and belongs to some clique—and don't say it's a lot of women!" She looked at him steadfastly. "Because it isn't, Luke." There was sincerity and conviction in her voice. She spoke quietly.

For a moment he was impressed, he was shaken.

"What do they say—specifically—"

"You better look, Luke. You and Dr. Runkleman. Before there's trouble. When everybody says the same thing—when they've been saying it for years—"

"Dr. Snider has a small private practice, you know . . ."

"I know. I heard all about it."

He sighed.

"I'll tell Dr. Runkleman," he nodded wearily. "There's probably some perfectly reasonable explanation for everything." He shrugged. "Otherwise—how was the day?"

"I didn't do much. There was only one baby—"

"I know—"

"He was awful cute—I'm used to so many—when you just see one, like that—but there was nothing for me to do." She paused, considering. "I looked in on the old men.—Lucas—you said once—would it be all right? If I wrote my father? If I asked him to come on?"

"Sure," said Lucas. "I don't care. Go ahead and write him." He remembered Carlile Emmons and he winced. "Go ahead! Write him!"

Three days later the afternoon office calls were interrupted by the arrival of a salesman from one of the medical supply houses. Dr. Runkleman promptly suspended work, closed the office door and sat back. Soon Lucas, too, was listening to the man with pleasure, inspecting his wares, relaxing in a recess.

He was a dapper little man, dressed somberly as befitted the dignity of calling on doctors and representing so great a house, he was plump, his shoes were a little shabby, he wore an Elks tooth on a vest chain and a Masonic emblem in his lapel. His scalp showed through his thin black hair, roached neatly back. On his plump wedding finger he wore a Knights of Pythias ring.

He brought them the news of the countryside. He mentioned doctors Lucas had never heard Dr. Runkleman mention, but whom Dr. Runkleman had met during his thirty-odd years of practice around Greenville, and all the news was somehow entertaining, some of it a little dull, but all worth listening to, a little exciting, even. It was the news of a large medical family, a family of which Lucas was part. Dr. Ames, over in Clarksville, had helped a farmer deliver a two-headed calf, probably see it at the county fair this fall if it lived—and how was the fair grounds coming and had Dr. Runkleman been able to get them to shelve the fair grounds and get a water works instead and stop the typhoid? And they told him about the mayor and the meeting and Dr. Runkleman told him proudly how Lucas had swung it—and the man grinned at Lucas, and nodded admiringly.

And put it away to tell it the next place he stopped, Lucas could hear him, Dr. Runkleman over in Greenville's got himself an assistant, bright young fellow from all accounts, Runkleman thinks a lot of him, says the feller put in just the right word and by jinks they're finally going to get a new water system . . .

And he had a tale to tell about a coroner in the next county who had spent five hours searching for a bullet in a murdered woman's head and of how the undertaker had found it in her hair. And he dropped cautiously his sorrow that Dr. Barnard and Mrs. Barnard seemed to be splitting up, all right, and a new doctor had come to Oraney, so far away that Dr. Runkleman could barely remember it, and there was some talk of abortions, some chiropractor feller in Wendelberg, him and his wife, and hadn't there been a little trouble of that sort around here? Seems he heard? And as one humbly connected with Medicine he shook his head wryly and smiled patronizingly at the very word "chiropractor."

There was a little more news, a little more gossip, and then, knowing to the infinite second how long a recess could be prolonged, he switched smoothly and apologetically to his wares.

"No," he said, "no use calling on Dr. Snider. They haven't bought anything up there at the County, why, you mightn't believe it, it must be a good ten years."

But he had a little something new he thought Dr. Runkleman and Dr. Marsh here might like to try—

"Same old arsenical," Dr. Runkleman grunted, looking at the bottle.

"Well, it's got a new twist to it—Dr. Brewster, now, well he swears by it—and Dr. Rankin, over in Lepton—"

Anyway here were a dozen samples— "Want more? Got lots more! Take all you want! And here's a lot more new stuff . . ."

The desk was littered with samples.

"By George, that stuff in prescriptions would cost a patient thirty dollars!" Lucas said suddenly.

Dr. Runkleman and the salesman looked at the desk.

"Nearer fifty," the salesman nodded complacently. "Lots more where that came from. Saves me carrying the weight of it around. Course, now, if you decide to *order* some—"

"What are we short of?" Dr. Runkleman asked Lucas.

And they ordered another five pounds of harmless "stomach pills," a few pounds of sore-throat tablets, two quarts of mild sedatives, oh, and the cough pills were running low—"Got one with a new flavor, now"—"No, no, we'll stick to the old . . ."

"And how about equipment? How's your X-ray?"

"No, we don't need a new X-ray—going fine—"

"Got a real buy this week—doctor over in Anadale died, widow wants to sell—cheap—"

"Hasn't got a good centrifuge, has he?" Lucas asked eagerly.

"That's right!" cried Dr. Runkleman. "You been wanting a decent centrifuge—"

"Well, now, he hasn't got a centrifuge, now, not that I think of—but how about this—have you seen our new line?"

And he riffled open a ten-pound catalogue.

"How's this one?" And he pointed to a page of centrifuges, then another and another, all exciting, all beautiful, all expensive.

Lucas sighed and shook his head.

"Too much money."

The salesman looked understandingly at Dr. Runkleman.

"Well, now, I guess—" he began.

"Which one?" Dr. Runkleman took the catalogue. He pored over it happily. "This one? This the one you want?"

"Yes," said Luke, "and I'd like a yacht, too!"

"Send it!" Dr. Runkleman bade the salesman.

"Yes sir! A man that wants a centrifuge wants the best! I know!"

But he knew his place, he never presumed to use medical language as if to lever himself thus onto a plane of equality with doctors, because he knew how that irritated doctors to hear a layman use their language, even if he was a medical supply salesman.

But Dr. Runkleman was already busy flipping the pages of the catalogue and the salesman winked at Lucas and nodded cheerily—

"I'd like to have one of these," Dr. Runkleman decided excitedly.

"By George, where have you been hiding this, Joe! This is just what I need!"

"Fine for hip work," the salesman said bending over the book, "new kind of nail, whole equipment." He looked up to Lucas. "You see this, Doctor?"

Lucas bent to look.

"They were trying them out at the hospital," he remembered. "I think they said they were pretty good—"

"No price on them," said Dr. Runkleman. "How much?"

"Eighty-four dollars. That's the complete set. Chisels, screws in a nice chrome rack all their own, easy to sterilize, set of nails, and a wire twister—"

Lucas whistled.

"I'll buy it!" Dr. Runkleman's eyes glowed.

"Yes, *sir*!" The salesman finished writing the order. "Why don't you keep that catalogue, Doctor? Nice to have around."

"This? Why, you don't want to go giving stuff like this away—must be a thousand shiny pages here—must have cost a fortune—"

"Did!" the salesman said cheerily. "Keep it. I guess it cost them twenty dollars and more to put that catalogue out. Glad to have you have it." He turned to Lucas. "You're good luck to me, Dr. Marsh. Didn't have a bit of trouble with Dr. Runkleman today." He grinned happily. "Now how about that X-ray—"

"Shoo!" said Dr. Runkleman. He looked quickly at his watch. "Look at the time! And the whole office full of patients . . ." His voice was hoarse again. He coughed.

Grinning, the salesman bent to cram instruments, pills, bottles, back into his huge bag.

"Wait a minute," Lucas exclaimed. He bent, he pulled a length of tubing out of the salesman's bag.

"Stethoscope tubing," the salesman said.

"I know! But look at the diameter!" He showed it to Dr. Runkleman, who looked at it blank-faced, smiling politely.

"That's the small diameter stuff!" Lucas cried. "They say you can hear a lot better with a smaller diameter tube—there was a piece on it not too long ago—" He tore the old tubing from his stethoscope.

"Wait! I'll help you!" The salesman got out a bandage scissors. He snipped twice. Lucas fitted the rubber tubing over the ear pieces, the diaphragm connections.

He looked at the salesman, he looked at Dr. Runkleman.

"Here!" he said. He walked to Dr. Runkleman, putting the ear pieces in his ears. "Let me see. Let me try them on you!"

"Me!" and Dr. Runkleman, embarrassed, began to fumble reluctantly with his vest buttons, but Lucas already had them open. The diaphragm was against Dr. Runkleman's chest.

Instantly he heard a diastolic murmur. The diaphragm moved. A heavy second aortic sound . . . thrill . . . dullness at the second intercostal space—it was plain, it was unmistakable—there was absolutely no doubt . . . none . . .

He straightened. He smiled delightedly at Dr. Runkleman.

"It's fine, sir! It's *much* plainer than the old diameter. Try it!" He offered him the stethoscope.

And Dr. Runkleman, smiling amiably, politely listened to Lucas' chest, widened his eyes, nodded his head, pursed his lips to show surprise, to show that he backed his assistant.

"Very plain, Joe! Much plainer!"

"By gosh, Doctor," the salesman sighed happily, "you sure keep up with things, don't you! Not many'd have known that! That new diameter tube isn't even out yet, you might say."

"How much," said Dr. Runkleman.

"Now, this is mine! This *I* pay for!" Lucas interrupted.

"I tell you what, Doctor, you just keep it. For being such a good salesman for me."

And he snapped his bag shut, shook hands all around, and was gone in almost the same wonderful, practiced movement.

Miss Snow put her head in the door.

"Children through playing?" she asked impassively.

"Got a lot of new toys!" Dr. Runkleman called jovially.

"I suppose."

She walked to the desk. She saw the samples. Her shoulders sagged.

"Oh, Doctor! Now where am I going to put this?"

"Take it home and set yourself up in business."

"You've already got a trunkful—there's cartons of samples down in the basement—"

"You take care of it," Dr. Runkleman said defiantly. "Come on, Doctor—"

They separated in the hallway. Lucas closed the door of a treatment room. Dr. Runkleman disappeared on the other side.

A woman of thirty-five, her hair dyed an uncertain yellow, her lean face heavily powdered, looked at him balefully.

"Do you know how long I been waiting?"

"I'm very sorry," said Lucas. "What seems to be the trouble?"

"The trouble? That's what I come here to find out! Keep a person waiting cooped up in a cubbyhole almost a half-hour—"Her eyes widened. "Why, I coulda died in that time!"

"Are you in pain? Does it hurt anywhere?"

She pointed to her abdomen.

"And I got headaches. Migraine. And I don't sleep nights . . ."

It was soon apparent that the reasons for her sore colon, her headaches, her insomnia did not lie in her colon, her brain, or her thalamus. As he wrote the prescription, which was composed of a mild sedative, and from a large bottle shook out a few mild laxative pills, and from another bottle shook out a dozen unmarked aspirin tablets, he wondered heavily how the leaves of this plant, the pulverized chemicals, could possibly solve this woman's real trouble, whatever it was. And he looked at her dull face and knew that she wasn't worth a miracle.

"I nearly died last Wednesday," she said aggrievedly, her eyes following the pills dropping into their little envelopes, her fingers taking the prescription reverently.

Nearly died, thought Lucas. You nearly died, did you? . . . Diastolic shock . . . diastolic murmur . . . heavy second aortic sound . . . hoarseness . . . cough—there wasn't any doubt, now—he was walking around with it—there was death in his chest and he was walking around. Did he know? Had he already guessed?

"Did you?" he asked the woman politely. "Was it that bad?"

"I thought for a minute I was actually going to die. I said to my husband—we were in bed at the time—" And the corners of her mouth drew down for an instant, her eyes flickered, it was all there, it was plain to see now, her voice went on, he rose, he smiled, he nodded to her encouragingly, the door closed behind her.

He went out into the corridor. Her husband probably bored her, whatever sex life remained, if there ever had been any for her, was a trial and an indignity. Sometimes she thinks of leaving him—but of course she couldn't do that—the neighbors—he'd be amazed to know she even thought such things. . . . They drifted together, they got married, neither of them ever mattered much to the other or the world, they were dull, meaningless people, they found each other dull, meaningless, they were trapped, stuck, enduring it out . . .

So she'll go on with her migraine, her insomnia, her sore colon . . .

And what difference does it make! What—in God's name—what difference does it make!

Biologically inadequate to begin with.

Meaningless.

Not even a real illness.

And all the time he was trying not to think of Dr. Runkleman. Because there wasn't anything to think about. Because there it was. Aneurysm of the arch of the aorta.

He went back to the office. He called Dr. Castle.

"You're right," he said. That was all he said.

At the other end of the line there was silence.

"How did you work it?" Dr. Castle sighed.

Miss Snow put her head in the door.

"I've got a lulu," she said.

"I'll see you tonight," Lucas said into the phone.

"I'm due at the mayor's. So are you."

"See that she takes two teaspoons every hour," Lucas said politely. He hung up.

"Come look at your lulu," Miss Snow led the way.

"Who is she?"

"Never saw her before. Stranger in town."

There were two of them, two girls. They were chewing gum. One looked up at him frightened and slid off the treatment table. The other sat in a chair and looked at him calmly, with interest.

"Which one of you is the patient?"

The frightened girl, the dark, thin one, pointed quickly, wordlessly at her companion.

"You come with me, dear," Miss Snow left, leading the frightened girl.

"What seems to be the trouble?" Lucas smiled, his eyes raced over her face, trying to miss nothing, missing little, aged about twenty, weight about one hundred and twenty-five, make it thirty, little sloppy, cheap clothes, calm, poised, healthy, chewing gum . . .

Possible slight chlorosis, moderate hyperpit, some extrusions centrals . . .

"Well," she said uncertainly.

She rose.

He stopped searching.

"Suppose you get up here," he stood aside, pointing to the table.

Her hands were clean. Her blond hair was tousled but clean. Her underwear was clean. Darned, too . . . I didn't know girls wore darned underwear . . . but clean. . . .

"I've got a pain," she said quietly. She was perfectly composed.

"Where?" he said. He pressed her abdomen. "Here?"

"Yes."

His fingers probed. She lay impassive. He straightened.

He looked at her levelly.

"You know what's the matter with you, don't you?"

She looked back at him, silent.

"You're going to have a baby. You knew that, didn't you?"

"I thought so," she said quietly. As if that had been solved now.

"You're pregnant. Those pains are labor pains. You're going to have a baby. Maybe tonight. You know where the hospital is?"

She shook her head.

"I'll call them. I'll tell them I'm sending you up." He looked at her card. "Now—Miss Townsend, is it? Oh, I see. You don't live here. You're not from Greenville, then?"

"Down from the southern part of the state," she said.

"I see . . . You'll have to give us your address, we have to have that."

She looked down. He waited. She raised her head slowly.

"Why?"

"Rules. If anything should happen to you—I'm sorry, but—"

"Beltville," she said expressionlessly. "RFD 1, Beltville . . . You figuring to tell my folks?"

"Not figuring to tell anything. Doctors don't 'tell.' Where's your young man? Why isn't he here?"

"Which way's the hospital?" she asked serenely.

"I'll call them," said Lucas. They walked down the corridor toward the office.

"You knew you were going to have a baby, didn't you?"

"I kind of thought so," she admitted. "The last week or so I was pretty sure. I didn't know how soon."

"Your girl friend know?"

"Her? Oh, gosh, no!"

"Sticking out like that—and she doesn't know?"

"She thinks I'm getting fat. She wouldn't know. We're both from the same place. We're looking for jobs together." She spoke to him slowly, calmly, friendlily.

"How about this fellow."

"Oh, *he* doesn't know."

"Aren't you going to tell him?"

She shrugged.

"What for?" She considered a moment. "He'd never admit it," she decided.

"I'll see you later tonight," he said. "Good luck to you . . ."

She thanked him gravely. She took her girl friend's arm. They left, the friend barraging her with questions, the pregnant girl answering calmly, slowly, expressionless. The word "appendicitis" floated back to him clearly.

Townsend, he repeated to himself. Elizabeth Townsend.

He called the private hospital.

A half-hour later the private hospital called back.

"She's going to have a baby, Doctor," the superintendent protested.

"I hope so," Lucas exclaimed.

"But she can't have it here! Not here, man!"

"Why not?"

"Doctor Marsh! Didn't she tell you how old she was? That girl's under age! She's twenty! We'll be stuck with the baby—"

"Her folks'll take it."

"You'll never find her folks in a million years! Chances are a hundred to one she's given the wrong address and wild horses won't pull it out of her—"

"Well, then, it'll be—"

"And she can't give it away. She can't give it away for adoption. She's under age—we don't want to be stuck with it, Doc. And another thing—I mean, I don't mind so much—but she hasn't got a dime, she and this girl friend ran away, they've got five dollars left, that's all they've got, that and an old jaloppy—what's the matter with the County?"

"Send her to the County," Lucas said coldly. He hung up.

The phone rang again ten minutes later. It was the superintendent again.

"Now the girl friend's gone!"

"What do you mean—'gone'!"

"Claimed she never knew it was going to be a baby, got hysterical, went to get something, came back and she was gone. Disappeared. She and the jaloppy."

"I'll come get her," said Lucas. He hung up.

"What's the matter?" Dr. Runkleman asked.

"Girl," said Lucas sardonically. "One of your Glorias. Young kid. Didn't know she was going to have a baby. Having half-hour pains. Nice kid," he said suddenly. "Damned nice kid. Clean as a whistle. Never turned a hair. Now, her girl friend's run out on her, and the Valley—"

"Couldn't take her there," Dr. Runkleman nodded. "She's a minor—"

"So I'm going over to pick her up and take her to the County."

"Old Dr. Stork himself," said Dr. Runkleman. He smiled surprise, approving.

As he walked into the County Hospital with the girl, Lucas met Kristina coming out. Her face was tired. Her eyes brightened at the sight of him.

"Still here?" he said, surprised.

"I'm just going home. I'll get supper right away. I got everything bought, all I got to do—"

"This is Miss Townsend. Miss Elizabeth Townsend. This is my wife, Miss Townsend. Will you take Miss Townsend to maternity, please? Will you say I sent her?"

Kristina saw, then. Her face softened. She smiled at the girl.

"Pleased to meet you," she said.

"Likewise," the girl smiled.

"You come along with me, I'll see you get everything nice, don't worry—"

"I'm not worried," the girl said calmly.

"You take care of her, Kris. I'm going back to the office."

"Thank you, Luke," she called after him. "Come on, dear," and she took the girl's arm, "look at the sun, what a nice day to have a baby," and they passed smiling fondly into the hospital.

Dr. Runkleman was at the office when Lucas returned. He was turning the pages of the huge catalogue the salesman had left. He looked up a little guiltily.

"All fixed up?"

Lucas nodded.

"Probably have it tonight. . . . Tired?"

"Oh . . . some . . . love to look at these catalogues." His voice was suddenly much hoarser. He cleared his throat. "What did you think of Joe?"

"Joe? Oh! He was quite a salesman, all right. Must make a fortune out of Binyon and Blake—"

Dr. Runkleman cleared his throat.

"Have you been getting a little hoarse, lately? Not coming down with a cold on me, are you?"

"Me? Lord, no! Healthy as a horse."

"You ought to know . . ."

"I sure do! What did you think of that X-ray business? That used X-ray unit?"

"I want to thank you for that centrifuge. That was certainly nice of you, Doctor . . ."

"Me? It's for the office, isn't it? No, no! I was just wondering about that X-ray." He coughed a little.

"Do you think we need a new X-ray?"

"Oh, I don't know. Ours is getting a little out of date, maybe . . . it's old as Methuselah. . . . Wonder who that doctor was? He didn't say, did he? Probably nobody we know. . . . I was just thinking, must be tough on the widow, all that stuff on her hands . . . probably didn't leave much . . ."

"One thing!" Lucas said. "She's evidently not selling the practice!" He said it with satisfaction.

Dr. Runkleman looked at him inquiringly.

"I hate to see those ads," Lucas burst out. "Damn it, every time I see it, I hate it! Selling practices, like toothpaste or onions or real estate!" He controlled himself. "How can you sell a practice?" He smiled. "Tumbling all over themselves, trying to outbid each other, like a bunch of merchants in a bazaar. What are they selling? Medicine? How can you sell the practice of Medicine?"

"I guess I never thought of it," Dr. Runkleman hesitated. "Seems like if a man spends his life building up a practice, good will, patients, I don't know—do you think he ought to give it away?"

"If we're scientists, then the ads should read: 'Scientist in town of 3,000, will sell his backers, and experiments, yearly gross $6,000,' if we're artists: 'For sale, thriving custom in town of 5,000, will sell rich sponsors, several large accounts, reputation, etc., should net $5,000'—"

"Maybe they put it wrong . . ."

"It shouldn't be hawked—"

"Still—they've got to sell it, somehow . . ."

"There's something wrong. I don't know what it is. But you can't sell the practice of Medicine. Not unless Cosgrove is really right. Not unless we're just tradesmen—I don't know . . . I can't figure it out . . ."

Dr. Runkleman watched him, troubled.

"End of the day," Lucas smiled tiredly. "Don't mind me."

"You're right in a way—"

"I'd like to look you over."

"Me?"

"I'd like to give you a thorough checkup."

Dr. Runkleman laughed heartily.

"Don't worry about me. I'm—"

"I know. You're sound as a horse! Please, Doctor—will you let me?"

"Sometime . . ."

"Now?"

"What did you hear today?"

"Hear? Hear when?"

"When you changed tubes so you could listen to my chest?"

Dr. Runkleman looked at Lucas, smiling.

"Listened to your chest? Listened to your—oh, yes! When the salesman was here! Now what in the world do you think I'd hear in fifteen seconds!"

Dr. Runkleman continued to smile, looked at him steadily.

"You're pretty hoarse lately," Lucas said soberly.

"All right . . . Get a pain in my chest occasionally."

"No harm looking," said Lucas.

Dr. Runkleman rose.

"Someday," he said mildly.

"Now?"

"No, I don't think so . . . Hey! Mrs. Marsh'll be looking for you!"

Lucas rose.

"There's nothing wrong. Don't worry, boy. I get a little tired sometimes, little hoarse, little chest pain, reached the age . . . Thanks for worrying . . ." He smiled broadly.

"There's going to be another meeting tonight," Lucas said levelly.

"I don't think I'll go," Dr. Runkleman sighed.

"No," said Lucas. "One of us is enough."

"You worried?" Dr. Runkleman asked suddenly.

Lucas eyed him squarely.

"Not a bit. I hope at your age I sound like you do!"

Some of the tension went out of Dr. Runkleman's face.

He left, taking the catalogue with him.

Lucas sat for a moment, trying to think but there was nothing to think about. He gave up. He opened the door of the second treatment room. He shut the door behind him. He was in his living room. He walked to the small kitchen. Kris was setting the table.

"She's got five brothers and five sisters!" Kristina began at once. "The girl! The girl who's going to have a baby!"

"Oh," said Lucas. "Big family, eh?" He took off his coat, tiredly.

"She and the oldest brother, they support the family. Then this happened. So she run away. She's a nice girl."

"She tell you anything?"

"I just been telling you—five brothers, five—"

"Where she came from? Whether that's her real name?"

"No," said Kristina. She turned away. "No, she didn't."

"What's she going to do with the baby?"

"I don't know," Kristina said in a low voice.

For a while they ate in silence.

"Luke? . . . If nobody wants the baby—I mean, maybe nobody wants it—do you think maybe I—maybe we—I mean—"

He set down his fork. He looked at her coldly.

"I know what you mean. I know exactly what you mean. And you know what the answer is. Don't you!"

"Yes," she said quietly.

He looked down at his plate. He stared at it, unseeing. He tried to control his rage. It grew too huge, too choking. He jumped up suddenly.

"God damn you!" he shouted. "God damn you to hell! You thick-headed imbecile! Couldn't you even let me eat dinner in peace?"

He trembled, on the verge of striking her.

She stared at him, he was pale, shaking with hate and rage. She looked away, she lowered her head.

He rushed from the room.

He drove through the night. When he was cooler he stopped the car, he looked moodily over the dim countryside. He remembered the meeting. He looked at his watch. He was late. He drove quickly to the mayor's house.

Dr. Castle had gone. Bemis Shedd was leaving. The mayor went to the kitchen to mix Lucas a drink.

"Sit here," said Harriet. She made room for him on the couch. "I'll tell you all about it. Nothing much happened, anyway."

"Thanks," Lucas said awkwardly. The moment he saw her his heart had begun to hammer. His lips felt thick.

"Is something the matter?" she asked. He moved and the back of his hand touched her thigh.

Her eyes were soft, suddenly, and brilliant, deep as a well, she leaned forward, her lips brushed his mouth. She sat back. She looked at him.

"I'll help Henry get you a drink," she said, rising as he reached for her. "You sit here. I'll be right back."

Lucas remembered little of the rest of the evening. He waited dumbly for the evening's end, waited to take Harriet home. He dared not think farther. He sat, waiting.

At eleven the phone rang. It was the County.

He rushed angrily into the night.

Two hours later Elizabeth Townsend was delivered of a baby boy. Lucas saw her to her bed. He patted her head.

He returned to the mayor's house. The house was dark. He drove away. He drove slowly past Harriet Lang's house. There were no lights. He drove past the house again. The house was dark. He parked the car. He sat uncertainly. He tried to think what to do. He made himself have courage. He got out of the car, he walked quietly to her door. He looked both ways. The street was empty. He knocked cautiously. There was no answer. He waited. He knocked again. He had to knock quietly. He waited. There was no answer.

He walked carefully into the shadows, walked quietly down the sidewalk, he got into his car, the noise of the starter was startlingly loud. He drove way.

After a while he drove reluctantly home.

⋆ CHAPTER 31

The town of Greenville, a named place on the earth's surface, lay deserted in the moonlight, deserted by the humans who had gathered there, and who with their rules, plans, concepts, resolves, habits, and history were now asleep. The town lay motionless, housing their sleep. Its earth was indistinguishable from the earth which composed its named edges; its trees, its air, its water, its earth, its elements, were the same trees, air, earth, water, elements as in the anonymous countryside which surrounded it.

But it was not countryside to humans for it had been named, it had been named Greenville, it had been defined, it had been bounded, it had been given shape, and time and usage had flavored it with distinction and character and individuality. And although some of these attributes were imaginary, they were accepted by all the humans who had elected to live there. The decision to abide in this pinpoint of geography had been followed immediately by the urge to name it, the compulsion to set it apart from anonymity, from wilderness, from the loneliness of space. And this handful of humans, pinpointed on a ball of mud spinning lonely in a universe without boundaries, despairingly conscious that they would go all their lives lonely in a place that was not home, having that secret fear, that sick knowledge born in them, distinguishable from other animals because of this knowledge, named an area of planet, gave themselves a point of reference, and for practical purposes, for a barrier against fear and a barrier against the desolation of knowledge, assumed the obstinate convention that they were not lost.

The area of their residence was named. Being named it acquired the first rule of men. The other rules followed rapidly, rules learned elsewhere, many necessary, many more unnecessary and indeed impeding, making living more difficult, but rules all the same, reassuring by their very complexity and volume, seeming to give purpose to the incomprehensible and the unknown.

Why am I here? the young asked.

And the old pointed to the rules.

Why should I be proud of this anonymous area where I was born, why am I born to defend it, to be homesick for it, to long to return to it, to feel the mother-feeling for it, to feel my roots here?

Because it has been named.

It is the place where you were born and it has importance and distinction and it is unique, it is the only place where you were born. And being born is a momentous thing, full of purpose, full of magic, alive with destiny, and this is the place where it happened. And this place has been named. And when you are choking with loneliness and doubt, and know yourself, sickly, and see no purpose, and discern no destiny, and howl to the uncaring heavens for a reason, a plan, a purpose, let this solid fact comfort you, in the end here is a place. And it is not anonymous. And it is named. That is solid. That is fact.

The humans who inhabited Greenville slept. And the town was deserted of their consciousness and the buildings, the streets were meaningless, they were arbitrary arrangements of wood and lines of cement and bits of metal beyond the understanding of other animals and alien to the earth itself.

And light came again, and the humans wakened, and the concerns of the community had meaning again, and the wood and the stone, the metal and all other objects and materials with which they designed living, again had significance, and relevance, and were important, as they had agreed upon.

Like all humans anywhere upon the planet these humans arose a day nearer death.

In the large house where he lived alone except for the furniture which companied him with presence, the presence of achievement, of things he had resolved one day to have, Dr. Runkleman rose early, made himself coffee, sat with it waiting patiently the hour when his fellow humans here who had not been shaped in the indelible habit of rising at five o'clock on a cold and barren North Dakota farm would be astir and he could be among them.

He thought briefly of the day in terms of its contents, of the operations scheduled at the County in the morning, the operations at the Valley, the dozen patients who would die this day or perhaps continue to live, the two or three who would almost surely die, and he reviewed automatically what had been done for this dozen and this two or three, to be certain that as far as he knew he had not left undone that which he ought to have done for them and that he had done for them that which he ought to have done, according to the rules of his profession in this society, and in this place.

He had practiced Medicine too long to be reassured by the knowledge man had amassed concerning himself and he knew that those would die whose dying condition had been described by his teachers long ago and by all he had learned since then, and that there were no miracles and that neither science nor discovery had materially altered their prospects. He knew he had done all that he was required to do.

He reviewed the prospects of those patients on whom he was to operate this day, ruminating again to assure himself that none would die on the table, that none would die immediately afterward, barring the completely unforeseeable.

And for the rest he thought almost indifferently and without interest of the small army of sick and ailing, of those organically ill and of those functionally ill, who would clamor for help with their voices, their tones, their eyes, their faces, this day. And this part of the day he estimated in terms of bulk, of volume, of time, and there might even be a triumph or two, a constantly used remedy which might produce startling betterment for someone, delighting himself and the patient, but for the most part it would be a steady, almost faceless procession, apathetic, dull, or excited by fear, or panicked by pain, one day nearer death, bearing with them organs he was powerless to reconstruct, bearing with them bodies that were slowly deteriorating, bearing with them bodies that neither he nor any man living fully comprehended or half comprehended, to which he would administer physical forces, chemicals, pressures, electricity, the result of which neither he nor any man living could absolutely guarantee and most of which he and all living men only partly understood.

And he knew that when they came to him they would come to a figure of mystery, awful in its ability to define what had gone wrong with them, awful in its knowledge of what to do to set things right, most awful of all in its knowledge of that greatest of all mysteries to man, the anatomy and the physiology of man himself.

This knowledge might be blighted by anger and disillusionment, by medicines which did not help. But then he would become a human who had failed them, just a human, a fellow human like themselves. And they would go to another doctor and perhaps even another and another, and in the end a hundred even, but their faith was obstinate, they would die believing that they had seen a lot of humans but that someone in the world, somewhere in the world, somewhere there was a man who could help them. And this man was a doctor.

He was indifferent to their criticism and their reproaches and even sometimes to their praises, for he knew that their praises had little to do with their gratitude. He found deference in himself for people of wealth or consequence and he treated their illnesses with greater concentration but in the end with the same physical forces at his disposal, the only means available for those he hated, those he loved, those to whom he was keenly alive or those to whom he was indifferent. Great poverty in his youth had taught him a respect for money and for those who possessed it.

He guarded his reputation with devotion and anxiety. He prized the grudged or freely given good opinion of his fellow physicians on the manner in which he practiced Medicine. He relished the delight of patients his ministrations had dramatically helped. He concealed from them always the nature of the prescription that had helped them.

He was entirely aware of the feeling of miracle evinced by patients, of their hunger for the miracle, of their reverence for it. And he was as entirely aware that this could be destroyed in an instant if the magic was removed from the substance, the essential magic of mystery, of the priceless, the unpronounceable, the unknown. If it became commonplace, if it became a thing familiar, known even to children, if it became aspirin, or a simple barbiturate, or phenacetin, or aloes, or buchu, or foxglove, or nux vomica, then, even if the cure had been sensational, the patient was disillusioned, if he became sick again the same medicine no longer would help him, he would become angry, even, knowing what had helped him, and to this greatest of all living fakers, this assemblage of frail cells and certain death faking a reason for living, faking a belief in himself, faking a sense of importance, the man who had helped him would be a faker, a hated man, a duper, a man to whom he had brought the true magic, the magic of living, and who had given him in return not magic at all, but a commonplace, a dirt, meant only for the living.

Dr. Runkleman viewed humanity through this knowledge, viewed them thus when he set his mind into the geared outlook of a doctor. He seldom had the time to view them as a fellow human. Most of the time he was a doctor. Those he viewed as fellows were Dr. Kauffman, Dr. Castle, grudgingly Drs. Binyon and Blake, the doctors in neighboring communities, dimly doctors everywhere. And Lucas Marsh. Lucas Marsh, the doctor.

He thought of Lucas fondly. As a doctor the young man was infinitely more than he expected to get when he advertised for a helper. He had his own views on Medicine, undeflectable views as Dr. Runkleman was well aware. But he practiced Medicine as Dr. Runkleman required it to be practiced, he apparently loved work, honestly loved it, and he was capable of it, he was strong, he was efficient, he was quiet, he was astonishingly able, he admired and respected Dr. Runkleman's judgment and he was excited and admiring of those techniques and abilities Dr. Runkleman knew he possessed and was proud of, himself.

When he thought of Lucas he thought of the reason he had advertised for a helper, he remembered his trouble. He was fairly sure of what was wrong with him. He was reasonably certain he had an aortic aneurysm. There was no particular point in confirming it. Someday he just might drop in on Dr. Snow down at the capital, just on the chance it just might be something else. Not that there was any real hope. Just on the chance.

There was no doubt about why he had an aortic aneurysm.

There was no doubt that Lucas had heard it.

There was no doubt that Castle knew it.

He was sorry they knew it.

He wondered what they thought about it.

He wondered how much time he had. How much, exactly.

He was comfortably aware, thinking of this, that he had ample time to quit, to go to Australia, to hunt, to fondle many gleaming, wonderful rifles. And after that the future faded easily into time and the unknown and the undisturbing.

He thought of his investments with a flash of exultation. He was rich, now, who had been a farm boy hating the farm, one day knowing its monstrous and horrifying future, unending labor, poverty, cold, insecurity, uncertainty, early death, early maiming, grimly setting out to study Medicine, to be rich, to be respected, to be secure, most of all, most of everything to be secret and secure. He was rich and the days ticked by, each day the stock market rose higher, each tide floated the boat to Australia an inch, a foot higher, nearer to departure, nearer to an end of work forever, to a chance to explore the world, the strange and exciting things in it, to diversions, to food, to people, to things he had never known.

And this boy, this Lucas, this nice young fellow of whom he was becoming more fond every day, was making all this easier for him, without him he would surely have to quit now, the time, the stock market, unripe. A thousand a week. A thousand a week—for life. And he was very close.

He would like to make Lucas a present of the practice. Just that. Give him the office, the house—everything. He toyed with the thought, seeing Lucas' eyes, savoring it, relishing it. His thoughts adventured very far, but at the end there was always the boundary and they returned reluctantly, one had always to think of oneself, there was prudence, oneself meant security, one was bound to stopper all bottles, close all cracks, he had better get something, a little something, something paid painlessly, but something. He sighed and put away the thought of the look on Lucas' face.

It would be better for him, anyway. He didn't know about money, yet. He didn't know how precious it was. He didn't know much about it, anything about it, he needed to be taught. He needed compromise in his armamentarium. He needed compromise badly. Time would give it to him but not easily as to other men, it would have to beat him down, he would get it painfully. He would probably rebel against compromise all his days. Nevertheless he needed to learn it. He needed compromise.

Dr. Runkleman shook his head over his cold coffee. That business at the County. That staying up all night with an old man who was bound to die anyway. That fierce fighting against the unbeatable. That fine fight—wasted. Fought for nothing. That black-and-white business—Snider was black, this was black, that was black, all the world was black and white. And they could be, that was the sad part of it, the part he had to learn, they could be just that, black and white. And it wouldn't make any difference.

You couldn't cure anybody with it.

It wouldn't make you richer or poorer.

And knowing that was the essence of compromise.

Not just saying it.

Really—really knowing it.

The world wasn't a hospital. And it wasn't a textbook. It was the way it was. And all this would wear off Lucas in time. He would forget Medicine as Medicine and it would become a way of life to him, casual as any other habit. And then his eyes would open, he'd *see* his wife, who was now just sort of a fixture to him, a sort of object. And he'd begin to get a little fun out of life now and then, maybe even hit on a dream or a hobby, as the vision of one day hunting in Australia. And he'd save for it. He and his wife, both. And life would have aim, then, that kind of aim, a reward you decided on. And life would be an easy, comfortable harness then, a pair of comfortable shoes, and he'd be happy, and things would be worth while.

That was the reward of Medicine.

You knew things as they were.

You saw them clear-eyed.

And you settled down to get what you could out of them.

Nobody was going to weep for you when you went. Nobody was going to be really glad you got what you wanted. You wouldn't be missed. And you could smile about it. And not care.

He sighed. He looked at his watch. He rose hurriedly. He left the house and walked toward the office to begin the new day.

In another part of Greenville, Harriet Lang prepared herself for her day's work by a swift and careless toilet, conscious that her other attributes of face, figure, and personality made a careful toilet unnecessary. She knew the day's program too well to reflect upon it, it was a day and its end would bring her a day nearer the day when she could have an atelier of her own, a never ending stream of concepts flowing from it under her skilled and all-knowing and incessant direction, and returning riches and in the riches submission, and unending admiration and acknowledgment.

She thought of life in Greenville with impatience. She remembered Lucas. She began to ponder their next meeting. She shook herself, she roused and prepared to go to work.

Dr. Castle's heart pained on rising and he took two pills from his bedside table and lay back waiting for them to work. He knew that these pills were keeping him alive nowadays and without them he would surely and painfully die quite quickly. He thought of Dr. Runkleman's heart, he had known what was the matter with Runkleman for some time but it was good to have Lucas confirm it. He wondered if Lucas was ruminating on the long-ago happening that had doomed Runkleman with an aneurysm of the aorta that would occur far in the future.

Lucas would know. He knew a great deal. He knew far more than anyone his years Dr. Castle had ever known. It was amazing what Medicine that young man knew. He and Runkleman had marvelled over it. But Runkleman really didn't know just how much Lucas did know. Runkleman didn't know why, either. Runkleman thought it would rub off in time. Runkleman thought it was the way young people were, fresh out of school, wanting everything perfect, everything like school. Runkleman was a good man. It was lucky Lucas had come to a man like Runkleman. Because Runkleman was kind. He might never know what it was all about, but he would be kind, just the same. And Lucas could learn from him. One thing Runkleman knew, he knew surgery. He got in and he got out. Quick. No fancy stuff, no pause, no indecision. No bleeders. No infection beyond the unavoidable. He worked as clean as the knife he held, sharp, shining, unhesitating. Oh, and there was knowledge, of course, the kind born of time, the sort of thing people called wisdom or experience, but they all had this, more or less, every man practicing that got to be as old as he and Runkleman. You couldn't avoid it. Not even if you wanted to. Even Snider in his dumb way, even Snider now and then would surprise you. The young knew all the rules. The old knew all the exceptions.

Runkleman should have done something about Snider long ago. But that was how Runkleman was. He wouldn't stick his neck out. He'd just let things happen. Splendid chap, really. He'd done his job. He'd done it well. Like some good faithful animal, really. Outlook other than Medicine pretty limited. What could a fellow like that do with all the money he must have piled up? Dr. Castle tried to picture Dr. Runkleman in English tweeds. Ordering a gourmet's dinner in Paris. Sipping beer on a terrace in Vienna. Lolling on a beach in Florida. Driving a foreign car. He wouldn't fit. He wouldn't fit, anywhere. Just a farm. And he wouldn't go back to a farm, any farm, anywhere, ever. . . .

It wasn't that he wouldn't fit, so much, he just wouldn't have any fun, he'd be apart, an onlooker, studying the program to be sure he was enjoying himself. Dr. Castle sighed.

Runkleman would have fun. He'd enjoy himself, he'd never know what there might be to miss, what he might be missing, whatever he did, he'd never be bored. Because he'd done so little. He should stop Medicine. He should stop right now. He should start getting some of the rewards he'd aimed at forty years ago. There was so little to do. There was so little time to do it in.

The pain in his heart eased somewhat. He took a sip of water. Time to be getting up, soon. Time for the first patients. Not many patients, now, thank God. No more than he could handle. Or could he handle them? Was he doing right by them? He nodded. They were getting along all right. And suppose Runkleman went off? How about surgery? Marsh would do the trick. They'd work together. No problem there. He'd go right on to the end. No problem there. He'd never be a cripple. One day he'd get it and it would knock him over and that would be that. No fuss. Just—over. He'd never know. In the meantime . . .

He thought carefully and with some anxiety about his patients. His heart swelled with pity for them. They were so helpless, they knew nothing about themselves, absolutely nothing, they went blundering about, getting into all kinds of messes, they were always frightened, they were helpless, completely helpless. And it took so little to help them. They thought it was so much, poor devils, tormenting themselves with how important they were and what a mystery they were and what magic there was inside them, and that's why they thought a doctor was a great thing, it was a shame, he'd tried to tell them always how simple things were and how little anybody knew, really, and they wouldn't listen. The poor devils—they'd just smile at him knowingly . . .

But they were strangers, still. After more than twenty years here, they were still strangers. And this place was alien corn. More and more lately he wished he could go back to Winnipeg, just for a visit, just to look around a bit, take a little trip, stroll around the college, see home again.

This Greenville, this was a dull hole, when you came right down to it. There was nothing here. Just people . . . That's all there ever had been. . . .

But Europe, now . . . maybe he could go back to Europe, see Paris again, stroll around the battlefields, the ones he remembered, stand there and go back twenty years, hear it again, live again through the shock of men damaging each other, it wasn't killing each other so much, it was the damage they did, the holes they made in each other, the absurd and awesome and unexpected and always horrible wounds, wounds that were so improbable no previous experience could help you, and yet you had to help them, they looked at you, their eyes implored you and you looked at the wound and it was impossible but you had to help them, all the same . . . the fellow who'd come into the aid station that day, his belly bayoneted open, a great smiling mouth of a slit, his guts drooling through the open lips, walking into the aid station, holding his guts in his hands, his inmost nakedness in his naked hands—the look of anxiety and wonder on his face, he must have walked a good mile, they were all the same, when they were sick or hurt they all had the look of a child in their eyes, bewildered and humble and expectant—right in his bare hands . . .

. . . Probably dead, now . . . long dead . . .

All but the look. The look lived on. There was something about the look . . . Dr. Castle frowned. Then his face cleared. Of course!

It was the look in Marsh's eyes occasionally, the look in young Marsh's eyes . . . the same look! The look in his eyes that night he trapped Henry Granite with all that Greek stuff and knew sickly that Henry was actually taking the bait, that a whole community's fate could hinge on anything so improbable as a tag out of Greek history. . . .

The look of his guts ripped out, holding them in his hands, begging someone to do something about it. . . . The look in his eyes for days after that episode of the old man dying at the hospital. . . .

How many more times had it been there? Because of people? Because of Medicine? Because of doctors?

He'd wear it often. He'd never lose it. He was a freak. He was something Runkleman never suspected. He was a specialized human. He was made that way. He was a stranger in the world. He was completely alone. He lived for nothing else, he thought of nothing else, there was no limit to him.

He was sick. There was no normal. There were just points of reference. And there were no points of reference, here. And as for the world, as for the fun there could be, as for the little, sighing vacations from pain and fear and doom, why, Marsh was as shut off as Runkleman.

He plucked idly at the lapel of his faded, once maroon bathrobe. The world was full of people to whom the pleasures of the world offered nothing. It was true, pleasure wasn't an end but a process, but here were all these wonderful things, music, concerts—except that everyone said concerts, said music, virtuously, and nobody really liked it much, no one except people who'd had a call to music, like Marsh to Medicine, not a call, exactly, born to it, someplace in the mind . . . he'd said concerts all his life, Dr. Castle reflected, and the only times he'd gone it'd been some damned woman or other who hadn't enjoyed it any more than he had, the both of them, posing for each other, music lovers, the hallmark of the intellect . . . it made sex all right, it made sex respectable if you went to a concert first. Then you weren't animals. You were just people pulled together by a natural love for something spiritual, like music, and that raised everything to an intellectual plane and you could go ahead from there . . . What would it be like, Dr. Castle mused, if someone were to try to explain sex to an animal? How would you go about it? How could you explain to an animal reasons for doing something that didn't need any reasons at all? Man is a reasoning animal. He thinks he's here for a reason and he's got to have a reason. For anything. Even for sex. Woman reasons mostly. When a woman saw a man she wanted—

He thought of Harriet Lang. So she'd fallen, finally . . . there wasn't much doubt about it . . . Young Marsh was going to have his hands full . . . I wonder, he mused whimsically, if he'll remember he's a doctor. I've got to remember! I've got to work around, somehow, to tell that wife of his, somehow, she ought to have a baby . . .

Time—there would be so much time—stretching thinly out—happening little by little, disappearing, something else happening . . .

His heart pained sharply again. He looked at his watch. Almost time to go to work. He took another pill. There would be Mrs. Appleby first, he thought, swallowing, taking a sip of water, she was going to lose a kidney, today was the day—he'd have to tell her today . . . and she'd be frightened—and he'd tell her he himself had only one kidney—though she needn't know his was a gunshot wound at Mons . . . the poor soul . . .

He heaved himself upright at the thought, swung his legs over the edge of the bed, wincing, felt for his carpet slippers. He was quite dizzy for a moment. The room reeled. He watched it, dispassionately. Then his head cleared. He rose with decision. She probably hadn't slept all night, waiting for this day. He was going to comfort her. He didn't know how, yet. But somehow he was going to be her Rock of Gibraltar. He went to the bathroom, dressed quickly, took another pill, and walked to the office.

The people of the town of Greenville roused, looked at their watches to see if it was time to be hungry, ate their first meal of the day, and eagerly or unwillingly, uncaringly, dully, sullenly, cheerfully, automatically, willy-nilly, left their shelters to do this day's measured struggle for survival.

Father O'Connor debated the marriage of a Catholic girl to a Protestant young man, reluctantly decided to marry them but to perform the ritual in an unritual side room and not before the ritual altar.

Bemis Shedd looked with pleasure at the waiting galleys of type his deaf and dumb linotype operators had produced and thought with satisfaction of the non-union salaries for which a deaf and dumb man would turn out half again as much work as a normal human. He went to his desk, cut four editorials out of a stock feature service, strolled next door to the drugstore for a second cup of coffee, asked the waitress, leering, why she looked so tired this morning, heard, shocked, of the illness of an old resident, contributed five dollars to a fund to get him a bed in the Valley Hospital, sauntered down Main Street, loosening the cork in his bottle of badinage, prepared to wheedle advertisements out of the harness store, two markets, two clothing stores, a filling station, and a small notions shop.

Bemis Shedd, born and brought up in Greenville. Knew every man, cat, and dollar in it. Delivered papers when they were almost as tall as he was. Went on to be printer's devil. Got to set type, after a while, time most kids were out playing baseball. Little by little learned the linos. Came that awful summer the new man organized the shop, the other linotyper, and a kind of crazy guy they kept for job printing, all three of them marching into Mr. Kuneo, looking foolish, telling him they wanted it to be a union shop, all closed, all union, asking first off for a raise.

All three of them out by nightfall, the dirty suckers, knowing it was press night, picking their time like a bunch of Bolshies and Mr. Kuneo always treating them so good, maybe he didn't pay so much, maybe he did like a good, hard day's work, but he always spoke good to them all, handing around free passes when the circus came to town and not keeping them for his own family and friends like some publishers,

And him and Mr. Kuneo putting out the paper by themselves. Just the two of them. And Mrs. Kuneo and one of the girls coming down around three in the morning with hot coffee and staying to fold.

But they got it out, all right. And the next day there were three new men, but old Mr. Kuneo hadn't forgotten. Bemis had got a dollar and a half a week raise. And in a little while he was out of the back shop, altogether, he was out selling ads. That was where he'd really learned. And when Mr. Kuneo died, why the widow put Bemis in. And today he owned it altogether, though of course Mrs. Kuneo never spoke to him, crossed the street when she saw him, but you couldn't hold it against her, that was the way women were and the fact was they didn't understand business, never did and never would.

Take advertising, for instance. You had to be sold on a thing before you could sell it, when you came right down to it anybody that walked down Main Street could see Charley Ferris had a sale on, there wasn't anything went on in town folks didn't know. But when you walked into Charley's store you knew you were going to sell him an ad saying he had a sale on. The only thing you didn't know was how much ad he'd stand for. But he'd take out an ad, all right. That was because you were so sold on advertising that you'd sold him, too. Everybody was sold on advertising. Everybody nowadays, knew you had to advertise.

He paused outside Charley Ferris' store front and smiled tolerantly. Oh, there were always a few that had to be educated, newcomers always, fellows that just couldn't see the light, didn't realize how good it was to have a friend at the newspaper office always ready to protect you by not printing about your boy getting drunk, or having a wreck, or about your wife giving a party, or your girl getting into the social column—and now and then there were even one or two you had to work a different way, fellows not taken into lodges, or blackballed, or kept out of the Chamber of Commerce, and so stubborn even then that you had to have a little talk with the health man, or the building inspector, or anybody else you'd helped elect and he'd have to pay them a little visit, and usually after that it was all right.

They just didn't understand. Usually turned out as nice as you'd ask for. Everybody had to live. That was the point they missed. Bemis had to live just the same as everybody else. And the only way Bemis lived was if everybody was sold on advertising. Maybe not as sold as he was. But sold, all the same. It was American. It was what was wrong with Europe and those other Bohunk countries, they didn't believe in it, it kept 'em backward, that's where they got all those Bolshie ideas and unions, foreign stuff, if you want to know.

You had to believe in it.

And you had to live and let live.

And you had to treat people right.

The days of his living ended and began again, each day a new thing arrived, a day was a thing, and if it was not always new, it was only slightly used, and if it was almost always only slightly used the face of it was almost never so worn that the face was undecipherable and anyway the shape was always there.

The nature of his means of survival gave him time for politics and he relished the unperspectived powers of his bailiwick, he revelled in presenting the presentiment of a man of caution, knowing more than he would utter, a Mona Lisa of village power.

He was invariably loyal to those who helped him make money, he had a genuine affection for them, a brotherliness; he believed in them, they were fine people.

The town of Greenville quickened, a community of any people, anywhere, bound automatically to the wheel of survival, born into rules legislating survival on simple agreements which had for basic philosophy the axioms that if a human liked a thing that thing became potentially dangerous in direct ratio to how much he liked it, and that which was natural for man must not be named, that the architecture and vector of his cells must be constrained, altered, educated, and constrained to rules which were designed for the protection of the whole man and which in the end made him their victim.

The miracle of life, an unvalued thing, a commonplace, an unregarded treasure since it was possessed by all and none could be more living than another, was used by each for the power to accomplish the day's concerns, for the living actions necessary to ensure the day's and the next day's survival, for the small actions of habit, they used life as the early caveman used fire and were content with it. To cook the day's meat, to ward off animals and to warm the cave, these and the hunt were all a man had time for, and no one here dreamed of turbines, steam, or civilization birthed by fire, of steel, a small trinket of fire, of the unimaginable sum of such trinkets not yet discovered. And in Greenville, where fire was a small trinket of life, life was unremarkable and commonplace and a man rose to the work of the day before and survived, and went to sleep again.

Henry Granite, who had been dazzled as a boy by the shining of the Golden Age of Greece, who long ago had discarded his impetuous love, his yearning for that golden day, and for many years had cultivated the recognition and admiration of his fellow men for his mere acquaintance with that unlikely period, saw now for the first time in his life an amazing, a totally incredible opportunity to link a hallowed attribute to a concrete civic improvement of the present, to make the unliving, unrelated, living, related, translated. Through the years his attribute, that which made Henry Granite a little different, had gradually become a little boring to him, he had begun tentatively to dabble in woodworking; now his early love, astoundingly about to be vindicated, renewed itself; like a new-found excellence discovered in a constantly used, once-prized gun it animated him with an itch to hunt again.

He knew his fellow citizens well. He knew they would not be won by describing the glories of ancient Greece. The town of Greenville would never put up the money to build a water system on the basis of the downfall of Athens, and if it had, Henry Granite would have been frightened by palpable insanity. He awakened, he began to think of ways and means with which to place the city council in an untenable position, in some position in which, if they did not vote for the new water system, they would be the butt of the electorate and the electorate would demand its rights angrily and instantly. He was exhilarated. He set every faculty into feverish activity. The effort would be epic, it would be Homeric, and he embraced the thought of the struggle fiercely and excitedly and with smiling confidence.

Ben Cosgrove had to appear in court that day and he dressed hurriedly, without interest, impatient, anxious to be in court, impatient to get a witness on the stand, to feel the heady contempt rise in him, choking him, as he rapiered the clod fate had provided him, glancing sidewise at uneasy opposing counsel, sneering sardonically at the rural judge on the rural bench.

Ben Cosgrove sneered automatically, sneered first, came in sneering in the same way a fighter automatically sticks out his left. He had long ago lost his mechanism of belief. He had beliefs, now, but he made no new ones and he accepted no new ones, and the beliefs he had were convictions born of the urgency not to be hurt, not to be let down, not to be smashed, not to be disillusioned ever, any more. He believed that men were stupid by agreement and by choice and that they had made their norm a standard they could all comfortably meet, and that they despised all who fell below this norm only a little less than they despised those who rose above it.

He believed that all men were inherently larcenous and that they had passed laws to make necessary larcenies legal so that all men might know what to expect and all would be defended from the unexpected. He believed there was no truth which was not untrue, and that there was no untruth which was not true. He had an unerring sense of the shabby and the imperfect and he had learned clearly and indelibly that sooner or later everyone he liked would exhibit a shabbiness or an imperfection which would embarrass him and make further respect for the liked one impossible, and indeed, rather horrible. He wanted no friends and he had none and he took a grating pleasure in demolishing those whom he might like before ever a friendship could ripen into a disclosure of the shabby, the stupid, the needlessly imperfect again.

He did not like being lonely and occasionally he was driven by loneliness to go to a party and he went to such occasions as fiercely and exultantly and expectantly as he now prepared to go to court. He saw himself clearly, a self-made outcast, a man who desired more than anything to be an outcast, who even sought deference by being an outcast; who knew he was cruel, who felt kindest to the most stupid, who would defend a stupid man against the most brilliant man in the room; while the evening lasted he was the stupid man's father and defender, he loved him fiercely and thereafter he would avoid him unless he got in trouble.

He was a communist now, not because he believed communism could permanently solve the world's problems but because it was the exact opposite to the religions, governments, and systems of belief by which men lived, and because communism made his fellows uneasy or angry. He had no illusions about men and the manner by which they would administer any system of government but he detested the world into which he was born with a hatred so implacable for what it had destroyed in him that he would give his life to smash it and to exult in the ruins and then prepare to smash the next one too.

It gave him something to live by, a hope, a substitute for faith, an antidote against belief, and this relief, this buffering against the corrosion of his own reactions to life as it was around him, against the despair that it would never change, against the hate that rose in him with this knowledge, had little by little grown into a mission and the mission was gradually becoming fixed, becoming a project, becoming a perfected case.

He belonged to communism because he did not belong to those around him and he would not belong to them, and there were no communists here to disillusion him as he knew they would, and he belonged to himself, actually, secretly, it was the last illusion he had and they would have to kill him to take it away from him. The tenets of communism fascinated his legal mind, he laughed aloud, delighted, at communism's contempt for justice, at its clear insight into organized religion, at its ridicule of the quality of sacredness as it applied to property. He was delighted with its forthright concept of man, seeing him without illusion. He undertook its case eagerly. He had diverted himself endlessly baiting the least likely, the bankers, the judges, his fellow lawyers, ministers, townspeople of substance. Their weapons were poor and dull and they had no real skill in the exercise of them, and the brains that directed them were ludicrously trappable and in the end they were pale with anger, or they mumbled, shattered, uncertain, uneasy, or they backed off, resentful and frightened. The sport had lost its luster. There were no new victims. There was the new doctor, Dr. Marsh . . . He would try him—but the end was foredoomed. There was no longer any real pleasure in it after the first few gambits.

Ben Cosgrove, building an intricate life within a life, planet within a planet, had conceived a new goal. It was more ambitious than argument. It was more exciting than words. It was a triumph that would rock the town. He wanted a convert. He began to appraise that new man, that Dr. Marsh. . . .

Tom Pierce, son of the janitor at the high school, pushed seventy-five cents through the teller's wicket at the Greenville Bank, then a thin, new savings bankbook. The teller, who had spent twenty-five years becoming teller, who had, himself, six hundred and twelve dollars on deposit, nodded at the boy approvingly.

"A penny saved is a penny earned—" he narrowed his eyes for emphasis.

"I've got eight dollars already," young Tom said proudly.

"You keep right on," the teller blessed him, "and never forget—you're worth what you saved!"

"My father says that a man who puts his money in the bank will always be a success because when a rainy day comes he's got an umbrella," Tom said, intoxicated by this interest in his affairs by so wise a man in a place so sacred as this bank.

"That's the ticket!" said the teller, and he stamped the book and handed it back. "You take care of that and it'll take care of you!"

There was no safer place in all the world than the Greenville Bank and anyone would know that if they had just once stepped through its doors, a Hottentot, who'd never seen a bank, would know that, he'd sense it somehow. This was the place where generations had put more than money, more than all that they'd saved, all that they represented in the community. This was the place where they put their faith, if you couldn't trust a bank there wasn't anything you could trust anywhere. Not that anybody ever thought about that or raised the question, and the teller permitted himself a ghostly small smile at the very idea. When it came to a bank, well, a bank was the national honor, when you came right down to it, it was the one thing you could trust like you trusted a church—and more than a man might trust many a church, if you happened to be passing by some of them and heard their goings-on. There was a whole generation of Tom Pierces coming along, now, learning what their fathers learned, and their grandfathers before them, learning that the best friend you had was money and the safest place to keep it was in a bank, learning the oldest, the most tried and true, the greatest rule of them all—one thing you can be sure of: put your money in the bank and when a rainy day comes you can be sure of protection. The teller patted the bank unobtrusively and admiringly. It was very real to him, it was living, and he loved it.

The September morning was warm. On the way to the County Hospital Lucas watched Dr. Runkleman think about the young girl who had come from nowhere and had the baby, was now steadfastly refusing to tell her real name or the address of her home.

"Of course the thing we ought to do," Dr. Runkleman sighed, "is notify the juvenile authorities, put the whole thing in their hands . . ."

"I like that girl—"

"She's a fine girl, isn't she! Clean!"

"I'd hate to turn her over to any authorities—"

"It's just that sooner or later we're going to have to do something about that baby. And the later we report it—well, they're just going to ask why we took so long. And I'll be damned if I know what we're going to say . . ."

"It's a nice baby," said Lucas.

"Isn't she though? No—it's a he—"

"Maybe today she'll say something."

"Let's see . . ."

Kristina, drying the dishes, heard the postman slither the day's mail under the door, without interest. The mail meant advertising circulars, patent medicines, and new medicines, printed ways to make money sent out by people who would be making it themselves if the ways were any good.

She finished drying the dishes. She tidied the kitchen smartly. She paused to look with pleasure over her kitchen and her handiwork in it. Then on her way through the living room she picked up the mail because it was a mess of paper by the tidy doorway.

She saw the letter from Minnesota almost immediately. The handwriting was strange. It was not from her father. It was from Mrs. Swenson, the practical nurse. It was about her father. Mrs. Swenson was nursing him. He was all right, now. But he had had a stroke. He was in bed and she was taking care of him, he got the stroke the day after her letter came, he was so excited, trying to pack everything at once, running around to say goodbye to people he had known all his life, well that was all there was for now and she would close, except that he spoke yesterday and he said her name, Kristina, plain as plain, and maybe it would be as well if now she came home.

Kristina packed. Her fingers trembled as she put things into a small bag, the bag she had carried from Minnesota to nursing school, to the state hospital, to the apartment she and Lucas went to after they were married, and then to this place. She shook her head a little trying to remember what it was she had to pack. This was her father, her father was going, a figure now, a man she had long since ceased to live with, but a man whose peril called up all the sum of love she had ever known for him, a being who knew her as no human knew her, now that her mother was dead, the last link of the other-self, and being born and protected, and loved and waited for in all the lonely world.

The bag was quickly packed. In the dresser drawer there was one hundred dollars. She took it out, put it carelessly in her bag. As she changed her dress she tried to decide whether to go to the County to tell Lucas, to phone him, or to leave him a note. If she went to the County he might be operating—if she phoned he might be operating, too.

But she could say it was urgent. If he was in the OR he would have to scrub again—it was urgent, just the same,

But then if she just left a note!

She tried to compose a note in her mind and failed. She picked up the phone. She called the County.

Lucas was operating. His voice, when it came, was amazed and irritated. When she told him he subsided guiltily.

"You go right on," he urged. "Don't worry about anything here. Let me know the minute you get there. Tell me everything you find. Have you got enough money? Now listen, Kris! If you need anything—anything at all, mind!—you just pick up the phone, understand? Pick up the phone and call me . . ."

She cried, then. She cried, she began to cry as she hung up, her eyes were red in the cab that took her to the station, she sat bolt upright in the dusty cab and looked out the window and the tears streamed down her cheeks.

The peace of mid-morning hung over Greenville, and people went about their waking habits, a day nearer death, and at the hospital, as he prepared to dress a burn, Lucas began guiltily to think of his now empty home, he thought of it with relief, and he thought of Harriet Lang.

On a sudden impulse, part gratitude for his freedom and part guilt for it, Lucas straightened, smiled at the patient, walked past the astonished nurse and the waiting treatment tray.

"I'll do this later," he called back, he was in the corridor, he was through the swinging doors, the door of his car slammed behind him, he was on his way to the station.

✶ CHAPTER 32

Lucas did not have complete freedom at once. He had only the sensation of freedom. He felt unbound, he felt immeasurably lighter, he felt free and alone. In that aloneness he was unencumbered by responsibility to any person except himself. In that aloneness his thoughts stretched, savoring this freedom. The censor eye looked elsewhere now that he had no wife to mark him, now that he was no longer a couple moving through the town, now that no one could guess his stature, his thoughts, his position in life, his social status, by observing the creature at his side.

And he knew, luxuriating in this release, that it was finest to be alone. Of all fates under the firmament the best fate for man was to walk alone.

I've always known this, he thought. It's odd how plain it is, now. To do what I want, to sleep as I want, to study as I want, to love when I want. That's the best that can happen to a man. Then he can do what he has to do, in the way he has to do it, then he can climb beyond the sun.

She's gone, now. And I'm alone among these people. She's gone, I'm free.

Of a sudden he wanted to shout. He had to master the impulse, his throat was tight with the beginning of it.

He felt as parted from Kristina as from a stranger with whom he had exchanged the rigmarole of statements having no meaning nor interest and which humans who have no meaning to each other exchange by convention when they must make sound because not to make sound is to be hostile.

Yet as the train receded, sadness suddenly diluted his happiness, he wanted the train to stop, time and the moment to stop with it. He winced, seeing again, seeing clearly now, Kristina's face, her eyes seeking in his face without much hope, seeing on his face a frown of intended sympathy, the face of a stranger with whom she was closely associated. There was nothing else she could see there, for that was the face he presented to her, there was nothing else beneath it. He knew this. He saw the scene again. He saw again her questing look. He saw her quest blunted, saw her eyes withdraw, saw her sorrow alone, unshared and unhelped.

He remembered her face then with a kind of love, an ache for its pain, an ache and a despair for what she felt, for his powerlessness to change himself, to give her anything but the presentment of sympathy.

He adjured himself, this was Kristina, this was the woman whom he had admired wholeheartedly for her skill and who put him through medical school and who had come to him gratefully, who was proud of him, who was devoted to him, who would keep him at any cost. And he could give her nothing but rejection. To every move she made toward him he fended an instinctive rejection.

And this human, prepared to do anything for him a human could do for another human, had a father. And she loved and was attached to this father. And the father was very sick and she had to go to him, and her heart was sick with her father's sickness and helplessness and loneliness and, inside, she must be maddened with grief.

He pictured all this to himself carefully, as simply as he could. And he tried to make himself feel the way Kristina felt. He tried to feel that way about his own father, Job, and promptly cast off the thought with almost a shudder. He tried to evoke the concept of father as Kristina's father, he sought to pierce himself with every maxim, every world convention concerning father, every attitude known, every logical next emotional step which the word "father" could conjure.

There was nothing in him for father.

All the maxims, all the conventions, all the phrases, words, attitudes, pictures, sounds, were a crowd of people confidently saying a word to him, waiting confidently for his response, looking at him. And the word they said with one voice, assured of the evocation, was a word in Urdu, a word in a foreign language, a sound, a word that evoked nothing.

He dropped this effort. He accepted her sorrow. He tried to recall his mother, Ouida, dying, dead. He remembered only his desolation. He tried to summon sorrow, he pictured Avery dead and he weighed his sorrow and he was amazed and heartsick that his sorrow was not boundless, he tried to imagine the death of the few people he knew, whom he liked. He discovered that his sorrow would be only regret.

He was staggered and frightened to discover that there was not a human whose death would cause him sorrow he could not contain. There was not a human whose death would cripple him with the sadness other humans felt, whose mortal illness could make him feel as Kristina felt, rushing to the bedside of her father.

He felt suddenly small, alone, alien to other humans. He envied her. He recollected her blue eyes, the small lines that had begun in her thin skin beside the eye corners, the smell of her face and of her skin as she kissed him, her high cheekbones of which he was fond, her wide mouth, for which he was lonely, her pointed chin, her warm neck. She was smaller, as he recollected her standing on the train platform, smaller than he thought of her, she was thinner than when he had married her, he felt a pang, a cruel pang remembering her dress, her old dress, the best she had.

He shook his head angrily, angry with himself. There was something he wished he could do for Kristina. He did not know what it was but whatever it was it would give her what she wanted. He wished with all his heart to do this.

Defeated, he looked out over the town. He saw the houses and as he looked they were not houses, they had separated as the letters of a word sometimes separate and unword, make a clump of letters without meaning. The houses were arrangements of wood, different sorts and shapes of wood, stacked thus and so, all having much the same sort of arrangement, wood laid on wood, not homes, not houses, even, but dropped wood.

And he saw the humans of Greenville going about their errands, walking resolutely, as if where they walked and how they moved had meaning and purpose, as if they were not dropped cells at all, and a sadness bound him, an infinite pity possessed him, a pity for them, he longed to put out his hand to comfort them, to pat them, to relieve the raking sadness, the intolerable sympathy that oppressed him.

Sadness, he said to himself, it is all sadness, just their being is sad, what they think, how they think, how they press on, doomed.

It is a sad thing to be a man. But even sad is a word and it is a word man himself has given meaning and he is the owner of it and what it means.

Is there something else to be?

Something to aim for? Something to change to? Something to become?

He sighed, suddenly anxious to be gone. He drove away. He had not once thought of himself as allied to these men or to any men or related to them and he was sad for them as beings for whom he had fondness.

He flinched, driving toward the office, at the thought of Kristina crying as the indifferent train clacked on and on, he fretted over his powerlessness to help her, he resolved that when she returned he would put his mind to discover what would make her life happier. He shook his head sharply to clear it of a wave of guilt. He parked the car. He walked into the office with a feeling of tenderness toward all whom he would meet.

In this tenderness he remembered Harriet Lang. He rejected the thinking angrily. He felt well to be alone. He felt complete. The office and all the equipment energized him and he felt embraced and secure. He thought of Dr. Runkleman. He rose quickly and picked a textbook.

He read hastily all that could be read concerning aneurysm of the arch of the aorta. There was little to be read. There were only a few paragraphs. Nevertheless he read on, on the chance that his mind might exploit a commonplace, might somehow discover something that had not been reasoned before.

He heard a rustling in the patients' waiting-room. He looked up, waited. Heard nothing further, began to read again. He paused. He frowned. He rose and opened the office door.

The girl faced him uncertainly.

"I'm sorry, this isn't office hours. Was there something you wanted to see me about? Come back this afternoon. See Miss Snow, she'll make an appointment for you. How did you get in?"

"I didn't want to come in office hours," the girl said.

Lucas looked at his watch. Dr. Runkleman was due.

"Was there anything seriously wrong? Couldn't you come in this afternoon?"

The girl looked at him silently.

"It's all right," she said at last.

She turned to go.

"You come in this afternoon."

"No," she said. "I wanted to see you alone."

He inspected her. She showed no illness. She was a slim, blond girl, pretty, quite young, there was a look of appeal about her, an inarticulate childish loneliness."

"All right," he said, "come in."

Pregnant—almost surely pregnant . . .

He turned and led the way to the examining room. She followed him docilely.

"Get up on the table," he said, and turned his back to her, hunted for the speculum, the lubricant jelly, the rubber glove. When he turned she was sitting on the edge of the table.

"Take your clothes off," he said, surprised. "I'm going to make an examination. How long is it since you had your last period?"

She reddened, got off the table, awkwardly began to remove her clothes.

"I didn't know," she apologized. Then in a lower voice, "My period? About a month ago."

He waited. She undressed in silence. She faced him, waiting.

"Get back on the table. Put your feet in the stirrups. No, no! Not your toes! Just your heels!"

She lay there, waiting; her knees stiff, her underlip in her mouth, staring resolutely at the ceiling.

He inspected her quickly, he started, he returned to the instrument cabinet for a smaller speculum. He came back to the table. She winced once at the touch of the instrument.

"Still!" he said. And after that she remained quite still.

He straightened, finally.

"We'd have to do other tests," he said. "But I can see nothing here to indicate that you're pregnant."

She continued to lie as he had ordered her.

"You can get up now."

She rose promptly.

"You can dress."

She began to dress.

"Have you actually *missed* a period?"

"I—I don't think so."

"What made you think you were pregnant?"
She said nothing.
"You'll have to tell me, you know."
She was silent.
"That's what you came here for, wasn't it? To tell me?"
He waited.
"My father," she said at last. Her words emerged slowly, left her mouth, were no longer part of her. She looked steadfastly at the door.
"Are you afraid your father will find out?"
And instantly he knew this was not so. She lifted her head. She looked down again.
"You mean your father—your father's been—" Then he looked at her narrowly. "But you're a virgin—you're still intact—"
"He never quite—"
"I see . . . he just—"
"Yes . . ."
"Why don't you scream out!" he cried angrily.
She began to talk. She talked in a low voice, a monotone. Long after she had finished, had shyly paid an office fee, had disappeared, Lucas sat, pondering. He pondered her problem, he remembered questions he could have asked her, he wondered whether her father had ever come in as a patient, what he looked like. He marvelled that what people did, what they thought, was never, never stamped on their smiling faces.
He tried to see her face again. He could not remember it. He had a memory of whiteness and thinness. He thought hard of whiteness and thinness. Her face flashed before him. It was a child's face.
"I'm sorry to be late," said Dr. Runkleman.
"I was beginning to wonder," said Lucas, rising. "I've already begun the afternoon, I just had a patient—"
"Excuse me for a minute." And Dr. Runkleman's bulk was passing between Lucas and the desk in the way of moving he had when there was something to be done which he must do. He picked up the telephone and called a number. His voice was a little hoarse.
"Have to make a call," he smiled apologetically, waiting.
And Lucas, who had begun to bring up the girl's case lightly and with professional offhandedness, nodded, confused, eager to present the appearance of concurring with the necessity for the call. He turned his back as Dr. Runkleman spoke over the telephone, and consulted the backs of the books in the medical-library shelves with what he hoped was elaborate disinterest. He could not help hearing what was said. But what he heard was without interest to him. It had to do with stocks and shares and a parcel of real estate, with holdings, with money, with accounts, with all the maze of activities in which people busied themselves and in which he was as disinterested as he was to dyeing processes or the mathematics of a pantoun. He heard Dr. Runkleman hang up, he kept his back to him a moment longer to emphasize the privacy in which Dr. Runkleman had spoken.
"That's done!" Dr. Runkleman cried joyously.
Lucas turned, smiling dutifully.
"Twenty-two more days, young fellow—and you'll have your dream!"

"Me?"

"You! I'll be on my way!"

"On your way—"

"I'll leave you the maimed, the halt, and the blind! I'll leave you the getting up when you'd rather sleep—the meals snatched on the run—the thankless and the thanking—the whole kit—the whole caboodle—I'll be on my way! Off! Write me care of Postmaster, Sydney, Australia!"

He rose abruptly, his heavy body tense, his lips stretched to their widest in a grin that only discipline kept from a shout.

"You'll have what you want! Admit it! That's what you've always wanted, my boy—that's it, isn't it?—a practice of your own—completely on your own!"

"What is it? Has somebody died and left you a lottery?" But Lucas' heart leaped and thudded for there was something here, there was something here, it was true, he felt it, it was an inevitable feeling, and whatever it was, and he dared not name it, sheered thought from it, it was coming true.

"Have you seen the market?" Dr. Runkleman looked at Lucas compassionately, knowing he had not, rushed on happily to communicate with him as if he had: "By God, boy, it's terrific! It's tremendous! Up, up and *up*! I'm over the top *now*! I've given my sell order. I'd dump today!—but there's no need dumping—we'll call the next ten days half of what I would have charged you. In twenty-two days—" he kissed the palm of his scrub-scurfed hand—"I'll be gone!"

"Twenty-two days," Lucas echoed, bewildered, trying to pace his thoughts with Dr. Runkleman's, this heavy, silent man behaving like an awkward schoolboy.

"I told you. I've been waiting for years. Buying a little, putting a little by, buying a little more, three years ago the market began to jump, it's been jumping ever since, up, up and up—do the same thing now! The minute you can!"

Miss Snow put her head in the door.

"What's all the shouting for?" she said severely.

"Meet your new boss, Miss Snow! Shake hands with Dr. Marsh! In three weeks I'll be on my way!"

"It's happened, has it!" She came into the room. "You're going to leave us. It's finally happened."

"Miss Snow knew it years ago. She was in on it from the first."

"It's a fact. I used to try to make him stop. All that stocks and bonds and stuff and good money going out to it."

"She's right, there! Pick good ones, boy. No fly-by-night stuff! I used to think to myself every time I mailed a check to the broker, Well, there goes five hundred night calls, five hundred times I got up in the middle of the night and took my reputation in my hands for a dollar bill—five hundred times I got up earlier than any farmer or any scrubwoman to look at pus, piss, or puke—that's what every check meant, that's what I was putting in an envelope and mailing to some stranger—you pick the good ones, I'll give you the name of my broker, I'll call him and tell him—"

"And now you're off to Australia. Now I'll hear the last of it! Morning, noon, and night—you, at your age, galloping around God knows where with a gun on your shoulder, killing whatever you lay your eyes on!" She shook her head. "I thought the day'd never come."

"You did, did you?"

"I did for a fact! At first I thought—well, and then I thought you were having a pipe dream, just another crotchet, a man's crotchet, something to talk about . . ."

"Twenty-two days!" Dr. Runkleman exulted. "I'll send you postcards—"

"You better send me postcards from the Valley Hospital! You're late, the both of you. Look at Dr. Marsh, thinks we're both crazy—"

"No, no!" Lucas protested. "I know what it means! You've been working all your life for this!" But he was a stranger. And he tried not to think of what it meant to him. And because he liked what warmed his heart about Dr. Runkleman he was uncomfortable, conscious of what Dr. Runkleman and Miss Snow shared, conscious of his exclusion.

"It means something to you, too, young fellow," Dr. Runkleman nodded, "I wish I had what you're getting, at your age."

"You're getting a wonderful practice," Miss Snow said reverently.

"She knows!" Dr. Runkleman nodded.

"He's worked all his life for this! I'm glad! I'm proud for you, Doctor!"

"I feel like I was sitting in on the reading of a will!" Lucas protested, laughing. Then his smile vanished. Dr. Runkleman had sat down. His lips had thinned. He was staring fixedly at the door. He was not hearing them at all. His hand had crept, offhandedly as it were, to his necktie. His forearm lay against his chest. And Lucas, become an instrument automatically, saw the pain, saw the process, saw the aneurysm, saw the aorta, catalogued the variety, all the variety of happenings,

"Here!" he said, and walked forward.

The phone rang. Miss Snow stepped between them. She picked up the receiver.

"It's the Valley," she said resignedly. She had seen nothing. She covered the mouthpiece. "They just wonder if you're dead, or what." She uncovered the mouthpiece. "He'll be right there," she said and hung up. Then she saw Lucas looking past her, looking fixedly at Dr. Runkleman. She looked at Dr. Runkleman in surprise.

"You all right?" Lucas asked, ignoring her.

Dr. Runkleman nodded. He waited a moment. He drew his breath in a sigh. His arm came reluctantly away from his chest.

"Heartburn," he nodded. Then he smiled. "Knew I shouldn't have had those hotcakes last night."

"What you need is a keeper," Miss Snow said severely. Dr. Runkleman grinned wryly and rose. "Now scoot—the both of you!" And as they rose and took up their bags and reached the door: "Who was in the treatment room this morning?"

Dr. Runkleman paused, looked inquiringly at Lucas.

"I'll give you the name later," Lucas promised. Dr. Runkleman followed him out the door.

"Later! Always later! Half the names I never get on the books and then you come around one day and ask me—"

Miss Snow's voice followed them, then the outer door closed, they were in the car, Lucas had managed to get in the driver's seat, they were on their way to the Valley.

"Quite a morning!" Dr. Runkleman sighed, his face a heavy mask of pure pleasure.

Should I ask him? Lucas thought. Should I just come out flatfooted and tell him I know what he has, or do we both keep on ignoring it? I can't say anything. I can't do a thing. I've got to wait for him. But—

"Excitement like that's not good for you!" he blurted.

"Not good for anyone," Dr. Runkleman assented calmly. "But the cause—that's something I'd prescribe for the whole world—"

"I suppose so," Lucas said mechanically. "Do you—feel all right now?"

"I'm fine," said Dr. Runkleman. And his tone discouraged further comment. It's my business, the tone said, and when I want your opinion I'll ask for it and no offense meant. "A little heartburn," he said carefully.

"That's all right with me," said Lucas, "but I'm standing there, you know, watching it—and if you were in my place—"

"I want to tell you something," Dr. Runkleman interrupted. "Drive slow. Take the long way around. I want to talk to you."

"We're late—"

"That's right—just about this speed. . . . The first thing I want to say is, I should have set these terms a long while ago. Things happened too fast. Now here's how I look at it: The office, the equipment, the house, they're worth about twelve thousand. Take them separately, the house eight thousand, the office four thousand. Complete."

"More than that! You couldn't replace the equipment alone—"

"Twelve thousand. That's what they're worth and that's what they'd bring—if you were my widow. Don't tell me how many thousands they cost. Or how much you'd have to pay for them. That's what they'd bring if you were my widow. The practice—I don't know. You want to cut it down. You probably will. You will. I know you definitely will. I don't know. I'm going to say—I'll tell you what. I'll tell you what we'll do. How does twenty-five thousand strike you?"

"If I thought you were serious I'd send you to an alienist."

"I mean it. That's what I want. You give me twenty-five thousand—we'll call it square!"

"In the first place I haven't got it. I haven't got twenty-five hundred. I don't know how much I've got. Kris knows. Maybe six hundred, at the outside."

"I came here, I had eighty-five dollars," Dr. Runkleman said complacently.

"I know. And nobody helped you. But I haven't got— Why, I don't begin to have anything like that. You could sell it for twice that—to somebody with cash—"

"I've got cash. I've got all the cash I need. I've got one thousand dollars a month for the rest of my natural life. One thousand dollars. Each month. Every month." He spaced the words carefully. He hugged them to him. "If I live to be two hundred." He turned and looked at Lucas intently. "And I don't want any money from you and I want you to understand that. You don't have to tell me how you're fixed because I know. I know who I'm dealing with. I know what kind of a hairpin you are."

"But—"

"I want twenty-five thousand dollars from you and you can pay me out of what you take in, however you want to do it, and I want the money to go to keep those youngsters in med school, part of it, and when they're out you just parcel it out among them so they can set up shop where they're a mind to. Now, that's how I've got it figured out. Now, what do you say?"

"Dr. Runkleman, I don't know *what* to say!"

Dr. Runkleman patted Lucas' knee and looked quickly away from the tears in his eyes.

"All right, then! Now, that's settled. Now we're all squared away. Now everybody's taken care of." Lucas swallowed. In this instant he loved this man at his side more fiercely than he had ever loved any living thing since he was born on the planet, this man who was, incarnate, this gift.

"I wish your wife was here," Dr. Runkleman grinned, as a child might. Then, soberly, "Was she all right?"

"Pretty bad. I guess they were close—she never said much—closer than I knew . . ."

"I guess she knows," Dr. Runkleman said soberly. "They get old. That's all. They just get old. And that's what happens. Did you tell her?"

"I said she mustn't expect too much . . ."

"That's right. She'll be all right—"

"Dr. Runkleman! If I could only tell you—"

"Never mind. I know all about it. It isn't the present I'm making you. You don't set much store by anything. I know that. I know what you are. I know what you have to be. I know this means letting you be what you have to—I know . . ." He sighed. "I wish it could have been that way for me . . ."

"But you love Medicine, too!"

"You don't have to be loyal. It's all right. I'm one of a million. We do our job. We're fitted for it. We're qualified. It's not a bad life. And I'll tell you something." He faced squarely around in the seat. "I wouldn't trade places with you for anything under the canopy!" He turned away. "No, sir!"

There was silence for a moment.

"Am I that bad?"

"Bad? I didn't say anything about bad! Lord, man! I don't mean it that way at all. It's just that well, *I* had a choice . . ."

"You don't think I had a choice?"

"Not any more'n being born with two heads," Dr. Runkleman said cheerfully. "And the patients can thank God for it. . . . Do you know something? I'm going to say something maybe I oughtn't, I don't mean to say anything to hurt your feelings—why, boy, you could be my own son and I couldn't be prouder . . . Don't take it wrong . . . But sometimes I can't help being a little sorry for Mrs. Marsh . . ."

"For Kris? No, I'm not angry, it's all right, but why do you say that? What is it you see in Kris? Why should you—or anyone—be sorry for her?"

"I know what you mean. She's a nurse and she married a doctor. And her husband's doing all right and she can hold her head up in the community and she's Mrs. Doctor Marsh. And you don't beat her and her time's her own—I know. I know . . . But take care of her, Luke. Will you do that? Just take care of her."

"Sure!" Lucas watched Dr. Runkleman, a mechanical smile on his lips, his forehead creased in perplexity.

"It's hard to tell you," Dr. Runkleman nodded. "I'm a bachelor myself, it's hard for me to make it clear . . . It's just what I've seen, living all this time, seeing all kinds . . . It's something that living will have to give you if you haven't got it, something that goes beyond rules, somebody you have if the whole world's wiped out and only you two are left. And you've only got her because she's set her heart on you. Not because of anything you— And because she loves you. That's what I mean. I don't say it very good. But that's about the size of it. And that's what you have to take care of. That's what I mean when I say take care of her . . . Bosh!" he cried suddenly. "Listen to me! What in the world time is it!"

Lucas whistled.

"We're late! We're *really* late!"

"Well, let's go. They'll keep. Nothing much this noon, was there?"

"Just that County appendectomy—Langer—peritonitis—and two Valley T and A's."

"We'll be through in an hour. I don't think Langer'll pull through. Do you? Anyway—do 'em good to wait. Make 'em appreciate us more."

"Sure! Only if Snider should ever decide we aren't coming—! And don't worry about Langer." Lucas was jubilation. At that moment he could have saved anyone.

"Snider? He'll never operate! Don't worry about that! He wouldn't know which end to begin. And don't think he doesn't know it!"

Lucas shook his head, his lips tightened.

"Thirty years' experience," he said with hate and contempt.

"No," said Dr. Runkleman quietly. "*One* year—thirty times . . ."

Lucas looked at Dr. Runkleman, startled.

"That's right," Dr. Runkleman nodded. "Just one year—thirty times . . . Well," he said self-consciously, "I guess there's a lot of others. Yes, sir! Who was in this morning?"

"It was a Miss Challis—"

"Irene Challis?"

"Blond girl, slim, about twenty-two—"

"I delivered her."

"You did?"

"Known her for years. Whole family. What did she want?"

"If you know her father you'd better speak to him."

"Tom? What's the matter with Tom? Is she worried about Tom?

That's a fine girl there. Teaches in Sunday school. The old man's kind of a rough diamond, but she worships the ground her mother walks on. Only got one arm. Not very well." His brows creased. "How did she happen to come in the morning like that?"

"He sneaks into her room at night."

Dr. Runkleman blinked.

"Tom?"

"When the mother's asleep the father sneaks into the daughter's room—"

"Tom? Tom Challis?"

"He sneaks into her room and he makes her lie still and she doesn't dare cry out because she'd die rather than let the mother know and then he—well, he hasn't broken the hymen yet."

"You're talking about Tom Challis? She told you that? You sure? You sure she said her name was Challis? Did she say her father's name was Tom? Thomas?"

"I'm sure."

Dr. Runkleman looked at Lucas helplessly. He tried to find words but he had no thoughts, he could find none. His face congested.

"God damn them!" he cried helplessly. "God damn their souls to hell! You mend them, you save them, you keep them going, you fight on even when it's hopeless! For what! What are you saving! What's all the effort about!"

"She didn't want to come to you. She didn't want you to find out. I tried to tell her you'd be the one to speak to him—"

"I'll speak to him! I'm going to tell him—I'm going to tell him jail's too good for him—I delivered that girl—I've taken care of the whole family for years—you know him, don't you? You've seen him? Big, bluff, hearty fellow, belongs to the Rotary Club, Lions, Chamber of Commerce, works for the post office—always going around like a man's man?"

Lucas shook his head.

"They're nothing to you. Not yet. Wait till you've lived here a while, when they all belong to you, when you belong to all of them—and then one of them goes and does something like that! I pulled him through typhoid once. I saved his life. I still don't know how I did it. And this is what he was spared for. This is what it's all come to. So he could take a nice, sweet, clean girl—his own daughter—and make her lie there and not dare to cry out because she loves her mother and the shock would kill her—"

"She was afraid she was pregnant."

"She could have been, too, you know! I'll talk to her." He brooded.

Lucas watched him, concerned about the effect of this excitement.

"I guess he's not the only one," he said pacifically. "Probably not worth getting upset about."

"No—I guess you're right . . ." He shook his head dejectedly. "You never know . . . You never know . . ."

They had come to the Valley Hospital. They alighted. Dr. Runkleman paused on the steps and Lucas paused obediently beside him. Dr. Runkleman gazed at the town, what could be seen of it, the roofs, the trees, the area it occupied. And Lucas, watching him, knew he was thinking of Australia, of the time come, of the hour of going, of release, of freedom, of an unknown continent and he an unknown in it.

Soberly, he followed Dr. Runkleman into the hospital.

A little later they were called to the County.

The difficult peritonitis-appendectomy finished, they made brief rounds.

"I don't see how you're going to save him," said Dr. Runkleman.

"I'll save him!" Lucas promised. "You'll see! Just so Dr. Snider does what I asked him . . ."

When they came to the women's ward they were met by Dr. Snider. His face was red, he was angry, he jerked a thumb toward the ward door.

"Better take care of your patient in there," he snarled. "First thing you know she'll be running the place!"

He went on before Dr. Runkleman could answer.

There was no question of which patient he meant. As they stepped into the ward Gloria hailed them loudly.

They walked to her, smiling.

"Where the hell's Agnes?" she demanded, oblivious of the other patients.

"Now, what have you been up to?" Dr. Runkleman chided mildly. "What have you been saying to upset Dr. Snider?" And all the time his hands were busy about her, Lucas helped him expose the stump of her leg, the flesh about the incision had begun to darken ominously. They avoided each other's eyes. They covered her. They faced her, smiling.

"She's in the nursery again!" Gloria inspected their faces as she spoke. "No use looking at you for anything. And if I asked you, you'd just lie—"

"You're doing fine."

"Go get Agnes, will you? She's in there with that kid again. We want to talk to you."

"I'll go," said Lucas. He left eagerly.

"Now, Gloria, you know better than to make so much fuss," Dr. Runkleman said diffidently.

"Snider see you? How would you like him to examine you?"

"He's the head of the County," Dr. Runkleman said mildly. He looked at her steadily.

"I know," she nodded, understanding. "And I'm a nurse, I'm still one of the team—think of the other patients. I know. Doc," she said earnestly, "I've lost my girlish protocol. I got a hunk of rotting meat on me, I'm one leg less, you know what he is and I know what he is. I don't want him fumbling around me."

Dr. Runkleman pulled up a chair and sat down.

"Stump bother you much last night?"

"Probably have to cut again, won't you!"

"What put that in your head?"

"Doc, that's the cutest baby, the one that little girl had, the one they can't get to talk—we want to talk to you about it, Agnes and I—"

"Throb much?"

"A little . . . Get your mind off my leg a minute. Listen, Doc! Here's what we've got in mind . . ."

In the nursery Lucas found Agnes sitting by a crib. She looked up as he entered, smiled absently at him and returned to her contemplation of the child. He stood beside her, watching it. The child, an anonymous assortment of humanoid features, its face expressing kinship with no friend, no relative, reflecting only a womb-time, alien to an outer world, kin to formation, stage, succession, and to all womb tissue everywhere, slept, deeply, in its sleep a stranger.

"It's beautiful, isn't it," Agnes murmured.

Lucas nodded. The child was neither beautiful nor unbeautiful, like all newly born, finished for the womb, it appeared unfinished in the world in which it had been ejected. His nod was an acknowledgment of the uterine reverence women expressed for that function of women which none of them ever quite believed.

"Not the first you've seen," he said dryly.

"I love them! They were the best part of nursing."

"Too bad you never had one."

"Yes," she said steadfastly, and she looked away, reviewing the years, reviewing the future, "yes, it's too bad."

He smiled politely. She rose, she inspected his smile, she removed the white gown in which she had been sitting. She threw it carelessly over the back of the chair. Lucas winced. He tried to think of a diplomatic way of telling her, who knew it already, that the gown ought to be hung up, ought really to be carried away. He inspected her covertly, she was wearing faded blue jeans, the pocket edges ravelled, the material shrunk, stretched, her man's shirt was torn, unpressed, wrinkled as it had come from the tub, her shoes were runover man's shoes, scuffed, her hands were none too clean, her hair was cut short, ragged, unkempt, and yet he did not want to hurt this entity, he was sorry for her and ashamed of himself for being sorry, there was some fellowship between them, she was a nurse, or once she had been a nurse, many of the things he had seen, she had seen, there was a sense of family in it.

"Well–" he smiled–"I guess we better get out of here before the baby nurse catches us."

She looked at him uncertainly, shrugged, followed him to the door.

"They don't pay much attention to that around here," she said scornfully. "I bet I'm the first one to wear a gown in there since the place was built."

"All the same . . ." he said gently.

She looked down at herself. She nodded.

"Guess I do look like a tramp," she said, her voice businesslike. She appraised him. "You'll get used to it. How do you like it here?"

Lucas looked into her eyes, looking away from the tattered clothes.

"Just fine," he said cordially. "Grand country–"

"What do you think of Dr. Runkleman?" she asked abruptly.

"You won't find any better," he said solemnly.

"That's what we think." She pursed her lips. She looked at him steadily and Lucas was uncomfortable.

"He's a fine man," he said strongly.

"And a fine doctor," she said emphatically.

"None finer," Lucas echoed.

She looked at him a moment longer. Then she shrugged.

"All right," she said, "don't mind me. I was just curious. Sometimes," she said apologetically, "I get curious about people."

"What did you expect me to say?" He grinned.

"Just what you said . . . It's all right . . ."

"Doing a little feminine intuition?"

"Maybe . . . I saw you looking at the baby . . . I've had my mind shut to people for so long . . ."

"I guess the war did a lot of that to you."

"I guess it did. One thing, it made us stop kidding ourselves about anything."

He nodded, accepting this.

"And what do you think of me?"

"I don't know." She looked at him reflectively. "A few years ago I'd have tried to find out. I guess you just remind me of how they were in war." She smiled disarmingly. "Gloria send you for me?"

"She's quite a character, isn't she?"

"Gloria's the only human I've ever really known—or loved." She said this quite simply, describing the country of which she had become a national, describing life as they had fashioned it.

"I suppose you know her condition."

"Yes."

"The prognosis—"

"She'll be dead in six months."

"Perhaps a year . . ."

"Maybe."

"And then—?"

"I'll think about it when I come to it."

Lucas nodded.

Agnes turned and faced the baby.

"We want to adopt it," she said.

"The baby? You mean you and—"

"The mother doesn't want it. What's going to happen to it? It'll just be a waif. Who wants a baby? We want to take it and bring it up and—"

"Haven't you got enough to handle now—you can't be serious—you two, living out there all alone, one of you hopelessly ill—"

"Gloria wants the baby."

"I see."

"When do you think we can have it?"

"Me? Oh, wait, now! I'm not the one you want to see—"

She looked at him intently.

"I know. But you're not going to say anything against it?"

"It's not up to me. Personally, I think you've got all you can handle—"

"Who wants a baby? You know what'll happen to him. You know! Don't you?"

"I guess we'd better go see Gloria," he said.

In the corridor he left her.

He went into the maternity ward. The girl, the mother of the baby, looked around brightly as he entered. She was sitting in a wicker chair beside her bed.

"And how are you today?" he asked mechanically.

"Fine," she said. She watched him intently.

"Everything all right?"

"Just fine," she smiled.

"I've just been to see your baby." She watched him silently, smiling. "Certainly is a fine-looking boy!"

She said nothing. Her silence disconcerted him. Her friendliness made him ill at ease.

"Made any plans?" he asked abruptly.

"Plans?"

"What you're going to do—notify your folks—where you're going to take the baby—if they let you keep him—"

"They won't let me keep him." She smiled, shaking her head wisely.

"They might—"

"Oh, no. I'm under age." She might have been discussing someone else.

"Why not give us your address, then? Come on. Why don't you do it! Your mother could take care of him—you could raise him yourself, that way—"

"Oh, no."

"Why not? Come on, there's no disgrace to this—we're all one family, here—"

"My mother's a drunk."

"Oh . . ."

Lucas looked away, embarrassed.

The girl nodded.

"There's six of us. Pop does what he can. But he gets drunk too."

He looked at her narrowly.

But she looked back at him serenely, one who knew facts, there was no sense blinking them, that was the way it was, and you had to begin from there. She sighed softly.

"One more kid . . ." she explained.

And you're not yet twenty, Lucas winced. And so old, so old, is that what it is? Is age just an absence of panic?

"How about the father?" he asked.

She shook her head. She smiled brightly.

"He'd never," she told him. "Never—"

"But the baby—"

"I know."

"It's your baby!"

She nodded.

"Don't you love it?"

She nodded again.

She continued to look at him, waiting, as if he might say something, something that would solve it, solve everything.

"Well," he said, not looking at her, "we'll see . . . We'll see . . ."

"I'm going to have to give him up," she said steadfastly. "It's mine

. . . It's the rule . . . They're going to take him from me . . . My own baby . . ."

"We'll see . . ." He edged toward the door. He tried to put confidence in his voice.

"Have you got a baby?" she asked suddenly. Her mouth had opened a little. Her smile had disappeared.

"No," he said. "Not me."

"You're married."

"That's right."

"I—I wouldn't mind your having him. He's a very nice baby. His hair's like yours. I saw your wife—she was very kind to us—I could work here, I could find work in the town and get to see him now and then—I mean I wouldn't be any trouble, I wouldn't have to see him so often—"

"Oh, now! Just a minute—!"

"Have you got a maid? I could be your maid, mister. I'm real good around the house—I could take care of the baby then, your wife wouldn't even have to take care of it—"

He looked at her face, tense with hope, not letting go, straining to make him see; he looked away, frightened, sorry, threatened, seeking escape.

"Now, what would I do—" he smiled, he tried to make his voice light —"what would I do if all you girls offered me all your babies! Me, a young doctor trying to get along!" Then his face became grave. "But thank you—I want you to know—I know what you mean—I know what it means to you . . ." He nodded, trying to make his nod say thank you, nodding quick, nodding hard. Then he smiled brightly and opened the door.

"I could pay you some way," she said. "I could work nights, maybe. Washing—is there a bowling alley here? I could set pins, there's all sorts of ways to make money—you like the baby, don't you? It isn't bad, is it? I know it's not much, but—"

"Now, don't you worry," he said loudly. "You just take care of yourself and get better—"

"I think your wife liked it," she said submissively. "She said it was a fine baby. She came quite a lot. I was sorry to hear her father's sick . . ."

"Yes . . . Well, now, you take care of yourself," he nodded hard at her, smiling.

She watched his face. She managed a smile. She looked down at her empty lap, looked quickly away. Then she sighed.

"I'm all right," she said in a low voice. And then, as the door closed, "Thank you, Doctor . . ."

In the safety of the corridor he walked quickly, he drew and expelled a deep breath, he saw Dr. Runkleman, he approached him, shaking his head.

"I've had *my* excitement for today," he said.

"Yes? You should have had mine! You know what those two want?"

Lucas nodded, smiling sympathetically.

"They want to adopt that baby! That one the girl—"

"I know," said Lucas. "Agnes told me—we had quite a talk . . ."

"What did you tell her?"

"I told her she'd have to see you."
"Thanks! Thanks very much!"
"I'm sorry—that's nothing to what I had! That girl—she wants to give *me* the baby!"
"Is that so?" Dr. Runkleman didn't seem surprised. He watched Lucas carefully. "What did you say?"
Lucas looked at Dr. Runkleman incredulously. He had expected him to laugh. He was not laughing. He seemed quite interested.
"Did she mention it to you?" he asked Dr. Runkleman, alert, now.
"She said something—what did you tell her?"
"I told her of course not."
"You did?"
"Of course. What in the world—what else—"
"I wasn't going to say anything to you. See how you took it. I tell you what, I think Mrs. Marsh likes that baby."
"Kris?"
"I think she'd love to have it. That's what I think."
"Oh, come on, now, Doctor!"
"I really mean it!"
Lucas shook his head. He chuckled to hide a spasm of anger.
"Someday, maybe," he said indifferently, "maybe we might have one of our own . . ."
"That's a nice baby," said Dr. Runkleman.
"Certainly is. And seriously—what do you think about your two old girls adopting it?"
Dr. Runkleman shook his head.
"Not much," he said shortly.
"That's what I told her. Aren't we due at the office?"
"I'm waiting for Agnes." And then, to Lucas' look of surprise, "She'll be back any minute. She went home to get out a couple of her old uniforms—pack a bag—I fixed it up with Snider to let her nurse here, a while. Take care of Gloria, mostly . . ."
And then, as Lucas stared at him:
"They can use her here! No sense her living off there all alone in the woods . . ."
"That's right. You're absolutely right—"
"Do the two of them good. And God knows they can use another nurse. You know that nurse? The one with the cancer patient? Cancer of the rectum?"
"The one who wanted to marry him?"
"Well, she's going to marry him, all right. She took him home today."
"Never!"
"Just came in, quit her job, told Snider what she thought of him, told everybody what she thought of them, waited for me a while to tell me what she thought of me, got tired of waiting and took him home."
"My God! How long's she think he's going to live? How could you fall in love with a cancer of the rectum patient? How could you marry him?"
"So we're one nurse short, anyway. Ten nurses short, if it comes to that . . ."

Lucas remembered Agnes, the tattered clothes, the scarecrow, independent figure.

"Wonder how she's going to like the harness again," he said discreetly.

Dr. Runkleman smiled.

"You don't have to worry about Agnes," he decided.

"Of course not," Lucas protested.

The outer doors opened and closed. In the anteroom there was the sound of voices.

"That's Agnes," said Dr. Runkleman.

The inner doors opened, a figure in white entered the corridor and walked toward them, Dr. Runkleman smiled, Lucas stared.

"All right, Doctor?" Agnes asked. She stood silently, her face expressionless, waiting.

"Fine!" Dr. Runkleman boomed. "Fine! Just fine!" He turned triumphantly to Lucas. "What do you think of our nurse, Doctor?"

Her shoes were white, her stockings were white, her uniform was spotless, her cape, her cap—

"For Heaven's sake!" Lucas managed at last.

"That's a nice cape you English girls wear," Dr. Runkleman admired.

"Is—is that an English cap?" Lucas asked helplessly, grateful for a lead to follow.

"Guys," Agnes said briefly.

"You've heard of Guys, Doctor," Dr. Runkleman explained.

"Yes, indeed!" Lucas said hurriedly. "One of the finest hospitals in London!"

"Used to be," said Agnes.

"Still is!" protested Dr. Runkleman.

"I guess the cap looks funny—compared to American caps—it's all what you're used to—the cape's a little wrinkled, maybe. I guess I didn't have to bring it, but—and everything's been put away so long—"

"You look like just exactly what you are," Lucas said happily. "A nurse! From head to foot!" A tingle of pride rippled at the back of his neck.

"Thank you," she said quietly.

"Absolutely!" said Dr. Runkleman.

"Well," she said, "I guess I'll go show Gloria . . ."

"You'll be all right!" Dr. Runkleman promised awkwardly. "If you have any trouble—if anything comes up—you just let me know . . ."

"Thank you, Doctor," she said gravely. She turned and walked surely down the hall, back in the fold again, a figure in pattern, a human belonging. She was in uniform and her cape billowed a little, billowed gracefully, reassuringly, reassuring to her and to the watchers, she did not look back, she opened a door and disappeared.

"Well?" said Dr. Runkleman. He drew in a breath.

"Amazing!" Lucas said sincerely. They grinned at each other. They left the hospital.

And in the car, driving to the office,

"Father knows best!" Lucas chuckled ruefully.

"They never lose it." Dr. Runkleman nodded. "No, sir! Never!"

• "I've got a lot to learn."

"No . . . But they never lose it. That's one thing they never lose." He swallowed. He winced. The pain passed. "Me—and you—and everybody— We're early. Let's go back to the Valley a minute."

The Valley was quiet, there were no operations, they made rounds, there were two new faces, slipped through a chink in the world, the outer world, into this other world, this hospital world, already capsuled, the shell of the hospital about them, living a new life, the other as if it had never been. Lucas memorized their faces, a gall bladder and a suspected mononucleosis, he made them part of him, he went out with Dr. Runkleman, they stood together on the steps of the Valley Hospital.

"Time on our hands!" Dr. Runkleman looked at his watch, surprised, happy. "Want to go for a drive?" he asked abruptly.

"I had sort of a halfway date with Dr. Castle," Lucas said, "I'd like to go, but—if you don't mind—"

"Go right ahead!" And he strode briskly to the car. "I'll see you back at the office—unless you want me to drop you?"

"No, no! I'd like the walk!"

"You know where I'm going, don't you?" He grinned like a small boy. "I'm going down to Sears, Roebuck!"

Lucas smiled at him politely, puzzled.

"To look at guns! I've got forty-five minutes and I'm going to look at every gun they've got!"

"Poor Australia!"

"Australia, here I come!" Dr. Runkleman cried. The car's wheels ground the dirt, spurted, the car lurched off.

Lucas watched it disappear. The smile faded slowly from his face. He sighed. He looked about him, sternly he put aside all thought of what he could not think of without hysteria, he thought of Dr. Runkleman, he bade his mind be cold and professional, he walked quickly down the street toward the offices of Dr. Castle. An autumn leaf fell golden, crimson, and brown across the sidewalk, blew a little, halted inquiringly, tentatively moved again. He stepped over it absently, oblivious, entered a tree-lined street, passed between the vague shapes, saw Dr. Castle's car parked at the curb, breathed with relief, walked faster.

As he entered the office a shapeless woman of forty, her face faded as her housedress, one of ten thousand faces in ten thousand housedresses, passed him on her way out. She glanced at him with a dull greediness, as if to milk the nature and the drama of his sickness from him, to cheek it like a horehound drop, to suck it on the way home. He looked at her coldly. She passed on unaware of his resentment, leaving a faint odor of musty closets and wet pots.

There was no one else in the waiting-room. Dr. Castle put his head through the door, saw Lucas, smiled warmly, surprised.

"Come in, come in! What brings you out? Nurse's gone to lunch."

"I had a little something I wanted to talk over. With you."

Dr. Castle looked at him keenly, the blue-gray eyes swept his face in an instant's detachment, the looking-for-signs look, found nothing, relaxed.

"Dave acting up? Take that chair, it's more comfortable. What's he been doing?"

"I think he's getting worse," Lucas said simply.

Dr. Castle nodded.

He's given me the office, Lucas wanted to shout, it's all mine, now! In a little while he'll be gone, he'll be off to Australia, I'll own it, I'll own Medicine.

"First of all," said Lucas, mastering himself, speaking word by word, "I want to tell you what's happened."

He spoke slowly, frowning, point by point going over a case, presenting it without emotion, with care, with precision. Dr. Castle listened without interruption. He narrowed his eyes a little, digesting each word. When Lucas had finished he turned from him and looked out the window.

"You know what you are, of course. You're the luckiest young fellow that ever lived."

"I never expected it. It's something I never even dreamed about. I thought, one day, maybe, maybe if all goes well, five, ten, a lot of years away—but to get all that, just given it, just to stand there and give another man your life's work—"

Dr. Castle nodded. His face darkened.

"By God Jesus!" he cried suddenly, "have you ever in your goddamned life heard anything worse? Have you? A thing like that to happen to such a man—to carry that all his days?"

Lucas looked down. He shook his head.

"If he could only get to Australia," he said, and the words strained heavily, and in the room the sound was self-conscious, betrayed.

"He'll never make it," Dr. Castle said. There was hope, though. And by saying it a man might buy off the odds, buy them off a little, make destiny careless, make destiny turn aside, the battle won.

"If he just takes care."

"You heard it. How long do you think? From what you heard?"

"Anytime. All right. But it could be months."

"You didn't palpate."

"I didn't have a chance."

"His voice is huskier than it's ever been. You wouldn't know that. And that cough—we're sitting around stabbing, stabbing, and we know and he knows—"

"He's taking potassium iodide."

"Openly? You mean actually openly?"

"I checked the bottle. We don't use it, much. I know when we do. It keeps going down, down . . . And I think bromides . . ."

"I wonder who she was?" Dr. Castle exclaimed.

Lucas looked down.

"I wonder who the son-of-a-bitch was!" Dr. Castle flipped a letter opener, flipped the point through a pile of envelopes, flipping them over, making them spin. "A life! A whole life! Blasted! Shut off! Walled out! Who gave him syphilis? That's what I'd like to know. I'd just like to see her once, just face to face, just so I could see—"

"It could have been something else. It could have been—say—well, it could have been—"

"Syphilis! What a thing for a man like that. You don't think it was anything else, do you? You know what causes aortic aneurysm as well as I do. You know that nine hundred and ninety-nine times out of a thousand that's what it is and I don't give a damn and you don't give a damn but think what it's done to him! Just think of it! He could have had a family. All these years he's known and lived by himself, lived like a monk, wanting a family, a man that ought if ever a man ought to have a family he's that man."

"How long have you known?" Lucas said at last.

"A long time."

And there was nothing you could do, Lucas brooded. You could know but you couldn't tell him you knew. You couldn't even tell him to take it easy for fear he'd know you knew. Most doctors—but this one, this one took it hard, this one was a pariah, inside himself, it was the way he was brought up, maybe, it set the impersonal aside, it set aside disease as just an entity and not a person, it made the disease the man, it was the way he thought, the way he lived, nothing could change it. Not even being a doctor. Not even Medicine. With him, syphilis was—syphilis.

Dr. Castle sighed.

"I've often wondered. I've gone over it in my mind. When he was a student, maybe. Maybe before. Young kid. And he'd have to hide it. And maybe after a while he sneaked away and treated it with what he knew—we didn't know much, then, don't know much now. And maybe it disappeared. Or seemed to. Only it didn't, of course. I've often wondered. I've sat here and I've thought to myself and sometimes I've thought, well, maybe it was worth it, dreamed things up, you know, maybe it was some girl he loved with all his heart, do you think he ever knew many girls? Maybe somebody he was crazy about, maybe that way . . ."

"One second of hard luck—"

"And so he's going off to Australia—another world. A world he never made . . . He's done it, though, has he? He's finally done it?"

"That's what he says. A thousand a month as long as he lives."

"Yes . . . And we've done all we can do—which is nothing. With all our might. Because no matter what we said and how much we all faced it, we couldn't alter for thirty seconds that stinking sacculation, we couldn't change it, we couldn't give him five more minutes."

"If he took it easy—"

"He wouldn't. You know he wouldn't. It's too late, now. The kindest thing—the kindest thing that could happen to that man. Yes. If he went mad. If that—if he quietly went insane. And we could strap him down. And he'd never mind it at all."

They looked at each other.

Dr. Castle nodded.

"It's a hell of a thing to work all your life for, isn't it?"

"I wonder how many haemorrhages he's had?"

"We'll never know. . . . I'll drop over, after a while. Maybe I can calm him down, some. I don't know. I'll drop over. You're going to the meeting tonight, aren't you? The big council meeting that'll probably vote down our water system again?"

"I planned to."

"You do that. I'll keep him from going. At least I can do that. I'll drum up a case—you notice that woman as you came in? Going out just as you came in?"

Lucas nodded.

"I can keep him talking on that all night. Chest pains. Occasional dizziness. Pains in the abdomen. A little anemic. Blood pressure a little low. What's your chief complaint? Doesn't know. Doesn't feel good. Just —all over. Hurt here? Yes—a little. There? Yes-s—now and then. Pains ever wake you at night? Maybe—sometimes . . ."

"Malingering?"

"No, no! Not malingering! Far from it. You see them by the thousands, by the ten thousands, by the millions. People always a little sick, always a little pain, blessed are the poor for they shall see God. Well, they can't see him soon enough. Because these are the really poor. These are the poor material. These are the ones. There's more of them in the world than anything else. Constitutional inadequates. The tissues—just poor material—poor kidneys, but not really sick, just poor, just inferior, just what they were given. Poor material. Everywhere. Stomach stuff below par, muscles, skin, eyes, arteries—bum tissues. Second-rate. Third-rate. Never sick. Never well. Never anything. Waste. Haven't you seen them? You will. It'll dawn on you someday."

"We had a beauty this morning. It didn't help him any. Someone he knew, apparently. Someone named Challis. Incest."

"Tom Challis? You mean to tell me—"

"He was pretty upset."

"Knowing Dave, think he would be! He delivered that girl. And Dave, with *his* notions—my God! To think of it! Tom Challis! My God! They keep surprising you, don't they!"

"Second incest I ever ran into."

"Oh, you'll run into it, enough. You'll run into everything, in time. Everything there is. About the fiftieth you're not surprised any more. It's all possible, you know—everything—it's all possible—the sensory system—I expect even a eunuch has aberrations—eunuchoid aberrations. Nothing to do with sex. Some other sensory excursion—something you'd never dream of . . ."

"Still," said Lucas. He shook his head. "In a little town like this—"

"Little town? There isn't any such thing as a town. It's all people. Let me tell you one I ran into, maybe it'll scale down everything you'll see for quite a while. I remember once. It was in England. It was during the war. I had a girl in to see me. A protty. One of those little protties chasing up and down Piccadilly. Nice enough young girl. Pretty. Couldn't have been more than twenty-five. I was treating her for—by God, I can't remember what I was treating her for. Nothing to do with her trade. Bunions, maybe."

Lucas laughed.

"Droll? That's probably what it was, though. Don't let me wander. Well, in the course of it, whatever it was, she told me this and that about her trade, which is always interesting. And then she told me about this fellow. He was Montgomery Welland."

"The—?"

"That's right! Son of one of the biggest bankers in England. Member of Parliament. All the rest. Picked her up on the street one day, took a fancy to her, bought her new clothes, set her up in a flat. Paid her five pounds a week. Five pounds and all expenses. All she had to do was to be there. And what do you think he did when he came to see her? The minute he came in she had to go to the stove and fry an egg. Hard. When it was cool she pinned it to her blouse. Hatpin. Over her left breast. Then he took out his fountain pen. He aimed it at the egg over her breast. He began to tremble. He shook the pen convulsively. A blob of ink hit the egg. He did it again and again, until there was no more ink."

"And then—?"

"That was all. He'd nod to her and put on his hat and leave without a word."

"That's all? That's absolutely all?"

"Five pounds a week, her own flat, the son of the biggest banker in England. That's all. That's absolutely all. Then he got tired of her. Then she went back to her trade again. I expect he got another one. Well—I just tell you. So when you run into one just take this one out and remember it."

"What did she say? Didn't she say anything? No reaction, I mean?"

"Oh, she thought it was an odd one. They run into odd ones all the time. They're like us."

Lucas recoiled, shocked. There was a gleam of laughter in Dr. Castle's watching eyes. Lucas relaxed.

"You don't like to hear anybody ride the profession, do you? You'll get used to it. Believe me. You'll get used to everything. After a while everything'll drop off you, all the excess baggage, all you'll carry is a smile, a smile and your bag. Well, boy, how does it feel? How does it feel to be on your own?"

"Almost."

"Almost."

"I can't tell you." Lucas shook his head. "I can't begin to tell you . . ."

"I know. I know how I felt. Dave probably felt the same way. Just—just don't expect—" He shrugged. "Nothing. We'll work together fine." He put out his hand. Lucas took it.

Dr. Castle gripped hard.

"We'll get him on the boat. Maybe get him to Australia—Hear you've got a loose baby up at the County?"

"It's loose, all right," Lucas said, on his way to the door. "If I'm not careful—you know that girl tried to give it to me? To me!"

"That so?" Dr. Castle said carefully.

"I'll see you a little later tonight," Lucas said. "I've got to scoot."

"You scoot," agreed Dr. Castle.

The door closed behind Lucas. Dr. Castle opened his bag. He took out a small bottle. He shook out a pill. He studied it. He put it carefully in his mouth. He took a small swallow of water. He sat down. He looked at his watch. He looked out the window at the autumn. His eyes wandered lovingly among the colors, among the leaves, caressingly over the limbs of trees, the haze, the yellowing grass. It was very peaceful. He sat very still. His eyes roamed the countryside. In a few minutes it would be time for afternoon rounds.

"They've been trying to get you," Miss Snow said.

"Which one?" Lucas said instantly.

"Do you have a peritonitis? Dr. Runkleman went to see that Glass woman—do you know where he was? He was down at Sears, Roebuck, looking at guns! I called Dr. Castle's but he said you'd left—"

They were standing beside the screened bed, Dr. Snider and two nurses. They were just standing there, they looked up as he came among them, then they looked back to the silent figure in the bed.

Lucas' stethoscope had come into his hand automatically, the black cone slipped over the chest wall, he heard the loudest sound of all, he heard nothing.

"Oh, he's dead," said Dr. Snider, "dead as a mackerel."

"I did just what I was told," one of the nurses protested, frightened.

"Hand me the chart," said Lucas.

"I don't know as I like your tone," Dr. Snider said mildly. "I don't make a point of it, I try to get along and make allowances. But I'm still head of this hospital. And that, by Jesus, doesn't entitle me to be low-rated in front of a bunch of nurses! You or anybody else!"

The thing he should have said was, "I'm sorry, Doctor. I didn't mean my tone to be offensive." There was a way to do it, this was an older man, he was right about the nurses, that, too. And the words choked in Lucas' throat. He could not apologize, even with the form of the words, only the empty form, to what this man fouled, what he was, this ignorant, dirty old man, somehow permitted in the world of Medicine.

He looked down at the bed to hide the raging of his eyes.

"I gave orders to stop the vomiting."

"We know every time one of your patients dies, we're going to have trouble, it's getting so people are afraid to breathe around here, any case you're connected with."

Well, now he was doing it, himself, right in front of the nurses, now he was as guilty. Lucas looked up. He controlled himself coldly.

"What's the matter?" Dr. Snider said indignantly. "This son-of-a-bitch had galloping peritonitis—you nor nobody else could have saved him—!"

Lucas waited. He doesn't even know. I don't know why I should find it incredible, only it's so simple. And he doesn't know. He doesn't know that nowadays when a peritonitis—that you have to stop a peritonitis from vomiting—that morphine's safer than vomiting—no matter how much morphine it's safer than vomiting, if he dies of morphine he'd have died of peritonitis, anyway. Only, there's a chance. If it's handled right, there's a chance.

"I gave orders that this man was to get enough morphine to stop any vomiting. I think I made that clear, Doctor."

Because here it was unchallengeable. Here he was within his rights, the protocol was right and he was right within the protocol. And he knew that all he said was going right over Dr. Snider's head, he didn't understand a word that was being said, it was almost like talking to a layman for all he'd ever heard of morphine and vomiting and peritonitis. But he'd said it right. And what he said was right. And there was a cold enjoyment in watching his indignation and bewilderment.

"He got morphine! Here!" And he wrenched the chart from one of the frightened nurses. "Gimme that chart! Look! Look at your goddamned chart! Morphine! See it? A quarter grain! And a sixth more!"

"I see," said Lucas. "There's vomit on the sheet. There's vomit in the kidney basin. The only way you can save him is to keep him from vomiting. You know that, Doctor? Don't you? Wouldn't you agree?" Because now he was going to destroy him. Once and for all, he was going to destroy him utterly.

And now for the first time Dr. Snider looked irresolutely at the nurses and meaningly at Lucas. He managed a forced smile. He looked to Lucas as if he would remind him of something, a look that tried to exclude the nurses.

"How much morphine you want, for Christ's sake, Doctor? God sakes, you didn't want *me* to kill him, did you? 'Stead of the peritonitis?" He said it as a joke.

"And opium," said Lucas.

"Two grains. Right there on the chart." He spoke confidently, now, it was all over, just a couple of doctors flaring up at each other, nothing the nurses hadn't seen now and then, before, nothing they'd better talk about if they knew what was good for them. Nothing serious.

"The point is, Doctor," Lucas said remotely, smiling in turn, "we wanted to get the respiration rate down to fourteen. We wanted to keep it there."

"I know." Snider nodded quickly. You know! Lucas looked at him with contempt. "That's what I did. You probably didn't notice. He got all the morphine he could take, he got two grains of opium, grain at a time, dropped on the tongue—you wouldn't want any more—"

"Because the respiration rate," Lucas said kindly, "is an index to the peristaltic rate. Peristalsis has stopped when the respiration's fourteen—"

"Of course!"

He never knew. If he ever knew he's forgotten. And the nurses know he doesn't know. He doesn't even know they know.

He looked at Dr. Snider intently, politely, waiting. He and the dead man, side by side, he and the man who needn't have died, unaccountably beside him, staring at Dr. Snider, knowing right from wrong. Waiting.

"Well," said Dr. Snider easily, it was all over, now, "well, I guess we can't save 'em all, you done what you could, nobody's blaming *you* for a minute—I guess we all know how hard *you* work, eh girls?" He twitched the sheet over the dead man's face. The embarrassment was covered. It was over.

"The point I'm trying to make," said Lucas, "I'm afraid I have to insist on it, Doctor—" Maybe he'd break, now, maybe this was the time, maybe he'd do something, say something, something that would be automatic, said and unrecallable. And in fact Dr. Snider's face was reddening again, slowly reddening, he looked at Lucas incredulous and beginning to anger, but more incredulous, oddly enough, than angry.

"The point I'm trying to make is—as I said in Dr. Runkleman's presence—keeping this man from vomiting was the only chance this man had. It was a desperate chance, that's true, at fourteen, breathing that slowly, just breathing—so somebody had to be here, somebody had to keep watching him, keeping him breathing, no more. You remember? Perhaps this is new to you, Doctor. I'm sure you've read—we don't measure the opium. We measure the respiration. And control the cumulative effect. Nowadays . . . That's what I meant . . ."

He's not through with it, Dr. Snider thought incredulously. The goddamned fool's going to keep right on. Is he crazy? And he stared at Lucas trying to decide, wordless, waiting, and he still kept looking at him with that same look, the look for a stranger, don't you know about mistakes, yet, about the two worlds, the world so far as the patient's concerned and we walking around in it knowing what they don't, and the world of mistakes, the thing we share together, the world where a man stands with his foot in his own bucket just like he was born to it, which he was, making the mistakes a man's got to make no matter who he is, big or little, as natural as breathing, a thing he's bound to?

Are you that dumb? Are you that unborn, yet, not part of everything that's moving around you, haven't you ever *seen* anything? Where you been, what's been happening to you that you ain't *seen,* that you don't know what anybody *knows,* big or little, knowing everything or forgetting half of it, lucky or unlocky, *no matter who*? You know mistakes, don't you? You know what a mistake is? You ain't passed your life perfect?

Well, then! Come into the club, join your kin, those you belong to, you're part whether you like it or not, you'll make 'em—and the dumbest of us will stick up for you—and you and the smart ones'll make 'em and the dumbest of us will look 'em right in the face and lie for you, look 'em in the face cold and contemptuous until they get confused and turn aside and maybe even apologize. And knowing we're making 'em, knowing it all the time. And they can't prove it. And they know it. And we know it, too.

The old man stood, looking at him, thinking this, one of a band, knowing himself, knowing how little he knew or pretended to, fretting, a little indignant, with this man who knew the rules and wouldn't play them, hadn't yet learned you had to play them. Because otherwise, because if you didn't, it was all up. It was dog kill dog. And he looked at Lucas with assurance, not guiltily at all, because it wasn't just the patient, now, it was the whole game, all the rules, everything. And a part of his assurance was having seen his betters on their day of disaster, the guilt and the shame in their eyes, the despair, the wanting to die and be buried from sight, for stupidity, for carelessness, for ignorance, for a moment's lapse. And the crowd around looking at him, then, not letting him off the hook a minute, just looking at him to let him know that they knew, and then, coldly, professionally, ignoring it, whether he was big man, little man, or nobody, and then going out to meet the public and the ranks closing, the solid, unbroken, unblinking front, and how you felt when that happened, and how the fellow who made the mistake felt, and how he felt forever after.

Because that was the way it had to be. After a while it wasn't even exciting, it was just normal and matter of course and you didn't even get a kick out of seeing a big man trapped, or a malice out of seeing a little one. You just closed in. All of you.

The only man who could convict you was your own.

And there never was a man who could take the witness chair guiltless, who wouldn't know, sitting there, that he could have been testified against, sometime or another past, present, or future, by the very men, maybe, waiting there for his testimony.

You were all in it together. Every one of you. There wasn't a one that hadn't made a mistake, wasn't making one now, maybe, wouldn't be making one tomorrow sure as God made men.

Stick together, you crazy bastards! Everybody knew that. Even the goddamned public knew it. Otherwise—where the hell are you?

"I guess I haven't been keeping up, lately," he said levelly. "We old fellows have to depend on you young ones." He said it impersonally, without any anger, now, knowing which side he was on, knowing what he must say, speaking for all of them, now, not for himself, for everybody, for every doctor that was. "We didn't use that in my time," he said quietly. "Maybe I should have kept up."

And Lucas' thoughts floundered. He looked down. He was amazed that Dr. Snider had that much discipline, that much wisdom, he was flustered by his sudden deadly poise. It was an old note, and he knew it well, and here it was again. And there was nothing he could say to meet it.

"Not at all, Doctor," he protested. He looked down. "I just thought we'd give it a try—I'm sure you've tried it yourself, often enough—"

And all this was for the nurses, now, there was nothing to be done, nothing . . .

He looked up and he managed a smile.

"Well," he said, "better luck next time—"

"You bet!" said Dr. Snider. He smiled back. Then he turned suddenly. "You girls shake the lead out of your ass! What are you going to do, stand there all day? Get this man ready! I have to tell you what to do?"

Lucas stood at the bedside a moment longer. The nurses pushed hurriedly past him, one of them bound the dead man's jaws with a strip of gauze, the other, never looking at her mate, tied off the dead man's penis with another strip of gauze, pulling the loop tight, then began to wad gauze into his rectum.

Lucas watched them mechanically, not seeing them. He swallowed.

"Well," he said. He moved off.

"See you tomorrow!" Dr. Snider said cordially.

"Right," said Lucas.

He drove back to the office. He's a doctor, the words pounded in his head, over and over, he's a doctor, he's a doctor. He reached the office, the words still pounding in a kind of panic, not to be faced, not to be seen, not to be heard,

"Trouble up at the County?" Dr. Runkleman looked up.
Lucas set his bag down.
"No," he said carefully, "the Langer case died . . ." He kept his back turned.
"Didn't have much chance," Dr. Runkleman said sympathetically.
"No," said Lucas, "he didn't . . ."
The first of the afternoon calls came into the temple.

⋆ CHAPTER 33

He sat beside Ben Cosgrove. On his other side was Dr. Kauffman and beside Dr. Kauffman sat Mrs. Kauffman and beside Mrs. Kauffman sat Harriet Lang.

"Is this your first town meeting? Have you ever seen a council meet before?" Mrs. Kauffman's eyes implored Lucas that this be his first, his virginal first, so that what was to happen would be her gift.

The council meeting room was filled with people and their tension and smoldering and purpose and anger. The people waited in this room, their feet shuffling, and their feet were the feet of a many-footed animal, of one person, many-footed. Of one person having many heads and many voices, and yet, unquestionably, one person. And not too many thousand years ago this family had gathered in forest clearings, its nerves twanging with the hate and the fear and the anger which the act of gathering, the being together, the waiting, the choice, the propinquity in mass had always lashed up in it.

Lucas felt the violence and retreated into scientific detachment.

"I don't know what you've seen before. But when you've seen our boys—when you've seen the noble citizens of Greenville—the way they've been whipped up the past week by Bemis Shedd—did you see his editorial yesterday?"

"You haven't seen anything till you've seen one of *our* town meetings!" Dr. Kauffman said with sorrowful satisfaction. A man in a seat ahead heard him and looked back at them and grinned happy affirmation.

"The masses," Ben Cosgrove said quietly. "The proletariat attending its own wake. Cattle in a pen, milling, unable to find their enemy, goring each other."

Here and there Lucas recognized the faces of patients. Some of them recognized him, recognition dawning slowly, tension pushing it aside almost immediately.

Before the massed seats was a wooden railing and beyond the railing at a long oak table sat the town's five councilmen and the mayor.

"Look at Granite," Cosgrove snorted. "Look at the bastard sweat!"

Lucas looked, then looked away embarrassed. This man, who had made a career of being mayor, whose mien was a habit made serene by previous knowledge of events, who reflected victory previously arranged, in whose eyes was the tolerant look of the winning side, now showed the face and behavior of nervous uncertainty trying to present confidence.

He rose, and as if in defiance, the shuffling and talking increased. He continued to stand, looking at the crowd, smiling patiently. The noise gradually abated.

"The council is aware that the principal subject for tonight's meeting will be a controversial one," he began. He paused. Now the noise ceased entirely. He waited a moment longer. "We will be glad to have your views. We ask only that you observe the usual rules of order, that you are recognized before you speak and that you confine your speech to three minutes."

He sat down. The noise began again. The clerk called the roll of councilmen. Mrs. Kauffman glared at the noisemakers. Harriet Lang watched, expressionless. Dr. Kauffman wore his consulting-room look. Cosgrove smiled contemptuously. Lucas began to be stirred by the tension.

Henry Granite reviewed the history of attempts to obtain a new water system for Greenville. His remarks were punctuated by occasional sounds of derision and mislike from the crowd and these sounds were attacked indignantly by those who favored the new water system or disliked those who opposed it.

The instant he finished a thin, old man, wearing a faded yellow toupee, jumped to his feet.

"How much is this gonna cost?" he demanded.

"It's been pretty well advertised," Granite said conciliatingly. "One hundred and twenty thousand dollars."

"It's been in the papers!" another voice shouted.

"I jist wanted to hear the bugger say it!" the old man said grimly. He sat down. He folded his arms.

The feeling of being a stranger, an observer, was waning rapidly in Lucas. Despite himself the effect of the crowd was invading him and he was slipping into it, becoming part of it, feeling its anger, its hate, its fear, its torment. Not knowing which side the old man favored he glared at him balefully. He looked anxiously at the council trying to estimate their reaction.

"I know we are all well acquainted with the reasons why it is felt we should have a new water system," Granite said. "But I think perhaps a word from one of our doctors might be in order—is Dr. Runkleman here?"

Heads craned, voices informed the chair that Dr. Runkleman was not present.

"Dr. Castle—?" Henry Granite was disconcerted. While the heads craned again to find Dr. Castle, Granite spied Dr. Kauffman. "Dr. Kauffman!" he cried, relieved.

Now the eyes all swung on Dr. Kauffman and he rose and Lucas, sitting only a few feet away, felt the eyes and a stab of fear, of panic.

"I think we've all gone over this problem of typhoid many times," Kauffman began confidently.

"Well, skip it then!" a woman cried from behind them.

Mrs. Kauffman whirled in her seat, her eyes slitting hate in the direction of the voice.

"That's Greenville's clarion," Cosgrove confided, "the loudest and the foulest-mouth woman in the state." Lucas looked straight ahead.

"What I would like you to consider this time," Dr. Kauffman continued imperturbably, "is the children." Someone made a small sound of derision, but now a wave of indignation drowned it out. "Children are particularly vulnerable to typhoid. Our school population is double what it was last time this matter was brought up. And there has never been a year within my memory when our school children didn't come down with typhoid. So far we have been lucky. I don't know how else it is—I think we have just been plain lucky. In the number. And I want to tell you, and I believe I reflect here the feeling of most if not all of Greenville's doctors, that this year—well—I'll only say this year I don't think we'll be so lucky."

He sat down.

The room was still.

"Just what do you base that on?" A woman's voice, shrill, angry, almost a shriek.

"The chair recognizes all of your rights to speak but will you please be recognized—"

"Just what do you base that on!" The woman rose, a stout woman in her forties, her eyes prominent, thyroid, Lucas noted grimly, noted it with happiness, anemic, probably going through change. He looked at her with cold hatred. Dr. Kauffman rose slowly.

"We're your doctors. We're trying honestly to point out to you all the factors available, what we know, what we believe—"

"You're not my doctor! Coming here trying to scare people—trying to frighten us by threatening our kids—!"

"If you please—" Granite rose.

"Who asked you to come here in the first place? Where's Dr. Runkleman, eh? Why isn't he here?"

"I have been empowered to speak for Dr. Runkleman and Dr. Castle." Dr. Kauffman flushed. He looked down at Lucas. "I believe I speak for Dr. Marsh, also."

Lucas nodded. The eyes swivelled upon him and he felt the hot wave of them, he nodded again and looked down.

"Folks, there's no use our getting all hotted up about this, I guess we can talk about it without losing our heads." A squat, gray-haired man was on his feet. "I guess we got to thank the doctors for telling us what they think—without charging us for it—" a ripple of laughter relaxed the room—"and all we got to figure is whether typhoid's cheaper than a new water system. I ain't saying either way. I come here like all the rest of you, to find out."

He sat down in a small buzz of approval.

"Amos Shockley," confided Cosgrove. "Shockley Street, Shockley Park—old-timers here. Gone to seed, now. Haven't got much. But old-timers. When he talks the tribe has to listen."

"How the hell do you know this is gonna cost a hundred and twenty thousand dollars? Who figured it?"

A red-haired man, burly, in his late thirties, glared from man to man about the council table. Granite rose and slowly began to read preliminary specifications and costs per item. The crowd listened heavily. Granite's voice droned on.

"What do you think of them?" Cosgrove jogged Lucas. "There you are! There's your human race in a nutshell. Look 'em over."

Lucas looked cautiously about him.

"There's Fowler, works for the gas company. How do you know what he wants or believes? He'll vote the way the gas company wants him to. He'll vote that way as long as he lives. No matter what. . . . There's Joe Barker, nice a guy as you'll want to meet, son of the man who owns the biggest farm in Greenville, has to drive a school bus between farming, father's dead set against spending a penny for anything and Joe's got four kids in school. . . . There's Ames, the town drunk, seen him lift a wagon off the road single-handed, he'll vote against whoever makes him the maddest. . . . Look at Mark Wilson, family old as the Shockleys, eats skunk—lots of people eat skunk, but he lets it hang, ages it—paints up like a woman, plucks his eyebrows. . . . See that old guy with the head like a Roman coin? That's Waverly, one of the men whose people founded this town, his wife's a setup for the hired men, at sixty, and his daughter's already had two bastards and nobody thinks the worse of him —and how'll he vote? . . . And Wilfred Hillman, who's in at every council meeting, keeps an open mouth on any subject. . . . And Jennifer Jessup, they elected her head of the PTA this year and the very first speech she made she said the girls were getting slack and hereafter when they had sandwiches the crusts had to be trimmed off . . ."

Granite read on.

Cosgrove speared human after human, a bite, a taste, the carcass thrown aside. . . .

All day Lucas had penned his thoughts, walling them, sealing them off from thoughts about the practice soon to be his. He could not bear to surrender, to think about it, the knowledge was a mountain of which he was piercingly aware, which he glimpsed from a corner of his mind's eye, started, and frightened, looked away. If he had looked on it fully, seen it fully, he knew he would not have been able to control himself, he would have shouted, he would have screamed with the glory of it, rolled on the floor, a human swelled by a thought the body could not contain, could only swell and swell and then express itself by bursting.

Now the mob energy, the impact of their emotions, was a sea of force that dashed against him and to that violence the violence within himself responded, beating back, having no target, no purpose, only response.

He stopped his thinking. He put it away fiercely.

A man had risen, he was interrupting Granite, eyes swung to him, he was saying,

"I lost a little boy last year." His voice was quiet. He spoke evenly. He paused. "If I had the money I'd build the system myself." He shook his head. "It isn't money, you might say. It's a little boy." He pondered this a moment. "Those of you that have them—I wish you'd think of that. What I mean is—it isn't much money—we've just got stubborn about it, maybe. But a little boy—for nothing—he didn't need to—I mean—let's consider that! No use Granite reading all that stuff . . ."

He sat down uncertainly.

The crowd shuffled its feet in embarrassment.

"We all know about Mr. Jeffers' tragedy," Granite said respectfully, after a pause. "And we know—I know—how he feels. Typhoid—it's all so needless, nowadays—today a child, tomorrow a grownup—there's those among us who've lost grownups, too . . . I know how ineffectual this cold report on costs must seem to such good people . . . But I hope you understand . . . It's my duty. I'll just read on. There's just a little more . . ."

They were all here, Lucas mused, all committed, most of those who favored the new water system not known to him, not even suspected, probably, by even the small leader group of which he was part. And outside the hall, in Greenville, the town went about its ways confident in the history of the past, confident that the number who waited here in this room would do as Greenville had always done, would vote it down. Or confident, from their own optimism, their own hopes which eclipsed any other possibility, that this time the measure must surely be voted in.

They were going to vote, that was the thing. They were actually preparing to submit to the whim of these inexpert livers, these vague humans who did not even possess the least notion of their own bodies, of their function, of the dangers, the peril they blandly and unconsciously faced hourly, they were here to let them decide whether it was better to spend money or bodies. Whether the peril was real or fancied. They were going to decide, this group in this room, whether all Greenville should be protected or whether all Greenville should willy-nilly take a chance on typhoid.

He looked about the hall incredulously, seeing these instruments, seeing these humans. Your fellows, he admonished himself. And the fellowship was meaningless. It was without relevance and without contact. They were humans with different purposes, with no purpose at all, most of them. Totally ignorant, totally indifferent to the glaring, blazing wonder of what they were. To the miracle of themselves, their Family, their Species, their incredible presence.

He drew away. He was remote, alone. He was sad with an almost unbearable sadness. He saw in that instant that the whole science of living which guides and buttresses a human man, his only protection, is a mended, amorphous structure of old errors, corrected. And the corrections, hoped to be valid—were they valid?—or was their force not truth but a vote, an agreement. And he was sick with a small and lonely voice whispering that on these hopes man built his hopes for a better world, man everywhere, and fed his hopes with his corrections, a Tower of Babel atop which he stood, keeping a hopeful eye on the Rewarder, to be remembered for having made corrections, wrong though they might be.

He shivered. His thoughts fled into the sanctuary of Medicine.

Henry Granite's list came to an end.

He looked up, waiting. The crowd murmured uncertainly.

The thin old man wearing the faded yellow toupee jumped to his feet.

"What I want to know," he repeated inexorably, "is how much is this gonna cost!"

Voices rose instantly, the owners with them.

"Sit down you old fool!"

"He's already told you, you goddamned old halfwit!"

"If you don't want to think of yourself, think of the kids!"

"Whose kids we gonna think about? Them Chinks and Wops down by the tracks? That who we're gonna make our kids pay for?"

"Where's your community pride, for Christ's sakes! Typhoid in this day and age!"

"You gonna pay for it?"

"There's folks in this town'd be *better* off dead!"

"Didn't kill my father—didn't kill me—"

"Think of the children, then."

"I haven't got any kids!"

"Me neither!"

"Goddamn you, if you're trying to infer—"

And the shocked murmur of women, the pious horror dutifully voiced.

"Gentlemen, gentlemen!" Henry Granite cried. He saw Cosgrove rise, acknowledged him gratefully.

"We're making a lot of fuss," Cosgrove said easily. "A great deal of noise we'll be sorry for tomorrow meeting our neighbors on the street, seeing them face to face—the main thing we've got to consider here is whether the new system is needed, how much it will cost, whether the cost is appropriate—"

"Nobody's gonna ram anything down our throats—"

"Nobody's trying to ram anything down anybody's throat. There's typhoid here. Nobody denies that. We all know it. Every year we've got typhoid. Every year we get a little more. Everybody knows that. Nobody denies it. We're going to have more and more until one day there's an epidemic. That's not scare talk. That's something you know. Or ought to. It's happened to every town around here. Wherever they had a bad water system. So that's something we know. There's no question whether we've got typhoid or not. We've got it. And sooner or later we're going to have an epidemic. Close the whole town down. Maybe quarantine for miles around. That's fact. We've seen it, and we know it, and that's fact!"

The room was quiet a moment.

"So we need a new water system. Have we got the money? Yes, we've got the money. This has been the best year in the nation's history. We've got money, and we've got plenty of it, all tied up nice and neat in bonds getting fatter every day the market rises. Well, let's spend it, then, for God's sake. For God's sweet sake let's spend it and get a new water system and get it over with!"

He glared around the room. He sat down.

"I think Mr. Cosgrove's got a point," Granite said smoothly. He spoke with assurance now. "As you all know whenever this issue has come up before I've thought twice about the costs, I've been inclined to minimize the danger, I've helped to vote it down. But this year—well, I've had a conference with our local doctors. I've talked to the county, I've talked to the state—the fact is we don't want to be a disgrace, a sort of state disgrace, not this town I've done so much—and you know how much I've done and whether I've done it well or ill—all right, well all I can say is this year—I've got no other course—it's the only thing to do—it's the right thing—not for the kids alone—for everybody—so I say: *put it through*! And I so cast my vote!"

The room sat silent.

A stout man in faded overalls rose slowly, ponderously. The people craned their necks.

"What's the matter?" Lucas said impatiently. "Who is it? What's happened?"

"It's Slocum. You don't know. He's Master of the local Grange. Half the Grange's convinced he stole three thousand dollars from the treasury. Nobody knows how he gets away with it. Now we'll have it! Now we'll have the fireworks! Now we've got a chance! If he just—if he—"

At the sight of Slocum, as the crowd recognized him, a low murmur swept the room.

"What I want to know is—along with brother Gilkey there—" he indicated the little old man with the faded yellow toupee—"what right we got spending all that money for something we never needed before and our fathers before us?"

He looked around indignantly, then sat down as ponderously as he had risen.

A short, spare man, his face pocked beneath his bushy brows, leaped to his feet.

"What I'd like to know is"—he grinned wolfishly—"what's brother Slocum so interested all of a sudden in how other people's money's handled?"

There were indignant protests, catcalls, a wave of laughter, angry laughter.

"There's been a lot of loose talk in this town—it's been going on long enough—" one of the town merchants rose threateningly, a grocer—"somebody's gonna go to law if they ain't careful—"

"Whose gonna be wearing the stripes?" a voice jeered.

Slocum rose ponderously again, his face brick-red.

"New schoolhouse last year—street lights year before—two new roads where they warn't any road needed—vote money here—vote money there—every time you think of something vote some more money—where are we gonna come to? Where's it gonna end? You people like to pay taxes? I don't! I been drinking that there water forty years, fifty years, my father before me—good-tasting water as any in the state—"

He was drowned out in a torrent of catcalls, a great wave of sound, part exasperation, part jeer, here and there indignation, mostly derision.

"You against it, Slocum?" The spare, pockmarked man rose, looked at Slocum, asked brightly.

Slocum's head nodded slowly.

"I am!" he said ponderously.

"That's enough for me!" the pockmarked man chirped, grinning. He sat down as if that had made up his mind.

"Three thousand dollars' worth, Slocum?" another voice prodded, seconding.

"What happened to the three thousand dollars, Slocum?" another voice called, behind them.

"I'm against it!" Slocum said slowly, red-faced, stubborn, inarticulate. He sat down.

"He's against it!"

"Old Slocum's against three thousand dollars!"

The hall rocked and groaned.

"Vote!" shouted Cosgrove suddenly above the uproar.

"Vote, vote!" other voices took up the cry.

"Three thousand dollars!" shouted Cosgrove. A wave of laughter and hatred swept the room again.

"Vote, vote!" A gray-haired woman rose up front, screaming.

Henry Granite smiled. He raised his hands in a gesture curiously like benediction.

"There's a motion for three thousand dollars–" he halted in mock dismay–"for a *vote*!" he corrected himself obviously. The hall roared. He smiled apologetically. He nodded. He sat down.

In the end it was not the rich against the poor, the intelligent against the animal, the feuds within the feuds aching for payment, striking out blindly, it was not the children, not the aged, not the health, not the pride, not even the simple evident necessity. It was none of these things. It was a little that this had been a good year, a safe, a secure, a wonderful, prosperous year. It was a little that the massed aggression inherent in a mob had boiled up and over. It was a little the realization by the small group of councilmen forced back by the tumult into the role of an observing group that these humans were incapable of thinking for themselves or even emoting themselves truly, an old realization, now, here, beautifully affirmed for them again.

It was a little of all these things and mostly it was the people against Jake Slocum, an old wrong, unproven, brooded over, come to a head at last, mostly this. And something of masochism, of doing what was presented to it because to do it would hurt, yes, it was that, that and Jake Slocum. And a laugh. The tough cruelty of the people, paying back, now, not to be forgotten, satisfying even those who were not members of the Grange. Yet when it came, when the result was made known, it was as if the result had always been clear, had never been a moment in doubt, had always been completely expected, completely predictable.

The crowd was polled.

The ayes were a hundred and seventeen for, and ninety three against.

The council voted.

The vote was four to one.

Greenville had voted against itself, against its own pocketbook, against the hard-held accumulation of individual survival, to protect itself against sudden death, by the construction of a new water system. Greenville had voted against Jake Slocum, who may or may not have stolen three thousand dollars from the Grange.

Cosgrove smiled happily, a smile of contempt. Mrs. Kauffman tried aimlessly to mend her disordered hair, blinked back her tears. Dr. Kauffman patted her shoulder and his breath came quickly with victory. Harriet Lang glanced at Lucas, her shoulders twitched slightly in a tolerant shrug, Lucas grinned at her.

"Well, and what do you think of them now?" asked Cosgrove. "What about your human race, what do you think of them?" *Yours,* he said. *Your* humans.

Lucas glared at him, resentment growing into anger, this small creature, this pincher, this *provocateur,* and what does he want of me? he thought, what is he probing for? What's he trying to find? What is it I've got that he wants to put his fingers on?

"I thought they did very well," he said shortly. "And why *my* humans?"

"Think they're worth saving? Think they're worth your work?"

Mrs. Kauffman wriggled through the hampering bodies, came close enough to them so that she could be heard.

"We're going to my place," she said. "All of us." She gestured her head toward Harriet Lang and her husband. Then she was gone before Lucas could demur.

"I was going home," said Cosgrove. "But I think I'll stay with you." He looked about him at the crowding faces, the bodies struggling toward the door. "I might as well drink this right down to the dregs."

When they reached the Kauffman home the lights were on everywhere.

"I've got to make a few calls first," Lucas said.

"I've already called him," Mrs. Kauffman cried. "Dr. Castle was there. I told him, he doesn't believe it! He said he'd tell Dr. Runkleman, he said there were no calls, to stay and enjoy yourself."

"I can't stay long." Lucas walked toward the living room.

"I can't either," said Harriet. He looked up and saw her, their eyes met and the impact almost made a sound, his ears rang, he looked slowly away.

"Democracy in action," said Cosgrove. He shook his head happily.

"I don't care what excuse they give," said Dr. Kauffman stubbornly, "they always seem to vote for the right thing."

"Like they've been doing the past seven years?"

"In the end."

"Yes, they sometimes blunder right. In the end. And then everybody rears back and shouts with delight over the way humanity's done it again —voted for their own best interests—known without words who was the best candidate—what was the best program—no matter what anybody says when you come right down to it, you can't fool the people—there's something inside them that knows—that's what you meant, wasn't it?"

"That's what I meant," said Dr. Kauffman agreeably.

"Well, you've got it now," said Harriet. "You've got what you wanted." She did not say "we." She said "you." But they would not have heard that, Lucas knew.

"We did it!" Mrs. Kauffman cried. She rose, she hugged her arms across her chest. "We did it!" Her voice was taut as her body.

They smiled, Lucas with embarrassment, Harriet with calm interest, Dr. Kauffman fondly, Cosgrove with raised brows. Mrs. Kauffman felt Cosgrove's taunting look.

"I can't say that we all seem pleased," she said, looking at him.

"Now, now—!" Cosgrove half protested.

"Well, you're not going to destroy my happiness tonight! You nor anyone else! This is a night I never dreamed to live to see!"

"The female," said Cosgrove mildly, "rejoicing over the safety of her children. Always the female—the *hysteros*—leading us on to better things—"

"You don't like women?" Harriet interposed mildly. Mrs. Kauffman had reddened, she had been about to speak.

Dr. Kauffman threw up his hands, mocking despair.

"I'll get the drinks," he said. "This I've heard before." He walked quickly out of the room.

"He doesn't like anything. Or anybody," Mrs. Kauffman said evenly. "He doesn't like it that we won tonight. He'd rather we'd lost. You would, wouldn't you? You'd rather we lost? Because then there would be a little more chaos, a little more despair, a day nearer the day when the people would rise and shake off all this and revolt and embrace communism? Say it! Don't be afraid! You can admit it! Do you think we don't know?"

"Freedom of political belief is not yet a—a man's still free to believe in any party he chooses, I believe—the Communist party so far as I know still has a right to be on the ballot—no, I'm not afraid, as you put it—not ashamed, either—I believe in communism—I believe in a way of life, not in a people. Do you think doctors are any different? Do you think doctors believe in people? They believe in ills, they believe in their equipment, they believe in the money that comes from the system that ensures they will grow rich on human misery—"

"But you were talking about women, Ben," Harriet said imperturbably. "Remember? Tell me about women."

Dr. Kauffman entered bearing a tray with glasses and ginger ale, a brown pint bottle of whiskey.

"He's going to tell us about women!" Mrs. Kauffman informed her husband significantly. Her husband smiled, put down the tray, sat down obediently.

"About Mrs. Everywoman," said Cosgrove. "Mrs. Majority. The great, lousy, animal middle class."

"Present company excepted," Dr. Kauffman postulated.

"All I want to do is talk about the animal who gives us our conscience, our morals, our manners, and our standards. The animal who raises us."

He turned to Lucas.

"You agree, don't you, Doctor, that our mothers shape us?"

"I'm listening," said Lucas. "I'd like to hear you define your terms, for once."

"If it isn't too long," Harriet said demurely. She looked at her watch.

"All right," said Cosgrove, "let's talk about Mrs. Stupid, then. And her daughter, Miss Stupid. Let's call her Mrs. Animal. Mrs. Vegetable would be better. But let's call her Mrs. Animal. Mrs. Average Animal.

First of all—she's a housewife. Almost her sole thoughts are her wifehood and motherhood. Giving life experiences a possible total of one hundred, her experiences add up to fifteen. She has no background, her life is a daily, narrow habit. She has a rigid moral and social code having the force of law. She judges everybody by this code and she is keenly aware that everybody judges her by the same statutes."

"In other words, she's a decent, law-respecting human, functioning as God made her," Mrs. Kauffman burst out.

"You don't have to defend her, yet—" Cosgrove looked at Mrs. Kauffman meaningly—"nor the God you claim made her." Mrs. Kauffman flushed. Cosgrove turned away. "She is afraid of the new because her friends are afraid of the new and the new brings criticism. She is mortally afraid of criticism. She lives all her days in fear of criticism. Especially by her own, her fellow tyrants. She is completely unimaginative because imagination has no part in her way of life, her daily rote, her life of rote. She is a fearing animal. She lives her days in fear, and she raises the human race in fear, and the fear she fears is what she has been told to fear. And that is what she teaches others to fear. Just live. Just get by. Don't raise your head. Just be the same. Buy what you're told to buy, buy what other people buy, speak like other people speak, dress as they dress, laugh at what they laugh at—and live your days in mortal fear of sin, the fear of offending the notions of other women. An animal!" He spat. "A functioning uterus, propelled about the world by a mind without a thought, in a body disguised as someone else's."

"My!" cried Harriet, admiringly.

"And on this teacher of the young the future of the world depends," Cosgrove brooded.

"How did we get off on this?" lamented Dr. Kauffman.

"I think you have to give her a sense of futility," Harriet said mildly. "Because I think you'll have to grant her that she knows her life is monotonous, and maybe even boring . . ."

Lucas looked down, flushing. Cosgrove's words seemed aimed at Kris. It seemed so plain to him, he was sure for a flustered moment that the rest must see it too.

"Well, perhaps because she is not defeated by it," said Dr. Kauffman. "She knows it's futile, the life she has to lead, but she keeps trying just the same. And she tries to get reward, satisfaction, out of filling her responsibilities—"

"That," said Harriet, "and the problems of looking after her husband and children—somebody has to do that—even communist mothers have to get meals three times a day, three hundred and sixty-five days a year—"

"You're not challenging anything else I've said," Cosgrove reminded her. "You still don't say that she's secure in any dealings outside her own little circle. All her hopes are vague and cautious and full of fear of criticism, her only goal is living up to the standards of wife and mother set by a billion others as like her—"

"Maybe she knows that," said Harriet. "Don't you think there's a kind of grace, there—knowing it and keeping on trying just the same? Don't you? I do!"

"Yes," said Lucas loyally. "Maybe it wouldn't do you any harm to watch a woman in labor, sometime."

"I've watched cows," said Cosgrove shortly. "Is the process any different? Any nobler? Are human births holy, maybe?"

"Here," said Dr. Kauffman. "Have a drink! Drinks, everybody! What got you started tonight, Ben? Tonight of all nights? And look at us! Letting you rope us in! When we ought to be tearing the roof off!"

"The people won a victory," Cosgrove admitted, conceding to himself as an adversary in his own thoughts, "the people won, all right. It was just the sight of them that got me suddenly. The sight of them, their dumb faces, their incredible irresponsibility—when all the time they've got the weapon right in their hands—" He gulped his drink. "Where'd you steal this, Kauffman? All right, let's relax, let's be happy, let's enjoy our victory!" He raised his empty glass. "Here's to women! Here's to the new water system! Here's to us!"

They left an hour later.

It had been surprisingly easy, almost as if the rest were trying to help them. He was driving her home now. He was sitting beside her, and her body was warm against his. She moved closer.

"They're nice people," she said idly. "A little mixed up. But very nice."

"I think I'd except Cosgrove from that."

"Ben? Oh, Ben's harmless! He's so harmless! Can't you see what he is? He's just a small-town lawyer fretting and smarting, trying to hold on to the ambitions a small town drags out of you—"

"Why doesn't he get out, then? Why doesn't he go to the city?"

"Why don't you?" she asked quietly.

"Me? You don't think I'm fretting and smarting, do you?"

She moved, so that his body felt her movement. He glanced at her sidelong.

"I don't think anything," she said languidly. "I just know you're wasted on a small town, wasted on people, really. Without people there wouldn't be any Medicine, would there."

"No . . . that's right . . . there wouldn't . . . I never think about it, that way . . ."

"Don't you?" she asked in a low, teasing voice. "How do you think about it?"

"I told Cosgrove tonight—my field is Medicine. Not sociology."

"You're the world's doctor . . . aren't you . . ."

"Yes . . . I am . . ."

"Don't drive home, world's doctor . . ."

"No . . ."

"Drive up in the hills a bit . . . just a little bit . . . before we go home . . ."

"Right," he said thickly. The pulse in his temples pounded. The highway was indistinct. He turned the car toward the hills.

"You do that," she said, her voice low in her throat. "Just," she said, "just for a little while . . ." She moved closer to him. She put her arm through his. Her flesh was warmer and the odor of her body, her scent, was suddenly sharp in his nostrils. He could go no farther. Dazed with desire, unable to see clearly, he pulled abruptly to the side of the road. The car crashed through underbrush. It came to a stop. He reached for her.

"What are you doing?" she said. "Is it safe here?"

He leaned toward her in the darkness.

"Over here," she whispered. She moved to make room for him. He fumbled for her, bearing her back, his hands were impatient.

"Wait," she whispered, "wait." In the darkness her voice was faraway, he felt her breath on his face. "Wait . . . wait—*there* . . ."

Suddenly all lay open to him, his fingers ravened over her bare flesh, she lay back, her body arched, her eyes blind, groaning, her hands seeking him, he drew back feverishly, groping, there was a pause, and in that last moment, suddenly animate, she fought her head free, she evaded him, with a tremendous effort she pushed him back, she sat up.

She slipped sideways, she grasped his hand where it reached again for her body, and held it tight. He looked toward her, still dazed, stupefied by this sudden turn.

"Shhh!" She sat forward, pretending to listen, pretending to be oblivious to him. Her fingers raced over her clothing.

"What is it, what's the matter?" His voice was confused, warming with anger.

"It's someone coming!" she whispered urgently. Then, before he could speak again, "Quick!" She pushed him away. "Quick! Luke! Hurry!" Her hands pushed him frantically back toward the steering wheel.

Still dazed he bumped and slid beneath it, his heel ground on the starter.

"Hurry!"

And alerted, now, he clashed the gears, the car spun back, lurched, was on the road again, was heading back toward town.

"Didn't you hear it?"

"I didn't hear anything—"

"Get me home in a hurry! Hurry, Luke! Maybe they're following us!" She turned her head to peer back into the blackness flowing behind them, her voice, her posture assuming worry and anxiety.

He drove in silence, looking apprehensively now and then through the rear-view mirror.

"Are you sure?" They were in town now, nearing her home.

She was arranging her clothing again, patting her wrinkled skirt.

She looked up at him demurely.

His breath caught in his throat. The car stopped before her house.

"I'll take you to your door," he said thickly. I'll get you inside. His voice said, I'll take you through the door and it will close behind us, and—

"No . . . No, Lucas! The neighbors! They watch every move—"

"But, darling—"

"Kiss me, Luke! Hurry! Hurry! Kiss me!"

She wrenched herself free. The car door slammed behind her.

"I'll go with you—just to the door—please—just to the door . . ."

"Go on! Hurry! Go on, Lucas! I'll call you tomorrow." She whirled, ran to the porch, waved to him and disappeared.

When the door closed behind her, she leaned her back against it, panting.

"Don't move!" she whispered fiercely to herself.

She heard the car start. She heard it drive away.

Slowly she began to undress. She smiled in the darkness.

When he arrived home, Lucas slumped in a chair, his face in his hands, breathing her body. Anger rose in him slowly, the anger of the balked. Had she really heard something? He rose abruptly. He went to the phone. He called her. He heard the phone ring, he let it ring, it rang again and again. There was no answer. He put it down, finally. He sat confused, staring at the phone, not knowing what to think, not daring to think.

He rose irritably. As he turned from the phone he remembered the County. He called the hospital.

There was no news. Everything was quiet. Only, the young girl, the one who wouldn't give her name, the one who had the baby—"gave her name, yes, not her *true* name, of course, Doctor"—well, she'd disappeared.

What's this? What's all this? What now?

"Just disappeared?" Lucas echoed. He forced himself to think, to understand.

Just up and disappeared. Vanished. Took what she had and left. No, she'd left the baby. Yes, it was all right, in its crib, everything was all right there. That new nurse, that Miss Agnes was calling for it, tomorrow. She'd take it home with her and that friend of hers, that Miss Gloria. Living all alone like that, two women, out in those woods.

"What are you talking about! Does Dr. Runkleman know—"

Yes, Dr. Runkleman knew. He said it was all right. He and Dr. Snider. Yes. She was sure. Positive. She had the orders. All written down . . . No, that was all . . . everything was very quiet . . .

Lucas hung up. He shook his head to clear it of bewilderment, shook it hard. It was the best thing, probably, the best thing for the baby, a little irregular, unquestionably, Dr. Runkleman might do it, he conceded reluctantly. But Snider! Snider jeopardizing his job? For what? For what? Because it was the right thing to do? Snider?

Why else? Why else? he thought finally. For there was no other reason. And yet—Snider—

Lucas sighed wearily. He sat down on the edge of the bed, suddenly incredulous. He had remembered that in a short time he would deal with Snider directly. This practice was about to be his. For however short or long a time he decided to remain in Greenville the opportunity was coming to deal with life on his own terms.

It was impossible to think of this explosive new fact yet. It was possible only to acknowledge it, that it had occurred, that it was impending.

He slipped into bed. He lay in the darkness. Harriet Lang came into the darkness. He thought of her and he thought of the practice about to be his. He made her all the things he wanted of a woman. He put her beside him. Greenville became another place, nebulous, not here, other-peopled. In this place he was alone, he was practicing Medicine, he was borne up, supported by a surrounding throng of doctors he loved and was proud of, they moved happily onward, an other-worldly confraternity, ecstatic with shining brotherhood, ecstatic with practice. They moved out of sight and he slept.

He thought of her often, next day. She was an alien to Greenville. She was an alien among all the women he had known. She was an alien aware of her foreignness, indifferent to Greenville, its men or its women. But not indifferent to him. There was a relationship between them and it was as if the relationship had previously existed, as if, unknown to each other, they had encountered in some vague middle ground before ever coming to Greenville.

When noon came and she had not called, the worst of waiting was over, he had become inured to it, he waited until the afternoon came to evening and he knew that she would be home and he was able to call her then with urbanity twitching his lips as he waited, poised, for her to answer. The phone rang on. She did not answer. He hung up, at last. He frowned uncertainly. He was not irritated. He was apprehensive. For a moment he had almost possessed this rare and desired entity, this somehow related and superior woman, this fellow.

But he did not call her next day, nor, stubbornly, the next.

The practice was his, now, almost his, he all but dominated this scene, this modality. He was hungry for her, he was afraid of losing her. But he did not call her. She waited serenely, smiling appreciatively, surprised and pleased.

The telegram from Kristina came interruptingly on the third day. Her father had died and she was on her way home.

⋆ CHAPTER 34

The platform's old wood, the cells of it burnt by wind and sun, was sib to cinders, and rust, and iron and dust and torn paper, alien as ashes. And on this wooden scaffold, waiting the execution of time and distance, Kristina stood beside her bags in the bleak September afternoon, now gazing hungrily at the flat countryside to cram the cupboard of her memory with a home-tree, a home-plain, a home-watertower, a home-sky, now seeing nothing, mindless with despair and loneliness, immobilized in mid-thought, paralyzed, transfixed by the lightning of realization.

The young woman beside her kept decorous silence, her eyes downcast, head slightly a-tilt, messaging sadness, and that stock grimace of the mouth which is not a smile but a parenthesis of the lips holding the consolation that grief is not timeless.

Conforming outwardly, the young woman awaited the arrival of the train with delight and impatience.

She might have been Kristina's younger sister, their eyes had an ethnic blueness, their hair was of the same flax, their cheeks were molded by the same decision of genes, their figures, their bones, their skin, their posture bespoke kinship.

Barely conscious of her, Kristina clung to this time before the train arrived, to the landscape about the station, now flat, now slowly rolling, the brush bending to the first frigid winds of Minnesota winter, a farmhouse, then emptiness, then faraway another, a wandering road, a puff of sandy loam, remote, gray-skied, inert.

The faces of cousins slipped through her mind, observers at grief, the faces of people, the faces of their children, memorized and looked at, and no longer part of her. The face of her father. The familiar face, the face of her father when she was a girl; and upon this face the face of her father when she was older, when she had left home; and upon this face of her father when she had returned the four days that were already a century ago, the stranger-face seized by age and disease and stroke and clapped on the face of death through which her father's eyes and the life that was still in them looked at her unseeingly. She tried again, hopelessly, that the essence of father be this face, the essence of love, the confirmation of memory, of home, of a thousand immutable recollections, of concept, of symbol, of a threshold that was safety and knew her running feet, of hands that had mended, that had stroked her hair, safe hands, secure hands, gnarled hands, and the foot's clump, the shoulders' breadth, the stooped figure, the mouth's grooved smile.

It was gone, now. And he had died, not knowing her, anonymous to her tears, her touch, her prayers, died impersonally, meditated, breathed a little slower, blinked and was gone. As ash to the burnt tree, as rust to the shining iron, so the man lay graved now, the soil above him new as this that had happened. The house, the rooms, that had been home, were empty of home. And the sight of it was a wince of agony for what would never be again.

The home was gone and the being who had fathered it, the ultimate refuge was no more and she was alone and now she belonged nowhere.

In the distance knelled the sound of the train.

Kristina shivered. She looked about her, dazed. The tears in her eyes were leaden as her heart, she swallowed, she looked down squeezing her eyes shut, the young woman beside her put a hand timidly on her arm.

"It's all right." Kristina nodded dully.

"I—I think it's the train . . ."

Kristina nodded, nerveless, helpless, despairing, her twisting consciousness chained to the slowing train, manacled to the next moment, to what was expected.

She mounted the steps, stupefied, incredulous at her own movement, her knees wading upward, heavy and slow against the current of reluctance, the tide of home, her feet dragging against the pull. The train lurched. Abruptly she was sitting. She looked anxiously about. And in that instant the train moved, gained speed, the station was moving, the platform was gone, the countryside fell back, let go, dwindled, was gone.

A bush, a field, a tree, a house, she held them a moment, she clutched them, the next moment they were vanished, implacably gone.

It was day. There was light where there should be blackness, there was emptiness pitilessly lit. She turned her dazed face from the window.

"Hasn't changed much, I expect," the young woman's voice deprecated the countryside she could not leave quickly enough. She spoke gently, for one bereaved.

"No," said Kris, dully, "it hasn't changed much."

The young woman swallowed. She thought of something. She brightened.

"Your husband'll be glad to see you!" She smiled fondly. "I bet he's been helpless! I can just bet he'll be glad to see *you*!"

Kristina turned. She looked at the young woman vacantly.

"Won't he?"

"What?"

"I can just see him standing there—if only I didn't have to get off before—is he as handsome as the picture you sent?"

"Oh, yes," Kristina nodded, hearing reluctantly. "Yes, that's true."

And she thought of Lucas, and he flashed before her, and the image was a new pain, the face familiar but not kin to her sorrow, grieving but ungrieved, the chest that would receive her, the arms that would hold her performing a rite, her man, hers for the comfort of the words. But not hers. And she clung to the image doggedly. Hers, all the same.

"I can just see him! Standing there helpless!" The young woman looked at Kristina respectfully, with admiration.

The ghost of a smile softened Kristina's mouth involuntarily.

"Not helpless," she murmured, her eyes faraway on Lucas, solitary in the world and glad to be so, needing nothing from any human, driving on in a world of his own.

"Oh, I know—he's a doctor, of course—I know that, but—

"Oh, I can't wait!" she cried suddenly. "I can't wait to be a nurse, myself!"

Kristina looked at her apathetically.

The young woman, abashed at her own outburst, looked away. But she continued doggedly, Kristina must not be allowed to think, she must be occupied, snatched from the grave, made to talk.

"I don't care what you say— Yes! Just where would he be without you!"

She stared at Kristina, knowing, triumphant.

"What?" Kristina looked at her.

"Oh, we know, Kristina! We know all about it! What you did! Your fath—the letters that came—we know all about it! He wouldn't be a doctor at all, would he!"

"That's not right," Kristina protested.

"Of course it's right! You don't give yourself credit! Everybody knows what you've done! I was only a little girl—I remember the day you graduated! That day—why, from that day there was nothing else but be a nurse like you—and when we heard—when you were made head operating-room nurse—when the *Svenska Bladet* printed your picture in that cape—!"

The young woman repressed herself contritely. She looked at Kristina with adoration.

A tremor of irritation stirred through the fog in Kristina's mind. "Do you think you buy a doctor?"

"I didn't mean that—I meant that without you—I mean you made it possible— Is your home nice, Kris? . . . Maybe I'll marry a doctor, too. One of the brothers. You never were religious, were you, Kris? It's different if your uncle was a minister. Will it be different to be a missionary nurse? Is it the same course?"

Home, Kristina meditated slowly.

And it waited. It waited expectantly as on the day she had made it, on the day it was complete; it was home, it was lived in, all the ingredients were there and it was a home. And it still waited. It remained a word. It remained treasured, expectant, waiting.

Would it ever be home for Lucas? Who had been homeless ever since he left, who was homeless now, for whom only a house seemed possible?

What would make it a home?

It would come to her. It would come to her, someday. . . .

And then . . .

They would come to see her, they . . . all of them . . . the other doctors' wives . . . the wives of patients . . . the rich and grand . . . and she would look at them, proud, proud with happiness—for she would be there, the mistress. And they would be in her home. . . . She would never be lonely again. They would get over the way she spoke, she would learn to speak better, they would chatter among themselves, happy full of laughter about nothing, about everything, like the women, the wives behind her, in the world in which she had been born and brought up and had laughed, too. They would be friends. The world would be full of friends. The whole world.

"It's the same course," Kristina heard herself say.

"What's he like? What do you call him?"

"Signe . . . it's hard to talk—"

"Try, Kris! Come on. Please."

Kristina sighed.

"Well . . ."

"Is he kind? Does he laugh much?"

"Oh, he's kind, Signe. Never worry about that! Sometimes I make him mad—I do something dumb—then his eyes, I can't look at them, I have to look away . . . I'm so dumb . . . and I hate myself!"

The young woman leaned forward impulsively.

"Are you lonely, Kris? Tell me! Are you lonely?"

"What he wants, I want, too!" And she pondered helplessly. How am I to give it to him, how can I help him, what can I do? "What do you think, Signe," she said irritably. "A doctor's wife lies in bed all day? A bed of roses?"

"No, no—"

"Her man is out—she waits at home. Her man is late—he's late. He has to get up—she prays to herself he won't get sicker than the ones who call him—"

Her man is getting sicker day by day, seeing what he sees, hearing what he hears, believing men can be holy, she thought bitterly, believing in doctors as he believes in his own soul, as men believe in ministers, in God. And she saw Lucas, believing Lucas, his faith steadfast, still steadfast, saw the days ahead enlarging the wounds of the present, the days when old discoveries must be repeated, new wounds made, shuddered for his faith, for the day—

He would be alone, then, she knew. She would be there, aching to help, ready to die to help, and she would be powerless. Then, when he needed her, there would be nothing for him to turn to . . .

Because if he let her . . . if he let her come inside him . . . and grow . . . and surround him . . . and make them one—

There, on that day,

When it would come,

She would be there.

How? How to make it come? How, when they were drifting even now, drifting imperceptibly apart, so you could tell only a month later and then it was too late, too late . . .

There was one thing.

What they needed was a child.

No matter what Lucas thought—a man doesn't know, how can he know, that's for the woman to know—

It had to be.

A child.

He would be mad and she would bow her head. He would scream, he would beat her, he would curse the day she was born. And she would bow her head. He would never speak to her, and she would wait on him patiently, unobtrusive, her head bowed.

Because it must be a child.

And the child would come and he would love it, part him, part her, part her father and mother . . . and it would be their child.

And she would give it to him.

And they would be together. . . .

"And do you nurse much, Kris?"

"I should do more. When I go back I will do more."

"I could never stop. Not even when I am married. No, I will be a nurse forever!"

Kristina nodded.

"Yes . . . Yes, you will. . . . You will never stop . . . Not if you are a true nurse. You will never be anything else. You will hang up your cape, you will fold away your uniforms. But you will wear them just the same. Your cape and your cap and your pin."

"I know," the young woman breathed. She looked down.

"That you will have always," Kristina said quietly.

"I know," said the young woman. Her eyes were bright. She looked quickly away.

"From God," said Kristina. She said it to herself and she looked out the window at the strange countryside rushing by, and the memory of her father, the worn floors of home, the face of Lucas, the baby to be, were one tide in her, rising, overflowing, until she could no longer see the window, and the young woman's arm slipped suddenly around her to hold her, to quiet the sobs. . . .

Very early next morning the young woman left, having prayed for herself and for Kristina. And then there were four hours and she sat and thought, numb thoughts, mostly, and then the conductor was beside her, pulling down her bags, smiling, and she smiled obediently back.

"It's Greenville," the conductor grinned.

The train was slowing.

And she started, and rose, and followed him, to look for Lucas.

This was the Kristina Lucas met.

He had come with sober face, averted eyes, and stern gravity, the lineaments of a husband meeting at the station his wife returned from burying her father.

He did not know what to communicate to her beyond the standard noises of sympathy for her grief and he was sure that his hypocrisy would be evident, his words false and his tone hollow. He dreaded her arrival.

But the Kristina who alighted from the train and threw herself upon him as if the sole purpose of her departure had been to return to him was a different Kristina than the woman to whom he had said goodbye less than a week ago. He perceived this instantly. He forgot his attitude in his astonishment, he forgot himself, looked at her, listened to her, confounded and relieved.

She had purpose, now. Purpose had marshalled her qualities, focussed them, aimed them, and now expressed her personality with substance that could be felt and an impressive new quality Lucas could not define.

It was she rather than Lucas who took initiative when she drew away from their initial embrace and after she had inspected him briefly and narrowly to ascertain whether he was as well as when she had left him.

"You been all right?" she asked to confirm her eyes.

"Fine, fine—but you! Poor Kris! I'm so sorry! So very sorry—"

"It's all right. It's done. He was an old man." Her eyes filled with tears briefly, her features softened. She dried her eyes with a quick, resolute movement of her hands, smiled faintly, inspected him again.

"You look thinner. You been eating in restaurants all this time. Never mind, I make it up to you." And she looked about her for her bags. Lucas intercepted her, snatched them up quickly.

"Well, Luke," she said abruptly, "I guess I'm alone in the world now. I guess you're all I got."

"That's not much," he said.

"It's enough, I guess. I guess not many girls got more."

She looked at him fondly.

"For your sake, I'm sorry. There's a way to act, now, things to say, a way to feel—all the things you need. I don't know what to say. I don't know what to do. All I can do is give you a sedative."

She patted his hand.

"I know, Luke. Don't worry. It'll come. Whatever you need, whatever's best for you, it'll come."

"This is the time a wife's supposed to need a husband—" He looked at her, helpless.

"I got you," she said. "That's all that matters. Whatever I want of you I make of it. That's up to me. Not up to you. Everybody's lonely, Luke. Nobody can feel what another person feels. All they can feel is what they feel. Nobody can join them. All you can do is do for them, like you said: giving me a sedative."

"He could have come to live with us. Remember? I told you, Kris—"

"We would have kept him like a pet. Like an animal, like an old horse. But the father . . . the father part was gone . . . gone long, long ago . . . That's what I knew on the train coming back . . . people grow away from each other, they do different things, they think different thoughts, what made them one is gone. They keep the names for each other. Like 'Father.' But what the names mean, that's gone . . . He was an old man, Luke . . ."

He put out his hand to her.

She smiled briskly through her tears.

"Now I got to take care of you! Now, we see!"

"I've got some news for you," he said, unable to contain it longer. And then, plunging in nakedly,

"Runkleman's quitting—"

"Lucas!"

"He'll be off to Australia in two weeks—"

"Two weeks!"

"And he's given me the practice!"

"Oh, no! No, no, no, no, no! No, never!"

"He's given me the practice—I have to pay him twenty-five thousand dollars for it—"

"Luke—"

"But just as it comes in—nothing down—just as I earn it—no strain—no worry—no—"

She flung her arms around him and the car swerved wildly. He straightened it, grinning at her.

They talked of it long after they lay abed that night, the crowded day still restlessly upon them: Kristina's tears and Dr. Runkleman's arm awkwardly about her, patting her, his own eyes moist, the conferences, the decision to take over Dr. Runkleman's house, also, and close off the office rooms they now occupied, the excited porings over the maps of Australia Dr. Runkleman spread over the table in the booth at the Chinese restaurant, the guns he had bought, the extra gun he had exuberantly bought for Lucas as a surprise that day, and Lucas holding it awkwardly and Dr. Runkleman showing him expertly from the books he had read how to load it, how to aim it, how it shot almost by itself, all the confused, kaleidoscopic events of that day rushed in on them. And as she lay beside him, feeling the warmth of his body, knowing what was about to come as between husband and wife and man and woman, Kristina licked her dry lips in anticipation and fright, quivering with the secret knowledge that she had deliberately not prepared herself, that she was open, now, open to conception, now and every night thereafter. Until it happened. Until that happened which was to make them one.

And he ceased talking, who was living it all anew, excited afresh from her excitement, he turned to her feeling her body's warmth, feeling her stiffen as she thought of the forbidden child-to-be, and he was ravenous suddenly with the hunger Harriet Lang had made to raven in him and beyond control and she was frightened at his ferocity. And then her body welcomed him, and she received him, hungry as he, new-hungry.

She was like a bride next morning, Lucas reflected. He watched her, perplexed, pondering the intensity of what had passed between them, wondering what had transformed her.

"I go to the hospital with you today," she decided.

"You do?"

She finished drying the dishes.

"First I help you operate—you got operations to do?"

"Just an appendectomy—"

"I be your OR—"

He did not know whether he was pleased at this or not. He drew back a little from her decisiveness.

"I'd better tell Dr. Runkleman not to call Miss Otis—"

"Oh, yes! Be careful there. Someday I might not be able to help—you might want her—I don't want to take any bread out of her mouth—"

"I don't know whether she really wants the money or helps us as a favor. I know she needs money badly enough. But she hates to leave her husband . . ."

"Keep her! Don't let her go. Don't let her think you don't need her any more—you gonna be head surgeon at the County when Dr. Runkleman—?"

"I suppose so. Yes. Sure. The County Board will have to appoint me. I don't suppose there'll be any trouble there. None of the rest want it. You've got to have a backlog of patients like Dr. Runkleman's to afford that kind of job."

"But it pays—?"

"Oh, sure! Five thousand dollars a year."

Kristina beamed with satisfaction.

"Soon—soon we going to have so much we never worry again!"

He smiled at her patronizingly.

"There's the little matter of my having my own practice. It's not just a possession. It's Medicine. On my own."

"I know, I know, Lucas!"

"Do you? Do you really, Kris?"

But she had raced to the bedroom, she flung her apron on the bed, she was out of her bathrobe, he strolled to the doorway, watched her slip expertly into her uniform, watched her pin on her pin, watched her gravely pin on her cap.

"There!" she said. She faced him.

"You look fine! Just like the girl I used to know!"

She went to the closet. She took her cape carefully from its hanger. She held it aloft a moment, let it settle slowly on her shoulders.

"Now," she said solemnly.

"Yes," he said.

"Now we go."

The difference, in the operating room, was astonishing. The barely trained assistants, for all they wore the uniforms of nurses, were not nurses. Each day they did what was required of them well enough, but there were always things to overlook, happenings to make allowances for, an awkwardness, a forgotten instrument, dressings to be gotten hurriedly from the autoclave while the operation waited. Sometimes Lucas and sometimes Dr. Runkleman did what had to be done, saying nothing for there was nothing to say.

But the operating room, with Kristina in charge, became in a twinkling a near-delight. The change was so profound and so complete that Dr. Runkleman's eyes above his mask peered at Lucas in grinning astonishment. Beneath his own mask Lucas watched in gratitude, pride, and amazement. Then they forgot Kristina and the operation commenced.

And in the next instant the instruments were slapping into their hands almost before their hands could leave the incision, the exact right instrument with never a need to turn the head, no matter what variation occurred the right instrument was always there, prescient, before they could speak and call for the variation. And the three of them fell into a pace, move, cut, pass, retract, cut, sponge, wipe, sponge, cut, needle, clamp, suture, sew, snip, sponge, cut, clamp, sponge, and in perfect rhythm the job was done, the area padded, the adhesive slapped—

They looked at the clock. Their heads swivelled like one head.

"Eleven minutes!" Dr. Runkleman cried, staring.

He looked at Lucas. They looked at Kristina. She looked down. They looked at the instrument tray. There was a fleck or so of blood. Otherwise it was as clean and ordered as when they had started.

"Hey!" cried Dr. Runkleman. He stripped off his gloves, gave way as the wheeled stretcher slid alongside the table. He undid his mask.

"Hey!" he cried to Kristina. "Where did *you* come from!"

Lucas, his gloves off, his mask untied, was grinning at her too. They saw a compact, trim figure in white, her head rigidly wound in a gauze turban, her eyes dropping before theirs in embarrassment and praise too sweet to hold.

"What do you think of her!" Lucas demanded, all pride. In that instant he loved her completely, needed nothing else.

"What do I think of her? Do you mean you've had that all this time? What's the idea? What—what—"

"There's the difference," Lucas boasted nakedly, "there's an operating-room nurse! Now you can say you've seen one in action!"

From Lucas? This from Lucas? Kristina turned quickly to hide her misty eyes. She began to bustle energetically with the spare instrument tray.

"Never mind fooling with that stuff!" Lucas commanded.

"Turn around here! And give an account of yourself!" Dr. Runkleman said mock-fiercely.

"What's the matter with you two," Kristina said defiantly, glancing sidelong at the other nurses.

"Boy, this is where you belong!" Dr. Runkleman said wonderingly. "You been sitting there at the house. With your hands folded. Never—" He turned to Lucas. "I never saw anything like that in my life. Oh, yes! Good ones. I've seen my share. But—did you see her work with us? Did you see it?"

"That's the first thing I saw when I first saw her!"

"No wonder!"

"Yes sir!"

"Mrs. Marsh give him up—and marry me!"

"Oh," said Kristina, "you—you're spoiled, that's all! You're getting this for nothing—and so you—wait till I tell Miss Otis! Girls! Get this tray into the autoclave, Mrs. Simpson will you pick up those gloves, please, before they step all over them—"

"Yes, Mrs. Marsh! Right away!" And the two helpers raced quickly, where yesterday they moved languidly, somehow seemed not to stumble, seemed to have new skill . . .

"Well," said Dr. Runkleman in the dressing room, "I don't know whether you know it or not, my boy, I guess you know it, all right, but—just to look at her—I never would have believed it! I mean, I've just *seen* it, but—"

"I know," said Lucas. "You should have seen her back at State. She didn't learn it overnight, I can tell you. She used to practice when the others were out dancing, dating, having fun. That's all she thought of, morning, noon, and night."

"She's sure got it down pat."

"That's all she ever did."

"She seems like a girl that likes fun—"

Lucas was silent for a moment.

"Well," he said diffidently, "she's got that Swedish accent, you know—"

"Oh, my God!"

"Yes . . . and the other girls, well they treated her like a bohunk or something, I guess it got to be a game with them, girls can be cruel . . ."

"Oh, no! I can't believe such a nice girl—"

"That was it, all right. That's what they did. They put her in a sort of Coventry. Even the probes used to mock her, sometimes not even behind her back—"

"I wish I had one of them here now! Just for a minute!"

Lucas looked up anxiously.

"Hey! Here, now! Take it easy!" He inspected Dr. Runkleman's flushed face rapidly. "It's all over and done with. And look what she got out of it!"

"You're right . . ." Dr. Runkleman splashed in the shower briefly. "I wish we could have her on regular," he called out.

"I think she'd like it." Lucas nodded. "For a while there I thought she'd hung up her cape for good—"

"She's not like other girls," Dr. Runkleman emerged dripping. Lucas handed him a towel. "Just marrying a doctor so they can settle down and never have to nurse again, read books and eat candy all day." He towelled himself quickly. Lucas watched him a moment before going into the shower stall, the strong body, the small genitals, the hairy skin, the belly potting from age, the big frame, the thick wrists on which he was flipping his wrist watch, the worn attachment to his body. The flush had disappeared from his features. He was calm, now, refreshed, the operating-room tension gone. He reached for his trousers. His billfold fell on the floor.

Lucas picked it up. It was almost too thick to fold. Lucas whistled. He handed it to Dr. Runkleman.

"Leave all that around here loose?"

"Here? Why not?"

"Lot of money."

Dr. Runkleman smiled sheepishly.

"Been buying things . . . No . . . you could leave it spread all over the floor. That's one thing about this place. One thing you got to hand Snider. In thirty years I been here I've never known but one theft. Somebody was snitching alcohol. The girls laid for him, caught him themselves. And it was a patient. No, sir! Every place, no matter what else you can say, has got one thing it's proud of. That's what it is, here. And this room—of all rooms—is safer than the Bank of England. Those girls outside never leave until they've seen us leave—and come in and inspect to see if we've left anything behind. I've left stuff here and had them rush all the way down to the office with it! A handkerchief!" He shook his head. "No sir! That's one thing!"

Lucas nodded.

When he had showered and dressed they went out together into the operating room.

They found Kristina in the nursery diapering a newborn baby.

"We're going to take you to lunch!" Dr. Runkleman said. He bent to peer at the baby. He straightened. "That's what you ought to be doing for one of your own!"

"Someday, maybe," Kristina said serenely.

Lucas smiled, said nothing.

"As soon as you get him ready—" Dr. Runkleman nodded.

"Me? Oh, I'm going to stay here, I'll eat here!"

"Dr. Runkleman wants to take you to lunch, Kris."

"No, no . . . Thank you, thank you very much. I got to catch up . . . today I better stay here."

And they could not move her, and after a time they shrugged, smiling helplessly, and left. And then the day swallowed them, the Valley, two emergencies, the deluge of office visits.

They met again at dinner that night. They went to Dr. Castle's office and captured him and brought him along.

"It's a pity," he said once, "that there's no place to celebrate but an eighty-five cent Chinese dive that thinks chop suey is Chinese food."

"Li!" Dr. Runkleman called at once. And the waitress relayed the call and a small Chinaman came in grinning from the kitchen. "You got any snails?" Li grinned, bobbing his head delightedly. "You got some fresh puppy dogs?" Li broke into a torrent of pidgin English. "You got octopus? Go get 'em. Dr. Castle here wants real Chinese food!"

"I'll fix you!" he said.

And a moment later the waitress sailed proudly in with four orders of chop suey and a bowl of rice.

It was a happy, merry dinner, and Chinese, and a celebration, the best available. And there were no emergency calls.

"I learned a lot today," Kristina said as they lay in bed hours later.
"What did you learn?"
"Oh, the girls talking. You know how a hospital is."
"Keep out of it. Don't be drawn into it . . ."
"I only listened . . . I never talk . . ."
"Don't—ever . . ."
"No. . . . You know that baby, that one the girl had? . . . The one who wouldn't give her name?"
"Oh . . . yes, yes . . ."
"Those two nurses took it—"
"I know—"
"It's against the rules. It's against the law, even . . . And Dr. Runkleman okayed it . . . and—Dr. Snider—"
"I know—"
"The girl's there, too."
"What girl?"
"The mother—the girl who had the baby—"
"Where?"
"Up there . . . up with those nurses—"
Lucas turned to Kristina, startled.
"They sent her on ahead of them—Agnes, the well one, helped her sneak out, told her where to wait, drove her up there when she left the sick one. She waited right there in Li's, where we ate tonight. And Agnes met her, and picked her up, and—"
"You mean to say she's living up there with them? Now?"
"That's right. The girl, the baby and all. One of the nurses tried to snitch to Dr. Snider and he hollered at her he didn't want to hear anything about it, swore at her and pushed her out of the room!"
"Well, I'll be damned!"
"It could cost him his job—"
"I don't know what the hell he's doing it for—"
"Oh, it's a pretty baby, Luke! Did you see it? Oh, it was darling! And that girl—she wasn't a *bad* girl—but that baby, Lucas! You know something?" She giggled. "I wanted it for my own!"
"Darned girl tried to give it to me!"
"No!"
"Yes, by gosh! I had all I could do—I've got a sneaking idea Runkleman was back of it, somehow—"
"He's so nice, Luke," she said reverently. "So clean, so sweet, so nice . . . He should have married, himself . . . he should have had a family . . . what a father he would have made . . . that's what he's doing—he's being a father to those boys he's helping through school . . . What happened, Luke? Do you think some girl—she died, maybe? She broke his heart?"
"Yes," said Lucas soberly.
"Died?"
"Broke his heart."
She stiffened.
"I wish I could just see her a moment! Face to face!" Kristina said fiercely.

"I wonder what Snider's up to?"
Kristina was silent.
"There must be something in it for him—or somebody's got something on him—"
"Ah, he's not that bad, Luke—"
"There's got to be something."
"He just did it because sometimes the law is wrong and doesn't cover everything and he took the law in his own hands. Dr. Runkleman, too, Luke!"
"Dr. Runkleman, I can understand. That's easy. That's what he *would* do. But Snider—risking his job—for somebody he never knew—a stranger that's got to be something—"
"He did it for the baby, Luke. And that young girl."
"Don't be a fool, Kris!"
"That's what he did . . . Once he bought a layette for somebody's baby . . . one of the girls told me . . . he was very mad when they accused him . . . threatened to fire them . . ."
Lucas sighed. Digested this, sighed, let his thoughts probe warily a moment, gave up, sighed again.
"Were you lonely when I was gone, Luke?"
"Not specially. Oh, sure! I missed you, but I was busy, as usual."
"I thought maybe Mrs. Kauffman would come over . . ."
"No, no. Nothing like that—I ate out—I saw Dr. Castle a couple of times . . . Dr. Runkleman's in bad shape . . . I don't think he knows how bad . . . tired, mostly," he corrected himself warily.
"I know . . . The girls told me . . ."
"The girls!"
"Dr. Castle's girl told one of the County girls . . ."
"My God! My good God!"
"It's a small town, Luke. You know what a small town is. Everybody knows everything. When they rake the lawn, even— We're gonna have a new water system, eh?"
"That's a miracle I still don't believe. You should have been there, Kris! You should have been there!"
"Yes . . . You took that Miss Lang home, Luke?"
Lucas raised himself on one elbow. He stared at her in the darkness.
"The girls tell you that?" he managed at last.
"Oh, sure. Someone always runs quick to tell you. Just as if it was nothing. Watching you. I told them you wrote me . . ."
Lucas sank back. He looked at the ceiling.
"We went to the Kauffmans' after the meeting," he said. "Dr. Castle stayed with Dr. Runkleman, we sat around for a while and that lawyer Cosgrove got off his usual vomit and the party broke up and I drove her home."
"I'm glad."
"Nothing to be glad about. I just drove her home."
"She's a nice girl."
"Yes, she is. She works very hard."
"A girl like that's got to be so careful . . . everybody watching her . . . a small town . . ."

"Well, they haven't got anything on her *that* night! We left the Kauffmans' at eleven o'clock, she must have been in bed before midnight! I came straight home . . ."

"It was good of you, Lucas. After such a day! Such a long, long day . . ."

"You don't know!" And Lucas, grateful for the interruption, told her all that happened, told her of the meeting, told her of Cosgrove. He paused at last, weary with it.

"Oh, Lucas! No calls? No calls, I hope!"

"I got to bed at one-thirty—"

She clucked sympathetically.

"And three-thirty they called me from the County!"

"Poor Luke!" She snuggled closer to him. "My poor, poor Doctor Luke . . ."

She kissed his neck. One-thirty . . . one-thirty . . . eleven and . . . one-thirty . . . Two and a half hours. Probably with her. He stirred. She held her arms open to him. He came to her, startled. It was like the night before . . .

And later, as he was drowsing peacefully off,

"You like her, Luke?" she whispered.

"Who?" he murmured drowsily.

"That girl—that Harriet Lang . . ."

"Go to sleep Kris . . . Go to sleep . . ."

"Yes," she whispered. And she snuggled closer to him. She put one arm across his chest. He fell asleep. She listened to his regular breathing. She thought of Harriet Lang. She thought of the baby. She sighed then, and relaxed, and fell asleep beside him.

Miss Otis was not available next day and Kristina helped again, this time they scrubbed together.

"So you got 'em all working, now!" They turned to Dr. Snider's voice. He was smiling his usual small mirthless smile, the corners of his thin mouth faintly stained with tobacco juice.

"Yes," said Dr. Runkleman, "got 'em all working. That's right."

Dr. Snider perched one hip on a table edge. He was wearing a white coat. It looked painfully clean.

"You won't need me, then."

"No," said Dr. Runkleman, "I guess not."

"Saw you had a gall bladder scheduled, thought you might be giving ether—"

"Yes," said Dr. Runkleman. "No, I think we'll do a spinal . . . Yup . . ."

Now they scrubbed in silence. Dr. Snider watched them.

"See they started digging already," he said suddenly. "Not wasting any time."

"No!" Dr. Runkleman turned to Lucas. "You hear that, Doctor?" He chuckled. "I guess Henry's not taking any chances."

"The way they're digging they might have the whole damn water system in before spring—pipes, pump, and all! That's something," he said grudgingly, "I never thought you'd see, Dave."

"No. I didn't either." He turned to Snider. "I won't, when you come to think of it."

"By God, no! You'll be in Australia, won't you! Clipping your bonds! You ain't the only one, by God! I got a few, myself!"

"I never knew you—"

"Oh, I got a few. Not like you, maybe. Enough to get out of this place in a few years if that market keeps on going the way it was going three weeks ago. How about you, Marsh? You started clipping yet?"

"I'm afraid not," said Lucas.

"He'll be all right," said Dr. Runkleman.

"Sure. Just take it easy, run things the way Dave did, first thing you know—" he waved his hand vaguely. "Not everybody gets things handed to 'em on a silver platter. No, sir! You got up a few nights for them stocks and bonds, didn't you, Dave!"

"I earned it," Dr. Runkleman said lightly.

"Yes, sir! Running all over creation in the middle of the night, snow to your armpits, skis, snowshoes, soaked to the skin, and all for seventy-five cents like as not you never got. Morning, noon, and night. Thirty years!"

He shook his head. He got down from the table.

"Things ain't what they used to be . . . Young fellows today're lucky . . ." He shook his head sorrowfully. He paused at the door. "Got any good tips, Dave?"

"I'm all through," Dr. Runkleman cried exultantly. "To tell you the truth I never liked that margin business—but in two weeks I'll be sold out, altogether!"

They rinsed their forearms in the basins ritually, one after the other. Dr. Snider watched them a moment longer. Then silently he was gone.

"Always buy yours outright," Dr. Runkleman said.

Lucas grinned.

Kristina looked quickly from one to the other, turned and entered the operating room. And now the smiles were over. They followed her. They stood silently, they put out their arms, were gowned, marched to another nurse, were gloved, took their places on either side of the table. The only human signs in that room of white tile, white sheets, white enamel, white figures and gleaming instruments were the rolling eyes of the patient, supine on the table, that altar of human knowledge, and the patient's body, whose mysteries were about to be explored by minds that did not know the ultimate mystery or even the greatest lesser mysteries but would do all they could.

Kristina nodded.

A nurse now turned the patient on his side. She put her arms around him, one arm over his shoulder blades, the other behind his knees. She drew him to her. His body arched. She held him fast in that bow. Kristina wet the skin over his lumbar vertebrae with antiseptic. Dr. Runkleman injected an area with novocaine. He stood back. They waited. Moments passed. The nurse stirred. She gripped the patient tighter. Dr. Runkleman's gloved finger tips prodded for the soft spot. He found it. He held his index finger on the place. As he put out his free hand Kristina slipped a syringe into it, tipped with a long needle. She extended a small bottle full of clear fluid. The needle pierced the bottle's rubber cap. The syringe drew up fluid. The needle was withdrawn. The syringe was removed. The needle hovered over the patient's flesh a moment, poised above his backbone. It touched the skin where Dr. Runkleman held his finger. It plunged in. Dr. Runkleman felt the feeling. The giving-way feeling. His eyes showed him feeling it. The room relaxed. From the open end of the needle, spinal fluid began to drop. It fell to the tiled floor. Dr. Runkleman counted. The drops fell. Lucas counted. They were silent, watching the drops fall.

"About right," Dr. Runkleman said finally.

Lucas nodded.

Dr. Runkleman fitted the syringe to the needle. He pressed the plunger. He pressed it slowly. In a few moments the syringe was empty. He pulled slowly on the needle and syringe. It was free. Kristina's hand was ready for it. The nurse holding the patient turned him on his back again.

"How do you feel?" Dr. Runkleman asked him in that artificial, raised tone in which he might address a stranger with an uncertain command of English.

The patient stared at him apprehensively.

"I feel fine," he said fearfully, but I won't feel fine in a moment, will I, you're going to do something to me, you're going to hurt me—

"Well, you just relax and take it easy, when you feel yourself getting drowsy just let me know, nothing's going to hurt you, you won't feel a thing—"

"Not a thing—" said Lucas.

"You'll be right as rain—" said Kristina.

"Just relax—" said Dr. Runkleman. He looked across the table. Kristina had the clamp ready.

"Feeling drowsy?" Lucas asked cheerfully.

Dr. Runkleman clicked the clamp, pinched belly skin lightly.

"Sort of—" the patient admitted unwillingly.

"Kind of sleepy?"

Dr. Runkleman pinched again.

"Kind of . . ."

"Feel that?" said Dr. Runkleman.

All eyes turned to the patient.

"Don't feel anything . . . kind of numb, like . . ." His voice buzzed a little, trailed . . .

Dr. Runkleman nodded briskly.

He put out his hand.

Kristina slapped a scalpel in the palm.

The knife descended, Lucas put out his hand, the flesh divided, Kristina slapped a clamp in the palm, the knife drew down, down, the blood welling, following it, Lucas put out his hand, she slapped a square of gauze in it, he drew it over the blood, the flesh gaped, the scalpel cut again, a new sponge, a wait, a clamp on the little squirting bleeder, sponge, muscle, now, cut . . .

The abdomen was open. The tough skin stretched between the heavy retractors clamping the cavity open, Dr. Runkleman's gloved hand groped wetly, half hidden in the body, he looked up, his hand in place,

"It's stones, all right!" he nodded to Lucas.

He lifted the gall bladder, exposing it. Lucas' fingers felt the stones.

"Let's see what it's like . . ."

He slit the sac. He spread the slit. The stones looked up at them, sharp, green-brown-black, three stones, one large—

The operating-room phone rang.

He halted. He turned his head, frowning. He turned back. The nurses looked uncertainly at each other.

"Let's see what we got here," Dr. Runkleman said.

Kristina handed him a sponge. Lucas put out a clamp. He grasped a stone. He drew it forth. It clinked in the basin. The dirty-surgical nurse stripped her gloves. She went to the phone. She said hello. She listened a moment.

Lucas reached for the second stone.

"But he's operating," the nurse said indignantly.

Dr. Runkleman was looking at the gall bladder.

"I don't know," he said. "That lining . . ."

"I can't help it!" the nurse cried. Her voice rose. "I tell you he's operating!"

"What is it? What is it?" Dr. Runkleman turned irritably. All eyes were angrily now on the short nurse, standing tiptoe at the wall phone.

She glanced at them, quailed.

"Just a minute," she shouted angrily into the phone. She looked at Dr. Runkleman. "It's for you, Doctor," she apologized. "I can't make out who it is—he's say to tell you it's your broker—he says all hell's broken loose—excuse me, Doctor—he says it's a matter of life and death—something about money, more money or—I told him you were operating—"

"Hang up!"

The nurse promptly fumbled the receiver back on the hook. She came back into the room. She began to put on another pair of gloves.

"Now, let's see," said Dr. Runkleman. He let out his breath. He turned to the nurse. "Who'd he say?"

"Something—your broker—I couldn't catch it—he was talking so fast—"

Dr. Runkleman grunted. He turned back to the open cavity.

"I think it's going to have to come out," he said, after a moment. He looked inquiringly at Lucas.

"I wonder," Lucas mused.

"I hate to do it."

"It's a pretty thin wall—"

"Yes . . . He's had trouble there . . ."

He studied a moment longer.

"Well!" he put out his hand.

Kristina's hand was already slapping a clamp into his palm. He clicked it open.

The phone rang.

This time as the nurse raced to it, her shoulders hunched defensively, he did not turn his head, he did not move, his hand stayed still, the open clamp rested around the sac's end, ready to close,

The nurse's voice came to them. She was arguing, her voice desperate.
"Well?" Dr. Runkleman cried suddenly. He had not moved his head.
"He says it's life or death," the nurse faltered. "He says you know what it is—and he won't be responsible for the consequences. He says—"
But Dr. Runkleman had straightened abruptly, turned from the table, was walking toward the telephone stripping off his gloves, dropping them as he walked.
"Hello," he said angrily, "hello, who's this, this is Dr. Runkleman, who's this?"
Then he listened.
In the room behind him there was silence. No one moved. Lucas looked steadfastly into the open cavity, his hands where they had been. Kristina stared steadily at her instrument tray. The other nurses looked at each other, then looked at the floor.
"When?" Dr. Runkleman's voice came out suddenly. Then,
"I heard you! I asked you when?"
His head turned quickly. He looked at the big clock on the wall. He turned back to the phone.
"I'll be there," he said. He hung up the receiver. He walked back toward the table. He began to untie his mask.
"Take over," he said to Lucas. Lucas looked up. "You take over. I think I'd take that out. Going to give him trouble, one day. I'll be back. I'm sorry. Have to go." He looked at the clock. Then back at the patient. "Manage all right?"
"You go ahead," said Lucas. He walked to the other side of the table, he stood where Dr. Runkleman had been standing. The clamp clicked shut. Lucas put out his hand. Another clamp slapped into it.
"Harder," murmured Lucas.
Dr. Runkleman nodded. His face was stunned.
"Sorry," he mumbled. "Damned fools . . ." He stood uncertainly a moment longer, then turned and walked abruptly to the dressing room.
Kristina moved the tray closer to the patient. She took the place Lucas had vacated. She did what he had done. And she passed for both of them. The minutes passed . . .
They looked up at last.
Lucas unfastened his mask.
There was a stir of activity in the room.
The stretcher headed toward the table.
"How do you feel?" Lucas said loudly. The patient murmured drowsily.
"He's asleep," a nurse said gaily. "Come on," she called loudly. "Come on, Mr. Grass! Help us while we get you off the table!"
The patient murmured drowsily. He was on the stretcher. He was gone.
"That was nice assisting," said Lucas.
"I've seen it enough," Kristina deprecated.
"It was nice work." He looked at her directly. "Thank you."
She flushed. She nodded and turned quickly aside to her tray.
Dr. Runkleman did not appear to join him at the Valley Hospital. Lucas made his rounds alone. He did not return for lunch.

"He's gone to the city," said Miss Snow. "Like the devil was after him. Never saw a big man move so fast!" she said admiringly.

He did not appear for afternoon calls. For a time Lucas attempted to cover them himself. Unobtrusively Miss Snow cancelled the least necessitous. Lucas plunged on, disappeared, buried beneath the volume of humans.

At three o'clock he took the extended receiver impatiently from Miss Snow's hands. It was Dr. Castle.

"Keep an eye on him," Dr. Castle began immediately.

"On who? I don't—"

"On Dave. Watch him like a hawk! I'm telling you!"

"What's the matter? Where is he? What's happened? I'm here all alone—we were operating and right in the middle of it—is he all right? What is it? Is he there?"

"The market."

"What's happened?"

"The market's busted wide open. He had every dollar in the world in it. He's down there, now. I don't know *what* he's doing! Selling his blood, probably . . . You don't know where he went, do you? The papers are full of it! Didn't you hear? If I knew where he was I could get down there, be with him—"

"We'll go together—"

"You stay where you are—"

"But—"

"Did he take his bag with him? Has he got something with him, at least?"

"I don't know! I think so. It's not here. I think he's got it in the car—"

"I got to find him. I'll keep on calling brokers' offices—it'll never stand it—it'll never stand it—"

He hung up abruptly.

But between them, filling the half-mile of space, was the bulging arch of the aorta as both men had seen a bulging aorta, thinning, rupturing, about to burst.

Lucas stared at the receiver. He hung it up. He put his chin on his hand. He gripped it hard. His heart beat fast, his eyes were wide with alarm. He rose. He began to pace the office. He walked faster.

The door opened.

"Miss Latimer," said Miss Snow.

The patient walked in reluctantly. She sat down.

"I've got heartburn," she said querulously, "seems to hit me here, I was feeling perfectly all right, I et some clams, all of a sudden I couldn't breathe . . ."

Lucas walked toward her slowly, he swallowed, his hand went automatically to his stethoscope, he looked at the woman blankly, he put the stethoscope in his ears.

"What—" he croaked, "when did this first begin to bother you . . . ?" He blinked. The woman answered something. He put the stethoscope against her chest. . . .

Late that evening, they were all there waiting, the lights were all on,

Dr. Castle, Dr. Kauffman, Miss Snow, Lucas, Kristina, the door opened, Dr. Runkleman came slowly in.

Lucas rushed a chair behind him. He sat down heavily. His ruddy face was gray, his eyes were dead, his skin was shrunk. He waved a hand listlessly. He let it fall back.

"It's gone," he said vacantly. "It's all gone . . ."

The bag was open and the syringe was filling fast, Dr. Castle and Dr. Kauffman were pulling his coat off, Miss Snow had his cuff undone, the sleeve up,

"It's gone," he whispered, the needle plunged home, Lucas rammed the plunger, "I'm finished," he said, "I'm finished," he whispered. He slumped. His eyes closed.

"Take him to the Valley!" Dr. Castle shouted. "Quick!"

"No ambulance!" Dr. Kauffman cried. "Never mind the ambulance," Miss Snow shouted into the phone.

"My car!" said Dr. Castle.

Kristina had his feet, Lucas was lifting the heavy shoulders, Dr. Kauffman brushed Dr. Castle's hands aside:

"No lifting for you!" Dr. Castle moved uncertainly back. "Don't want *two* patients!" Dr. Kauffman's voice shook.

"He's breathing," said Kristina, they lifted him, they staggered with him through the door, Miss Snow held the outer door open.

"He'll be all right," they told each other.

"He's breathing better," said Dr. Castle.

"The shot's taking hold," said Lucas.

All their words were empty words, desperate, meaningless, the sounds of reassurance without faith, without meaning, only desperate, only hope.

"Easy!" they said. And they got him into the car, they got him to the Valley, they got him into bed.

And there they stayed.

They stayed all night.

And in the morning he opened his eyes and his eyes were bewildered, and then he saw them, and then he remembered. And then he closed his eyes again.

⋆ CHAPTER 35

He hovered for three days, neither alive nor quite dead, breathing slowly, breathing as they let him, inert, suspended.

And on the afternoon of the third day he breathed more easily toward evening, his tired heart adjusted sluggishly to this new demand, this disordered-order, in his heavy body the blood pressure fell reluctantly, the pain in his chest dulled, he lay still, thinking.

He had no desire to move. Anger, fright, despair were remote strangers. He lay, disembodied, conscious, he looked at nothing, seeing nothing, hearing nothing, alive in a quiet watchfulness. He lay content, wishing for nothing.

Lucas found him thus.

He sat by the bedside, he sat down quietly, divining the desire, the fixed state of the body, in his first all-measuring glance, for it was very plain, it emanated from the body, it was a finger raised to the lips. He sat by the bedside and thought, long thoughts, thoughts as slow as the breaths the man in bed was drawing.

There was no doubt now. There was not the slightest, lingering justification for hope. For a time between Kauffman, Castle, and himself there had been the unsaid hope of a tumor. Now there were X-rays and there was no doubt, there was diastolic shock and ringing, there was second aortic sound, the fingers of hope, each hold vanishing, gripped upon nothing, unclenched, fell limp and useless.

There was no hope. There was only Time and the unknown. And the unknown now was a tender comfort, a sanctuary. There was no slightest possibility that he would ever get well. But it was unknown when he would die. It would not be long. But not-be-long was a possible month, a vague unmonthed longer time, it was an hour, a day, a little time, a little-long time, it was unknown.

Dr. Runkleman lay in the bed, his bulk outlining the smooth covers, he looked quietly and watchfully at nothing, he breathed slowly. Occasionally his eyelids blinked. He was alive.

After a time Lucas cautiously tiptoed from the room. He looked at the chart. There was nothing to be read. There was nothing to be added. He looked at it, waiting. He put it down, nodded to the nurse, and went to Dr. Castle.

Dr. Castle presented inspecting eyes, Lucas offered his reporting face, Dr. Castle dropped his eyes, nodding.

"Well—he's alive." He sighed. He sat down. "How long do you think?"

Lucas shook his head. He did not answer.

"Oh, hell! Sometimes they live for years," Dr. Castle said vacantly.

Lucas nodded.

"Seen any? Like that?"

Dr. Castle averted his eyes. He shook his head.

"Book says so."

"Well," said Lucas, "he's read the book."

And between them, unspoken, was the memorized text, the remembered sentence. An aneurysm sufficiently advanced to produce symptoms causes death within thirty months.

"Two and a half years," said Dr. Castle. "Wonder how long he hasn't let on?"

"I don't know," said Lucas. "The other day in the shower you could actually *see* pulsation . . ."

They sat a while in silence.

"Do you think—" Dr. Castle's voice trailed.

"I don't know," said Lucas.

"He wanted to make Australia . . ."

Lucas shook his head.

But on the next day he was stronger. The vitality of his large body seemed to accrue, lying still. In the evening Dr. Castle and Lucas sat beside him and let him talk.

"Market still bad?" he asked mildly, without much interest.

"Still bad," said Castle. "There's talk of it going up. You weren't the only one."

Dr. Runkleman smiled assent.

"Quite a few in this town busted to their socks."

Dr. Runkleman nodded.

Throughout the world, their survival and the destiny of their bodies and the harvest of their minds anastomosed to the veins of ink that pulsed unordered and quixotic in the world's play marts, men faltered, contemplated death, lay lifeless, walked blinded, their bones dissolved in fear by that poisoned flow to which they had linked their very blood.

"It'll go up again," said Dr. Castle.

Dr. Runkleman nodded without interest.

His lips moved. The words came slow and thick.

"I got twelve thousand left," he whispered with satisfaction. He said it almost with content, who in an afternoon had seen the whole yield of his lifetime vanish and buy nothing.

He began to talk of Australia.

"They got fields there," he said once, looking through the room, out into space, "flat, level, going away and away into nowhere . . ."

"Emus," said Dr. Castle. "Kangaroos."

"It's a wonderful country," said Dr. Runkleman. And he spoke of it as a place to which he would return, who in all his life had seen only four states and who had been in this tiny town for more than half his life. He spoke of it as home.

"Birds," he said softly, and his eyes saw their plumage, "birds and animals," and his eyes saw their strange shapes, "mulga scrub," he said, to tell them, "tall grass, eucalyptus, mountains and plains . . . sunset . . . like a sea . . .

"Gold," he said softly.

"Opals," said Dr. Castle.

"Gold and opals . . . and euros . . . and dingoes . . . and cockatrice . . ."

He shook his head slowly, he smiled at them shyly. He sighed.

"You'll be there!" Dr. Castle assured him.

He smiled.

"You wait and see!" said Lucas.

Dr. Runkleman turned his head.

"Things all right?"

"Couldn't be better!" said Lucas. "Don't even think of it. Office running along, everything's taken care of, not a thing to put your mind on. Not a thing. Not one earthly thing. You just get well."

Dr. Runkleman nodded.

"I'll be all right," he said mildly.

"You bet you will! We'll start again. We'll have that place going like a factory. In no time you'll load those guns and be on your way, just as you planned."

Dr. Runkleman said nothing then. He nodded pleasantly, he shut his eyes.

"It's all flat," he said. He shook his head dreamily. "Stretching out flat . . . as far as you can see . . ."

And he opened his eyes and they were golden with the wonder of it, the wailing hunger hidden in the mind of a man, keening to him softly, keening forever, honing its appetite on sorrow and disillusionment and compromise and bitter loss for empty gain, the wailing hunger of man who knows he is man and jailed and dreams of sunlight and escape. All his life. All the man of him.

And the two men at his bedside, the young man and the old man, their hearts, their minds, the secret place within them, stirred; they who were sib to this man, the sound of his voice, the burden of his words, the far-roaming of his sick eyes was a hand stirring in their tender, closed and secret places. And Lucas moved restlessly, in his imperfect world he tried to imagine Australia before he closed his thoughts to watch the sick man's face. And Dr. Castle's thoughts stayed with Dr. Runkleman's. What do you see Dave? What is it? Is there a place for me, too, an island maybe, a lonely place, far off to sit and rest a while, to remember and dream and rest . . . the Blessed Isles, Dave . . . is a continent your Blessed Isle? . . . And for me . . . what do I want? Where is it? Where is the place for me? Where do I want to go? . . .

And the hunger of man for a far place, the old, old hunger, the indomitable hunger, the jogging, reminding hunger of all men, strangers in a place that is not home, the dim soul memory of a place that is not here and is somewhere, some nameless place not here, that troubled faith of the far home place was in the old eyes of Dr. Castle, in the sick eyes of Dr. Runkleman; that look, the soul's look, naked with an old pain.

He rested for a week.

He talked of Australia.

And the visitors came, tiptoed in, tiptoed out, Bemis Shedd, his soft, fat face wreathed with a halo of concern, his eyes large to see a man in mortal peril, so great a man, a little surprised not to see blood, a little disappointed; and Agnes, scolding in a whisper, her lips clamped in grief, and,

"Yes, the child's fine, the mother's helping me, you just get well—"

And returning his heavy, conspiratorial wink, winking obediently back, walking out quickly to hide her wet eyes, back to the hiding woods and the loneliness.

They all came, Dr. Kauffman, silent with knowledge and kinship; Mrs. Kauffman silent, uncertain and compassionate; Miss Snow—"Does he need any money, Dr. Marsh? I've got twelve hundred dollars I don't know what I even saved for . . ."; Dr. Snider—"I guess we all got to go sometime . . . I thought I'd be the one, first . . ."; and Kristina, every day, to read to him about Australia.

They all came. Even a few patients.

"Had one of them come in to me—what do you think he wanted to know?" Lucas grated angrily.

"He wanted to know what he was going to do for a doctor, now that Dr. Runkleman was sick," Dr. Castle said equably.

Lucas looked at him, nodding, outraged.

Dr. Castle shrugged.

He stayed thus for a week and at week's end the prodigy had declined, the news had staled, the lashed waves of sympathy had settled tranquilly, and in the world outside the hospital, life went on, there was a new tension in the air, the tension of money moving in far-off places, of ominous things, of money, of survival, of unease, of a toy become a deadly weapon.

They caught him toward noon one day in the second week standing shakily by the side of his bed. After that he could not be controlled. He grinned at them, shamefaced, but they could do nothing with him and by the end of the second week he sat in a chair, he walked a little, and they watched him helplessly.

They came in grinning one night.

"He did a beauty today!" Dr. Castle jerked a thumb at Lucas.

"He helped me," Lucas reminded.

Dr. Runkleman looked at them eagerly.

"Mrs. Ferdinand," said Lucas.

"The neurotic!" said Dr. Runkleman.

"That's right!"

"You talked her into it!"

Lucas nodded.

"She's had two nervous breakdowns already," Dr. Runkleman reminded Dr. Castle defensively. "Precipitate menopause . . ."

"I know—"

"Well, what did you do?" He leaned forward eagerly. "Who did you get?"

"It was a woman by the name of Kellogg—"

"Kellogg—"

"A new patient."

"Sarah Kellogg?"

"That's the one. How did you—"

"Had her when she was first married. Menstrual."

"Well, she had a fibroma."

"So that's where you got it!"

"Dr. Castle helped me—and we had Kris—I took out the ovaries—"

"Beautiful job!" Dr. Castle shook his head.

"Hegar's. And we put them in Ringer's solution, body temperature—" He shrugged, and paused.

"And then we took on Mrs. Ferdinand—and he did an ovarian graft."

"We both did!"

"You know who did it, Dave!"

Dr. Runkleman beamed.

"I've learned a lot from you," Lucas said simply.

"I don't doubt that," said Dr. Castle.

"He doesn't need to learn from anybody," said Dr. Runkleman.

"I saw him work," Dr. Castle said.

"I've seen it before," Lucas said, embarrassed. "It's amazing. Even if it doesn't take, it seems to stimulate something, seems to excite latent cell 'rests' in the broad ligament, maybe . . ."

"I'll be darned!" Dr. Runkleman said. His face was a broad, proud grin. And he looked admiringly at Dr. Castle who had possessed the confidence in Lucas to assist him.

"She'll be fine," Dr. Castle said.

"What a job!" Dr. Runkleman whistled softly.

"Two hours and forty minutes." Lucas nodded.

"And what do you think was the first thing she asked us?" Dr. Castle demanded.

"Well, knowing Lottie Ferdinand—" Dr. Runkleman waited.

Dr. Castle chuckled.

"She wanted to know if the donor was a Methodist or an Episcopal!"

"Oh, no!"

"That's right!"

"And she meant it! She was really concerned. I thought a moment, I couldn't remember what *she* was, I told her the woman was an atheist! You should have seen her face!"

"Poor Lottie . . ."

"Oh, we fixed her up. We found out she was a Methodist—I can't remember half the time what they are—and I told her the woman was a Methodist, and now she's happy—"

"I'd have told her it was a cow," said Dr. Runkleman.

"The things they go through." Dr. Castle shook his head.

"The laws they make to keep them unhappy," marvelled Dr. Runkleman. "The way they make rules, the way they stick to them long after they're meaningless, hedge themselves in, invent new ones . . . and all the time there they are . . . naked in the world, staggering along under the terrible things that happen to them just because they're humans—"

"Their own jailers," said Lucas. "In the jail of their own body—"

"And not knowing it!" cried Dr. Castle. "Going along just as if the rules they're all the time cutting themselves on are the important things—and when you think of all that can happen—of the body's imperfections—that everybody's born sick . . . and everybody's born, dying . . ."

"Just to survive," Dr. Runkleman said hoarsely.

Lucas' eyes, Dr. Castle's eyes, widened alertly. Their faces became expressionless. Dr. Castle rose. Lucas copied him instantly.

"That's enough for today, Dave."

"I'm fine. Honestly!"

"I know . . . come on . . ."

And between them he moved reluctantly back to bed.

He seemed to mend.

"I've run out of things to read about Australia," Kristina said one day. "What should I do?"

Lucas thought a moment.

"Take him a gun book," he decided. "Get something on guns. From the library."

"That's right!" Kristina sighed. "The poor, poor darling . . . Lucas! Does he ever ask—does he want to see the paper—the stock market—does he say anything—?"

"Not a word. He's never mentioned it. Not once."

"You'd think that those who owe him—now that they know—now that they've got a chance to do something—I bet there's thousands and thousands on those books!"

Lucas shook his head.

"Not one? One, even? I bet I could collect it! I bet I—do you want me to try, Luke? Shall I?"

He shook his head.

"You know better than that . . . No . . . He mentioned money once . . . He and Castle got to talking . . . They figured out the best pay was a teacher. A teacher who couldn't ever pay more than a hundred dollars for an operation without going in the hole and having to do without something . . ."

During the third week he seemed to mend rapidly.

"I feel fine," he assured Dr. Castle one afternoon.

"I think you're walking too much."

"I know when to stop—I know how to control it—I've been out in the corridor—"

"I know. You've been all over the hospital."

Dr. Runkleman looked down guiltily.

"No stairs!" he said defensively. He looked at Dr. Castle earnestly. "Can you sit a while?"

"I just had a minute. I thought I'd drop in. Luke been by yet?"

Dr. Runkleman looked at his watch.

"He's doing office visits. Up to his neck. Sit down, Henry. I want to talk to you."

Dr. Castle sat down. Dr. Runkleman sat back. He pursed his lips. He thought a moment.

"What's on your mind, Dave?"

Dr. Runkleman stared at him.

"Henry—I haven't got long . . ."

Dr. Castle flushed. But his eyes did not move from Dr. Runkleman's.

"We're not kidding anybody. You know. And I know."

"What's on your mind, Dave?"

"Henry—I want to go to Australia."

Dr. Castle smiled. He looked diffidently aside.

"I know—I know what you're going to say—"

"You *ought* to know, Dave—"

"I know. I know all about it. I'm the one that's got it."

"If you take it easy—and rest—"

"That, too!"

"Dave, I know what you mean. And if I—"

"But you can't. There isn't anything you can do, there isn't anything anybody can do. And I could go any minute. You don't know when and Luke doesn't know when and Kauffman doesn't know when. Nobody knows when. I don't know when. All we know is—I haven't got long . . ."

He gazed at Dr. Castle's down-bent head, waiting.

"What's on your mind, Dave?" Dr. Castle studied the floor.

"I want to give the boy the practice."

"You could sell it—there's a lot wrapped up there—"

"I want to give it to him. I've got enough. It isn't much. It's all I'll live to spend, though."

"You don't know—"

"It's all I'll live to spend."

"You've got two boys in school to think about—"

"The boy'll take care of them. Out of the practice."

"Haven't you got some kin to think about? Somebody?"

"I've got some cousins, someplace. Somewhere, I guess . . . Nobody! Not a soul—and Henry—I don't know how you're fixed—"

"I'm all right—"

"Watch it! I know what's coming—"

"Me, too."

"We've been through it before—"

"Nineteen-seven—that was a beauty, wasn't it!"

"Nineteen-seven! How about eighteen-ninety-three? How about nineteen-one? How about nineteen-twenty? Nineteen-twenty-four?"

They looked at each other across the years, the scarred years, remembering incredible chaos, remembering calamity, remembering those great dates when humans starved and sickened and went mad, when there was no help, no succor anywhere, no Ark, only the screams of the drowning under the insane, planet-drowning oceans of depressions.

They looked at each other, veterans of horror, who had known, who knew what they knew.

"It's coming again," said Dr. Runkleman.

"I know—"

"That first shake—that was only a shake—"

"I believe it—"

"In a month—in two months—"

Dr. Castle nodded.

"Well, you know. We both know. We've been through it. We know what a depression's like. And we know what a practice is worth—during a depression . . . I'm not giving him, anything, Henry . . . I'm—I'm sorry for him . . ."

Dr. Castle brooded. He looked up.

"All right, Dave? What's on your mind?"

"Australia."

"Be serious—"

"I'm serious."

"You know better."

"I want to go. I want to start. See, I'll be on my way. Going to it. You don't know—I don't know—I may even make it!"

"Never!"

"I may!"

"You know you can't!"

"I may! And if I don't—even while I'm going—I'll know, I'll be on my way, going . . ."

"But Dave—but how?—don't you see—"

"That's what I've dreamed about—nights when I was wet in the snow—it's warm there . . . it's always warm—it's been my dream, Henry . . . I've dreamed it . . ." And his pleading eyes were soft, and he standing on the boat, alone in the prow, and the blue ocean, and the wide sky, and there ahead, flat, golden, magic, the land of Australia.

And the dream. The dreaming land.

Dr. Castle looked away.

He thought, he pondered, he chewed his lip.

"I've got it all figured out," Dr. Runkleman said softly.

"You may not even get out of town . . ."

"I'll be on my way. Just give me another week, and—"

"Suppose the boy finds out—"

"He'll never know. Till it's too late."

"You're getting excited now!"

"I'm not!" He leaned back obediently. "Henry! Look! Here's what we'll do—I'd do it for you, Henry." They looked at each other levelly. "If that's what you wanted, I'd do it!"

"Go on," said Dr. Castle. His voice was very low. Dr. Runkleman leaned forward again.

"Look!" he said. He talked slowly, carefully, surely. Dr. Castle began to make notes. Once or twice he asked a question. In a few minutes it was over. In half an hour it was all done. Dr. Castle sighed. He rose. He looked down at Dr. Runkleman. His mouth smiled uncertainly.

"It's my funeral," said Dr. Runkleman.

"All right, Dave . . . It's your funeral . . ."

And one day, late in the fourth week, he asked Lucas to take a call for him, a call far in the country.

In the late afternoon of the day he stood with Dr. Runkleman beside the train in the Greenville station. He kept his arm about him. The porter put two bags aboard, a heavy suitcase and a faded, scuffed physician's handbag.

"I guess we got everything," Dr. Castle said awkwardly. The porter moved to help them. Dr. Runkleman turned. They faced each other. From down the track came the trainman's warning cry.

"Easy on the steps!" Dr. Castle admonished.

Dr. Runkleman put out his hand. It was a thinner hand now, the clothes, the coat, bagged on him grotesquely.

"I thank you," Dr. Runkleman said simply.

"You send me a postcard," Dr. Castle said angrily. "Now, don't you forget! You hear?"

"Goodbye, Henry."

". . . Dave . . ."

Their hands gripped.

"Goodbye, Dave . . ."

They helped him up the steps. He turned once, to wave.

Dr. Castle nodded. He swallowed. He waved back.

The train gained speed.
It was gone.

Each day there was a wire, a jubilant, reassuring wire, each day past the first astonishment, the first indignation, amazement, stunned acceptance, each day a wire. And then one day passed. And there was no wire. And Lucas and Dr. Castle looked at each other, it was a week, now, they called the telegraph office, no, there was no wire . . .

The wire came next morning.

Dr. Runkleman had died at sea. He died quietly, in his bed, hearing to the last the confident, throbbing engines bearing him nearer and nearer to Australia . . .

That far place.

He died at sea. They buried him there.

And he was gone.

⁎ CHAPTER 36

In a month the people of Greenville no longer spoke of Dr. Runkleman. The past received him and he was buried there, not as a body, not even as a whole memory, but as substance dispersed out of contact, vanished, the scene of the vanishing passed by, forgotten.

With each day the rising sun distinguished implacably that which was real from the night's phantoms, the light divided that which was old from that which had yet to be endured. And in this procession of days he was buried, and in that obligation of rising he was forgotten.

His pattern vanished and men walked through the paths he had made in living. And what they owed him was no more, and what he had done for them had no monument, and what they needed of him they took to someone else, and the days passed and it was a month and their lives were a month shorter.

Lucas watched this bitterly. He watched a sense of loss, the impact of shock, the wariness and amazement over a fellow marcher struck and fallen, he watched this fade in them, watched with incredulity and finally with hate as they went their ways in a final indifference, grateful to be alive now that he who had helped them live was dead.

For what he did, for what he would do, for what he had done, he wanted no gratitude. That they would one day treat him thus in his turn evoked in him conviction and simultaneous indifference. He could not forgive them for forgetting Dr. Runkleman, and he summed them for forgetting him and he regarded that sum with nausea and then with anger and then with cold and indelible contempt.

The practice had begun to dwindle. The depression whose first days had wiped out Dr. Runkleman now came on quickly. A few stores were already vacant. The pottery plant had laid off a tenth of its workers. Men of substance had become penniless overnight, calamity was becoming the order of the days and consternation was a dawning habit.

"Folks are getting scared," Bemis Shedd conceded.

"Are they?" Lucas shrugged.

"You feel like I do, don't you! This is just a phase. Sure! They're always getting scared, ain't they!"

Lucas smiled politely.

"I been up and down this street for three hours and there ain't a human being but what's shivering in his boots! Afraid to advertise! Afraid to spend the money! Why this country—" Bemis Shedd gestured valiantly to the vague cosmos which had always provided him with a newspaper and the means to operate it—"this country's been through a *thousand* such things and never fazed it! Look at it today, I tell 'em! What's changed? Ain't nothing changed! Little trouble a thousand miles away, few fast boys mixing in what don't belong to them—why those bankers, you take Morgan, you take those big boys, those bankers ain't going to let anything happen! Why, how could they?"

Lucas watched him silently, noted his flushed face without curiosity, appeared to listen.

"That's what I tell 'em! That's what I say! Why they ought to be ashamed of themselves!"

"And what do they say?" asked Lucas politely.

"You ought to hear them," said Bemis Shedd. "They're scared to death. Keeps on I may have to lay off a pressman, maybe a printer." He looked at Lucas, incredulous.

"Too bad," said Lucas. "But you're all right, aren't you?"

"Me? Sure I'm all right! You don't catch me killing myself over them like Dr. Runkleman did, like we both know, although I was always scared of that stock market myself, the poor soul! I bet they didn't break any legs running in to pay a few dollars back bills, have they?"

"I closed the books," Lucas said levelly. "The way he told me to. So far as he's concerned, they're free and clear."

Bemis Shedd shook his head.

"He was a fine man," he said piously. "Never got to know him the way I should. He served this town mighty well. Everything all right?"

"Fine."

"Good! You and me'll have to go hunting one of these days—you ever go hunting? Go every year. Me and the crew. Take the whole crew and off we go, I cook the best pancakes you ever ate."

"I'll have to do that, sometime. Pretty busy, now—"

"Season ain't open yet. I'll let you know. You come along, Doc. You'll have fun. No . . . I ain't worrying. I got me a house and I got me a garden, there's plenty of deer around, plenty of game, worst comes to the worst, glad to hear you're getting along all right, saw Harriet Lang the other day, she was asking for you, understand they laid off quite a slew up at the pottery—"

"So I understand."

"Well, you got a good woman there in that Miss Snow. She'll take care of you. I was going to call her, today. You been up to the supervisors yet? Anybody contact you?"

"Supervisors? You mean the board? No. What for?"

"Saw Henry Granite a while ago. Understand they're trying to get in touch with you. Doc's job, probably. Up at the County. Well, I gotta be going. Don't forget, now! About our hunting trip! Take it every year! Man only lives once. Does a man good!"

A week later the board of supervisors sent for him, four strangers, they waved him easily to a chair, surveyed him curiously.

"It's about that job," one said finally. "Head surgeon. Up at the County."

Lucas waited.

"The point is—do you want it?" another asked abruptly.

"Do I want it? I've been doing it—"

"That's right. Right at the start we want to say: we're perfectly satisfied. Doc picked you and that's good enough for us, let alone Snider says you're all right. The point is—do you want it?"

"Why—why I guess so. I hadn't thought about it. I took it that—"

"Well, that's all we wanted to know. We have to draw it up legal style, all formal, the way it's done. There's one thing, Doc." He cleared his throat. "I guess you know how times are. Getting, anyway. Now, when he started we paid Doc Runkleman thirty-five hundred a year, a lot in them days, don't say it ain't worth more today, but the way things are going—"

"You just speak out free and clear. We got a job to do and—"

"'Course in the future we'd see our way clear to raise you—"

"We all got to work together—"

"You want me to take Dr. Runkleman's job as head surgeon for thirty--five hundred dollars a year? Is that what you want?"

"Like I said, we're open to suggestion—"

"You know yourself how things are, Doc—"

"I'll take it," Lucas said briefly.

"Glad to hear it!"

"And anything you need—within reason, of course—"

"Hate to do this to you, Doc. We just got a job to do. Soon as ever we can we'll jack it back where it was. It ain't only us. But you understand that. No use going off half cocked like the township, voting in a water system one minute, starting work like the devil was after 'em if they didn't get through by sunset—and then calling the whole thing off with less'n fifty feet of pipe laid—"

"They've stopped?"

"Hain't you heard? Sure—the whole thing's been called off. Town had its money in bonds—been gettin' sassy investing here and there—woke up one day and found its bonds had more water in 'em than the water system! Sure! Whole thing's called off!"

"Damned foolishness in the first place!"

Lucas swallowed, trying to digest this, wordless.

They rose awkwardly, one by one they shook hands with him.

"It's all formal now, Doc. You're the head surgeon."

"Soon as we can, like I say—"

"Somebody better call Bemis and tell him—"

"Well—we'll be dropping in on you, one of these days . . ."

Lucas drove slowly back to the office.

He had made few changes. The medical supply salesman passed on his rounds and Lucas had bought a few instruments of a type he had used during his internship to replace a few older instruments Dr. Runkleman had probably used during his internship. He had changed the function of the rooms on either side of the long office corridor so that now one side was entirely for women and children.

Kristina had gone timidly through the huge old home Dr. Runkleman had used in the rear of the office. She had inspected its rooms tentatively, a little dismayed and a little excited by their number and their size and by their almost unused condition.

They might have moved there. Lucas had begun to consider using their present rooms as a laboratory, stocking it with equipment when they moved to the big house, hiring a technician.

But the bank one day sent men who explored the big house, made inventory and deprecatively locked the doors and departed. It stayed locked, thereafter, owned by the bank now, waiting a buyer, one of the securities Dr. Runkleman had thrown in to avert the calamity that had wiped him out.

"Make a nice place for you," Mr. Henderson, the banker, said hopefully one day. He peered at Lucas over his rimless glasses. "You could have it cheap. How does twelve thousand strike you?"

"It doesn't strike me," Lucas said bluntly. "I haven't got twelve thousand dollars." He frowned. You know how much I've got, he thought resentfully. You know every cent I've got. It's all there, in your bank. What are you pretending you don't know, for?

"Doesn't have to be cash, you know. I'm not saying credit's not tight. But you're a doctor. One thing about doctors: they're good for it. We know that."

"If we could pay it off like rent—" Kristina said hopefully.

"Why not?" said Mr. Henderson. "I don't see why not?"

"No," said Lucas.

"No investment on your part—"

"No."

"Hate to sell it to somebody else. Have somebody living there you mightn't like—"

"No," said Lucas.

Kristina looked down. The banker spread his hands helplessly.

"Thanks," said Lucas. "Thanks all the same."

"Don't you want it?" said Kristina when they were on the street.

"Sure I want it. You know damned well I want it."

"He said we could have it like rent—"

"I don't want to buy it from the bank. I want to buy it from Dr. Runkleman. Every payment—not to Dr. Runkleman but to the bank. Every month—reminding us. And I want it like he had it. Cash. No debts. Straight cash. That was his way. And it's his house."

She nodded.

He looked at her uncertainly.

"Do you see what I mean?"

"Sure," she said. He looked at her, surprised. She looked back at him steadily. "Sure, I see. It'll be there," she said. She patted his arm. "No matter who buys it."

But no one bought it. No one rented it. There were many homes for rent now. Many homes for sale. The big house stayed quietly empty, its doors locked, it sat as it had always sat, in the rear of the office, sat indifferent to time and men, and waited. You could not tell a house Dr. Runkleman was dead. Once a week, although Lucas did not know it, Kristina swept its porch.

"I'll do that," Miss Snow said one day.

"You got plenty to do," Kristina said.

"Not so much as you think."

"No?" Kristina stopped sweeping.

Miss Snow shook her head.

"Times are very bad. You wouldn't believe it."

Kristina nodded.

"Why, there's folks going to the County now, for free, who wouldn't have set foot on the grounds three months ago!"

"Lucas says the County's pretty full." Kristina waited.

"Why, one family I know—I went to school with the girl—why, he had a big job, he worked at the pottery, he was a foreman—now he can't get a job as a janitor. I took them some food last week. They're *hungry*. Can you imagine? He can't get a job—they're eating the furniture—they're actually *hungry*!"

"What's going to happen?"

"I don't know. I've never seen anything like this before. There was something like it five years ago, only it only lasted a few months—"

"I remember—"

"And then four years before that—"

"That, too—"

"I was only eight when the bad depression—the 1907 one—"

"I wasn't born," said Kristina.

They looked at each other, their eyes wary, frightened, waiting to be instructed, to be prepared, to know, to fend, the immemorial look of women seeing in the distance the men returning empty-handed, seeing and frightened and automatically estimating the larder, the stretching, the times ahead, quickened to fight for life, the cave's life, women and mother and children and men.

"A few fell away when Dr. Runkleman passed on," Miss Snow said delicately.

"Bound to." Kristina nodded. "I told Lucas—"

"A few he was just waiting to send elsewhere."

"Sometimes he's impatient—"

"I don't blame him. I'd have got rid of them years ago. Just keep coming—there's nothing to do for them, really—you know—"

"I know—"

"Take up time—there's nothing wrong with them—all they need is money, or a new husband, or a new wife, or a better job—and they come in with a bellyache, a pain here, this and that—and you tell them—"

"Lucas never could see why Dr. Runkleman let them come—so many really sick ones—"

"Well . . ." Miss Snow shrugged. "Dr. Runkleman . . ."

She sighed.

"Anyway—he's cleaned them out. It was quite a day. Some of them were pretty mad. Funny . . . the ones with the longest-outstanding bills . . . they were the maddest . . ." She sighed again. "But now—even with the ones we've got left—the bills come in very slow . . . And not many new ones . . . Hardly any, at all . . ."

They were silent a moment.

"Thanks for telling me," Kristina said.

"Oh, it's not bad yet. Nothing to worry about, really. It'll be all right, Mrs. Marsh . . . They say it's going to get worse . . . And then again," she shrugged, "some say it's going to get better! What's the matter with them, anyhow?" she burst out suddenly. "Honestly! If I could just get my hands on some of the men who are doing this! People suffering and—decent, thrifty, able-bodied men thrown out of work and can't get a job and their children hungry—children, mind you—"

The two women looked at each other. Kristina shook her head. Miss Snow sighed.

"Well," said Kristina, "it never looked like much before, but we always got the County to fall back on . . ."

"Yes. If they don't close the County—"

"My God! Would they do that? Honest?"

"No, no. They'd never do that. I just meant—"

"I know . . . Maybe Lucas shouldn't turn so many away—"

"I don't know . . . I've tried to tell him—"

"I'll talk to him!"

"Don't say I said so."

"Never! Never, Miss Snow!"

"And—I'd sort of bring it up easy—you know Dr. Marsh . . ."

"I know. Well, I know! He's too honest—"

"I don't have to tell you, Mrs. Marsh—he's a—a fine doctor! I've never seen a better—no, it's true—not even Dr. Runkleman!"

"He's a good man," said Kristina stoutly. "It's just—well, him and money . . . I'll—I'll tell him." She nodded. "I'll be careful . . ."

At the County Hospital Marie Paget—Marie Glaimer now—was waiting with her husband.

As Lucas looked at them, surprised, Dr. Snider walked in. He sat casually on a corner of the desk.

"What's the trouble?" Lucas asked.

"The same trouble," Mrs. Glaimer said sullenly.

"Having a great deal of pain, Mr. Glaimer?"

"Getting worse," the man said glumly.

"I've got to have a job," Mrs. Glaimer said.

"You mean you want your job back—here?"

"I always gave satisfaction, didn't I?"

"Made enough trouble, if that's what you mean," observed Dr. Snider.

"I did what the rest did. You never fired me—"

"Things are a little different now," said Dr. Snider. "Jobs ain't growing on bushes any more. We ain't standing around with our hats in our hands hoping none of you'll quit—"

"I wouldn't need to stand here asking you. If what ought to be done had been done—I might be—we might be—"

Dr. Snider glanced inquiringly at Lucas. Lucas felt the bright, malicious glance, instantly restrained a sharp retort.

"What's the matter with the shop?" he asked carefully.

"The shop!" She spat the word.

"Might as well close," Glaimer said glumly. "Can't collect for what you do, and the business there is you can just forget."

"Things sure is bad," Dr. Snider shook his head. He rolled his tobacco from one side of his mouth to the other. "Sure bad," he said dispassionately. "Lots of folks around here going to get what's coming to 'em. Folks that never had more'n one shirt to their backs or their fathers before 'em, buying radios, new cars, every damned thing they lay their eyes on—they got it coming to 'em! Bound to happen! Now they got it coming!"

"I don't know about radios nor new cars," said Glaimer sullenly. "All I know is I worked for Murchison before me since I was that high, got up at five and worked past sundown, worked for my board and keep to start with, didn't see a dollar's pay until I was past fourteen, never got but four dollars a week till one day I was about to quit having heard of what kids in the city was getting—"

"He bought the shop out of what he earned!" Mrs. Glaimer said hotly. "He saved every dollar of it. Four dollars a week, ten dollars a week, saved nearly four hundred dollars—"

"Then the old man died. I remember like it was yesterday. He didn't have none saved, just a couple hundred dollars for buryin'. Just that and the shop. I kep' old Mrs. Murchison nearly five years, paying her every week out of what the shop brought in. Until she died. And then I had to keep paying five years more. Some cousin. Never even seen the place. Bound to some man I never even seen, never even seen me, hadn't no more claim to the money, and the sweat I earned it with, the worrying I did, the working night after night to keep a-going—just dropped in his lap."

"Money don't care who it's owed to," said Dr. Snider.

"I paid it. I paid every last cent of it. And then it was mine. And just about the time I was getting the good out of it—"

"You came up here once for the piles," said Dr. Snider. "We told you what had to be done. Why didn't you let us do it? Two weeks you'd have been good as new! No—you had to let it go—let it drag on . . . We told you . . . I remember Dr. Runkleman standing right here! Telling you!"

"Two weeks! And how was I going to—what was I going to do? Shut the shop? Stop the payments? He didn't care! All he wanted was his money! He only wanted an excuse. He'd a sold the shop the minute I closed it! Two weeks! Why, two weeks—and all I put into that place—my whole life, you might say—!"

"Well, just don't go blaming people that tried to help you! Hell! You didn't expect Dr. Runkleman or me to go down and run your shop for you while you was laid up, did you?"

"I ain't blaming nobody." He looked at the floor.

"Nobody told you to quit, either," Dr. Snider turned to Mrs. Glaimer. "Flouncing out of here like a ball of fire, telling everybody in the place where they got off, marrying a man you knew didn't have a chance, all bold and sassy figuring you had a meal ticket—"

"What you're after is your job back, isn't it?" Lucas said quickly.

Mrs. Glaimer, whose face had paled paper-white, whose eyes glittered with frustrated rage about to overspill, swallowed with a great effort, looked at the floor, found her voice.

"That's all," she said hoarsely.

"What about it, Dr. Snider?" Lucas turned to the older man.

"That—and treatment for Oscar here," Mrs. Glaimer added, her eyes steadfastly lowered.

"Well, I don't know," said Dr. Snider. "What do you think? Seems like we got a couple of Socialists or Bolshies here, don't it? Seem to think the world owes them a living or something? Like to go blaming everybody for what they done themselves? Blaming Dr. Runkleman for—"

"Well, it's bad luck. I guess we can't tell people how to take it—we could use another nurse, didn't I hear you say?"

"We can use somebody that's going to work, if that's the way you want it. Personally—"

"That's fine, then. That takes care of you, Mrs. Glaimer. I think you owe Dr. Snider an apology for the things you said when you left—"

"Oh, don't bother about me. I've seen 'em come, I've seen 'em go. I'll be here long after the last of 'em—"

"I—I'm sorry I said what—I did. I—I apologize . . ."

"You get back to work and you stay with it! Minute I see you slacking off, grumbling, making trouble—"

"You understand that, Mrs. Glaimer?"

She nodded. She did not raise her eyes.

"I understand." Her voice was muffled.

"You report tomorrow morning, then." He turned inquiringly to Dr. Snider. "That all right?"

"Up to you," shrugged Dr. Snider.

"And now as to Mr. Glaimer—"

She lifted her face. They were both staring at him.

"Can you do something? Anything?"

"Let's have a look," said Lucas.

Dr. Snider slid off the edge of the desk.

"Well," he said, "guess you won't need me any more."

"Thank you, Doctor," Lucas nodded. "Thank you very much."

"Thank you," murmured Mrs. Glaimer. She looked at him and then quickly looked away. Dr. Snider went out as if he hadn't heard.

The cancer was plain now, very plain, plain to the finger tips. The mass had grown greatly. And there was no hope. There was absolutely none. In all the knowledge of Medicine there was only blankness for this, there was nothing to say, nothing to do, there was only to wait.

They watched him as he sat down at the desk. They watched every movement, they watched his face, they watched his eyes, they watched his mouth.

"It's gone pretty far," he said at last.

"You can do it!" Mrs. Glaimer cried. "We know you, Doctor Marsh! You can do it!"

Lucas said nothing. There were many things he could say, he reflected. There were the words for the dead. There was a phrase he had once heard an older man use, "You have lived so long together . . . you have shared so much . . . now you must share this . . . why don't you share this, too?" But they had not lived long together. What they had suffered they had suffered apart. There were many things, there was a careful explanation, the mass is too large, you've been around a hospital long enough to know some things are inoperable, I hate to tell you . . . but this is one of them . . . There were so many things. Things to be said.

He looked up at last.

"I'm sorry—"

"You can do *something*!"

It was the woman crying out, tense, pleading. The man was at bay, alert, almost calm.

"You mustn't ask the impossible, Mrs. Glaimer. The mass is just too large . . ."

"Operate! Will you do that? We want you to—don't we, Oscar?—just operate! That's all we ask! We know you! Just operate!"

"There's no use."

"But you can do it! If we ask you? If we take all the blame? You can put it in writing—you can say you warned us—"

"The first thing to do," Lucas rose, "is to put this man to bed—"

"But will you? Will you do it?"

"We'll see," Lucas conceded reluctantly.

"Oh, you will! You will!" She grabbed his hand. She kissed it. "Oscar!" She turned to her husband wildly. "Oscar! He will! He will!"

"I don't mind, Doc," Glaimer said gruffly.

"It'll be all right now, Oscar!"

"Might as well go one way as another—"

"Excuse me if I ever said anything, Doctor—I didn't mean it—forgive me—!"

"Never mind, now," said Lucas. "You just behave yourself—I'm not promising you anything. I want you to know this: I want you to know it, now. There's no real hope. There's no such thing as miracles. If I do it—it'll be against my better judgment—I have no right to—you may have months left you—"

"We understand," Mrs. Glaimer said humbly.

"It would have been the same if Dr. Runkleman had operated," Lucas warned.

"Yes, sir," she said obediently.

"You're the doctor," said Glaimer.

"No," said Lucas. "I'm not the doctor, here. But I'll do what I can."

And when they left, he waited a moment, waited for them to get clear of the corridor, then walked quickly into the operating room.

"Get rid of them?" Dr. Snider asked incuriously.

Lucas nodded.

"They want me to operate," he confided reluctantly.

"Damned fool if you do," Dr. Snider said promptly. "If Runkleman wouldn't do it, you can bet your bottom dollar he'd have died on the table. Old Dave had a nose for 'em. He never failed. He could spot one coming a mile away."

Lucas winced. It was true, though. And Snider was proud of him for it.

"Thanks for taking her on again."

"Nothing to me—one way or the other. I thought it was something you wanted."

"I guess I felt sorry for them."

Dr. Snider grunted.

"That's up to you . . . You got a tonsillectomy this morning. Want me to help?"

"If you don't mind . . ."

Because there was no help for it. Because from now on whenever another doctor would be needed it would have to be Snider. No matter what it was like—it would have to be Snider. There was no one else.

The patient was wheeled in. The anesthesia began. There was no difference, it was like the first time, Dr. Snider slapped the mask over the boy's face, he began to dribble ether on the gauze.

"A little slower, Doctor," Lucas burst out at last.

"You want to do it?"

"No, no. It's fine. I just like it a little slower."

Dr. Snider shrugged. Obligingly, he dripped the ether more slowly.

The stupid, ignorant fool! The imbecile! The grinning yokel fool! How could he know so little? How could any human forget so much? Not keep up? Not try, at least! This—*this* was a doctor!

"Thank you, Doctor," he said quietly.

Did he hear me? Did he hear me say "Doctor"? If I keep on will it mean something, will his vanity—maybe—a little . . . ?

"Always glad to hear another man's ideas," Dr. Snider said imperturbably.

Midway, the suction apparatus failed. One of the nurses fumbled with it helplessly.

"Get away from it!" Dr. Snider cried at last. "Get me something else!"

"What should I—"

"Goddamn it, don't just stand there! Get me anything!" He turned to Lucas. "Don't bother trying to fix it. Washer's rotten, or something. Always something wrong with the goddamned thing!"

"Can we get a new one?" Lucas looked up hopefully.

"A new one? You mean, ask the board?"

"But we need one—if we told them—"

"Need one! Good God! What's that got to do with it! Costs money, don't it? Got a laboratory in there, too, ain't we? Built it right when they built the building. Got a complete laboratory. Everything but a microscope. Somebody told 'em doctors always had microscopes. Got everything but a microscope and a centrifuge and an incubator—got a box of slides and eight stains and a laboratory. I told 'em long ago—there! You got her! What the hell'd you do? She's coming now. . . ."

At the office that afternoon the third patient was Cosgrove.

"I want something to sleep with," he said abruptly.

"What seems to be the trouble?"

"If you look you'll find it. I don't want any trouble. All I want is some sleeping pills."

Lucas began to look through the patient file.

"What are you looking for?"

"I'm trying to look you up. See if you can take sleeping pills—"

"Don't bother. You won't find me in there. I don't—as the locals say—'doctor.' When I need something I go to a drugstore. I can't get sleeping pills. Not without a prescription."

"What's all the hostility about?" Lucas asked mildly. Within himself he was indifferent. He moved toward Cosgrove. "Just take off your coat a minute."

"Just my usual good nature, my state of being with the world as the world goes—"

"You're intelligent enough to know you might have some condition sleeping medicine might aggravate—there might be something that would contra-indicate one kind of medicine and indicate another—"

"Go ahead and listen," Cosgrove said resignedly.

Lucas moved the stethoscope deftly and quickly about Cosgrove's chest. He stood back.

"All right," he said. "What kind of medicine did Dr. Runkleman prescribe for you?"

"You never could read the gibberish he scrawled. He didn't want you to know. All part of the sacred mumbo-jumbo, eh?"

"Maybe," Lucas said. "It isn't always good for patients to know what they're getting."

"It's their bodies, isn't it?"

"That's true. But it's our care."

"You think it's right to keep a grip on their minds? To enlarge on the poor fools' hunger for magic?"

Lucas sighed.

"Cosgrove, a few months ago I would have gotten angry. I would have argued. I would have tried to answer you. I know you've got a chip on your shoulder. I know that every time you see me I'm like a red rag—I'd appreciate knowing what's on your mind. Is it just me? Or is it all doctors?"

"Forget it."

"I'd like to know."

"You and Harriet Lang—she was asking for you, the other day—she asked me the same thing."

Lucas started.

"You people with brains. Walking around in a fool's paradise. The kind of people the world needs. Just as dumb, just as blind as the dumbest. Sure I pick at you! You've got brains. You've got a weak spot. Your God is Medicine. Maybe if I pick at it long enough, get you mad, get you thinking—don't you ever think? Don't you ever think at all?"

"About what?"

Miss Snow put her head in the door.

"In a moment, Miss Snow." She shrugged. The door closed.

"You're a doctor. Let's begin there. I'm not going to take long. Because I don't have to. You're a doctor and if there's misery going, you see it. None better. Where do you think it comes from?"

"I know where it comes from!"

"You know! All right, let's hear it!"

"It comes from an imperfect body in an imperfect environment. If you could only see each other stripped naked this instant—if everybody could see everybody else, just as they are, naked—"

"And that's it, eh?"

"That, my friend, is it."

"You're a fool. There's an answer. And you won't see it. Look around you! There's a depression on! Whose depression? Is it yours? Is it mine? Is it the poor slob's in the street? You know who it belongs to! A handful have been exploiting the millions ever since this country was founded, ever since capital began in the world! Is there order anywhere? Is there rhyme or reason for what you see?"

"What do you propose? What's your answer?"

"My answer? My answer is the only answer there is. That's my answer. Where you cure dozens, my answer can cure millions."

"You think your answer will solve the problems of human beings?"

"There isn't a human problem my answer can't solve. It's the one answer—the only answer—for humans on this earth. If you'll see it—if you'll just see it—"

Lucas looked at Cosgrove and his heart filled with pity. There was no doubting this human's utter sincerity.

"There isn't an evil we know that doesn't spring from the tyranny of capital. It fetters even you. Yes, it fetters you. You can't think of pure Medicine—you can't think of Medicine for Medicine's sake. You have to think of money. What do you think of Binyon and Blake?"

"I really don't know them—"

"You know them, all right. Are you proud of them? Money does that. The tyranny of money. Capital. Capital serves the interest of capital. Only of capital. And the men who have the capital rule the country. And the depression is your answer. The water system!"

"I'll have to think about it," Lucas said tiredly.

"Think about it! My God, man! Haven't you read about it?"

"If you mean Marx and Engels—I've read about it."

"Then you've got to see—you've got to listen—you've got to let me show you—"

"I can help *you,*" Lucas said suddenly.

"You can help me?"

"I've got a patient—you might say: he's ripe! Would you like to meet him?"

"Is this some kind of a joke?"

"I'll give you his name—I don't think it's anybody you know. His name is Glaimer—"

"The fellow who runs the shoe shop?"

"You can't see him now. He's at the hospital. I'll tell you when. And you mustn't tire him—a half-hour a day, to begin with—"

"Why, he's as Methodist as they come! I know all about him! I knew you were up to something—I knew just by looking at you—"

"You're wrong," Lucas said quietly. "I'm telling you the truth. He's had a hard life. Maybe you've got the answer for him."

Cosgrove studied Lucas a moment longer. Then he rose jubilantly. He put out his hand. He took Lucas' hand and he shook it hard.

"Then I thank you! God damn it! I'll defend your next malpractice—free!"

"I'll let you know when you can see him—"

"Think it over! Think it over yourself!"

"I have thought it over. A long time ago. I've read about every sovereign remedy for the ills of mankind I've ever heard about—"

"Then you'll come our way, yet!"

"Wait! Here's your prescription."

But Cosgrove was gone.

"You think you'll need me tomorrow?" Kristina asked that night.

"I probably will—what's tomorrow got to do with it?"

"I thought maybe I clean the house."

"Can you get it done in time to help me?"

"I don't know," Kristina said vaguely.

He stared at her, incredulous.

"What do you mean, you don't know! You know I'm stuck with Snider! Which do you think comes first—the house or the practice of Medicine?"

She nodded thoughtfully.

"God damn it, Kris! You can get so addlepated—don't you think I have enough stupidity all day without coming home to—"

"All I was thinking was maybe someday we could get a maid."

"Well, get a maid, then! If that's what you wanted in the first place, why the hell—"

"I didn't know whether we could afford it. I didn't know whether the practice was making money enough—"

"You've been talking to Miss Snow!"

"Luke—I—I just happened to—"

"You've been talking to Miss Snow! Damn you, Kris, I won't have you meddling, prying, gossiping around the office! How dare you put your stupid nose in what's none of your business."

"Luke! You're wrong! Don't blame Miss Snow! We just happened to be talking—"

"You 'yoost' happened to be talking—and you 'yoost' happened to find out that I'm getting rid of the deadwood and the deadheads—and you 'yoost' thought you'd put your fine Swedish wits to work 'yoost' to see how much money you could keep rolling in. And that's been the extent of your interest in Medicine ever since I married you!"

"You're tired. We talk about it sometime else."

"It's true, isn't it!"

"I was only thinking of the family. A woman's got to think of the family. She's got a right."

"What family!"

"You and me," she said hastily. "That's all. But someday—"

"Kristina, I'm going to tell you this—and I'm going to tell you for the last time: There isn't going to be any family! Understand? Can you get that through that thick head of yours?"

She lowered her eyes on a sudden fear.

"All right, Luke . . ."

"And stay away from Miss Snow!"

"We were just talking, Luke. She just happened to mention how hard times were all of a sudden and—"

"And all of a sudden you just happened to find yourselves talking about the patients I was throwing out right and left!"

"It's true," she said humbly.

"Well, just mind your own business."

"You're awful smart, Luke. You see right through me. Only, don't get mad . . . I know you're right . . . I just don't understand . . ."

"All you understand is: Every time I cut out a patient I'm throwing away good money."

"Yes," she said humbly.

"I can't take care of them all, Kris! Can't you understand that? Don't you know even Dr. Runkleman had to call for an assistant? Did you ever stop to think a practice that big might have helped kill him?"

"I thought you might get an assistant."

"I don't want an assistant. I want this all to myself. You weren't thinking about me at all, were you! You were just thinking about money!"

She flushed.

"You don't think of such things, Luke. Somebody's got to think—it's a wife's place to—"

He felt the coldness grow in him. He watched her bleakly. He inspected her face with a defeated and fatigued curiosity. The blur of familiarity faded and he saw her features sharply, each feature distinct, known and yet alien, seen clearly now, as he had seen her on the day he averted his head and married her.

He shook his head slowly in helpless protest. The face remained. He stared at her, fascinated. This was a stranger. She had no part in his life whatsoever. She had only contact. She had no least inkling of Medicine, she had no knowledge of his inner life, of his dreams, of his thoughts. And she had never had. And she never would. He stared at her, hoping against hope.

"Just tell me," she said gently. "If you'd just try to tell me, sometimes —you know more than I do—just tell me—try . . ."

"Do you know what a constitutional inadequate is?" he said reluctantly.

She shook her head.

"You know that everybody is made of tissue, cells, fluid. Well . . ." He paused. He shook his head helplessly. "Just think of materials. For a dress. No material is perfect. But there's good material and there's bad material. And there's material in between. And some material is just shoddy. It looks like material. But it's shoddy. Human beings are cut from that material: good, middling, and shoddy. A constitutional inadequate is a human being who happens to be made of shoddy material.

And there are millions of them. Every doctor's office has them. They don't show any definite ailment. They wander in and they complain listlessly or accusingly that they're weak, always weak and tired, always got pains, full of pains, nothing definite, just pains here and there, some days here, some days there, never well, never happy, always ailing."

He looked at her, considering.

"Do you understand that?"

"Maybe it's their minds—"

"It isn't their minds. It's their bodies. They're biologically inferior. And no surgery and no treatment of any kind can do much for them. They can't stand up under the stresses and strains of normal life. They're inadequate. And the only thing you can prescribe is rebirth or a better set of forebears."

"And nothing can be done?"

"I won't take their money. There's hundreds of sick people to treat, people you can really do something for—"

"But they're sick too. If it can't be cured they need a doctor worse than any of them—"

"I'm not a witch doctor, Kristina."

"But if they get comfort—if they're willing to pay—"

"There are plenty of doctors who will take them," he said bitterly. "Plenty, it seems . . ."

"But Dr. Runkleman—"

"I don't think Dr. Runkleman ever had the time to fully diagnose—I think he just did the best he could in the time he had—treating a symptom here—treating a symptom there—popping pills like popping candy into kids' mouths to keep them quiet. I can't do that."

"If they get the good out of it—if what they pay lets you do charity work for the ones that need it—"

"There's no such thing as charity work," he said wearily. "There's only Medicine. Just one Medicine."

He turned away.

"You'll never understand, Kristina. I might as well be talking to a laundress, or a shopkeeper, or a Senegambian. It's not in you. You understand money. Medicine's not money."

"I know, Lucas! I know how you feel! That's how I want you to feel! But you got to have money—a little money—just enough to—"

"To what!"

"To be . . . to be happy . . ."

He looked at her with dislike and contempt.

"To buy things you need! To do the way you want!"

"I've got what I need. And I'm doing what I want. And if it's money you want—you've got all you need. Do you want more money? Haven't I paid you back?"

He spoke quietly. He discovered with sick wonder that he was not even angry.

"Ah, don't, Luke! Don't say things like that! I'm only trying to help and things are getting bad and you don't understand—"

"I've tried to explain it to you. I can't begin to make you understand what Medicine really means. I've tried to show you just one simple thing: why I'm getting rid of those that don't need doctors. There aren't enough doctors, as it is. If you were Cosgrove, you'd tell me that the Czars of Medicine keep a permanent shortage because an adequate supply might start a price war, the performance of unnecessary services, and a rat race for the dollar that would rush past ethics without a backward glance. Just hold out a ten-thousand-a-year bait, Cosgrove would say, and the majority will stay in line. And that's why we have our quotas. And that's why a man in a free country can't even get a chance to be a doctor even though we haven't got enough doctors—"

He paused suddenly. The sardonic look disappeared from his face. He frowned.

"Maybe he's right," he said uncertainly.

"You don't listen to me. All I mean is, do it gradual—"

"Maybe the powers that be know best. Maybe it's ruthless. But maybe it's the only way. They know their humans. They've got no illusions. If you want a man to behave like a doctor—if you want to keep him bound by anything so frail and noble and foreign to humans as a code of ethics—you'd better keep him well fed. Because the minute competition starts—the apes scramble and bite and howl on the floor of the forest. For the biggest pieces. Doctor-apes just like any other apes."

He was still. He was sick for a moment, thinking. Then he turned to her. When he spoke his words were lifeless.

"If you wanted money, Kristina, you were right to marry a doctor. But you should have married a carpetbagger like Binyon or Blake."

"Luke!"

"That's what you should have done," he sighed. "Hard luck, Kristina."

"You never said a thing like that in your whole life! You? Talking bad about doctors?"

"Maybe it's time I woke up," he said tiredly. He looked at her emptily, not even unfriendly. "I'll need you in the morning," he said. "We've got a kidney and two hernias." He walked toward the bedroom.

"All I said was—" she followed, pleading.

"Never mind, never mind, Kris . . . I understand . . . Let's go to bed . . ."

He fell asleep almost instantly.

She lay awake, staring toward the ceiling, bewildered, guilty, going over and over what she had said, what he had replied, how she had been stupid again. His helpless slumber, his exhaustion, made her wince suddenly with guilt, with anger at herself, with disgust for whatever she had done.

Tomorrow, she rowelled herself silently, tomorrow he don't have to move a little finger! Tomorrow I help him like he never seen a nurse before in his life! I make it up! And he looked at me—he looked at me like . . .

She fell asleep. She slept smiling, dreaming of the way he had looked at her in the operating room . . . the day when like a clap of thunder he loved her . . . and what she had was theirs . . . and safe. . . .

She did brilliantly next day. But when they were done, he only nodded absently and thank her and went off to change and make rounds.

I do better tomorrow, she told herself stoutly. With practice I get much better. Much!

When he reached the Valley Hospital two calls were waiting for him. He picked up the telephone.

"Didn't expect *you* yet!" Miss Snow exclaimed. "How'd you get there so soon? Thought you had two hernias and a–"

"I did."

"You're getting faster than Dr. Runkleman! Wait a minute . . . All right. You got two calls. The first one was a baby, she swallowed a spoon. They called a few minutes ago and said they'd found the spoon . . . The second just came in. It's a little boy out in the country–Orcutt farm –fell out of an apple tree. Sounds like he broke his arm. May be smashed up the way the woman talked."

"All right," he said. He looked at his watch. There was plenty of time. "That's all?"

"That's all–wait! A Miss Lang called–"

"Oh, yes."

"Nothing particular, she said. Just called to say hello."

"Thanks," he said gruffly. His heart thumped. His wrists tingled. He hung up. He debated only a moment. Then he called her.

He heard the phone ring.

Then he heard her voice.

"Busy?" he said, at last.

"Busy?" she echoed. "Who is this–?"

"I got your call–"

"Oh! It's you, is it? Finally?"

"How would you like to see a farm?"

"Now? Today?"

"I have to take a run out, I thought you might like to see a country doctor at work–"

"Right now? Right this minute?"

"I just thought I might catch you at an odd moment–I thought I'd buy some sandwiches–we could eat on the way–"

"Wait!" she begged. "Wait a minute!"

He heard her voice, muffled, talking to someone in her office. He breathed heavily, waiting.

"It's all right!" she came back. "Drive by the front gate! You know where the pottery is? Drive by the front gate. I'll be waiting!"

He did not remember what kind of sandwiches he ordered. He barely remembered ordering them. He remembered standing and waiting and the wait was interminable.

She was walking to the front gate of the pottery plant as he drove up. She got in. The car swept them away.

They drove in silence.

"Whatever happened to you?" she said finally.

"I've had my troubles," he protested.

"I know, I know!" She put her hand gently on his forearm. "But I thought you'd call–" She disengaged his fingers from the wheel– "Let me hold your hand–or just say something–'hello'–anything . . ." She took his hand to her lap, held it there. "I waited and waited—where are we going?"

"Someplace to eat our sandwiches." His eyes searched the countryside.

"Are you hungry?"

"Not very."

"Well, find a place, then."

"Over this next hill," he said, and then they were over the hill, he saw the vague road, they were bumping the ruts, the highway behind them disappeared, they were hidden in the firs.

"Where in the world—!"

The car jounced to a stop.

"Old logging trail," he reached for her.

She was in his arms, the feel of her lithe body, the familiar odor of her skin, the smell of her hair, swept over him. After a time she moved, he pulled her tighter, she lay back a little longer, and she moved again, and this time her lips were free.

"Now, look at me," she whispered. "You're naughty . . . naughty . . ."

Her hands drifted slowly over his shoulder, feeling the harsh fabric, then to the softness of his neck below his ear, his jaw, his skin, the man feel.

He reached for her, seeing her dimly.

"Are we safe?" she whispered, fending her mouth, "is it safe here?"

Then his hands found her body, and her head rolled, helpless, she groped for his hand, she put it over her breast. She felt his body convulse, felt his weight, she lay a moment longer, then she pulled herself away with a tremendous twist.

"Luke!" she panted. For he was reaching for her and would not be denied. "Luke!" She hit his shoulder, pounded hard.

"Lie still!" he mumbled.

"Listen to me! Luke! Do you hear me?"

His eyes focussed slowly, reluctantly.

"Luke!"

"I hear you," he said thickly.

"Not here, darling. Not here."

He sat up, anger showing in his eyes.

"No, no," she whispered. "Not like this—"

And then as he reached for her again,

"Wait! . . . I'm not ready . . . And you've got your patient! Luke! Remember? Your patient!"

He looked at his wrist automatically.

"You're a bad, bad boy," she said.

The car backed, bumping, over the abandoned road. They were on the highway again. She smoothed her skirt.

"Sure you know where we're going?"

"We won't be long." He looked at her and drove faster. "Kid fell out of a tree—broke his arm."

"I've got to be back, you know—"

"It won't be long."
"I've got to get back to work. And you're a monster."
"You know, in a way, you're kind of a monster yourself." He said it matter-of-factly.
"I know," she whispered. "And you love it, don't you!" She drew her hand hungrily and slowly along his leg. She clenched her teeth. She pinched him, hard.
"Hey!" he cried.
"Ah, but that's not half the way you'd like to hurt me . . ."
He put his head out the window. "We've got to start counting mailboxes."
They turned into the long farm driveway.
"You could say you were just giving me a lift and the call came and I asked if I could go along with you . . ."
"You can stand by. You can hand me things."
The car stopped in front of the farmhouse. Lucas got out, he lifted his bag from the back, his face set as he lifted it.
The farm wife led them quickly into the bedroom. A ten-year-old boy lay on the bed, his face wet with tears, twisted with pain.
"What have we got here?" Lucas said, he smiled, and bending as he spoke he went quickly to work. His fingers probed. The boy screamed, tried to escape.
Lucas straightened.
"Ribs all sound," he smiled. "Just a greenstick—"
"Busted? I've told him fifty times to stay out of that apple tree! He had to go up, he fell like a stone—"
"Incomplete break," Lucas explained. "He'll be all right. We'll just put a little cast on . . . and . . ."
"Wonder he didn't kill himself!" The woman shook her head angrily. "And Mr. Orcutt gone to Annivale—"
The cast finished, the boy in bed, the green pills shaken from the small vial, the bag closed, the directions given, Lucas stretched his arms and smiled at the farm woman.
"Like to set a spell? Have a cup of coffee? 'Bout dinnertime—"
"Why, no. Thanks, Mrs. Orcutt—"
"We don't have anything fancy—" Mrs. Orcutt was eyeing Harriet uncertainly.
"No, no. I tell you what, I was just about to drive Miss Lang back from the hospital when your call came and I asked her if she'd like to go along. So I whisked in and grabbed a couple of sandwiches—"
"We wondered if it would be all right to look around—"
"Miss Lang's never seen a real farm—"
"Why, help yourself!"
"And we could eat them while we walked."
"Go right ahead. Go where you're a mind to. We got some new heifers down at the barn—" she pointed toward a broad roof almost hidden by a hill some distance behind the house.
"We'll drive down," said Lucas. "You take care of the boy."
"All right to feed him?"

"Give him anything he wants."

"And me right in the middle of baking! I don't know what his pa'll say—I declare, you turn your back a minute and—"

"He'll be all right," Lucas called cheerily. "You bring him in this evening, we'll take an X-ray."

The car moved slowly ahead. The front door of the farmhouse slammed. A chicken scurried across their path. Then they had rounded the hill, the farmhouse disappeared. A country barn stood before them. From an open window yellow hay spilled fatly. On one side of the barn was a split-rail-fenced enclosure and from this enclosure a young mare watched them nervously.

"Now, let's have our picnic!" said Lucas. He took her arm.

"Where are you going?"

"Why, we can eat in the barn," he said innocently. "Sit on the hay and eat and have a real picnic!"

"You!"

She looked around apprehensively.

"Someone will come!"

"Come here!" And he held her tight against him, feeling her whole body, now, her knees against his.

She had been watching the hill.

"Wait!" she said. And as he turned his head to look she darted away.

"Come on," he pleaded.

"Come on up here for a minute." And she climbed the fence and sat on the top rail. Reluctantly, he climbed beside her.

"Now, you're out of mischief," she said smugly.

"You think so, do you?" And he reached for her.

"Careful! Wait! . . . What's that?"

He looked where she was looking.

"What's what?"

"That noise—hear? That—drumming noise!"

From the barn came faintly the imperious sound of a horse whinnying. The mare lowered her head. She straightened. She began to trot aimlessly. Suddenly she whinnied in return.

"That's a horse. That's a stallion whinnying. He's kicking the barn apart. He wants to get out."

"Can he get out? Maybe we better get down—"

Lucas was peering at the mare more closely.

"Why she's in heat!"

He grinned at Harriet.

"That's what it's all about!"

"He can't get out, can he?"

He glanced at the stoutly fastened side door.

"No," he turned back to her, reassuring, "he can't get out."

She was staring at the side door. The drumming of the stallion's hooves was louder.

"Come on," he said. "Let's have our picnic . . ."

He put his arm around her. Before them the mare wheeled, wild-eyed, whinnied again. Beneath his hand Lucas felt Harriet's body stiffen. From the barn screamed again the clamor of the stallion.

She turned to him, hypnotized. She moistened her lips.

"Lucas," she whispered. Her eyes were luminous. "I've never seen . . ."

He jumped from the fence, raced to the side door, pulled the bar. The door swung slowly open. He raced back to sit beside her. For a moment the enclosure was quiet. The mare stood, her neck arched, listening, scenting. She moved her feet nervously. Suddenly the doorway was filled with the head and shoulders of a huge stallion. Then the doorway was empty and he was thundering to the mare. The mare reared, screaming she slashed down at his back with her forefeet. As quickly the stallion reared, his forefeet bowled her over. She staggered up. He was at her, his teeth seeking the back of her neck.

Lucas glanced at Harriet. She was hypnotized, her face pale, her eyes wide.

The mare dashed to escape. There was no escape. Again the stallion sank his teeth in her neck. She trembled.

Instantly he reared. He plunged on her. His loins moved convulsively, his hips aimed, drew back suddenly.

"Oh! Oh, my God! He'll kill her!"

She clung to Lucas, her body twitched, with each movement of the stallion she gave a little moan, Lucas gripped her tighter, the stallion screamed, driving the mare almost to her knees.

It was over. The stallion dismounted slowly and at the sound and sight Harriet, swaying, shut her eyes.

Lucas watched her. Then he slipped from the fence, she was in his arms, he was half running with her toward the open door of the barn.

"Luke!"

She twisted free, she stumbled, she almost got away.

"Luke! Luke!"

But he dragged her to the barn. She clung to the door. Then with a brutal, tremendous tug he yanked her inside.

"Luke! For God's sake!"

In a corner was a vast pile of hay.

And he dragged her, stallion-blind and deaf, never feeling the wild flailing of her free arm, he knelt in the hay, he pulled her down beside him,

"Luke! For the love of God!"

She beat at him.

She felt the prick of hay on her bare body.

She stiffened.

She cried out suddenly.

Then she moaned and was still.

"We've got to go," she said later. She sighed. She snuggled against him. "We'll be missed . . ."

"I suppose so." He lay quietly, not moving. "I didn't know," he said, remembering, "I didn't know you were—intact—" He stopped delicately. He was silent.

"What did you think? Why do you suppose I fought you so."

"I didn't know . . ."

"I've got to get out of this hellhole," she said suddenly. She sat up. She clasped her knees.

"It's not all easy for me, you know." He sat up.

"You! You've got your work—you're doing what you want—you've got a nice little niche—"

"Wait a minute—"

"In a nice little town—"

"What's the matter with your job? You're doing what you want, aren't you?"

She stared at him scornfully a moment.

"Is that all you think of me? Do you think I belong here? In a hick town, with a hick tile factory—and the things I ache to do just beyond my finger tips? I spent four years at art school!" she stormed suddenly, "I was a bright kid, I was the brightest in my class—big men, men you never heard of—said things about my work—"

"They say you've done wonders down at the pottery—"

"The pottery! Do you know what I was doing when you called? I was —I'm ashamed to tell you." She was silent. "I was decorating ash trays!" she cried. "That's what I was doing! Cheap ash trays. For cheap people. Well—and that's played out, now. That's about to end. They're going to let me go. Now, whether I like it or not, I'm going to the city, I'm going to New York and now I'll have my chance and now I'll follow my star. I'll never leave it. Never again. I'll starve. But I'll never leave it!"

"I didn't know," Lucas said at last, troubled.

"Of course you didn't know. How could you?"

They were silent.

"We're not too different," he said at last.

She nodded.

"For you it's a little town, little ash trays . . . But you've got your pottery," he said quietly, "you've got your designing, your art, it isn't sullied, it hasn't been touched. . . . Runkleman," he said evenly, and his voice came to him from a distance, "Runkleman was a fine man. Runkleman was a doctor you could look up to—but he sold it wholesale, he got what he could, and he ran away from death and he never took a chance. . . . And he was a doctor. . . . Oh yes, and beside him there's Snider . . . And I don't know how many he's killed and I don't know anybody more ignorant, more contemptible, and maybe he's a grafter, too . . . I couldn't prove it, but they say he's got his fingers in the County till. . . . And there's Kauffman, who's a Jew first, and a doctor second—because they've made him that way, my brothers in Medicine—and he's here, he's through, holed up, getting by. . . . And there's Binyon and Blake, the medical department store, doctors of Medicine, service our specialty, the latest equipment and let us remove that fee for you. . . . And there's Dr. Gordon, over in Lepton, who's got a secret remedy he won't give out. . . . And there's Dr. Castle—and he watches it all—and he doesn't care—and he's ready to go. . . . The best of the lot of them. And I'm afraid to get closer. I'm afraid of what would happen about him. . . . I'm afraid to think of other doctors. I'm afraid to think of the men I went to school with. That's my Medicine . . . One by one . . . illusion after illusion . . . that's my world, the only world I want, that's what it's come to. . . ."

They were silent a long time.

"We could get along pretty well together," Harriet said slowly.

"A fresh start," he sighed.

"I'm lonesome," she said suddenly. "I've been lonesome all my life."

He nodded.

"How did I get here? I've got to get out of this hellhole!" she cried. She began to pound her knees. "I've got to get out of here!"

"A fresh start," he said again.

They stared at each other.

"Soon!" she cried fiercely.

They rose. They brushed each other. They drove silently back to town.

It was still quite early.

It was late.

But it was still quite early.

The town was much the same.

⋆ CHAPTER 37

The weeks passed, full of days, crammed with days, men who had not been conscious of days shrank from them now, aware of each day, shrinking from the next. The community which had been a placid settlement of humans surviving easily and pacifically now woke daily to doubt survival, to find its standards and its rules, its beliefs and its faith without meaning, or mockeries, or falsehoods. There was no rule to which to turn, no counsel, the book of living was suddenly blank of these and filled instead with astonishment and calamity and panic and despair.

There was no real hope and confidence was replaced with anxiety to exist, to pass another day, the downfall of a neighbor was a pang of terror but it was also an ugly comfort that all men were in like case and a furtive hope that calamity might by so much be appeased. Dignity and pride, those two luxuries of the unsuffering and the unfrightened, fell first and in a month were almost forgotten. The unreal and the unbelievable became commonplace. Hunger and want, those two social embarrassments which now and then revealed themselves among the unemployable poor or among Greenville's handful of foreigners, were now the respectable comrades of all. Actual hunger and actual want had come to a few of Greenville's wealthiest families. And then the days passed, astonishment faded, it became apparent that there was hunger and want and shame to comrade every man and woman and child, hunger and want and shame, waiting.

Then the habit of depression settled upon the community. And this became commonplace too, became in time as if it had always been. And survival was every man's problem, and anxiety and terror were every man's eyes, and wherever the eyes looked they saw hunger and want and wherever the senses raced to escape they faced the ominous and naked image of themselves, intent on survival. This dreadfulness became commonplace and the placid past vanished, and no man thought of it.

"And now," said Dr. Castle, "the worst is about to begin."

"Can it get worse?" Lucas doubted.

Dr. Castle sprawled back on the couch in the Valley Hospital dressing room.

"How's everything going? How's your volume of office calls, collections?"

"Well, they're not what they were, of course. But I cut down a lot, you know."

"I heard you did. In fact, I got a couple of dozen you cut out. Kauffman did too. And of course, I suppose Binyon and Blake—"

"I could have been mistaken on the ones I cut out, on some of them—"

"No, no. Not if I know you. Which I think I do. You were probably right to the last decimal point. Just a bunch of chronic inadequates . . ."

Lucas waited, his face expressionless.

"But they've got to go to somebody," Dr. Castle said mildly. "I always did think Dave's practice was too big, too unwieldy—"

"It was getting so I didn't have time for the really sick—"

"And it was a man killer, too. But they've got to go to somebody. Dave didn't want them either. He just didn't want them going to quacks—"

"They go anyway—"

"Oh, sure! . . . Next time just let a fellow know in advance before you open the floodgates!" He nodded. "I give them short shrift. I tell them they're wasting their money and my time, I give them pills for occupational therapy. I can't do any more."

"It's not getting any better," Lucas admitted. "We've had to let Miss Ables go. She's gone to live with her sister in Annivale. Miss Snow keeps the books now—what books there are to keep, as she puts it."

"Templeton's folded up this morning," Dr. Castle said.

Lucas started.

"They did, though. Oldest and biggest dry-goods store in Greenville, been in the family for three generations, old man came here with a pack on his back. It's gone. Vanished."

"It doesn't seem possible. Stern's you could expect, Elder's never was much, a dozen little stores I never could understand—but Templeton's!"

"I don't know whether you've noticed, but half the stores in town are empty, boarded up, padlocked."

"Would you say half?" Lucas deprecated.

"Oh, yes! Half, all right. What are you doing with your proteins, your baby foods, the samples of stuff they keep sending us?"

Lucas looked uncomfortably away.

"Well, there's a few of my patients, people really down and out—"

"That's right! That's what to do with 'em. And your drugs too. All the samples you can get your hands on." He shook his head reminiscently. "Druggists were sore as hell, last time. Claimed we were taking bread out of their mouths. Don't know but what they had a point. At that."

"They're getting enough," Lucas said shortly.

"I know it. Always have. Fifteen cents for a dozen aspirin! They don't ever seem to get rich, though. That's the darndest thing. Ever see a rich druggist?"

"I never saw one starving."

"And I guess that's true, too. . . . Collections?"

Lucas shrugged.

"Miss Snow says they're pretty poor."

"They'll get worse . . . It's coming . . . Now we've got to lay in against the malnutritions, the accidents and breakdowns from men taking unfamiliar jobs, insanity's going to start creeping up, bad teeth, operations will be put off and what we'll get will be emergencies—here and there the contagious diseases'll begin again . . ."

Lucas looked at him, bewildered.

Dr. Castle stuck out his lower lip consideringly.

"Never seen a depression, have you?"

"There was what they called a shakedown, I can remember my father calling it a shakedown, something in nineteen-twenty, twenty-four—I was a little young—"

"I've been through four of them. And I couldn't tell it to you if I tried. Time, time, my God! how it slips away from you! The human wail: 'Wait! Wait a minute!' " His eyes were dark, remembering. "You'll have to see it yourself, Marsh. You've got an experience coming to you."

"I'm like Agnes and Gloria," Lucas shrugged. "I went to see how they were making out— 'We never had much,' said Gloria. 'We've always got along on next to nothing. Hell! Everybody's just coming down to our level!' I've never had much, either."

"It's not just losing what you had," Dr. Castle pondered. "That's the first thing that happens, that's always a shock. You get over that. No . . . it's what it does to *people*. Not just a man or two here and there—but people! Society is the clothes they put on, all sewed up neat with little rules, cut according to the fashion of the locality, made out of the fabric woven by a civilization—and in that suit of clothes man looks pretty good! He doesn't look like an animal at all! . . . And then a depression comes along. There's something lytic about it—there's something—the stress, the terror, the bitter sweat of the First Law—and all of a sudden—the Emperor hasn't got any clothes on!"

"You think we're in for a crime wave?"

"Oh, God, sure you're in for a crime wave. Shedd isn't printing half what goes on now! People have to live, you know! They'll steal, they'll do anything. But those are acts, transients, like shock. I don't mean that. I mean the condition. The day-to-day condition. The naked animal confronting other naked animals. No rules, no nothing. And their bellies empty, and the wife sick and the kids crying at home. No pretensions any more. No pride in anything but the victory that means a dollar that means a meal. Just a quick pride. Soon over. Soon hungry again. Just man. Forlorn on a planet where he probably doesn't belong. Inadequate, one of the weakest animals, not pretending any more, nakedly out to survive. Which one of the banks do you think will go first?"

"The banks? You don't think the banks—!"

"We've never needed two banks. One of them's bound to go. Then, if they don't keep their heads—maybe both. You got a safe?"

"There's one in the office—but, really, Doctor—"

"If you've got any savings draw them out gently, put them in postal savings, keep what you need in your safe. Believe me! I was caught twice! I know."

"Money!" Lucas shook his head.

"Yes," said Dr. Castle. "Always money. How's Gloria? That kid doing all right up there?"

"I think the other leg's started. She's put up a long fight. It's going, all right. And then—" He spread his hands helplessly. "The child's fine—happy—they play with it all day long—"

"A baby without a wedding is a better guarantee of love than a wedding without a baby," Dr. Castle nodded. And then, as Lucas' eyes lighted with admiration, "Listen to me! The old Doc! I'm getting into my anecdotage! My mementopause! Christ! The last thing in the world I ever want to be is the kindly old village doctor, full of wise saws and courage, and character. That old son-of-a-bitch! God help me, I'm a man with a bad heart, crawling up the side of every day and stubborn as hell about getting to the next one. And why, I swear to God I don't know. I've got to admit it. I just like to live, that's all. And don't ask me why . . . What did you ever do about those two kids Dave was putting through school?"

Lucas flushed.

"I'm sending them the County money—"

"Understand you took a little cut there."

"Twelve hundred apiece will pay their tuition, anyway. When I can make it, I'll send them more."

Dr. Castle leaned forward and looked at Lucas intently.

"Are you clearing a hundred and fifty dollars a week?"

"Just about."

"Don't be embarrassed. Did I embarrass you?"

"Well—no—"

"Well, don't be. Dave . . . well, you're kind of a legacy, you know."

"I'm all right," said Lucas.

"Yes . . . You're all right . . . You'll take a while getting used to life. You'll have to find out that whatever animates you is carried in a cheap clay pot . . . you'll have to learn to put up with what never should be put up with . . ."

"Why?"

"Why?"

"Yes! Why, sir?"

"I don't know why. All I know is you can't buck it. It's the time element. You've got so little time. You can't win. You can't change people."

" 'Eppur si muove.' "

"Yes, it moves all the same. That's all very fine and heroic. But don't miss the point. Old Galileo had sense. He didn't waste his life bucking the system. He knew what he was made for. And dying at the stake wasn't part of it."

"I've no interest in trying to change people. You and I and every other doctor are just spectators. I know that's all we have time to be. I look around Greenville, today. It's a disaster town. But wind hasn't done it, there's been no flood, no fire, the earth hasn't changed—the town of Greenville, its houses, its soil, its climate is just the same as it was before the depression hit. We're the physical refuge of precocious children and their games, and the injuries they suffer in them are something we can't change. I know that. But because of what we know, and because of what made us want to know, we're a people apart. And the thing to which I can't reconcile myself—and to which I'll never be able to reconcile myself—"

"Is Medicine practiced by human beings."

"I'm afraid I don't understand. If you're saying that doctors are, after all, human beings, aren't you saying that diamonds are, after all, carbon?"

"I'm trying to tell you that you'll have to put your faith in wanting. Just wanting. And keeping your wanting clear and bright. Hell, I can remember—did I ever tell you when I was in the Army?"

Lucas looked guiltily at his watch.

"We live by the clock, don't we. We'll steal fifteen minutes and everybody will be looking for us and crying 'stop thief'!" Dr. Castle pursed his lips.

"It was the Canadian Army. In those days I was like you, I guess. Doctors were a people apart and all I lived for was Medicine. The Army took a lot of that out of me. I don't know just how. I couldn't stomach a lot of things in the Army. I fought them. So they shoved me clear down to the bottom of the list. Where I could help the least people. This hit me hard, one day. I was treating an enlisted man back of the lines. A shell hit nearby and he reared up on one elbow and he said to me anxiously, 'Don't bother about me, Doc. Look after yourself. You'll be here after I'm gone.' "

He paused, remembering. Feeling it again. It was a thing that had made its impression on him. The words echoed in Lucas' mind. You'll be here—you doctors—after we're gone. . . . Snider, then? And Binyon and Blake?

"That was one time . . ."

"But that's just what I mean!"

"I know . . . But I wasn't helping any on the bottom of the list—being right . . . The things you fight! The things you remember! . . . I remember a fellow—I had a little trouble, there was a fellow just had to be operated on, nobody could see it, nobody would listen to me. I walked right into the commanding officer.

" 'I want that man operated on!'

" 'What for?'

"What for, my God I saw red! He was a big surgeon. If anybody knew, he knew!

" 'Because I say so!'

" 'Not by me, he won't be.'

" 'Then I want him transferred to base hospital!'

" 'You do and I'll have you court-martialled.'

" 'Go ahead!'

"I walked out and I slammed the door. They had me! He knew it and I knew it. If I operated myself—I wasn't qualified for that particular operation and if the man had died they were just waiting for something like that! They'd have had me! The head man wouldn't operate—and everybody just waiting to back him up. And if I bulled ahead and transferred the patient to base—they'd court-martial me. And I'd be guilty."

"How in the name of God—what do you mean, 'guilty'!"

"The reasoning being—not, were you justified, but did you obey orders. If the CO says black is white—black is white. . . . And then, later on, I found out it wasn't only the Army . . . it was Medicine in general . . ."

"What happened to the patient!"

"He died . . ."

"Christ!"

"Yes, he died . . . slipped away next morning . . . And you know something? Today, that commanding officer is a knight, he's president of the Royal College, he's got every honor known to man."

He laughed. He shook his head wryly.

"What do you do!"

Dr. Castle looked up, startled. Lucas' eyes were pinpoints, his nostrils were white,

"What do you do—about that!"

"Do?" Dr. Castle began to smile gently, Lucas' eyes bored grimly into his, the smile faded, he looked away, looked out the window, into the past.

"Do?" he said to no one, "well . . . I'll tell you. . . . You've got to do this . . . you've got to make believe that you're the only doctor in the whole world . . ."

He turned to Lucas.

"That's what you've got to do."

There was a knock at the door.

"Call for you, Dr. Marsh!"

"Somebody's got to help them!" said Dr. Castle. His eyes searched Lucas'. "Just get 'em by. Somebody's got to!"

The call was at the County. Lucas raced there, his mind sifting Dr. Castle's words, and the nurse at the County: "Somebody's cut his throat—"

He lay on the table. Kristina stood behind his head, her fingers about his throat, her white uniform blood-soaked, her face, even her cap, spattered.

"Where's Dr. Snider?" Lucas was out of his coat, his eyes on the patient.

"He's not here," another nurse fluttered. "We tried and tried to get him—"

"We tried everywhere," Kristina said shortly.

Lucas pulled a treatment table nearer, he listened rapidly to the man's heart,

"Better give him a little adrenalin," he said to the second nurse. He picked up a clamp. All else went from his mind but the tissues before him. The cut was deep. It extended from one point of the underjaw to the other. It was deepest where—

"You can let go," Lucas said.

Kristina removed her pressing fingers.

Instantly a stream of blood spurted high as their heads. In the next instant Lucas had clamped, clamped again. And then again. And again.

"Got the jugular, all right!"

"Used a razor, thank God!" Kristina looked angrily down at the man. "What did you do it for! Haven't you got any better sense?"

The man had been staring at the ceiling. He closed his eyes. "Polish!" Kristina shrugged. "Laborer, probably. Can't understand a word they say. Something about money—stocks—his brother-in-law! Him! Stocks! Can you imagine?"

Lucas did not hear her.

The neck, its characteristic integrity gone, its smooth, even column, the design of so many million cells, now disordered by the wanton slash, was a confusion of sticky blood, gaping edges, a welling pool of crimson, the pink of muscles, the white thread of an occasional nerve.

And it was to this disorder that Lucas addressed himself. Automatically, as the gauze sponge mopped the wound, the tissues showing startling clear, then drowned in blood again, he sought the vessels which had been cut. As always, with the first movement he was alone within himself, uplifted, remote, the world gone, presiding at that to which he had been born, secure and exalted in a cosmos in which his brain and all his sentient being flowered in triumph, functioned in ecstasy, sure and invincible.

The cells of his memory, unasked, visioned for his mind's eye the internal structure of the neck, he saw its every muscle, its least nerve and blood vessel. His hands, moving before his conscious will could direct them, went surely to the anatomical landmarks. He found the flat ellipse of the internal jugular—the descendens hypoglossi, it was close to the thyroid, it was a near thing. And the divided sheath of the thyroid was white suddenly, then red again, and his fingers had clamped the anterior jugular and the common facial, the posterior external jugular—

"That's got it," he said silently, absently.

The bleeding had stopped.

He mopped again. Now the tissues lay bare, moist, hiding nothing. They showed themselves mutely. The gaping edges of the sterno-hyoid, the omo-hyoid, the sterno-mastoid, showed as slit muscles, helpless, accusing. The ligaments that bound them showed their white edges, and there were the divided ends of the anterior cutaneous nerve, and another —the superior thyroid? No . . . he had missed that . . . the vagus was intact . . . the laryngeals . . . what accident, what irony had slid the mindless razor harmlessly past the thyroid, the descendens hypoglossi . . .

He paused to wonder. And marvelling, anger rose in him, incredulity and outrage.

He looked up at Kristina. She quailed.

He touched the handle of a clamp over the severed nerves, arteries, the complex welter severed from miracle and logic and pattern.

"Do you know what he's done?"

She nodded.

"Do you know?"

"I don't know what you do—but I know—"

She looked down, sickened.

He looked down at the neck. He saw the field again. His eyes cleared.

He began to sew. He united the cut ends of the jugular and the tube in his fingers was three tubes, each layer a functioning entity, to the eye a single tube, and his mind visioned the cells of each layer, each tube within a tube, cells functioning in perfect order, dying and regenerating and never their function ceasing, mindless cells having perfect intelligence, their destiny created when this man was conceived, when two cells met and became one and mysteriously divided and became two, and became four . . . and then a hundred . . . and then a thousand . . . and now no longer cells multiplying, but cells multiplying in a suddenly perceived pattern, identical cells in a pattern, identical cells in a plan.

Cells become an egg shape. And from the inmost egg the cells, deciding to pattern anew, guided by no brain, triggered by no known direction, began unerringly to be the skin of all the glands, the alimentary tract, the bladder, the respiratory tract. And as the entoderm did this the next layer, the mesoderm, began to divide and multiply infallibly in the pattern of lymph, and spleen, and middle ear and the pulp of teeth, and the heart, and the arteries and the veins and the blood to fill these—that blood drying there, caking on the man's neck, those muscles, those arteries, those veins, those membranes—

And the outer layer of the egg, the ectoderm, divided and multiplied, to form nerves—those cut nerves—to form skin—that cut skin—

And all this in an egg, of identical cells beginning with no form, having no resemblance to skin or arteries or blood or tendons or muscles or bone or any tissue, proceeding unerringly, each cell knowing its function, selecting its undirected destiny, until at last there was form, there was a human, there was an entity which spoke and laughed and dreamed and one day cut its throat.

And the human used the mind these cells had made in their turn and operated all the moments of their life, directed it through an incredible basketwork, a spidery filament of nerves to raise the beautiful, the flawlessly functioning musculature of the arm, the fingers to pick up a razor invented by that mind, and to draw the razor pitilessly, wantonly, through millions of perfectly arranged and functioning cells—

And the skin gaped, split, discontinuous—

Through another miracle of cells being an architecture of tubes—

And the veins and arteries opened, mutilated—

And the precious blood gushed wild and useless—

And the muscles parted, the intricate billions of cells arranging of their own intelligence myriad bundles of fibers, showing as disciplined muscle—

The human had picked up a razor.

And he had cut his throat.

Lucas snipped the end from the final stitch. He bandaged the neck. His eyes cleared. He looked at the man stonily.

"You don't know what you've done," he said. "And you're not worth what you are." He remembered the mysteries, the inexplicable, the cells which were even now implacably moving, each according to its mindless miracle of intention, repairing, fighting invaders, making nerve and blood and muscle and sinew and blood vessels again, knowing when to begin, what to make, when to stop, until all was perfect again, intricate and smooth-functioning and magnificent and whole,

"You did this because somewhere in this insane world you designed—somewhere a drop of ink—on a piece of paper—formed a pattern you didn't like!"

The man looked at him blankly. The doctor was angry. He was very angry about something . . . He shut his eyes. He had done something to make the doctor very angry. Also he had cut his throat, and there would be trouble. He was indifferent. Let the police . . . Could there be more trouble than a brother-in-law who said hold on, hold on—and then the numbers on the money page went to nothing—the numbers . . . and all the money, all the grand paper, the heavy coins, all a man had . . . gone—all gone. . . .

A tear welled slowly out of his closed eyes.

"I called the police," said the nurse.

Lucas nodded.

He turned from the priceless mechanism on the table, he washed his hands, obliterating his thoughts as he did so.

"Did you call anyone else?" he demanded.

"We did, Doctor Marsh! Honest! We tried just about everybody! We couldn't get you—we tried twice—"

"I was at the Valley."

"We tried there. We called Dr. Castle—"

"He was with me."

"Dr. Kauffman was out on a call—" Her voice trailed.

"Did you try Dr. Binyon or Dr. Blake?"

"Yes, sir," she said in a low voice.

"They were in?"

She nodded.

"And they wouldn't come?"

"I told them, Doctor—"

"Did you tell them it was an emergency? That a man had cut his throat? That it was an emergency?"

"I told them." She swallowed. "They said—they said they were busy . . ."

In Dr. Snider's empty office Lucas found his hands on the receiver were shaking.

"Dr. Binyon?"

"Why, yes—" The voice hummed, pleasant and baritone and smooth. "This is Dr. Marsh."

"Glad to hear your voice, I was just saying to Blake the other day—"

"Do I understand you were called to the County within the past half-hour—for an emergency?"

"I believe I was. Yes. Just what seems to be the—"

"You deliberately refused to answer an emergency?"

"Just what seems to be the trouble, Doctor?"

"Do you mean to tell me that you—that you, a doctor—that you actually refused to answer an emergency?"

"I don't know who you think you are, Doctor, or what right you think you have to dictate my conduct. I know of no law requiring a physician to answer an emergency call! Do you? Is there a law on the books? Some law?"

"I want to tell you this, Dr. Binyon. I want you to listen to me closely. If you ever refuse to answer an emergency again I'm going to the County Society—"

"I'll be glad to go with you—"

"And if the Society doesn't discipline you—if a profession without ethics is what you want—I'll give the story to the newspapers—"

"Ahah! Doctor! And who's unethical now?"

"And you won't be able to answer, you smug, money-grubbing disgrace to the profession—because I, personally, will give you something you'll never forget!"

He waited a moment, breathing hard.

"Are you all through, Doctor?" Dr. Binyon asked politely.

Lucas slammed the receiver on the cradle. The phone rolled off the desk. He picked it up, he set it down carefully. He looked at it. When he could breathe evenly again he rose and went to look for Dr. Snider.

As he passed through the doorway Dr. Snider appeared, walking toward him.

"What's going on," he called irritably, "what the hell's happening here?"

"We were looking for you a while ago, Doctor."

"I've been right here! I've never budged!"

Lucas turned then, and looked at the nurse.

"We—we looked for you, Dr. Snider—we tried everywhere—"

"Goddamned blockheads! Can't trust you a minute! Can't even trust you to find somebody! I haven't been out of this building! One of these days some of you imitation nurses are going to be right out of here on your ass!" He stared at her. He nodded ominously. "Just remember that!"

"I'm sorry, Doctor—"

"I was right here every minute." Dr. Snider ignored her, turned to Lucas. "Why, Mrs. Gaunt can tell you! I was talking to Mrs. Gaunt! No reason on earth why they shouldn't have found me!"

Lucas looked at him. Then he nodded and walked on. The head nurse would say whatever Dr. Snider wanted her to say. He walked on, numbly, defeated, sick.

"What's it all about?" Dr. Snider called after him.

"A man cut his throat." Lucas did not pause or turn.

The operating-room doors closed behind him.

He heard faintly Dr. Snider's voice demanding,

"Now, what the hell did he do that for? Who was it?"

The nurse's reply was lost.

He walked into the operating room. Lying waiting on a stretcher was Oscar Glaimer.

Lucas managed a smile.

"Be right with you," he said with all the reassurance he could intone.

"Is it gonna be all right?" Glaimer asked.

"Seems to me you've asked me that before," Lucas smiled. "Nothing's changed, if that's what you mean—"

Glaimer peered at him uncertainly.

Shall I say, "We'll see?" Shall I say, "We'll do the best we can?" Shall I say, "At least we can try?" Lucas tried to decide. He discarded them all. There was nothing to say.

He nodded cheerily, smiled confidence, waved and departed for the dressing room.

Moments after he made the first incision, laid bare his first landmarks, Lucas halted, stared thoughtfully at what he saw, probed with his finger, straightened, shook his head rejecting the instrument Miss Otis offered, asked for needle clamps, needles, sutures.

Twenty minutes after Oscar Glaimer had been wheeled into surgery he was wheeled out again. His wife, waiting in the room, jumped up in surprise as the stretcher pushed in, looked quickly at her watch, then at her husband on the stretcher.

"You opened him and closed him," she said slowly.

"He's full of it," Lucas said quietly. "It's everywhere."

She stared at her husband.

"I guess that's that, then," she said tonelessly, words without intention or meaning. She stared on.

Lucas slipped quietly from the room.

She rushed to the door after him.

"How—how long—?"

"Two weeks—two months—maybe, at the outside, even three months."

"Opened and closed him, hey?" Dr. Snider stood beside them. "Well, that's the way it goes. That's the way I figured. Old Dave was seldom wrong. He always had the law and the dogs on his side."

Mrs. Glaimer listened a moment, head bent, then turned and reentered the room. The door closed gently behind her.

"Now, a lot of fellows, they find a setup like that, they'll just leave a few bleeders, get what I mean? Just forget, like forget to tie off three or four. Just enough. Get what I mean?" Dr. Snider peered at Lucas, his expression ready to change to righteous censure or sly approval.

"I've heard of it," Lucas said levelly.

"Never seen it, huh? Sure! That's what they do. Saves 'em suffering. Can't save 'em, after all, nothing you can do, might as well save 'em torture, let 'em linger a few days, say their goodbyes, maybe they got a point . . ."

"Nobody would know about it," Lucas said gravely.

"Who'd want to know?"

"And it would make a bed for the next one."

"Right!"

Dr. Snider waited eagerly.

Lucas nodded.

"He's good for at least a month—maybe three," he said pleasantly. He nodded and walked on. Now he did not even feel anger. The cup had overbrimmed.

At the Valley Hospital next day Dr. Castle was waiting for him.

"Got a friend of yours in here."

He led the way. Tucked neatly in bed, where the white sheets made alien contrast with his yellow skin and Mongolian features, was Li. His head was bandaged. He smiled widely as Lucas entered.

"Car hit him in front of his restaurant last night. Knocked the hell out of him. What are you grinning about, Li?"

Li grinned more broadly in appreciation.

"Skull?"

"Doesn't seem to be. Concussion, of course. Bad scalp rip. . . . Your head hurt, Li?"

"Head feel fine."

He smiled at them, his eyes watchful.

"He's worrying about his leg," Dr. Castle said in a low voice.

"What did you do to yourself!" Lucas scolded.

"Do nothing! Stand there, car come along—boom!"

"Patella—whole joint—look here—"

The X-rays showed the kneecap hopelessly smashed, shivered into fragments. Lucas' mind visioned the tendons, those taut guy-wires released now, sprung back, the hopeless snarl of torn muscles, ripped networks, the chaos of the unattached.

They looked at each other. The next step was in the minds of both.

"Doesn't want me to cut it off," explained Dr. Castle.

"That's a pretty bad leg there, Li. You'll have a good new one. Good as the old!"

"No cut!"

Li said this as a fact. He smiled as broadly as before.

"They've got notions. Got that burial chest of yours almost full, Li?"

"Almost full," Li smiled.

"I'm going to give you another little shot now. This time quit grinning and try to sleep." The needle slipped home. "He had one less than an hour ago," Dr. Castle said. "They've got an extra tolerance . . ." He shook his finger at Li. "Opium! You close the shop, you sneak out back, you smoke chandoo? Eh? Too much chandoo!"

"No chandoo," Li grinned happily. His eyelids lowered a little. The morphine was finally taking hold.

They watched him a moment.

"You go sleep, now!"

Li looked at them in turn. He smiled. He sighed and closed his eyes. He began to breathe evenly.

"Sit a minute. You don't mind?"

"I'm cleaned up. We get through amazingly early nowadays."

"That's one virtue of a depression. Haven't had a chance to sit like this in weeks. Getting a little more rest every day. He doesn't want to lose his leg."

"I don't blame him. But–"

"They save up their money and when they die the money goes to ship their bones back to China. The things you have to know about patients! So if the bones get there, and there's a leg missing–I don't know the rest of it. It's something so important, not arriving complete, that the poor devil–"

He shook his head.

"Did you tell him? That he'd have to lose it?"

"Little devil's probably lying there playing possum. Listening to every word we say. Funny! So long as we're here, he doesn't worry. I think he's got an idea that if we leave strangers will come in and take him out and–"

"Of course there's one way," Lucas mused.

"Plates? I've heard of it–I don't think–"

"I was thinking of ankylosis . . ."

Dr. Castle's face cleared in a wide smile.

"Of course he'll have one straight stiff leg, hip to heel–"

"God! Do you think *he'll* care? Li, you devil! Did you hear that?"

Li opened his eyes sleepily.

"No hear anything," he murmured. His face relaxed. His eyes closed again.

"I'm not much as an orthopod . . ." Dr. Castle said, troubled.

"There's a fellow over in Annivale, isn't there? A new man? Somebody named Morgan?"

"Horgan! That's right! He's a brand-new orthopod! You want to call him in?"

Lucas shifted a little. "It's all right with me, of course. . . . This private room must be costing him a lot already. Can he afford–Horgan?"

"I don't think so," Dr. Castle meditated. "Not without tapping that burial fund . . ."

"We could shift him over to the County. I could call Horgan and tell him it's a County case–"

"Will you do it?"

"Of course! I'm not saying the ankylosis is bound to work, you know–"

"Popliteal's not involved. That much you've got."

"It's worth a try. Between the three of us–"

"Right! You hear that, Li?" Li's eyelids quivered almost imperceptibly. From his lips came a gentle snore. "He's heard every word! Now he's happy."

"Oh, it's just an idea, I just happened to think–"

"I kind of like this old devil. Always grinning! I don't know what he's got to grin about . . ."

"Or anybody else."

"Trouble this morning?"

Lucas took a deep breath. Speaking evenly, he told his call to Dr. Binyon.

"I'd heard something," Dr. Castle said at last. He looked away, shaking his head.

"About not making night calls—but this was an open refusal to come to an emergency. In broad daylight!"

"Have to talk to him," Dr. Castle sighed.

"I'd like to take it to the County!"

"I know . . . Wouldn't do any good . . . Like he says: there's no law on the books . . . Can't be . . . Who's going to testify what's an emergency? . . . First thing you know everybody'd be in a public dogfight. . . . No . . . I'll call him. I'll take care of it . . . there's always ways—"

"I've heard that ever since I came into Medicine! Excuse me! I'm not angry at you. I've just heard that until I'm sick of it. That vague 'there's always ways'! What ways? What, specifically, can be done? What can be done to make a doctor behave like a doctor? You know the answer as well as I do! There's not one damned thing!"

"I could always call the County Society secretary . . . He could just talk to him unofficially, put the fear of God in him—"

"This is a new crop. The old laws are gone. I had a few of them for classmates. They know the score, they know the answers, they know where they stand. I know this type. Why, he'd simply look at you and laugh! Laugh right in your face! Because what could you do, actually? After he told the secretary politely to go to hell? If it was the big city, and we had medical politics, we could perhaps take him off the hospital rolls, pass an open vote of censure at a county meeting, see that he got no referrals. He'd get by. It would hardly touch him! But what can we do here? Here—multiplied by a million other communities?"

"There's one thing every sensible doctor has to depend on," Dr. Castle said quietly. "And that's the testimony of his fellows. We're all wide open to suit. Every day of our lives. We've lobbied through a law that says we don't commit malpractice unless we fail to do something we ought to have done, or do something we ought not to have done—all measured to the way Medicine is practiced where the offense occurred. Legally, poor judgment doesn't enter into it. But nobody—not even Binyon or Blake—wants to be the loser in a law suit. And the only expert testimony is the testimony of fellow doctors . . . So it settles down to our permanent standard—the least common denominator—the lowest third in practice . . ."

He paused, significantly.

"If it comes down to that, I'll remind him," he said. "I think he'll listen to reason."

"And I think he'll laugh in your face," Lucas answered quietly. "Because he knows who he's dealing with. He knows the last thing we'd ever do would be blacken our own profession. That we have no right to decide for the profession, setting its good name at stake . . ."

"I'll speak to him. It'll come out all right. I'm going to amaze you.

I've seen worse. Now, let me try . . . And don't take it so hard! He's sleeping soundly, nights. If you're looking for a world with justice . . ." He brooded a moment. He looked at Li. "You asleep, you heathen devil?"

The old Chinese did not stir.

Dr. Castle moved his thumb to point at the slender form.

"There's a people that probably invented it. An old, old people, very cynical, mature young—bear happily—die easily . . ."

Lucas flushed.

"Maturity—" he said.

"Now wait! I wasn't suggesting for a minute—"

"I know . . . But maturity—maturity's a very loose cloak," Lucas said a little bitterly. "It means you concede that justice is possible but doesn't exist. That men make a lot of pious noises about it and even get roused up, now and then. But like the apes they sprang from, their attention is easily diverted, they soon bore, they'll settle for a lot less. That's maturity, isn't it? Facing that!"

"They haven't got time for much justice, much self-improvement. It takes a lot of a man's time to survive. Just to find food to nourish the brain that can ponder these things."

"All right, and survival's the First Law. And it's man's prime problem. And if he's in trouble today it's because the tribe, the Species, the Family—even though they know this is man's most important problem—won't abandon every other human pursuit—drop everything and once and for all, solve it. No . . . we've got brains to discover radio—and automobiles—and every wonderful toy of locomotion, or sense projection—but not to solve this one problem, the problem of survival, the naked, simple question of food, safety, and shelter— the *sine qua non* of human existence."

"I don't say it's perfect. Is there a perfect setup? A perfect government?"

"There is for us—the custodians. And for all our kind. And you can start with the soma! The soma and the psyche! The body and the mind. Life without consciousness. And consciousness on borrowed life. The perfect intellect of the body—having no consciousness. And the perfect consciousness of the mind owing its life to the body. Those two."

He looked at Dr. Castle defiantly.

"You're not going to propose government by doctors!" Dr. Castle begged.

"I'll propose government for the soma," Lucas said steadfastly. "Government which has for its basic aim the feeding, the safety, the protection of the soma. Take from the psyche the job of minding the baby—free it from that sad, elementary, lifetime doom—isn't that all civilization comes to? Isn't civilization simply the progress of man in solving the obligations of the soma?"

"You're leaving out a lot of statuary and literature and—"

"Yes, but those are triumphs of the psyche—in spite of the obligations of the soma. Was the wheel invented for the psyche? The pin? Fire? The high art points in civilizations are encouragements to the psyche, hints of what could be done—if only it didn't have the baby to mind. No . . . every invention and most of our science has one aim . . . push-button care of the soma . . . and the freedom of the psyche . . . and someday . . . some wonderful day in the future of man—those thirty-five miles of unused brain pathways—pathways he dies with, unused—will be the basis of a world we can't guess at . . . a world as alien to us as Heaven itself . . . and if there is a destiny for man—he will know it, there. . . ."

Dr. Castle was silent. He sighed.

"I don't know . . . I don't know, anymore. . . . They'd get ahold of that notion, next thing we'd have some kind of Spartan society—some physical-culture government. They'll do anything with a notion! Maybe —maybe Dave had the right idea . . ."

"Maybe he did," Lucas nodded tiredly. "When you see it as clearly as we can see it—what they do with themselves has to sicken you. Maybe he was right. Maybe you just have to work for the day when you can get away. Turn your back on it. Get away and go hunting. Start over. A clean man in another part of the forest. Pure because he's alone, proud because he survives and content because—aging—dying—only Time and Chance and Death, antagonists who are not enemies, could vanquish cleanly a full life, lived strongly and with honor."

"Will you settle for that?"

"It's not the answer to the First Question. It's just a concept. And the concept tells the body and the body shrugs and goes along . . ."

"What is it you want, Luke? What is it you must have? What will you settle for? Have you asked yourself that yet?"

"I want to be a doctor," Lucas said simply.

"Well, of course you *are* a doctor—!"

"No . . . But you gave me something . . . I remember what you said . . . 'You've got to make believe you're the only doctor in the whole world—and practice accordingly . . .' "

"You know Thomas Aquinas says Charity can exist independent of Faith and Hope. That's something else, as long as you're remembering things—"

He prodded Li gently with his forefinger.

"You asleep, Li? You listening to all this?"

The Chinese snored softly.

"I don't know," said Lucas. "If you mean a clear aim—I don't know any longer. You could sum it up—you could say—just Medicine."

And he knew what he could not say, that whatever his dreams or his aims he was bound to the events of the day, bound to people by their mischances, no longer an actor but a reactor. And that force which was not mortal and which had directed his birth and which had one day made him exalted and free now bound him irrevocably to the earth and to the next moment for its fulfillment.

And all he had said returned to him, and it was true, and he was bound in all his actions to the actions of those about him, involuntarily the servant of man, himself and his life force and his dreams, linked to all men as all men were linked to each other. Belonging to all men, nourished by all men, crippled by all men, and his nights bleak with this knowledge in a place that was not home, and rising, lifting again the links of the chain that bound him to the next man in the endless linkage, he must be bound to the path they would walk, bound to the next event. And of this event he and those to whom it would happen were ignorant and helpless and only bound.

"After a while," said Dr. Castle, "you look up one day and it floors you. You're a minor character in a tale of which you're the hero."

"If you're not careful," Lucas said quietly, "that can happen."

Dr. Castle looked away.

"That wife of yours—she's quite a help."

"Tell me something!" Lucas said impulsively. "I know her qualities —at least I think I do—but what is it you and Dr. Runkleman see? What is it about her that makes you jog me from time to time—is it something I'm overlooking? Something I don't see?"

"Oh, well—we old bachelors—we doctors don't have much time for our women, you know—"

"It must be something! Something you see and don't want to point out—"

"You've got a mighty fine woman there."

"And that's all?" Nothing specific. A mighty fine maid. And a mighty fine nurse. But was there something? Something else?

"I like that woman," said Dr. Castle. "The more I see her the better I like her." He stared directly at Lucas.

"She has her points," Lucas nodded. He could say no more. He felt embarrassed suddenly. "You should see what she's done to the County OR—I mean the way she's—"

"I've heard about it. I see you've been reading up Cytology—what do you do—read it together?"

Lucas looked at Dr. Castle amazed. He hid his incredulity swiftly. Does he really think she could understand the implications of a cell? That I who ache for it so endlessly could talk to her about the things that are in my heart? Can he really, really be so blind?

"We don't get much time together," he said smoothly. "I haven't had a chance for a talk like this since—since school."

"I thought you'd been reading up."

"No . . . I don't have much chance for that, either . . . that cut throat this morning set me thinking. Sometimes for an instant in a busy day you see it clearly. And then you can't help marvelling. That damned intellect without consciousness. Making decisions . . . sometimes even deciding remorselessly against themselves. Deciding to disappear."

"Like the appendix, the tail, the pineal gland—"

"How do they decide? Is it use? Some purely local decision? Or a total conference, organ and substance messaging needs and opinions? And do the messages themselves compose a new intelligence, deciding the fate of organs, the next physical factor to be improved?"

"Why are we right-handed! Why don't we have a sloping brow any more, a barrel chest, a suit of hair, a tail!" Dr. Castle nodded tiredly.

Lucas shook his head, brooding.

"No . . . we don't even know the location of mind. But our subconscious knows. Our cells know. And maybe we can discover . . . For there is mind, there, greater than any mind we have conceived . . ."

Dr. Castle sighed.

"Maybe so," he said resignedly, for he was not beginning. He laced his knotted knuckles. "Maybe so . . ."

Lucas rose. He looked at Dr. Castle apologetically.

"I'm sorry . . . I'll get a soapbox . . ."

Dr. Castle's old frame straightened. He rose slowly. He waved his hand.

"Good for you to get it off your chest. . . . No . . . There's nothing wrong in what you say . . . As a matter of fact maybe that's why fellows like you get born . . . Maybe that's another intelligence of the cells, a sort of supreme effort to achieve for celldom what the normal man they make doesn't give them . . ."

"I didn't know I was abnormal—I mean—"

"Something like that funny business of heart specialists dying of heart disease—and brain men dying of brain trouble—maybe the cells *do* know where their weakness lies. And sort of shape things so the man's bent for a specialty in which he may learn something to save himself."

Lucas smiled deprecatively.

"It doesn't seem to explain obstetricians, does it . . ."

"By God, it doesn't disprove it, either! Maybe a born OB just represents another effort—another cellular survival project! Lord God, look at the time! I wouldn't have missed a minute of it! You, Li! You, pretending to sleep! We're going to save your leg, do you hear? You go back to China all okay!"

The old Chinese opened his eyes.

"Half a grain of morphine and heard every word, didn't you!"

Li smiled.

"No cut," he whispered trustingly, his eyes closed, this time he slept.

As they walked down the corridor, as they neared the admission desk, they saw the clerk hand a man a receipted bill.

"That's Garvey," said Dr. Castle. "How's your new baby, Garvey?"

"Fine, Doc—hello, Dr. Marsh—I just paid for her, I guess I own her, now." His lean face, deeply lined, looked at them unsmilingly. "Whilst I'm at it, I'd like to start paying *you* off, Doc Marsh. Mind if I kind of pay you in payments? Guess there's got to be a first time for everything," he said apologetically. He extended a bill. "Tain't much. Just five dollars—"

"Perfectly all right—what did you do to your hand?" Lucas put the bill on the desk, took Garvey's hand, peered at the base of his thumb where a long gash sloped.

"Hurry to get here—damned carving knife—"

"Get me a bottle of mercurochrome, will you? And a gauze sponge?" Lucas called to a passing nurse.

"It's nothing—" Garvey protested.

"No charge," Lucas said cheerfully.

"How's the grocery business, Garvey? Ready to retire yet?"

"Ready to retire, all right. What cash business there is don't pay for having babies. Everybody's charging—nobody's paying, the pottery's just laid off a hundred more men—I got to *give* credit, but there's a limit to the credit I can *get*—"

"Pottery's laid off a hundred more!"

"That's right. And the end ain't yet. I hear talk they'll close it altogether!"

"Never!"

"I don't know, Doc—if it's the same with them I don't see how they stood open this long—"

The nurse brought the bottle of mercurochrome, the square of gauze. As she walked away the five-dollar bill on the desk fluttered. Lucas put the open bottle of mercurochrome quickly on it. With the wet gauze he sponged the gash on Garvey's hand.

"I don't know what folks here are going to do if the pottery closes," Dr. Castle said soberly.

"It isn't definite," said Lucas. "It isn't definite, is it?"

Garvey shrugged.

"Well, I guess you don't need *my* assistance." Dr. Castle moved off.

"I'll phone Horgan this afternoon," Lucas called after him. Dr. Castle waved and was gone.

"There, now!" said Lucas. "If that acts up, you come and see me! Go tell the nurse I said to put a dressing on it. Keep the dirt out. Here! Take this with you—"

He lifted the bottle of mercurochrome, capped it, handed it to Garvey. He picked up the five-dollar bill. Where the bottle had rested the bill now showed the broad outlines of a red square. They looked at it, surprised.

"Guess it didn't hurt it any," Garvey hazarded at last.

Lucas put the stained bill in his wallet.

"Took a few germs off," he said indifferently.

"Thanks, Doc . . . sure sorry it's so little—"

Lucas nodded abstractedly.

Pottery closing? He thought about it, moving toward the entrance. He stopped, he turned abruptly, he went to a telephone booth.

"I can't take the time," Harriet said. "I can't come all the way into town—"

"There's a little place right by the plant—"

"So close? . . . All right . . . all right, then—"

He drove out quickly, past the scarred earth of the abandoned water system, a little distance past the pottery.

They began to sip their coffee. The counterman moved off.

Harriet looked about uneasily.

"It's all right," he said quickly.

"It's so close . . ."

"Forget them! I just heard something—I heard the pottery was about to close—"

"The plant?"

"Garvey. The grocer. He said he heard—"

"They laid off a hundred men this morning—"

"He said that too."

"Close the plant? I'd have heard—" She paused uncertainly.

"Better keep your ear bent." His face softened. "Miss me?"

"What? Of course! You know I do! . . . Luke—I'd better get back—"

"Stay a minute! Finish your coffee. You'd have heard—"

"I'm a luxury . . . I'm expendable . . . the whole department—I've got to know—" She moved her head angrily. "These rumors, nowadays! Nothing but rumors!"

His eyes misted, watching her.

"It won't last forever . . ."

"What have you been doing?"

"I've been with Dr. Castle—talking about man and cells—and come to think of it, about Kristina!"

"You don't think he knows anything, do you? About us?"

"Good Lord, no! Castle?"

"Why was he talking about your wife then?"

"Oh, I don't know . . . He and Runkleman think—"

"What did he say?"

"He didn't say anything. He just said that I had a very valuable wife there and be sure I didn't forget it."

"He knows something!"

"He doesn't know anything! Ever since I've known them he and Runkleman have always said the same thing, a sort of oblique hint that I have a real treasure there if only I'd realize it."

"How did he happen to just say it this morning?"

"Harriet! For goodness sake—stop looking under the bed—"

"I'm sorry. I guess I'm edgy. I've got to go, now, Luke!" She drank the last of her coffee. She stood up. Her eyes were absent, harried.

"When you move," she said, abstracted, "you've got to move fast—you've got to have plans—"

He got off the stool reluctantly.

"I'll see you tonight?"

"Tonight? Yes . . . tonight—"

"I'll pick you up—"

"Not too early—" She looked at him, her eyes luminous for a moment. In his chest was a hot, hard lump. She lowered her eyes. Lucas walked to the cash register.

He handed the counterman a bill.

"What's this?" The counterman turned it slowly.

"What's—Oh! Just a little mercurochrome. Doesn't hurt it a bit—"

"Even dough's goin' in the red these days!" the counterman said sourly. He put the bill in the cash drawer, handed Lucas his change.

They stood outside.

"I'll walk back," said Harriet.

"I have to drive that way anyway!" Lucas protested.

But Harriet waved and was on her way.

At the office, Miss Snow was ready with a book of checks. She stood beside him as he signed. As he finished he looked at the balance stub.

"Getting low," he murmured, impressed.

"Not like the old days," sighed Miss Snow. "I better start working on some of these delinquents."

"They'll come in," Lucas shrugged.

She picked up the signed checks.

"It doesn't bother you, does it," she marvelled.

"We're all right—"

"I know. But money! Doesn't it mean anything to you? Honestly, Doctor?"

Lucas looked at her steadily.

"Do you think that's what I'm working for?"

"But people have to be paid, too. A man doesn't just work for nothing! What's the matter with money?"

He looked away from the cold eyes of Alfred into the pitiless eyes of the bursar. He was homeless and the eyes of friends were wary and alien, he ran the gauntlet of that shame, sick with an old terror, outcast and alone.

"You're hating the wrong thing," Miss Snow said quietly.

"Nobody has to work for it," he said, his voice low and hard. "Not just for money." He shook his head, his lips tight. "Nobody!"

Miss Snow looked away.

"I'll start sending them in," she said softly.

"I've got a call to make. Give me five minutes."

She nodded and shut the door behind her.

Dr. Horgan's voice was a soothing, cultivated baritone.

"I'd be happy to assist you, Doctor!" And his voice was suddenly eager, the cultivated tone threadbare.

"It's your line, of course—I've been meaning to run over to meet you, anyway—"

"Yes, yes! Yes indeed! It's high time we met! Yes . . . I've got my boards, you know—"

"No, I didn't."

"Very recently! Yes! Yes, I'll be very happy to cooperate with you—" his voice paused significantly—"always! I'm sure we can work out a mutually advantageous arrangement—Dr. Binyon may have spoken of me? Or Dr. Blake?"

"You'll have no trouble making an—arrangement—with the patient," Lucas said coldly.

"Oh? Ah, yes . . . I see . . . These patellar cases—in my experience they tend to be complex . . . Yes . . . Now, what would you say, the, Doctor—or, rather I should say, what are the patient's circumstances?"

"I'm afraid your fee will have to be small—"

"Oh, Doctor! I wouldn't scrub for less than a hundred dollars—"

"People are pretty hard pressed—in my own practice I find that I have to temper the wind to the shorn lamb nowadays—" Lucas forced himself to speak evenly, lightly.

"I've spent years, Doctor, acquiring my diploma, my boards, costly, costly years—if my services are not worth my minimum fee I would rather do it for nothing!"

"Fine!" said Lucas instantly.

"I beg your pardon?"

"I said: 'fine'! Thank you, Doctor! This man deserves it!"

"What I intended to imply was—"

"I agree with you absolutely. We all have to do them for nothing now and then, don't we. Tomorrow, then, at nine o'clock."

"I must say—I wish you had informed me of these circumstances earlier, Doctor! Naturally, if my services are required and the man is an absolute pauper . . . If you should care to attempt it yourself there is a procedure I could easily describe to you—I'm sure you'd have no trouble—I've heard quite a bit about you, Doctor."

"I think I'll have to depend on the best man qualified," Lucas said pleasantly. "It's fortunate that as you told me you have the hour so conveniently open—I'm looking forward to assisting you with great interest!"

"Good day, Doctor," the voice said coldly.

"Good day!" Lucas echoed cheerily.

The door opened.

"Here's Mrs. Cunningham," said Miss Snow. "What are you so happy about all of a sudden?"

"I'm always happy to see Mrs. Cunningham," Lucas said exuberantly. He rose. "Come in, Mrs. Cunningham!"

"You'll want Room A," said Miss Snow. They walked down the corridor. They entered the first room.

"It's getting bigger," Mrs. Cunningham said dully.

"It does seem to be, doesn't it!" Lucas considered the huge, swollen belly. His eyes flicked briefly over the pendulous breasts, the mottled thighs. "Sit down, Mrs. Cunningham—no—right there. That's right . . . Now, if you'll get a bucket, Miss Snow, I think we'll do a little tap . . ."

"Gonna let some of it out?" the gray-haired woman asked incuriously.

"That's right—won't hurt a bit."

"Where's it all come from!" She shrugged her lank shoulders. She folded her heavy hands in her lap. "Dr. Runkleman, he used to give me liver stuff—"

"That's right. It's your liver—and other things."

". . . that's what he said . . ."

"Yes . . . Now, Miss Snow, if you'll just hand me that trocar—now this isn't going to hurt a bit, Mrs. Cunningham, just a moment's discomfort, just a—"

The tip of the long trocar dimpled the swollen belly, its sharp tip moved harder, disappeared, the thick body of the needle followed, half its gleaming steel disappeared in the woman's belly.

Deftly, Lucas removed the stylet. The broad-bored steel was now a hollow tube. And instantly from the end outside her body a trickle of cloudy, thin fluid began to fall. Miss Snow hastily moved the pail to catch it.

"Well, look at that," the woman murmured with mild interest.

"That's what you don't excrete, Mrs. Cunningham. You see, your body—"

"Comin' out in a regular stream ain't it." She straightened and leaned back, satisfied.

"Yes . . . Well . . . You'll call me, Miss Snow, in about five minutes?"

Miss Snow's lips twitched. They exchanged wry, confounded smiles. Miss Snow nodded. She turned back to her patient.

"You just go right ahead and leak away, Mrs. Cunningham," she encouraged.

Lucas walked down the corridor. After a moment he shrugged.

The man in his office twisted his hat nervously.

"Why aren't you on the farm?" Lucas smiled. "Nothing the matter with you, is there?"

"No, no! I'm all right . . . I, uh, I come here on something else . . ."

"Well, sit down. What's on your mind? Wife all right?"

"She's a-comin' . . . The point is, Doc—"

"I've got to get out to that fine farm of yours. Just for the pleasure of it!" The farm rose in his mind, the sea of white chickens.

"It's about that bill, Doc." He twisted his hat.

"Is something wrong?"

"It ain't but twenty dollars . . . It ain't you . . . The fact is, Doc, I'm broke!"

"Well, take it easy! I haven't dunned you, have I?"

"I'm a man that pays his bills. I lived here forty years now, and my father afore me, and can't nobody say any of us ever owed a nickel. Not a penny! All my life . . ."

"It'll be all right. I appreciate the way you feel, but—"

"I ain't got but a dollar."

The man fumbled two coins from an old snap purse.

"Wait!" Lucas cried. He remembered something. "I'll tell you what you do!" He saw an old woman, and this room, and Dr. Runkleman, and an old woman, and on the desk—"You pay me off in chickens! How'll that be?"

The man looked at him. He laid the two half-dollars quietly on the corner of the desk.

"Hain't got no chickens," he said.

Lucas stared at him.

"Couldn't buy the feed."

Memory of the white sea of feathers, clucking, rippling, limitless, thrust at Lucas.

"No, no! You don't understand! I don't mean a lot! I mean what you can spare! A half-dozen—three—anything—*one*!"

The man looked at him steadily. He swallowed.

"I ain't got one."

He left, and Lucas sat motionless at his desk, the man's flat voice eddying its hopeless echoes: ". . . ate the last one three days ago . . ." But all those thousands . . . every one . . . every last one . . .

He heard a baby crying.

The door opened.

Miss Snow entered.

"Here's a little patient," she grinned. She looked at the bundle in her arms, straightened the clean, worn blanket. "Listen to him!"

The mother followed. She looked at Lucas anxiously.

"Not much more than a baby yourself!" Miss Snow said. "Going and getting married and having babies! I can remember when Dr. Runkleman delivered you—"

They walked down the corridor. . . .

Toward the end of the day a woman rose to leave,

"How much'll that be?" she asked uncertainly.

"That'll be three dollars," said Lucas, "but you can give it to Miss Snow.—Hey! Wait!" He picked up the bill. It was a five-dollar bill, in its center a familiar square, red stain.

"Where did you get this?"

"What's the matter?" the woman asked apprehensively.

"It's all right. There's nothing wrong. I was just wondering where you got this bill—"

"I don't know," she said, worried. "I been to the drugstore, bought a pair of socks, bought some thread—it's all right, isn't it? Is it counterfeit?" Her voice rose, despairing.

"No, no, no! It's perfectly all right. I just wondered—it's just that I—never mind!" He put the bill in his wallet. He gave her two bills. "I think I'll just keep this as a souvenir."

She smiled uncertainly, left hurriedly.

When the door closed behind her he took out the bill again. It was the same bill. There was no possible doubt of it. The same bill, the bill from Garvey, the grocer . . . handed to him this morning . . . he paid me . . . I put it in my wallet . . . and then I—the man at the counter—for the coffee . . . He heard the woman's voice . . . And then to the druggist, or the children's wear . . . or the dry-goods . . . and then . . .

He stared at the paper. It returned his stare with the indifference of the inanimate.

He fingered the bill wonderingly. He put it carefully in his wallet.

The door opened.

"Last patient," said Miss Snow.

A boy walked in, holding his side.

And on that side hung the appendix, the faultless transparent apron of mesocolon, the white slender beauty of the ureter, the ileocolic artery and its network of perfect crimson branches . . . it could be colic, of course, it could be anything . . .

"Well, now, let's just see," said Lucas. "Have you been vomiting? Throwing up? Is it here? Right here . . . ?"

The door closed at last. Miss Snow left for the night. Lucas stretched wearily. He looked about the room for the ended day's last time. He blinked tiredly, content. He turned out all the lights. In the darkness he found his way to the connecting door, stepped through it and was home.

For an instant he thought he was mistaken.

Then, distinctly from the living room beyond, he heard voices. He heard Kristina's voice. And then, stiffening, horrified, incredulous, he heard the other voice again. He walked into the living room.

"Hello, there!" said Job.

They had been smiling, laughing. Kristina was suddenly sober.

Lucas stared at his father. Job was shrunken. His forehead stretched tightly, a wide and high dome from which the thin, still blond hair had retreated. His nose was now huge in his face, the lines deep on either side of the nostrils, and though his cheeks were thin, folds of unshaven skin were at the rim of his jaw and his neck where it disappeared into his dirty collar.

His hands were now long claws and at the end of his yellowed fingers his nails were long and black.

His shoes were cracked and broken, he wore an old and shiny serge coat, the cuffs ravelled, and odd trousers, stained, wrinkled, and threadbare.

His eyes, set more deeply in his skull, beamed blue and cheerily, small wrinkles at the corners indefatigably carrying their tale of amusement, delight in the implausibility of any human concern, and a sly and indomitable resolve to make a profit out of it.

"Where'd you come from?" Lucas asked, swallowing.

"Oh, I been here, I been there, I been everywhere," said Job. "I'll bet I've been over half the United States." He surveyed his clothes ruefully. "One way or another."

"You just get in?" Lucas asked warily.

"Sit down, sit down," Job urged. Lucas sat reluctantly. "No, I been in town a few days—"

"Here?"

"Just looking things over. Thought I might see a thing or two—"

"In harness?"

"Oh, no, no. Not harness. That's gone. Gone the way of all flesh, as the feller says. No, I been out of harness years now—still a fortune in it, though, smart fellow wanted to make a small investment, South America, Africa, Australia, places like that." He looked at Lucas appraisingly.

"What have you been doing? Going around telling everybody you're my father? Using me as a reference?"

"Never said a word," Job said cheerfully. "Figured it might be bad for your—ah—line. Nope. Happened to be going through the capital the other day, looked you up at the university, thought I'd drop by—" He winked at Kristina. "That's some wife you got there," he leered. "Chip off the old block! Always wanted to get better acquainted with some of those pretty Swedish girls—"

Lucas started, peered at Kristina. She dropped her eyes.

"You've been here before, then—"

"Now, don't go blaming her. I just dropped in one day, you weren't here, figured you might have a place for me to sleep—"

"So she gave you some money—"

"Just a few dollars, Luke!" Kristina said helplessly.

"And next day I just didn't happen to be in, again, and—"

"This depression can make a smart man a millionaire," Job nodded.

"Small towns like this, sometimes a smart man can jump in, people all paralyzed with fear, pick up something for a song—there's no limit to it."

"There is in Greenville," Lucas said steadily. Now he was no longer frightened, he was no longer angry, shame no longer choked him.

Job appraised him again. He moved his lips consideringly. He smiled cheerfully.

"All right, if you say so," he nodded. "I can't say there's much pickings here." He shrugged. "Figured to drift down past Milletta, see how things are going, maybe drop by your mother's grave—you got a nice place here—glad to see you doing so well—"

"I wouldn't go near Milletta if I was you. No. Not Milletta."

"I could use a few dollars—if you could spare it—"

Lucas glanced at Kristina significantly.

"You've already got a few dollars."

"I mean, to eat on," said this stranger.

"I'm sure you do," Lucas said, hate rising in him past the fingers of pity probing old loves, old ties.

"It's your father, Luke!" Kristina cried.

"Behind my back," he nodded to her. "You're a good pair. You knew what you were doing, didn't you. You knew what I'd say, you knew how I'd feel—"

"Now, that's no way to talk—it's not her fault, it's mine—I don't know what's so terrible about all this—I did the best I could for you when I had it—"

Lucas drew out his wallet as if it were a gun.

His fingers shook, his eyes blurred, he was almost unable to count.

"If you could spare a little—" Job said, watching.

In the wallet there was almost eighty dollars. Lucas took out fifty, pushing back the red-marked keepsake bill.

"Well!" said Job, pleased.

"There it is," said Lucas. "It's the last."

"Well," said Job, "much obliged."

"That's all right," said Lucas, and he walked to the door. His father rose. He found his battered hat on the floor beside his chair. He grinned at Kristina.

"I'm glad I met you. Always knew my son was a picker. Just keep him in line and don't forget that story I told you about the widow woman." He chuckled, leering. "She's been telling me all about her father," he turned to Lucas. Lucas stared stonily at Kristina's white, beseeching face.

"Well," said Job, in the silence. "I guess if I hustle I guess I can catch one of the night trains." He put the money negligently in his torn pocket. "Heard about a deal up in Philadelphia—way it sounds there ought to be a fortune in it—"

Lucas opened the door.

"Never can tell," Job said cheerily.

"Well, so long, Kristina," he said. "Glad to have had the chance to have met you—"

Kristina smiled wanly.

"Good night, Luke," Job said. He put out his hand. Lucas hesitated. He took the offered hand.

Job nodded. He stepped over the threshold.

"Take care of yourself!" he cried buoyantly. "Pomme de terre—and likewise—pross de toot!"

The door closed behind him.

Lucas stood numbly. He wiped his right palm slowly over his trousers.

"He's an old man, Luke," Kristina pleaded. "I didn't mean any harm—I couldn't turn him away—he's a father—"

She had betrayed him. And she had been the witness of his shame.

"I've got nothing to say to you."

"It was just a few dollars—just to sleep—"

"You knew what you were doing. You knew every step of the way. You knew how I'd feel—"

"I was afraid—"

"Afraid I'd get rid of him? Do you know what he means to me? Do you want me to make a picture of it for you? Is there anything else you can do to me? Anything? Have you got something else in mind?"

She pleaded with her eyes, then lowered her head.

"Yes, Luke."

He looked at her, burned free by anger and outrage and hot shame, and in that flame the last straw of obligation shrivelled.

He turned to the door.

"Where are you going?" she asked timidly.

"Where I won't see *you*."

"But the calls—"

"I'll call the operator."

"Luke! Please, Luke! Don't go—tell me where you're going, at least—"

He looked at her coldly.

"I may go over to Annivale," he said deliberately.

"To Annivale—!"

But he didn't mean that. He was telling her. He was deliberately telling her.

There was no doubt, now.

She remembered a bag of stale sandwiches she had found cleaning the rear of the car. Found, stared at a heart-cold stillness, disposed of. Burned the bag but not the sight, numbly watched the implication blackening to shapeless embers, saw the bag there still, walked away, walked heavily, bearing the bag, bearing its intolerable weight, bearing it in her heart, silent, frightened, bore it like a death and said no word. And the days passed. And she watched. And she remembered little things. And she hoped. And now it was open. Now it was open and he looked at her defiantly. And she remembered the bag.

Her face reddened. She stared at him.

"Don't shame me, Lucas," she said steadily.

Shame? he thought, do you know what it is to be shamed? Do you know how you have shamed me? Do you know what it is to be married to you?

But he said nothing. There was no use in saying anything.

He shut the door and was gone.

He drove impatiently. Harriet was waiting. In a few moments they were in the quiet hills.

And afterwards, in the hills, silent together, brooding, Lucas spoke out suddenly.

"There must be another way of life, a right life—somewhere . . . Somewhere! Is it asking so much?"

She turned abruptly, anxious.

"You don't think I've waited too long, Luke? It hasn't really been wasted, has it? I *have* been creating—I *have* been working—I don't think I've got rusty—"

"You?" He appraised her, disconcerted. "I don't know . . . I shouldn't think so . . . I—I don't know your line so well, you see . . . I was thinking . . . I guess I was thinking of myself . . ."

"That's right! That's the one to think of, Luke! That's the one you have to! Always!"

She was silent then and they watched the sky, the dark, mothering night sky, sending their dreams to it, sitting side by side, silent, absorbed, bodiless, yearning.

As the door closed behind Lucas, Kristina sat stunned, the minutes passed, she sat immobile, lost.

What had she done? Where had she erred?

There's something I'm supposed to do . . . something a woman should do . . . I've done what they do . . . Her mind stumbled over the thoughts and acts of her life with Lucas, examining, appraising, testing them against speculation of what another woman might have done, what another woman would do, now . . .

He doesn't love me . . . he never has, really . . . once I could help him . . . and he even hated me for that . . . it's natural . . . that's the way a man . . . I'm so dumb . . . and I can't learn . . . what do they do . . . What does a woman do . . . what should I do . . .

. . . always wrong . . . if I wouldn't move . . . wouldn't talk . . .

. . . an old man like that . . . God help me, I knew it was wrong . . . oh, he's right, he's right, he's always right . . .

. . . what do other women do . . . there's got to be something . . . what would they do . . . in my place . . .

. . . he knocked at the door and I opened it and he said . . . but I shouldn't, I shouldn't, I shouldn't . . . Oh, God, Luke! forgive me . . . and so he's going to her, now . . . I'll never, never, never again . . . he's gone to her . . . and this time I know . . . this time it's over . . .

Now there was no real hope, perhaps there had never been much, enough to work on, to try with, to keep patching, to hope. She closed her eyes at the memory of Luke's face.

Now there was another marriage and what there was had to be endured. There was a new basis, now. If there was anything. And if she saw nothing, now, kept her eyes resolutely averted, heard nothing, saw nothing, walked her ways in meekness, kept out of the way, spoke only when she was spoken to . . .

A day might come. A time of days. A sort of truce. A weariness, a scar, and then another life. If she held on lightly, never seen, never heard, ah, but lightly—

She stiffened.

She remembered the child in her womb.

An hour ago . . . an hour ago he would have been angry when he found out . . . he would have been furious . . . but when he had seen it—naked and beautiful and his . . .

And now . . . now if he knew he would not be angry. It would be the end.

Just that. . . .

She rose heavily.

In the closet, in a shoe box hidden by her cape—

She found the box. She went into the bathroom. She locked the door. She opened the box. She dumped the contents on the laundry hamper. There was not much here. A pair of bootees, a cap, a sweater, a bit of lace for a small coat. She stared at them dully. The sweater seemed to sag on one side, she had knitted poorly there, she stretched the wool carefully, straightening it. She looked at these things a moment longer. Then she opened the door of the medicine chest. She took out a pair of scissors she had worn as a nurse. She lifted the toilet lid. She took one of the bootees. She fought a craving to press it to her mouth. She shut her eyes. The scissors opened. She cut down. She opened her eyes. She opened her mouth to keep back the tears brimming her eyes. A tiny snip of soft wool floated in the toilet bowl. She held the bootee over the bowl and snipped again. When it had been cut in small pieces, when there was no more left and her hands held only the scissors, she flushed the toilet. She picked up the other bootee. She put it quickly back. She snatched the sweater, put it down, picked up the cap, picked up the sweater again.

The scissors cut down.

In a little while it was all done. The bootees were gone, the sweater, the tiny cap, the bit of lace. She put back the scissors she had worn as a nurse. She closed the cabinet. She turned and stared at the empty toilet bowl.

Suddenly her heart leaped.

How much time? How long had she been here?

For there was something else. There was that other . . . she had to do . . . And he might be coming back! He might be back any moment! He might be on his way right now! Now!

She fumbled the locked door open.

She listened.

Terror dried her tears.

There was not a doubt in her mind of what she had to do. She had to do the most terrible thing a woman could do. Not a woman, only. A nurse. And she faced this. It was a shadow moving grimly, moving swiftly over her mind. For there was no question. There was Luke. There was the Luke that was hers and the Luke to whom she belonged. And she meant to keep him. And there was only one thing to do.

If she had time—

If there was time! Time, only!

She stumbled to the office next door. She turned on the light. She went, lagging, to the dispensary cabinet. She rummaged through the bottles.

The name leaped at her.

Grudgingly, she took out the bottle.

She shook out four pills. She raised her hand toward her unwilling mouth.

Her hand stopped in midair.

She stayed thus, frozen.

There was something else.

If it doesn't work.

If I get sick.

If it half works.

If I have to be scraped.

But if I don't—

She was panting. She began to cry, helplessly. She beat her temples softly. What should a woman do? What? What? Ah, God, why don't you tell me! . . . Lucas, Lucas. . . . She saw his face again. She shivered.

She put the pills into her mouth then, and the next instant she had swallowed them.

She stared at the bottle. Her ears hummed with the room's stillness. Her heart beat more slowly. She sat down.

There was a loud rapping at the front door.

She jumped. She put her hand to her mouth in mindless panic.

The rapping began again. And then louder.

She went numbly to the door. She trembled, she fought down the nausea of terror. She opened the door a crack.

She heard her voice say,

"Dr. Marsh is not in—"

"Oh, hello, Mrs. Marsh," said Dr. Kauffman.

And then she had to open the door.

She stared at him, her eyes round with terror, despairing with criminal guilt.

She backed away.

"He isn't here, Dr. Kauffman." Her voice croaked.

He came in, his eyes on her terror. He smiled, his eyes expressionless.

"Oh, dear!" he said helplessly. "I've got to see him. Do you mind if I wait?"

She looked at him stupidly. She swallowed.

"Come in," she heard herself say. "Please come in."

Dr. Kauffman walked into the office. She followed him. He put his bag on a chair, he dropped his hat and coat over it. He looked casually around the office. He saw the open door of the dispensary cabinet. His eyes did not pause.

"You've got so much more office room than I have. Dr. Marsh hasn't changed anything, has he. No . . . Many's the night I've sat here, talking to Dr. Runkleman. When I was new here. Dr. Marsh is out late tonight, isn't he?"

"He got a call," said Kristina.

"Nothing serious, I hope?" His eyes missed nothing, her heaving breast, the mortal terror in her eyes, her shaking hands, her dry lips. He smiled pleasantly.

"I—I don't know when he'll be back—"

"I see," he said gently. He looked away from her white face.

At the movement of his eyes Kristina remembered suddenly, she stifled a gasp, she walked to the desk, leaned against it, facing him.

His eyes flicked over her, noted the bottle behind her, he looked at the floor, digesting this, he looked up, expressionless, his mouth smiling gently.

"How many did you take?" he asked quietly.

She said nothing.

He glanced at the bottle. Then he looked at her, waiting.

Her lips moved, her face was chalk, no words came.

She stared at him.

"Mrs. Marsh . . ."

His eyes waited. He smiled gently.

Her tongue moved in her dry mouth.

She could not look away from his eyes. His eyes spelled her, sure, compassionate, waiting.

From a great distance she heard her own voice.

"F-four," she said thickly.

She had said it.

She was done, now. She hung her head. She was weary. She was past even shame.

He had taken her arm. She looked up dully.

"We'll get rid of it," he said gently. She felt herself led to the bathroom. She felt herself kneel, felt his fingers down her throat.

Later, he led her back to the office, silently gave her an injection, sat down then, watched her gravely.

"Anybody could take the wrong bottle," he said.

She looked up once, then quickly looked away from him.

Lucas, nearing the office, saw the lights and came in.

Dr. Kauffman rose.

Kristina bowed her head.

"Your wife seems to have eaten something that disagreed with her," she heard Dr. Kauffman say deprecatively. "I took the liberty of prescribing a little pet remedy of mine."

"Well, thank you, what in the world—"

"She'll be all right now, I think."

Kristina rose.

"I'm all right now," she said. "I'm sorry—"

She could say no more.

She nodded and walked from the room.

"Sorry I wasn't home." Lucas watched her go.

"That's all right. I didn't want to talk over the phone. I've seen the others."

"That so?"
"I just wondered if you've had any typhoid, lately."
Lucas looked at him blankly.
"In the last week or two."
Lucas sat down.
"Yes," said Dr. Kauffman, "I've had three cases in the last week . . . Castle's got one . . . and Binyon and Blake aren't sure . . . you know, it's a little hard to diagnose if you haven't seen much of it . . . I just thought I'd drop around—"
"Four!"
"Six, probably—"
"Six!"
"Six!"
Dr. Kauffman nodded.
"Yes," he said quietly, "it looks as if we're in for it. . . ."

CHAPTER 38

Dr. Maurice Horgan was a tall man in his late thirties, the car he drove was expensive, he alighted from it, immaculate, well tailored, carrying a costly bag.
He shook Lucas' hand coldly. From behind his tortoise-rimmed glasses his eyes appraised Lucas' clothes.
"You're rather younger than I expected," he said, expressionless. "You seem to have made quite a reputation for yourself, Doctor." He scanned Lucas' vest. "Are you Nu Sigma Nu by any chance?"
"I hadn't the money," Lucas said shortly. "Nor the time, I'm afraid."
"Ah, yes. I must say the old fraternity ties have stood me in good stead now and then—"
"I'm sure they have—"
"Yes. Now, you say this patient is a pauper? I'm sorry to hear that. You're quite sure? Of course I do my share of charity cases, but you'd be surprised how many are outright fakers—"
As they walked toward the dressing room a stretcher entered through the swinging doors. On the stretcher lay Li. Dr. Horgan raised his brows questioningly. Lucas nodded. They stepped into the dressing room. The door closed behind them.
"A Chinaman, eh! Well, now, that's one kind you've got to be careful of. They've usually got pots of it buried away somewhere, burial money or something—"
"Don't you think that's just a superstition?"
"You've got to watch them." He shook his head. He placed his clothes very carefully on a chair, removed his shoes. "There's no limit, apparently, to the dodges dishonest people will try—"

They came to the table at last.

"No cut!" Li called cheerfully.

"No cut bad," Lucas reassured.

"No cut off leg."

"Now remember—we talked it all out. Remember?"

"No cut off leg?"

"That's right. We're going to save it. Dr. Horgan here is an expert—big man—"

"You be here."

"I'll be right here. I'm going to help."

"No ether."

"I'll be right here, Li."

"No ether."

"Are we ready?" asked Dr. Horgan.

"I guess we can give him a spinal, all right."

"If you don't trust us, how would you like us to operate without giving you anything?" Dr. Horgan said coldly.

"All right." Li smiled happily.

"He means it, too," Lucas said.

"I have no doubt. Shall we get going?"

Li rested quietly under the spinal, feeling nothing, forcing his eyes half open to watch Lucas.

Dr. Horgan exposed the knee joint.

He reached for the instrument, his elbow struck Miss Otis. She dropped a retractor.

"Clumsy!" he cried. He looked at the tray. "Is this your best layout?"

"County—" said Lucas.

"I wouldn't use such stuff on a horse."

It was necessary to see nothing and to hear nothing. Nothing really mattered except Li's leg.

"Miss Otis is good enough to come in and assist us from time to time," Lucas said mildly.

Dr. Horgan grunted.

"Look at that mess! We've got to get that bone out of there, first—"

Lucas' fingers raced to help. The shattered fragments of the kneecap were lifted out or dissected free.

"Where's that set of mine!" Dr. Horgan cried suddenly.

Miss Otis pointed to the tray where a few tools gleamed in opulent contrast to the scarred and old-fashioned hospital instruments.

"Yes," said Dr. Horgan. He looked at them proudly, greedily. "You'd be surprised what those things cost! I paid forty dollars just for those pliers. Now, how about a saw—"

"We'll have to use a Gigli," Lucas said.

"You use it then!"

Lucas obediently took up the flexible chain of saw, looked inquiringly at Dr. Horgan.

"You see, it's all very simple, just as I told you it would be," Dr. Horgan said irritably. "I could have told you the whole procedure over the phone. Just here—" he pointed to the end of the femur—"cut here, and take a slice off the top of the tibia—"

Lucas worked silently. He finished sawing.

"I'm sorry. I thought there might be something new—"

"Nothing new! Absolutely nothing! You didn't need me at all. Just take off enough to make sure of union, wire the cut ends together—"

He worked deftly.

"You're a great deal faster than I would have been," Lucas murmured.

"Nonsense! You didn't need me at all. All you needed was instruments—I'd have rented you mine—"

He tightened the last wire.

"Now close him up. And if he doesn't infect—in about six weeks—how old is he? Looks a hundred—say eight weeks—ought to last him the rest of his unnecessary life."

Lucas finished the last suture.

"No cut off leg."

The voice came drowsily.

"Everything's fine, Li! You'll be hobbling around good as new."

Dr. Horgan stripped off his gloves and walked toward the dressing room. Lucas lingered.

"You'll be all right, Li," he repeated. He turned to Miss Otis. "I'm sorry about today—"

"That's all right, Doctor—"

"Save those bone fragments, will you?"

"These?"

"That's right. I mean it! He'll want them. Just wrap them up in a piece of gauze and send them in with him. Tell the nurse."

Halfway to the dressing room he halted.

"Be careful of Dr. Horgan's instruments."

"I will, Doctor."

"That's right. And say—was that his wire we used?"

"Yes, it was."

"I want to replace it," Lucas nodded.

"Got something for you," said Dr. Snider. He stood in the doorway. "Something you ought to see."

Lucas glanced uncertainly at the dressing room, then walked to Dr. Snider and followed him into the corridor.

"Seen much typhoid?" Dr. Snider asked conversationally. They turned the corner. They entered a room. The air of the room was heavy with the odor of mice and the fetor of cadaver. Two patients lay in the room's two beds and it was from these humans that the smell was emanating. In the bed nearest him Lucas saw an eight-year-old girl. Her upper lip was drawn back and a dried trickle of blood from a fissure in the cracked lip lay on her dry teeth. The child's hair, once flaxen, lay now in lifeless strands, corpse-tawny about her pinched face. From her nostrils and beside her mouth, dried blood traced thin rivulets, curving over her small lower jaw and reappearing on the pillow on either side of her neck.

The child's face was apathetic, its lines obliterated, the eyes gaped at the ceiling, the neglected windows of an empty house. Her small form in the bed was covered with a thin coverlet and this rose and fell in small, quick, indifferent response to her breathing.

Lucas took up her chart. Dr. Snider watched him alertly, on his mouth the sardonic smile, the *risus sardonicus* which was the shape of his thin lips. His eyes missed no movement of Lucas', no expression of his features.

The fever line was a jagged step. It had reached one hundred and four degrees. The pulse was slow.

Dr. Snider twitched back the coverlet. Brusquely he pulled up the child's nightgown. From the emaciated body the smell of mice and of cadaver rose in a thick and languid cloud. On the gaunt-ribbed chest were scattered clumps of lentil-shaped, rose-colored raised spots. Her abdomen was taut and swollen.

Lucas replaced the coverlet.

The child coughed. The dry, papery sound did not move the mouth, the tiny teeth; from her throat came a hoarse wail. Her sightless eyes did not change.

"Goner," said Dr. Snider.

Lucas turned to him quickly.

"You can smell it," Dr. Snider grinned without mirth. "She'll be dead in forty-eight hours." He thought a moment. "Or if she lives—" He shrugged.

"Hits some of 'em quick. Look at this one."

In the other bed lay a young man, twenty-five, his frame wide and long.

"How you feeling, George?"

The young man's eyes were tightly closed. He breathed loudly through his open mouth. His lips were dry and caked, and a crusted filth of dried saliva, food and epithelium showed on his yellow teeth and bleeding gums. His hand alternately waved weakly, fell back, the fingers picked at the bedclothes. His neck was rigid. Occasionally he slowly ground his teeth.

"George Newcomb. Scoutmaster. Big husky fellow, ain't he! Seems like they take it worse. That's what you get for leading a clean outdoor life, ain't it, George?"

The tendons in the young man's neck leaped briefly. His legs contracted, lifting the coverlet. Dr. Snider forced an eyelid open. The opened eyelid disclosed a gray eye, cloudy, unseeing, mirroring a strange vigil.

"Doesn't hear a goddamned thing!" He lifted the coverlet. "You stink, George!" He turned to Lucas. "He stinks worse'n the other one." He grimaced. "Bed's probably full. Look!" On the sheet, between the young man's uneasily twitching legs, a thin, green, pea-soup dejecta clamored a nauseating stench blending with the odor of mouse fur and the sweet, rotting odor of corpse.

The young man's body was emaciated.

"Don't take long to gaunt 'em out. George, here, by God, he was one of those physical-culture guys. Two weeks ago, anyway. You stink, George," he said, and replaced the coverlet.

Lucas pried open the stinking teeth. The tongue was dry, small, and fissured, here and there it bled through a thick brown fur. The throat was swollen, granular, and eroded.

Lucas stepped back.

"Gotta clean him up," Dr. Snider nodded. "Told 'em once, told 'em forty times George here has to be restrained. Got to strap him down. Bugger'll be out the window and far away . . ."

Lucas took up the chart. The fever peak read one hundred and six. The pulse was fifty.

"This one'll be nuts," said Dr. Snider. "Probably crazy right now. May stay crazy long as he lives—if he don't die in the next couple of days from haemorrhage or perforation or what the hell."

"What will you give them?" Lucas swallowed.

"Ain't a thing! Not one goddamned thing! Just keep feeding 'em and wait and see what happens. That's all there is. There isn't any more." He shrugged. "Seen enough?"

"There isn't anything whatever?" Lucas tried to remember.

"You show me the textbook gives a remedy—any medicine for relief, even—I'll buy you a new car."

The child had begun to breathe stertorously.

"Ought they to be in here together?" Lucas asked uncertainly.

"Just here for the time being. They won't bother each other any. Old George, there, he won't even open his eyes. He's afraid of the light. Christ! I gotta put 'em someplace! Away from the others. Until we get more. And figure things out." He paused at the door. "Funny—old George there, he had it once—and by God, he was vaccinated, too! Did it myself!"

They stood in the corridor a moment. Lucas was bemused with what he had seen, remembering, classifying, storing away.

"Beats reading all hollow, don't it!"

Lucas shook his head.

"Well—" Dr. Snider grinned—"now you can say you seen one!"

Lucas walked thoughtfully back to the operating room. In the operating room Miss Otis was unwinding her turban, preparing to go home.

Lucas walked quickly to the dressing room. He opened the door. The room was empty.

"Where's Dr. Horgan?" he called, surprised.

"Oh, he left, Doctor. He went out soon after you did. I think he was in a hurry."

"That's too bad. I wanted to thank him."

He undressed, showered, dressed in his street clothes.

He was good with those wires, he thought. I wouldn't want to see him again, but he knew his stuff. He twisted them first, then he . . . yes . . . Lord! The types you meet . . . Well, anyway he did it . . .

He remembered the wire.

And I've got to pay him. I'll pay him for that wire if it's the last thing

I do. Two dollars ought to cover it. I'll give him five . . . I'll borrow an envelope from Snider and mail it right here—"

He brought his billfold from his back pocket as he walked from the dressing room. He opened it. He halted. A sensation of cold enveloped his shoulders. His eyes stung. He looked again. The billfold contained three ones.

"Something the matter, Dr. Marsh?" Miss Otis called.

"No—anybody been in the dressing room?"

"Not a soul. I've been here all the time. Nothing's missing, is there? My God, Doctor! Is something missing?"

He looked at her shocked face. He managed a smile.

"I thought I'd put a keepsake here," he said. "I guess I left it home."

"Oh, yes! Because not a soul has—"

"It's all right," said Lucas. "And thank you, Miss Otis. Husband all right?"

"Same as ever," she sighed.

"He'll be all right," he said mechanically. The operating-room doors swung behind him.

He stood on the front steps. He saw again the billfold, saw himself extract bills, reserve the red-marked five-dollar bill, a ten, three ones, saw himself hand fifty dollars to Job. The mercurochrome-stained five-dollar bill had been in the wallet. And a ten.

He walked slowly to his car. He sat a moment, trying not to think. His thoughts moved in remorselessly. He saw Dr. Horgan's face again, heard his voice, had again a hazy memory of the locker room at school, of something not to be spoken of. He shivered.

"A doctor is a thief," he said aloud.

"A thief," he said again, hearing it.

He looked miserably at his lap.

At the Valley Hospital he avoided the corridors, waited until he was sure Dr. Castle had gone. Then, apathetically, he made his rounds.

In the morning the County Hospital had received its first two typhoid-fever cases. By noon it had five. Before the day ended an entire ward had been set aside and eight cases were isolated there.

They were all adults with the exception of the little girl. Greenville's schools were not closed until the fifth day, but the official closing was a formality, for after the second day, when twenty-two children collapsed in the classroom, attendance dropped steadily. The third day eleven more sickened. The fourth day twenty-seven were downed, and on the fifth day, although only fourteen more children were stricken, the classrooms were almost empty, two of the teachers were victims, and few of the remaining staff appeared.

By the fifth day one hundred and seventeen persons, of whom eighty-one were children, lay helpless in their beds, hosts to a deadly plant occurring in short, plump rods having twelve threadlike filaments with which the healthy plant propelled itself through the blood stream, feeding ravenously, seeking lymph, reproducing by binary fission each twenty minutes, then more slowly, an army of millions of marching plants, their numbers becoming so huge that their deadly wastes began to sicken a number of themselves.

Before this new invasion the community of Greenville retreated, dispersed, flung away habits, codes, and its individual connections with each other. The depression, stripping them of the practiced tools of survival, of money, of reserves, of the logic of work and saving, had left them single-minded in a will to survive, those who had nothing were driven on by the implacable acids of hunger, those who had a little fought to keep that little, those rare few who were untouched straddled what they had, prepared to die for it. They lived in fear, they lived in terror, many of them lived without hope, many were stripped of any obligation but the ruthless necessity to survive and to take what was necessary, to do what was necessary, abandoning any pretense of law, custom, or social behavior. But they lived, and the considerations that faced them were still the considerations of man's historic attempt to survive on the basis of rules laid down for each generation. There were even dim rules for calamity, there were the memories of other calamities, there was a subconscious sense that what was happening was man's doing and what man had done man could undo and that if a depression lasted forever man could adapt to that, too.

But before this new assailant the community overnight lost all semblance of communal life. This was not man-made. This was not an enemy of a way of life, of a blueprint for living, of any convention of hope, or agreement of thought. This was an enemy of the body. This was an enemy against which no man knew a sure defense. No woman knew whether her child was protected. No one knew, moving in terror, whether battle had been joined in their tissues as they walked, slept, talked, or looked wide-eyed at each other.

Panic and rumors began on the fourth day. The hospitals were now filled, the sidewalks were almost empty, hardly a street in Greenville but had at least one house bearing the white placard of isolation. The school janitor, an elderly man, died in the County Hospital of heart failure. News of his death raced through the town with stunning speed. A family of five was stricken simultaneously. Two died before the day ended.

Without conference, struck in unison by a single idea, dozens deserted the safety of their houses and rushed to the doctors' offices, most of them had never been immunized, they crowded the offices, spilling over onto the steps outside, filling the sidewalk, demanding vaccination.

When this onslaught began no doctor was in, all were scattered treating the sick, leaving hasty orders, rushing to the next case. Recalling this, dozens left their siege posts, drove frantically through the streets looking for the doctors' cars. When they found these some waited beside the cars, some rushed into the placarded houses demanding to be vaccinated, some pulled the doctors from the bedsides.

Lucas had been out in the countryside. When he returned to his office he was amazed to see a crowd waiting on his steps. His car was instantly overwhelmed. Women who had brought their children pushed them out of the way to offer their own bared arms. Men pushed savagely past the women. They invoked him with meaningless cries:

"Remember me, Doc! I'm the one fixes your car—!"
"Doc, Doc! Here's the money . . ."
"I'll give you fifty—"
They screamed their claims, they invented claims, they beseeched him in the name of God, a minister implored him in the name of professional brotherhood, they buffeted him, they tore at his clothing, women fell at his feet, scrabbling to find his legs, clutching them, were trampled upon, were dragged away by stronger women, one held her child overhead, shaking it to catch his eye, her eyes blind, her mouth open, screaming sound without words.
He reached the steps, finally. He clutched his bag with both arms from the hands that strove to tear it from him. He had begun yelling for their attention at the top of his voice at the first onslaught. "Wait!" he yelled. "Wait! Listen to me!" Over and over, unheard.
Now they heard him, suddenly. Those nearest him became aware that he was yelling something. Their clamoring stopped. The rest clamored on. But in that small diminution of sound, his voice roared out, a few more heard him,
". . . the worst possible thing you could do . . . the quickest way to get it is mobbing up . . . crowds . . . some of you may be passing it on right now . . ."
Suddenly there was silence. Now they were all listening. They were holding their breath. The screams of the children began again but over their terror and protest and pain Lucas' voice carried easily.
". . . vaccination's no guarantee—it's no guarantee . . ." He heard his own voice shrieking in the sudden quiet. "It's no guarantee!" he said in a hoarse voice more nearly his own. They listened, drinking every word, scanning every line of his face. "If one of you has it—every one of you has been exposed. That's what you've done! That's what you're doing!"
The mob moved uneasily.
In another instant it would have scattered.
"I'll take you as long as you're here. The damage is done. Make a line. Stay four paces apart. Women with children first. Children next. Then you men . . ."
Kristina was at the County, Miss Snow was nursing in a private home. An hour later Lucas stood, needle poised, waiting the next bared arm. But the office was empty. He had vaccinated perhaps half the throng. The rest had vanished. Some had slipped away, pricked by a new rumor that vaccination itself might bring on typhoid. Some had stood their ground as long as they could, then pelted off, terrorized by the proximity of the others. Once the flight had started the full exodus followed swiftly.
Lucas stared at his last patient. The woman watched him anxiously.
"You next?"
She reached behind her, extricated a child clinging to her skirts, pushed him forward.
Lucas examined the child.
"He doesn't seem marked up."
The woman looked at him, bewildered.

"One of the few kids that wasn't all scratched and bruised—"

"Wasn't it awful?" the woman cried. "Did you see them? Some of those women—why, I know some of those women!—actually pushing away their own kids to get to you first! And the men—!"

"I was there," Lucas said dryly.

"You might expect it of some of the men," the woman said, angry, now. "But women! Mothers! Their own children!"

Lucas bandaged the child's arm and pulled down his sleeve.

"He's all right now. How about you?"

"I was vaccinated a year ago," she said. She shook her head. "That I should have lived to see the day! Foreigners, maybe—but our own women!—our own Greenville women—why, I went to school with some of those girls!"

Lucas rose tiredly.

"He might be a little under the weather for a day or so—" He patted the boy's head. "You all right, little fellow?"

"He's an angel," the woman said. She swept him up in her arms. "He's like his father. Never opens his mouth and wouldn't cry if his teeth were falling out. Aren't you, darling?"

Lucas smiled obediently.

The woman paused in the doorway.

"We aren't all like that . . ."

Lucas nodded.

The door closed behind her.

He looked at his hands. They were trembling. He discovered that his whole body was trembling. He rose abruptly. He was anxious to leave this scene. He escaped to the County Hospital.

There was order, here. It was a feverish, crowded plague world, but there was order. He saw Kristina almost at once. She was at a patient's bedside, helping Dr. Snider. Her eyes were dark with fatigue, she looked at him wordlessly for a moment, she washed her hands and turned to the next patient.

"I been trying to tell her to take it a little easy," Dr. Snider said mildly.

"How long have you been on duty?"

"Since this morning only—I'm all right—"

"You quit at five!"

"But Luke, I'm strong, it's nothing—!"

"Five! You're nurse enough to know what fatigue can do—"

"The others—"

"Never mind the others! Dr. Snider will take care of the others!"

Lucas turned away. Dr. Snider followed.

"I been trying to tell her," he said.

Lucas glanced about the ward. What he saw surprised him.

"You seem to be doing all right!"

"This is old stuff to me."

"Except for the crowding you'd never know you were handling an epidemic."

"You don't have to look so surprised."

"I am surprised! This is a good job, Doctor!"

"What you fellows forget now and then is there's things we know too. We old-timers know a thing or two. Maybe not what you fellows know—new stuff—but you take typhoid—"

"There isn't much typhoid any more, you know."

"Nobody ever found a cure for it, either."

"Just prevention—"

"Sure! The water supply. Damned near wiped it out, didn't we! All you have to do is keep the water clean, have good sewers, eliminate the backhouse, watch your food handlers—and vaccinate!"

"But here it is—"

"That's right, here it is! How many people you know get vaccinated today? Right here in Greenville, knowing we get a little every year? No, by God! No typhoid—no vaccination. And just let a catastrophe come along, mess up the water system—take any big city—and where the hell's your medical profession! Bare-assed! That's where they are. I bet ninety percent of the buggers graduating today never even seen a case of typhoid! Just to name one! To say nothing of typhus, erysipelas, diphtheria, smallpox, God knows what else."

"You've done a fine job, Dr. Snider. A fine, fine job . . ."

"Can't get over it, can you?"

He peered up at Lucas, pleased, his mouth corners stained with tobacco juice escaping in his excitement, his rumpled and soiled white coat unbuttoned.

"Once I saw damned near a whole township wiped out—Christ, it was an old story, then. Castle get ahold of you? We're supposed to meet here tonight. My office. Six o'clock. Got a Board of Health man coming probably never saw a case of typhoid either—some young squirt . . . Christ, I don't know, you can smell it—"

"You mean—smell it? Actually—"

"Sure you can smell it. You get so you can smell it a mile away. And they get a funny look in their eye—"

Lucas sighed. He smiled politely.

"You'll hear tonight! Don't worry! Castle'll tell you."

He waved, and grinning happily, bumbled off down the corridor.

The five men gathered in Dr. Snider's office had witnessed an almost identical day. They spoke of the mobs with affected humor, warily, and they added the cases, and there had been another death. Lucas glanced surreptitiously at Dr. Binyon and Dr. Blake. Their urbanity and their aloofness were gone tonight, and they sat as Lucas sat, their pads before them, waiting for Dr. Castle to begin.

He rose and began without preamble.

"I'm going to be saying things you already know. It looks like we're in for it." He paused. Then he began rapidly: "Fifty percent of your cases will be between fifteen and twenty-five years. Typhoid's a disease of the lymphatic tissues. Peyer's patches in the intestine, those are the worst hit. And when they break down they'll be the biggest killers. Always figure they've waited a week before coming to you. They'll have a dull headache, no appetite, general aching, daytime drowsiness, nighttime restlessness. At that time the organism's in the blood. Watch for bronchitis. That's very common with typhoid. Watch for nosebleed. That's fairly common too. And, of course, a swollen, tender spleen. And you've always got fever. Always. Sometimes after a few days all symptoms will go away, there won't be any swollen spleen, no rose spots, not even a positive Widal. And they'll have it just the same—"

"You can smell it!" Dr. Snider cried.

"There are doctors who say they can smell it. It may be so. Not all of us have had a chance to develop a selective sense of smell. Not for typhoid. One of the best signs is slow pulse and fever. One hundred and five fever and a pulse of less than a hundred. When you get a marked rise in pulse rate—watch out! It's probably a complication. Embolus, pneumonia, haemorrhage, perforation of the intestine. You'll get a dicrotic beat—"

"I've felt a pulse with a quadruple beat!" Dr. Snider said proudly.

"It's true. But dicrotic is by no means rare. But at the end of the first week you'll get the rose spots. Pale, circular red spots, shape of a lentil, somewhat elevated, somewhat firmer than the surrounding skin. And they fade on pressure. And most of them will be on the abdomen and chest. When they're numerous you'll find them on the back and even on the extremities and face. You'll get rose spots in more than ninety percent of all cases. The thing about these is that they're croplike. And a crop lasts from three to five days."

"How about the hair?" asked Dr. Binyon.

"That comes later. Loss of hair almost always follows a severe case. But only from the head, and of course it grows back. Sometimes they lose their nails too. But that comes later."

"There's the tongue," Dr. Kauffman said diffidently.

"Yes. In the early stages it's moist, covered with a gray fur. But the border, extending from a triangular area extending from the tip, is bright red. Clean at the border—furred in the middle. That's typhoid tongue."

"You can see it in their eyes," said Dr. Snider.

"I've heard that, too. You'll get a tremor of the lips and tongue at the height of the disease and the speech will be hesitating and trembling. You've got to watch them like hawks. You'll almost always have delirium. And there has to be someone to watch them."

"They're foxy—they're just waiting until your back is turned—goddamn I had one jump out of a six-storey window once!" Dr. Snider cried.

"It's best to tie their feet down. They're very shrewd in their delirium. They'll wait until your back's turned, they'll knock you down. Sometimes they start right in being maniacal. You can pretty well figure the blood's carried the bacteria to the meninges of the brain. In infancy—watch for vomiting. Watch for convulsions."

He paused.

"A lot of this you already know. You want to figure that the complications are the killers. Seventy-five percent of typhoid deaths come from complications. And complications are the rule of typhoid. And not the exception. Intestinal haemorrhage—and you know the signs of haemorrhage—the chill, rapid pulse, low blood pressure, collapse. You won't get much pain with haemorrhage. And about twenty-five percent will die. Perforation—usually the onset is sudden, severe pain over the whole abdomen—it gets worse and deep breathing or changing position accentuates it. The face gets a pinched look, the look of anxiety. The heartbreaking thing is there's not a single sign or symptom characteristic of typhoid perforation. You'll have to weigh the evidence. You'll get perforation in about three percent and my rule is—when in doubt, operate."

He paused again. He looked inquiringly at Dr. Kauffman, then at Dr. Snider.

"That's about all. The rest is in your textbooks too. You'll want to watch for hoarseness. Ulceration of the larynx is pretty frequent. So far as the heart's concerned, myocarditis is the most frequent cardiac complication of typhoid—an edema of the feet, a markedly slow pulse, a faint heart tone, usually a mitral systolic murmur. They usually get away with it. Unless, like Charley, the school janitor . . . The picture is one you have to weigh as a whole . . . Even the Widal isn't much good to you, it won't be positive until the end of the first week—maybe not till the third. And a single negative test never excludes the possibility. And don't forget—the vaccinated get it too, and if they've been vaccinated there goes your Widal! . . . Isolation, vaccination, disinfection of stool, of everything handled by the patient—tell your nurses, your families, to watch for swollen bellies, hiccups . . . and vaccinate . . . And remember, vaccination ought to be repeated every three years . . . Wherever you go . . . vaccinate! . . . I guess that covers it."

"Try not to get overtired," said Dr. Kauffman.

"That's very important—"

"Feed 'em plenty of milk," said Dr. Snider.

"Would you say so? I think experience has been that milk—"

"We always fed 'em milk till it came out of their ears!"

"It's a question whether the curd doesn't decompose enough in the intestine to swell the gut and predispose to perforation. I think a high-calorie diet—I wonder if you wouldn't try that, Dr. Snider?"

"Try anything!" he shrugged.

Dr. Castle nodded.

"Drugs—well, nothing we've got is much good—maybe hexamethylenamin after the second week to keep the bacteria out of the urine . . . Keep up the fluid output . . . Keep up their strength. They'll burn up half a pound of muscle daily. . . ."

He nodded. He sat down.

"How about us?" Dr. Blake asked. He cleared his throat. Lucas looked at him quickly, then looked away, dreading what was to come.

"The state, of course, will cooperate with all the needed vaccines—will continue to cooperate I should say—"

"I mean us—personally. I mean, going from case to case, wide open to everything—"

"We all know one can't be morbid about things like that. I don't know why, but doctors don't seem to come down with it like the others, we're not immune, of course—but sensible precautions, ordinary care—"

"What are you afraid of?" Dr. Snider demanded. "I been through dozens of these things! I'm like the fellow who had the clap ten times, cured every dose but the last." He waited for a laugh that did not come. "You got nothing to be scared of," he said contemptuously. "Nothing the rest of us ain't got!"

"I'm not thinking of myself so much," Dr. Blake licked his lips. "It's the patients I'm thinking of—some of us might be carriers, for all we know."

"It's all right, John," said Dr. Binyon. "We know what you mean."

"Of course!" said Dr. Castle.

"And you, Castle, take a little of your own advice about taking it easy," said Dr. Snider. "You with that heart of yours."

Lucas assembled his notes and rose with the rest. And with the rest he departed without ceremony for his home, his dinner, and the night's case load.

"I don't like the way you're looking," he said suddenly during dinner.

"I'm all right," said Kristina. "Just not used to working so much," she said apologetically. But her heart bounded at his concern. "Just tired," she said. "Just tired, that's all."

He inspected her face narrowly.

"I appreciate all you're doing. I want you to know that. But there's no need killing yourself. You're not helping me, you're not helping anybody—"

"Tomorrow I be fine," she said steadfastly. She kept her eyes down lest he be troubled at the joy and gratitude in them.

The town was a thousand houses, each in a state of siege, during the next three days. Rumors multiplied. There were no further disturbances on a scale to match those of the fourth day. On the ninth day a new rumor, the rumor of possible carriers, swept the houses. A few humans diverted from universal fear eagerly focussed on the idea of a human foe. On this day a small group outside one of the garages looked up from their speculation on this new rumor to see Agnes marching down the street with a basket of fresh bread she had come to sell. They watched her warily. She came closer. Suddenly a sixteen-year-old boy screamed,

"There she is! That's the one! There's your carrier!"

They looked at each other, dumfounded.

Moments later, given a victim, the crowd surrounded Agnes. Her eyes flickered from face to face, bewildered.

"Got a backhouse, ain't ya!"

"Sure! Live in the woods in some filthy hole—!"

"Lookit the bread! Bringing it right in with her!"

"By God, I'll bet you—! I'll bet you—!"

They moved in. The bread scattered. She swung the basket at them wildly, an instant later they had torn it from her hands, one of them knocked her to her knees. From the *Greenville Clarion* across the street Bemis Shedd came running, he reached her first, others came, the crowd dispersed, shouting defiantly, watchful, still ready to pounce.

Shedd brushed at Agnes' faded overalls.

"They don't know any better," he said, red-faced, ashamed.

"It's all right, Bemis!" She pushed his hands away. "It's all right," she said, trembling. "I know them. I know their kind. None better."

"Don't be scared—"

"I'm not scared. But if I had a gun—"

He looked quickly away from her eyes. Her bread lay scattered and trampled, worthless. Someone picked up her basket, brushed it awkwardly, handed it to her.

She got back in her old car and without another word drove back to the woods. On the way she began to estimate the time necessary to turn out a fresh batch. The canned milk and the medicines the bread had not bought still had to be purchased. When she arrived home she was quite calm. She had not time for amazement or anger. Gloria and the child were sleeping.

Lucas called the pottery plant that evening.

"I can't go anywhere with you now," Harriet began.

"I just wanted to make sure you're all right," he protested.

"I've been vaccinated."

"Within the past three years? If you haven't you'd better let me give you another—"

"Two years ago. I'm fine . . . You've got your hands full, haven't you?"

"We've been pretty busy—typhoid on top of everything else—"

"You sound tired."

"I just thought I'd drop by for a few minutes."

"Here?"

"No, no! Home, maybe—"

"Oh, Lucas!" Then her voice tightened with anger. "Is that all you think of me? Are you really serious—?"

"What do you mean? I could meet you, then, no one could see us—"

"See us! You actually mean to stand there and say you'd come over—you'd—you've been handling them and saturated with them—you'd deliberately expose me like that?"

"Harriet! Listen! And you've been vaccinated, anyway!"

"And is that positive protection? Didn't you tell me yourself—"

"All right, Harriet. Never mind. Don't get excited."

"I'm not excited! It's you that—oh, I'm sorry, darling—it's what we've been going through—I am a girl you know, I think of my hair falling out, the blotches, maybe being crippled . . . I'm sorry . . . You come over. You think it's all right? All right, then. Come over."

"No, no. You're right. You're right, Harriet. We can wait."

"Why take any chances—"

"Absolutely. Will you take care of yourself? Will you do that?"

"Like a tiger!"

"For me?"

"For you, darling . . . For us . . ."

On the twelfth day, Tom Yannis, janitor at the Greenville Bank, lay in his home, alone and delirious. A small group gathered outside the bank doors, chatting easily.

"We've had it before and lived through it—"

"Never this bad, though!"
"More, that's all. Give it another week, say two—"
"Lot of people in this town going to have pretty red faces—going all to pieces like that—"
"What's keeping old Tom, I wonder?"
"First time he's been late opening up in thirty years! Yes sir! I'll bet it's all of thirty—"
"None of you boys got the key?"
The clerks looked at each other helplessly.
"Where's Mr. Wedekind?" The speaker looked at his watch. It was twenty past nine.
"He's late," said one of the women, a teller, "sometimes he doesn't get here till nine-thirty—"
"Wonder where old Tom is!"
New faces had arrived to whom the delay was explained and who frowned and looked at their watches. A few loafers wandered up to watch and listen and offer advice.
"Somebody else ought to have a key—"
"The old boy's probably off drunk—"
From nearby stores heads began to appear looking curiously toward the gathering group before the bank doors. People on other errands stopped uncertainly and watched.
"For Heaven's sake!" One of the bookkeepers tossed her head exasperated.
"Go call Mr. Wedekind, Helen," a clerk bade. "Go ahead! Hurry!"
"And I'll go see what's happened to Tom!" another clerk cried.
They ran off in opposite directions.
Seeing them run those who had been watching promptly rushed to the bank.
From up the street, seeing this new movement, a woman screamed. She dropped her bundles. She screamed again.
"The Bank!"
She joined those running. The cry was taken up. Shops emptied. Those who ran into the streets saw the crowd rushing toward the bank. They ran after them, shouting as they ran.
Within fifteen minutes the news had reached every house in Greenville.
"The bank is closing!"
"Which bank!"
"The Greenville Bank!"
Long before the last depositor arrived on the run, the clerk who had rushed off to telephone Mr. Wedekind arrived in Dr. Castle's car, flourishing the key overhead,
"It's all right," he shouted, "I've got it! It's all right! Mr. Wedekind's sick—Tom's sick—I've got the key—"
They engulfed him. He was lifted off his feet, borne bodily to the doors, jammed against them, he worked desperately, the key shot home, the doors opened and he fell forward and was trampled underfoot in the onrush.

Dr. Castle stood as close as he dared to the plunging stream pouring into the bank.

"It's all right," he called over and over again. "Mr. Wedekind's sick —I've just come from him—your money's safe—why do you think I drove back with the key—"

They rushed past him, unhearing.

"You fools!" he shouted, as the bank filled. "You know a crowd's the best way to pick up typhoid—the man you're pushing against may have it—typhoid, you fools! Typhoid!"

A few drifted fearfully away, watched from a small distance.

The run was soon over. The bank closed before noon. The crowd still lingered, quieter now, reluctant to go home, hoping for a miracle. Police dispersed the last of them near nightfall.

"It's a good sign," Dr. Castle said. "You put your money where I told you?"

"What there is of it," said Lucas. "What's good about it!"

"Money's got the upper hand again," Dr. Castle said quietly. "Now they're back to worrying more about their money than about dying."

"I hadn't thought of that," said Lucas after a shocked pause. "I—I guess you're right—"

"Sure! How many new today?"

"Twenty-two."

"I've got eighteen . . . How's Snider?"

"Twelve more, ten from my twenty-two—"

"Kauffman's got fifteen. Binyon and Blake got twenty-four— Valley's jammed—"

"County, too—"

"Hope we don't get any more from today . . . You can't isolate the bastards . . . you could a couple of days ago . . . money or no money . . ."

"Are you taking care of yourself?"

"I'm watching . . ."

"I mean it!"

"Think you can help me with a gall bladder tomorrow?"

"Won't hold?"

"I don't think so . . . we're short an anesthetist, too . . ."

"No!"

"Died this morning."

"I'll be there. One-thirty?"

"Right!"

The next days were the worst. Now all lives interlaced, intertwined upon a framework of fever and delirium, of nursing and death and exhaustion.

The tale of death by a little telling lost the syllables of flight. The tale was freighted with terror, the horror passed in sick flashes between the eyes of the teller and the hearer. It was a horror and a terror too great for grief. But the legs no longer trembled to flee.

A primal center, a center evolved with man himself, functioning through the trumpetings of terror and the deafening keen of panic, continued to send its imperturbable message and now was dimly heard by the other centers. And this center asserted that man was innately organized to adapt to anything life could marshal, anything, anything whatever. And that he would endure this too. And the principle of his species would live through it. And that a prodigy lived with becomes commonplace.

And the terror gave way to fear, and the panic became apprehension. And the rules of tribal living slowly returned to precedence over the rule of survival, and it was like a storm lingering, its surprise endured, its violence become familiar, and the people of Greenville drew together again.

At the County Hospital Kristina worked long days and she would have worked nights if Lucas had not prevented her. Miss Otis was ill, her crippled husband was early stricken, and as he moved into the third week, she who had nursed him constantly day and night fell ill also, he died and she did not know it, they took him from the house and she was not aware, staring at the ceiling in mindless stupor. Kristina took her place in the operating room. There was typhoid, but other illness, other mischance, did not stop. They operated daily, the acute cases, those that could not be put off; babies were born, bones cracked, split, tissues were sundered in all the mischances of living. There was typhoid but these others did not stop.

"I don't like the way you're looking," Lucas said one morning. "I don't like what's happening to you."

Now Kristina held her breath, knowing what grew within her body.

"I'm tired," she said. "But you're tired too. We're all tired."

"Maybe I'd better look you over. Maybe you ought to have a complete check."

She looked at him numbly.

He was caring for her as a mechanism, there was little love or hate or any sentiment in his mind, she knew. It was his duty and he was caring for her. But he had not put her away. And chance was helping her, there was too much to do, his every moment was for the sick, what had happened blotted out for this armistice of time even the other woman, the woman who lived with them, now. The stranger who was present at their bed and board and in all their living together. For this time she was cancelled too, she could make no gains. What Kristina had of Lucas was hers.

"You got enough to do," Kristina said. "If I need a doctor you need a doctor too." She must shift his attention. Luke was incredibly sharp. Sometimes his eyes went right into you. He missed nothing. "Look at you," she said carefully. And his eyes were black-rimmed, his cheeks sunken, and a pang smote her but she knew that somehow healing healed, that a doctor and a nurse unaccountably did not sicken, no, not very often, because they healed, and healing somehow held them up and healed them. Until the heart gave way.

"Sleep doesn't seem to rest you," Lucas said. And now he was looking at her fully, the look he had when all of him was his eyes and the body was a book. "Your cheeks are puffy—"

"You better take care of Dr. Castle. Did you see how he looked yesterday? Can he keep this up much longer? I don't think that girl of his helps him enough—"

Lucas frowned. She had succeeded. He was thinking of Dr. Castle.

"He's going to drop right in his tracks," he said.

"You better talk to him. Why can't he do like Dr. Binyon or Dr. Blake? Why can't he send most of his cases up here? Or out of town if they got the money?"

"There isn't room up here. He knows it." Lucas' face darkened.

She watched him, waiting. She was safe, his attention was diverted.

And what would she do? What would happen? The baby grew steadily. The baby was a little lump of tissue, having form now, nested in the uterus, cell to cell, it was a living thing. And it was more than blind multiplication, it was an idea, it was a concept, a whole myriad of rules surrounded it. Her child and Lucas'. It was a fact now. Nothing could alter it. One day it would be born. One day it would be noticed. And on that day—

"If you don't need me now I better go into the wards," Kristina said resolutely.

"Yes," said Lucas. He put out his hand.

"Wait. I want to tell you something . . ." He looked at her tired face, the familiar face of the woman he had married, the symbol of the human of whose limitations he despaired, the wall he could not penetrate, could not interpenetrate with his thoughts and his dreams. His heart winced. "I want you to know something. I want you to know that I appreciate what you've done during all this. Wait! . . . And you're the best operating-room nurse I've ever seen—and I don't believe there's a better one!"

She lowered her head.

"That's all," he said. "I want you to know that. Because it's true."

He looked at her a moment longer. She raised her head.

"I go into the wards now," she said, her voice low.

He looked after her. Then the day grasped at him, snatched him up, whirled him away in the human tide which had become a current.

"Now, what do you want me to do?" Dr. Castle asked irritably when they met for a moment at the Valley Hospital. "You want me to just quit and let them take care of themselves?"

"You're not going to be much good to them, dead."

"I never felt better in my life—"

"Or looked worse—"

"What the hell has looks got to do with it! The layman thinks we're working like hell, why, all we are is in motion, that's all. We're just in motion. Rushing from house to house—but it's the car that's doing the work—and when we get there what do we do? Wrestle with 'em? Hell, we don't lift anything heavier than their wrists, we look at them, we shake something out of a bottle—"

"You should have been a lawyer. And by the way, what do you think your friend Cosgrove's doing?"

"I know what he's doing. He's up at the County every day. I sent him up there."

"You did! I thought it was a little experiment of mine—"

"He wants to help the common man, the County's the place for him and I told him so."

"Well, that's what he's doing. He's emptying bedpans, and being a glorified orderly, and the only complaint he's making is that the poor ought to have the same treatment as the rich. I told him the Eberthella makes no distinctions. He snarled something about capital—I think he thinks the government ought to step in, something about all these humans belonging to the state . . . By God, I'll say this for him: he's practicing what he preaches."

"I'm a great believer in catastrophe. Once they get over the shock, people always show up at their best in a catastrophe."

"I can't say I've seen much change."

"Well," said Dr. Castle reflectively, "they haven't failed me yet. You still working alone?"

"Sometimes Miss Snow comes in for an hour or so—I can use her better nursing patients."

"Mine's afraid."

"No!"

"Yup! . . . Granite came in to see me, wanted to know what he could do . . . I told him to borrow some money. Mrs. Kauffman's working night and day, your friend Agnes is on her fifth case—"

"And three from me—and she's got that young girl working with her, you'd think they'd be afraid for the baby—"

"So you think I ought to lie down and let them take over?"

"But just take it easier. I don't have to tell you about that. You can do that, can't you?"

"We need room. That's what we need. More room—some big building, someplace—a house . . ."

"A house!" Lucas cried.

"What is it?" Dr. Castle clutched at Lucas' sleeve.

"I'm stupid! I'm just plain, blind stupid! Dr. Runkleman's!"

"That big house!"

"Right next to the office! Right where we could keep an eye on them!"

"The bank—"

"That's where I'm going!"

Thomas Epperly was a bachelor. He was a meek man for a banker, Lucas pondered, shaking his thin hand, a meek, bald little man in his early fifties, and his story was a simple one. Greenville knew it well. Forty years ago he had gone into the bank and soon after his father had died and on his thin shoulders had fallen the responsibility for his mother and three sisters. After a few years he had buried his mother. Then one by one he had supplied the trousseaux for his sisters. It was then too late for marriage. So Thomas Epperly accepting his long troth one day had quietly and imperceptibly married the bank.

He sat down at his desk when he had seated Lucas and smiled diffidently. He heard Lucas through. He tapped his teeth reflectively.

"It would be ideal, wouldn't it," he mused.

"Right next to my office, centrally located—and we wouldn't have to use it long—"

"That's right . . . just until the worst of this is over . . ."

"It would be a fine thing," Lucas said warmly. For there was no doubt in him now but that his mission had succeeded, all that remained was to impart to this fine little chap some of the jubilation this boon for the sick had roused in himself. And some of the praise he richly deserved.

"There's no doubt of it," Mr. Epperly sighed. He shook his head sadly. "I wish we could do it . . ."

"But it's yours! It's the bank's! Why, you don't even have to think twice!"

"That's it. It's the bank's. It's something we own—something whose value would forever after be marred—'that's the place they used as a pesthouse during the typhoid'—you know how people are . . ."

"But it could be fumigated, completely cleaned, safe as a church—why half the houses in Greenville are under that blight right now! Do you mean to say they couldn't be sold because of that?"

"It's a little different," Mr. Epperly said shyly. "Using it as a sort of hospital . . . Knock its value clear to smithereens . . . and it's such a shame . . . such a shame . . . just standing there, idle . . . and people needing it so bad . . ."

"But it's the bank's!" Lucas cried incredulously. "You can do as you please with it, Mr. Epperly!"

Mr. Epperly shook his head gently.

"No . . . not the bank's . . . one of my sister's young ones, her only son, died last week . . . understand . . . I know . . ."

"But all you have to do—"

"I know. I know how it seems to you. But a bank is a building. That's all it is. Just a building. A building with books in it. And people who keep the books. And that house—why, that house belongs to the depositors, Dr. Marsh. Do you see? It belongs to everybody who's put their money in this building—and if there were just a few of them maybe we could even ask them—but they're not all in Greenville—and some of them are companies, and that's more people—and in the end there's nobody to ask. Do you see, Dr. Marsh? Do you see?"

"No, I don't! There's this perfectly empty building and people sick and dying—"

"There's one or two other empty houses in Greenville, Dr. Marsh. Nothing like this one! Not nearly so convenient or so big and all. But you couldn't just walk down the street and walk up to one of those empty houses and say: 'I'll take this one—or that one.' You couldn't do that . . . those houses belong to somebody . . . it would be . . . Well, it would be stealing, wouldn't it!"

The little man looked up at Lucas forlornly. His eyes were full of sorrow. His mouth twitched wretchedly.

"I know . . . I know what you're going to say. 'It might be a good idea.' I know . . . It's your job. You got to look after their bodies. And fight for them no matter what. And they gave me the job of looking after their possessions . . . and fight for them the same way . . ."

There was no answer. Lucas' lips drew thin.

"You realize, Mr. Epperly, that one of your own, another of your sisters' children—"

Mr. Epperly looked at him steadily.

"I know," he said. "I been thinking of that . . . and there's just nothing I can do . . ."

Lucas rose.

"You'll forgive me for saying that," he said gruffly.

Mr. Epperly smiled.

"I know," he said.

There was no time for puzzling an answer. I'm sworn to protect the cell, Lucas mused helplessly, and he's sworn to protect the depositor. He drove back to his office, a dairyman was waiting for him, he had come to donate milk, he had a truckful parked outside, where should he deliver it.

"Pasteurized, of course?"

"Good raw milk! Best in the county! Pure Jersey!"

The man waited pridefully.

"I see . . . Of course there's one thing we've got to watch—"

"There's no typhoid in *this* milk!"

"Of course not . . . No . . . Only, we don't give milk the way we used to—"

"Don't give milk for typhoid?"

"Well, not like we used to. No . . ."

"You mean to tell me you don't give milk for typhoid? Why, that's all anybody's ever given—!"

"Well, you see—"

"By God, I drive all the way in here, hundred and fifty gallons of the purest high-butterfat milk man ever drank—I'm offering it to you free—you understand that? Free!"

"I understand. And don't think I'm not grateful. I know what that means in times like these—it's just that—"

But the man had flung out angrily.

Late in the afternoon, his nostrils thick with the mousy, cadaverish scent of the typhoid in house after house he had entered, Lucas made his way to a shack in Greenville's poor section, his last house call for the day. He sighed wearily. He knocked and opened the door. He entered the dim interior.

"How are you today, Mr. Sarginelli?" he said. And then he stopped abruptly. The filthy interior had been cleaned. The bed with its burlap and rag covers had been tidied. And there were three boys standing in the gloom as startled by the sight of him as he had been by them.

"What's all this?"

"Theesa boys—" Mr. Sarginelli wheezed apologetically.

There was a broken chair beside the bed and a glass of water upon it.

"We were just helping out a little," one of the boys said uneasily.

They were wearing uniforms.

"Why, you're Scouts!"

"Yes, sir. And—"

"Have you been vaccinated?"
"Yes, sir!"
"Sure, now!"
"A year ago, all three of us—and we kind of thought—"
"Old Mr. Sarginelli here—he's the junkman—"
"And we got to talking—"
"And we remembered we hadn't seen him lately—"
"So we thought we'd come down—"
"Do your parents know you're here?"
"No—but—we weren't doing anything—"
"We didn't think it'd be wrong—"
"We were going to tell our folks, all right . . ."
They stared at Lucas waiting.
"I see," he said gruffly. He put down his bag. "Well, we'll just have a look at Mr. Sarginelli here. . . . You've got some pretty good nurses, Mr. Sarginelli." Mr. Sarginelli bobbed his head feebly but energetically and made noises around the tube of the thermometer. "About three times as many as any other patient in town!"
He read the thermometer. He nodded.
"The County for you. Now, don't look so upset. That's the best place for you. The ambulance'll be here directly—"
"We can take care of him, Dr. Marsh—"
"Feed him, and everything—"
"You're going with me."
They followed him silently.
"Did we do something wrong?" one of them ventured after the car had travelled a few blocks.
"Wrong? Listen! If you ever get sick—no matter what happens to you—long as you live—you come to me! Understand? And there'll be no bill!"
"What are you going to tell our folks?" the youngest quavered.
"That's what I'm going to tell them."
From the last house he drove directly to the *Clarion*. He told Bemis Shedd the story.
"By the Jesus!"
"Now, you print it, Bemis! You tell people—"
"By the Jesus Christ!"
Bemis' story said more. And he added a front-page editorial.
The last wavering panic seemed to leave the town. Dozens of humans had been quietly helping their own, and now these and dozens more volunteered, the miasma of typhoid, the smell of it, still hung over the town but there were tales of courage with which to defy it, now, and courage and defiance and service and help, these also became commonplace. And one day a small band of volunteers began to dig where the new water system had been abandoned. And word spread and more came. And a few fell away and a subscription was begun and the poor gave mightily and it became a shame not to give and there were angers on the giving and angers on the work, on who was working and who was not working and who giving and who not, and all these things were not typhoid and they ended gloriously on a day a month later when Henry Granite, hav-

ing browbeaten the council into maneuvers among the town's bonds that guaranteed all of them easy prosecution, announced that the new system would be completed after all.

There was still typhoid. There was still an endless succession of homes cursed with the mouse smell, the winter stayed mild, the undertakers blessed the soft ground, the doctors cursed the temperate weather, life was a fragment of many cases, of the dying, the hairless, the weak, the mouse smell, always the mouse smell, house after house, the mouse smell, the battering days went on, the brief nights, the endlessly battering days, lifetimes lived in a week, in a month, seen for an instant, then passed on. And there was never room. There was never room enough. The homes, the hospitals were crammed, the beds begged for room. In the end the living solved the problem by dying. The dead gave up their beds. And there was room.

The snow fell.

There came a day when there had been no new case for a week.

And another week passed.

And it was over.

Those who were sick began slowly to mend. Some of them died. Some mended and were mindless. There were no new cases. The cold was bitter. Reports of coal thefts began, then became commonplace. A grocery was robbed. The bacillus typhosus, a healthy plant seeking only to live, dwindled, died of its own poisons and of immunizing substance mysteriously decided and manufactured by untaught cells. It dwindled and waited for another time.

One hundred and eighty-four humans had been swept away, lay dead, now, gone to nothingness, presences stopped, were laid away, buried, the earth smoothed above them, obliterated.

Among their number in the quiet, life-alien cemeteries of Greenville lay Henry Granite, Gloria, Mrs. Kauffman, Miss Otis, and Miss Snow.

Oscar Glaimer lingered on.

And so did the rest of Greenville.

And it was over.

⁎ CHAPTER 39

The snow faded quickly, then came on again, there was a little rain and that snow went also and then it was cold and the ground froze. The mouse smell was gone, there were still patients with typhoid and the mouse smell, but it was not all the smell there was, there was every smell of the winter and most of all it was too cold to smell, and it was hard to live, fuel was short, food was very cheap and there was no money to buy it, and when they ate, people pulled the shades down.

Typhoid was not even a fear word now. It was a history word, a tombstone word, a very bad winter turning toward spring. It was not gone yet but there were colds, now, vicious, paralyzing invasions that kept a jobless man bedded when he should be looking for the work that was not there, looking at least, and not bedded. A mixed cold, a mixed virus, a mixed staphylococcus, a chemical that reproduced and mutated, adapting themselves obedient to the changed life condition humans provided them. And the community was full of colds, mild colds, bad colds, pneumonias, a few weak chests surrendered quickly, the waiting-rooms echoed now with coughs and sneezes and thickened nasal voices.

It was the usual winter round, the lot of humans at this season, an old and familiar enemy, the thing that happened to humans when it was winter. But this year the enemy marching onto its familiar battleground found unexpected booty, the weapons left behind in the skirmishing of depression, the siege and the flight of typhoid. And the enemy found the humans weaker.

So it was respiratory infections now, and not typhoid.

In the spring it could be anything, Lucas reflected. When the depression got worse malnutrition would be serious. The external forces of the life man had arranged for his external self, the world he could see and hear and taste and touch and smell was a constant threat, whether man was at work surviving or at dangerous play celebrating it. And the danger of this external world was that it consistently and never-endingly weakened the resources with which the body had to meet its normal seasonal dooms, and the dooms which came from nowhere and were only logical after they had passed and the reasons for them had become clear from the fact that they had occurred.

This cold spell, he estimated, ought to be over in three weeks. And then it would be spring and it was hard to think what it would be then but there would be colds enough, certainly, and of course the winter thaw would release the exuberant plants of childhood diseases. And there would be falls and broken bones because it would be slippery, and hearts slowed by the winter would be commanded to double their potential, and a predictable number would collapse and a predictable number would fail totally.

And then there would be summer.

And the things that lay in wait for man in summer would be—

Kristina made a small noise with her cup and he looked up irritated.

"Did I do something wrong?" she asked anxiously.

"Why do you keep asking me that? It's nothing. You rattled your cup, that's all."

"I'm sorry."

"And don't be sorry! Nothing happened! I was thinking and you rattled your cup and it doesn't matter and there's nothing to be sorry about."

"I didn't know you were thinking."

"It doesn't—oh, the hell with it!"

She looked down.

His irritation faded, her helplessness disarmed him, trapped him, he was angry with himself. Just sitting there, taking it, day in, day out. And doing a goddamned good nursing job, keeping the house up too, if it came to that, doing more than anybody had a right to expect. And when it came to typhoid—

Well, Kristina was used to typhoid. It wasn't so bad when you were used to it. And no matter what—thank God Harriet had kept out of it.

"We've got a full day," he said, making amends.

It was easy. All he had to do was talk, just say anything. Kristina would respond eagerly. No rancor, no hard feelings.

"That mastectomy—I don't see how you're going to do it!" Kristina said.

"That? Oh, you and I'll breeze through that like nothing!"

"Honestly, Luke?" She looked up at him, credulous and respectful.

"Look! It's easy!" He took out a pencil. "Now where the hell's a piece of paper—"

"Use the tablecloth," she said quickly.

"Really?"

"It doesn't matter. Washes right out. Go ahead. Show me."

"Well, we'll start here—" he sketched quickly. "From the axilla . . ."

"Yes," she said. She leaned forward, absorbed, watching the pencil, listening to his voice. "Yes . . . and then . . ."

"And then we go here . . ."

It went very smoothly at the County Hospital that morning. He looked up at the clock and he was surprised at the time they had made. He looked at her, exhilarated.

"We'll have to do that more often! Sketch them out first, at breakfast. Like we did this morning."

"Oh—would you? Really?"

"I'd be doing myself a favor. Look at the time! And I'll tell you something else, Kris. You're getting so you assist pretty good—I don't mean the OR—I mean the assist!"

"I've seen enough—"

"You're getting damned good in there with those clamps—"

"We use to suture sometimes, you know—"

"Really?"

"Sure. Sometimes—even in training—one of the doctors would say: 'All right, nurse. You go ahead and try your hand at a little stitching.' "

"Nobody likes to suture. I don't mind it. I like it. Especially when you're a team—singlehanded, I don't know—"

"When I do wrong you tell me! Don't worry! You just tell me!"

"You just keep on the way you're going," he said. He stripped off his gloves. "You're doing fine, Kris."

He beamed at her. She smiled back, then flustered, turned to the instrument table, watching him from the corner of her eye as he walked out, dropping robe and cap and mask for the dirty surgical to pick up, picking a coat from the linen closet as he went.

In the corridor he saw Dr. Snider and stopped briefly for the day's summary.

"Three more left this morning," Dr. Snider began without preliminary. And "three more" meant three more typhoid. "Two went walking. And Sanderson came for the other. Little Wop girl—Wops sure can't take typhoid."

"She died?"

"Didn't you hear it? From the way that family carried on you'd think they'd lost the Virgin Mary. I thought you'd hear it clear in the operating room."

"I didn't think she'd die."

"Well, she did. About four o'clock this morning."

"I didn't notice any—did she perforate? What happened?"

"I don't think she perforated. I think she just died. Don't worry. There was nothing you could have done about it. When they're going to go—they go."

"I'd rather thought that was why we were around," Lucas said pleasantly.

"You want to do an autopsy?"

"I'll take your word for it." It's a little late to do anything about it now. I don't even want to know what the autopsy would tell me. It wouldn't tell me about her. It would tell me about you. And I know about you. And I don't want another instance. Just let me alone. This, too, was one of the things that lay in wait for humans. This accident. This diploma.

He turned to go.

"Oh, and you can call off your friend now," he said stiffly.

"Who do you mean?"

"That lawyer friend of yours—" his face wore the look it wore when someone had been baiting him—"we don't need him any more. And if you don't mind my saying so—thank God!"

"Cosgrove?"

"Friend of yours, ain't he?"

Lucas shrugged.

"Has he been making trouble? I'll tell him . . ."

Dr. Snider turned abruptly and went into his office.

Lucas passed through the wards swiftly, paused for a moment to pat Li's knee gently, to joke with him while the other patients jealously pretended not to watch. He inspected a woman in labor. He passed quickly through the women's wards.

He went to the room where Oscar Glaimer lay. Before he reached the door Mrs. Glaimer stopped him.

"How's everything?" Lucas asked gently. This was a human tangle it was difficult even to think about. Did she love this man? Or was she in love with his sickness, was it a focus for a whole life of protest and defiant mumbling?

"About the same," she said in a low voice.

"Does he know?"

"My God, no!" she said, shocked.

"You do as you please," he said after a moment.

"I wouldn't tell him for anything!"

"And you—what are you going to do . . . after . . ."

"I haven't thought. I don't know. I know one thing. There's one thing I'm going to do. I'm going to get out of this town as fast as a train will carry me." She shuddered with hatred and distaste.

"You've got folks? You can go to them? I can see that you keep your job here—"

"Here! My God! These lice! I hate every stick and stone, every human that draws breath in this foul hole!"

"I'm sorry—"

"And if you're smart—that's what you'll do too! Get out of here! Get out before it gets you! Break away! Go clean! Because if you don't—it's going to get you too! Yes! You!"

He turned away.

"Let me know," he said. "When you decide—let me know. I wish there was something—"

"There's nothing. So don't bother your head about it. Not that I'm not grateful to you, Doctor. For doing what a doctor ought to do. But don't mind me. It's not only that. You're not like the rest."

"Are you going in?"

She nodded.

"That fellow Cosgrove's with him," she said jealously.

They opened the door, they went in, Glaimer smiled at them from his waxy, yellowing face, the Hippocratic face, the shadows of the facies already there, this human who was planning and hoping, sleeping and rising and the facies already there. Cosgrove rose from a bedside chair.

"I was just going," he said.

"It's time, I think." Lucas looked at his watch.

"Don't worry about me." Cosgrove was smiling at him strangely, there was exultation in it.

"He has to rest," Mrs. Glaimer said angrily.

"You want to see me?" Oscar Glaimer asked Lucas hopefully.

"No," Lucas smiled cheerily. "I'll leave you to your own doctor!" He nodded at Mrs. Glaimer. "She tells me you're doing fine."

He held the door open for Cosgrove. They walked down the corridor together.

"Let's get a cup of coffee," Cosgrove said genially.

Lucas looked at his watch.

"I've got to be at the Valley—"

"We'll get a cup on the way. You can drop me."

"All right," said Lucas. His heart sank. He would have to call Harriet later. The noontime was best. There was always a chance she could get away for a long lunch.

"Well," said Cosgrove, "how's tricks? How's misery paying, boy?"

"Oh, for God's sake, don't start on that. You're not going to start on that, are you?"

"I am not. I am not going to start on anything."

"What are you so happy about?"

"Am I happy? Would that be your diagnosis, Doctor?"

"You're acting like a shyster that's just found a well-forged will—the last time I saw you like this was when I first came here and you had just sprung a guilty child-rapist on a flaw in typing that let him go free until they caught him the next time. Whose justice have you made your water on this morning?"

"I'm above you."

"That still leaves me pretty low—"

"You're not a bad fellow, Marsh. And I want to tell you something—I'm grateful to you! You don't know it! But I am!"

"What are you grateful about."

The car stopped outside a small café.

"Let's go inside," Cosgrove bubbled. "I'll tell you about it!"

They sat in a booth. When the waitress had gone, Lucas looked at his watch.

"You don't like me very much, do you?" Cosgrove smiled.

"Because I looked at my watch? Sometime between now and six o'clock I have to remove two sets of tonsils and adenoids, tend twenty-seven bedridden patients, treat thirty more on office calls—and any emergencies that crop up."

"I used to be like you, you know. That's why I say that. I used to think the law was the purest concept of which humans were capable. And those who practiced the law were its high priests. And now I know that the law is what the judge says it is."

Lucas stirred his coffee.

"That isn't what's made you so happy this morning."

"No, that's not what made me so happy this morning. But when I found out that it was men that governed justice and not justice that governed men—and when I knew that the concept was unchanged—then I knew that there had to be a system in which truth could function."

He waited, looking at Lucas.

"And then you found the system."

"I found the only system. It's so clear, so evident, so perfect that a blind man could see it. What do you do when you describe an ailment to a patient, describe the remedy, and he looks at you blankly and won't take it? Won't accept it? How do you feel, then? You, to whom the body's sacred?"

"I don't see that often. Because I prescribe what has been tested, what his neighbor has used. And to him I'm a man who has been tested by the rules of his fellow men—and *he* comes to *me*—"

"But if he was sick you'd go to him, anyway. That wouldn't stop you. The world's sick, man! Look at it! Look at the horror we're going through now, the senseless, needless horror of depression in the midst of plenty!"

"My remedy is based on a demonstrable truth, on a chain of reasoning, each link having been tested—"

"Oh, man, man, man! The great doctors before Harvey discovered the circulation of the blood—all their remedies were based on just that kind of reasoning—only it was based on the false premise that blood didn't circulate. The great doctors who went step by step through a flawless chain of logic—and then Vesalius discovered that all those years doctors had been blindly following Galen. And Galen's anatomy was based on the cadavers of monkeys!"

"But that was demonstration! Harvey and Vesalius proved what they proved, upset what they upset, by proof! Not an idea—not a vague concept of government but the blood circulating, the pattern of tissues, the visible evidence of government!"

"I'm going to forbear to mention the function of mind, which falls within the province of Medicine. The fact is that the world is sick today, and its political doctors are blind as the medical doctors who said syphilis and gonorrhea were the same disease; the world is sick and there is a remedy crying to be picked up as ether was in the days when patients screamed on the table and that centuries-old discovery then being used as fifteen drops in a glass of water for stomach complaint lay within easy reach, begging to be used for what it was. I know the remedy. I've known it for ten years. And for ten years in this town I've tried to make somebody see it. First I wanted everybody. Then I'd settle for a hundred. Then for a dozen! Just a dozen! All this time . . . Knowing the answer . . . Going crazy with it. And then, finally . . . For One! Just *one*! One convert!"

The bitterness was gone from his face now. The frustration lines, the lip curl, these were smoothed away. His eyes shone. He was younger. He leaned tensely across the table.

"You've got one," Lucas said quietly.

"Yes. I've got one."

"You've got Oscar Glaimer."

A slow smile relaxed Cosgrove's mouth. His eyes glowed.

"You gave him to me—"

Lucas nodded.

"Is he happy now? Do you think it's made him happy?"

"He's more rabid than I am. I have to hold him down. Now that he sees it—"

"You mustn't let him get too excited."

"Oh, I'm careful! He's a fine man, that Glaimer!"

"But he hasn't got the answer."

"He's got the answer to every human problem on this earth."

"Not communism."

"Yes, my friend, my poor, blind friend, yes, communism."

"The problem of man is life."

"The problem of man is man!"

He smiled at Lucas with complete tolerance, full friendship, with gratitude, with affection.

He was almost boyish in his elation. It was another Cosgrove. Lucas felt ill at ease before Cosgrove's dropped guard, his ingenuous joy, his gratitude. He dropped his eyes, remembering the basis of Cosgrove's present rapture. He tried to say something that would spare him, to think of some simple beginning that Cosgrove would accept and extend and thus cushion for himself the inexorable abyss waiting beneath his happy soaring.

He could think of nothing. It was too late now. There were no simple beginnings. He looked steadily at a point below Cosgrove's chin. He saw Cosgrove's collar was frayed. He saw that his tie, dull and worn, was set in a knot in which he had first tied it when it was new. He saw that his suit was nondescript, from the rack of some Greenville merchant, badly fitting, pressed thin. He saw what he had never seen before, a unit of humanity, legally trained, here with him now because he was possessed of an idea, a thin man, meager, wiry, perhaps constitutionally inadequate, intense, heedless of his clothes, his food, his person. He had never seen Cosgrove before. He had only heard him. He was shorter than he would have thought. And what he saw made Lucas' despair keener.

He could not spare him. Nothing could spare him. Cosgrove waited, his eyes were on Lucas, his mouth was friendly, he waited compassionately, he thought Lucas was pondering his last sentence, ready to yield.

He's so happy, Lucas writhed, and I started this, and there's no way out. He's got a twopenny dangle of knotted thoughts on a frame of phrases and he believes that human beings can be made whole by political government. Redeemed by ownership, mended by dialectic, maintained by doctrine. As if man were anything less than his cells, as if the cells were not the basis of democracy, as if any government which was not founded on the cell and its needs, its improvement and its repair and its protection, was not a fantasy, another heartrending evasion of the obvious and the true.

Lucas sighed irritably. Get it over then.

"Well," he said evenly, "anyway you've got a convert."

"Right under my nose! He's a fine fellow, Marsh! Treat him good! How is he! How's he doing?"

"You've solved all his problems—"

"When'll he be out? When are you going to let him go home?"

Lucas rose.

"My Lord!" he said. "Look at the time!"

"You're a good loser, Marsh! I want you to know I'm grateful." He rose. "It's all right to keep seeing him?"

"I wouldn't excite him—maybe shorter visits—"

"When is he going home? What's his trouble, Marsh?"

"He's got cancer," Lucas said levelly.

Cosgrove recoiled. His mouth opened.

"Cancer!"

"I'm sorry. He's got two months to live. Three at the most."

Cosgrove sat down.

"You son-of-a-bitch!"

"It isn't me, man. I gave you your convert—"

"You dirty son-of-a-bitch!"

Lucas' anger flared, died as quickly, he looked tiredly at the hatred and bankruptcy and fear that glared from Cosgrove's eyes.

"But you're dying too," he said quietly. "You know that . . ."

"I'll get even with you, Marsh! It may take me to the day I die—"

"You've got years where he's got weeks—don't you understand? Can't you see that? Your cells can. Did you convert his cells to communism? When you solved his problems?"

"All right, Marsh. You know where we stand—you and I . . ."

"All right," said Lucas tiredly. "You're dying, you planners, you men with the answers, no matter what laws you make, no matter how loud you shout—you're dying—dose yourself with dialectic—

"I'm sorry," he said awkwardly.

He walked out.

He paused irresolutely on the steps of the Valley Hospital. I hope I didn't worry him, he winced. I shouldn't have said he was dying. Now he'll think he's got cancer too. He shrugged. Maybe he has. . . . And if it's not that it's something else. . . .

He went into the hospital to remove the scheduled tonsils and adenoids, an operation man had been performing efficiently for something less than a hundred years. He inspected a hysterectomy, the first of which had been successfully performed fifty-one years before. He examined a woman in labor, the basis of conception having been discovered fifty-four years before this day, and the physiology of the menstrual cycle having been discovered in 1903. He checked a kidney patient, the first kidney having been removed by man sixty years before, and he paused by an old man and inspected the catheter through which his water passed after a successful prostatectomy, the first of which had been performed successfully in man's history forty-two years ago and twenty-six years before his own birth, brand-new when the man on whom it had been performed was twenty-five years of age. He viewed a number of X-rays which man, tens of thousands of years old, had discovered some thirty-four years ago. He checked a gall-bladder patient recovering after an operation which had first been performed in human history sixty-two years before. He signed a release permitting a man to go home after a hernia operation, which his species had first executed forty years before. He gave a hypodermic injection with a needle invented fifty-one years before his own birth.

He was leaving the hospital when a nurse caught him at the door. He did not recognize the voice on the telephone.

"I'm Dr. Binyon's nurse!" he heard, finally.

"Yes, yes!" he said immediately.

"Can you come over, Doctor? Can you come right away? It's Dr. Blake—I'm calling for Dr. Blake—oh, my God!" she cried, and he heard the receiver fall.

His car had never seemed so slow. His tires screeched to a stop outside the Binyon and Blake office. He was out, he was flying up the steps, bag in hand he flung into the reception room, he opened the office door, the room was empty.

"In here!"

He wheeled and ran to a treatment room.

On the floor beside a couch lay a young woman. On a chair in a corner sat Dr. Blake, his head in his hands. He did not look up. Beside the young woman kneeled the nurse. Her uniform was spattered with blood. Blood drenched the young woman's neck. There was a great pool of it beneath her hair. Her shoulders and chest were covered with blood. The towel which had been tucked beneath her dress's neckline was wet and red, it was not white in any part.

Lucas was on the floor.

"She's bleeding to death—she's bleeding to death!" the nurse screamed. Dr. Blake groaned. His head sank lower.

"Shut up!" Lucas shouted. He slapped her across the face. "Shut up and get me a clamp!"

She reached wildly in the direction of an instrument tray. At the same instant Lucas found two haemostats, one clamped uselessly to the skin, the other dropped in panic nearby. He snapped them, they crushed tissue blindly.

"More!" he shouted. And then to Blake: "You! God damn you! Get on your feet!" Dr. Blake shook his head. He kept it buried in his hands.

The nurse handed him a handful of haemostats. She whimpered.

"It wasn't his fault," she cried. "It was just a little thing and she kept bothering him and he finally said come over and he'd take it out—just a local—"

Lucas' fingers jumped. The bleeding would not stop. The young woman was unconscious. Her face was white. Her skin was cold. Her breathing was almost imperceptible. His fingers raced on, probing, pressuring, clamping,

"Just a cyst," the nurse wailed, "just a little cyst—"

The bleeding seemed to stop. Lucas paused. His free hand reached bloodily for the young woman's lower leg. It was cold. He stared at her. He watched. He watched for the slightest sign. There was none. She had stopped breathing. He removed his fingers reluctantly from the tissues of her neck. A little blood flowed languidly. There was no pulse. There was no breathing. The young woman was dead.

Lucas rose. He stared at Dr. Blake. He swallowed.

"That was a branchial cyst," he said huskily.

Dr. Blake did not move. Lucas walked over the body of the young woman. He struck at the hands Dr. Blake held over his face. He tried to pull them away.

"Did you know that? Do you know what a branchial cyst is? Get up you yellow bastard!"

"He just used a little forceps and pulled it forward and snipped the base—" the nurse screamed. She pulled at Lucas' arm.

"And half an inch of jugular vein with it!" Lucas shouted. "Look at her! Take your hands away and look at her! She's dead! And you sat here and let her die! You got scared—you didn't know what happened—you yellowed out! You! You son-of-a-bitch! A doctor! You yellowed out!"

"Doctor, Doctor—!" the nurse pleaded.

"Don't you know anything? Don't you even know the sheath of a branchial cyst? Don't you even know it's always one with the large blood vessels of the neck? Didn't you even learn that? She's dead! Look at her! Come on, you ignorant yellow bastard! Look at her! You that sat there and let her die!"

Lucas tore at Dr. Blake's hands. He tried to pull them from his face.

"Dr. Binyon!" the nurse screamed suddenly.

Lucas turned.

"Here's some of your work!" Lucas shouted. "Take a look at it! Do you know what he's done?"

Dr. Binyon stood in the doorway. His face was white. He was staring at Dr. Blake.

"I heard it," he said.

"Cover this up if you can! Just try!"

Dr. Blake had removed his hands from his face. His cheeks were wet with tears. He looked at Dr. Binyon.

"Oh, Bert, Bert," he moaned.

"That's what you did," said Dr. Binyon tonelessly. He did not ask it, requiring confirmation, he put it as a fact, he spoke quietly, he waited, there might be one more fact.

"Out of nowhere," Dr. Blake wailed, "just a little cyst, Bert, I snipped and—" His bewildered eyes dropped to the dead young woman. "Oh, my God!" he cried brokenly. He buried his face in his hands again.

"And he sat there," said Lucas. "He sat there. And he let her bleed to death!

"Go on!" he said. "Say something! Defend him!"

But Dr. Binyon was looking steadily at Dr. Blake.

"I'll give you two hours to get out of here," he said.

"Oh, Dr. Binyon!" the nurse whispered. She clapped her hand to her mouth.

"Remember that. Two hours. If you're here two hours from now I'll call the police." He looked steadily at his classmate. "I hope I hear of you practicing Medicine again," he said levelly. The room was very silent. "That's all I want to hear!"

He turned to Lucas.

"Thank you, Doctor—"

"If I could have been here five minutes earlier, even—"

Dr. Binyon nodded.

"Two hours," he said. "Remember that, John."

He walked from the doorway. Lucas looked at Dr. Blake again. He looked at the nurse.

"Take care of her"—he nodded to the body of the young woman. He stepped over the body.

"Dr. Blake," the nurse was saying, "come on, now, Dr. Blake . . . Dr. Blake—"

He reached the corridor and followed Dr. Binyon.

"I'll take care of the calls," Dr. Binyon said. He kept his head averted.

"All right," said Lucas.

Dr. Binyon's voice was dead.

"Don't worry. He'll never practice again."

Lucas waited.

"I'll call you," said Dr. Binyon. "He'll be out of town in two hours. I'll call you, tonight."

"I'll be waiting," Lucas said quietly.

Dr. Binyon did not say anything more. He did not turn his head.

Lucas walked out. When he drove away he noticed that his hands were sticky. The steering wheel was wet. He looked at his fingers. He had not washed his hands.

He drove to Dr. Castle's office.

When he had finished talking he sat as he was, leaning forward, listening expectantly.

Dr. Castle studied him a moment, holding the moment, summing the man, summing himself, summing the world, holding back the moment of speech.

The young man leaned forward tensely, he was a young-old man now, he was as old as the illnesses he knew and the remedies and operations conceived to prevent them. He was as long ago as man had begun Medicine, and all the years between were in that age, and the present. That time and that knowledge were in him, and the lines of his face curved in the arcs of age in young tissue.

And he sat forward now, leashed, waiting to be unleashed and to destroy what had happened and to make that part of Medicine whole again.

"Too bad," Dr. Castle said tiredly. "Too bad, too bad . . ."

Lucas' hearing brushed the sound aside, sound to fill space, meaningless. He waited.

"I didn't think it would come to this," Dr. Castle nodded. He sighed, emptying himself, breathing out the last of the waiting. "He's been having trouble with him lately," he said diffidently.

"What are we going to do."

"Something during an operation . . . Dr. Rankin told me . . . and I heard rumors before . . . of other things . . ."

"He's killed a woman."

"Of course he should never have been graduated . . . I don't know how you can tell, though . . . they pass their examinations . . . one or two always slip through . . ."

"Do we go to the county first? Or the police. It should be the police, shouldn't it?"

"I don't know whether I ever told you . . . Rankin was last in his class . . . I didn't? . . . Somebody has to be, you know . . . last, next to last, and on up . . . of course there's the basic minimum . . . even the last one's got that. . . . The police? Did Binyon call the police?"

"I don't know. He said he'd call me. I don't think Blake's had time to clear out yet—"

"They were classmates, you know—"

"How sure are we about Binyon?"

"He kicked him out, didn't he?"

"He practiced with him. Blake was his choice. He picked him for a partner. If anybody knows him, Binyon ought to know him. And he's been working with him. He'd be working with him yet—if Blake hadn't killed somebody."

"He kicked him out."

"We've got nothing to charge him with. Maybe that's it. His skirts are clean. He's cleaned them."

"They were classmates. And before that they went all through school together. They were farm boys, really. Came from some little place in Ohio. Smaller than Greenville."

"We can still head him off—"

"All that English country-gentleman stuff—God, how many times I've seen it—the thick soles, the heavy tweeds, the manicured manner, the childlike belief that now they were rounded human beings with a strong streak of art in them and a deep appreciation of all the arts—and not just humans like you and I who never had a chance to learn anything else—my God, they're embarrassing! And these two—all they wanted was to put that small town in Ohio into oblivion and be reborn. That's what all the tweeds were about and the fancy equipment and the fancy prices."

Lucas waited, silently, his eyes patient.

"But you know, they went all through that, together. That's the thing about it. They were closer than brothers. Do you see what I'm getting at?" he demanded abruptly. "That's what Binyon threw out! Did you see his face? Was he scared of you?"

"No," Lucas said reluctantly.

"He wasn't scared. That's what I'm trying to make you see. The thing in Binyon that makes him a doctor—that's what threw Blake out." He leaned forward. "Can you see that?"

For this was very important. He said nothing more. He simply looked at Lucas and waited.

"Supposing you're right," Lucas said at last.

"Why did you call me in? Why did you come over here?" Dr. Castle leaned back. He uncapped a vial and slipped a pill in his mouth. Lucas watched him, looked at his face, searched it for sign. "Because you wanted a conference. That's why you didn't go directly to the police department. You weren't sure. You're not sure yourself—what's the right thing to do—it's the human in you, coming up against the doctor—what would you have done two years ago?"

Lucas blinked, troubled, suddenly guilty.

"All right," he said, the words came from his mouth with difficulty, "but we can't let him off Scot-free—"

"He'll never practice Medicine again."

"More of those vague channels? A man like that loose in the human community, with what he knows—"

"Are you going to disgrace every man in his class and the men who taught him—disgrace all of us—disgrace Medicine—with a public trial? Who are you trying to punish? The woman who distrusts doctors and is on the verge of reporting a queer swelling in her breast? Every death we've ever had, our faults or not? Every family that's ever known a death?"

"Who's going to take up his license?"

"It can be done quietly. I know. I've seen it done. He'll never practice again." He touched the telephone lightly with his finger tips, folded his hands in his lap.

"I'm not worried about Blake, son. I'm not thinking about Binyon. It's you I'm thinking about."

"Can I adjust to it, do you mean? Your young freak friend? Does what we're doing shock me and shame me so I want to vomit? Yes, I can adjust to it. I'm getting to be a veteran now. A veteran adjuster. It doesn't change me, though. If you think it changes what I know Medicine is—"

"That's all I meant."

"I didn't mean to bark out at you—"

"I know what you're barking out against. Be a schizoid! Can you do that? Be a schizoid!" He raised his hands and let them drop tiredly onto his lap. "Hell, man—I can't tell you anything else . . . I wish I could . . . I don't know any more . . . there's no real pattern . . . Most of us spend our lives trying to match our fathers instead of trying to improve ourselves . . . All I can give you is old . . . old, old stuff . . ."

"Just go home—and wait for him to call me—?"

"And let him handle it. He knows you! He'll handle it! And I'll check with him . . ." He put his hand on the telephone again. "Along," he said, "along with—the rest . . ."

Dr. Binyon called before Lucas was through with his afternoon office calls. Dr. Blake had left town. He would not practice Medicine again. He would not be heard from again. The young woman's family had been notified. Dr. Binyon had assumed full responsibility. There might be a suit. There might not. Dr. Castle had called the family, also. And Dr. Kauffman. Dr. Binyon had signed the death certificate. Did Dr. Marsh want anything else? Then, was there anything else at all, anything, Dr. Marsh would want?

"No," Lucas said dully. "No, that's all."

He waited. At the other end of the line Dr. Binyon waited also. I've done what I had to do, each man was saying mechanically to himself, and in their separate ways each was saying, I've done what the rules, what the situation called for. And for both there was limitless sadness and despair. And for both there was another patient at the door.

"I think that is all, then, Doctor," said Dr. Binyon.

"I think that covers it," said Lucas.

They hung up.

Kristina ushered in the last patient, ushered her out. They went in to dinner together. She was very quiet. She saw that something had happened. She was subdued, he observed irritably and then with a pang of gratitude, as if there had been a death in the family. Maybe she sees, he thought helplessly. Maybe she's not far from right.

"What are you subdued about, Kris?" he asked idly, trying to blot out thinking.

She gave a small cry. He looked at her, then at the small hallway of their home. He walked forward and picked up the telegram.

He looked at her as he opened it. Poor sod, he shrugged, she's afraid of telegrams.

"Wonder why they didn't leave it next door," he said irritably.

"Drop us a line," it said. "Typhoid or no typhoid. Worried."

"It's from Avery!" he cried.

"Is he all right?" Kris clasped her hands before her chest. He thrust the telegram at her.

"I've got to call him!" he said as she read it.

"I want to say something too!" she begged. He had been about to go to the office. He sat down by the home phone.

And a few minutes later they were talking. Avery's familiar voice was coming over the line and Lucas clung to it, he laved himself with it and all the past with which it was compounded. He yearned to be all his secret thoughts, his life, to be in his voice, in his words, telling Avery everything, laying it before him in a syllable.

"What the hell's going on up there?" Avery was demanding.

"I guess you heard we had a little typhoid—"

"I didn't know whether you were dying, or dead, or what. I thought about it a while then I decided to put the money for the movie I won't see next week into a telegram—"

"Why didn't you send it collect?"

"I couldn't think of anything that'd run more than ten words—how are you? Everything all right? How's Kris?"

Lucas looked at her. She was beaming. He had not seen her smile so in many days.

"She's right here! Grinning her head off. She wants to talk to you—"

"Are you happy, boy?"

"I guess so . . ."

"Everything's okay now?"

"You mean what we talked about?"

"That—and the rest . . ."

"I'll tell you when I see you—"

"You're going to stay there, aren't you? You're not up to something? We talked all that out—"

"When am I going to see you?"

"You're sure you know what you're doing?"

"Give me the news! Tell me what's happened!"

"Nothing's happened. I'm still an assistant professor, the same old grind, new ones coming in every term—that's one of the things I wanted to see *you* about—wait till you see me, will you, Luke?"

"If I can—"

"What do you mean—if you can! Does Kris know? Listen, Luke—"

"I want what I've always wanted. I've never changed, Avery. I'm going to have it. No matter what. I know that, now. Now, I know."

"Put Kris on—"

"Tell me about the others! How's Aarons?"

"This is costing you a fortune—"

"Is he a dean yet?"

"He's gone."

"Aarons?"

"He's teaching at a Negro school—he was passed over—I'll tell you about it—"

"My God!"

"And your friends—you know, the two lab gals? They're out in the Midwest, somewhere—they split up—they had a big fight one day—I think one's in Kansas, one's in Michigan. Your pal Alfred, your roommate, I guess you heard—his folks went bust in the crash—he had to come back from Europe, I don't know what he's doing, his father shot himself, I understand the mother and the girls had to go to work. And you know who—the guy who taught in the high collar—he's been fired—the same faces, though . . . mostly . . . the same old faces—let me speak to Kris!"

"My God!" Lucas said softly. He handed the phone to Kristina.

He sat for a while, thinking, what he had heard capered through his thoughts, would not make a picture, he went over the pieces of news with delight again, only dimly aware of Kristina's voice.

"I understand," she was saying. Her eyes were glowing. "No, no . . . I understand . . ."

She bit her lip on a smile.

"I have," she said quietly.

". . . no . . . no, he doesn't . . ."

There was a spate of talk from the other end. She nodded.

"Yes," she said quickly. "Oh, no! I understand—"

She handed the phone to Lucas.

He looked at her, surprised. Her eyes were glowing.

"He wants to talk to you," she said.

"I'll be free in three weeks," said Avery. "Shall I come up there? Or will you come down here? We'll have a long weekend."

"That'll be wonderful," said Lucas. "What did you say to make Kristina so happy?"

"It doesn't take much to make Kristina happy. You come down here. All right?"

"I'll be there—"

"And until then, you'll sit tight!"

"A lot's happened, Avery. It's not me, any more."

"Kiss Kris for me—"

The line was dead. Lucas hung up the receiver reluctantly. He stared at the phone.

"He's a real friend," Kristina said.

"What were you two chinning about?"

"He wanted me to do something. And I told him I already done it."

"Did it . . . What did he want you to do?"

"See that you got regular meals," Kristina said steadily. "I guess I lied, didn't I?"

"Not really," he relaxed. "I wouldn't worry about it, Kris . . ."

The call sustained him for days. He had never worked so well. There was a day when Dr. Kauffman and Dr. Castle joined him at the Valley to watch him operate. And they sat in the dressing room afterwards and took a cap and stitched it and did the stomach resection, the new insertion of the oesophagus, upon it all over again. He revelled in each day, free and unfettered and crowded with precision and diagnosis and at night he read as he chose and one night Kristina woke him in the office, it was after three o'clock, he had been reading, waiting for an obstetric call that came as she woke him. Kristina the nurse he did not forget. The nurses at the Valley were expert but Kristina at morning surgery at the County was clean satisfaction, precision past astonishment.

"You're practicing!" he accused her one morning. "You were never this good!"

He'd caught her, as usual. Kristina nodded. She shrugged.

"Once I did it for the hospital," she said shyly. "Now I do for my husband."

He looked at her admiringly, not hearing.

For some days Kristina had been nagged by a doubt, a thought that had stubbornly become conviction. She had examined it patiently, warily, carefully. Manual expertness was one thing. But to surprise him—to be not dumb, for a minute—

She took the plunge.

"What do you think, Luke? It comes to me that anybody can pass. In a few hours I could teach a layman. There's nothing to passing. You pick something up—you hand it to somebody!"

She looked at him earnestly. She flushed.

"There's the little matter of knowing what to pick up—" he was still smiling. The Heavens had not opened.

"But when they watch a little—when they learn the names of instruments—"

"Actually, we don't use many instruments—mostly the same things, over and over," Lucas said thoughtfully.

"Sure! And a little practice—the hands go awful fast! You don't have to think, even. A layman—"

"Why do you keep saying 'layman,' Kris?"

"A good nurse—just standing there, passing—when she could be nursing—and nurses so short . . ."

Lucas looked at her and blinked.

"By God, Kris! I believe you've got something!"

She looked away, embarrassed, thrilled to her marrow.

"I just thought—" she said deprecatively.

"And you're right! You're absolutely right! By gosh, Kris! Sometimes—"

"You about through?"

Lucas turned. Dr. Snider was standing by the swinging doors.

"Got a friend of yours out here." He grinned.

Lucas walked toward him, Kristina watched him go, nursing the fragment. He disappeared.

In the hall was Bemis Shedd. He stared at Lucas' gowned figure uneasily.

"You look like a Ku-Kluxer!" he said reproachfully.

"What's on your mind?" Lucas laughed.

"Get outa them things so you look like a human being again and I'll tell you."

"I've got to make rounds," Lucas said. He tried to guess what Bemis wanted.

"Snider says you already made rounds—go on! Shoo!"

When he reappeared Bemis took him by the arm and began to walk toward the side door.

"Where you going?" Lucas protested. "I've got work to do!"

"You got five minutes, too! I got orders!"

"What kind of orders?"

But Bemis had taken over his car, he drove Lucas to the center of Greenville, they got out in front of the *Clarion*.

". . . so now you know whose orders—so now you're here, I want you to take a look at the place—"

"But Dr. Castle was just kidding you—"

"He called *me* up! I didn't call him! Come on! You ever seen a newspaper plant before? We got some place here! Won't take a minute!"

Lucas followed him reluctantly.

He entered a room that seemed to overflow with paper. Bits of paper, whole newspapers, covered all available flat surfaces, hiding desk and chairs; there were strips of paper hanging from hooks on the wall, paper underfoot, paper everywhere covered with print or pencil marks.

"This here's Miss Shallop." Bemis pointed to a long counter. Miss Shallop rose from a seat before a typewriter. She appeared to be seventy years old, she was birdlike, flustered, she smiled timidly.

"Meet Dr. Marsh!" Bemis said proudly. "Come to look us over! Miss Shallop's our society and classified-ads editor!"

"Pleased to meet you, I'm sure," Miss Shallop whispered.

"Anytime you got anything at all—taking a trip—mow your lawn—the missus has some folks in to tea—you just call Miss Shallop. Miss Shallop, anytime Dr. Marsh or his missus calls anything in—!" Bemis nodded his head sharply.

"Old maid," he confided to Lucas out of the corner of his mouth as they walked on. "Been here forty years. There's folks in this town'd give their right arms to get in the *Clarion* society column—she knows 'em all, she weeds 'em out—anytime you or your missus got anything social, you just call her. I'll see it gets in!"

"Well, thanks, but—"

"Don't mention it. No trouble at all. This here's my desk—what you can see of it!" He surveyed its immense disorder proudly. He turned. "We got a sports editor and reporter and what-not—he's out probably getting a big scoop I'll have to cut down to a paragraph—likely boy, father's Charley Henderson—not the undertaker, the mailman!"

He led the way to the back shop.

"Watch yourself," he warned. "Don't get your clothes dirty—"

"And this is where you print it!"

"No, no! We run it off in the back. This is where we set it up—in type!"

Two men at the linotype machines flipped their fingers over a bank of keys. A thin man in an ink-stained apron looked up from a type-laden turtle and grinned at them.

"This is the gang!" Bemis said proudly. "Art—come here. I want you to meet somebody."

He spoke in an ordinary tone and although Lucas wondered how he could hear above the clamor of the press and the linotypes, the thin man promptly walked to them.

"This is Dr. Marsh, Art," Bemis said.

"I'm glad to meet you, Doctor," Charley said promptly. He rubbed an ink-stained palm apologetically on his apron.

"Art's deaf but he can hear good as you and me."

Art grinned.

"Deaf—but not dumb," Bemis explained carefully.

"From birth?" Lucas asked.

Art shook his head.

"Reads your lips," Bemis confided.

He turned to face the two linotypers.

"I want him to meet the boys. Doc here is going hunting with us—"

"Now, I didn't say that—"

But Art had turned, he tapped the nearest man's shoulder, both the linotypers turned to him, his fingers raced in the air, they turned, beaming, to Lucas.

"I told them," said Art. His voice lacked the flat, atonal quality of one who had never heard speech. He talked quite normally. "This here is Fred—" he pointed to the nearest worker, a blond, stocky man in his late twenties—"and this is Phil," and a lanky, lean man in his late thirties bared discolored teeth to smile at him.

"Dummies," said Bemis. "Can't hear a word you say, read lips a little but not as good as Art—and can't say a word. Born that way. Art here's our interpreter—sort of a go-between you might say."

Art's fingers flickered again. The two turned back to their machines. Their fingers raced again.

"Best damned linotypers you can get!"

"Never distracted by anything," Lucas nodded.

"You betcha. And they'll work for peanuts—average shop doesn't want 'em. How the hell's a deaf and dumb guy gonna earn a living like ordinary folks? Swell gang!" Bemis said happily. "Been with me for years! Art here—he's got a wife and two little kids! Yes sir! Wife's deaf and dumb. Kids perfectly normal. Yes sir! All live together, sort of, got three little houses out on the edge of town, I want to tell you they're neat as pins! Okay, Art, you can go back to work now."

"It's been very interesting," said Lucas, "look at the time! I've got to get back to work, myself!"

"Now, you're not going anywhere until you've made me your promise!"

"But I don't know the first thing in the world about hunting!"

"Hunted when you were a kid, didn't you?"

"Never," Lucas was about to say.

"Very little," he protested. "Almost never—"

"Sure! Everybody's hunted sometime or other! It's only natural! Hell, we don't care whether we get anything or not! We just go hunting. I'm the cook—you never tasted pancakes like I can cook 'em—we take a bunch of bacon I been curing just specially for this—and a pot of beans—by God, one thing! I don't remember ever coming home empty-handed!"

"It sounds fine, but—"

"Beautiful pine woods—you never saw country so wild as this—clean air—we go up four thousand feet, real wilderness, the genuine article—place hardly anybody even knows about—we go up in the truck and you can sleep in the truck bed, or on a nice mattress of pine boughs—and a nice campfire—just a bunch of guys out alone—free from everything—there's nothing like it! Never! Nothing!"

They were in the front room again.

"You got a gun?" Bemis asked suddenly.

"Yes . . ." Lucas remembered the gun Dr. Runkleman had bought for him. "But the trouble is, a doctor can't just decide he wants to go hunting—"

"Does the idea appeal to you!"

"It sounds fine, but—"

Bemis promptly picked up the battered telephone on his desk. He called a number, he turned and handed the phone to Lucas.

"It'll do you good," said Dr. Castle.

"What are you trying to do?" Lucas demanded. "What's going on . . . ?" He smiled to hide a little irritation.

"I'm trying to get you two days' rest," said Dr. Castle. "Got any objections? Like to tell me you don't need it? Now go ahead and go on with the man. I went once—it's something you'll never forget. And stop making a fuss about nothing. I've already arranged with Dr. Kauffman. Between us, we'll take over your two days."

As he spoke, Lucas felt himself becoming excited. The thought of the woods and a gun in his hands made his pulse beat faster. The thought of the rest, the clear solitude—

"Just tell him yes!" said Dr. Castle. He hung up.

Lucas put the receiver back on the hook slowly. Bemis peered at him eagerly.

"Well—if you don't mind taking a greenhorn—"

"That's the stuff!" Bemis smote his back.

"An absolute greenhorn, mind—!"

"Christ! We'll sit you where you can't miss! We'll all go in the truck! Don't worry about the wardens! Not with the press, boy! Are we going to have a time! A week from today, now! We'll leave four o'clock Saturday morning, we'll all meet here, bring a couple of blankets, never mind your comb and razor . . ."

Lucas rushed to the Valley Hospital. He was delighted. When he made rounds he called Harriet.

"I'm going hunting! What do you think about that? Me, going hunting! Where do you go nights? I've been trying to reach you all week!"

"I've been here," she said. "What's all this about hunting—"

"Sounds like an expedition! Bemis Shedd asked me, and Castle and Kauffman are going to take over for me—do you know this is the first vacation I've ever had! I'll tell you all about it—tonight."

There was a pause.

"All right," she said. Her voice was reluctant.

"What's the matter!" he flared. "Don't you think the typhoid has worn off me? I'm safe! You won't lose your pretty hair!"

Then, instantly, he was frightened. But when she answered, her tone was as before.

"It's not that," she said guardedly.

But it was that, Lucas knew. It had been that. And now it was something else.

"What's the matter?"

"Nothing—nothing . . . I'll tell you when I see you."

"You all right? You're all right, aren't you?"

"I've got to hang up," she said. "Somebody's coming. Eight o'clock."

At intervals during the afternoon he heard her voice again, he was disturbed, there was nothing here to comprehend. Toward the middle of the afternoon a patient said to him, grinning respectfully:

"Hey, Doc! What's this I hear—understand you're going hunting!"

Lucas startled, halted his bandaging of the burned arm.

"Where on earth did you hear that?"

He was a small man and he looked up, his eyes had that hint of awe and devotion in them Lucas had begun to notice in his patients lately, it was a look that discomfited him, a personal look, familiar and yet respectful.

"Oh, you're in the big time now, Doc. You're in the *Clarion*. Just come out. How you and the editor and the crew're all going hunting—you like to hunt, Doc?"

Now, this was a man, talking to another man.

"Why, yes," said Lucas. He had a desire not to disappoint him. "I've never done much. But I like it. I suppose you hunt all the time?"

"I wish I could. You work for the power company you don't get much chance. Once a year—but then when vacation comes, what the hell, the missus has been working all year, too—"

He grinned at Lucas. His look said, You know how it is.

"You got a dog, Doc?"

"A dog?"

"Something to hunt with?"

"Well, no . . . I haven't had much chance . . ." He taped the bandage gently. He made small, useless motions. He wanted to prolong this. He wanted this man to think of him as having a gun and a dog. He did not know what to say next. He might blunder.

"I suppose you've got one," he said, trying to smile wisely.

"Labrador. Best damned hunting dog in the world and all he does is stay tied up all day." He cleared his throat. "I was gonna say, Doc—if you'd like to use him—"

Lucas kept his eyes down.

"Why, thanks!" he said. Then he looked squarely at the patient. "Thanks a lot!"

"Oh, hell! Just remember—if you want to use him—God! You know what some people are doing, lately? Eating dog food! Yes, sir, right out of the can! By God, times are getting bad, aren't they, Doc!"

"They'll be better soon—"

"You think so? That your opinion, Doc?"

"They've got to be."

"I guess that's right—say! That looks swell! How much I owe you, Doc?"

"If you should happen to go hunting this fall I'll take a brace of ducks—"

"Come on! We know about you! You can't live on that! How much!"

"A dollar."

"For all that? Come on, Doc—"

"One dollar—"

"Doc, I'm not as bad off as most folks, I got a job, you know, I get paid regular—so far—"

"That's all! Now come on! I got another patient waiting—"

The man laid two one-dollar bills carefully on the desk and walked toward the door.

"Don't forget about that dog," he admonished.

Lucas walked to the window and watched him drive off. He turned at a noise behind him. The next patient was walking in briskly, a familiar figure, a dumpy little woman in her early forties.

"Mrs. Cornell!" The surprise left his face and he flushed. Irma Cornell was one of the constitutional inadequates he had weeded out from Dr. Runkleman's heavy case load. She sat down heavily, defiantly.

"Well, here I am!" she said.

"I thought you were going to go to Dr. Castle. I thought we agreed that—"

"I want to go to you!"

"But I told you, Mrs. Cornell—you remember? I told you, distinctly—"

"Somebody's got to treat us, don't they? Answer me that! Just answer me that! Don't they?"

Lucas raised his arms, let them drop to his sides.

"But what can I treat you for?"

"Well, I got pains, you know—just the same as anybody else. I don't feel good—where do you go, then, but to a doctor? That's what I want to know! And it happens you're the doctor I want to go to—"

"But why me, Mrs. Cornell! Any doctor can—"

"We know all about you!" She nodded briskly. "Yes, sir! You can't fool folks! Not long, you can't. We know what you are. I don't care what you want to say to me—here I am and here I stay! You're my doctor!"

"Well," sighed Lucas. He shrugged.

The woman's eyes filled with tears suddenly. With her fist she smote them angrily away. She looked up at him helplessly.

"I can't help it, Doctor Marsh—I do get pains—even if I'm what you said—"

"Sure I'm your doctor. You bet I am. You come back anytime you want. And don't worry about that other. If you understand it—that's the main thing."

"Whatever made me so? I don't mean to be ailing all the time. What did I do?"

"It's just this way, Mrs. Cornell. Nature—or our forefathers—just made some people who aren't strong enough for the load of life—and no matter how many sicknesses you can put your finger on in them—and cure—you still can't make them over."

She shook her head sadly.

"That's a nice thing to look forward to, isn't it."

"Well, look at me! Look at me, Mrs. Cornell! How do you think I'd make out trying to make a living as a prize fighter?"

"Isn't there anything can be done? Do I have to blow my brains out?"

"Well, I'm not blowing my brains out because I'm inadequate as a prize fighter—or because I'm constitutionally inadequate to be a strong man in a circus. Just face it, Mrs. Cornell. That's all. Just face it."

"But I have pains—"

"I know you have pains. And you get tired easily. And you get faint. And your digestion's poor, you're constipated—I know all that. It's true. You have these things. They aren't all imaginary. But when they come, you've got to tell yourself you know what the trouble is. And try to put up with it. You take Robert Louis Stevenson, there's a fellow who had tuberculosis, he never passed a day free of pain—and he said something I want you to remember. He said a man has good health if he can only do without it uncomplainingly."

"I used to read him in school."

"Well, you remember that. Now I'm going to give you some pills."

"The same old pills—"

"Yes, the same old pills. They won't hurt you. And they'll make you more comfortable when you feel worst."

"He wrote some pretty pieces—"

"You bet he did! And remember! These pills won't make you over. Don't be peevish with me—because I can't cure you. And don't be peevish with the pills. They're your friends and they're all I've got to give you. And you don't have to come in every other day—once a month is plenty."

"Pays a person to do a little reading now and then." She got up. She took the pills. She started to take bills from her worn purse.

"That's fifty cents, Mrs. Cornell."

She looked up swiftly, silent.

"That's all. That's all they're worth. And you remember, now. And don't fight it. Or me, or anybody else. Just mold your life accordingly, and—"

"Fifty cents!"

"Just give it to Mrs. Marsh on the way out. And will you tell her to send in the next patient?"

She looked at him a moment, then walked out.

Lucas walked to the window. They'll come back, he thought. One by one, they'll come back. And I'll have to take them. As long as I'm here. And some will understand, as she did, and some won't. And I'll just have to do my best. Tell them the truth, straight out. And he saw their familiar faces, saw a procession of them, saw the anxious faces, the dull, apathetic faces, the twitching faces, the mutinous faces. And his heart was very heavy. For he could do nothing. And when a doctor sees tissues and cells and not the individual he is seeing all men and he is seeing himself and all that can happen to a man and all that prisons a man and tethers him and compels him and shapes him, his life and his death.

Mrs. Cornell walked to Kristina, where she sat at her desk.

"Office calls two dollars, aren't they?"

Kristina nodded.

"You feeling better, Mrs. Cornell?"

The woman put two dollars before Kristina.

"Wanted to charge me fifty cents!" she said indignantly.

Kristina looked at the bills dubiously.

"If Doctor said fifty cents—"

"I don't want any nonsense from you, either. You're his wife, aren't you? Ought to know enough about a man's foolishness by this time. You better start watching after him or we won't have a doctor. What do you expect to live on! Fifty cents!"

She snapped her worn purse shut, fisted it stiffly into her handbag. She looked up, she sniffed briskly, her head jerked in a little nod. She turned and stalked out, her back straight.

Lucas laughed mirthlessly when Kristina told him about it at dinner.

"There's one specialty that's wide open and nobody's formed a board for it, yet. Sooner or later there's going to be a specialty in the treatment of constitutional inadequacy. God knows there's enough patients waiting."

"I told her if you said fifty cents—"

"That's all right. Maybe paying me four times what it's worth is part of her treatment. I hate to take their money . . ."

"But somebody's got to be their doctor—"

"I know, I know . . . they go from one man to another . . . most of them won't believe the truth if you tell them . . . if they'd face themselves as they are, maybe you could help them . . . before they spend all their money—for nothing."

"Aren't they really sick?"

He looked up.

"I mean—I guess I don't understand—"

"Sure, they're really sick. I've told you. And some of them show symptoms a man is justified in—I'll tell you a case—a woman—she went to a big clinic—everybody had a shot at her. She had painful menstruation. The gynecologist swooped on that. She had headaches. The neurologist was confident her troubles were due to migraine. The orthopedist figured she had a twisted spine, and the endocrinologist traced everything to a pituitary-ovarian source, and she had pain in her abdomen so the gastro-enterologist said colitis. And the surgeon said appendix."

"Which one? Who was right?"

"Well, they resected her presacral plexus. That fixed up the menstrual pain. They just disconnected the nerves. But she still had the headaches. So they gave her ergotamine. That stopped the headaches. She was always tired, so she gave up her job and got married. Still had back pain—and physical therapy took care of that. Still had abdominal distress, so they put her on a diet and gave her enema instructions. That took care of that. And the surgeon took out her appendix."

Kristina waited. Lucas struck the table suddenly.

"But she didn't get well! She went right on having just as much misery as she ever had! She was just as tired as she ever was! And that's how she is today! All that for nothing!"

"That's—"

"That's Mrs. Cornell."

"My God!"

"Multiply her by a hundred thousand—by a million. And only when it was all over did it dawn on them that all her troubles were just manifestations of constitutional inadequacy."

"If somebody'd only told her—"

"She probably wouldn't have believed them. She'd have shopped around until finally everything would have been done to her that she had done. That's the trouble with them in your practice. They're always trouble—and you can almost never do anything for them—it all comes to nothing in the end—and they take up time you should be giving those you can help. It's—messy. It's—unprofessional, somehow. Taking money from them—everything!"

Kristina sighed.

"And I bet they're the first ones to go around saying doctors are no good."

"Of course they are!"

"You're right." She nodded. "Like always." She nodded. "I just remembered something. When he couldn't do anything for a patient—that's how Dr. Runkleman used to act. Remember? When they were hopeless?"

Lucas started. His brows knit. He glared at her suspiciously. She looked back at him innocently. He rose, still watching her uncertainly.

"This has got nothing to do with Dr. Runkleman!" he snapped.

"I only meant—"

"I don't care what you meant!"

"What did I say? Luke, I'm sorry! What is it?"

"Never mind! It just seems like every time I relax a minute, try to talk to you—"

"But Luke—!"

"To hell with it!"

He put on his coat and hat and flung out of the house. He reached the car. He looked at his watch. It was not quite seven. He still had an hour. He drove slowly into the hills.

He sat a long time. He looked at the lights of the town of Greenville. He thought about Dr. Runkleman. He stirred uncomfortably. It's not the same at all, he said once, angrily. He thought about Dr. Runkleman again. He thought a long time. After a while he nodded. His eyes were miserable. He sighed. He looked over the town of Greenville. He watched it, hardly seeing it.

When he remembered to look at his watch he jumped.

It was after eight. He was late.

⋆ CHAPTER 40

She was waiting for him a block from her house. He scanned the dark street frantically, at first he did not see her in the shadows. Then she moved slightly. She was in the car. Two blocks away she slammed the door shut.

"You're late," she said evenly.

"I'm sorry—I got tied up."

He turned the car into the narrow road, the branches closed behind them, they were in their trysting place.

"Getting your hunting gear ready?"

"I said I was sorry, Harriet—no, dear, I wasn't getting my hunting gear ready—I don't have any hunting gear . . ." He reached for her.

She allowed him her mouth.

He sat back, bewildered.

"What's the matter?"

"I just don't like hiding on dark streets and standing there like a thief wondering what's happened—that's all. All right, it's done. Forget it."

"That hunting business—it's just a whim—I took a sudden notion, as they say here—I'll only be gone two days—"

"You hunt. You need the rest. You look terrible. You ought to take care of yourself, Luke."

"I don't really have to go—"

"You go. I may not be here."

"May not be here!"

He recoiled, stupefied, fear draining his heart.

"Put your arm back. There . . . Now listen. Try to listen to me . . . We knew it had to come, didn't we?"

"What are you talking about?"

"Put your arm back. The job . . . It's finished—done—*kaput*! Today!"

"But you don't have to leave—you can wait for me—!"

"Be quiet, now. Try to think. There's nothing for me, here. You can always join me, later . . ."

"Harriet—listen! You can't! You mustn't!"

"Mustn't what?" She stroked his hair.

"Mustn't leave! Don't you see? I'm not ready, yet! You can't leave, Harriet!"

"Luke, I want to talk to you . . . No, lean back—just like you were . . ." She stroked his hair. "You're a person who needs help. We're the same people. What drives me drives me just as hard as what drives you . . . I think you need help worse than I do . . . Maybe instead of helping me, I'd spend all my time helping you. . . . Maybe I need somebody stronger than myself . . . Somebody *I* can lean on . . ."

He listened numbly, hardly breathing.

"Do you see?" she asked gravely. "Don't be upset, Luke! I'm just talking, trying to think things out, trying to see . . . help me . . ."

"Just a month," he whispered.

She turned her head. She looked in his direction a long moment. He turned to her.

"You're what I've always wanted," he said steadily.

She said nothing. He drew her to him.

For a moment as his hands roved hungrily over her she stiffened, she put her hand on his chest.

"Please," he whispered.

After a while, as he lay breathing heavily, she patted his cheek gently.

They spoke no more of leaving. They spoke little. And after a while she stirred and he sat up, and the car moved out, onto the road again, through the dark streets warm with the perfume of her. The car stopped. She took his head between her hands. She kissed his face.

"I'll call you tomorrow," he whispered. She nodded. Then she was gone.

His mind was very tired. He was soon home. He could think no longer. He drew a deep breath. He went into the house. He lay down on the sofa. He fell asleep almost immediately.

Early in the morning, while it was still dark, the phone rang. He wakened on the sofa. Sometime during the night Kristina had covered him with a blanket. The call was from a farm on the outskirts of town. He struggled sleepily into his coat, found his hat, picked up his bag, the front door closed behind him.

The wine-cold air drove the blood from his face, stung his eyes, cleansed his skin, the dark was a new day, cold-minted as the stars and the night, and the cold and the stars were alone with him. His footsteps echoed in the silence, he heard the sound with pleasure, it was good to be alone, it was sanctuary. The empty streets, the stars and the night were his old friends. On the horizon there was a faint lightness, a dark that was not dark as the earth or dark as the sky, a new day was in it.

In this darkness the farmhouse windows interrupted suddenly with alien light. The patient was a seventeen-year-old boy. He lay atop his bedcovers, his pajamas were open, his pulse was rapid, his skin wet and clammy with evaporation, his forehead was hot, his eyes were glazed with pain, his knees drawn up. Over a point between his umbilicus and the tip of his hip there was marked tenderness, the muscles were rigid, the skin was tender, there was tenderness on rebound.

Lucas looked about the bedroom. It was very plainly furnished. He went into the living room. The furniture was old, it had been poor furniture when it was new, he spoke briefly with the worried parents, he called the County Hospital, he ordered an ambulance.

Until the ambulance arrived he waited beside the boy, who breathed more quietly, now, his pupils and his pain diminished by morphine. When they heard the ambulance they went quickly to the door, it opened, Lucas stepped out, the night was gone. The light was gray and nothing was hidden, nor lit, either, and where the light slid film over the distance reluctant mists clabbered and sank upon the hills.

"Getting you up early!" the driver called and his voice was thin in the still empty day.

"That's right," Lucas smiled obediently.

"Whatcha got? An appendix? Good weather for hunting, Doc—oughta be perfect in a couple of days!"

"Hunting? Oh, yes! That's right—yes, it looks like it might be perfect for hunting." So the whole town knew, apparently. And they all seem so happy to learn I'm doing something they do.

They came out with the stretcher. He walked beside it to the ambulance.

When they left he felt, as he drove away, an unwillingness to go home, a desire to hold time still, to keep the day as it was, stationary. The car bowled inexorably on, the town was awake now, there was movement, there were people, traffic had begun, there was no sun, but the day was lighter, it was on its way, nothing could any longer hold it back. He drove past his house. He saw lights. Kristina was up. He drove on. He had a cup of coffee in the Greenville Café. He drank it slowly, surreptitiously watching the clock. Someone tapped his shoulder. He looked up, Art smiled at him, Lucas smiled back recognition, made his mouth an O. Art pointed to his bag. Lucas looked at the bag, then looking up at Art nodded quickly.

"Night call," he shaped the words carefully with his lips. He shook his head, smiling ruefully.

Art nodded. He pointed at the clock. He patted Lucas' shoulder gently, he shook his head in understanding sympathy.

"Time for me to go to work," he said. Lucas was shocked to hear him talk in the instant before he remembered Art was not dumb but only deaf. He watched him walk to the door and it occurred to him that Art himself probably forgot this momentarily.

He looked at the clock again. It was all right to call. He went to the phone booth.

Harriet's voice had none of the drowse of sleep.

"You up so early?"

She hesitated a moment.

"Of course!"

"I thought you'd sleep late, today—now that you're no longer tied to the clock."

"No, I got up early. Where are you?"

"I'm in a café—I just had a cup of coffee—it's good to hear you—"

"It's good to hear you, too. You've been up all night, I'll bet. You take care of yourself, Luke!"

"I'm all right. Kid had an appendix—we'll take it out this morning—what about afterward? What about lunch? In Annivale?"

"I can't—"

"Oh, come on! You don't know anybody in Annivale—"

"I can't." He heard noises at the other end. "Luke—there's somebody at the door—I've got to go—"

"Tomorrow!"

There was a faint pause. He was about to speak.

"We'll see," she said.

"Goodbye! Go let him in!" He hung up exultantly.

He returned to the office. Kristina was ready. Her white uniform rustled cleanly as she got into the car beside him.

"I had to go out," he said.

"I heard you."

"Appendix. Seventeen-year-old boy. Name is Albert Rapper. Farm folks."

"This morning?"

"Right away."

"We've got that hernia—"

"It'll wait."

"Is it bad?"

"I don't think it's burst. I think it's about to."

"Get some breakfast, Luke. The cook will make you an egg—at least have a cup of coffee. By the time you're through I'll have everything ready."

"I hate that hospital coffee," he said.

They walked through the familiar doors together.

"A glass of milk—"

He nodded and walked on. She looked after him, turned and went quickly into the operating room. For here was where they were married.

Here was where they were husband and wife. And it was better than home, to her. This table, these shelves of instruments, this autoclave and stands and trays with the furniture of home, the home she shared with her man. The rest was just a waiting, a time, a waiting-room.

The patient had been prepared. His mother rose from his bedside silently. Lucas winked at him reassuringly.

"This'll teach you to get folks out of bed all hours!" he scolded playfully.

He sensed someone beside him. He turned. Li hunched over a pair of crutches, grinning triumphantly.

"You, again!"

"Me!"

"You want to go home, I suppose. Walk a few steps. Let's see how you walk. You don't need both of those crutches. Put one down—no, the other one. That's right. Now let's see how you walk."

Li hesitantly took four paces, his left leg stiff, a single member from hip to heel. He turned laboriously, gazed at Lucas inquiringly.

"See? That's all you need. Pretty soon no more crutch. Just cane. Want you to use cane. Understand?"

Li nodded brightly. He stood waiting.

"All right. You can go home tomorrow."

"Today?"

"Tomorrow!"

Li limped off happily.

"I'll see you in a minute, young fellow," Lucas said. The boy smiled uncertainly. "He'll be all right, Mother."

"You just lie still," the woman said, reassured.

He walked past the women's ward. Dr. Snider stepped out.

"We're gonna have trouble."

"Delivery?"

"No, it's one of those goddamned typhoids. We're shut of all but two. One of 'em's acting up."

Lucas followed him into the women's ward. He looked down at the woman.

"Why, hello there!"

She looked up at him blankly, a young woman, married, two children, a café—

"Don't you remember me? Dr. Runkleman—you waited on us—you paid Dr. Runkleman part of your bill—"

A sluggish flicker of recognition stirred briefly in the young woman's eyes. Then they were blank again.

Lucas took her limp wrist. Her pulse was rapid, her temperature low, her skin pallid—relatively rapid, relatively low, relatively pallid . . .

"What do you think?" Dr. Snider demanded.

"Her abdomen is a little distended."

"Not too bad, though—"

"Not too bad . . . No . . . I don't get much dullness . . ."

Dr. Snider shrugged.

"Long as I got you here I wish she'd make up her mind."

Lucas studied the woman.

"What do you think?"

"Better watch her . . ."

"Ah, I'll bet she isn't perforating any more'n I am! I've seen 'em like this before. When they're haemorrhaging you can smell it! Every time! She looks better now than she did ten minutes ago! Yes sir!"

"I'd watch her—"

"Hate to take a nurse off—"

"She ought to be watched."

"Okay," Dr. Snider sighed. "I wish to hell we'd seen the last of these!"

Lucas looked at his watch. He went quickly to the operating room. Kristina was ready and waiting. She stood beside the patient. One of her two assistants stood at the tray. Lucas undressed, showered, donned white pants, scrubbed quickly. A few moments later, gowned and gloved, he advanced on the operating table. Kristina's other assistant had bent the boy's body around her.

Lucas looked at the three, surprised.

"Pretty fast this morning!"

The needle slipped smoothly home. The boy lay back on the table.

"How do you feel, Albert? Do I look funny to you in this mask? Like Halloween, eh?"

"Yes, sir," the boy muttered.

"Now you just tell me when you feel anything. Here . . . ?" Albert shook his head drowsily. "Here . . . ?" The boy shook his head.

Lucas looked up at Kristina. Their eyes traded the immemorial look. He nodded.

"Ready," he murmured.

He put out his hand. The nurse at the tray slapped a scalpel into his palm. He looked at her sharply. He looked at Kristina.

"Would you rather I passed?" she said gently.

He looked back at the other nurse. Above the masks their eyes were on him. He capitulated.

"All right," he said. "A little harder, please."

The other nurse nodded.

He cut.

Kristina mopped the flow. She held out her hand. The nurse slapped a haemostat in her palm.

"There." Lucas pointed his gloved finger.

Kristina clamped the squirter. She mopped again.

He cut.

Now they both clamped. She swabbed, they waited, the area was clear, she put out her hand, the nurse slapped her palm with forceps, Kristina lifted the lining, the nurse slapped Lucas' palm with the cleaned scalpel,

"Getting pretty sharp around here." Lucas cut. His eyes twinkled. The nurses stirred. Then they were absorbed again. The muscles were bared.

Now the rhythm began, the movement of hands, of instruments, of response, of timed wait, of juncture, of beat, of pauses, unhurried, unhalting, and the three blended and became a trio, interdependent and whole.

The edge of the first layer of muscles was retracted. In this gap the broad, thin sheet of the next layer showed its fanlike fibers, was split, disclosed a final muscle layer, fanlike as the layer above it. Lucas moved the retractors, included it. Kristina cleared the obscuring seepage of blood. Lucas paused. The nurse wiped a clamp, held it ready. Kristina dropped the bloodstained square of gauze, seized a new one. They watched the area. It stayed dry. Lucas put out his hand. The nurse slapped the clamp in his palm. He split the fibers of the last layer, held the new gap open. Kristina moved a retractor, included the new layer. With her right hand she swabbed the white band of fascia beneath. The nurse had taken the clamp from Lucas' extended hand. His hand stayed extended. She slapped home a scalpel. At one edge of the gap a small artery suddenly spurted. Kristina clamped. As she handed the clamp back, the nurse slapped her palm with forceps. Lucas divided the fascia. An instant later he divided the membrane of the peritoneum. Now the abdomen was open. The inmost man, the viscera, lay bare. There was no pause. Tenderly, Lucas stripped the filament of the apron-edge of mesocolon from its juncture with the appendix. He ligated. He ligated again. He delivered the appendix.

"Just in time," he said. The sound was an alien thing in the white room.

The appendix showed swollen, angry red.

He put out his hand. The nurse slapped a clamp in his palm. He crushed the stump. He extended his hand. The nurse slapped home a clamp. He set the second clamp beside the first. Around the stump he needled an in and out weave of suture, leaving the ends free. He was about to put out his hand.

"Doctor Marsh!"

Their heads turned, indignant, outraged.

A nurse stood in the doorway ten paces away. She wheeled a stretcher on which lay a dishevelled, blood-spattered man, his trousers about his ankles, his underwear crimson, on the side of his leg a steady flow of blood, a moving sheet to the ankle.

". . . and they just brought him in and we can't find Dr. Snider—" with her right hand she was pressing fumbling fingers in the man's groin —"and he keeps bleeding—I think it's—"

The man's face was gray-white. His head dropped, lolled.

It was the femoral, there was no doubt about that, "Put him on the fracture table!" Lucas cried, it was the femoral and he had minutes, maybe less, "Hurry up!" and he reached across the open patient to the instrument tray as the nurse pushed the man forward, he grabbed a handful of clamps, he looked at the appendix, the opening, the swollen appendix, "Take over," he said sharply, he looked up at Kristina, the words and the movement were simultaneous, in the next instant he was running toward the next room, his gown flapping as he ran.

They watched him go. They stared at each other. From behind the tiled wall partly separating the two rooms they heard a rip, ". . . terrible accident," they heard the nurse say. ". . . Truck and this fellow, and he—"

Kristina looked into the cavity. What was there stared back at her.
"Take over."
The room still echoed with it.
Kristina stared, paralyzed.
From the next room came Lucas' voice, sharply.
"All right, Kris?"
She nodded numbly.
"All right!" she cried, obedient. Her voice tugged at her. She licked her lips.
Take over, he said. Lucas said. Lucas said take over. Do what he said. He knows. He knows—hurry!
She walked around the patient's head to the other side of the table. The operator's side. She looked down at the appendix again. It seemed larger, redder. Lucas said. She drew a deep breath. She held it. She put out her hand. The nurse wavered. She put a scalpel in Kristina's palm. She put it gingerly. Kristina grasped, almost lost it, recovered.
Kristina looked down. There it was. There was the appendix. And there were the two clamps. And between the jaws of those clamps showed an eighth inch of appendix. And in her hand was the scalpel. For a moment her panic clamored to throw it down, to run from the room. Her eyes cleared. There it was. Still waiting. Lucas said—
She drew the scalpel between the two clamps. The appendix was free. And then,
Then lift a clamp. She lifted it. The appendix dangled from its jaws. She dropped it on the tray. The nurse stared at it, picked up the clamp, clicked the jaws open, the appendix dropped on a square of gauze, she wiped the clamp dazedly, stared at Kristina.
Then,
Next,
The ends of the suture, the purse-string suture.
Her fingers grasped the ends.
Take up the slack,
She held the ends in her left hand. She extended her right hand. The nurse fumbled, found a swab, jiggled a bottle open, Kristina swabbed the cut stump gaping from the jaws of the remaining clamp. She dropped the swab.
Then,
Next,
They,
Pull the ends tight,
She pulled.
Then they—
The clamp. They opened the clamp.
The clamp was open. The stump was free, its end bound by circling suture.
And now—
They pushed the cut end in—
She clicked the clamp shut and used its tip, pushing hard against the pressure of the circling suture—one edge—a tag stayed out—
It was in!

And instantly she pulled the purse string shut, she tied, her fingers raced, she made a square knot, she pulled hard, another—

The breath left her body in a great gush. She felt her mask billow from it. Her muscles uncoiled. Her shoulders slumped. She looked down. It was done. She stared at it, unwilling to move.

"Give me some sutures!"

They jumped at Lucas' call.

"Chromic sixes—and skin—"

The nurse looked uncertainly at Kristina. Kristina nodded sharply at her.

"Right away!" she cried.

She nodded her head hard again. The nurse groped clumsily in the suture jar, Kristina stirred, the nurse seized half a dozen vials, rushed them dripping to the other room.

From the other room Lucas' voice called out again.

"Keep going!"

She looked dazedly at the canoe-shaped opening.

"Do you hear me, Kris?"

She swallowed.

"All right," she managed. "All right!" she said, louder.

"Keep going!" he cried peremptorily.

And then,

"Be right with you—"

She looked into the cavity.

First,

First the peritoneum.

They—

She took the suture from the tray, shook it out, the needle dangled from it. She clamped the needle in the needle holder. Now it was ready to pass. Now she would pass it. She passed it to herself.

Now they did—

She poised the curved needle over the cut lining.

She halted, but the point descended, she hesitated, but her left hand moved, the first stitch was through, she studied it.

But her right hand was moving again, her left hand drew the free end, the clamp clicked, the needle was free, the clamp clicked on it again, wait, she said, wait,

But the needle was moving,

Her left hand pulled suture. The needle clamp clicked, the needle was free, was clamped again, she reached for the free end,

There was a click. She started. She looked up, dazed. Across the table stood Lucas. He had clamped the free end of the suture. He drew it taut. He was not looking at her. He was looking steadily into the area. He had come in. He was standing where she stood. He was assisting her.

He looked steadily into the area.

"Don't you want to—"

"Go ahead," he said.

She finished the suture line. His hands were ahead of her, unerring, unobtrusively tightening, shifting a fraction—and assisting. Always assisting. The line was finished. She looked up at him incredulously.

He lifted his head at her movement. His eyes smiled.

"That's right," he said. "You've seen enough of them, haven't you. I'll bet you could do it blindfolded."

But his hand was already out for the next suture, he remembered, he found it himself on the tray, the needle holder clamped again, he had slapped it into her palm,

She had begun the next layer.

She had no chance to waver, a moment later she had no chance for doubt, her fingers were moving and his amazing fingers were ahead of her, making all clear, she stitched as she had seen him stitch, they came to the end, she tied, he snipped, ligature slipped over haemostat, drew tight, haemostat slipped free, there was a brief clash, a small rattle, the retractors were gone, she hesitated, the clamp was poised at her, waiting, it was in her hand, the interrupted ones had begun.

And then the skin.

She looked up. She took a pace back.

"Have to hang out your shingle," said Lucas. He was laying a pad of gauze over the incision. He put on a larger pad, reached for a long strip of adhesive. "Didn't think you could do it, did you!"

Hurriedly she pressed one end of the adhesive to the patient's side. Lucas drew the other end tight. They repeated this.

"Did you?" said Lucas.

The other nurse had come in.

Kristina swallowed. She looked numbly down at the patient. She shook her head.

"Everything all right?" Lucas asked the nurse.

"He's gone," she nodded.

"Gone!"

"I mean gone to his room—they're giving him a transfusion."

"Don't scare me like that," said Lucas.

"I'm sorry—"

"Look what your girl friend's done here!"

He untied his mask. He kept his eyes on the nurse. She was staring at Kristina, awed.

"Why, Mrs. Marsh—!"

"He was right here!" Kristina felt her face hot. "I didn't—he was—just the first—"

"All by herself," said Lucas. And now he looked at Kristina. And from his gaze, from the pride, the tense pride, the claiming bond in his eyes, Kristina drank one intoxicating gulp, choked, turned aside.

"What do you think of her?" Lucas demanded.

"Why, Mrs. Marsh—!" the nurse echoed.

"That's right, Mrs. Marsh—what do you say to that?"

Kristina untied her mask. Her fingers shook. She looked at her hands, she plucked at the sheet over the patient.

"You—you going to leave him here all day?" she stammered.

The nurse hastily began to strip the laparotomy sheet from the patient, the doors opened, a nurse entered wheeling the Gurney, Kristina stepped out of the way, she walked to her husband, where he stood she began to unfasten the tapes of his gown, safe behind his back. Her knuckles, as if accidentally, touched the substance of him beneath the gown, felt his warmth. He shook the gown free. He faced around. She felt her husband's hands on her shoulders. He had whirled her. He was undoing her gown tapes. She pulled hastily free. She faced him a few feet away.

"I got work to do!" she protested. And she began to gather up instruments, making a deal of clatter.

"I'll do that, Mrs. Marsh," the other nurse protested.

"You get those there cleaned up—put them in the autoclave—" Kristina flustered.

"You come on with me!" Lucas ordered. "You come on with me and put your patient to bed!"

And Kristina, not knowing which way to look, her hands clasping, fidgeting, took her place beside him and they walked side by side out of the operating room, following the nurse pushing the stretcher, into the corridor, into the ward.

"And now," said Lucas, his face hardening, the smile, the pride, the softness gone, "now I've got to have a little word with Dr. Snider."

They walked together to the door of the ward.

"Don't get mad, Lucas," Kristina pleaded gently.

"It was that close," he said grimly. "It was just—that—close . . ."

But Dr. Snider was not in the hospital.

They called his house.

"I think he just went downtown for a minute," the head nurse said.

"You told me he was here!"

"I thought he was! I could have sworn—"

"Now you say he's gone downtown."

"I remember now, he told me to tell you—"

"Why didn't you remember while that patient was bleeding to death?"

"You're always here when we need you, Dr. Marsh. That's one thing Dr. Snider was saying the other day. I'm sure he just intended to be gone a minute—he's never gone more than five minutes. He was saying about you just the other day—"

"I'll be at the Valley," Lucas said coldly. "When you're through, Kris, you go back to the office."

"I hear Mrs. Marsh—" the woman began, fawning.

"That's all," Lucas said coldly.

He rushed on to the Valley Hospital. He made two calls. When he reached the office Kristina was waiting. The reception room was full. He sat down. She sent in the first patient. Smoothly, the afternoon calls began, the treatment rooms ready, the patients shunted deftly, the setups always at hand.

The call came in the middle of the afternoon. Lucas rushed to the County. In the women's ward Dr. Snider stood beside the bed of the typhoid patient. A nurse was putting up screens.

"Went out, by God!" said Dr. Snider. His jaws worked, a small dribble of tobacco juice came to the corners of his mouth.

"Just like that!" he snapped his fingers.
The abdomen was grossly swollen.
"Was there somebody here watching her?"
"Every goddamned minute!" Dr. Snider clucked.
"Well," he shrugged, "that's how they go. I didn't think she had much chance, anyway."
Lucas picked up the chart. He looked at it. He started.
"Who ordered this?"
"What? Who ordered what? That? You mean the physic? *I* ordered it! She hasn't moved her bowels in damned near ten hours—that's what I always do! What's the matter? What's wrong?"
Lucas stared at him, stupefied.
"She's perforated!"
Dr. Snider looked at the body.
"Wouldn't be surprised—" he nodded.
Lucas was about to speak, he checked himself, he opened his mouth again. He closed it.
"You—you gave her a physic . . ."
"Pull them screens closer!" Dr. Snider directed the nurse.
"All right, Snider," Lucas said.
"All right, what?"
"This is the last," Lucas said evenly.
"What—"
"You'll never kill another one," Lucas said quietly.
They watched him go. He walked quickly from the room. He called Kristina, cancelling the rest of the afternoon's calls. He got in his car. He drove to Annivale, to the office of the chairman of the County Medical Society.
This time there would be no turning back.
This time there was only one thing to do.
This time, and he pressed the accelerator fiercely, this time he was doing it. Once and for all. And forever.
He found the building. He parked his car. He mounted the stairs, unshackled, ready, purified at last.
The dusty glass showed the faded gold letters: "Dr. Bruce Gillingham, M.D."
There was an honesty, a plainness, here. There was the incorruptible in this dust, the unassuming in this bare door. This was the office of the chairman of the county society. Lucas stepped over the threshold, a man who had come home.
A dozen golden oak chairs stood stiffly about the walls, the floor was bare except for a small rectangle of worn carpet, in the middle of the room was a long table offering old, well-worn magazines. There were two windows and between them stood a kerosene heater. On the wall at the far side of the room was a door. Lucas halted, respectful, irresolute. He listened. There were no sounds of occupancy. He looked at the inner door. He sat down.
A moment later the inner door opened. Lucas rose instantly. A tall, broad-shouldered man in his sixties, quite bald, his brows bushy, his

mouth wide and thin, stood in the doorway. He wore a white coat. He peered at Lucas, unsmiling, waiting.

"Dr. Gillingham?"

"I am Dr. Gillingham."

"I'm Dr. Marsh—from Greenville."

Dr. Gillingham's heavy face relaxed. He did not smile. He inclined his head courteously. He opened wider the door behind him.

Lucas entered a smaller room. It contained a bookcase, a treatment table, a cabinet of instruments, a desk and two chairs. Dr. Gillingham had been reading a medical journal. It lay open on the desk. On a corner of the desk was a pile of the same publication.

Dr. Gillingham went to his desk and when he was seated Lucas sat also.

They looked at each other.

Runkleman's protégé, pondered Dr. Gillingham . . . nice-looking boy . . . got that old look already . . . This is the one that's smart . . . looks like a comer . . . nerved up . . . looks like that typhoid put him through the wringer . . . He's on edge about something. Just barely holding it in. What's happened, now? What's happened in Greenville. What's he done? What's he here for?

If I could have drawn the man, Lucas thought grimly, that face, that figure, this is the man I would have drawn. This is authority. This might have been my professor. And when I tell him—

"You took over Dr. Runkleman's practice," Dr. Gillingham nodded.

"He often spoke of you, sir. I'm sorry to have come over so abruptly, but—"

"I've heard of you. Not only from Dr. Runkleman. I've heard some nice things about you. Glad to have you with us."

Hold him back, thought Dr. Gillingham. Set the proper tone. Later he'll be glad if everything said was said decorously.

"I wish my errand today was a happier one—"

"I see Dr. Castle occasionally. Quite a bout you had with typhoid this year."

"Yes, sir," said Lucas. He sat back. This was the way he wanted it, then. His own time, his own order. It doesn't matter. It has to come. And when it does . . . Sit back, then. Do it the way he wants. Let him ask the questions.

"Yes," said Dr. Gillingham. He nodded slowly. He cleared his throat. Might as well have it. "Well, Doctor," he said quietly, "I don't suppose you've come as a patient."

"No, sir."

"You wish to see me as the chairman of the County Board."

"Yes, sir."

And it was good, thus. For there was order, there was method, there was dignity, and this was the law of the profession, and this man was its court.

"You have a matter you wish to bring up with me?"

"I have, sir."

Dr. Gillingham nodded gravely. He's calm, now. He'll speak as a doctor.

"Proceed, Dr. Marsh."

"I am here, sir, to charge Dr. Alpheus Snider with malpractice."

Dr. Gillingham's expression did not change. Lucas watched it intently. Dr. Gillingham gazed at him, he seemed to be waiting.

Snider again? What was it this time. What was it Runkleman once hinted? And Castle . . . Castle said something, too. . . . Snider . . . that sorry excuse for a doctor—that long-ago graduate of a defunct fourth-rate school . . . that bumbling old man . . . Malpractice, though! That could mean abortion!

"This is a very serious charge, Doctor."

Now it has come. Now I will tell him, I will confide everything. And when he knows, when he hears what this man has done to Medicine—

"Dr. Gillingham, I am here directly from the deathbed of a young woman. I came here from the County Hospital. She was one of our last typhoid cases."

It was not an abortion, then. Thank God, it wasn't an abortion . . . Mismanagement . . . I don't doubt that, knowing Snider . . . Or is this a grudge . . .

Dr. Gillingham's eyes narrowed slightly.

"This morning I saw this patient at Dr. Snider's request. We both looked at her. She was semicomatose. Her pulse was relatively rapid. She was pale. Her temperature had dropped. Her abdomen was somewhat swollen. We looked at her together. It was evident that if these symptoms increased the patient would have to be explored for possible perforation and haemorrhage. It was borderline."

Lucas waited. Dr. Gillingham nodded.

"Less than an hour ago I got an emergency call from the County. When I arrived, the patient was dead. She now showed obvious signs of perforation and internal haemorrhage."

Dr. Gillingham sighed.

"Haemorrhage in those cases is frequently very rapid. I think you did all you could, Doctor."

"To this patient, knowing she was a borderline case, Dr. Snider had given a purge."

He halted now. It had been said. In his mind, as in Dr. Gillingham's, was a full picture, a picture of a human abdomen, of the viscera made frail by inflammation of infected lymphatic patches, distended by gas, of a patient on the probable verge of explosion, of perforation, of this patient given, of all the medicines in the pharmacopeia—a physic. The one medicine best calculated to kill her. It had been said, there was no equivocation, there was no possibility of ambiguity. Murder had been done. By a doctor. Now the vindication of Medicine was in the guarding hands of its judges.

And Dr. Gillingham watched Lucas, brooding.

That's it, is it? That's all? Was there a fight? Did they shout at each other? Does half the town know it?

"You brought this to Dr. Snider's attention?"

"I don't understand. Did I tell him formally—did I say, 'You killed this woman by giving her a physic'? There was no point in saying anything. I said to him, 'This is the last.' Then I came straight here. I am at fault there. I should have come before. But—this is the last."

"I see," said Dr. Gillingham. Thank God. No scandal. And he killed her, all right. Oh, yes, he killed her. I wish I could tell you that. I wish we could do something, just the two of us. And you're outraged. You've got a right to be. But you don't know. You don't know what you're asking. You'll be outraged by more than this by the time you're my age. You'll think this was nothing. And you'll do what I have to do. . . . I'm going to break you, now . . . I'm going to break your heart . . ."

He looked at Lucas. He put on an impersonal look.

"You feel Dr. Snider mismanaged this case?"

A faint misgiving shook Lucas. But this might be process, the question might be orderly process.

"I feel," he said levelly, "that Dr. Snider is responsible for this young woman's death. That he killed her. And I have come here—"

Oh, he killed her, all right. No doubt about that! And how many more, young man, that you nor I have ever heard about? Snider in Greenville, Toftus in Lepton, Grismer right here in Annivale, seven DC's and warning or no warning I'll bet he's still at it . . . only three of them, thank God, three in the whole county . . . And before them . . . But this was now!

"Dr. Snider has handled a great many typhoid cases."

It had to be done. It had to be done this way.

"Inevitably, when one handles a great many such cases—"

"I'm afraid I didn't make myself clear, Doctor. I should have added that this morning I also ordered this patient watched. Dr. Snider agreed to put a nurse there. If she had been watched—even though a physic was exploding her—I would have been called—she might have had a chance. I forgot to mention that."

Lucas spoke almost with anxiety, now. He must omit nothing.

"There are no absolute rules for typhoid, Dr. Marsh. I think we both know that."

"But a purge—surely, Doctor—!"

"In your experience, Dr. Marsh, are you prepared to say that a purge is never indicated in such circumstances?"

"Never, sir! Never!"

"Have you treated much typhoid?"

It was all coming now, the gambit, the old, familiar gambit, it was cruel, it was unfair, but it had to come. It had struck home. Now he knew. He was flushing.

"We have just been through an epidemic—" Lucas' eyes widened. He denied himself thought.

"And prior to that?"

Lucas stared, said nothing. His heart began to beat faster.

"Dr. Snider has been through many such epidemics. I suspect many of our young men being graduated today have never even seen a case of typhoid. And as to the perforation and haemorrhage—the *possible* perforation and haemorrhage—I think you yourself used the word 'possible'?"

"Dr. Gillingham, that woman died of perforation and haemorrhage!"

"Are you prepared to say she would not have died if she had not been given a purge?"

I'm sorry, young man, I'm sorry, indeed I'm sorry! I can't tell you any other way. You have to see. There's only this way to show you. It's not just Snider. It's a doctor. He's got his diploma. He's one of us. A part of you and a part of me. A part of all the men the Society must protect. But you won't see. Not until you've been steam-rollered. Not until I've done what I have to do. And then maybe you won't. Until it's too late. Until we've had to deal with *you*. A fine young doctor like you! For a Snider! Yes, look at me—I've betrayed you, haven't I . . .

"We're all liable to errors in judgment, Doctor. All of us."

I haven't betrayed you. You're going to have to learn that. You're going to have to be one of us.

"Errors in judgment?" Lucas echoed stupidly.

"Errors in judgment."

"Are you trying to tell me, sir, that Dr. Snider didn't kill that woman?"

" 'Kill' is a bad word, Doctor. A bad word in Medicine. A hard word to prove. You, for instance, have come to me with very grave charges—"

"I have come to the Society to report a disgrace to Medicine!"

"In your opinion, Doctor—"

"Dr. Gillingham—do you know Dr. Snider?" Lucas demanded incredulously.

"Very well."

"In your opinion does he represent a standard of Medicine you are prepared to endorse?" For *God's* sake, man! For *God's* sake!

"He has been licensed to practice Medicine. It is not my opinion that is at issue here. If you have facts—facts, Dr. Marsh—which would justify the State Board of Examiners in suspending his license—"

"I see," said Lucas. He licked his lips. "I see," he said numbly.

It was the priesthood. The old, old priesthood, the priesthood that had never died. It was no myth. It was real. The parallel was exact. The priesthood did not try for murder. It tried for heresy. It did not execute. It turned the defendant over to the secular arm. And the priesthood protected. It protected its own. Not Medicine. But the priesthood. It was real. It sat here in the room with him. And Dr. Snider was a Priest. And the ranks had closed.

"As chairman of the County Board I do not represent you or Dr. Snider. I represent Medicine as it is practiced in this county. If he has offended against the ethics or the canons of Medicine—if it can be proven that he has behaved in any way such as to bring Medicine into disrepute . . . Tell me, Doctor! What have been your relations with Dr. Snider?"

Lucas heard him dimly. But at the last, at the question, he stirred.

Let the ranks close, then. Let be what must. He's going to hear it all. He's going to know. And I know what's right. And I'm going to tell him.

That much I'm going to do. Whatever he does—whatever he says—I'm going to do that. And then—

He looked at Dr. Gillingham steadfastly.

"I have told you of one death this man has caused. I do not think that any panel of doctors sworn to uphold the highest ideals of Medicine as an art or a science—" He mastered himself with an effort. "I am unable to tell you how many deaths this man has caused. I think if you had to practice with him you would find his practice incredible. I don't think you would believe it."

Oh, yes, young man. I would believe it. Only you don't know. You don't know what you're attacking. This is organized Medicine we're protecting—not just one man. A scandal—a stink—and the public revelling . . .

You're an enemy, young man. You don't know it. But you're dangerous. You're an enemy.

"Has there been bad feeling between you and Dr. Snider?"

"No," Lucas said slowly. "You're wrong. If you think this is a personal feud—"

"No offense intended. It has happened."

"My introduction to Dr. Snider—as a doctor—came when I first came to Greenville. I want you to consider this, also," Lucas said deliberately. "One day I saw two beds waiting in the corridor outside the X-ray room. The X-ray room is not heated. In each of these beds was an old man. In the X-ray room itself—protected only by a sheet and counterpane—lay another old man. They were some of the county aged. When Dr. Snider judged the senile were near death it was his long custom to expose them to pneumonia to hasten their end."

"You have proof of this?"

Someone would definitely have to talk to Snider.

"Any nurse at the hospital will testify—"

"Any doctor?"

"Dr. Runkleman knew it. He knew it well! He persuaded me not to report it. He gave me to understand that he would see that Dr. Snider stopped this."

"And Dr. Runkleman is dead."

I'm sorry, young man. I'm very sorry for you. But we'll take care of this. In our own way. If I could only tell you . . .

"Dr. Runkleman is dead," Lucas assented. Rage welled in him. He tried in vain to fight it down. "And so are all the old men exposed to death to make room for more patients!" For an instant he could barely see the man before him. "Do you know that we don't allow him to give ether? That he gives it with a dead cigarette in the corner of his mouth? Do you know that? Do you know that Dr. Runkleman whom you respect has thrown him out of the operating room—bodily? Do you know that the nurses gossip that he pockets county money, that he extracts fees from charity patients? That twice, now—that dirty, ignorant man—has been absent from his post when patients were bleeding to death?"

His voice had risen. He confronted Dr. Gillingham, his hands trembling.

Dr. Gillingham nodded. Now you've said it. Now it's off your chest. This is the time, then. Now . . .

"Have you ever been protected, Dr. Marsh?"

"By whom!"

"Have you ever, since your graduation in Medicine, committed an error in judgment? Something for which you were grateful for the protection of your fellow physicians?"

"Never!"

"Something—we are all made of meat, Dr. Marsh, we are all human, none of us is beyond error, we must make mistakes before we die—something for which your fellows could have denounced you, denounced you publicly—and which they did not, but closed around you protectively, keeping it in the family, knowing we are all made of meat, knowing the thousands you would save? The error you would not commit again?"

"The immunities and privileges?" Lucas said bitterly. "The magic words on the diploma? Is that what you mean, sir? The immunities and privileges that save a bad doctor from prosecution for manslaughter? That covenant with the law?"

"That covenant with humanity, Doctor. Perhaps you are one of the fortunate ones. I have heard excellent reports about you. Perhaps you have not yet made an honest mistake. Perhaps you have not yet in a moment of fatigue or tension or human weakness been careless. You have a long life ahead, Dr. Marsh. No man is perfect. Medicine without that law would be impossible. Of ten doctors five might testify that a death was unavoidable, five could as honestly say it was manslaughter. The public has a right to its faith in us. We have worked for it with all our might. And it is our duty to keep that faith whole. Would you prefer not to have those privileges and immunities? Do you think any doctor would take his liberty in his hands to operate on a dying man? On a man with a fifty-fifty chance? On a one-in-a-million chance? Why should he!"

He sat back. It was almost over. He looked at Lucas sternly. His eyes hid compassion. You are trapped, young man. You are trapped.

Lucas smiled, a small, a cold, a steady smile.

"McDowell did," he said evenly.

"I beg your pardon?"

Dr. Gillingham stared.

"You asked me if I could imagine a doctor operating with a noose dangling over his head. McDowell did. Ephraim McDowell."

Dr. Gillingham was silent. That was one I hadn't expected. There's a brain here. Fencing is dangerous. And he summoned the Society behind him, he began what could wait no longer.

"Dr. Marsh, you expect the Society to act in this matter?"

There would be no sparing, now.

"I do."

"You realize that if what you say is true you are asking the Society to recommend the suspension of Dr. Snider's license?"

"I do."

"Dr. Marsh, I have a duty. It is a duty to yourself, and to Dr. Snider, and to every doctor practicing in this county, and to every doctor practicing in America. It is not *your* Medicine, Dr. Marsh. It belongs to all of us."

He waited. Lucas said nothing.

"I refuse to entertain your charges."

Lucas swallowed. His heart hurt, the hurt in him was sick, paralyzing with betrayal, with revulsion, his heart supine beneath the fallen altar.

He waited numbly. There was no hope anywhere. The words crashed in his ears anew.

"And now, hear me!" Dr. Gillingham said coldly. "I am not speaking to you now as the chairman of the County Medical Society. I am speaking as your elder, your senior in Medicine. Say I agree with you. Say that all these things are true. These things you can never, never prove. Say they are true. The woman is dead. No power on earth can bring her back. You are new at this. You are young. What would you do differently?"

He waited. Lucas said nothing. He could not speak.

"You are young, you are on edge after an exhausting epidemic, you see black as black and white as white, Dr. Snider is not the doctor he once may have been, it is very irritating—it is an outrage."

He pursed his lips.

"But he is a doctor. And you are a doctor. And I am a doctor. We are all doctors. We are all in this together. And Dr. Snider is old. His days are numbered. I am not going to do to you what I could do—to ask you what pneumonia is and how it can be recognized—to ask you how to treat pneumonia in the aged—to ask you how you would prove that those patients were not already suffering from pneumonia at the time of what you call their exposure. I am not going to ask you why Dr. Runkleman did not report these things immediately—or to remind you that his name must be smirched if this should ever be brought up." He drew a deep breath.

"I am going to suggest this to you . . . that if you press this—if you persist in bringing formal charges—if you force us to act—then, whatever the result—be very sure of one thing!"

He leaned forward. He shook a long forefinger slowly. He stared at Lucas intently.

The words cracked out.

"Don't ever make a mistake!"

He paused. The words crashed again, clipped and harsh.

"Don't you ever—as long as you live—make a single mistake!"

He sat back. His eyes were implacable.

"Because if you do—" he said softly. He let the sentence trail. The room was very still.

"Now, Doctor—" he said.

Lucas rose. His bones were lead. For a moment he thought he would be sick. He swallowed. He heard the words as in a cave, echoing, his head was the cave.

There was no sanctuary. None. Anywhere.

Dr. Gillingham had risen.

"Sometimes it is my duty to be harsh," he was saying. "You will think about this. You will understand. You will see that as the guardian of Medicine I cannot think of individuals or even of myself. I am glad you came here. Our talk is between ourselves. It will go no further. You're doing fine work, Dr. Marsh. You've won the respect of your seniors. We're glad you've come here. You have a long and useful life ahead."

He put out his hand. Lucas took it mechanically.

"Good luck to you. Goodbye, Doctor. I'd like to see you at our meetings. Once a month, you know—last Tuesday." Outside, there was the tinkle of the office bell. He nodded. "Come in anytime!"

Lucas nodded. He went out. He walked past the patient in the reception room. He opened the outer door. He stood in the empty hallway. He had been to the County Medical Society. He had come here on behalf of Medicine. And this man had confronted him, on behalf of Medicine.

He walked down the shabby steps, the steps of things as they are, the afternoon was unchanged, his car's familiar shape waited at the curb, he was an alien, a doctor of Medicine in a strange place. And there was nothing he could do.

It was through, here. It had finally ended. The Medicine he knew, the practice of the only Medicine he knew, that was over here.

He shuddered.

Organized, official Medicine. The chairman, the chairman himself, the chairman of the County Society—

"I could have told you that," Dr. Castle said sadly. "If you'd come to me, I could have told you—"

"No. I never would have believed you. Never."

"I could have told you."

"If you could have heard him. And he believes it. He believes he's right . . ."

"I know. I know. And if it wasn't Gillingham it would have been somebody else."

"There's no defense, then. Is there? You have to catch him red-handed—with a knife in his hand—and the blade in the heart—and six witnesses—"

"And what would you do? What good would it do? What guarantee would we have that a worse Snider wouldn't take his place? I know. I know the answers. I was like you are, once. I could have told you. I'm sorry. I know what it means to you."

"But if it had been Cosgrove!" Lucas could not shake off his incredulity. "What do we know? it summed up to. How can you be sure? How are any of us sure of anything? And then that horrible bit at the end—that blackmail—you keep still, or we'll catch you, too!"

"We don't know much," Dr. Castle said humbly. "It's God's truth. We—and all the other sciences. When you come down to it, what do we know? Of the very basis on which a science operates. Engineers don't know why cement sets. Electricians don't know what electricity is. What good is that shaky table of atomic weights and valences to a chemist in a condition without gravity. We—we don't even know what life is. Go down the line. What do we know?"

"We know one thing! We know what Medicine is!" Lucas' eyes were faraway. "And if we know—and suffer anything else—"

"It all comes down to what I told you before."

Lucas looked at him.

"You've got to practice Medicine as if you were the only doctor in the world."

"All right," said Lucas. He rose. "The only Medicine there is."

"And this is a good place to practice it."

"I don't think so."

"You will."

"You know better."

"Maybe I do . . . Maybe I do . . . you sleep on it . . ."

"I'm going to be alone," said Lucas. "I guess my mind was made up before I went there. I came out, I came out of school taught what we were all taught. I've never had much to do with humans. And they've never had much to do with me. There was one thing that never let you down, that never betrayed you, and that was Medicine. That's something finer than all of us, and it is, now, and it always will be. Fine and pure—and maybe holy. And the men who practiced that—the doctors—I can remember since I was a kid how I worshipped a man who was a Doctor of Medicine. And I knew that once the concept became the man—a Doctor of Medicine was Medicine itself. Beyond reproach."

He stared through Dr. Castle. His face was very pale.

"And one by one—like the leaves of an artichoke—I've watched the illusions stripped away . . . A doctor is a thief . . . A doctor is a murderer . . . A doctor is a merchant . . . A doctor is dishonorable . . . A doctor is yellow . . ."

He drew a deep breath. It sighed out of him.

"No . . . there's more . . . There's more and more . . . You know it all. You've seen it. You've been through it . . . I won't . . ."

"You can't be alone. Ever."

"I'll be alone. I'll do it my own way. I'll be alone. I'll treat their diseases. I'll work in a hospital . . . I'll practice Medicine . . . I'll work in a laboratory . . . I've had enough . . ."

"We're not all bad—"

"Not you! God no!"

"I know you didn't mean me. I mean there's a lot more of you and me. Working along, day in and day out, doing the best we can, stepping over what we have to step over and trying not to notice, keeping our own ideas, our own ways. . . . You think a bit—I know how you feel—you'll feel better. . . . Snider won't be there long . . ."

"Gillingham will. Or somebody like him."

"And you won't have time to think. Or be troubled. The patients—they just keep right on coming—all they know is, they're sick . . ."

He put out his hands.

"Look at these!"

Lucas saw the long hands, the long fingers, the knuckles knotted with arthritis, stiff, ungainly.

"Would you believe it? I was pretty clever with these, once! Yes, sir!

It's enough to frighten a patient away, isn't it! . . . Well, you put up with them when you're young and I guess they look at these hands and figure they'll put up with me when I'm old . . ."

"You ought to quit. You know that!"

"Why, once—I can remember at McGill—why, they came from miles around to see me that day—I was really hot, I had a new idea for an oesophagus resection, went in from the back—by God, I *still* think—!" The memory cleared from his eyes. He smiled. "No . . . I can't quit . . . and neither can Kauffman, and neither can Rankin—first in the class, last in the class— Did you know Kauffman was a hell of a man when he graduated? They wanted him to be a neurologist, Wyeth himself wrote him—"

"Kauffman hasn't got your heart. How much longer do you think you're going to keep this up? Tell me!"

Dr. Castle smiled fondly.

"I'll die in harness, boy."

Lucas looked down.

"You've got a rest coming to you," said Dr. Castle. He took Lucas' arm. "You go home, now, and get that good wife of yours to cook you up some dinner—when you come back from your trip I may have something to tell you!" He smiled and nodded his head significantly. "You'll see!" he promised.

The nurse put her head apologetically in the door.

"Ready, Doctor?"

"Send 'em in!" Dr. Castle cried.

Lucas drove slowly home.

Kristina was not smiling.

"There was a call," she began haltingly.

"What's the matter, Kris? What's happened?"

"She left a message—"

"Who? Who are you talking about?"

But his heart had grown cold. Kristina's face was strange. She was sorry for him, there was compassion in her eyes.

"She had to go," Kristina said in a low voice. She looked away. "That Miss Lang. She left this afternoon. She said to tell you goodbye. It was very sudden . . . I guess you didn't know . . ."

"No," said Lucas. He heard his voice from a distance. "No, I didn't know . . ."

"She had to go," Kristina murmured.

"Yes," said Lucas. "I guess she did . . . Did she say where?"

"She didn't say."

She'll write, maybe she'll write . . . What could she say to Kris? After all, what could she say? . . . She'll write . . .

"I guess she got a job in the city," he said, dry-mouthed. "I guess that's what she did. She heard of some job in the city. Jobs are pretty scarce these days! Yes sir! You've got to jump!"

He nodded brightly.

Kristina walked to him. She put her hand hesitantly on his arm.

"I'm sorry, Luke."

Her face, her simple face was sad, there was nothing else there, sincerity, sadness, and compassion.

"About what?" he said loudly. "What in the world are you sorry about?"

Kristina dropped her eyes.

"She was a nice girl," she said steadily. She took her hand from his arm. "You were friends—I'm sorry—you didn't get to say goodbye to her . . ."

Lucas managed a shrug.

"Here today," he said, "and gone tomorrow."

"Yes," she said.

He turned and walked blindly toward the closet.

"You want dinner?" she said. "Where you going?"

He opened the closet door.

"I'm going to take this gun apart," he said, "and see if I can learn something about it."

"I'm glad you're going, Luke. I'm glad."

"Me too." He slid back the bolt, inspected it, unseeing. "Maybe I can bring you back a deer." He appraised the gun absorbedly.

Kristina watched him a moment longer. She turned to go to the kitchen. She nodded.

"I make dinner," she said.

In the kitchen she lifted her head, she shut her eyes prayerfully, then she relaxed with a long sigh of thanksgiving.

"I'm not very hungry," he called out.

"No," she answered humbly.

CHAPTER 41

On either side of the road the mountains began, there were no houses anywhere. The truck labored up the long grades and the four men watched silently, the mountain mass streamed past, Lucas watched the towering green wave dividing from their passage, curling past on either side, suspending his thought, he was one with the passing, borne dreamlessly onward.

Each was silent, watching the limitless mountains, resting indolently, adrift in the onward movement, their guns bidding their pulses beat faster. And they were the more silent.

Lucas rode in front with Bemis Shedd and on the flat bed behind them Phil and Art stretched, and they had been travelling thus for two hours. The sun was up, it scattered a shrill, lifeless light through the overcast, and the pearly winter sky was an ancient thought, obscure and remote.

And as the road unrolled, so did the life of this human, sitting among these three, alien to them, conscious of his difference, a small boy waiting to carry a doctor's bag while other children played, children he never knew, games he never played. Children he never missed, games he never missed, parents he lost early, people to be ashamed of. Ouida. Ouida and Job.

What mattered was Medicine. Only, there were people in Medicine. People to dilute it. And they were not his people. There was Avery. There was Castle. There was that one professor. Perhaps there were a few more. And the rest of the people of Medicine, they were alien too. There was only Medicine, really. For his mind and soul there had never been any other purpose. And for his needs as a human—

He shut his eyes. He remembered Alfred, he remembered the time of his crucial, perilous, desperate need, he remembered that everyone he had turned to had made his need a chasm suddenly between them, he sickened again, looking across that chasm. He remembered his marriage, it was monstrous again, the gun to his head, the self-revulsion of that ruthless, helpless, deliberate deed. Kristina was the victim. Life would be kinder to her. Life would find her someone else. She would have that. There was no doubt of this. Because Kristina—

And the sum of Kristina came to him vaguely, Kristina the nurse, Kristina the uncomplaining, Kristina the stable, unastonished, accepting without challenge, without protest, grateful to be permitted, flustered by praise, grateful to be ordered. . . . What did Kristina want, anyway? What was she getting out of this? Was that enough, he marvelled? Just a husband? A marriage? Kristina . . . Kristina the stranger . . .

She would fare better. And she had earned it. He remembered her face, her eyes raised to him over the appendix patient. He saw her again. . . . There was something else . . .

There was something else about Kris, these days. There was a change, there was something his memory or his subconscious was trying to tell him . . . some physical thing . . . and yet not physical, either—it eluded him. . . . The truck had topped a rise . . . Ahead was another. The hills ascended steadily. He felt alien again, he was conscious of the three men, he remembered the life that was waiting for him. He was not one of them. He was a passenger. He was free. He was alien.

Yet, now, in this pilgrimage there was grateful union.

Ahead of them the road stretched, the black ribbon unwound endlessly, they saw fewer cars, then for a long time none at all. The region of the towns was past. The truck sped on, they were borne onward, passengers, the black ribbon dwindled behind them, flowed away, a Lethean blur, bearing backward the bobbing flotsam of everyday, fled to a vanishing point, their homes vanished, their daily lives, the hour's custom, the day's convention. And they were loosed, they were bound to nothing, four men in the wonder of freedom, inert, bemused, passive to the sweet twinges of their guilt, escaped, hugging the import of their destination, men with their guns, companying into an old domain, men alone, bound for the hunting grounds.

And Lucas feeling this, moved by this, one with the rest, kept cautious silence lest a green word break him from his union with the others.

On either side the mountains began straightway, soared up, ridged, ridged again, thick with oak and pine. Lucas started. Bemis had elbowed him. He was pointing. Far ahead two figures leaped across the road.

"Spike and doe!"

Lucas peered excitedly. There was only a flash, a movement, then they were gone, swallowed up.

"Buck country," said Bemis. Lucas nodded diligently. "Kind of stuff where you jump a buck, get a running shot at him slipping through, and if you're gonna get him you better squeeze and pray."

"I don't think I've ever seen it this dense. Not like this."

"Makes you feel good, don't it. Out here. Leaving everything behind. This is the only life. This is what a man needs." He nodded grimly. "He can be a hundred yards away and you not see him. He can just stand there looking at you, twenty yards away, right under foot!—and scare the heart out of you—and before your gun's up, he's gone."

There were no more cars now.

"We got an hour to go," Bemis said. They passed two foxes, they passed dozens of fat porcupines, each time the glass panel behind them resounded with the flat palm poundings of Art and Phil, grinning enormously, mouthing, pointing excitedly.

"We're here," said Bemis. Two does jumped across the road, the truck lumbered off the summit, pitched and swayed into a roadless meadow. Branches slapped at the windshield. The road behind them disappeared. There was a small clearing. The truck stopped.

In an hour the camp was ready. Lucas watched respectfully as Bemis bustled through the gambits of camp making. He joined the absorption of finding the right rocks for a campfire, the setting up of two crates for a food locker, the gathering of pine branches for a mattress on the truck bed. The first fire was ritually made.

And then, denying themselves no longer, the four men got their guns. The plump, heavy cartridges were lovingly loaded.

"Well," said Bemis, "I guess we're ready."

They looked at each other, grinning. Phil stepped forward. He tapped Lucas' chest. He stepped back. He raised his gun, shaped his lips, made a soundless bang, flipped his gun between his knees, put his thumbs to his temples and waggled his fingers. He pointed delightedly at Lucas. His fingers flew.

"He says you're going to get a five-pointer," Art interpreted. Phil nodded vigorously. He made urgent sounds in his throat. He held up five fingers.

"One thing," said Bemis, "they know this country. It's wilder than hell. They got eyes. They sure use 'em. They'll see a deer before you can say it."

Lucas tapped Phil's chest. He pointed to Phil. He aimed his gun. He moved his lips in a soundless bang. He pointed at Phil, again. He pointed to himself. He pantomimed carrying a burden. He gave up, laughing at his ineptness. Phil watched him, grinning amiably.

"I'm trying to tell him—if he kills one, I'll carry it," Lucas explained.

Art's fingers flew. Phil's head bobbed in exaggerated nods of comprehension, he smiled, he winked appreciatively.

"I'll go with Phil," Bemis said. "We none of us'll go far." He planted himself in front of Art. He articulated carefully. "Me and Phil are going over this way—west. You and Doc—you go east." He looked at his watch. Art nodded. His fingers flew, telling Phil. "It's eleven o'clock. We all oughta be back here by four. No later." Art looked at his watch and nodded soberly. "All we're going out for is a brief little hunt, sort of to keep our hand in and get acquainted with the country. Art—you watch it, now!" He gestured to the forest. "Take care of Doc!"

They set out together. In thirty paces they had left the tiny clearing. There was a faint trail and they struck into this, single file. The branches closed behind them. The green ocean swallowed them.

Overhead, fragments of sky could be seen through the treetops. The trail mounted steeply. Lucas breathed harder. He tried to hide the sound, abashed. He could see Art's back, ahead of him, he could hear Bemis and Phil thrashing, invisible, a few yards ahead. Abruptly the steep grade turned, climbed again, then ended. They had come into another clearing. It was smaller than the one in which they had made camp. The trees were larger. The earth was visible in patches, brown, splintered with pine needles. At the left of the clearing was a huge boulder.

"Take a look," said Bemis. Lucas put his gun against a tree, he clambered up the smooth face of the boulder, found a footing on a tough shrub, he inched his way precariously upward. At the top he looked down twenty feet at the three below, at this height partly hidden by the branches.

"Look around," Bemis called. The three peered up at him. He turned. Ahead he could see only trees, the deep green of the pines, thick, impenetrable, the tops of oak and beech and hickory. To the right and the left he saw the same. He turned. He looked back in the direction from which they had come. The camp had vanished. He looked at his watch. They had been gone twenty minutes. Ahead of him the green stretched to infinity, the mountains had disappeared, they had become an undulating sea of unbroken green. The vastness was absolute.

He climbed down. He jumped. Art picked him up. Phil dusted him industriously.

"See how they work?" Bemis said. "Straight up and down and crawl around, wind here and there, one mountain ends where another mountain begins, every ridge looks just like the next."

Lucas nodded. They watched him carefully.

"You stick close to Art today," Bemis said offhand. "Okay, Art?"

"Okay!" said Art.

"Let's go, then."

He turned and Phil followed him, they struck off to the right, a moment later the clearing was empty of them, Lucas heard the swishing of branches. Almost immediately these sounds became fainter. Then they ended.

He smiled, amazed. Art watched him, nodded happily.

"Like smoke!" Lucas shaped the words carefully.

"We'll go this way," said Art. He pointed to the left. "We'll circle. We'll keep ten feet apart."

They were out of the clearing. They fought a sky-hiding jungle of bush and brush. They plunged through. They were in the forest. Lucas strode gratefully through the spaces of the tall trees. He watched Art closely. He eyed landmarks, memorized twisted trees, rocks, cups in the terrain.

Art stalked carefully. Lucas mimicked him. He maintained a distance from Art. He lifted his feet high to clear dead branches. They walked slowly, as silently as they could. Lucas noticed his heart beating. He was a hunter, stalking in the woods, alert for a patch of brown fur, a white tail, an antlered head. His eyes strained for the sight of a deer. His gun became heavy with significance, he yearned to swing it to his shoulder, to pull the trigger. In his imagination he saw a deer leap out, pause, his gun flew to his shoulder, he heard the sharp report, he saw the deer drop. He licked his lips. He glanced at Art.

They stole on.

They were climbing steadily now. Lucas breathed heavily. They were climbing, it must be a mountain, the trees never stopped, the subdued light was soft and dim on the gray-brown trunks, his breathing was a pain in his chest. He looked at Art. Art pointed to a fallen tree. They reached it. They sat down.

Art was breathing easily.

"Hard climb!" He smiled.

"My second wind," Lucas gasped.

"Bet old Bemis is puffing." Art grinned at the thought. "You see anything?"

Lucas shook his head.

"Nice country."

"Wouldn't want to get lost," Lucas gestured, made a sign of apprehension.

"Not here. Couldn't get lost, here. Out there—!" Art gestured northwest. He raised his eyes piously. He drew a forefinger across his throat. "Plenty deer here, though. Last year I got two." He held up two fingers.

Lucas was breathing more easily.

"Getting hungry?"

Art looked at a faint patch of sky overhead. Lucas looked at his watch. They had been gone more than two hours. Art rose.

"Guess we'll start back," he said diffidently.

It was downhill now. For a few minutes the going was grateful. Once again Lucas' eyes bored through the foliage, his fingers gripped his gun. Then the inexorable downhill pull, the aching of his calves as he began to slip and flounder, stripped from his mind any thought but the next step, and the step after, and the step after that. They rested. They went on. Lucas gave up hoping it would end in the next hundred yards, the next ten minutes, the next time they turned, the next bush, the next tree. He stopped looking for landmarks. The forest was an infinity of trees, anonymous, identical. He no longer had any idea where he was. He depended entirely on Art. He followed him blindly, uncaring. His knees bent. The gun was a clumsy, branch-tangling weight. He started violently. A rifle had exploded a few feet away.

And as Lucas' ears rang the gun crashed again. Lucas saw a flash of brown, a bobbing of white. His gun was pointing at the brown movement, his fingers jerked the trigger, there was a roar, the stock punched his shoulder, he had fired again, and then a third time.

They looked at each other. Lucas' heart pounded, his lips were dry, his shoulder hurt.

"I think we got him!" Art cried. And they were pelting off, leaping over tree trunks, flinging themselves through bush and brush heedless of branches. They found the spot where the deer had been. They circled wildly. There was no sign.

They looked at each other, panting.

"Sometimes they lay under a bush, look so damn much like the ground you can walk on 'em and not see 'em and they'll never move!"

Lucas nodded eagerly.

"I think I winged him," Art said. He gazed uncertainly ahead, to either side.

"I know damned good and well I got him!" Lucas cried. "I couldn't have missed!"

"See if he left any blood."

They searched the ground, the leaves. Lucas peered everywhere, absorbed, incredulous. He looked up at last to see that Art had stopped looking.

"Twenty miles from here by now." Art nodded.

"I swear we got him!"

"Maybe so. Hard to tell—"

"Don't you think we got him?"

"Branch probably threw the bullet off—"

"Honestly?"

"I guess he's gone."

Lucas' face fell. He stared at the dense foliage. He was amazed, heavy with disappointment.

"Well . . ." Art moved off. Lucas reluctantly followed him. Now he walked tensely, his gun ready, all his senses alert. He saw deer everywhere. An instant later they were branches, or patches of brown earth, a split second before he could raise his gun to his shoulder. He stalked with infinite care. He had never been tired.

"One more ridge to cross," Art called.

Lucas grinned at him. His heart was light, the camp-thought wrestled with the lingering to hunt, a few minutes longer, just a few more minutes.

They walked around a dense, head-high clump of deer brush. Unaccountably there was a clearing there. It was a small clearing, there was something vaguely familiar about it, there was a rock, no it was more than a rock, it was a boulder, a high boulder—

They were back at the clearing from which they had split up.

"Smell the bacon!" said Art. He was unloading his gun. Lucas hastily copied him. They went on.

The underbrush, the branches, the trees swallowed them again. He plodded after Art. He put the branches aside, they swished behind him, he took a step, he pushed at more branches, he ducked the branches rebounding from Art, he took another step, there were more branches, he stumbled, recovered, pushed through more branches, ducked, plunged on again, suddenly the branches were gone, the bushes were smaller, they were walking through them easily. Ahead was the camp clearing. Bemis was squatting over the fire. He held a pan in his hand. Phil was putting plates along a log.

Bemis heard them, he looked up, he rose, the pan in his hand.

"What'd you get?" he shouted. At his movement Phil had looked up also. Now he ran toward Art, his fingers flying as he ran.

"What the little boy shot at," Art grinned. His fingers were flying for Phil. Phil laughed suddenly, put his arm around Art's shoulders, hugged him, walked him back to the fire.

"I could have sworn we got one!" Lucas protested.

"Heard your shots," said Bemis. "Where the hell were you? Where'd you see him?"

"We were up there," said Lucas. He turned and pointed, realized he didn't know where he was pointing, "about there," he said. He turned inquiringly to Art.

"Up in the woods aways," Art explained. "About half a mile from the take-off clearing—"

"To the left?"

"Where that old mine digging is—you know where those dead hemlocks make a tepee holding each other up?"

"Yes—sure—"

"Right there! About fifteen, twenty yards south!"

Comprehension spread over Bemis' face.

"Big one?"

"Just got a flash—"

"Can't eat flashes," Bemis chided.

"Doc, here, got in a couple of shots—"

"That's the stuff!"

"I could have sworn I hit him!"

"Yup—I know just what you mean. Maybe you did, at that. . . . Lookit them two talk! Lookit 'em go!"

He squatted over the fire again and he and Lucas watched Art's fingers flashing, Phil's eyes intently on them, Phil's fingers fluttering an interruption, an inquiring look, a nod from Art, and the fingers flashing again.

"Be lost without each other," Bemis chuckled.

"I guess they would at that," said Lucas.

"Must be a funny world they live in. All shut up, sealed away, you might say. Folks in town shy away from them, think they're freaks, I guess they embarrass people. Old Phil, there, he'd be lost without Art."

"What happened to the other one?"

"His wife got sick at the last minute. Had to stay and nurse her. Guess nobody else'd know what she wanted."

It was dark quickly. The sizzling eggs, the pungent bacon were devoured, they were full at last, the tin dishes cleaned, the fire burned orange and yellow. Bemis spread a blanket on the ground.

"Might as well play a little poker," he said elaborately.

He produced a dirty, limp deck of cards.

"These here are our hunting-poker cards. Been using them ten years now, just about. You play poker, Doc?"

"Not much," said Lucas. Art and Phil watched, grinning.

"Watch him, boys!" Bemis cried. "He'll take your eye teeth! He says he's a beginner!"

Art's fingers flashed. Phil opened his mouth and nodded understanding. He waggled a warning finger at Lucas.

"Just for matches!" said Bemis. He shook a box of wooden matches over the blanket. "Everybody take twenty-five."

They played for a clamorous hour. They stole each other's matches, the tiny clearing was noisy with cries of upbraiding, swaggering male gambling, with Phil's hoarse throat noises, mewling protest, squealing delight, with pointing, with flashing fingers.

They lay in the truck bed, at last.

"Wait'll you hear the dummy snore," Bemis murmured reminiscently. Then, as Lucas turned quickly toward the other two, "They can't hear you. They can't hear a sound."

Lucas lay back. He sighed. Overhead, through the trees, he saw a vagrant star twinkle.

"Polaris."

"No," said Bemis. "Over there." His arm moved. "Fools you, don't it. Sometimes they all look alike. Especially when this is all you see. Cassiopeia's a W. All of a sudden there's W's everywhere. They fool you."

"This place is wild."

"They don't come any wilder. That's what I like about it. Everything but Fork Flats."

"Was that where Art was pointing? We sat down for a while, he pointed to his right, he drew his finger across his throat."

"Art knows. You get in there—you're through. Blooey."

"What is it? What's the matter with it?"

"Never been mapped. God! You could hide the United States Army in there and never find 'em in a hundred years. Hide nor hair."

"Wild—as this?"

"This is a front lawn compared to it. Why, there's been folks lost in there—the last man lost in there was four years ago—they never *did* find him. Not even his bones. It just winds and overlaps, winds and overlaps, range after range, country a buck can't get through. You'd have your clothes ripped off in a hundred yards."

They considered this.

"We'll just work around here. There's all the game anybody wants right underfoot."

They were silent, watching the night.

"Kinda new to you, ain't it, Doc?"

"I never thought I'd like it this much."

"It's a man's game! Good to get away from the women for a while."

"Yes," said Lucas. The hunting fever fled. He remembered Harriet. With a sudden sag of apprehension and dismay, he wondered where she was, what she was doing, whether she had written, whether the letter was home, now, waiting for him.

"You like it here, Doc? Greenville?"

"It's all right . . ."

"Good place to make money? You know that was one trouble with old Doc Runkleman, I always thought he carried too many free-loaders. You want to watch yourself. Some of these people here in town are pretty slick. A good man can make money here if he watches himself."

"I suppose he can . . . I never worry too much about money . . ."

"That's what I heard."

"You heard!"

"Oh, God, a small town—you hear everything. Specially if you're running a newspaper. See your friend left the other day—"

"Who's that?"

"That Lang girl. Damned nice, kept to herself, minded her own business—"

"Why do you say *my* friend?"

"Just a way of speaking. Nobody's friend, from all I hear, though there's those— Your friend Blake was buzzing around before you came. Sure left in a hurry, didn't he!"

"I was a little surprised."

"Yeah."

"Probably heard of a better connection."

"I think Binyon did the right thing."

"What do you mean?"

"Scandal doesn't help. You couldn't bring the girl back to life. Best, all around."

"So you know," Lucas said finally.

"Not much I don't know. Have to."

"Does anybody else know?"

"Far as I know, not a soul. Tell me, Doc! What makes a fellow like that? A doctor?"

"You mustn't be misled by Blake. There's fellows like that in every line—one or two . . ."

"But just sitting there—"

"He knew what to do. He just lost his nerve."

"You think he knew what to do?"

"Bemis, one thing you must never forget. You'll run into a lot of doctors—"

"I've run into some beauties!"

"Maybe so—but I don't care who, I don't care how little he seems to know, he's had it pounded into him for five years, a sort of set of cardinal rules, something he'll never forget—the ways of recognizing mortal illness and what to do about it in a hurry. He may not know where this nerve is, or he may have forgotten the branches of that artery, he may have forgotten everything he ever learned. But that set of rules he never forgets. The signs of internal haemorrhage, of shock, of poisoning, of cyanosis—"

"They all know it."

"They couldn't forget if they tried. They have the hell scared out of them for five straight years, every week, every month, a detail here, a detail there—and if you forget you're in trouble. Quick! Bad, bad trouble."

"So if he'd kept his nerve—"

"That's all he had to do."

"What can we do about stuff like that, Doc? We can't do nothing. You fellows got us hog-tied."

"Wherever there's a monopoly there's bound to be abuses."

"You know, Doc, I don't mean anything against you, but deep down, people resent doctors."

"You're in our power, Bemis. And nobody likes to be in anybody else's power. It's a double tyranny. Your own body is one autocrat. And Medicine's another."

"But we got no appeal!"

"There's groups you can appeal to—"

"Oh, come on, now, Doc! We know a medical board'll prove a doctor right in spite of hell. They've got to. You can't fool people. And even if it's open and shut the guilty doc is only going to get a slap on the wrist."

"I'll tell you what it is, Bemis. What I think it is. The people need their own board."

"Like the telephone company. There's another monopoly. They're smart. They do their best to keep resentment down. And they know if they get too snotty the people can always appeal to a railroad commission or a power commission that's just waiting for something like that—"

"Maybe if there were state boards—if people knew they were protected—if they knew they'd get a square deal—if they could only see the results of their appeal—get a hearing—"

"They'll never do it. The big guns want the old hush-hush. You know what they'd say? They'd say people'd lose confidence in doctors—"

"They might for a while. But who else are they going to go to?"

"You got a point there, Doc. You're pretty strong for people, ain't you."

"I'm pretty strong for Medicine, Bemis. There'd be better Medicine if there were that kind of board. Everything'd be in the open. A long time ago Medicine was run by priests. There's no magic in Medicine. Maybe a priest has to be omniscient. But a doctor doesn't. And he isn't. And it's time people accepted that. It's time we stepped out of the special-citizen class. We've got work to do. And there's nothing more important than doing it right."

"You know, Doc, the town's lucky we got a young fellow like you."

"I don't know how lucky you are. I've got a life to consider, too, Bemis."

"You're happy here, ain't you?"

"Why do you ask?"

"You don't want to be disappointed on account of money, Doc. Don't forget there's a depression on. There's a mint here if you'll only play your cards right. Why, you've just started, Doc!"

"I'll tell you something, Bemis. I didn't get into this for money."

"You stick around a while. Pretty soon old Snider'll drop dead or the board'll retire him—you'll have the whole place to yourself. Put your wife on the payroll—everything."

"It isn't money."

"I'll tell you something. I said to myself when I got out of the last war: What's in it for you, Bemis? I was just like you are, once. Because, honestly, is there something else? Except what's in it for you?"

"It doesn't have to be money. From salvation to satisfaction there isn't anything else but what's in it for me. But it doesn't have to be money."

"You sound a little bitter, Doc. Like one of these what they call the Lost Generation. Hell, there's never been a generation that wasn't a Lost Generation. We get all nobled up and we tell the kids a lot of things we wish was so and they find it ain't and you got another Lost Generation. Hell, they ain't lost! A fellow that's lost don't know where he is. They know where they are. They just don't want to *be* there."

He sucked his teeth meditatively.

"And after a while they find out there isn't anyplace else to be. Then they settle down and before they're through they got a nice new goldbrick to make suckers out of the next generation. Did somebody sell you a bill of goods, Doc?"

"No, Bemis. Nobody's sold me a bill of goods. And I'm not bitter."

"You want to be like me. You weren't in the last one, were you?"

"I was too young."

"You'll be in time for the next one. Be like me, Doc. You're a smart, intelligent man. You know the score. All you have to do is keep a straight face and go along with it."

"Did you say *I was* bitter?"

"Hell, *I'm* not bitter, Doc!" Bemis was honestly shocked. "I got the third-biggest newspaper in the county—even today I could sell out tomorrow for forty thousand dollars—"

"That much!"

"Twenty-five, anyway. Rock bottom twenty-five! You might not think it but the governor himself has been to see me that time I was thinking of running for Senate. And I would have run, too, only who'd have run the paper while I was in jail from all the money I expected to make as Senator?"

Lucas laughed. His laugh died away to a mirthless chuckle.

"You're all right, Bemis . . ."

"No, sir, Doc! What taught me was the Army. That last war was a war to end war. And before it was over—and sure as hell while we were on the way home—we knew they'd made suckers out of us. It took a while to get over that and I guess a lot of fellows never did. Most of us just woke up one day and saw the war was just part of a long drink of sheep dip we'd been swallowing all along and felt sheepish for not seeing it sooner. Hell, they make suckers out of a human from the minute they can start pumping the sheep dip into him. They start right in telling him to be honest and noble like everybody else is and when he's full of it, right up to the neck, his eyes shining with it, they break it off in him."

"That must have been some war, Bemis."

"It always is. They tell you you're fighting for Democracy and a better world to raise your kids. And ten years later it turns out nobody was bothering Democracy—nobody was within a million miles of Democracy—some halfwit started blowing a bugle and all of a sudden people got so whipped up they forgot what they really were and in the hysteria everybody got feeling noble—and the next thing you know they were confusing *feeling* noble with *being* noble—and all of a sudden there we were, convicts, tramps, tax dodgers, business crooks, everybody noble."

He groaned reminiscently, resignedly.

"And we came home, the same people we'd always been, not feeling noble any more, to the same people we left—and they weren't noble either. And there we were. Gypped again."

He raised himself on one elbow.

"We stuff our kids full of it! I swear to God I don't know what for—because the only problem is how to get the other guy to give you something for less than you give him. And the kid isn't out in the world five minutes before he learns it. And then he knows all about you, too."

They were silent thinking of this, each in his own world. Bemis sighed easefully. You've been aching to tell me this, haven't you, Lucas smiled in the darkness. It's the story of your life. Your personal history. You want to show me yourself—you and the others—you and everybody . . . that damned compulsion on you to grab the next man's arm, to tell him the story of your life . . . And now you're empty of it, it's like a bowel movement, isn't it, you feel better. Until life has filled you again . . . Life—or whatever the hell it is you lead . . . You spend half your lifetime doing that, don't you. Rushing around telling each other the story of your lives . . . You all know the answers . . .

And he was sad, he was wretched, cold, lonely as space, thinking an old, old thought. All that science can do, all that minds can dream, all that men can give their lives for is being done, is being dreamed, is being given, night and day, to preserve your existence, Bemis; men are dying, men are sacrificing their lives so that you can live longer. Because your life is so precious. That life you lead. Those thoughts you think. That sorry purpose you have created for yourself. You, Bemis. You and almost every human being I have ever met.

And it won't be long . . . Because now I'm going to get away from you . . . from the reminders of you . . . from the heartbreak of patching what you might be, knowing what you are. . . .

And he thought, brooding and sad, of quiet laboratories, of specialties that were pure science, of patching that was pure Medicine, he thought of himself, alone, and his solitary heart beat faster.

Because, when this trip was ended—

When they came back to Greenville—

Because now it was settled.

"Take religion," Bemis said. "You're not religious, are you, Doc?"

Oh, God, no. Not religion, now . . .

"Not Catholic, are you?"

"No. Not Catholic."

"What's all this stuff Catholics go by? You know about that, Doc?"

"Ritual is the tendency of organisms to repeat their own actions. Then legends are invented to explain the ritual, and rules are laid down —it's common to all of us, Bemis—"

"I mean Catholic doctors. The special rules they have to follow. You run into any of that? You hear stories—"

"They've got their rules. And I guess some of them live up to them. Birth control, sterilization, childbirth anesthetics which might damage a child, save the child at the expense of the mother—they have whole books of special rules governing every case where Medicine and Religion might conflict."

"I heard something like that."

"That doesn't mean they don't practice Medicine as well as the next man—and maybe even better. I don't agree with all of it, but one thing you can say for them: a human life in the vilest criminal, in a freak or a savage or a monster, is so stupendously noble to them—"

"You don't go to church much, do you, Doc."

"When do I ever get a chance to go to church—"

"You got to go, though. Stick your nose in the door once in a while. Looks good. Especially for a doctor."

"I'll go with you."

"Hell, *I* go! I go all the time!"

"I'll bet!"

"I'm not kidding, Doc! Hell, I know this town inside out. I know every human being in it, where he came from, what he's doing, how much he owes at the bank, what the town thinks of him. I got to. And I'm glad you're here, Doc. We need somebody like you. And I tell you—you could make a mint here, pay no attention to how things are now, it's right here waiting for you, all you got to do is listen to an old-timer like me and go along with the bunch and by God, before I'm done, I'll make you a millionaire!"

"Why?"

"Why?"

"What would you want to do that for, Bemis?"

"I don't know. Maybe I like you. That's why. You don't mean nothing to me. Maybe I just like you."

"I appreciate it, Bemis." And you'd like to make me one of you, too . . . I know, Bemis. I know . . .

"You stick around, Doc. And anytime I can help you—Jesus God! I promised Castle I'd see you got some rest!"

"You don't have to worry about me sleeping tonight."

"Wait'll you taste my pancakes tomorrow morning! Five o'clock, Doc! Bright and early! And no telephones all night. . . . Good night, Doc . . ."

Lucas watched the stars float above the small patch overhead. He thought of Harriet. He thought of freedom. He moved fretfully, a weight upon him, impatient to be gone. The night's sweetness blew cold and promising, stilling his face, stilling his thought, he burrowed deeper in the quilt, he closed his eyes, he thought of Harriet, he fell asleep.

When Bemis awakened him, he looked about, bewildered.

It was still dark. He heard the snapping fire, he recollected where he was, he rose unwillingly.

"I thought the smell of them pancakes'd wake the dead!" Bemis complained.

It was cold, there was frost on the ground, his muscles ached, the thought of hunting was meaningless. Art and Phil stood over the fire, warming their hands, they lifted grinning faces.

"Today we get 'em!" Art's fingers raced.

Phil nodded vigorously. He held up two fingers, pointed at Lucas, pointed at Bemis, pointed at Art, held up five fingers, pointed to himself. Art waved a scornful hand.

"He says he's going to get five," Bemis obliged.

Phil tugged at his sleeve. He made a noise in his throat. He brandished his gun.

"Wait until it's light," said Bemis. He pointed to the dark overhead. "Tell him when we can just about see our front sights—" Art's fingers flashed. Phil groaned. He sat down.

"We've got to get Doc a deer," said Bemis.

"You bet!" said Art. His fingers told Phil. Phil rose instantly. He patted Lucas' arm. He nodded vigorously. He made a noise in his throat.

"We'll get you one!" said Bemis. "Come on! By the time we get to the first clearing it'll be light enough."

In the first clearing Lucas leaned against the high boulder.

"You get your breath," said Art. Phil eyed him solicitously.

"I'm fine!" Once again the hunt held him, the gun in his hand was alive.

"We'll go the same way you and Art took yesterday. Maybe we can see your friend again. The one you shot at."

And Lucas' heart pounded faster. They spread out, they walked softly, their eyes bored ahead, they were on the hunt. Lucas walked better now. They stopped for a breather. They went on. Bemis waved his hand. The signal passed along. They stopped again. The woods were not so strange. Lucas stalked confidently. They came at last to the fallen tree on which he and Art had sat the day before. They pushed on again.

"Know where you are?" Bemis asked.

Lucas nodded confidently.

Art pointed. "That's as far as we went yesterday." Lucas saw the tree trunk on which they had rested before starting back. He nodded again. Phil waited, watching them.

"We're going to set you on point," said Bemis. "Okay? Gonna give you the cream of the hunt. All you have to do is sit here. Whatever we start up'll come sneaking back this way." He swept his arm toward the northwest. "We'll make a wide circle. We'll drive 'em back."

"One of you fellows ought to sit here," Lucas protested halfheartedly.

"You sit here," said Bemis.

"You're the one we want to get a deer," said Art. His fingers explained to Phil. Phil nodded, mewling vigorously.

"Just be careful," said Bemis. He grinned. "Don't mistake one of us for a deer, now!"

"You all look too tough to me," Lucas grimaced.

"And when you hear shots—you'll know we got one. Understand? So just get up and come in. Go on back to camp. And if we hear you shoot—we'll do the same. Okay?"

He watched them go. His throat was thick with sudden affection for them. He was one of them. They spread out. Now, they spread much wider. They slipped away to his right. They were gone. He heard them moving. The sounds diminished. The forest into which they had disappeared was still. It was silent and it was empty. It was as empty as if they had never been there. The trees watched him. He sat down on the log.

He held his gun across his lap. He kept his finger on the trigger. His heart was thumping hard. His eyes sentinelled the forest. He heard a sound. He started, he flung his gun to his shoulder, his finger tightened on the trigger, he waited, rigid. He saw nothing. Nothing moved. He kept his gun trained. He was ready. He was waiting. If it should be a deer—if he shot—if he missed—

His arms ached. Hesitantly, his finger still on the trigger, he lowered the gun. There was nothing. Nothing but silence. High overhead the trees towered. There was not a bird. There was that of the gray sky which filtered the forest, the grudged half-light that made the forest motionless. He was alone. Silence thickened, silence moved, crept before him, slipped behind his back. Silence was a presence, waiting, unlidding the eyes of the forest, the limbs, the earth, the trunks, the stones, watching him.

Cold moved his head, finally. He dared to move, he looked slowly around. There was nothing. The woods on either side, the woods back of him, were still and empty. He stood up. Cautiously he stepped a pace from the trunk. He walked back. He stood irresolutely. It was very cold. He looked at his watch. They had been gone half an hour. He put down his gun. He strode up and down, breaking silence, warming himself. He sat down again. He waited. The silence crept back. Silence enveloped the forest. His ears strained for a sound. His eyes patrolled the trees. He waited.

The moments passed, the minutes, the sections of hours, they lagged, they raced incredibly, they lagged again, then there were intervals when he was alert, desperate and tense to some sound, the movement of a branch. He sat watchful. Then he hoped against hope. Then he no longer cared. He sat indifferently, resigned, enduring.

. . . Avery had what he wanted . . . Or did he? Had he found out too? Is he going to tell me that? . . . Not teaching, either? . . . There was a fellowship somewhere . . . there was a field, there was some field . . . was that why Aarons had picked Pathology? But not pathology . . . It's hidden, it's true. You're alone. No one but the cadaver. But in that cadaver over and over again the intruding evidence of preventable failure, jeering from maimed tissue, from body deprived of life. And the invisible presence of the doctor who had done this.

Not, not pathology . . .

Surgery was good . . . surgery was an unconscious patient and your own intellect and your trained fingers . . . only surgery was mechanical. A surgeon was a mechanic. There was mechanics in Medicine. But Medicine was not mechanics . . . Medicine was the quick diagnosis he loved, the logic of pharmacology, the fellowship with the cell, with all cells, with the healthy, criminal bacteria, the clues of an internist, the impersonal facts of a laboratory, the virtuous service of birth, the greeting wail of the newborn, the hesitant, trusting face of a child, the look on the face when the door opened and the doctor came in and smiled and set his bag down.

He turned in revulsion from that last. Not that. That was magic. That he would never see again. There were specialties. And in one of these, stripped of people, stripped of their lives but not their bodies . . . Avery will know . . . we'll find it out together. . . .

It would be easy to find Harriet . . . She had gone to New York . . . wherever there was a pottery . . . an art school . . . and the letter was home now . . . He could see it, see his name in her writing. . . .

He looked at his watch.

It was past noon when he heard the first shot. It came from his right. It was very faint. He stood up. He craned toward the far sound, uncertainly. There were two more shots. There was no mistaking it. The sound was faraway. But those two sounds were shots.

Pent breath left his body. He smiled. It was over. The log which had been his base and his companion these many hours he looked at with disdain, needing it no longer, seeing it as a dead log in a dead forest. He walked back in the direction from which he had come here. His legs were stiff, he walked quickly, careless of noise, the hunting accomplished, impatient to be back, to see the deer. The great forest was prosaic trees, the masking bushes were malicious barriers where he wished to run. He walked steadily in the direction from which he had come, ignoring enticing trails, easier walking; once he fell, and even falling, kept his eyes alertly fixed ahead.

When he had made his way downhill for forty minutes he slowed, went on a few paces more, halted. He was breathing hard. He looked about uncertainly. He had come to a tiny plateau. He did not remember a plateau. For an instant, digesting this, his abdomen tensed, the woods blurred, he looked wildly. He saw a leaning tepee of trees. His eyes closed with relief. He had approached it from the left side. He put his hand on it. He breathed there a moment. He went on jubilantly, confident, proud of himself. Then there was a free space and he looked around surprised, he was in the clearing. Gaily, he was off again, the trail was clear, crushed bushes, broken boughs, the marks of passage, the true trail, the trail home; he floundered impatiently on, he pushed aside the last branches, the camping place lay before him.

Bemis and Phil were standing beside a tree. Their backs were to him. Between them hung the carcass of a deer.

"You got one!" he cried.

Bemis whirled. He put his hands on his hips, his heavy red face beaming. "How do you like it? Ain't that a beauty?"

Phil did a quick-step. He ran his fingers over the body. He made sounds deep in his throat, he wrenched them out high-pitched, his throat straining, his face reddening with the effort. Lucas winked at him, nodding quickly.

"He's trying to tell us something," Bemis said. "What are you trying to tell us, boy?" He jerked his chin up inquiring. Phil fell to patting the deer. He pointed to himself.

"Go on!" cried Bemis. "You didn't shoot it! Soon as we find the bullet I'll tell you who shot it!"

"My God, that's a beautiful deer," Lucas marvelled.

"Lugged him over half the county!" Bemis was back at the deer again, his hunting knife slitting expertly. Phil tugged at Lucas' arm. He nodded his head up and down, great slow motions, he pointed to a tree with an overhanging branch.

"Yes." Lucas nodded, "Yes, Phil! The tree!"

"Trying to tell you something," said Bemis. "God knows what. Probably saw a tree like that where we shot him."

"Where's Art?"

"He's probably gone farther'n we did. He'll be in directly. What time is it?"

It was twenty minutes after one.

"He'll be all right," said Bemis. He began to peel the hide off. "Don't worry about old Art."

Phil tugged Lucas to a basin. He patted his belly.

"Deer liver for supper? You ever eat fresh deer liver?" Bemis asked. "You never lived until you've ate real deer liver! He knows, don't you, boy! He spotted him."

"Phil?"

The deaf and dumb man watched them.

"Eyes in the back of his head," Bemis said proudly. "That's one thing about a dummy. See things you couldn't see in a million years. You got bright eyes for a dummy, haven't you!" he said fondly.

"Bet he misses Art right now."

"He'll be along," Bemis said comfortably. He went to the truck, rummaged for a steel, began to sharpen his knife. "You could do this better'n I could, Doc."

"Not a deer, I couldn't. No, sir, you go right ahead—"

There was a sound of crashing in the direction of the trail. Bemis stopped sharpening his knife. They turned to look. They waited. The crashing came again, this time far off.

"Probably a fawn," said Bemis. He looked at his watch. Lucas looked at his own. It was twenty minutes to two.

"He'll be along," said Bemis. He returned to the deer. "Make a fire, Phil." He made chopping motions. He pointed to the embers. Phil nodded quickly. He moved into the underbrush. He disappeared. From a few yards away came the sound of his chopping.

"Didn't see a thing, eh?" Bemis asked.

"Not a thing. I heard your shots and I came in."

"Think you were going to freeze to death? Hold that a minute, will you—" he spread the slit belly open, Lucas held the edges for him, "got to clean him out dry—" he swabbed the cavity with a flour sack—"then I'll tell you what you can do, you can get some water out of the can, we'll start a little coffee, set the plates out, and I'll finish wrapping Buster."

When he had finished, Lucas sat down beside the fire. Phil struggled through the bushes. He staggered, his arms loaded with wood. He dropped it near the fire.

"That all you got?" Bemis cried indignantly. He gestured at the wood, raised his brows, spread his palms wide.

Phil shook his head vehemently. His forefinger stabbed at the bushes. He walked quickly away. The brush swallowed him again. Bemis sat down beside Lucas.

"I feel guilty," said Lucas. "You must be dead—"

"I ain't what I used to be. I'll say that. Be glad when we can start eating."

"I could eat that whole deer raw!" Lucas said fervently. Suddenly he was ravenously hungry.

Phil crashed through with a second load of wood, went back for another.

"You'll never have an appetite like you get here. Fellows get awful hungry. Which'll kill you first, Doc? Hunger or thirst?"

"Thirst, Bemis! Thirst'll kill you quick."

Phil stumbled toward them with another load of wood.

"Christ! That's enough!" Bemis protested. Phil looked at him blankly. He started back. Bemis grabbed his sleeve. Phil halted. Bemis released his sleeve. He pointed to the log. Phil nodded. He sat down next to Lucas.

"Wish I could make my hands go the way they can," Bemis complained. "You ever see fingers move so fast? One of the dummies told me once he knew a fellow stuttered in sign language just like a fellow would stutter talking. You believe that?"

Lucas was about to answer but he felt Phil's hand tapping his shoulder. He turned. Phil's face was inquiring. He pointed to his watch. Lucas looked.

"Hey!" he cried.

"What's the matter with him?" said Bemis.

"It's half past two," said Lucas. He looked inquiringly at Bemis.

Bemis looked at the fire.

"Misses Art," he said.

"It's nearly two hours," said Lucas.

"He should be in by now," said Bemis. He turned his head. He looked in the direction of the trail. He looked back at the fire. "Art's okay," he said. "He'll be along."

Lucas smiled reassuringly at Phil.

"He'll be along," he mouthed carefully.

"Doesn't know what the hell you're saying," said Bemis.

Phil grinned doubtfully. He made a deprecative motion with his head.

"He's trying to tell us he's making fun of himself for worrying," said Lucas.

"Or else he's hungry. Or else that he's tired lugging that deer in. God knows. God only knows."

"Seems like he ought to be here by now," said Lucas. "He knew about the shots. Would he be that far?" He remembered. Art couldn't hear.

"He knows these woods like the back of your hand," Bemis said quickly. "He likes to go off by himself. I never worry about Art. He's due back any minute. This ain't the first time. By God!" he burst out suddenly, "if he don't come back with a deer I'm gonna tell him something! Keeping us all hungry like this!"

Phil watched them. He watched every move they made. He watched them talk. When they stopped he looked back at the fire again, where they were looking.

At fifteen minutes past three Bemis rose. Instantly they rose with him. Bemis faced the trail.

"Well . . ." he said. He waited. "I don't know whether to eat or look for him!"

"He might have got hurt," Lucas murmured.

"I'm beginning to wonder," Bemis said quietly.

The clearing was darkening. Phil darted in front of them. He looked from face to face.

"He could have started a deer, rushed after it, not noticing," Bemis said, watching the trail. "He could have wandered off, gone west, got into the brush country, the edge of Fork Flats. He might be there now."

"I guess we better look."

"And if he's there, if that's where he is he can make less'n four hundred yards an hour . . . less'n he's got into the draws and ravines, full of boulders, full of trees, so full of brush you can't see ahead and you can't see back and most of the time you can't even see the sky . . ."

"Should we start?"

"And if he's down someplace, hurt . . . seems like he'd fire his gun . . . the way these mountains twist you mightn't even hear him . . . seems like he'd build a fire—it's too dark, now, to see the smoke . . ."

He looked at Lucas.

"Start? God, man! There'd be three of us lost! Why, you could bust through the woods hollering, firing guns, and he'd be two feet away and never hear a sound.

Phil watched them intently. He made a mewling noise in his throat. Bemis pursed his lips. He nodded at Phil soberly.

"Come on," he said. He walked to the truck. "Guess it's time to get the warden."

They drove over the crest, they drove a long way, the truck stopped finally at a tiny town. They found the warden's house. His wife opened the door.

"Sorry to bother you, ma'am," said Bemis. "But we come for Sam. Got a fellow lost."

"Fork Flats?"
"I'm afraid so."
She put a hand to her breast, stepped aside to let them in. "Sam's out," she said. "Gone clear to Martinville."
"You think maybe you could find him, ma'am?"
She went to the phone on the wall, cranked hard, picked up the receiver.
"See if you can get Sam for me, Lorna Belle," she said. "Bemis Shedd's here and two other fellows. Got a man lost in Fork Flats . . . I know . . . Try Painter's. He said he was going to Martinville."
She waited a long time. Occasionally she spoke to the operator. She hung up, finally. She came toward them, shaking her head.
"No luck," said Bemis.
"I'll tell him, Bemis."
"Thanks. Well—"
"You fellows want any coffee?"
"I don't think so," Bemis said delicately, "not right now. But how about you, Doc? This here is Dr. Marsh, one of our Greenville doctors and this is Phil Acton, one of my helpers."
"No thanks," said Lucas. He thought of Art, lost in the woods.
"One of your deaf and dumb help?"
"One of 'em—"
"Bemis! Is the one that's lost—?"
"Not dumb. Just deaf. Bad enough. Well, thanks," he nodded. He backed to the door. "Better be getting back."
"I'll tell him the minute I get him. He'll round up the boys—they'll find him, Bemis. You know that fellow might be setting there waiting, when you get back!"
"That's true."
"Not much use looking at night—"
"That's right."
"That place could swaller every one of you!"
"We're much obliged," said Bemis.
"Now don't you go hunting off on your own! Don't go crazy, Bemis. That ain't gonna help!"
"We'll wait."
The truck started back.
"Another thing," Bemis said suddenly, "they can smell. I bet if Art smells that deer—let alone the fire—"
The fire was chilling embers. The clearing was empty. They built the fire again. Phil sat beside them. His face was pale, his eyes were lost.
"Want to eat?" Bemis slapped Phil's shoulder. He motioned to his mouth.
Phil shook his head.
"You, Doc?"
"None for me," said Lucas.
"We got to cheer him up," said Bemis. "It's bad for us. Think what it must be for him. Him and Art . . . and even so, Art's his only contact

. . . He's in a world of his own, now. He can't talk, he can't hear. He's kind of locked away."

"And his pal's lost," said Lucas. "Lost and deaf. And he knows what that means—"

"So let's eat! Come on! We'll get him to eat!"

It was black night now. It was barely possible to see the truck, a blacker mass fifteen yards away. The fire lit a small circle. Beyond the circle was blackness.

Bemis rose. He cuffed Phil's shoulder, grinning. Phil looked up. He tried to grin back.

"Gonna eat!" Bemis said loudly.

Phil looked at Lucas. Lucas smiled at him confidently. Phil shook his head. Bemis was plopping the liver into a frying pan. "Gonna eat if I have to choke it down you!" he vowed. Lucas put his arm around Phil's shoulders.

When they were through eating they put their plates away, almost untouched.

"Now, by God, we're going to play a little poker!" Bemis spread the blanket on the ground. He pulled Phil up. He led him to the blanket edge. He made dealing motions. Phil nodded obediently. He slumped down.

They played close to the fire. It was very cold. Bemis waved his arms, made barefaced attempts to steal Phil's matches. Sometimes Phil smiled a little. Afterward he would rise, put another stick on the fire, stand motionless, staring in the direction of the trail. Then Bemis would lean to pull at his trouser leg, he would come back and sit down.

Toward midnight a wind began. They looked up.

"He can get branches, wrap all up in pine boughs," said Bemis. "If he can cut 'em. If he ain't hurt . . ." He looked up. "Hey!" he cried.

Phil was staring at the deck in his hands. He was motionless. His face was wet. Tears were streaming down his cheeks.

"Hey!" shouted Bemis.

"He can't hear you," said Lucas.

"I know it," Bemis said. "Hey!" he shouted again. He shook Phil's shoulder. Phil looked up dully. His lips moved, he was trying to smile. "Go ahead and deal!" Bemis gestured. "I'm gonna murder you—I'm gonna strip you clean!

"I know it," Bemis repeated. He picked up his cards and pushed a handful of matches in the center. He drew his finger across his throat and stabbed his finger at Phil. He pointed to the pot. Phil nodded. He pushed in the last of his matches.

"He's seen you, Bemis," Lucas said.

"Seen me, has he! I'll ruin him!"

Phil laid down his cards. He had a pair of sevens.

"I'll be damned," Bemis cried. He threw his hand down with exaggerated disgust. He shook his fist in Phil's face. "I'll get you!" he cried. "I'll take the hide offa you!"

"Take it in!" Lucas clapped Phil's shoulder, raking with his other hand.

When it was near five o'clock Bemis rose to make coffee. The stars were paling. The edge of the clearing was visible. Lucas went to the edge, stared at the just visible bushes, the faint gray light. The night was over. Somewhere in the wilderness, if he was alive, if he was conscious, Art was watching it too.

They drank their coffee. In the night Phil had aged. His thin face was shrunken. His eyes were lifeless. The posse arrived as they were rinsing out the cups. They came in trucks, in the trucks four horses, saddled. There were fourteen men.

They descended silently from the trucks and immediately began to unload the horses. The warden walked to Bemis. The other men clustered around the fire. They said nothing. They held out their hands to the blaze.

"Have some coffee," said Bemis.

"I guess we ought to get started," said the warden. "Unless some of you men want—"

"We had some, thank you kindly," one of the men said.

"Breakfast?" said Bemis.

"No," said another man, "I don't believe we will. I thank you, though. We had a snack before we left."

There was a small chorus of thanks.

"I guess we got a-plenty," the warden said.

There was a silence.

"This here is his pal," Bemis said. He pointed to Phil. The men looked briefly at Phil. He sat on the log by the fire. His head swung from side to side, he looked from man to man, he looked at the trail, he looked at the horses, he looked humbly from man to man again. The men looked gravely away.

"He's deaf and dumb," said Bemis. "The other fellow's name is Art. He can talk. But he can't hear. They ain't feebleminded or anything. Just can't talk to you and can't hear you. They're the ones that set it up in type when we run a little story about the warden here, or you fellows."

The warden shifted his feet.

"Wife told us," he said gently.

"Well," said Bemis, "if you fellows don't want any coffee—"

"All right, fellows," said the warden.

They left the campfire, they picked up their guns, four men went for the horses, passing Phil a man stepped heavily on his foot. Phil made a mewling noise in his throat, looked up quickly, nodded his head, managed a grimace of understanding.

"Excuse me!" the man said, flustered.

"He can't hear you," said Bemis.

The man's face was red.

"Excuse me, anyway," he said.

"I'll take you where we last saw him," said Bemis.

"I guess we're ready," the warden said. He collected the men with his eyes.

Lucas, holding his gun, was about to join them. The weight of the gun in his hand halted him. He went to the truck. He put down his gun.

He got his bag from the seat. He started toward them. They were waiting for him.

With the horses it was easier. Lucas walked behind Phil and Bemis and they were walking behind the warden's horse. Attached to the saddle were two coils of rope and on the other side was the warden's gun in a worn leather scabbard.

"I don't like the way the dummy's acting," Bemis said. Lucas glanced sidelong at Phil. His thin face was pinched and anxious. His gentle, intelligent eyes were remote. He was drawn deeply within himself, into a world deeper even than the pit his deafness and his speechlessness had dug when he was born. He was suffering but he could not cry out. He needed the sympathy of his fellow men but he could not hear it. As he walked he stumbled frequently. For a time his eyes had probed the forest endlessly. Now he no longer searched. From time to time he looked at Lucas, then at Bemis. Then he stumbled and looked down again.

They reached the scene where Bemis had last seen Art.

Lucas scanned Phil again, his lifelessness, his gaunt face, the prodigious change the past fifteen hours had extracted.

"Like *he's* lost," Bemis nodded. "Like he's lost, himself. How do you explain it, Doc? When a man's lost? You ever seen one, Doc? Sam here can tell you. Maybe the doc can tell us, Sam."

"It's pretty bad," Sam said.

"Some can stick it out a few days. Some don't last hardly any time at all."

"What happens?"

"That's what we want to know. You find 'em sometimes, food and water right beside 'em—remember that fellow Crow, Sam?—food and water right beside 'em, not hurt anyplace, not frozen or anything—just dead. Kind of shrunken and dead. What happens, Doc? What kills 'em?"

"Fright, maybe—"

"No sign of fright. No sign of nothing. What is there in being lost that kills a man?"

"I don't know," said Lucas.

The men looked down.

"It could be stress—if there's no mark of any injury, if he's got plenty of food and water—it could be shock, and stress—there's the will to live, you know—that's important—that's very important—we don't know the mechanics, exactly—but you can understand how morale—" Lucas was silent. "I've never seen a case," he said at last.

"Happens every time," Bemis watched Lucas hopefully. "You find 'em and they're dead. Or they're so far gone you just bring 'em back to bury 'em. Ain't it so, Sam?"

"I don't know," said Lucas. "I don't think we'll have to worry about Art, though. He hasn't been lost that long. I don't think he could die of exposure or anything else in that time."

"Don't take long for some," said the warden. "You take a fellow like your friend, knowing he can't hear and all, works on him harder, you might say he's sort of half lost to begin with."

"Look at the dummy." Bemis pointed. They looked at Phil. He

looked down the line of men, face to face. They looked away. "He's been warm and he's been fed—look at him. You stay with me, Phil. Understand?" He pointed to Phil and then to himself. "Me and you." Phil nodded apathetically. "You think there's much chance, Sam?"

The warden shrugged.

"If he didn't get into Fork Flats . . . if we can find him soon . . ."

"I don't want to be the one that tells his wife."

The men's heads came up.

"He's married?"

"He's got two kids, normal as you and me."

"I guess we're ready," said the warden.

"Who do you want me to go with?" Lucas demanded.

"Don't think it exactly matters, do you, Bemis? Can't tell who's gonna find him."

"No sense him not looking too. When you hear three shots, Doc, you follow the sound. Case you get separated."

"All right, you men," the warden said. "You all know what to do. We're going to spread out, we're going to make a long line, anybody sees anything holler to his neighbor. Try to keep contact, spread out and let's get going. Once you're under way we aim to swing out, fan northwest, circle back."

He turned his horse and started forward. The line spread out slowly. Bemis and Phil stayed next to the warden. Lucas took his bag, turned to the left, walked next to the last man in the line.

"Maybe you better go in the middle, Doc," the warden called. Lucas nodded. He crossed six men and walked in the middle of the line.

"Remember!" the warden called. "Two quick shots. Then a third, an even minute after." The men murmured assent. The long line had already spread out.

"Think we'll find him, Doc?" the man on his left called. He was twenty yards away, working farther left, the man on his left turned to hear the answer, the man beyond could not hear, the rest, the end of the line, were already out of sight, spreading out, pushing forward through the forest.

"I'm a little worried about pneumonia," said Lucas. He no longer had any doubt that they would find Art. There were too many men searching for him. And these were men who knew these mountains, they were rugged outdoor men, experienced members of a posse.

"I think he's dead," the man confided. "I don't think we're ever gonna find him. Not even his bones."

Lucas struggled over a huge log. His bag bumped his knee. "We'll find him," he called. He freed his bag. He looked toward the man on his left. The man had disappeared.

Lucas licked his lips. Then he heard the reassuring sound of men crashing through the underbrush, men on all sides. He walked resolutely onward, bearing to his left, bearing steadily to his left, to his left and forward.

He walked on. It was uphill and at last he panted to a halt. He leaned against a tree. For a time he simply leaned and panted, his legs aching with fatigue, his chest aching with his breathing. Gradually, he recovered his breath. He looked up. Far overhead, through the treetops, he could see a few wisps of clouds in a small window of sky. He looked at his watch. They had started only twenty minutes ago. He shook it and held it to his ear to make sure. His breathing was quiet now. And slowly be became aware of something else. The woods were silent. The noise of crashing had disappeared. There was no sound anywhere. There was no movement. There were only the trees. He straightened. He looked about again. He waited uncertainly. And then he called. He waited. There was no answer. He called again. The forest was silent.

Instantly he fled.

Slipping, stumbling, forcing himself through underbrush, grasping any handhold to haul himself upward, he clawed his way up the side of the mountain. Quickly his lungs ached again, he panted helplessly, his feet dragged, his bag weighed heavily, caught incessantly, he wrenched it free, he struggled upward. He dared not stop. Time and distance ceased. He crawled over a log, plunged headlong into a clump of bushes, struggled upright, through the dim forest light saw the crest ahead, saw a clearing. He shambled into the clearing at a staggering trot, he saw a high mass of rock, he put his bag down, he clambered weakly to the top. Ahead the mountain he had climbed sloped steeply. The treetops merged at the bottom with a ravine of treetops, and without interruption ascended the slopes of another mountain five miles away. Beyond the ridge of the next mountain was an unbroken line of mountain ridges, distant, travelling to infinity. To his right the ridge on which he stood stretched on to other ridges, the ravine at his feet crisscrossed by intersecting mountains and as far as he could see the treetops outlined mountains. Behind him was a sea of green. Somewhere, miles back, he knew there was a highway. There was no sign of a highway anywhere, there was only an unbroken, heaving mass of mountains and not even a ravine or cleft or any division showed where a highway might begin. On his left there was a short ridge and then another, and as he stared helplessly he saw a movement. He shouted. He waved his arms frantically. The figure halted. He heard, infinitely faint, an answering shout, his straining eyes saw a movement that might have been a wave.

Lucas shut his eyes in a slow smile of thanksgiving. He made his way slowly down the rock. He picked up his bag. He walked along the ridge top in the direction of the man on his left. He walked confidently now. The ridge was easier walking. When he found the man this time, he would stay close to him. He would not let him out of his sight for an instant. Even if he had to walk beside him. He had a goal now. He walked toward it steadily, rested by the easier walking, reassured and made strong by that gift, that boon, the sight of that man. He thought of him with affection, he remembered his face well, the competent way he strode, his heart lifted buoyantly remembering the other men, the whole group, strung out somewhere in these mountains, come without question and without thought of reward to search for someone they had never seen, someone who was lost.

And Art—

He tried to imagine himself deaf, he used only his eyes, denying himself hearing.

"I might be walking beside him," he said aloud. He was grateful for the sound of his voice. *"I might be walking five feet from him. And he'd never hear me."* The sound of his voice died in the silence of the forest. There was only the thrashing of the branches as he pushed steadily on. The ridge dipped. Art lying on the ground, his leg doubled under him. . . . Art unconscious, his skull fractured . . . Art lost, utterly alone, thinking in agony, the deaf and dumb Phil thinking in agony, the invisible bond of agony stretching between them, deaf and dumb, trying to find each other . . .

The ridge mounted again, he kept to the left, his eyes bored every bush, every tree, he never stopped looking. Art, and his eyes were everywhere, he walked faster, his eyes strained to penetrate the foliage, all his senses were vigilant and alert, he forgot everything but finding Art, finding him beyond the next bend, the next tree, the next clump of bushes. Twice he came upon deep rectangular pits. Old shafts. Art could have fallen into one of these. He might lie there with a broken leg. Unable to hear, and now, out of sight. Unable to get out. Lucas walked faster.

He had to stop.

He rested. He lay on the ground, staring up at the sky, panting.

And who'll break the news to his wife? Who'll tell her? Will they write it? And the kids . . . when she starts crying . . . making that mewling noise . . . And Phil would tell her . . . she would watch his hands . . . and then she would look up at him . . . and then—

He scrambled to his feet. The ridge ended. He kept steadily to his left. The man was ahead, somewhere. It didn't matter. He was there. Nothing mattered now. Nothing but Art. He made a system. Walk fifteen minutes, rest five. He found another ridge. His feet walked nothingness suddenly and he plunged, clutching at bushes, jarring into a fallen tree, spun, stopped, lying there, looking down. He was facing head down, on the downslope. He got up slowly. His wrist stung. It was bleeding from a rock cut. He made his way slowly up to the ridge again. He had not let go of his bag. He tried to think of a way to carry it slung over his back. He looked up at the sky. It was less bright now.

He began to take longer rests. He looked at his watch. It was past noon. The second hand was not moving. He shook the watch, he held it to his ear. It had stopped. He remembered his fall. He tried to estimate how long ago that had occurred.

"About an hour," he said aloud. "Yes," he said deliberately, "about an hour."

He had been on the hunt for seven hours. In that time he had covered perhaps a dozen ridges. Uncounted thousands of ridges stretched remotely about him. Perhaps five thousand, he estimated. Perhaps ten. And twice that many mountainsides. And twice that many ravines. Seventeen into ten thousand—say sixteen, it wasn't fair to count Phil—

Now, the forest stretched before him, the mountains stretched endlessly, the sum of them presented themselves and not the few familiar feet on either side,

"We'll never find him," Lucas said suddenly.

"No," he said carefully to his own voice, "we'll never find him."

A breeze stirred gentle and cold.

"He's lost," he told the trees.

And the immense silence swallowed the words and they were part of the endless mountains, the idle breeze, and the infinite.

He looked through the treetops at the sky. The light was not so bright. He looked about him for the last time. His eyes searched the ridge, the ocean of mountains beyond. There was nothing. There was only silence and distance. It was time to go back.

He scanned the sky again. It should be brighter to the west. Wherever it was brightest, that was the west. There was little sky to judge by. Only a patch the treetops framed directly overhead. It was brighter to his left. He started down the slope. He halted.

It was too late. It was time to get back.

"I have to get back," he said apologetically.

He started down again.

In the camp clearing far below Kristina and Dr. Castle sat before the campfire. Kristina's cape-covered arm circled a four-year-old girl. The girl's seven-year-old brother played idly with a pile of sticks. At the edge of the clearing a slight young woman stood, her back to them.

"I better go get her to sit down," Kristina said. She straightened her white cap. "Maybe she'll come for a cup of coffee." She released the little girl, who ran straightway and kicked down the pile her brother was building. Her brother promptly pushed her. She sat down hard. Her voice soared up in a loud wail. Kristina looked up from the coffee making. Her eyes darted anxiously to the woman. The woman stayed motionless, her back to them.

"She can't hear," Dr. Castle reminded. "She can't hear a sound." He rose and set the little girl on her feet.

"You don't want to push your sister," he said mildly, "your daddy wouldn't like it."

"My daddy's lost in the woods," the boy said proudly.

"Lost inna woods—lost inna woods—" the little girl capered gaily.

"It's all right," said Dr. Castle. "They don't know—what are you building there, son? You see if you can get her to drink some coffee, Kris."

"I'm building a new house for my daddy. We're gonna live right here. Only she pushed it down."

"You build another one," said Dr. Castle. "You're a big boy. You've got to take care of her."

Kristina turned aside. When her features were composed she turned again to Dr. Castle. He was bent over the pile of sticks, helping the boy.

"Luke doesn't know anything about woods," she said. She kept her voice even.

"Lucas'll be all right." Dr. Castle did not look up. "He's with the others."

She thought a moment.

"He's never hunted before," she said.

"I'm glad he was here," said Dr. Castle. "Those backwoods telephone operators—from the way she talked—I tell you for a while there I didn't know who or what or which or—"

"Yes," said Kristina.

She went quickly to the woman. She touched her shoulder. The young woman whirled. Her thin face stared frightened at Kristina. Then her eyes sought the children, reassured she looked questioningly at Kristina. Her gray eyes were huge, her lips were bloodless. Kristina took her thin arm. She tugged gently.

"Coffee!" She shaped the word with her lips.

The woman put a preventing hand on Kristina's arm. Against the white uniform the hand was rough, the knuckles reddened, the bones ridged beneath the thin skin, on her finger a wedding ring was a large, worn hoop of gold.

Kristina put her arm about her. The woman shook her head quickly. She pulled back, resisting.

Dr. Castle walked to them. He smiled, he patted her shoulder. He took her other arm. The woman shook her head harder. She made a mewling noise in her throat, a sound of anguish and of protest. With her chin she gestured toward the trail.

"I know," Dr. Castle nodded, "I know. But you've got to have a little coffee. You're ice-cold."

And he and Kristina put their weight against her, began to move her toward the fire. She slipped from their grasp, she wriggled free, she fell to the ground. She made sounds deep in her throat. She began to cry. She clasped her hands. She shook her clasped hands at them. Her tears came soundlessly. She begged with her hands again, her arm flew out in an anguished gesture toward the trail. They helped her to her feet. She put her head on one side. Her eyes apologized for her violence. She clasped her hands again. She turned her back and faced the trail. From her throat issued a low strangle. Her shoulders shook.

Kristina returned to the fire. She got a cup, poured it full, brought it back. The woman took the cup. Her eyes gazed gratefully at Kristina. She nodded. She held the cup in her hands and watched the trail.

"You watch the kids," said Kristina. "If this is where she wants to stand, let her stand here."

"What are you going to do?"

"I'm going to stand here with her. I got a man out there too."

"All right," said Dr. Castle. "Luke's all right, Kris."

He waited a moment, she said nothing further, he returned to the children.

"My daddy's been gone a long time," the boy said.

"Lost inna woods—lost inna woods," the girl sang happily.

Kristina put her arm about the young woman's thin shoulders. After a while the young woman's arm stole about Kristina's waist. They stood thus, gazing steadfastly at the wilderness, and they could not speak, for one was dumb, and there was nothing to say, there was only the wilderness and the silence and the unwived, and death and terror and waiting. And the man who belonged to them and who was needing. And it was an ancient tale for two hearts old with the tale and their arms tightened about each other, and they were alone and they waited.

The light ebbed steadily. Lucas mounted another ridge, it was a short ridge, he started down the other side. He was staggering a little. He plodded down the slope in the direction he had set for himself. Halfway down he paused and leaned against a stump, he looked up at the sky. Through the high treetops the light was yellowing. It was a dirty yellow-gray. It was getting colder. When he started again the sweat was cold where his clothes touched his skin. The downslope gradually levelled. He stopped again.

I mustn't think, he said to himself.

He circled with his eyes the space where he stood. Around him were tall trees. There would never be anything but trees. Ten yards, and he could see no farther, ten yards and more trees. Suddenly a desire gripped him to run into them, run straight ahead, smashing at them with his fists. The rage passed. He shook a little. His eyes cleared. He looked at his useless watch. He looked at the sky. It was getting darker. He should have been back in camp. He should be back, by this time. He looked about him. There was nothing but woods. He began to shake again.

"Stop it!" he cried. His voice rose angrily. *"Stop it! You hear me? Stop it!"*

He drew a deep breath.

All right, he said to himself, now let's face it. Let's think calmly. You're not lost. You couldn't possibly be lost. And if you're lost just keep going and you won't be lost long. Just keep going.

The level ended abruptly in another ridge. He looked over the edge. It angled sharply twenty feet to the bottom. He gripped his bag. He started down. He slipped, recovered, clutched at a bush, the roots pulled out, he toppled and rolled to the bottom. His head hurt where a branch had slashed it. A stone had banged his ribs. He felt them cautiously. Nothing was broken.

He lay where he had fallen. He looked up at a dirty patch of fading sky. He looked at the bushes, the stones near his face, saw their details, absorbed. Suddenly he was very tired. It was more than a weariness of his long-exhausted muscles. It was an absolute fatigue. He was tired of thinking. He made himself get to his knees. He heaved himself erect. He started up another alien, nameless ridge. He plodded fifteen steps. He stopped. When he had breathed again he plodded fifteen more. He stopped. He climbed the ridge. There were three hundred and fifty-seven steps. He counted carefully. For this was the ridge. There could be no more. He kept his eyes resolutely down. He had reached the top. He raised his eyes.

The ridges kept on. There were ridges everywhere.

He stared at them dully, lying across a leaning tree, gasping for air. He was finished.

The time had come to give up. He could move no farther. The light was dimming now. His breath came slower. He straightened slowly.

When he was erect he stumbled back, he put his back against a tree. It was very still. It was all over. It was done.

He was lost. Somewhere in his head began a quiet thumping. He stayed motionless. He had no wish to move. He wanted to stay where he was. Motionless. Eternally. Through the dying light the trees loomed, rotting and stern. Nothing was familiar. Nothing was in the right place. Nothing inside him said go anywhere. He knew now that they would never find him. He was lost. And they would never find him. And in a few moments this became old too, and he bowed his head and he was alone.

There was only himself. There was no other world. The world was gone. There was no other life.

The cold reached him. He bent apathetically. He picked up his dropped bag. He might as well keep moving. Because there was nothing else to do. He appraised the forest dully. The nape of his neck prickled. Utter terror gripped him. The trees stood stiffly in the gloom. The place was evil, suddenly. And in the gloom was peril. The forest was waiting for the darkness, chill as a sepulcher. He forced his paralyzed legs to move. He felt the forest at his back, felt the nameless, grasping for him, he ran, he fell crashing, picked himself up, an agony of horror flung him on again. He fell again, crashed headlong, and this time he did not rise. He kept his face against the earth.

When he could breathe evenly again, the horror had left him. In the gloom he propped himself against a tree. The gloom was kind now. The chill was a soft blanket against his cheek. His tired legs lay along the earth gratefully. He pulled his bag toward him. He remembered the day he had bought it. It was a good bag, it was full of medicines, medicines to cure or help almost anything. But there was no medicine here for him. He remembered the bags he had carried for doctors. He was a man now . . . he had always followed that bag . . . and a man is a number of things . . . he is the boy he was and the way he grew up and the love he got . . . he is the people he knows . . . he is the man some woman loves . . . and he is a myriad of other things that he must become . . .

And he knew he was lonely, that he had been lonely all his life, only he was not lonely now. There was too much to think about and too much to remember. Because all his life he had been the loneliest man, it was not his fault, it was what was given a man, the man with vector beyond his fellows, of all men on earth the least at home. And he summed it, now, remembering, and remembering that man, and he saw that he must be bewildered and frustrated and disillusioned every hour of his existence and that the price may not be worth it but willy-nilly such a man must pay.

And there were people, he peopled the gloom with them, there was Runkleman and Castle and Avery and Kris—and if Kris, ah Kris—he shivered a little with the cold—if Kris knew he was lost she would crawl through these woods on her knees—she would never stop—and the men . . . the men who had started out . . . He saw their chiseled faces again, grim-set to find a fellow man, he saw their faces lovingly, there was that about people, there was that you couldn't deny, they are at their best in catastrophe, they are at their best when they are looking for one of their number who is lost . . .

And he yearned for them. And he needed them.

He saw them fumbling their untaught way through life, sure of no goal, having no measurement but themselves, the daily prey of mischance and agony and bewilderment and death, knowing no better, groping blindly toward a Heaven they must believe, bound to each other from their first cry to the grave's edge.

And he was weak for them, weak with longing and understanding.

And he knew now, he knew what killed a man, a man who was lost. A lost man was a dying man, he could not live without his fellows, there was a poison in it, a deadly sickness, the sickness of a newborn and the cord ripped, and the man lost, and he must die.

He must die.

It was a wasting melancholy of lifeless life. The will went. The mind gave up. The spirit would not go on. The soul escaped from stasis. Uncaringly, the man died.

And he would die, also. He, who had wanted so bitterly to be alone. And now he would die of it. The unerring poison of his family and his species.

"My species," he said aloud, seeing himself.

And it may not be the best species, but it's the best species I've got.

And my people.

And they may not be the best people but they're the only people there are. . . .

He stumbled erect. He would walk a little longer. Because it didn't matter. But a man should walk. The light was almost gone. He stared in the direction of the living. He stared fondly. Between the living and the dead the essence of man.

He stared yearningly.

He is not alone . . . He is one tragedy and one joy, and one purpose and one life and one death and one soul. . . .

He walked slowly and aimlessly and lost into the darkening void about him. His shoulder struck a tree, and rebounding he plodded on again. A slope descended beneath his feet and involuntarily he ran a few paces, he fell suddenly, his body crashed through the bushes. He staggered slowly to his feet. He knew that if he sat again he would never rise. He toppled against a tree. He fought for breath.

"Seen anybody?" a voice demanded.

He whirled. Across a small clearing he could discern the man who had started on his left. The man had topped a rise. He was standing there, watching him. He watched the man walk toward him.

"Heard somebody crashing around," he said mildly. "Thought it might be one of the boys."

Lucas swallowed. His eyes stung.

"Guess they got him," said the man. "Hear the shots?"

Lucas wet his mouth.

"No," he said humbly.

"Long about three o'clock. Started back soon as I heard 'em."

"I didn't hear them," Lucas murmured.

"That's these god-blasted hills for ya. I know places you could fire a gun and a man stand a hundred yards away and not hear—branches, foliage, way the hills turn—"

He looked sharply at Lucas.

"You all right, Doc?"

Lucas turned his head. He brushed at his clothes.

"Took a tumble," he said.

"I bet I took fifty," the man said. He smiled. The smile spread over his grim face. "Guess we better get going," he said. "They'll be needing you."

They pushed aside a tall clump of brush. They struggled through. They were in a small clearing. Lucas halted, uncertainly. He gazed at a tall boulder.

"Look familiar?" the man grinned. "Want to rest a bit, Doc? Want me to carry your bag for you?"

"No," said Lucas. He averted his head. He compressed his lips. He fought for his voice. "No," he said. "I'll carry it . . ."

They were past the clearing. Ahead loomed the trail. The foliage was sparse now, mashed and trampled and hacked away by the man who had preceded them.

"That's them!" the man cried.

Lucas lifted his head.

Far down the hill he saw a procession breasting the bushes, two men in advance lurching with a stretcher of poles and coats. As he looked a woman raced to meet them, she threw herself beside the litter, she was crawling beside it on her knees, her hands fluttering, touching Art everywhere.

The group halted. They helped her to her feet. They moved on again. When they had passed he saw Kristina.

She was standing on a little hill. She looked tall, standing motionless, standing very erect, facing the trail, capped and caped and waiting.

He broke into a run. She looked up then. She saw him. He heard her cry out.

Then he was racing through the bushes, rushing to her.

⋆ CHAPTER 42

It was quite dark when they reached Greenville.

"I'll go home," said Bemis, "and let you boys start work. You sure he's all right?" Kristina was leaning against Lucas' shoulder. His arm was about her. Bemis looked hastily back to the road. "I'll take the dummy home." He cleared his throat.

"He'll be fine," said Lucas. "You just drop us at the County and we'll have him fixed up in no time."

"We're not going to any County," Bemis said shortly. He looked in the mirror to be sure Dr. Castle was still following.

"No man that works for me is going on charity."

"I'm glad to hear it, Bemis," Lucas said gravely.

The truck drew up before the Valley Hospital. Dr. Castle's car pulled up behind.

"You coming in?" Lucas asked, from the sidewalk.

"I hate hospitals," Bemis said. He stuck his arm from the truck window and waved it violently. Phil looked up, reluctantly left Art, got in the truck beside Bemis. "Got to take him home to his folks. See you later."

The truck drove hastily away.

Art lay in bed. His hair was very black against the white hospital pillow. The lights, now that they could see him well, accented his gaunt face, his gray weariness, his sunken eyes. His wife leaned above him feeding him, oblivious to everything but his face, his mouth, the spoon and the soup.

He tried to smile. His movement spilled the spoon of soup. The children, who had been watching the feeding absorbedly, suddenly broke off to tug at their mother's skirt.

"Hungry!" the little girl screamed. She hopped up and down.

Her brother pushed her out of the way. His small fingers fumbled the hand language. He pointed to his open mouth. He rubbed his stomach.

"I want my dinner!" he cried.

"They're hungry," said Art. His wife waited with the soup. Her eyes never left his face.

The nurse took the children to the diet kitchen.

"Not as hungry as you, I'll bet," said Lucas.

"I wasn't hungry," said Art. "I had a couple of chocolate bars."

His wife looked at them pleadingly.

"Don't talk any more, Art," said Dr. Castle.

"Followed this damned deer," Art murmured. His eyes were blank, remembering. His wife put her finger on his lips. "That's all I remember."

"Save it for tomorrow," Lucas said.

"They found you sitting against a tree," said Kristina.

He nodded.

"Fired shots . . . no more bullets . . . made a fire, smoke couldn't get above the treetops . . ." His eyes closed.

At this his wife's face jerked up startled, white with terror.

Dr. Castle patted her shoulder. He nodded. He smiled reassuringly. He put his hands at the side of his cheek in the gesture of sleeping. She looked at them uncertainly. Dr. Castle took out his prescription pad and his pen.

"He'll be all right tomorrow," he wrote. "All he needs is the med. we gave him and little sleep. You can go home, now."

She read the square of paper eagerly.

Dr. Castle pointed to the last sentence. She shook her head quickly. She turned to watch her sleeping husband. She watched him steadfastly.

After a while they tiptoed into the corridor.

A nurse beckoned to Dr. Castle.

"We'll wait for you at the desk," Lucas called. He took Kristina's arm. "What are you frowning about?" he asked, at the desk.

"What was it, Luke? He didn't fall, he wasn't hurt, he had food, he had a fire—"

"That's what happens, Kris."

She scanned his sober face.

"Was it fear? Some kind of shock?"

He shook his head.

"No," he said gravely, gently, "no, not fear."

She waited.

"He was lost, Kris . . ."

"But—"

"I'll tell you sometime. All right? Sometime I'll tell you all about it."

"All right," said Kristina. She took his arm shyly.

"Wonder what Castle's got?" Lucas said.

"He's been gone a long time. I want to get you home and feed you and give you a hot bath. Phew! You smell!"

"Wood smoke—"

"Yes—and *you,* too!"

Dr. Castle was walking down the corridor.

"All done?" Lucas called to him.

"Meningitis," said Dr. Castle. His mouth wried. "First of the season."

Kristina groaned.

"Epidemic type?" Lucas waited.

"I wonder—" Dr. Castle said at last.

"How about Kauffman? Isn't he our neurologist?"

Dr. Castle strode to the telephone.

". . . he doesn't think it's epidemic," he put his hand over the mouthpiece. "He got two cases. He said to tell you the Gross baby was a false alarm." He hung up.

"Are we in for it?" Lucas demanded.

"I don't know," Dr. Castle said wearily. He rubbed his forehead. "But this is the season . . ."

"Child?"

Dr. Castle nodded.

"Playing around the dump, got bit by a rat, mother thought it was ratbite . . ."

He rose and walked them out to the car.

"Might have been. Might have lowered her resistance. . . . I don't know . . . we'll see in the morning . . ."

"I don't like that ratbite." Lucas helped Kristina into the car.

"I don't like that dump, either."

"Have we got a dump problem, too? What's the matter with this town!"

"Like any other town. It's got a dump. When Granite was alive he promised to clean it up every election. But meningitis—she must have got it somewhere . . ."

He sighed.

"When I get home I'll call Binyon, see if he's got any."

"If there's any going we'll have it at the County," Lucas said grimly. He and Kristina alighted.

"Keep your fingers crossed," Dr. Castle called. He drove off.

They walked through the familiar doorway. The door shut behind them. Lucas took a deep breath. He looked about him. He was home.

"Kris!" he called.

"I'm coming," she said. She hung up her cape, unpinned her cap. She came back to the living room.

"You look nice in your uniform."

"I got it dirty." She brushed industriously at a smudge.

"I like it." He stepped toward her. She lifted her head quickly. "Come here, Kris."

And his arms were about her. He kissed her ears, his mouth brushed her neck, his mouth was on hers. He paused a moment to see her again. She looked back at him, dazed. Her body was warm and swelling against him. Her breasts—

His mind was suddenly still. A cell of memory tapped clearly. A cell of association chimed. The thing that had puzzled him, that vague something-changed—

The data marched into place. And now he knew. His startled mind totted the facts again. Kris was going to have a baby. And she almost surely knew it. And she never said—because—

But he put away the thought of the days when she might have said. Now he was only thunderstruck, close to her, holding her, home. And his heart soared.

He drew back, his face expressionless.

"What's the matter?" she said.

"Getting kind of chesty, aren't you?"

She looked quickly down at her breasts, her eyes searched his apprehensively.

"I like chesty Swedish girls," he said evenly.

"Go! Take your shower!" She wrenched free.

As his arm reached for her his lips twitched at a sudden thought, and as she drew back:

"Stand still," he said. His thumb and forefinger plucked at her waist.

"What is it?" she cried.

He looked up, frowning, sober.

"Why, it's a tick, Kris!"

"A tick—!"

"You must have got it in the woods."

"My God, Luke!" Her fingers flew. Her uniform opened, dropped to her ankles. She kicked it gingerly. "Did I get any on you? Look, Luke! Look quick!"

"How about your slip?" he frowned.

"My God!"

She raced to the bedroom, pulling at the slip. Her body was lovely. Her white skin, the pale blue veins, the curve of her legs, her panic,

His mouth was suddenly dry.

"I'll help you." Her flesh was warm and incredibly smooth. He yearned to rub his stubbled chin against it. His fingers fumbled. He turned her around.

Her breasts were larger. The pink areola now circled the nipple no longer pink but brown. She was pregnant.

He shook his head.

"Nothing there," he said dubiously.

She gazed at him helplessly, her arms across her chest.

"Sometimes, Kris–"

He walked toward her. She saw his face.

"Now wait, Luke–Luke!–you mustn't–you're tired–"

"Kris," he said thickly, "Kristy–"

"Luke! Later–somebody'll come in–"

His body was hot against her skin.

"Ahh, God . . . I don't care, Luke . . . I don't care . . ."

Afterward, long afterward, they lay lazily silent. Her hair was a blonde disorder on the pillow. Her legs were wanton. They lay indolently, looking upward, their hands clasped.

"We haven't had dinner yet," he mused.

"I'll get it," she said, not moving.

They were silent again.

"Do you think it'll be a boy, Kris?"

Her body tensed. She lay stupefied.

He knew.

"I hope it's a girl," he said. "She'll be a good nurse . . ."

"Lucas–my Lucas–"

"Yoost like her mama," he said serenely.

She raised on one elbow. She peered at him. Then her mouth was soft, open against his, her cheeks were wet, he turned to her, she fell back, her arms strained him to her offering body.

It was eight o'clock.

"I'll make some eggs," Kristina said. Her cheeks glowed, her lips were ripe.

"No dishes–will you have dinner with me, nurse? You little tramp?" He walked to the telephone.

"Where are you going–"

"I'm going to call Kauffman. We'll go to the Chinese place. Maybe he hasn't eaten yet, either."

He made the call.

"He'll come," he said. "Where'd you get that dress, Kris?"

"I always had it. That was a nice thing to do, Luke. She was such a nice woman. He must be terrible lonely now."

"Nice! I've *got* to butter up to him!" He glared at her. "Who do you think's going to deliver you?"

She gaped at him. Then she giggled.

"Not me, woman!" Lucas said. He seized her arm. He marched her to the car.

"I like that Bemis," she said irrelevantly. The motor started. The car moved off.

"Because he paid for Art's room and nurse?"

"He didn't have to, Luke. And I always thought—"

"And you were right," he said. "This is the same man—I can see his gleeful face the day he told me how he always hired the handicapped so he could pay them less than a union wage."

"No!"

"That's the truth, Kris."

"But he paid for it—"

" 'No man that works for me is going on charity'—"

She snuggled closer to him.

When they were seated, Li stumped out of the kitchen to complain about his leg.

Dr. Kauffman grinned as Li stumped away again.

"A grateful patient is always glad you didn't do any worse," he comforted.

"Patients!" sniffed Kristina.

"I hear we're going to have a lot more," said Lucas.

"Meningitis?"

"How does it run here? Do you think we're in for it?"

"I don't think Castle's case is epidemic—more lymphocytes than polys. Tell better tomorrow. We usually get a few cases this time of year. With the depression and the typhoid I wouldn't be surprised but this year we may have a handful."

"We're in for it."

"I wouldn't be surprised."

"One thing or another—it never stops, does it."

"No, it never stops."

"You're not eating anything," Kristina complained.

"I've had my dinner, really," Dr. Kauffman said. He looked away. "I was just sitting home, nothing to do, waiting for calls—"

"They don't come till two o'clock in the morning," Kristina reminded.

"I was glad you asked me," Dr. Kauffman said.

"I wish you'd come up to the County sometime and show me some neurosurgery," said Lucas.

"It's a long time since I've done any." But Dr. Kauffman straightened a little.

"You keep up with it?"

"Oh, yes! I keep up with it. It's what I wanted to do." He smiled. "Only—I guess you knew Dr. Aarons pretty well, didn't you?"

"He was a good man!" Kristina said fiercely.

"Well," said Dr. Kauffman, "neurologists' jobs are even scarcer . . ."

"I'd be grateful if you'd help me out," said Lucas.

Dr. Kauffman nodded. His eyes had brightened.

"That ratbite Dr. Castle mentioned—meningitis is respiratory spray, isn't it? He felt the ratbite infected her, lowered her resistance."

"It seems to be spread from the respiratory tract. It's definitely proven contagious. And he's probably right about the ratbite. That dump is a disgrace."

"Isn't there anything we can do about it? Castle and Binyon and you and I?"

"We've tried—"

"Couldn't we try again? All four together?"

"I don't know who'd back us, now that Granite's gone. He always let us down before. But I think this time— Say! Why don't you see Bemis? He's a friend of yours, now. You're practically blood brothers!"

"He's paying that printer's hospital bill—" Kristina reminded.

"That's right," Lucas grinned. "Maybe he's loosening up."

"Wouldn't cost much—"

"Not a cent more than an epidemic."

"No harm in trying—"

"I'll see him tomorrow," Lucas promised. He leaned back. "Now tell me. If we're in for meningitis, what do you do on babies? Cisterna or lumbar?"

"I'll tell you what!" said Dr. Kauffman. He hitched his chair closer to the table. "You can use the cervical, too."

"The poor little things!" Kristina said reproachfully.

Under the table Lucas pressed her hand. Dr. Kauffman had taken out his pen. He was drawing on his prescription pad.

"Look," he said. His pen moved eagerly. "Say here's your third cervical . . ."

When they were home they undressed wearily, slipped groaning into bed. Lucas reached for her and Kristina slipped into his arms. He held her quietly, her familiar body, the comfort of its contact. His hand caressed her hip, wandered slowly over her belly.

"Three and a half months, Kris?" he asked drowsily.

"Three months and three weeks," she murmured.

He moved closer to her. Her arms tightened about him. Almost instantly they were asleep.

In the morning there was a single case of meningitis at the County Hospital. It was a young man and he had been carefully isolated. His chart hung neatly at the foot of the bed. The bed had been scrubbed. The utensils shone.

Lucas' eyes widened.

"Oh, they'll do their work if you sit on them hard enough," said Dr. Snider. His jacket was fresh, pressed and white. His mouth was empty. He looked subdued. "Yes, sir! I want to tell you something, Marsh! I gave those nurses hell about that typhoid! By God, I told them they'll keep on their toes now or they're out on their ass! Yes, sir!" he said, chastened, "no excuse for that! No excuse at all! Specially after you telling her to stay, the way you did! I said to her, 'Who the hell do you think's gonna sign that death certificate!' " He eyed Lucas cautiously. "She said it wouldn't happen again . . ."

"Good!" said Lucas.

"I told her it better not!"

So Gillingham had called. And whatever he said—

"We all have our limitations," Lucas nodded.

"No use buckin' 'em!"

So now they knew, he and Snider. Now it was settled. Now things would be smooth, he could relax . . . Until the next time . . . And when it came he could handle it.

"That's four—" he pointed to the patient.

"Binyon thinks he's got one. That'd be five. You want to know what I think? I think we're in for it!"

They walked into the corridor.

"Looks like you got a free morning," said Dr. Snider.

"I know. It isn't often that operating room's empty this time of day. One little T & A—"

"They'll fall off the roof on you tomorrow."

"Kauffman said he'd help me out now and then—do you mind?"

"Okay by me!" Dr. Snider said vigorously. "We'll do our best to make him to home. And Marsh!" he called, as Lucas reached the door. He walked to him quickly. "One thing," he confided from the corner of his mouth, "I wouldn't say anything to that nurse—I already told her plenty . . ."

"Right!" said Lucas, straight-faced.

He drove to the *Clarion*. He passed his office, saw behind it the house that David Runkleman had built. They would need more room.

He passed the bank, frowning.

Mightn't do any harm to drop in . . . one thing about it, it was furnished . . . and if that banker thought he was going to get away with any price like that in times like these . . .

He stopped in front of the *Clarion*. Bemis came out to meet him.

"Come on and have a cup of coffee, Doc! I called the warden, he wanted to be remembered to you, him and the boys, Art's looking fine! You know that damn wife of his stayed there all night? By God, what do you think of them letting her!"

"Bemis—"

"You know we go fishing, too? We'll go fishing this summer—whole slew of us—"

"Bemis, I've got a little news for you. There's five cases of meningitis—"

"I heard four!"

"Five. Are you running it?"

"There you are! There you see! If I don't run it, you fellows will drive me nuts. And if I do run it I'll have the Chamber of Commerce down my neck, business'll fall off, the merchants'll quit advertising— I'll put a little warning in. Just say you fellows warned parents to be careful."

"I don't know whether you heard, Bemis. But that little girl got bit."

"What was she playing around there for in the first place? What business parents got letting little kids play around the dump? What gets into people, anyway?"

Lucas smiled. He dropped his hand on Bemis' shoulder.

"How about that dump!"

"Doc—let me give you a piece of advice—"

"Rats, Bemis. Typhoid, typhus, paratyphoid, plague—"

"You leading up to meningitis?"

"How do we know? I'm leading up to that dump."

"Because I already called Castle—"

"Don't be so sure it wasn't rats, Bemis. How about it? How about that dump?"

"Not a chance in the world."

"And you say that—remembering the epidemic we've just been through? You? My friend? The editor of this big paper?"

But Lucas' eyes were grave.

"Doc, it ain't my dump. It belongs to the town. And I want to tell you something. Newspapering and politics is the science of the possible. This just ain't possible. We'll be years paying off the water system. There's a slight depression on. Business is shot to hell. The pottery plant's barely open. The town just hasn't got the money."

"Back us up," said Lucas. "It won't cost much. Just try it. You know what it means to the town. Will you do that? Will you do it for me?"

"I wouldn't do it for God Almighty," Bemis said sincerely.

Lucas took a deep breath. The color returned to his face. He nodded. He got back in his car.

"What about that fishing trip?" Bemis cried. "You're coming, ain't ya?"

Lucas made himself smile.

"I'll try," he said. "We'll see . . ."

Nothing had changed.

He drove to Dr. Castle's office.

Dr. Binyon's case was definitely meningitis.

"Which serum do you like best," Dr. Castle sighed. "Flexner's or Jobling's?"

"Or just puncture?" said Lucas.

His eyes narrowed. Dr. Castle had risen stiffly, plodded to the bookcase, returned to his desk with a heavy book. He was panting a little. His lips were gray-blue. He opened the book and riffled the pages to meningitis.

"How did you sleep last night?" demanded Lucas.

"Oh, fair—just fair—let's see, here it is, now—"

Lucas rose, walked to the desk and took his pulse.

"Little fast?" Dr. Castle asked mildly.

"You know it's fast. You had an attack last night, didn't you."

"This morning," Dr. Castle turned back to the book.

"Will you take a pill? Now?"

"What's got into you?" He took the pills out, slipped one into his mouth.

"I'm going to be in the midst of the afternoon calls one day. And a call is going to come in. It'll be from your nurse. And she'll say, 'You haven't seen Dr. Castle, have you? I can't imagine what's keeping him.' And she'll give me the address you went to. And I'll drive out there. And your car will be parked beside the curb. And you'll be over the wheel."

"And the woman'll come running out of the house where I was supposed to call and demand to know why I'm late—"

"And I'll say, 'He's dead.' And she'll say, 'Well, what am I supposed to do, then?' And before night she'll be going to another doctor."

"I know," Dr. Castle sighed. "I've heard it often enough." He looked at his gnarled knuckles. "Funny, how you hate to quit . . . I couldn't any more quit now. I want to keep going . . ."

"When I think of what you gave that heart up for—"

"Nobody asked me to, you know," Dr. Castle said. "Even if you're right. Which I'm not admitting you are—"

"When I think of the people you spent that heart on—"

"Nobody asked me to," Dr. Castle said tiredly.

He was silent, thinking of the years, the lifetime.

Yes, Lucas thought, you don't want to think of it, it's true, my friend.

And there is this, also. This glacial fact that it is necessary to ignore their aims, their ambitions, their occupations, their standards. It is necessary to ignore whether they will enrich the world, or their nation or their community, or breed a better or a worse generation. It is vital not to ponder whether they are so useless that to help them live is a defiance of the value of life for then comes the abhorred madness with the sound of leaves blowing dryly in a hidden place, the madness in the grotesque thought of succoring everything living because it is living, of rushing here and there, to this one and that one, all of them faceless, now saving an idiot, now a great mind, now a near-moron, now a savior. Because they are living.

—*"All my life I have yearned and schemed to get that one single button. If I had that one button in my collection I'd be willing to go, then. I'd die happy." . . . "The thing is, Doc, do you think I ought to keep on making electrodes for spark plugs? When all my life I've had my heart set on being one of these telegraphers?"*—

It is necessary never to consider what they do, or what their terms of time are spent upon, the terms you help make longer, nor to accommodate your mind to what they dream of in return for the power to dream, or that with which they destroy their bodies in return for the gift of life; you must not judge, nor weigh, nor translate, nor form opinions; if you wish to be sane you must keep your mind far away from such thinking and you must address yourself and your science and your art steadfastly to the life that is within them and to the spark of divinity with which they were equipped when they were born.

If you do not keep your mind resolutely from these things, if you once dwell upon what these imbeciles are doing in the miracles they inhabit, if you perceive these sad, mad, reeling, blundering, haphazard, hysterical adults, senile at thirty, childish, committed, prodigiously absorbed in their own characters at any amusement park or novel with an enlarging mirror, convinced of their current importance as they are convinced of their past absurdity, if you analyze even so fragmentarily as this what you are keeping alive, what you serve with the profoundest mysteries and the greatest inventions man has been permitted to discover were in his hands all the time, then that so newly evolved brain rostral to the motor area will become anonymous tissue beneath the weight of incredulity and the compression of sorrow and the pressure of hate and rejection.

"I don't do OB any more . . . I take it easy . . ." Dr. Castle looked out the window. He drummed his fingers gently on the open book. "I don't think I hurt anybody . . ."

His ear lobes were pallid. Lucas winced. A tremor of protest, of fear, wrinkled his heart. He shut his jaws tightly. He drew a deep breath. He plunged.

"What about an assistant?"

Dr. Castle continued to look out the window. He said nothing. Lucas compressed his lips miserably. He had hurt a man he wanted least to hurt.

"Don't misunderstand me—" he pleaded.

"I don't," Dr. Castle said quietly. He gazed out the window.

"Some smart young fellow—"

Dr. Castle turned slowly. He gazed at Lucas. He opened his lips to speak. He closed them. He opened them again.

"There isn't enough practice left to tempt a smart young fellow," he said evenly.

He pursed his lips. He looked down.

"I don't want any bums in here," he said.

But Lucas had placed the call. And in a few moments he was talking to Avery.

"How'd you like to come up here and go into practice?" he demanded without preamble.

"Where the hell are you? How did you get drunk this time of day?"

"Are you going to do it, or not? With that Dr. Castle I told you about!"

"Are you serious?"

"He's sitting right here. I want to know. Now. You can practice the kind of Medicine we always talked about—we'll be living next door to each other—"

"Luke! Listen!"

"I'm listening—"

"I'm *practicing* the kind of Medicine we always talked about," said Avery.

The line was silent.

"I wanted to tell you that," said Avery. "I made up my mind when I last saw you. I thought over what you said. After you left, I knew. And Luke! I want to tell you about Kris—now, don't get excited—"

"I know," said Lucas.

"Good God! You *do*?"

"You've got to come! We need somebody! Bad!" He knew it was no use. And he kept his eyes resolutely from Dr. Castle. "There's hunting here and—"

"Not me. . . . How would you like a nice, bright, young man! New-hatched. Just through his internship." Avery paused. "There's only one drawback," he sighed. "He's got the same ideas you have . . ."

"Ask him if he'll take two hundred and fifty a month," Dr. Castle said mockingly.

"Will he take two hundred a month?"

"He'll jump at it," Avery promised.

"When can he come up?"

"When do you want him?"

"Yesterday," said Lucas.

"He's on his way," Avery hung up.

"Well," said Lucas proudly, "it looks like you've got yourself a boy."

Dr. Castle peered at him, incredulous.

"What's the hitch?"

"The only drawback is," Lucas said steadily, "he looks at Medicine the way I do."

Dr. Castle swallowed.

"What's taking him so long?" he asked mildly. Lucas drew a deep breath and exhaled it. Dr. Castle cleared his throat. "What's his name?" he said gruffly.

"Good Lord! I forgot to ask." A thought stilled him. "Does it matter?"

"Matter! *I* don't care what his name is. If he hasn't got a name we'll give him one!"

The pottery plant's noon whistle shrilled.

"I suppose you're happy now!"

"If I wasn't married I'd kiss you!" Lucas exulted.

"You doctors!" Dr. Castle snorted. "You're all alarmists! I've got longer than that!"

He walked to the window. Lucas followed him.

"It's a sight I always like to see," Dr. Castle said.

Lucas watched the working people of Greenville trickling into the streets, peopling the sidewalk, homing for the noon-day meal.

"Half a day gone," said Dr. Castle. "And there's that many safe."

"You always come to look?"

Dr. Castle nodded.

"Yes," he said, "there they go, they don't know it but meningitis is hanging over their heads, the new season, the new enemy is waiting for them . . ."

They were silent, watching.

And Lucas saw them clearly, saw himself, saw the mortally ill man at his side, saw the dying pass before him resolute and undismayed. And his mind saw clearly, yearned to them, and his heart wept seeing irrevocably that the noblest thoughts of man and his highest resolves are helpless inmates of a prison camp that is his body. For they survive or perish, are shaped or blunted, made mean or whole at the mercy of the blind dooms that warp their jailer. And in the body's war there is no armistice with chance, no warning of assault, and torture and fear and disease and death tighten the vigil of their eternal siege with every sleep and every waking. And over the surest leers the chance that need and peril drop an iron curtain between that which is noble or divinely missioned in him and that which must survive at the expense of any life but its own.

That man is the Passion of man, and man is his Crucifixion, he must be his own redeemer, ignorant of his purpose, never knowing any other resolve but human resolve, any standard but a human standard.

And like a blind man who cannot see the light but feels its force he gropes for Truth, lives for it, dies for it, knowing indomitably that although he cannot name it, glory waits it, and although he cannot prove it, glory is his birthright, and that to be better than man, to be not man, is the highest endeavor of which he can dream.

He dreams on. Dreams ever braver dreams, more sure, more shining,

God-led by a vision which is vague, which is boundless and which death will not stop.

The streets were nearly empty now.

Behind them on the desk, the phone trilled.

Dr. Castle walked heavily away, lifted the receiver. He listened.

"It's for you."

Lucas nodded. He walked to the desk, a man who had gone a far journey.

As he listened, his eyes cleared, he frowned once, he spoke soothingly, he hung up.

"I think we've got another one," he said. He started for the door.

"Here we go again!" sighed Dr. Castle. "Good luck! . . . And thanks!" he called to the shut door.

Lucas drove headlong back to the office.

Kristina was filing cards beside the reception room.

She rose instantly.

"Get ready, Kris! I want you to come with me! We've got another one!"

She had fled to the next room before he had done talking.

"We'll be back in time for office calls!" he shouted.

He called the operator.

He heard Kristina's running feet.

He stood up. He walked into the reception room. She was waiting.

Capped and caped, Kristina held the door open for him.

The sick were waiting. The maimed and the dying, the stupid and the brilliant, the lucky and the blind and the world in which they lived in the shadow of their doom.

Ahead was the future.

Ahead was all a man can be.

He picked up his bag and went out in the world and began the practice of Medicine.